Praise for *A Widow for One Year*

"Stunning...Powerful...Sophisticated...It is comic without being condescending, ironic without being bitter, satiric without descending to sarcasm. Although the narrative is steeped in immorality and betrayal, it is essentially a moral story about how the hidden pulse of love and the yearning for it has the power to redeem every lost soul, no matter what the previous damage.... Irving has produced a wonderful, sumptuous, entertaining antidote to the nihilism of superficiality, a novel of genuine character that reminds us how deeply we may yet love one other, even when we think we don't."
The Ottawa Citizen

"*A Widow for One Year* re-establishes John Irving as a premier storyteller, master of the tragicomic and among the first rank of contemporary novelists."
Los Angeles Times Book Review

"*A Widow for One Year* casts a spell...The plot of this novel is Shakespearean. Characters appear and disappear. Astonishing interventions occur. Serendipity rules characters' destinies. Everything about this plot is as satisfying as one of Shakespeare's romances.... It's also a novel rich in perfect details. *A Widow for One Year* is a comic fantasy about missing persons. Sometimes these departures and returns are coincidences, and sometimes they seem foretold. In John Irving's hands, they are miraculous events, the sort that are longed for and cherished, the sort that sustain the imagination when reality becomes too disappointing."
The Financial Post

"[*A Widow for One Year*] is a deeply moving and often magical story that spans almost half a century."
The Daily Telegraph

A Widow
for
One Year

A WIDOW
FOR
ONE YEAR

A Novel

John Irving

VINTAGE CANADA
A Division of Random House of Canada Limited

First Vintage Canada Edition, 1999
Copyright © 1998 by Garp Enterprises, Ltd.

All rights reserved under International and Pan-American Copyright Conventions. Published in Canada by Vintage Canada, a division of Random House of Canada Limited, Toronto. First published in Canada by Alfred A. Knopf Canada, Toronto, in 1998, and simultaneously in the United States by Random House, Inc., New York. Distributed by Random House of Canada Limited, Toronto.

Grateful acknowledgement is made to the following for permission to reprint previously published material:

PENGUIN USA: Excerpt from *Madeline's Christmas* by Ludwig Bemelmans. Copyright © 1956 by Ludwig Bemelmans. Copyright renewed 1984 by Madeline Bemelmans and Barbara B. Marciano. Copyright © 1985 by Madeline Bemelmans and Barbara B. Marciano. Reprinted by permission of Viking Penguin, a division of Penguin Books USA, Inc.
A.P. WATT LTD. ON BEHALF OF MICHAEL YEATS: "When You Are Old" and excerpt from "He Wishes for the Cloths of Heaven" from *The Collected Poems of W.B. Yeats*. Reprinted by permission of A.P. Watt Ltd. on behalf of Michael Yeats.

Canadian Cataloguing in Publication Data
Irving, John
A widow for one year

ISBN 0-676-97194-6

I. Title.
PS3559.R8W52 1999   813'.54   C98-932389-7

Random House website address:
www.randomhouse.com

Printed and bound in the United States of America

10 9

Book design by Victoria Wong

For Janet,
a love story

"… as for this little lady,
the best thing I can wish her is
a *little misfortune.*"

—WILLIAM MAKEPEACE THACKERAY

Acknowledgments

I am grateful for my many visits to Amsterdam during the four years I spent writing this novel, and I'm especially indebted to the patience and generosity of brigadier Joep de Groot of the District 2 police; without Joep's advice, this book couldn't have been written. I'm also indebted to the help given me by Margot Alvarez, formerly of De Rode Draad—an organization for prostitutes' rights in Amsterdam. And most of all—for the time and care that he devoted to the manuscript—I want to thank Robbert Ammerlaan, my Dutch publisher. Regarding the Amsterdam sections in this book, I owe these three Amsterdammers incalculable thanks. For what I may have managed to get right, the credit belongs to them; if there are errors, the fault is mine.

As for the numerous parts of this novel *not* set in Amsterdam, I have relied on the expertise of Anna von Planta in Geneva, Anne Freyer in Paris, Ruth Geiger in Zurich, Harvey Loomis in Sagaponack, and Alison Gordon in Toronto. I must also cite the attention to detail that was ably demonstrated by three outstanding assistants: Lewis Robinson, Dana Wagner, and Chloe Bland: I commend Lewis and Dana and Chloe for the irreproachable carefulness of their work.

An oddity worth mentioning: the chapter called "The Red and Blue Air Mattress" was previously published—in slightly different form, and in German—in the *Süddeutsche Zeitung,* July 27, 1994, under the title "Die blaurote Luftmatratze."

—J.I.

Contents

III. FALL 1995

I

SUMMER
1958

The Inadequate Lamp Shade

One night when she was four and sleeping in the bottom bunk of her bunk bed, Ruth Cole woke to the sound of lovemaking—it was coming from her parents' bedroom. It was a totally unfamiliar sound to her. Ruth had recently been ill with a stomach flu; when she first heard her mother making love, Ruth thought that her mother was throwing up.

It was not as simple a matter as her parents having separate bedrooms; that summer they had separate houses, although Ruth never saw the other house. Her parents spent alternate nights in the family house with Ruth; there was a rental house nearby, where Ruth's mother or father stayed when they weren't staying with Ruth. It was one of those ridiculous arrangements that couples make when they are separating, but before they are divorced—when they still imagine that children and property can be shared with more magnanimity than recrimination.

When Ruth woke to the foreign sound, she at first wasn't sure if it was her mother or her father who was throwing up; then, despite the unfamiliarity of the disturbance, Ruth recognized that measure of melancholy and contained hysteria which was often detectable in her mother's voice. Ruth also remembered that it was her mother's turn to stay with her.

The master bathroom separated Ruth's room from the master bedroom. When the four-year-old padded barefoot through the bathroom, she took a towel with her. (When she'd been sick with the stomach flu, her father had encouraged her to vomit in a towel.) Poor Mommy! Ruth thought, bringing her the towel.

In the dim moonlight, and in the even dimmer and erratic light from the night-light that Ruth's father had installed in the bathroom, Ruth saw the pale faces of her dead brothers in the photographs on the bathroom wall. There were photos of her dead brothers throughout the house, on all the walls; although the two boys had died as teenagers, before Ruth was born (before she was even conceived), Ruth felt that she knew these vanished young men far better than she knew her mother or father.

The tall, dark one with the angular face was Thomas; even at Ruth's age, when he'd been only four, Thomas had had a leading man's kind of handsomeness—a combination of poise and thuggery that, in his teenage years, gave him the seeming confidence of a much older man. (Thomas had been the driver of the doomed car.)

The younger, insecure-looking one was Timothy; even as a teenager, he was baby-faced and appeared to have just been startled by something. In many of the photographs, Timothy seemed to be caught in a moment of indecision, as if he were perpetually reluctant to imitate an incredibly difficult stunt that Thomas had mastered with apparent ease. (In the end, it was something as basic as driving a car that Thomas failed to master sufficiently.)

When Ruth Cole entered her parents' bedroom, she saw the naked young man who had mounted her mother from behind; he was holding her mother's breasts in his hands and humping her on all fours, like a dog, but it was neither the violence nor the repugnance of the sexual act that caused Ruth to scream. The four-year-old didn't know that she was witnessing a sexual act—nor did the young man and her mother's activity strike Ruth as entirely unpleasant. In fact, Ruth was relieved to see that her mother was *not* throwing up.

And it wasn't the young man's nakedness that caused Ruth to scream; she had seen her father and her mother naked—nakedness was not hidden among the Coles. It was the young man himself who made Ruth scream, because she was certain he was one of her dead brothers; he looked so much like Thomas, the confident one, that Ruth Cole believed she had seen a ghost.

A four-year-old's scream is a piercing sound. Ruth was astonished at the speed with which her mother's young lover dismounted; indeed, he removed himself from both the woman and her bed with such a combination of panic and zeal that he appeared to be *propelled*—it was almost as if a cannonball had dislodged him. He fell over the night table, and, in an effort to conceal his nakedness, removed the lamp shade from the broken bedside lamp. As such, he seemed a less menacing sort of ghost than Ruth had first judged him to be; furthermore, now that Ruth took a closer look at him, she recognized him. He was the boy who occupied the most distant guest room, the boy who drove her father's car—the boy who worked for her daddy, her mommy had said. Once or twice the boy had driven Ruth and her babysitter to the beach.

That summer, Ruth had three different nannies; each of them had commented on how pale the boy was, but Ruth's mother had told her that some people just didn't like the sun. The child had never before seen the boy without his clothes, of course; yet Ruth was certain that the young man's name was Eddie and that he *wasn't* a ghost. Nevertheless, the four-year-old screamed again.

Her mother, still on all fours on her bed, looked characteristically unsurprised; she merely viewed her daughter with an expression of discouragement edged with despair. Before Ruth could cry out a third time, her mother said, "Don't scream, honey. It's just Eddie and me. Go back to bed."

Ruth Cole did as she was told, once more passing those photographs—more ghostly-seeming now than her mother's fallen ghost of a lover. Eddie, while attempting to hide himself with the lamp shade, had been oblivious to the fact that the lamp shade, being open at both ends, afforded Ruth an unobstructed view of his diminishing penis.

At four, Ruth was too young to ever remember Eddie *or* his penis with the greatest detail, but he would remember her. Thirty-six years later, when he was fifty-two and Ruth was forty, this ill-fated young man would fall in love with Ruth Cole. Yet not even then would he regret having fucked Ruth's mother. Alas, that would be Eddie's problem. This is Ruth's story.

That her parents had expected her to be a third son was not the reason Ruth Cole became a writer; a more likely source of her imagination was that she grew up in a house where the photographs of her dead brothers were a stronger presence than any "presence" she detected in either her mother or her father—and that, after her mother abandoned her *and* her father (and took with her almost *all* the photos of her lost sons), Ruth would wonder why her father left the picture hooks stuck in the bare walls. The picture hooks were part of the reason she became a writer—for years after her mother left, Ruth would try to remember which of the photographs had hung from which of the hooks.

And, failing to recall the actual pictures of her perished brothers to her satisfaction, Ruth began to invent all the captured moments in their short lives, which she had missed. That Thomas and Timothy were killed before she was born was another part of the reason Ruth Cole became a writer; from her earliest memory, she was forced to imagine them.

It was one of those automobile accidents involving teenagers that, in the aftermath, revealed that both boys had been "good kids" and that neither of them had been drinking. Worst of all, to the endless torment of their parents, the coincidence of Thomas and Timothy being in that car at that exact time, and in that specific place, was the result of an altogether avoidable quarrel between the boys' mother and father. The poor parents would relive the tragic results of their trivial argument for the rest of their lives.

Later Ruth was told that she was conceived in a well-intentioned but passionless act. Ruth's parents were mistaken to even imagine that their sons were replaceable—nor did they pause to consider that the new baby who would bear the burden of their impossible expectations might be a *girl*.

That Ruth Cole would grow up to be that rare combination of a well-respected literary novelist *and* an internationally best-selling author is not as remarkable as the fact that she managed to grow up at all. Those handsome young men in the photographs had stolen most of her mother's affection; however, her mother's rejection was more bearable to Ruth than growing up in the shadow of the coldness that passed between her parents.

Ted Cole, a best-selling author and illustrator of books for children, was a handsome man who was better at writing and drawing for children than he was at fulfilling the daily responsibilities of fatherhood. And until Ruth was four-and-a-half, while Ted Cole was not always drunk, he frequently drank too much. It's also true that, while Ted was not a womanizer every waking minute, at no time in his life was he ever entirely *not* a womanizer. (Granted, this made him more unreliable with women than he was with children.)

Ted had ended up writing for children by default. His literary debut was an overpraised adult novel of an indisputably literary sort. The two novels that followed aren't worth mentioning, except to say that no one—especially Ted Cole's publisher—had expressed any noticeable interest in a fourth novel, which was never written. Instead, Ted wrote his first children's book. Called *The Mouse Crawling Between the Walls*, it was very nearly not published; at first glance, it appeared to be one of those children's books that are of dubious appeal to parents and remain memorable to children only because children remember being frightened. At least Thomas and Timothy were frightened by *The Mouse Crawling Between the Walls* when Ted first told them the story; by the time Ted told it to Ruth, *The Mouse Crawling Between the Walls* had already frightened about nine or ten million children, in more than thirty languages, around the world.

Like her dead brothers, Ruth grew up on her father's stories. When Ruth first read these stories in a book, it felt like a violation of her privacy. She'd imagined that her father had created these stories for her alone. Later she would wonder if her dead brothers had felt that *their* privacy had been similarly invaded.

Regarding Ruth's mother: Marion Cole was a beautiful woman; she was also a good mother, at least until Ruth was born. And until the deaths of her beloved sons, she was a loyal and faithful wife—despite her husband's countless infidelities. But after the accident that took her boys away, Marion became a different woman, distant and cold. Because of her apparent indifference to her daughter, Marion was relatively easy for Ruth to reject. It would be harder for Ruth to recognize what was flawed about her father; it would also take a lot longer for her to come to this recognition, and by then it would be too late for Ruth to turn completely against him. Ted had charmed her—Ted charmed almost everyone, up to a certain age. No one was ever charmed by Marion. Poor Marion never tried to charm anyone, not even her only daughter; yet it was possible to *love* Marion Cole.

And this is where Eddie, the unlucky young man with the inadequate lamp shade, enters the story. *He* loved Marion—he would never stop loving her. Naturally if he'd known from the beginning that he was going to fall in love with Ruth, he might have reconsidered falling in love with her mother. But probably not. Eddie couldn't help himself.

Summer Job

His name was Edward O'Hare. In the summer of 1958, he had recently turned sixteen—having his driver's license had been a prerequisite of his first summer job. But Eddie O'Hare was unaware that becoming Marion Cole's lover would turn out to be his *real* summer job; Ted Cole had hired him specifically for this reason, and it would have lifelong results.

Eddie had heard of the tragedy in the Cole family, but—as with most teenagers—his attention to adult conversation was sporadic. He'd completed his second year at Phillips Exeter Academy, where his father taught English; it was an Exeter connection that got Eddie the job. Eddie's father ebulliently believed in Exeter connections. First a graduate of the academy and then a faculty member, the senior O'Hare never took a vacation without his well-thumbed copy of the *Exeter Directory*. In his view, the alumni of the academy were the standard-bearers of an ongoing responsibility—Exonians trusted one another, and they did favors for one another when they could.

In the view of the academy, the Coles had already been generous to Exeter. Their doomed sons were successful and popular students at the school when they died; despite their grief, or probably because of it, Ted and Marion Cole had funded an annual visiting lecturer in English literature—Thomas and Timothy's best subject. "Minty" O'Hare, as the senior O'Hare was known to countless Exeter students, was addicted to breath mints, which he lovingly sucked while reading aloud in class; he was inordinately fond of reciting his favorite passages from the books he'd assigned. The so-called Thomas and Timothy Cole Lectures had been Minty O'Hare's idea.

And when Eddie had expressed to his father that his first choice for a summer job would be to work as an assistant to a *writer*—the sixteen-year-old had long kept a diary and had recently written some short stories—the senior O'Hare hadn't hesitated to consult his *Exeter Directory*. To be sure, there were many more *literary* writers than Ted Cole among the alumni—Thomas and Timothy had gone to Exeter because Ted was an alumnus—but Minty O'Hare, who had managed only four years earlier to persuade Ted Cole to part with $82,000, knew that Ted was an easy touch.

"You don't have to pay him anything to speak of," Minty told Ted on the telephone. "The boy could type things for you, or answer letters, run errands—whatever you want. It's mainly for the experience. I mean, if he thinks he wants to be a writer, he should see how one works."

On the phone, Ted was noncommittal but polite; he was also drunk. He had his own name for Minty O'Hare—Ted called him "Pushy." And, indeed, it was typical of Pushy O'Hare that he pointed out the whereabouts of Eddie's photographs in the 1957 *PEAN* (the Exeter yearbook).

For the first few years after the deaths of Thomas and Timothy Cole, Marion had requested Exeter yearbooks. Had he lived, Thomas would have graduated with the class of '54—Timothy, in '56. But now, every year, even past their would-be graduations, the yearbooks came—courtesy of Minty O'Hare, who sent them automatically, assuming that he was sparing Marion the additional suffering of asking for them. Marion continued to look them over faithfully; she was repeatedly struck by those boys who bore any resemblance to Thomas or Timothy, although she'd stopped indicating these resemblances to Ted after Ruth was born.

In the pages of the '57 *PEAN,* Eddie O'Hare is seated in the front row in the photograph of the Junior Debating Society; in his dark-gray flannel trousers, tweed jacket, regimental-striped tie, he would have been nondescript except for an arresting frankness in his expression and the solemn anticipation of some future sorrow in his large, dark eyes.

In the picture, Eddie was two years younger than Thomas and the same age as Timothy at the time of their deaths. Nevertheless, Eddie looked more like Thomas than like Timothy; he looked even *more* like Thomas in the photo of the Outing Club, where Eddie appeared more clear-skinned and confident than the majority of those other boys who possessed what Ted Cole assumed was an abiding interest in the outdoors. Eddie's only other appearances in the '57 Exeter yearbook were in the photographs of two junior-varsity athletic teams—J.V. Cross-Country and J.V. Track. Eddie's leanness suggested that the boy ran more out of nervousness than for any apparent pleasure, and that running might possibly be his only athletic inclination.

It was with feigned casualness that Ted Cole showed these pictures of young Edward O'Hare to his wife. "This boy looks a lot like Thomas, doesn't he?" he asked.

Marion had seen the photographs before; she'd looked at all the photos in all the Exeter yearbooks very closely. "Yes, somewhat," she replied. "Why? Who is he?"

"He wants a summer job," Ted told her.

"With *us*?"

"Well, with *me*," Ted said. "He wants to be a writer."

"But what would he do with you?" Marion asked.

"It's mainly for the experience, I suppose," Ted told her. "I mean, if he thinks he wants to be a writer, he should see how one works."

Marion, who'd always had aspirations of being a writer herself, knew that her husband didn't work very much. "But what exactly would he *do*?" she asked.

"Well." Ted had a habit of leaving his sentences and thoughts unfinished, incomplete. It was both a deliberate and an unconscious part of his vagueness.

When he called back Minty O'Hare to offer his son a job, Ted's first question was whether Eddie had his driver's license. Ted had suffered his second drunk-driving conviction and was without a driver's license for the summer of '58. He'd hoped that the summer might be a good time to initiate a so-called trial separation from Marion, but if he were to rent a house nearby, and yet continue to share the family house (and Ruth) with Marion, someone would have to drive him.

"Certainly he has his license!" Minty told Ted. Thus was the boy's fate sealed.

And so Marion's question regarding what Eddie O'Hare would *do*, exactly, was left standing in the manner that Ted Cole frequently let things stand—namely, he let things stand vaguely. He also left Marion sitting with the Exeter yearbook open in her lap; he often left her that way. He couldn't help noticing that Marion seemed to find the photograph of Eddie O'Hare in his track uniform the most riveting. With the long, pink nail of her index finger, Marion was tracing the borders of Eddie's bare shoulders; it was an unconscious but intensely focused gesture. Ted had to wonder if *he* wasn't more aware of his wife's increasing obsession with boys who resembled Thomas or Timothy than poor Marion was. After all, she hadn't slept with one of them yet.

Eddie would be the only one she *would* sleep with.

A Sound Like Someone
Trying Not to Make a Sound

Eddie O'Hare paid little attention to the many conversations in the Exeter community concerning how the Coles were "coping" with the tragic loss of their sons; even five years after the fact, these conversations were a mainstay of the faculty dinner parties given by Minty O'Hare and his gossip-hungry wife. Eddie's mother was named Dorothy, but everyone—except Eddie's father, who eschewed nicknames—called her "Dot."

Eddie was not a gossip maven. He was, however, an adequate student; the boy prepared himself for his summer job as a writer's assistant with the kind of homework he imagined was more essential to the task than memorizing the media accounts of the tragedy would be.

If Eddie had missed the news that the Coles had had another child, this news did not escape Minty and Dot O'Hare's notice: that Ted Cole was an Exeter alumnus ('31), and that his sons had both been Exeter students at the time of their deaths, was sufficient to give *all* the Coles an Exeter connection forever. Furthermore, Ted Cole was a *famous* Exonian; the senior O'Hares, if not Eddie, were egregiously impressed by fame.

That Ted Cole was among North America's best-known writers of *children's* books had provided the media with a specific angle of interest in the tragedy. How does a renowned author and illustrator of books for children "deal with" the deaths of his own children? And with reports of such a personal nature, there is always the attendant gossip. Within the faculty families at Exeter, possibly Eddie O'Hare was the only one *not* to pay this gossip much attention. He was definitely the only member of the Exeter community to have read everything that Ted Cole had written.

Most members of Eddie's generation—and of a half-generation before and after his—had read *The Mouse Crawling Between the Walls,* or (more likely) they'd had it read to them before they were old enough to read. And a majority of the faculty and most of the Exeter students had also read some of Ted Cole's other children's books. But truly no one else at Exeter had read Ted's three *novels;* for one thing, they were all out of print—in addition to being not very good. Yet, as a faithful Exonian, Ted Cole had given the Exeter library a first edition of each of his books and the original manuscript of everything he'd written.

Eddie might have learned more from the rumors and the gossip—at least "more" in the sense of what might have prepared him for the labors of his first summer job—but Eddie's appetite for reading was a testimony to the earnestness with which the boy studied to be a writer's assistant. What he didn't know was that Ted Cole was already becoming an *ex*-writer.

The truth is, Ted was chronically attracted to younger women; Marion had been only seventeen, and already pregnant with Thomas, when Ted married her. At the time, Ted was twenty-three. The problem was, as Marion grew older—and although she would always be six years younger than Ted—Ted's interest in *younger* women persisted.

The nostalgia for innocence in the mind of an older man was a subject that the sixteen-year-old Eddie O'Hare had encountered only in novels—and Ted Cole's embarrassingly autobiographical novels were neither the first nor the best that Eddie had read on this subject. Yet Eddie's critical assessment of Ted Cole's writing did not diminish the boy's eagerness to be Ted's assistant. Surely one could learn an art or a craft from someone who was less than a master. At Exeter, after all, Eddie had learned a great deal from a considerable variety of teachers, most of whom were excellent. Only very few of the Exeter faculty were as boring in the classroom as Eddie's father. Even Eddie sensed that Minty would have stood out as a representative of mediocrity at a *bad* school, let alone at Exeter.

As someone who'd grown up on the grounds and in the nearly constant environment of a good school, Eddie O'Hare knew that you could learn a lot from older people who were hardworking—and who adhered to certain standards. He didn't know that Ted Cole had ceased to be hardworking, and that what remained of Ted's questionable "standards" had been compromised by the unendurable failure of his marriage to Marion—this in combination with those unacceptable deaths.

Ted Cole's children's books were of more intellectual and psychological (and even emotional) interest to Eddie than the novels were. A cautionary tale for children came naturally to Ted; he could imagine and express *their* fears—he could satisfy children. Had Thomas and Timothy lived into adulthood, they would doubtless have been disappointed in their father. And it was only as an adult that Ruth Cole would be disappointed in Ted; as a child, she loved him.

At sixteen, Eddie O'Hare was suspended somewhere between childhood and adulthood. In Eddie's opinion, there was no better beginning to *any* story than the first sentence of *The Mouse Crawling Between the Walls:* "Tom woke up, but Tim did not." In Ruth Cole's life as a writer—and she would be a better writer than her father, in every way—she would always envy that sentence. And she would never forget the first time she heard it, which was long before she knew it was the first sentence of a famous book.

It happened that same summer of '58, when Ruth was four—it was just before Eddie came to stay with them. This time it was not the sound of lovemaking that woke her—it was a sound that she'd carried into wakefulness from a dream. In Ruth's dream, her bed had been shaking; when she awakened, *she* was shaking—therefore, her bed seemed to be shaking, too. And for a second or more, even when Ruth was wide-awake, the sound from her dream had persisted. Then it abruptly stopped. It was a sound like someone trying not to make a sound.

"Daddy!" Ruth whispered. She'd remembered (this time) that it was her father's turn to stay with her, but her whisper was so soft that she couldn't hear her own voice. Besides, Ted Cole slept like a stone. Like most heavy drinkers, he didn't fall asleep, he passed out—at least until four or five in the morning, when he could never get back to sleep again.

Ruth crept out of her bed and tiptoed through the master bathroom to the master bedroom, where her father lay smelling of whiskey or gin—as strongly as a car smells of motor oil and gasoline in a closed garage.

"Daddy!" she said again. "I had a dream. I heard a sound."

"What sort of a sound was it, Ruthie?" her father asked; he hadn't moved, but he was awake.

"It got into the house," Ruth said.

"The *sound*?"

"It's in the house, but it's trying to be quiet," Ruth explained.

"Let's go look for it, then," her father said. "A sound that's trying to be quiet. I've got to see this."

He picked her up and carried her into the long upstairs hall. There were more photographs of Thomas and Timothy in the upstairs hall than in any other part of the house, and when Ted turned on the hall lights, Ruth's dead brothers seemed to be begging for her attention—like a row of princes seeking the favor of a princess.

"Where are you, sound?" Ted called.

"Look in the guest rooms," Ruth replied.

Her father carried her to the far end of the hall; there were three guest bedrooms with two guest bathrooms—each with more photos. They turned on all the lights, and looked in the closets and behind the shower curtains.

"Come out, sound!" Ted commanded.

"Come out, sound!" Ruth repeated.

"Maybe it's downstairs," her father suggested.

"No, it was upstairs with us," Ruth told him.

"I think it's gone, then," Ted said. "What did it sound like?"

"It was a sound like someone trying not to make a sound," Ruth told him.

He put her down on one of the guest-room beds; then he took a pad of paper and a pen off the night table. He liked so much what she'd said that he had to write it down. But he had no pajamas on—hence no pockets for the piece of paper, which he held in his teeth when he picked Ruth up again. As usual, she took only a passing interest in his nakedness. "Your penis is funny," she said.

"My penis *is* funny," her father agreed. It was what he always said. This time, with a piece of paper between his teeth, the casualness of his remark seemed even more casual.

"Where did the sound go?" Ruth asked him. He was carrying her through the guest bedrooms and the guest bathrooms, turning off the lights, but he stopped so suddenly in one of the bathrooms that Ruth imagined that Thomas or Timothy, or both of them, had reached out from one of the photographs and grabbed him.

"I'll tell you a story about a sound," her father said, the piece of paper flapping in his teeth. He immediately sat down on the edge of the bathtub, still holding her in his arms.

The photograph that had caught his attention was one that included Thomas at the age of four—Ruth's age exactly. The photo was awkwardly posed: Thomas was seated on a large couch upholstered in a confused floral pattern; the botanical excess appeared to completely overwhelm Timothy, who, at the age of two, was unwillingly being held in Thomas's lap. It would have been 1940, two years before Eddie O'Hare was born.

"One night, Ruthie, when Thomas was your age—Timothy was still in diapers—Thomas heard a sound," Ted began. Ruth would always remember her father in the act of taking the piece of paper from his mouth.

"Did they both wake up?" Ruth asked, staring at the photograph.

And that was what set the memorable old story in motion; from the very first line, Ted Cole knew this story by heart.

"Tom woke up, but Tim did not."

Ruth shivered in her father's arms. Even as a grown woman, and an acclaimed novelist, Ruth Cole could never hear or say that line without shivering.

"Tom woke up, but Tim did not. It was the middle of the night. 'Did you hear that?' Tom asked his brother. But Tim was only two. Even when he was awake, he didn't talk much.

"Tom woke up his father and asked him, 'Did you hear that sound?'

" 'What did it sound like?' his father asked.

" 'It sounded like a monster with no arms and no legs, but it was trying to move,' Tom said.

" 'How could it move with no arms and no legs?' his father asked.

" 'It wriggles,' Tom said. 'It slides on its fur.'

" 'Oh, it has fur?' his father asked.

" 'It pulls itself along with its teeth,' Tom said.

" 'It has teeth, too!' his father exclaimed.

" 'I told you—it's a monster!' Tom said.

" 'But what exactly was the sound that woke you up?' his father asked.

" 'It was a sound like, in the closet, if one of Mommy's dresses came alive and it tried to climb down off the hanger,' Tom said."

For the rest of her life, Ruth Cole would be afraid of closets. She could not fall asleep in a room when the closet door was open; she did not like to see the dresses hanging there. She didn't like dresses—period. As a child, she would never open a closet door if the room was dark—out of fear that a dress would pull her inside.

" 'Let's go back to your room and listen for the sound,' Tom's father said. And there was Tim, still asleep—he still hadn't heard the sound.

It was a sound like someone pulling the nails out of the floorboards under the bed. It was a sound like a dog trying to open a door. Its mouth was wet, so it couldn't get a good grip on the doorknob, but it wouldn't stop trying—eventually the dog would get in, Tom thought. It was a sound like a ghost in the attic, dropping the peanuts it had stolen from the kitchen."

And here, the first time she heard the story, Ruth interrupted her father to ask him what an attic was. "It's a big room above all the bedrooms," he told her. The incomprehensible existence of such a room terrified her; there was no attic in the house where Ruth grew up.

" 'There's the sound again!' Tom whispered to his father. 'Did you hear that?' This time, Tim woke up, too. It was a sound like something caught inside the headboard of the bed. It was eating its way out—it was gnawing through the wood."

And here Ruth had interrupted her father again; her bunk bed didn't have a headboard, and she didn't know what "gnawing" was. Her father explained.

"It seemed to Tom that the sound was definitely the sound of an armless, legless monster dragging its thick, wet fur. 'It's a monster!' Tom cried.

" 'It's just a mouse, crawling between the walls,' his father said.

"Tim screamed. He didn't know what a 'mouse' was. It frightened him to think of something with wet, thick fur—and no arms and no legs—crawling between the walls. How did something like that get between the walls, anyway?

"But Tom asked his father, 'It's just a mouse?'

"His father thumped against the wall with his hand and they listened to the mouse scurrying away. 'If it comes back again,' he said to Tom and Tim, 'just hit the wall.'

" 'A mouse crawling between the walls!' said Tom. 'That's all it was!' He quickly fell asleep, and his father went back to bed and fell asleep, too, but Tim was awake the whole night long, because he didn't know what a mouse was and he wanted to be awake when the thing crawling between the walls came crawling back. Each time he thought he heard the mouse crawling between the walls, Tim hit the wall with his hand and the mouse scurried away—dragging its thick, wet fur and its no arms and no legs with it.

"And *that*..." Ruth's father said to Ruth, because he ended all his stories the same way.

"And *that*..." Ruth said aloud with him, "that is the end of the story."

When her father stood up from the edge of the bathtub, Ruth heard his knees crack. She watched him stick the piece of paper back between his teeth. He turned out the light in the guest bathroom, where Eddie O'Hare would soon be spending an absurd amount of time—taking long showers until the hot water ran out, or some other kind of teenage thing.

Ruth's father turned out the lights in the long upstairs hall, where the photographs of Thomas and Timothy were perfectly all in a row. To Ruth, especially in that summer when she was four, there seemed to be an abundance of photographs of both Thomas and Timothy at about the age of four. She would later speculate that her mother might have preferred four-year-olds to children of any other age; Ruth would wonder if that was *why* her mother had left her at the end of the summer when she was four.

When her father had tucked her back into her bunk bed, Ruth asked him, "Are there mice in this house?"

"No, Ruthie," he said. "There's nothing crawling between our walls." But she lay awake after he'd kissed her good night, and although the sound that had followed her from her dream didn't return—at least not that same night—Ruth already knew there was *something* crawling between the walls of that house. Her dead brothers did not restrict their residence to those photographs. They moved about, and their presence could be detected in a variety of unseen ways.

That same night, even before she heard the typewriter, Ruth knew that her father was still awake and that he wasn't going back to bed. First she listened to him brushing his teeth, then she heard him getting dressed—the *zip* of his zipper, the *clump* of his shoes.

"Daddy?" she called to him.

"Yes, Ruthie."

"I want a drink of water."

She didn't really want a drink of water, but it intrigued her that her father always let the water run until it was cold. Her mother took the first water that ran from the tap; it was warm and tasted like the inside of the pipe.

"Don't drink too much or you'll have to pee," her father would say, but her mother would let her drink as much as she wanted—sometimes not even watching her drink.

When Ruth handed the cup back to her father, she said, "Tell me about Thomas and Timothy." Her father sighed. In the last half-year, Ruth had demonstrated an unquenchable interest in the subject of death—little wonder why. From the photographs, Ruth had been able to distinguish Thomas from Timothy since she'd been three; only their pictures when they were infants occasionally confused her. And, by both her mother and her father, Ruth had been told the circumstances surrounding each of the photos—whether Mommy or Daddy had taken this one, whether Thomas or Timothy had cried. But that the boys were *dead* was a concept that Ruth was newly trying to grasp.

"*Tell* me," she repeated to her father. "Are they dead?"

"Yes, Ruthie."

"And dead means they're *broken*?" Ruth asked.

"Well ... their bodies are broken, yes," Ted said.

"And they're under the ground?"

"Their bodies are, yes."

"But they're not all gone?" Ruth asked.

"Well ... not as long as we remember them. They're not gone from our hearts or from our minds," her father said.

"They're kind of inside us?" Ruth asked.

"Well." Her father left it at that, but this was more than Ruth would get, in the world of answers, from her mother—her mother would never say "dead." And neither Ted nor Marion Cole was religious. Providing the necessary details for the concept of heaven wasn't an option for them, although each of them, in other conversations with Ruth on this subject, had referred mysteriously to the sky and to the stars; they had implied that *something* of the boys lived somewhere other than with their broken bodies, under the ground.

"So ..." Ruth said, "tell me what *dead* is."

"Ruthie, listen to me ..."

"Okay," Ruth said.

"When you look at Thomas and Timothy in the photographs, do you remember the stories of what they were doing?" her father asked her. "In the pictures, I mean—do you remember what they were doing in the pictures?"

"Yes," Ruth answered, although she wasn't sure she could remember what they were doing in *every* picture.

"Well, then ... Thomas and Timothy are alive in your *imagination*," her father told her. "When you're dead, when your body is broken, it just means that we can't see your body anymore—your body is gone."

"It's under the ground," Ruth corrected him.

"We can't *see* Thomas and Timothy anymore," her father insisted, "but they are not gone from our imaginations. When we think of them, we see them there."

"They're just gone from *this* world," Ruth said. (For the most part, she was repeating what she'd heard before.) "They're in *another* world?"

"Yes, Ruthie."

"Am I going to get dead?" the four-year-old asked. "Will I get all broken?"

"Not for a long, long time!" her father said. "*I'm* going to get broken before you are, and not even I am going to get broken for a long, long time."

"Not for a long, long time?" the child repeated.

"I promise, Ruthie."

"Okay," Ruth said.

They had a conversation of this kind almost every day. With her mother, Ruth had similar conversations—only shorter. Once, when Ruth had mentioned to her father that thinking about Thomas and Timothy made her sad, her father had admitted that he too was sad.

Ruth had said: "But Mommy's sadder."

"Well ... yes," Ted had said.

And so Ruth lay awake in the house with *something* crawling between the walls, something bigger than a mouse, and she listened to the only sound that would ever succeed in comforting her—at the same time that it made her melancholic. This was before she even knew what "melancholic" meant. It was the sound of a typewriter—the sound of storytelling. In her life as a novelist, Ruth would never be converted to the computer; she would write either in longhand or with a typewriter that made the most old-fashioned noise of all the typewriters she could find.

She did not know then (that summer night in 1958) that her father was beginning what would be her favorite of his stories. He would work on it all that summer; it would be the only piece of writing that Ted Cole's soon-to-arrive writer's assistant, Eddie O'Hare, would actually get to "assist" Ted with. And while none of Ted Cole's books for children would ever enjoy the commercial success or the international renown of *The Mouse Crawling Between the Walls,* the book Ted began that night was the one Ruth would like the best. It was called, of course, *A Sound Like Someone Trying Not to Make a Sound,* and it would always be special to Ruth because she was its inspiration.

Unhappy Mothers

Ted Cole's books for children could not be categorized with respect to the age of his audience. *The Mouse Crawling Between the Walls* was marketed as a book to be read aloud to children between the ages of four and six; the book succeeded in that market, as did Ted's later books. But, for example, twelve-year-olds often experienced a second appreciation of Ted Cole. These more sophisticated readers frequently wrote to the author, telling him that they used to think he was a writer for children—that is, before they discovered the deeper levels of meaning in his books. These letters, which displayed a variety of competence and incompetence in penmanship and spelling, became the virtual wallpaper in Ted's workroom.

He called it his "workroom"; later Ruth would wonder if this didn't define her father's opinion of himself more sharply than she'd perceived it as a child. The room was never called a "studio," because her father had long ago stopped thinking of his books as art; yet a "workroom" was more pretentious-sounding than an "office," which it was also never called, because her father appeared to have considerable pride in his creativity. He was sensitive to the widely held belief that his books were merely a business. Later Ruth would realize that it was his ability to *draw* that her father valued more than his writing, although no one would have said that *The Mouse Crawling Between the Walls* or Ted Cole's other books for children were successful or distinguished because of the illustrations.

Compared to whatever magic existed in the stories themselves, which were always scary and short and lucidly written, the illustrations were rudimentary—and there were too few of them, in every publisher's opinion. Yet Ted's audience, those millions of children from four to fourteen, and sometimes slightly older—not to mention the millions of young mothers who were the principal *buyers* of Ted Cole's books—never complained. These readers could never have guessed that Ruth's father spent much more time drawing than he spent writing; there were hundreds of drawings for every illustration that appeared in his books. As for his storytelling, for which he was famous ... well, Ruth was accustomed to hearing the typewriter only at night.

Imagine poor Eddie O'Hare. In 1958, on a summery June morning, he was standing near the Pequod Avenue docks in New London, Connecticut, waiting for the ferry that would bring him to Orient Point, Long Island. Eddie was thinking about his job as a writer's assistant, never suspecting that there would be precious little *writing* involved. (Eddie had never contemplated a career in the graphic arts.)

Ted Cole was alleged to have dropped out of Harvard to attend a not very prestigious art school—truly, a design school that was chiefly populated with students of mediocre talent and modest ambitions in the commercial arts. He never gave etching or lithography a chance; he preferred just plain drawing. He used to say that darkness was his favorite color.

Ruth would always associate her father's physical appearance with pencils and erasers. There were black and gray smudges on his hands, and eraser crumbs were a constant accessory to his clothes. But Ted's more permanent identifying marks—even when he was freshly bathed and cleanly dressed—were his ink-stained fingers. His choice of ink would change from book to book. "Is this a black book or a brown one, Daddy?" Ruth would ask him.

The Mouse Crawling Between the Walls was a black book—the original drawings were in India ink, Ted's favorite black. *A Sound Like Someone Trying Not to Make a Sound* would be a brown book, which was responsible for the prevailing *odor* of the summer of 1958—Ted's favorite brown was fresh squid ink, which, although more black than brown, is sepia-like in tone and has (under certain conditions) a fishy smell.

Ted's experiments with keeping the squid ink fresh were a strain on his already strained relationship with Marion, who learned to avoid the blackened jars in the refrigerator; they were also in the freezer, where they stood perilously close to the ice trays. (Later that same summer,

Ted tried preserving the ink *in* the ice trays—with comedic, if harrowing, results.)

And one of Eddie O'Hare's earliest responsibilities—not as a writer's assistant but as Ted Cole's designated driver—would be to drive three quarters of an hour each way to Montauk and back; only the fish store in Montauk would save squid ink for the famous author and illustrator of children's books. (When the fishmonger himself was beyond hearing distance, the fishmonger's wife would repeatedly tell Eddie that she was Ted's "biggest fan.")

Ruth's father's workroom was the only room in the house where not a single photograph of Thomas or Timothy adorned the walls. Ruth wondered if maybe her father couldn't work or think in the sight of his departed boys.

And unless her father was in his workroom, it was the only room in the house that was off-limits to Ruth. Was there anything that could hurt her in there? Was there an infinite number of sharp tools? There were countless (and swallowable) nibs for the pens, although Ruth was not a child who ever put strange objects in her mouth. But regardless of the dangers of her father's workroom—if, indeed, there *were* dangers—it was unnecessary to impose any physical restraints on the four-year-old, nor was there need for a lock on the workroom door. The smell of squid ink was sufficient to keep the child out.

Marion never ventured near Ted's workroom, but Ruth would be in her twenties before she realized that it was more than squid ink that had kept her mother away. Marion didn't want to meet, or so much as see, Ted's models—not even the children, for the children never came to model without their mothers. It was only after the children had modeled a half-dozen times (or more), that the mothers would come to model alone. As a child, Ruth never questioned why so few of the drawings of the mothers with their children were ever printed in any of her father's books. Of course, since his books were for children, there were never any *nudes* in his books, although Ted drew a lot of nudes; those young mothers accounted for literally *hundreds* of drawings of nudes.

Of the nudes, her father would say: "A requisite, fundamental exercise for anyone who draws, Ruthie." Like landscapes, she at first supposed, although Ted did few of those. Ruth used to think the reason for his relative lack of interest in landscapes might be the sameness and the extreme flatness of the land that lay like a tarmac running to the sea, or what seemed to her to be the sameness and the extreme flatness of the sea itself—not to mention the huge, frequently dull expanse of sky above.

Her father appeared to be so unconcerned with landscapes that it later surprised her when he would complain about the new houses— the "architectural monstrosities," he called them. Without announcement, the new houses would rise up and intrude upon the flatness of the potato fields that had once been the Coles' principal view.

"There's no justification for a building of such experimental ugliness as that," Ted would pronounce over dinner to anyone who'd listen. "We're not at war. There's no need to construct a deterrent for parachutists." But her father's complaint grew stale; the summer people's architecture in that part of the world called the Hamptons was not of comparable interest—to either Ruth *or* her father—as the more abiding nudes.

Why young *married* women? Why all these young *mothers*? When she was in college, Ruth was in the habit of asking her father more direct questions than at any other time in her life. It was also when she was in college that a troubling thought first occurred to her. Who *else* would be his models, or, more briefly, his lovers? Who *else* was he always meeting? The young mothers were the ones who recognized him and approached him, of course.

"Mr. Cole? I know you—you're Ted Cole! I just wanted to say, because my daughter is too shy, that you're my daughter's favorite author. You wrote her absolutely best-loved book...." And then the reluctant daughter (or the embarrassed son) would be pushed forward to shake Ted's hand. If Ted was attracted to the mother, he would suggest that the child, together with the mother, might like to model for him— maybe for the next book. (The subject of the mother posing alone, and nude, would be broached at a later time.)

"But they're usually *married* women, Daddy," Ruth would say.

"Yes ... I guess that's why they're so unhappy, Ruthie."

"If you cared about your nudes—I mean the *drawings*—you would have chosen *professional* models," Ruth said to him. "But I guess you always cared more for the women themselves than for your nudes."

"This is a difficult thing for a father to explain to his daughter, Ruthie. But ... if nakedness—I mean the *feeling* of nakedness—is what a nude must convey, there is no nakedness that compares to what it feels like to be naked in front of someone for the first time."

"So much for professional models," Ruth replied. "Jesus, Daddy, do you *have* to?" By then she knew, of course, that he didn't care enough about his nudes, *or* his portraits of the mothers with their children, to keep them; he didn't sell them privately or give them to his gallery, either. When the affair was over—and it was usually over quickly—Ted Cole would give the accumulated drawings to the young mother of the moment. And Ruth used to ask herself: If the young mothers were, generally, so unhappily married—or just plain unhappy—did the gift of art make them, at least momentarily, happier? But her father would never have called what he did "art," nor did he ever refer to himself as an artist. Ted didn't call himself a writer, either.

"I'm an entertainer of children, Ruthie," he used to say.

To which Ruth would add: "And a lover of their mothers, Daddy."

Even in a restaurant, when the waiter or the waitress couldn't help staring at his ink-stained fingers, this never elicited a response from Ted of the "I'm-an-artist" or the "I'm-an-author-and-illustrator-of-children's-books" kind; rather, Ruth's father would say, "I work with ink"—or, if the waiter or waitress had stared at his fingers in a condemning way, "I work with squid."

As a teenager—and once or twice in her hypercritical college-student years—Ruth attended writers' conferences with her father, who would be the one children's book author among the presumed-to-be-more-serious fiction writers and poets. It amused Ruth that these latter types, who projected a vastly more literary aura than that aura of unattended handsomeness and ink-stained fingers which typified her father, were not only envious of the popularity of her father's books; these ultraliterary types were also annoyed to observe how self-deprecating Ted Cole was—how enduringly modest a man he *seemed*!

"You began your career writing *novels,* didn't you?" the nastier of the ultraliterary types might ask Ted.

"Oh, but they were terrible novels," Ruth's father would reply cheerfully. "It's a miracle that so many book reviewers liked the first one. It's a wonder it took me *three* of them to realize that I wasn't a writer. I'm just an entertainer of children. And I like to draw." He would hold up his fingers as proof; he would always smile. What a smile it was!

Ruth once reported to her college roommate (who had also been her roommate in boarding school): "I swear you could hear the women's panties sliding to the floor."

It was at a writers' conference where Ruth was first confronted with the phenomenon of her father sleeping with a young woman who was even younger than she was—a fellow college student.

"I thought you'd approve of me, Ruthie," Ted had said. When she criticized him, he often adopted a self-pitying tone of voice with her—as if she were the parent and he the child, which in a way he *was*.

"*Approve* of you, Daddy?" she'd asked him, in a rage. "You seduce someone younger than *I* am, and you expect me to *approve?*"

"But, Ruthie, she's not *married*," her father had replied. "She's nobody's *mother*. I thought you'd approve of *that.*"

Ruth Cole the novelist would eventually come to describe her father's line of work as "Unhappy mothers—that's my father's field."

But why wouldn't Ted have recognized an unhappy mother when he saw one? After all—at least for the first five years that followed the death of his sons—Ted lived with the unhappiest mother of them all.

Marion, Waiting

Orient Point, the tip of the north fork of Long Island, looks like what it is: the end of an island, where the land peters out. The vegetation—stunted by salt, bent by the wind—is sparse. The sand is coarse and strewn with shells and rocks. That June day in 1958 when Marion Cole was waiting for the New London ferry that was bringing Eddie O'Hare across Long Island Sound, the tide was low and Marion indifferently noted that the pilings of the ferry slip were wet where the fallen tide had exposed them; above the high-water mark, the pilings were dry. Over the empty slip, a noisy chorus of seagulls hung suspended; then the birds veered low over the water, which was ruffled and constantly changed colors in the inconsistent sun—from slate-gray to blue-green, and then to gray again. The ferry was not yet in sight.

Fewer than a dozen cars were parked close to the slip. Given the sun's reluctance to linger—and the wind, which was northeasterly—most of the drivers waited in their cars. At first Marion had stood outside her car, leaning against the front fender; then she'd sat on the fender, spreading her copy of the 1958 Exeter yearbook on the hood. It was there, at Orient Point, on the hood of her car, that Marion took her first long look at the most recent photographs of Eddie O'Hare.

Marion hated to be late, and she invariably thought less of people who were. Her car was parked at the front of the line where people waited for the ferry. There was a longer line of cars in the parking lot, where people taking the return ferry to New London were also waiting; but Marion took no notice of them. Marion rarely looked at people when she was out in public, which she seldom was.

Everyone looked at her. They couldn't help themselves. That day at Orient Point, Marion Cole was thirty-nine. She looked twenty-nine, or slightly younger. When Marion sat on the fender of her car and attempted to hold the pages of the '58 *PEAN* steady in the unruly gusts from the northeast, her pretty legs, which were also long, were mostly hidden from view in a wraparound skirt of a nondescript beige color. There was, however, nothing nondescript about the *fit* of Marion's skirt—it fit her perfectly. She wore an oversize white T-shirt that was tucked into the waist of the skirt, and over the T-shirt she wore an unbuttoned cashmere cardigan that was the faded-pink color of the inside of certain seashells—a pink more common to a tropical coast than to the less exotic Long Island shore.

In the stiffening breeze, Marion tugged the unbuttoned sweater snugly around her. The T-shirt fit her loosely, but she had wrapped one arm around herself and under her breasts. That she was long-waisted was apparent; that her breasts were full and pendulous, but well contoured and natural-looking, was evident, too. As for her wavy, shoulder-length hair, the on-and-off sun caused it to change color from amber to honey-blond, and her lightly tanned skin was luminous. She was almost without a flaw.

However, upon closer inspection, there was something distracting in one of her eyes. Her face was almond-shaped, as were her eyes, which were a dark blue; yet in the iris of her right eye was a hexagonal speck of the brightest yellow. It was as if a diamond chip, or a shard of ice, had fallen into her eye and now permanently reflected the sun. In certain light, or at unpredictable angles, this speck of yellow turned her right eye from blue to green. No less disconcerting was her perfect mouth. Yet her smile, when she smiled, was rueful—for five years, few people had seen her smile.

As she searched through the Exeter yearbook for the most recent photographs of Eddie O'Hare, Marion frowned. A year ago, Eddie had been in the Outing Club—now he wasn't. And last year he'd liked the Junior Debating Society; this year he was no longer a member, nor had he advanced to that elite circle of those six boys who comprised the Academy Debating Team. Had he simply given up the outdoors *and* debate? Marion wondered. (Her boys hadn't cared for clubs, either.)

But then she found him, looking aloof among a smug and cocky group of boys who were the editors of—and the principal contributors to—Exeter's literary magazine, the *Pendulum*. Eddie occupied one end of the middle row, as if he might have arrived late for the photograph and, feigning a fashionable lack of concern, had slipped into the frame at the last second. While some of the others were posing, deliberately showing the camera their profiles, Eddie was staring the camera down. As in his 1957 yearbook pictures, his alarming seriousness and his handsome face made him seem older than he was.

As for whatever was "literary" about him, his dark shirt and darker tie were the only visible factors; the shirt was of a kind not normally worn with a tie. (Thomas, Marion remembered, had liked that look; Timothy—younger or more conventional, or both—had not.) It depressed Marion to try to imagine what the contents of the *Pendulum* might have been: obscure poems and painfully autobiographical coming-of-age stories—artsy versions of "What I Did on My Summer Vacation." Boys of this age should stick to sports, Marion believed. (Thomas and Timothy had stuck to nothing but sports.)

Suddenly the breezy, cloudy weather chilled her, or she felt chilled for other reasons. She closed the '58 *PEAN* and got inside her car, then once again opened the yearbook, resting it against the steering wheel. The men who'd noticed Marion getting back inside her car had watched her hips. They couldn't help themselves.

Regarding sports: Eddie O'Hare was still running—period. There he was, a year more muscular, in both the photographs for J.V. Cross-Country and J.V. Track. Why did he run? Marion wondered. (Her boys had liked soccer and hockey and, in the spring, Thomas had played lacrosse and Timothy had tried tennis. Neither of them had wanted to play their father's favorite game—Ted's *only* sport was squash.)

If Eddie O'Hare had not risen from the junior-varsity to the varsity level of competition—in either cross-country or track—then he couldn't have been running very fast or very hard. But, regardless of how fast or hard Eddie ran, his bare shoulders once more drew the un-conscious attention of Marion's index finger. Her nail polish was a frosted pink; it matched her lipstick, which was a kind of pink shot through with silver. In the summer of 1958, it's just possible that Mar-ion Cole was one of the most beautiful women alive.

And, truly, there was no *conscious* sexual interest in her tracing the borders of Eddie's bare shoulders. That her compulsive scrutiny of young men Eddie's age might *become* sexual was, at this point in time, strictly her husband's premonition. If Ted trusted his sexual instincts, Marion was deeply unsure of hers.

Many a faithful wife has tolerated, even accepted, the painful be-trayals of a philandering husband; in Marion's case, she put up with Ted because she could see for herself how inconsequential his many women were to him. If he'd had *one* other woman, someone who'd held him under an enduring spell, Marion might have been persuaded to get rid of him. But Ted was never abusive to her; and especially after the deaths of Thomas and Timothy, he was consistent in his tender-ness toward her. After all, no one but Ted could have comprehended and respected the eternity of her sorrow.

But now there was something horribly unequal between her and Ted. As even the four-year-old Ruth had observed, her mother *was* sadder than her father. Nor could Marion hope to compensate for an-other inequality: Ted was a better father to Ruth than she was a mother. And Marion had always been so much the superior parent to her *sons*! Lately she almost hated Ted for absorbing his grief better than she could absorb hers. What Marion could only guess was that Ted might have hated her for the superiority of her sadness.

Marion believed that they had been wrong to have Ruth. At every phase of growing up, the child was a painful reminder of the corre-sponding phases of Thomas's and Timothy's childhoods. The Coles had never needed nannies for their boys; Marion had been a complete mother then. But they had virtually nonstop nannies for Ruth—for al-though Ted demonstrated a greater willingness to be with the child than Marion demonstrated, he was inadequate at performing the nec-essary daily tasks. However incapable Marion was at performing these, she at least knew what they were and that *someone* responsible had to perform them.

By the summer of '58, Marion herself had become her husband's principal unhappiness. Five years after the deaths of Thomas and

Timothy, Marion believed she caused Ted more grief than their dead sons did. Marion also feared that she might not always be able to keep herself from loving her daughter. And if I let myself love Ruth, Marion thought, what will I do if something happens to *her*? Marion knew that she could not go through losing a child again.

Ted had recently told Marion that he wanted to "try separating" for the summer—just to see if they might both be happier apart. For years, long before the deaths of her beloved boys, Marion had wondered if she should divorce Ted. Now *he* wanted to divorce *her*! If they'd divorced when Thomas and Timothy were alive, there could have been no question about which of them would have kept the children; they were *her* boys—they would have chosen her. Ted could never have contested such an obvious truth.

But now ... Marion didn't know what to do. There were times when she couldn't bear even to talk to Ruth. Understandably, this child would want her father.

So is that the deal? Marion wondered. He takes all that's left: the house, which she loved but didn't want—and Ruth, whom she either couldn't or wouldn't allow herself to love. Marion would take her boys. Of Thomas and Timothy, Ted could keep what he could remember. (I get to keep all the photographs, Marion decided.)

The sound of the ferry horn startled her. Her index finger, which had continued to trace the borders of Eddie O'Hare's bare shoulders, bore down on the page of the yearbook too hard; she broke her nail. She began to bleed. She noticed the groove her nail had left in an area of Eddie's shoulder. A pinpoint of blood had spotted the page, but she wet her finger in her mouth and wiped the blood away. Only then did Marion remember that Ted had hired Eddie on the condition that the boy had a driver's license, and that Eddie's summer job had been arranged *before* Ted had told her that he wanted to "try separating."

The ferry horn blew again. It was so deep a sound that it announced to her what was now the obvious: Ted had known for some time that he was leaving her! To Marion's surprise, her awareness of his deceit failed to rouse any anger in her; she could not even be sure if she felt sufficient hatred for him to indicate that she had ever loved him. Had *everything* stopped, or changed for her, when Thomas and Timothy died? Until now, she'd assumed that Ted, in his fashion, still loved her; yet *he* was the one who was initiating their separation, wasn't he?

When she opened her car door and stepped outside to have a closer look at those passengers disembarking the ferry, she was as sad a woman as she'd been at any moment in the past five years; yet her mind was clearer than it had ever been. She would let Ted go—she would even let her daughter go with him. She would leave them both before Ted had a chance to leave her. As Marion walked toward the ferry slip, she was thinking: Everything but the photographs. For a woman who'd just come to these momentous conclusions, her step was inappropriately steady. To everyone who saw her, she seemed positively serene.

The first driver off the ferry was a fool. He was so stunned by the beauty of the woman he saw walking toward him that he turned off the road into the stony sand of the beach; his car would be stuck there for over an hour, but even when he realized his predicament, he couldn't take his eyes off Marion. He couldn't help himself. Marion didn't notice the accident—she just kept walking, slowly.

For the rest of his life, Eddie O'Hare would believe in fate. After all, the second he set foot on shore, there was Marion.

Eddie Is Bored—and Horny, Too

Poor Eddie O'Hare. To be in public with his father always caused him complete mortification. The occasion of Eddie's long drive to the ferry docks in New London, or of his seemingly longer wait (with his dad) for the arrival of the Orient Point ferry, was no exception. Within the Exeter community, Minty O'Hare's habits were as familiar as his breath mints; Eddie had learned to accept that both students and faculty unashamedly fled from his father. The senior O'Hare's ability to bore an audience, *any* audience, was notorious. In the classroom, Minty's soporific approach to teaching was renowned; the students whom the senior O'Hare had put to sleep were of legendary numbers.

Minty's method of boredom was never ornate; simple repetition was his game. He would read aloud from what he judged to be the significant passages of the previous day's assignment—when presumably the material was fresh in the students' minds. The freshness of their minds could be seen to wilt as the class wore on, however, for Minty always located *many* passages of significance, and he read aloud with great feeling, and with repeated pauses for effect; the lengthier pauses were required for sucking on his mints. Little discussion followed the ceaseless repetition of these overly familiar passages—in part because no one could argue against the obvious significance of each passage. One could only question the *necessity* of reading aloud such passages. Outside the classroom, Minty's method of teaching English was so frequently a matter of discussion that Eddie O'Hare often felt as if he'd suffered through his father's classes, although he never had.

Eddie had suffered elsewhere. He was grateful that, since early childhood, he had eaten most of his meals in the school dining hall, first at a faculty table with another faculty family, and later with his fellow students. Therefore, school vacations were the only times when the O'Hares, as a family, dined at home. Dinner parties, which Dot O'Hare gave regularly—although there were few faculty couples who met with her reluctant approval—were another story. Eddie was not bored by such dinner parties because his parents restricted his presence at them to the briefest of polite appearances.

But at family dinners during school vacations Eddie was exposed to the stultifying phenomenon of his parents' perfect marriage: they did not bore each other because they never listened to each other. A tender politeness passed between them; the mom would allow the dad to speak, at length, and then it was the mom's turn—almost always on an unrelated subject. Mr. and Mrs. O'Hare's conversation was a masterpiece of non sequiturs; by not participating, Eddie could best entertain himself by trying to guess if *anything* of what his mother or father had said would ever be remembered by the other.

Shortly before his departure for the ferry to Orient Point, an evening at home in Exeter became a case in point. The school year was over, the commencement exercises recently concluded, and Minty O'Hare was philosophizing on what he called the indolence of the students' behavior in the spring term. "I *know* that they are thinking of their summer vacations," Minty said for perhaps the hundredth time. "I *realize* that the return of warm weather is itself an invitation to sloth, but not to slothfulness of such an advanced degree as I observed *this* spring."

His father made these same statements *every* spring; the statements themselves brought forth a deadening torpor in Eddie, who'd once wondered if his sole athletic interest, running, wasn't the result of trying to flee his father's voice, which had the predictable, ceaseless modulations of a circular saw in a lumberyard.

When Minty had not quite finished—Eddie's father never seemed to be finished—but he had at least paused for breath, or for a bite of food, Eddie's mother would begin.

"As if it weren't enough that, all winter, we were witnesses to the fact that Mrs. Havelock chooses *not* to wear a bra," Dot O'Hare began, "now that the weather is warm again, we must suffer the consequences of her refusal to shave her armpits, too. And there is still no bra in sight. Now it's no bra *and* hairy armpits!" Eddie's mother declared.

Mrs. Havelock was a new young faculty wife; as such, at least to Eddie and the majority of the boys at Exeter, she was of more interest than were most of her counterparts. And Mrs. Havelock's bralessness was, for the boys, a *plus*. While she was not a pretty woman, but rather plump and plain, the sway of her youthful, ample bosom had fully endeared her to the students—and to those uncounted men on the faculty who would never have confessed their attraction. In those prehippie days of 1958, Mrs. Havelock's bralessness was both unusual and noteworthy. Among themselves, the boys called her Bouncy. For lucky *Mr.* Havelock, whom the boys deeply envied, they demonstrated unparalleled respect. Eddie, who enjoyed Mrs. Havelock's bouncing breasts as much as anyone, was perturbed by his mother's heartless disapproval.

And now the hairy armpits—these, Eddie had to admit, had been the cause of considerable consternation among the less sophisticated students. In those days, there were boys at Exeter who seemed not to know that women *could* grow hair in their armpits—or else these boys were deeply distressed to contemplate why any woman *would*. To Eddie, however, Mrs. Havelock's hairy armpits were further evidence of the woman's boundless capacity to give pleasure. In a sleeveless summer dress, Mrs. Havelock bounced *and* she was hairy. Since the warm weather, not a few of the boys, in addition to calling her Bouncy, had taken to calling her Furry. By either name, the very thought of her gave Eddie O'Hare a hard-on.

"The next thing you know, she'll stop shaving her legs," said Eddie's mother. The thought of *that* admittedly gave Eddie pause, although he decided to reserve judgment until he saw for himself if such a growth on Mrs. Havelock's legs might please him.

Since Mr. Havelock was a colleague of Minty's in the English Department, it was Dot O'Hare's opinion that her husband should speak to him about the disturbing inappropriateness of his wife's "bohemianism" at an all-boys' school. But Minty, although he could bore with the best of bores, knew better than to interfere with the clothing or the shaving—or the lack thereof—of another man's wife.

"My dear Dorothy," was all that Minty would say, "Mrs. Havelock is a European."

"I don't know what *that's* supposed to mean!" Eddie's mother commented. But Eddie's father would already have returned—as agreeably as if he had never been interrupted—to the subject of student indolence in the spring.

In Eddie's unexpressed opinion, only Mrs. Havelock's mobile breasts and furry armpits could ever relieve the sluggishness he felt—and it wasn't the spring that made Eddie feel indolent. It was his parents' unending and unconnected conversations; they left a veritable wake of slothfulness, a trail of torpor.

Sometimes Eddie's fellow students would ask him: "Uh, what's your dad's *real* name, anyway?" They knew the senior O'Hare only as Minty, or—to his face—Mr. O'Hare.

"Joe," Eddie would reply. "Joseph E. O'Hare." The *E.* was for Edward, the only name his father called him.

"I didn't name you Edward because I wanted to call you Eddie," his father periodically told him. But everyone else, even his mom, called him Eddie. One day, Eddie hoped, just plain Ed would do.

At the last family dinner before Eddie left for his first summer job, he had tried to interject some of his own conversation into his parents' endless non sequiturs, but it hadn't worked.

"I was at the gym today, and I ran into Mr. Bennett," Eddie said. Mr. Bennett had been Eddie's English teacher in the past school year. Eddie was very fond of him; his course included some of the best books that the boy had ever read.

"I suppose we can look forward to seeing her armpits at the beach all summer. I'm afraid I just may *say* something," Eddie's mother announced.

"I actually played a little squash with Mr. Bennett," Eddie added. "I told him that I'd always been interested in trying it, and he took the time to hit the ball with me for a while. I liked it better than I thought I would." Mr. Bennett, in addition to his duties in the English Department, was also the academy squash coach—quite a successful one, too. Hitting a squash ball had been something of a revelation to Eddie O'Hare.

"I think a shorter Christmas vacation and a longer spring break might be the answer," his father said. "I know the school year is a long haul, but there ought to be a way to bring the boys back in the spring with a little more pep in them—a little more get-up-and-go."

"I've been considering that I might try squash as a sport—I mean, next winter," Eddie announced. "I'd still run cross-country in the fall. I could go back to track in the spring...." For a moment it seemed that the word "spring" had caught his father's attention, but it was only the *indolence* of spring that held Minty in its thrall.

"Maybe she gets a rash from shaving," Eddie's mom speculated. "Mind you, not that I don't get a rash occasionally myself—but it's no excuse."

Later Eddie did the dishes while his parents prattled away. Just before going to bed, he heard his mom ask his dad: "What did he say about *squash?* What *about* squash?"

"What did *who* say?" his father asked.

"Eddie!" his mom replied. "Eddie said something about squash, and Mr. Bennett."

"He coaches squash," Minty said.

"Joe, I know *that!*"

"My dear Dorothy, what is your question?"

"What did Eddie say about squash?" Dot repeated.

"Well, you tell me," Minty said.

"Honestly, Joe," Dot said. "I sometimes wonder if you ever listen."

"My dear Dorothy, I'm all ears," the old bore told her. They both had a good laugh over that. They were still laughing as Eddie dragged himself through the requisite motions of going to bed. He was suddenly so tired—so *indolent*, he guessed—that he couldn't conceive of making the effort to tell his parents what he'd meant. If theirs was a good marriage, and by all counts it seemed to be, Eddie imagined that a *bad* marriage might have much to recommend it. He was about to test that theory, more strenuously than he knew.

The Door in the Floor

En route to New London, a journey that had been tediously over-planned—like Marion, they'd left much too early for the designated ferry—Eddie's father got lost in the vicinity of Providence.

"Is this the pilot's error or the navigator's?" Minty asked cheerfully. It was both. Eddie's father had been talking so much that he'd not been paying sufficient attention to the road; Eddie, who was the "navigator," had been making such an effort to stay awake that he'd neglected to consult the map. "It's a good thing we left early," his father added.

They stopped at a gas station, where Joe O'Hare made his best attempt to engage in small talk with a member of the working class. "So, how's this for a predicament?" the senior O'Hare said to the gas-station attendant, who appeared to Eddie to be a trifle retarded. "Here's a couple of lost Exonians in search of the New London ferry to Orient Point."

Eddie died a little every time he heard his father speak to strangers. (Who but an Exonian knew what an Exonian was?) As if stricken by a passing coma, the gas-station attendant stared at an oily stain on the pavement a little to the right of Minty's right shoe. "You're in Rhode Island" was all that the unfortunate man was able to say.

"Can you tell us the way to New London?" Eddie asked him.

When they were back on the road again, Minty regaled Eddie on the subject of the intrinsic sullenness that was so often the result of a sub-par secondary-school education. "The dulling of the mind is a terrible thing, Edward," his father instructed him.

They arrived in New London in enough time for Eddie to have taken an earlier ferry. "But then you'll have to wait in Orient Point all alone!" Minty pointed out. The Coles, after all, were expecting Eddie to be on the later ferry. By the time Eddie realized how much he would have preferred to wait in Orient Point alone, the earlier ferry had sailed.

"My son's first ocean voyage," Minty said to the woman with the enormous arms who sold Eddie his passenger ticket. "It's not the *Queen Elizabeth* or the *Queen Mary*; it's not a seven-day crossing; it's not Southampton, as in England, or Cherbourg, as in France. *But,* especially when you're sixteen, a little voyage at sea to Orient Point will do!" The woman smiled tolerantly through her rolls of fat; even though her smile was slight, one could discern that she was missing a few teeth.

Afterward, standing at the waterfront, Eddie's father philosophized on the subject of the dietary excesses that were often the result of a subpar secondary-school education. In one short trip away from Exeter, they kept running across examples of people who would have been happier or thinner (or both) if they'd only had the good fortune to attend the academy!

Occasionally Eddie's father would interject, at random, sprinkles of advice that, out of nowhere, pertained to Eddie's upcoming summer job. "Don't be nervous just because he's famous," the senior O'Hare said, apropos of nothing. "He's not exactly a major literary figure. Just pick up what you can. Note his work habits, see if there's a method to his madness—that kind of thing." As Eddie's designated ferry approached, it was Minty who was suddenly growing anxious about Eddie's job.

They loaded the trucks first, and the first in line was a truck full of fresh clams—or, empty, it was on its way to be filled up with fresh clams. It smelled like less-than-fresh clams, in either case, and the clam-truck driver, who was smoking a cigarette and leaning against the fly-spattered grille of the clam truck while the incoming ferry docked, was the next victim of Joe O'Hare's impromptu conversation.

"My boy here is on his way to his very first job," Minty announced, while Eddie died a little more.

"Oh, yeah?" the clam-truck driver replied.

"He's going to be a writer's assistant," proclaimed Eddie's father. "Mind you, we're not exactly sure what that might entail, but it will doubtless be more demanding than sharpening pencils, changing the typewriter ribbon, and looking up those difficult words that not even the writer himself knows how to spell! I look at it as a learning experience, whatever it turns out to be."

The clam-truck driver, suddenly grateful for the job he had, said: "Good luck, kid."

At the last minute, just before Eddie boarded the ferry, his father ran to the car and then ran back again. "I almost forgot!" he shouted, handing Eddie a fat envelope wrapped with a rubber band and a package the size and softness of a loaf of bread. The package was gift-wrapped, but something had crushed it in the backseat of the car; the present looked abandoned, unwanted. "It's for the little kid—your mother and I thought of it," Minty said.

"*What* little kid?" Eddie asked. He clutched the present and the envelope under his chin, because his heavy duffel bag—and a lighter, smaller suitcase—required both his hands. Thus he staggered on board.

"The Coles have a little girl—I think she's four!" Minty hollered. There was the rattling of chains, the chug of the boat's engine, the intermittent blasts of the ferry horn; other people were shouting their good-byes. "They had a new child to replace the *dead* ones!" Eddie's father yelled. *This* seemed to get the attention of even the clam-truck driver, who had parked his truck on board and now leaned over the rails of the upper deck.

"Oh," Eddie said. "Good-bye!" he cried.

"I love you, Edward!" his father bellowed. Then Minty O'Hare began to cry. Eddie had never seen his father cry, but Eddie had not left home before. Probably his mother had cried, too, but Eddie hadn't noticed. "Be *careful!*" his father wailed. The passengers who overhung the rails of the upper deck were all staring now. "Watch out for *her!*" his father screamed to him.

"*Who?*" Eddie cried.

"*Her!* I mean *Mrs.* Cole!" the senior O'Hare shouted.

"*Why?*" Eddie screamed. They were pulling away, the docks falling behind; the ferry horn was deafening.

"I hear she never got over it!" Minty roared. "She's a *zombie!*"

Oh, great—*now* he tells me! Eddie thought. But he just waved. He had no idea that the so-called zombie would be meeting his ferry at Orient Point; he didn't yet know that *Mr.* Cole was not allowed to drive. It peeved Eddie that his dad had not allowed him to drive on the trip to New London—on the grounds that the traffic they would be facing was "different from Exeter traffic." Eddie could still see his father on the receding Connecticut shore. Minty had turned away, his head in his hands—he was weeping.

What did he mean, a *zombie?* Eddie had expected Mrs. Cole to be like his own mother, or like the many unmemorable faculty wives who comprised almost everything he knew about women. With any luck,

Mrs. Cole *might* have a little of what Dot O'Hare would call "bohemi-anism" in her nature, although Eddie hardly dared to hope for a woman who gave such voyeuristic pleasure as Mrs. Havelock so amply provided.

In 1958, Mrs. Havelock's furry pits and swaying breasts were ab-solutely all that Eddie O'Hare thought about when he thought about women. As for girls his own age, Eddie had been unsuccessful with them; they also terrified him. Since he was a faculty brat, his few dates had been with girls from the town of Exeter, awkward acquaintances from his junior-high-school days. These town girls were more grown up now, and generally wary of the town boys who attended the acad-emy—understandably, they were anticipating being condescended to.

On Exeter dance weekends, the out-of-town girls struck Eddie as unapproachable. They arrived on trains and in buses, often from other boarding schools or from cities like Boston and New York. They were much better dressed, and seemingly more like women, than most of the faculty wives—excepting Mrs. Havelock.

Before leaving Exeter, Eddie had leafed through the pages of the '53 *PEAN,* looking for pictures of Thomas and Timothy Cole—it was their last yearbook. What he found had intimidated him greatly. Those boys had not belonged to a single club, but Thomas was pictured with both the Varsity Soccer and the Varsity Hockey teams, and Timothy, lag-ging not far behind his brother, was captured in the photographs of J.V. Soccer and J.V. Hockey. That they could kick and skate wasn't what had intimidated Eddie. It was the sheer number of snapshots, throughout the yearbook, in which both boys appeared—in the many candid pho-tos that make up a yearbook, in all those shots of the students who are unquestionably having *fun.* Thomas and Timothy always appeared to be having a ball. They'd been *happy*! Eddie realized.

Wrestling in a pile of boys in a dormitory butt room (the smokers' lounge), clowning on crutches, posing with snow shovels, or playing cards—Thomas often with a cigarette dangling from the corner of his handsome mouth. And on the academy dance weekends, the Cole boys were pictured with the prettiest girls. There was a picture of Timothy not dancing with but actually *embracing* his dance partner; there was another of Thomas *kissing* a girl—they were outdoors on a cold, snowy day, both of them in camel-hair overcoats, Thomas pulling the girl to him by the scarf around her neck. Those boys had been *popular*! (And then they had died.)

The ferry passed what looked like a shipyard; some naval vessels were in a dry dock, others floated in the water. As the ferry moved away from land, it passed a lighthouse or two. There were fewer sailboats farther out in the sound. The day had been hot and hazy inland—even earlier that morning, when Eddie had left Exeter—but on the water the wind from the northeast was cold, and the sun went in and out of the clouds.

On the upper deck, still struggling with his heavy duffel bag and the lighter, smaller suitcase—not to mention the already-mangled present for the child—Eddie repacked. The gift wrapping would suffer further abuse when Eddie shoved the present to the bottom of the duffel bag, but at least he wouldn't have to carry it under his chin. Also, he needed socks; he'd begun the day in loafers with no socks, but his feet were cold. He found a sweatshirt to wear over his T-shirt, too. Only now, his first day away from the academy, did he realize he was wearing an *Exeter* T-shirt and an *Exeter* sweatshirt. Embarrassed at what struck him as such shameless advertising of his revered school, Eddie turned the sweatshirt inside out. Only then did it occur to him why some of the seniors at the academy were in the habit of wearing *their* Exeter sweatshirts inside out; his new awareness of this height of fashion indicated to Eddie that he was ready to encounter the so-called real world—provided that there really *was* a world where Exonians were well advised to put their Exeter experiences behind them (or turn them inside out).

It was further heartening to Eddie that he was wearing jeans, despite his mother's advice that khakis would be more "appropriate"; yet although Ted Cole had written Minty that the boy could forget about a coat and tie—Eddie's summer job didn't require what Ted called the "Exeter uniform"—Eddie's father had insisted that he pack a number of dress shirts and ties, and what Minty called an "all-purpose" sports jacket.

It was when he repacked on the upper deck that Eddie first took notice of the fat envelope his father had handed him without explanation, which in itself was odd—his father explained *everything*. It was an envelope embossed with the Phillips Exeter Academy return address, and with O'HARE written in his father's neat hand. Inside the envelope were the names and addresses of every living Exonian in the Hamptons. It was the senior O'Hare's idea of being prepared for any emergency—you could always call on a fellow Exeter man for help! At a glance Eddie could see that he didn't know any of these people. There

were six names with Southampton addresses, most of them from graduating classes in the thirties and forties; one old fellow, who'd graduated with the class of 1919, was doubtless retired and probably too old
to remember that he'd ever gone to Exeter. (The man was only fifty-
seven, in fact.)

There were another three or four Exonians in East Hampton, only a
couple in Bridgehampton and Sag Harbor, and one or two others in
Amagansett and Water Mill and Sagaponack—the Coles lived in
Sagaponack, Eddie knew. He was dumbfounded. Did his dad know
nothing about him? Eddie would never dream of calling upon these
strangers, even if he were in the most dire need. Exonians! he almost
cried aloud.

Eddie knew many faculty families at Exeter; most of them, while
never taking the qualities of the academy for granted, did not inflate
beyond all reason what it meant to be an Exonian. It seemed so unfair
that his father could, out of the blue, make him feel that he *hated* Exeter; in truth, the boy knew he was lucky to be at the school. He
doubted that he would have qualified for the academy if he *hadn't* been
a faculty child, and he felt fairly well adjusted among his peers—as
well adjusted as any boy who bears an indifference to sports can be at
an all-boys' school. Indeed, given Eddie's terror of girls his own age, he
was not unhappy to be in an all-boys' school.

For example, he was careful to masturbate on his own towel or on his
own washcloth, which he then washed out and hung back in the family
bathroom where it belonged; nor did Eddie ever wrinkle the pages of
his mom's mail-order catalogs, where the various models for women's
undergarments provided all the visual stimulation his imagination
needed. (What most appealed to him were the more mature women in
girdles.) Without the catalogs, he had also happily masturbated in the
dark, where the salty taste of Mrs. Havelock's hairy armpits seemed on
the tip of his tongue—and where her heaving breasts were the soft and
rolling pillows that held his head and rocked him to sleep, where he
would often dream of her. (Mrs. Havelock doubtless performed this
valuable service for countless Exonians who passed through the academy in her prime years.)

But in what way was Mrs. Cole a *zombie*? Eddie was watching the clam-
truck driver consume a hot dog, which the driver washed down with a

beer. Although Eddie was hungry—he'd not eaten since breakfast—the slightly sideways drift of the ferry and the smell of the fuel did not incline him toward food or drink. At times the upper deck would shudder, and the entire ferry swayed. And there was the added factor of where he was seated, directly downwind of the smokestack. He began to turn a little green. It made him feel better to walk around the deck, and he decidedly perked up when he found a trash can and seized the moment to throw away his father's envelope with the names and addresses of every living Exonian in the Hamptons.

Then Eddie did something that made him feel only a little ashamed of himself: he strolled over to where the clam-truck driver sat suffering the agonies of digestion, and boldly apologized for his father. The clam-truck driver suppressed a belch.

"Don't sweat it, kid," the man said. "We all got dads."

"Yes," Eddie replied.

"Besides," the clam-truck driver philosophized, "he's probably just worried about you. It don't sound easy to me, being no *writer's* assistant. I don't get what it is you're supposed to *do*."

"I don't get it, either," Eddie confessed.

"You wanna beer?" the driver offered, but Eddie politely declined; now that he was feeling better, he didn't want to turn green again.

There were no women or girls worth looking at on the upper deck, Eddie thought; his observation was apparently not shared by the clam-truck driver, who proceeded to roam the ferry, looking intently at *all* the women and girls. There were two girls who had driven a car on board; they were full of themselves, and despite being not more than a year or two older than Eddie, or only Eddie's age, it was evident that they regarded Eddie as too young for them. Eddie looked at them only once.

A European couple approached him and asked in heavily accented English if he would take their picture as they stood at the bow—it was their honeymoon, they said. Eddie was happy to do it. Only afterward did it occur to him that the woman, being a European, might have had unshaven armpits. But she'd been wearing a long-sleeved jacket; Eddie also hadn't been able to tell if she was wearing a bra.

He returned to his heavy duffel bag and the smaller suitcase. Only his "all-purpose" sports jacket and his dress shirts and ties were in the suitcase; it weighed next to nothing, but his mother had told him that his "good" clothes, as she called them, would be sure to arrive unwrinkled that way. (His mom had packed the suitcase.) In the duffel was everything else—the clothes *he* wanted, his writing notebooks, and some books that Mr. Bennett (by *far* his favorite English teacher) had recommended to him.

Eddie had not packed Ted Cole's entire *oeuvre*. He'd read it. What was the point of carrying it with him? The only exceptions were the O'Hare family's copy of *The Mouse Crawling Between the Walls*—Eddie's father had insisted that Eddie get Mr. Cole's autograph—and Eddie's personal favorite among Ted's books for children. Like Ruth, Eddie had a personal favorite that was *not* the famous mouse between the walls. Eddie's favorite was the one called *The Door in the Floor;* it frankly scared the shit out of him. He hadn't paid close enough attention to the copyright date to realize that *The Door in the Floor* was the first book Ted Cole had published following the death of his sons. As such, it must have been a difficult book for him to write at all; it certainly reflected a little of the horror that Ted was living in those days.

If Ted's publisher hadn't felt such sympathy for Ted because of what had happened to his children, the book might have been rejected. The reviewers were almost unanimously *un*sympathetic to the book, which sold about as well as Ted's other books, anyway; his popularity appeared to be of that unassailable kind. Dot O'Hare herself had said that it would be an act of indecency bordering on child abuse to read that book aloud to any child. But Eddie was thrilled by *The Door in the Floor;* which, in fact, enjoyed a kind of cult status on college campuses—it was *that* reprehensible.

On the ferry, Eddie thumbed through *The Mouse Crawling Between the Walls*. He'd read it so many times that he didn't read a word of it again; he looked only at the illustrations, which he liked more than most book reviewers had. At best reviewers would say the illustrations were "enhancing" or "not obtrusive." More often the commentary was negative, but not *that* negative. (Such as: "The illustrations, while not detracting from the story, add little. They leave one hoping for more next time.") Yet Eddie liked them.

The imaginary monster was crawling between the walls; there it was, with its no arms and no legs, pulling itself along with its teeth, sliding forward on its fur. Better still was the illustration of the scary dress in Mommy's closet, the dress that was coming alive and trying to climb down off the hanger. It was a dress with one foot, a naked foot, protruding below the hem; and a hand, just a hand with a wrist, wriggled out of one sleeve. Most disturbing of all, the contours of a single breast seemed to swell the dress, as if a woman (or only some of her parts) were forming *inside* the dress.

Nowhere in the book was there a comforting drawing of a *real* mouse between those walls. The last illustration showed the younger of the boys, awake in bed and frightened of the approaching sound. With his small hand, the boy is hitting the wall—to make the mouse scurry away. But not only is the mouse not scurrying away; the mouse is disproportionately *huge*. It is not only bigger than both boys together; it is bigger than the headboard of the bed—bigger than the entire bed *and* the headboard.

As for Eddie's favorite book by Ted Cole, he removed it from his duffel bag and read it once more before the ferry landed. The story of *The Door in the Floor* would never be a favorite of Ruth's; her father had not told it to her, and it would be a few years before Ruth was old enough to read it for herself. She would hate it.

There was a tasteful but stark illustration of an unborn child inside its mother's womb. "There was a little boy who didn't know if he wanted to be born," the book began. "His mommy didn't know if she wanted him to be born, either.

"This is because they lived in a cabin in the woods, on an island, in a lake—and there was no one else around. And, in the cabin, there was a door in the floor.

"The little boy was afraid of what was under the door in the floor, and the mommy was afraid, too. Once, long ago, other children had come to visit the cabin, for Christmas, but the children had opened the door in the floor and they had disappeared down the hole, under the cabin, and all their presents had disappeared, too.

"Once the mommy had tried to look for the children, but when she opened the door in the floor, she heard such an awful sound that her hair turned completely white, like the hair of a ghost. And she smelled such a terrible smell that her skin became as wrinkled as a raisin. It took a whole year for the mommy's skin to be smooth again, and for her hair not to be white. And, when she'd opened the door in the floor, the mommy had also seen some horrible things that she never wanted to see again, like a snake that could make itself so small that it could sneak through the crack between the door and the floor—even when the door was closed—and then it could make itself so big again that it could carry the cabin on its back, as if the snake were a giant snail and the cabin were its shell." (*That* illustration had given Eddie O'Hare a nightmare—*not* when Eddie was a child, but when he was a sixteen-year-old!)

"The other things under the door in the floor are so horrible that you can only imagine them." (There was an indescribable illustration of these horrible things as well.)

"And so the mommy wondered if she *wanted* to have a little boy in a cabin in the woods, on an island, in a lake—and with no one else around—but especially because of everything that might be under the door in the floor. Then she thought: Why not? I'll just tell him not to open the door in the floor!

"Well, that's easy for a mommy to say, but what about the little boy? He still didn't know if he wanted to be born into a world where there was a door in the floor, and no one else around. Yet there were also some beautiful things in the woods, and on the island, and in the lake." (Here there was an illustration of an owl, and of the ducks that swam ashore on the island, and of a pair of loons nuzzling on the still water of the lake.)

"Why not take a chance? the little boy thought. And so he was born, and he was very happy. His mommy was happy again, too, although she told the little boy at least once every day, 'Don't you ever, not *ever*—never, never, *never*—open the door in the floor!' But of course he was only a little boy. If *you* were that boy, wouldn't you want to open that door in the floor?"

And *that*, thought Eddie O'Hare, is the end of the story—never realizing that, in the *real* story, the little boy was a little girl. Her name was Ruth, and her mommy *wasn't* happy. There was another kind of door in the floor that Eddie didn't know about—not yet.

The ferry had come through Plum Gut. Orient Point was now clearly in sight.

Eddie took a good look at the jacket photographs of Ted Cole. The author photo on *The Door in the Floor* was more recent than the one on *The Mouse Crawling Between the Walls*. In both, Mr. Cole struck Eddie as a handsome man, suggesting to the sixteen-year-old that a man of the advanced age of forty-five could still move the hearts and minds of the ladies. A man like that would be sure to stand out in any crowd at Orient Point. Eddie didn't know that he should have been looking for Marion.

Once the ferry was secured in the slip, Eddie scanned the unimpressive gathering on shore from the vantage of the upper deck; there was no one who matched the elegant jacket photos. He's *forgotten* about me! Eddie thought. For some reason, this inspired Eddie to think spiteful thoughts about his father—so much for Exonians!

From the upper deck, however, Eddie did see a beautiful woman waving to someone on board; she was so striking that Eddie didn't want to see the man she might be waving to. (He assumed that she must have been waving to a man.) The woman was so distractingly gorgeous, she made it difficult for Eddie to keep looking for Ted. Eddie's eyes kept coming back to *her*—she was waving up a storm. (From the corner of his eye, Eddie saw someone drive off the ferry into the stony sand of the beach, where the car instantly stalled.)

Eddie was among the last of the stragglers to disembark, carrying his heavy duffel bag in one hand, and the lighter, smaller suitcase in the other. He was shocked to see that the woman of such breathtaking beauty was standing exactly where she'd been when he'd first spotted her, and she was still waving. She was dead-ahead of him—and she appeared to be waving at *him*. He was afraid he was going to bump into her. She was close enough for him to touch her—he could smell her, and she smelled wonderful—when, suddenly, she reached out and took the lighter, smaller suitcase from his hand.

"Hello, Eddie," she said.

If he died a little whenever his father spoke to strangers, Eddie now knew what it meant to *really* die: his breath was gone, he couldn't speak.

"I thought you'd never see me," the beautiful woman said.

From that moment on, he would never *stop* seeing her, not in his mind's eye—not whenever he closed his eyes and tried to sleep. She would always be there.

"Mrs. Cole?" he managed to whisper.

"Marion," she said.

He couldn't say her name. With his heavy bag, he struggled to follow her to the car. So what if she wore a bra? He had noticed her breasts nonetheless. And in her sleek, long-sleeved sweater, there was no knowing if she shaved her armpits. What did it matter? The coarse hair of Mrs. Havelock's armpits that had once so thoroughly engaged him, not to mention her floppy tits, had receded into the distant past; he felt only a mute embarrassment at the very idea that someone as *ordinary* as Mrs. Havelock had ever stirred an iota of desire in him.

When they arrived at the car—a Mercedes-Benz the dusty red of a tomato—Marion handed him the keys.

"You can drive, can't you?" she asked. Eddie still couldn't speak. "I know boys your age—you love to drive every chance you get, don't you?"

"Yes, ma'am," he replied.

"Marion," she repeated.

"I was expecting Mr. Cole," he explained.

"Ted," Marion said.

These weren't Exeter rules. At the academy—and, by extension, in his family, because the *atmosphere* of the academy was where he had truly grown up—it was "sir" and "ma'am" to everyone; it had been Mr. and Mrs. *Everybody*. Now it was Ted and Marion; here was another world.

When he sat in the driver's seat, the accelerator and brake and clutch pedals were the perfect distance away from him; he and Marion were the same height. The thrill of this discovery was immediately moderated, however, by his awareness of his immense erection; his hugely evident hard-on brushed the bottom of the steering wheel. And then the clam truck drove slowly past—the driver had noticed Marion, too, of course.

"Nice job if you can get it, kid!" the clam-truck driver called.

When Eddie turned the key in the ignition, the Mercedes gave a responsive purr. When Eddie stole a look at Marion, he saw that she was evaluating him in a way that was as foreign to him as her car was.

"I don't know where we're going," he confessed to her.

"Just drive," Marion told the boy. "I'll give you all the directions you need."

A Masturbating Machine

For the first month of that summer, Ruth and the writer's assistant rarely saw each other. They did not meet in the kitchen of the Coles' house, largely because Eddie ate none of his meals there. And although the four-year-old and the writer's assistant slept in the same house, their bedtimes were considerably different, their bedrooms far apart. In the morning, Ruth had already eaten her breakfast, with either her mother or her father, before Eddie got up. By the time Eddie was awake, the first of the child's three nannies had arrived, and Marion had already driven Ruth and the nanny to the beach. If the weather was unsuitable for the beach, Ruth and her nanny would play in the nursery, or in the virtually unused living room of the big house.

That the house was vast made it immediately exotic to Eddie O'Hare; he had first grown up in a small faculty apartment in an Exeter dormitory—later, in a not much larger faculty house. But that Ted and Marion had *separated*—that they never slept in the same house together—was an unfamiliarity of far greater magnitude (and cause for speculation) for Eddie than the size of Ted and Marion's house. That her parents had separated was a new and mysterious change in Ruth's life as well; the four-year-old had no less difficulty adjusting to the oddity of it than Eddie had.

Regardless of what the separation implied to Ruth and Eddie about the future, the first month of that summer was chiefly confusing. On the nights when Ted stayed in the rental house, Eddie had to go fetch him with the car in the morning; Ted liked to be in his workroom no later than ten A.M., which gave Eddie time to drive to the Sagaponack General Store and post office en route. Eddie picked up the mail, and coffee and muffins for them both. On the nights when Marion stayed in the rental house, Eddie still picked up the mail but he got breakfast only for himself—Ted had eaten earlier with Ruth. And Marion could drive her own car. When he wasn't running errands, which he did frequently, Eddie spent much of his day working in the empty rental house.

This work, which was undemanding, varied from answering some of Ted's fan mail to retyping Ted's handwritten revisions of the extremely short *A Sound Like Someone Trying Not to Make a Sound.* At least twice a week, Ted added a sentence or deleted one; he also added and deleted commas—he changed semicolons to dashes and then back to semicolons. (In Eddie's opinion, Ted was going through a punctuation crisis.) At best, a brand-new paragraph would be raggedly created—Ted's typing was terrible—and then instantly and messily revised in pencil. At worst, the same paragraph would be cut entirely by the next evening.

Eddie did not open or read Ted's mail, and most of the letters that Eddie retyped for Ted were Ted's replies to children. Ted would write to the mothers himself. Eddie never saw what the mothers wrote to Ted, or Ted's responses to them. (When Ruth would hear her father's typewriter at night—*only* at night—what she was hearing, more often than a children's-book-in-progress, was a letter to a young mother.)

The arrangements that couples make in order to maintain civility in the midst of their journey to divorce are often most elaborate when the professed top priority is to protect a child. Notwithstanding that the four-year-old Ruth would witness her mother being mounted from behind by a sixteen-year-old boy, Ruth's parents would never raise their voices in anger toward, or in hatred of, each other—nor would her mother or her father ever speak truly ill of the other to Ruth. In this aspect of their destroyed marriage, Ted and Marion were models of decent behavior. Never mind that the arrangements concerning the rental house were as seedy as the unfortunate dwelling itself. Ruth never had to inhabit that house.

In the real estate parlance of the Hamptons in 1958, it was a so-called carriage house; in reality, it was an airless one-bedroom apartment that had been hastily assembled and cheaply furnished over a two-car garage. It was on Bridge Lane in Bridgehampton—not more than two miles from the Coles' house on Parsonage Lane in Sagaponack—and, by night, it sufficed as a place for Ted or Marion to sleep far enough away from the other. By day, it was where the writer's assistant worked.

The kitchen of the carriage house was never used for cooking; the kitchen table—there was no dining room—was stacked with unanswered mail or letters-in-progress. It was Eddie's desk by day, and Ted took his turn at that typewriter on the nights he stayed there. The kitchen was supplied with all sorts of booze, and with coffee and tea— period. The living room, which was simply an extension of the kitchen, had a TV and a couch, where Ted would periodically pass out while watching a baseball game; he never turned on the television unless there was a ball game or a boxing match. Marion, if she couldn't sleep, would watch late-night movies.

The bedroom closet contained nothing but an emergency ration of Ted's and Marion's clothes. The bedroom was never dark enough; there was an uncurtained skylight, which often leaked. Marion—both to keep out the light and to restrain the leak—tacked a towel over the skylight, but when Ted stayed there, he took the towel down. Without the skylight, he might not have known when to get up; there was no clock, and Ted often went to bed without knowing when or where he'd taken off his watch.

The same maid who cleaned the Coles' house would stop at the carriage house, too, but only to vacuum it and change the linen. Maybe because the carriage house was within smelling distance of the bridge where the crabbers fished for crabs—usually with raw chicken parts for bait—the one-bedroom apartment had a permanent odor of poultry and brine. And because the landlord used the two-car garage for his cars, Ted and Marion and Eddie would all comment on the permanence with which the odor of motor oil and gasoline lingered in the air.

If anything improved the place, albeit slightly, it was the few photographs of Thomas and Timothy that Marion had brought along. She'd taken the photos from Eddie's guest bedroom in the Coles' house, and from the adjoining guest bathroom, which was also his. (Eddie couldn't have known that the small number of picture hooks left in the bare walls was a harbinger of the greater number of picture hooks that would soon be exposed. Nor could he have predicted the many, many years he would be haunted by the image of the noticeably darker wallpaper where the photographs of the dead boys had been hung and then removed.)

There were still *some* photographs of Thomas and Timothy left in Eddie's guest bedroom and bathroom; he looked at them often. There was one with Marion that he looked at the most. In the photo, which had been taken in the morning sunlight in a hotel room in Paris, Marion is lying in an old-fashioned feather bed; she looks tousled and sleepy, and happy. Beside her head on the pillow is a child's bare foot—with only a partial view of the child's leg, in pajamas, disappearing under the bedcovers. Far away, at the other end of the bed, is another bare foot—logically belonging to a second child, not only because of the sizable distance between the bare feet but also because of a *different* pair of pajamas on this second leg.

Eddie could not have known that the hotel room was in Paris—it was in the once-charming Hôtel du Quai Voltaire, where the Coles stayed when Ted was promoting the French translation of *The Mouse Crawling Between the Walls*. Nevertheless Eddie recognized that there was something foreign, probably European, about the bed and the surrounding furnishings. Eddie also assumed that the bare feet belonged to Thomas and Timothy, and that Ted had taken the photograph.

There are Marion's bare shoulders—only the shoulder straps of her slip or camisole are showing—and one of her bare arms. A partial view of its armpit suggested that Marion kept her armpits cleanly shaven. Marion must have been twelve years younger in the photograph—still in her twenties, although she looked much the same to Eddie now. (Only not so happy.) Maybe it was the effect of the morning sunlight slanting across the pillows of the bed that made her hair appear more blond.

Like all the other photographs of Thomas and Timothy, it was an eight-by-ten enlargement that had been expensively matted and framed under glass. By removing the photograph from the wall, Eddie could prop it on the chair beside his bed in such a way that Marion was facing him as he lay on the bed and masturbated. To enhance the illusion that her smile was meant for him, Eddie had only to remove from his mind the children's bare feet. The best way to accomplish this was to remove their bare feet from his sight as well; two scraps of notepaper, which he affixed to the glass with Scotch tape, did the trick.

This activity had become his nightly ritual when, one night, Eddie was interrupted. Just as he'd begun to beat off, there was a knock on the bedroom door, which had no lock, and Ted said, "Eddie? Are you awake? I saw the light. May we come in?"

Eddie, understandably, scrambled. He jumped into a still-wet and exceedingly clammy bathing suit that had been drying on the arm of the bedside chair, and he hastily rushed into the bathroom with the photograph, which he crookedly returned to its place on the bathroom wall. "Coming!" he cried. Only as he opened the door did he remember the two scraps of notepaper that were still taped to the glass, hiding from view the existence of Thomas's and Timothy's feet. And he'd left the door to the bathroom open. It was too late to do anything about it; Ted, with Ruth in his arms, was already standing in the doorway of the guest bedroom.

"Ruth had a dream," her father said. "Didn't you, Ruthie?"

"Yes," the child said. "It wasn't very nice."

"She wanted to be sure that one of the photographs was still here. I know it isn't one that her mommy took to the other house," Ted explained.

"Oh," said Eddie, who could feel the child staring right through him.

"There's a story to every picture," Ted told Eddie. "Ruth knows all the stories—don't you, Ruthie?"

"Yes," the child said again. "There it is!" the four-year-old cried, pointing to the photograph that hung above the night table, near Eddie's rumpled bed. The bedside chair, which had been pulled close to the bed (for Eddie's purposes), was not where it should have been; Ted, holding Ruth, had to step awkwardly around it in order to look more closely at the photograph.

In the picture, Timothy, who has skinned his knee, is sitting on the countertop in a large kitchen. Thomas, demonstrating a clinical interest in his brother's injury, is standing beside him, a roll of gauze in one hand, a roll of adhesive tape in the other, playing doctor to the bloody knee. Maybe Timothy (at the time) was a year older than Ruth. Maybe Thomas was seven.

"His knee is bleeding, but he's going to be all right?" Ruth asked her father.

"He's going to be fine—he just needs a bandage," Ted told the child.

"No stitches? No needle?" Ruth asked.

"No, Ruthie. Just a bandage."

"He's just a *little* broken, but he's not going to die—right?" Ruth asked.

"Right," Ted said.

"Not yet," the four-year-old added.

"That's right, Ruthie."

"There's just a *little* blood," Ruth observed.

"Ruth cut herself today," Ted explained to Eddie. He showed Eddie the Band-Aid on the child's heel. "She stepped on a shell at the beach. And then she had a dream...."

Ruth, satisfied with the skinned-knee story and with that photograph, was now looking over her father's shoulder; something in the bathroom had caught her attention.

"Where are the feet?" the four-year-old asked.

"*What* feet, Ruthie?"

Eddie was already moving to block their view of the bathroom.

"What did you did?" Ruth asked Eddie. "What happened to the feet?"

"Ruthie, what are you talking about?" Ted asked. He was drunk; but even drunk, Ted was reasonably steady on his feet.

Ruth pointed at Eddie. "Feet!" she said crossly.

"Ruthie—don't be rude!" Ted told her.

"Is pointing rude?" the child asked.

"You know it is," her father replied. "I'm sorry to bother you, Eddie. We have this habit of showing Ruth the photographs when she wants to see them. But, not wanting to intrude upon your privacy ... she hasn't seen much of them lately."

"You can come see the pictures whenever you want," Eddie said to the child, who kept scowling at him.

They were in the hall outside Eddie's bedroom when Ted said, "Say 'Good night, Eddie'—okay, Ruthie?"

"Where are the feet?" the four-year-old repeated to Eddie. She kept staring right through him. "What did you did?"

They went off down the hall with her father saying, "I'm surprised at you, Ruthie. It's not like you to be rude."

"I'm *not* rude," Ruth said crossly.

"Well." That was all Eddie heard Ted say. Naturally, after they left, Eddie went straight to the bathroom and removed the scraps of notepaper from the dead boys' feet; with a wet washcloth he rubbed any trace of the Scotch tape off the glass.

For the first month of that summer, Eddie O'Hare would be a masturbating machine, but he would never again take Marion's photograph off the bathroom wall—nor would he again consider concealing Thomas's and Timothy's feet. Instead, he masturbated almost every morning in the carriage house, where he thought he would not be interrupted—or caught in the act.

On the mornings after Marion had slept there, Eddie was pleased to discover that her scent was still on the pillows of the unmade bed. Other mornings, the feel and smell of some article of her clothing would sufficiently arouse him. In the closet, Marion kept a slip or some sort of nightie that she slept in; there was a drawer with her bras and panties. Eddie kept hoping that she would leave her pink cashmere cardigan in the closet, that one she'd been wearing when he first met her; he often dreamed of her in it. But the cheap apartment above the two-car garage had no fans, and the stifling heat of the place was unrelieved by any worthwhile cross ventilation. While the Coles' house in Sagaponack was usually cool and breezy even in the warmest weather, the rental house in Bridgehampton was claustrophobic and hot. It was too much for Eddie to hope that Marion would ever have any need of that pink cashmere cardigan there.

Notwithstanding the drives to Montauk and back for the evil-smelling squid ink, Eddie's job as a writer's assistant amounted to an easy nine-to-five day, for which Ted Cole paid him fifty dollars a week. Eddie charged the gas for Ted's car, which was not nearly as much fun to drive as Marion's Mercedes. Ted's '57 Chevy was black and white, which perhaps reflected the graphic artist's narrow range of interests.

In the evenings, around five or six, Eddie often went to the beach to swim—or else to run, which he did infrequently and halfheartedly. Sometimes the surf casters were fishing; they raced their trucks along the beach, chasing after the schools of fish. Driven ashore by the bigger fish, minnows were flopping on the wet, hard-packed sand—yet another reason why Eddie had little interest in running there.

Every evening, with Ted's permission, Eddie would drive to East Hampton or Southampton to see a movie or just eat a hamburger. He paid for the movies (and for everything he ate) out of the salary that Ted gave him, and he still saved more than twenty dollars every week. One evening, at a movie in Southampton, he saw Marion.

She was alone in the audience, and she was wearing the pink cashmere cardigan. It was not a night when it was her turn to stay in the carriage house, so it was not likely that the pink cashmere cardigan would end up in the closet of the seedy apartment above the two-car garage. Yet after that sighting of Marion alone, Eddie would look for her car in both Southampton and East Hampton. Although he spotted it once or twice, he never saw Marion in a movie theater again.

She went out nearly every evening; she rarely ate with Ruth and she never cooked for herself. Eddie presumed that if Marion was going out to dinner, she was eating in a better class of restaurant than he usually chose. He also knew that if he started looking for her in the *good* restaurants, his fifty dollars per week wouldn't last long.

As for how Ted spent *his* nights, it was clear only that he couldn't drive. He kept a bicycle at the rental house, but Eddie had never seen him ride it. Then one night, when Marion was out, the phone rang in the Coles' house and the nighttime nanny answered; the caller was the bartender of a bar and restaurant in Bridgehampton, where (the bartender said) Mr. Cole ate and drank almost every night. On this particular night, Mr. Cole had looked atypically unsteady on his bicycle when he'd left. The bartender was calling to express his hope that Mr. Cole was now safe at home.

Eddie drove to Bridgehampton and followed the route he guessed Ted would take to the rental house. Sure enough, there was Ted, pedaling at first in the middle of Ocean Road, and then—as Eddie's headlights illuminated him—veering off the road onto the soft shoulder. Eddie stopped the car and asked if he wanted a ride. Ted had less than a half-mile to go.

"I *have* a ride!" Ted told him, waving him on.

And one morning, after Ted had slept in the carriage house, there was another woman's smell on the bedroom pillows; it was much stronger than Marion's scent. So he has another woman! Eddie thought, not yet knowing Ted's pattern with the young mothers. (The pretty young mother of the moment came to model three mornings a week— at first with her child, a little boy, but then alone.)

In explanation of his and Marion's separation, all Ted had said to Eddie was that it was unfortunate that his coming to work had to coincide with "such a sad time in such a long marriage." Although the statement implied that the so-called sad time might pass, the more the boy saw of the distance that Ted and Marion maintained, the more he believed that the marriage was finished. Besides, Ted had claimed only that it was a "long" marriage; he hadn't said the marriage was ever good or happy.

Yet, if only in the many photographs of Thomas and Timothy, Eddie saw that something *had been* both good and happy, and that the

Coles had once had friends. There were pictures of dinner parties with other families, couples with children; Thomas and Timothy had had birthday parties with other children, too. Although Marion and Ted made infrequent appearances in the photographs—Thomas and Timothy (even if only their *feet*) were the main subject of every photo— there was sufficient evidence that Ted and Marion had once been happy, if not necessarily happy with each other. Even if their marriage had *never* been good, Ted and Marion had had a multitude of good times with their boys.

Eddie O'Hare could not personally remember as many good times as he saw excessively depicted in those photographs. But what had happened to Ted and Marion's friends? Eddie wondered. Excepting the nannies, and the models (or model), there was never anyone around.

If, as a four-year-old, Ruth Cole already understood that Thomas and Timothy now inhabited another world, as far as Eddie was concerned, those boys had *come* from another world as well. They'd been loved.

Whatever Ruth was learning to do, she was learning it from her nannies; for the most part, the nannies had failed to impress Eddie. The first one was a local girl with a thuggish-looking boyfriend who was a local, too—or so Eddie, from his Exonian perspective, assumed. The boyfriend was a lifeguard who possessed the essential imperviousness to boredom that all lifeguards must have. The thug dropped the nanny off every morning, glowering at Eddie if he chanced to see him. This was the nanny who regularly took Ruth to the beach, where the lifeguard was tanning himself.

In the first month of that summer, Marion, who usually drove the nanny and Ruth to the beach and later picked them up, asked Eddie to perform the chore only once or twice. The nanny had not spoken to him, and Ruth—to Eddie's shame—had asked him (once again), "Where are the feet?"

The afternoon nanny was a college girl who drove her own car. Her name was Alice, and she was too superior to Eddie to speak to him— except to say that she'd once known someone who'd gone to Exeter. Naturally he'd graduated from the academy before Eddie had started, and Alice knew only his first name, which was either Chickie or Chuckie.

"Probably a nickname," Eddie had said stupidly.

Alice had sighed and looked pityingly upon him. Eddie feared that he had inherited his father's penchant for saying the obvious—and that he would soon be spontaneously dubbed with a name like Minty, which would stick to him for the rest of his life.

The college-girl nanny also had a summer job in one of the restaurants in the Hamptons, but it was not a place where Eddie ever ate. She was pretty, too, so that Eddie could never look at her without feeling ashamed.

The nighttime nanny was a married woman whose husband had a daytime job. She sometimes brought her two kids, who were older than Ruth but played respectfully with Ruth's innumerable toys—mostly dolls and dollhouses, which were largely ignored by the four-year-old. Ruth preferred to draw, or to have stories read to her. She had a professional artist's easel in her nursery; the easel had the legs sawed off. The only doll Ruth was attached to was a doll missing a head.

Of the three nannies, the nighttime nanny was the only one who was friendly to Eddie, but Eddie went out every night. And when he was home, he tended to stay in his room. His guest bedroom and bathroom were at the far end of the long upstairs hall; when Eddie wanted to write letters to his mom and dad, or just write in his notebooks, he was almost always left alone there. In his letters home, he neglected to tell his parents that Ted and Marion were separated for the summer—not to mention that he regularly masturbated to Marion's scent while clinging to her slinky clothes.

On the morning when Marion caught Eddie in the act of masturbating, Eddie had elaborately arranged upon the bed a veritable reassembly of Marion herself. There was a peach-colored blouse of a thin, summer-weight material—suitable for the stifling carriage house— and a bra of a matching color. Eddie had left the blouse unbuttoned. The bra, which was positioned roughly where one would expect a bra to be, was partially exposed but still caught up in the blouse—as if Marion were in this specific stage of undress. This gave to her clothes the appearance of passion, or at least of haste. Her panties, which were also peach-colored, were placed the right way (waist up, crotch down) and they were the correct distance from the bra—that is, if Marion had actually been wearing the bra and the panties. Eddie, who was naked— and who always masturbated by rubbing his penis with his left hand against the inside of his right thigh—had pressed his face into the open blouse and bra. With his right hand, he stroked the unimaginable silky softness of Marion's panties.

Marion needed only a fraction of a second to realize that Eddie was naked, and to recognize what he was doing—and with what visual and tactile aids!—but when Eddie first spotted her, she was neither entering nor leaving the bedroom. She was standing as still as an apparition of herself, which Eddie must have hoped she was; also, it was not exactly Marion herself but rather her reflection in the bedroom mirror that Eddie saw first. Marion, who could see Eddie in the mirror *and* Eddie himself, had been given the unique opportunity of seeing *two* of him masturbate at once.

She was gone from the doorway as quickly as she'd appeared. Eddie, who had not yet ejaculated, knew not only that she'd seen him, but also that, in a split second, she'd understood everything about him.

"I'm sorry, Eddie," Marion was saying from the kitchen, as he struggled to put away her clothes. "I should have knocked."

When he'd dressed himself, he still didn't dare leave the bedroom. He half-expected to hear her footsteps on the stairs down to the garage—or, more mercifully, to hear her Mercedes driving away. Instead she was waiting for him. And since he hadn't heard her footsteps come *up* the stairs from the garage, he knew that he must have been moaning.

"Eddie, it's *my* fault," Marion was saying. "I'm *not* angry. I'm just embarrassed."

"I'm embarrassed, too," he mumbled from the bedroom.

"It's all right—it's *natural*," Marion said. "I *know* boys your age. . . ." Her voice trailed away.

When he finally got up his nerve to go to her, she was sitting on the couch. "Come here—at least *look* at me!" she said, but he stood frozen, staring at his feet. "Eddie, it's *funny*. Let's call it funny and leave it at that."

"It's funny," he said miserably.

"Eddie! Come here!" she ordered.

He shuffled slowly in her direction, his eyes still downcast.

"Sit!" she commanded, but the best he could do was perch rigidly at the far end of the couch—away from her. "No, *here*." She patted the couch between them. He couldn't move.

"Eddie, Eddie—I *know* boys your age," she said again. "It's what boys your age *do*, isn't it? Can you imagine *not* doing it?" she asked him.

"No," he whispered. He started to cry—he couldn't stop.

"Oh, don't *cry!*" Marion insisted. She never cried now—she had cried herself out.

Then Marion was sitting so close to him that he felt the couch cave in, and he found himself leaning against her. He kept crying while she talked and talked. "Eddie, listen to me, *please,*" she said. "I thought one of Ted's women was wearing my clothes—sometimes my clothes looked wrinkled, or they were on the wrong hangers. But it was *you*, and you were actually being *nice*—you even *folded* my underwear! Or you tried to. I never fold my panties or my bras. I knew *Ted* wasn't touching them," she added, while Eddie wept. "Oh, Eddie—I'm *flattered*. Really, I *am!* It's not been the best summer—I'm happy to know that *someone* is thinking about me."

She paused; she seemed suddenly more embarrassed than Eddie. She quickly said: "Oh, I don't mean to assume that you *were* thinking about me. Goodness, that's rather conceited of me, isn't it? Maybe it was just my clothes. I'm *still* flattered, even if it was just my clothes. You probably have lots of girls to think about..."

"I think about *you!*" Eddie blurted out. "Only you."

"Then don't be embarrassed," Marion said. "You've made an old lady *happy!*"

"You're not an old lady!" he cried.

"You're making me happier and happier, Eddie." She stood up quickly, as if she were about to go. At last he dared to look at her. When she saw his expression, she said, "Be careful how you feel about me, Eddie. I mean, take care of yourself," she warned him.

"I love you," he said bravely.

She sat down beside him, as urgently as if he'd begun to cry again. "*Don't* love me, Eddie," she said, with more gravity than he'd expected. "Just think about my *clothes*. Clothes can't hurt you." Leaning closer to him, but *not* flirtatiously, she said: "Tell me. Is there something you especially like—I mean something that I *wear*?" He stared at her in such a way that she repeated, "Just think about my *clothes*, Eddie."

"What you were wearing when I met you," Eddie told her.

"Goodness!" Marion said. "I don't remember..."

"A pink sweater—it buttons up the front."

"*That* old thing!" Marion shrieked. She was on the verge of laughter; Eddie realized that he'd never seen her laugh. He was totally absorbed by her. If at first he hadn't been able to look at her, now he couldn't stop looking. "Well, if *that's* what you like," Marion was saying, "maybe I'll surprise you!" She stood up again—again quickly. Now he felt like crying because he could see that she was going to go. By the door to the stairs, she took a tougher tone. "Not so serious, Eddie—not so serious."

"I love you," he repeated.

"*Don't*," she reminded him. Needless to say, he would have a distracted day.

And not long after their encounter, he returned one night from a movie in Southampton to find her standing in his bedroom. The nighttime nanny had gone home. He knew instantly, with a broken heart, that she was *not* there to seduce him. She began talking about some of the photographs in his guest bedroom and bathroom; she was sorry to intrude, but—out of respect for his privacy—she didn't allow herself to come in his room and look at the pictures unless he was out. She had been thinking about one of the pictures in particular—she wouldn't tell him which one—and she had stayed to look at it a little longer than she'd intended.

When she said good night, and left him, he was more miserable than he'd thought humanly possible. But just before he went to bed, he realized that she'd folded his stray clothes. She'd also taken a towel from its customary position on the shower-curtain rod, and she'd returned it, neatly, to the towel rack, where it belonged. Finally, although it was the most obvious, Eddie noticed that his bed was made. He never made it—nor, at least at the rental house, did Marion ever make her own!

Two mornings later, after he deposited the mail on the kitchen table of the carriage house, he started to make coffee. While the coffee was brewing, he entered the bedroom. At first he thought it was *Marion* on the bed, but it was only her pink cashmere cardigan. (*Only!*) She had left the buttons unbuttoned and the long sleeves of the sweater pulled back, as if an invisible woman in the cardigan had clasped her invisible hands behind her invisible head. Where the buttons were open, a bra showed itself; it was a more seductive display than any arrangement of her clothing Eddie had made. The bra was white—as were the panties, which Marion had placed exactly where Eddie liked them.

Come Hither . . .

In that summer of '58, Ted Cole's young mother of the moment—the furtive Mrs. Vaughn—was small and dark and feral-looking. For a month, all Eddie had seen of her was in Ted's drawings. And Eddie had seen only those drawings where Mrs. Vaughn was posed with her son, who was also small and dark and feral-looking, which strongly suggested to Eddie that the two of them might be inclined to bite people. The elfin features of Mrs. Vaughn's face and her too-youthful pixie haircut could not conceal something violent, or at least unstable, in the young mother's temperament. And her son seemed on the verge of spitting and hissing like a cornered cat—maybe he didn't like to pose.

When Mrs. Vaughn first came to model *alone,* her movements—from her car to the Coles' house, and back to her car again—were especially furtive. She shot a glance toward any sound and in every direction like an animal anticipating an attack. Mrs. Vaughn was on the lookout for Marion, of course, but Eddie, who didn't yet know that Mrs. Vaughn was posing *nude*—not to mention that it was Mrs. Vaughn's strong smell that he (*and* Marion) had detected on the pillows in the carriage-house apartment—mistakenly concluded that the little woman was nervous to the point of derangement.

Besides, Eddie was too consumed by his thoughts of Marion to pay much attention to Mrs. Vaughn. Although Marion had not repeated the mischief of creating that replica of herself so alluringly arranged on the bed in the rental house, Eddie's own manipulations of Marion's pink cashmere cardigan, which was redolent of her delectable scent, continued to satisfy the sixteen-year-old to a degree that he had never been satisfied before.

Eddie O'Hare inhabited a kind of masturbatory heaven. He should have stayed there—he should have taken up permanent residence. As Eddie would soon discover, to have more of Marion than what he already possessed would not content him. But Marion was in control of their relationship; if anything more was to happen between them, it would happen only upon Marion's initiation.

It began by her taking him out to dinner. She drove, without asking him if he wanted to drive. To his surprise, Eddie was grateful to his father for insisting that he pack some dress shirts and ties and an "all-purpose" sports jacket. But when Marion saw him in his traditional Exeter uniform, she told him that he could dispense with either the tie or the jacket—where they were going, he didn't need both. The restaurant, in East Hampton, was less fancy than Eddie had expected, and it was clear that the waiters were used to seeing Marion there; they kept bringing her wine—she had three glasses—without her having to ask.

She was more talkative than Eddie had known her to be. "I was already pregnant with Thomas when I married Ted—when I was only a year older than you are," she told him. (The difference in their ages was a recurrent theme for her.) "When you were born, I was twenty-three. When you're my age, I'll be sixty-two," she went on. And twice she made a reference to her gift to him: the pink cashmere cardigan. "How did you like my little surprise?" she asked.

"Very much!" he stammered.

Quickly changing the subject, she told him that Ted had not really dropped out of Harvard. He'd been asked to take a leave of absence— "for 'nonperformance,' I think he called it," Marion said.

On every book jacket, in the part about the author, it always stated that Ted Cole was a Harvard dropout. Apparently this half-truth pleased him: it conveyed that he had been smart enough to get into Harvard and original enough not to care about staying there. "But the truth is, he was just lazy," Marion said. "He never wanted to work very hard." After a pause, she asked Eddie: "And how's the work going for you?"

"There's not much to do," he confided to her.

"No, I can't imagine that there is," she replied. "Ted hired you because he needed a driver."

Marion had not finished high school when she met Ted and he got her pregnant. But over the years, when Thomas and Timothy were growing up, she had passed a high-school equivalency exam; and, on various college campuses around New England, she'd completed courses part-time. It had taken ten years for her to graduate, from the University of New Hampshire in 1952—only a year before her sons were killed. She took mostly literature and history courses, many more than were necessary for a college degree; her unwillingness to enroll in the other courses that were required had delayed her getting a diploma. "Finally," she told Eddie, "I wanted a college degree only because Ted didn't have one."

Thomas and Timothy had been proud of her for graduating. "I was just getting ready to be a writer when they died," Marion confided to Eddie. "That finished it."

"You were a *writer*?" Eddie asked her. "Why'd you stop?"

She told him that she couldn't keep turning to her innermost thoughts when all she thought about was the death of her boys; she couldn't allow herself to imagine freely, because her imagination would inevitably lead her to Thomas and Timothy. "And to think that I used to *like* to be alone with my thoughts," she told Eddie. Marion doubted Ted had *ever* liked to be alone with his. "That's why he keeps his stories so short, and they're for children. That's why he draws and draws and draws."

Eddie, not realizing how sick he had become of hamburgers, ate an enormous meal.

"Not even love can daunt the appetite of a sixteen-year-old boy!" Marion observed. Eddie blushed; he wasn't supposed to say how much he loved her. She hadn't liked that.

And then she told him that when she'd displayed her pink cashmere cardigan on the bed for him, and especially as she'd chosen the accompanying bra and panties and was arranging these in their respective places—"for the imagined act," as she put it—she had been aware that this was her first creative impulse since the death of her sons; it had also been her first and only moment of what she called "pure fun." The alleged purity of such fun is debatable, but Eddie would never have questioned the sincerity of Marion's intentions; it hurt his feelings only slightly that what was love to him was merely "fun" for her. Even at sixteen, he should have better understood the forewarning she was giving him.

When Marion had met Ted, Ted introduced himself as a "recent" Harvard dropout who was writing a novel; in truth, he'd been out of Harvard for four years. He was taking courses in a Boston art school. He'd always known how to draw—he called himself "self-taught." (The courses at the art school were not as interesting to him as the models.)

In the first year they were married, Ted had gone to work for a lithographer; he'd instantly hated the job. "Ted would have hated *any* job,"

Marion told Eddie. Ted had learned to hate lithography, too; nor was he interested in etching. ("I'm not a copper or stone sort of man," he'd told Marion.)

Ted Cole published his first novel in 1937, when Thomas was a year old and Marion was not yet pregnant with Timothy. The reviews were mostly favorable, and the sales were well above average for a first novel. Ted and Marion decided to have a second child. The reviews of the next novel—in '39, a year after Timothy was born—were neither favorable nor numerous; the second book sold only half as many copies as the first. Ted's third novel, which was published in 1941—"a year before you were born," Marion reminded Eddie—was hardly reviewed at all, and only *un*favorably. The sales were so low that Ted's publisher refused to tell him the final figures. And then, in '42—when Thomas and Timothy were six and four—*The Mouse Crawling Between the Walls* was published. The war would delay the numerous foreign translations, but even before them it was clear that Ted Cole never had to hate a job or write a novel again.

"Tell me," Marion asked Eddie. "Does it give you the shivers to know that you and *The Mouse Crawling Between the Walls* were born in the same year?"

"It does," Eddie admitted to her.

But why so *many* college towns? (The Coles had lived all over New England.)

Ted's sexual pattern was behaviorally messy. Ted had told Marion that college and university towns were the best places to bring up children. The quality of the local schools was generally high; the community was stimulated by the cultural activities and the sporting events on campus. In addition, Marion could continue her education. And *socially*, Ted told her, the faculty families would be good company; at first Marion had not realized how many young mothers could be counted among those faculty wives.

Ted, who eschewed anything resembling a real job on the faculty—also, he wasn't qualified for one—nevertheless gave a lecture every semester on the art of writing and drawing for children; often these lectures were sponsored jointly by the Department of Fine Arts and the English Department. Ted would always be the first to say that the process of creating a book for children was *not* an art, in his humble opinion; he preferred to call it a craft.

But Ted's truest "craft," Marion observed, was his systematic discovery and seduction of the prettiest and unhappiest of the young mothers among the faculty wives; an occasional student would fall prey to Ted, too, but the young mothers were more vulnerable game.

It is not unusual for love affairs to end bitterly, and as the marriages of the more unfortunate of these faculty wives were already frail, it was not surprising that many couples were permanently parted by Ted's amorous adventures.

"And that's why we were always moving," Marion told Eddie.

In the college and university towns, they easily found houses to rent; there were always faculty on leave and there was a relatively high rate of divorce. The Coles' only home of any permanence had been a farmhouse in New Hampshire that they used for school vacations, ski trips, and a month or two every summer. The house had been in Marion's family since she could remember.

When the boys died, it had been Ted's suggestion to leave New England and all that New England reminded them of. The east end of Long Island was chiefly a summer haven and a weekend retreat for New Yorkers. For Marion it would be easier *not* to talk with her old friends.

"A new place, a new child, a new life," she said to Eddie. "At least that was the idea."

That Ted's love affairs had not abated since leaving those New England college and university towns was not surprising to Marion. In truth, his infidelities had *increased* in number—if not in any observable measure of passion. Ted was *addicted* to love affairs. Marion had a bet with herself to see if Ted's addiction to seductions would prove stronger or weaker than his addiction to alcohol. (Marion was betting that Ted could more easily give up the alcohol.)

And with Ted, Marion explained to Eddie, the seduction always lasted longer than the affair. First there were the conventional portraits, usually the mother with her child. Then the mother would pose alone, then nude. The nudes themselves revealed a predetermined progression: innocence, modesty, degradation, shame.

"Mrs. Vaughn!" Eddie interrupted, recalling the little woman's furtiveness.

"Mrs. Vaughn is presently experiencing the *degraded* phase," Marion told him.

For such a small woman, Mrs. Vaughn left a big smell on the pillows, Eddie thought; he also thought it would be imprudent, even prurient, for him to voice his opinion of Mrs. Vaughn's odor to Marion.

"But you've stayed with him all these years," the sixteen-year-old said miserably. "Why didn't you leave him?"

"The boys loved him," Marion explained. "And I loved the boys. I was planning to leave Ted after the boys finished school—after they had left home. Maybe after they'd finished college," she added with less certainty.

Overcoming his unhappiness on her behalf, Eddie ate a mountainous dessert.

"That's what I love about boys," Marion told him. "No matter what, you just go on about your business."

She let Eddie drive home. She rolled her window down and closed her eyes. The night air blew through her hair. "It's nice to be driven," she told Eddie. "Ted always drank too much. I was always the driver. Well . . . almost always," she said in a whisper. Then she turned her back to Eddie; she might have been crying, because her shoulders were shaking, but she didn't make a sound. When they arrived at the house in Sagaponack, either the wind had dried her tears or she hadn't been crying at all. Eddie only knew, from the time he had cried in front of her, that Marion didn't approve of crying.

In the house, after she dismissed the nighttime nanny, Marion poured herself a fourth glass of wine from an open bottle in the refrigerator. She made Eddie come with her when she checked to see if Ruth was asleep, whispering that, despite every appearance to the contrary, she had once been a good mother. "But I won't be a *bad* mother to Ruth," she added, still in a whisper. "I would rather be *no* mother to her than a bad one." At the time, Eddie didn't understand that Marion already knew she was going to leave her daughter with Ted. (At the time, Marion didn't understand that Ted had hired Eddie *not only* because he needed a driver.)

The feeble night-light from the master bathroom cast such faint illumination into Ruth's room that the few photographs of Thomas and Timothy were difficult to see; yet Marion insisted that Eddie look at them. She wanted to tell Eddie what the boys were doing in each of the pictures, and why she'd selected these particular photos for Ruth's room. Then Marion led Eddie into the master bathroom, where the

night-light illuminated those photographs only a little more clearly.
Here Eddie could discern a water theme, which Marion had found appropriate for the bathroom: a holiday in Tortola, and one in Anguilla;
a summer picnic at the pond in New Hampshire; and Thomas and
Timothy, when they were both younger than Ruth, in a bathtub together—Tim was crying, but Tom was not. "He got soap in his eyes,"
Marion whispered.

The tour continued into the master bedroom, where Eddie had
never been before—nor had he seen the photographs, each one of
which summoned a story from Marion. And so on, throughout the
house. They traveled from room to room, from picture to picture, until
Eddie realized why Ruth had been so agitated by the little scraps of
notepaper covering Thomas's and Timothy's bare feet. Ruth would
have taken this tour of the past on many, many occasions—probably in
both her father's *and* her mother's arms—and to the four-year-old, the
stories of the photographs were doubtless as important as the photographs themselves. Maybe *more* important. Ruth was growing up not
only with the overwhelming presence of her dead brothers, but also
with the unparalleled importance of their absence.

The pictures *were* the stories, and vice versa. To alter the photographs, as Eddie had, was as unthinkable as changing the past. The
past, which was where Ruth's dead brothers lived, was not open to revision. Eddie vowed that he would try to make it up to the child, to reassure her that everything she'd ever been told about her dead brothers
was immutable. In an unsure world, with an uncertain future, at least
the child could rely on that. Or *could* she?

More than an hour later, Marion ended the tour in Eddie's bedroom
—and, finally, in the guest bathroom that Eddie used. There was an appropriate fatalism to the fact that the last photograph to inspire Marion's background narration was the picture of Marion herself, in bed
with the two bare feet.

"I love that picture of *you*," Eddie managed to say, not daring to add
that he had masturbated to the image of Marion's bare shoulders—*and*
to her smile. As if for the first time, Marion slowly considered herself
in the twelve-year-old photograph.

"I was twenty-seven," she said, the passage of time, the melancholy
of it, filling her eyes.

It was her fifth glass of wine, which she finished now in a perfunctory fashion. Then she handed her empty glass to Eddie. He remained standing where he was, in the guest bathroom, for a full fifteen minutes after Marion had left him.

The next morning, in the carriage-house apartment, Eddie had only begun his arrangement of the pink cashmere cardigan on the bed—together with a lilac-colored silk camisole and matching panties—when he heard Marion's exaggerated clomping on the stairs leading up from the garage. She didn't knock on the door—she *beat* on the door. She wasn't going to catch Eddie in the act *this* time. He had not yet undressed to lie down beside her clothes. Nevertheless, a moment of indecision overcame him, and then there wasn't time to put Marion's clothes away. He'd been thinking about what an unwise color choice it had been for him to put pink and lilac together; yet the *colors* of her clothes were never what motivated him. He had been drawn to the lace on the waist of the panties, and to the lace in the fabulous décolletage of the camisole. Eddie was still fretting over his decision when Marion beat on the door a second time; he left her clothes on the bed and hurried to answer the door.

"I hope I'm not disturbing you," she said with a smile. She was wearing sunglasses, which she removed when she came into the apartment. For the first time, Eddie noticed her age in the crow's-feet at the outer corners of her eyes. The night before maybe Marion had had too much wine—five glasses of anything alcoholic was a lot for her.

To Eddie's surprise, she moved directly to the first of the few photographs of Thomas and Timothy she'd brought to the rental house, proceeding to explain her choices to Eddie. The pictures were of Thomas and Timothy when they were more or less Eddie's age, which meant the photos had been taken shortly before the boys died. Marion explained that she'd thought Eddie might find photographs of his contemporaries familiar, even welcoming, in what might be *un*familiar and *un*welcome circumstances. She'd worried about Eddie, long before he arrived, because she knew how little there would be for him to *do*. And she had doubted that he would have an easy time of it; she'd anticipated the nonexistence of any social life for the sixteen-year-old.

"Excepting the younger of Ruth's nannies, who were you ever going to meet?" Marion asked. "Unless you were especially outgoing. Thomas was outgoing, Timothy was not—he was more introspective, like you. Although you *look* more like Thomas," Marion told Eddie, "I think you *are* more like Timothy."

"Oh," Eddie said. He was stunned that she'd been thinking about him before he arrived!

The photography tour continued. It was as if the rental house were a secret room off the guest-wing hall, and Eddie and Marion had *not* ended their evening together; they had merely moved on, to another room, with other pictures. They traipsed through the kitchen of the carriage-house apartment—Marion talking and talking all the while— and back into the bedroom, where she continued talking, pointing to the one photograph of Thomas and Timothy that hung over the head-board of the bed.

Eddie had little difficulty recognizing a most familiar landmark of the Exeter campus. The dead boys were posed in the doorway of the Main Academy Building, where, under the pointed pediment above the door was a Latin inscription. Chiseled into the white marble, which was offset by the great brick building and the forest-green double door itself, were these humbling words:

HVC VENITE PVERI
VT VIRI SITIS

(The U's in HUC and PUERI and UT had all been carved like V's, of course.) There were Thomas and Timothy in their jackets and ties, the year of their deaths. At seventeen, Thomas seemed almost a man—at fifteen, Timothy seemed very much a boy. And the doorway where they stood was the photo background most commonly chosen by the proud parents of countless Exonians. Eddie wondered how many un-formed bodies and minds had passed through that door, under that stern and forbidding invitation.

COME HITHER BOYS
AND BECOME MEN

But it hadn't happened for Thomas and Timothy. Eddie was aware that Marion had paused in her narration of the photograph; her eyes had fallen upon her own pink cashmere cardigan, which (together with her lilac-colored camisole and matching panties) was displayed on the bed.

"Goodness—not pink with lilac!" Marion said.

"I wasn't thinking of the colors," Eddie admitted. "I liked the...
lace." But his eyes betrayed him; he was looking at the décolletage of
the camisole, and he couldn't remember the word for it. *Cleavage* came
to his mind, although he knew that wasn't the right word.

"The décolletage?" Marion prompted.

"Yes," Eddie whispered.

Marion raised her eyes above the bed to the image of her happy sons:
Huc venite pueri (come hither boys) *ut viri sitis* (and become men). Eddie
had suffered through his second year of Latin; a third year of the dead
language loomed ahead of him. He thought of the long-standing joke
at Exeter about a more fitting translation of that inscription. ("Come
hither boys and become *weary*.") But he could sense that Marion was in
no mood for a joke.

Looking at the photograph of her boys on the threshold of manhood, Marion said to Eddie: "I don't even know if they had sex before
they died." Eddie, remembering that picture of Thomas kissing a girl
in the '53 yearbook, would have guessed that Thomas had. "Maybe
Thomas had," Marion added. "He was so...popular. But surely not
Timothy—he was so shy. And he was only fifteen...." Her voice trailed
away and her glance fell back to the bed, where the pink and lilac combination of her sweater with her lingerie had earlier caught her eye.
"Have *you* had sex, Eddie?" Marion asked abruptly.

"No, of course not," Eddie told her. She smiled at him—pityingly.
He tried not to look as wretched and unlovable as he was convinced
he was.

"If a *girl* died before she had sex, I might say she was lucky," Marion
continued. "But for a *boy*...my goodness, it's all boys want, isn't it? Boys
and men," she added. "Isn't it true? Isn't it all you want?"

"Yes," said the sixteen-year-old despairingly.

Marion stood by the bed and picked up the lilac-colored camisole
with the incredible décolletage; she picked up the matching panties,
too, but she pushed the pink cashmere cardigan to the far side of the
bed. "It's too hot," she said to Eddie. "I hope you'll forgive me if I don't
wear the sweater."

He stood there frozen, his heart pounding, while she began to un-
button her blouse. "Close your eyes, Eddie," she had to tell him. With
his eyes closed, he was afraid he might faint. He felt himself weaving
from side to side; it was all he could do not to move his feet. "Okay," he

heard her say. She was lying on the bed in the camisole and the panties. "My turn to close *my* eyes," Marion said.

Eddie undressed clumsily—he had to keep looking at her. When she felt his weight on the bed beside her, she turned on her side to face him. When they looked into each other's eyes, it gave Eddie a pang. In Marion's smile, there was more that was motherly than what he had dared to hope he *might* see there.

He didn't touch her, but when he began to touch himself, she gripped the back of his neck and pulled his face against her breasts, where he hadn't even dared to look. With her other hand, she took his right hand and firmly placed it where she had seen him put his hand the first time—against the crotch of her panties. He felt himself explode into the palm of his left hand, so quickly and with such force that he flinched against her. Marion was so surprised that she flinched in response. "Goodness—*that* was fast!" she said. Holding his cupped palm in front of him, Eddie ran into the bathroom before he made a mess.

When he'd washed himself, he came back to the bedroom, where he found Marion still lying on her side, almost exactly as he had left her. He hesitated before lying down beside her. But without moving on the bed or looking at him, she said, "Come back here."

They lay looking into each other's eyes for what seemed to Eddie to be a never-ending time—at least he never wanted the moment to end. All his life, he would hold this moment as exemplary of what love was. It was not wanting anything *more*, nor was it expecting people to exceed what they had just accomplished; it was simply feeling so *complete*. No one could possibly deserve to feel any better.

"Do you know Latin?" Marion whispered to him.

"Yes," he whispered back.

She rolled her eyes upward, above the bed, to indicate the photograph of that important passage, which her sons had not navigated. "Say it in Latin for me," Marion whispered.

"Huc venite pueri ..." Eddie began, still whispering.

"Come hither boys ..." Marion translated in a whisper.

"... *ut viri sitis,"* Eddie concluded; he'd noticed that Marion had taken his hand and again placed it against the crotch of her panties.

"...and become men," Marion whispered. Again she gripped the back of his neck and pulled his face against her breasts. "But you *still* haven't had sex, have you?" she asked. "I mean not *really*."

Eddie closed his eyes against her fragrant bosom. "No, not really," he admitted. He was worried, because he didn't want to sound as if he were complaining. "But I'm very, very happy," he added. "I feel *complete.*"

"I'll show you *complete*," Marion told him.

The Pawn

Regarding sexual capacity, a sixteen-year-old boy is capable of an astonishing number of repeat performances in what Marion, at thirty-nine, would attest was a remarkably short period of time. "My *goodness!*" Marion would exclaim, to the perpetual and nearly constant evidence of Eddie's erections. "Don't you need time to ... *recover?*" But Eddie required no recovery; paradoxically, he was both easily satisfied and insatiable.

Marion was happier than she'd been at any time she could remember since her sons had died. For one thing, she was exhausted; she was sleeping more soundly than she had in years. And for another thing, Marion took no pains to conceal her new life from Ted. "He wouldn't dare complain to *me*," she told Eddie, who was nonetheless anxious that Ted *might* dare complain to *him*.

Poor Eddie was understandably nervous about the obviousness of their thrilling affair. For example, whenever their lovemaking had marked the sheets in the carriage-house apartment, it was Eddie who was in favor of doing the laundry—lest Ted should see the telltale stains. But Marion always said, "Let him wonder if it's me or Mrs. Vaughn." (When there were stains on the bedsheets in the master bedroom of the Coles' house, where Mrs. Vaughn could not have been the cause, Marion said, more to the point, "Let him wonder.")

As for Mrs. Vaughn, whether or not she knew of the strenuousness of Marion's exertions with Eddie, her more subdued relationship with Ted had changed. While Mrs. Vaughn had once epitomized furtiveness by her hesitant and darting movements in the driveway—both on her way to model and on her way back to her car—she now approached every new opportunity to pose with the resignation of a dog submitting to a beating. And when Mrs. Vaughn left Ted's workroom, she staggered to her car with a carelessness that implied her pride was irretrievable; it was as if the particular pose of the day had defeated her. Mrs. Vaughn had clearly passed from the *degraded* phase, as Marion had called it, into the final phase of shame.

Ted had never been in the habit of visiting Mrs. Vaughn at her summer estate in Southampton more than three times a week. But the visits were less frequent now, and of notably shorter duration. Eddie knew this because he was always Ted's driver. *Mr.* Vaughn spent the workweek in New York. Ted was happiest in the Hamptons during the summer months, when so many young mothers were there without their commuting husbands. Ted preferred the young mothers from Manhattan to the year-round residents; the summer people were on Long Island just long enough—"the perfect length of time for one of Ted's affairs," Marion had informed Eddie.

It made Eddie anxious. He had to wonder what Marion thought was "the perfect length of time" for her affair with *him*. He didn't dare ask.

In Ted's case, the young mothers who were available in the off-season were more troublesome to break up with; not all of them were as ongoingly friendly (*after* the affair) as the Montauk fishmonger's wife, whom Eddie had heretofore known only as the ever-faithful provider of Ted's squid ink. At the end of the summer, Mrs. Vaughn would be back in Manhattan—where she could fall apart about a hundred miles from Ted. That the Vaughn residence was on Gin Lane in Southampton was ironic, considering Ted's fondness for gin and posh neighborhoods.

"I never have to wait," Eddie observed. "He's usually walking along the side of the road when it's time for me to pick him up. But I wonder what she does with her kid."

"Probably tennis lessons," Marion had remarked.

But lately Ted's trysts with Mrs. Vaughn were lasting no more than an hour. "And last week I left him there only once," Eddie reported to Marion.

"He's almost finished with her," Marion said. "I can always tell."

Eddie assumed that Mrs. Vaughn lived in a mansion, although the Vaughn property, which was on the ocean side of Gin Lane, was walled off from his view by towering hedges. The perfect pea-size stones in the hidden, disappearing driveway were freshly raked. Ted always told Eddie to let him out of the car at the entrance to the driveway. Maybe Ted liked the feel of walking to his assignations on those expensive stones.

Compared to Ted, Eddie O'Hare was a mere fledgling at love affairs—a rank beginner—yet Eddie had quickly learned that the excitement of anticipation was *almost* equal to the thrill of lovemaking; in Ted's case, Marion suspected that Ted enjoyed the anticipation *more*. When Eddie was in Marion's arms, the sixteen-year-old found this possibility unimaginable.

They made love in the carriage-house apartment every morning; when it was Marion's turn to spend the night there, Eddie would stay with her until dawn. They didn't care that the Chevy *and* the Mercedes would be parked in the driveway for anyone to see. They didn't care that they were seen having dinner together in the same East Hampton restaurant every night. It was an unconcealed pleasure for Marion to watch Eddie eat. It also pleased her to touch his face or his hands or his hair, no matter who was looking. She even went with him to the barbershop to tell the barber how much to cut or when to stop cutting. She did his laundry. In August, she began to buy him clothes.

And there were times when Eddie's expression as he slept would so keenly resemble an expression of Thomas's or Timothy's that Marion would wake him up and bring him (still half asleep) to the specific photograph—just to show him how he had suddenly appeared to her. Because who can describe the look that triggers the memory of loved ones? Who can anticipate the frown, the smile, or the misplaced lock of hair that sends a swift, undeniable signal from the past? Who can ever estimate the power of association, which is always strongest in moments of love and in memories of death?

Marion couldn't help herself. With every act she performed for Eddie, she thought of everything she'd ever done for Thomas and Timothy; she also attended to those pleasures that she imagined her lost sons had never enjoyed. However briefly, Eddie O'Hare had brought her dead boys back to life.

Although Marion didn't care whether Ted knew of her relationship with Eddie, she was puzzled that Ted hadn't said *something*, for surely he must have known. He was as amiable to Eddie as ever; lately Ted was spending more time with Eddie, too.

With a large portfolio of loosely held-together drawings, Ted had asked Eddie to drive him into New York. They took Marion's Mercedes for the hundred-mile trip. Ted directed Eddie to his art gallery, which was either on Thompson near the corner of Broome, or on Broome near the corner of Thompson—Eddie couldn't recall. After delivering the drawings, Ted had taken Eddie to lunch at a place he'd once taken Thomas and Timothy. The boys had liked it, Ted had said. Eddie liked it, too, although it made him uncomfortable when Ted told him—on the drive back to Sagaponack—that he was grateful to him for being such a good friend to Marion. She'd been so unhappy; it was wonderful to see her smiling again.

"He said that?" Marion asked Eddie.

"Exactly," Eddie reported.

"How odd," Marion remarked. "I would have expected him to say something snide."

But Eddie detected next to nothing in Ted that was "snide." There was one reference that Ted had made to Eddie's physical condition, but Eddie couldn't tell if Ted's remark had or had not insinuated his knowledge of Eddie's daily and nightly athletics with Marion.

In his workroom, by the telephone, Ted had posted a list of a half-dozen names and numbers; these were his regular squash opponents, who (Marion told Eddie) were Ted's only male friends. One afternoon, when one of Ted's regular opponents had canceled a match, Ted asked Eddie to play. Eddie had earlier expressed his newfound interest in squash, but he'd also confessed to Ted that he was a player of less-than-beginner status.

The barn adjacent to the Coles' house had been restored; in the loft, above what served as a two-car garage, an *almost* regulation-size squash court had been built to Ted's specifications. Ted claimed that a town ordinance had restricted him from raising the roof of the barn—hence the ceiling of the squash court was lower than regulation size—and dormer windows on the ocean side of the barn had caused one side wall of the court to be irregular in shape and offer notably less playing surface than did the opposing wall. The resulting peculiar shape and dimensions gave Ted a distinct home-court advantage.

Actually, there had been *no* town ordinance restricting Ted from raising the roof; he had saved a considerable sum of money, however, and the eccentricity of a squash court of his own specifications had

pleased him. Among the local squash players, Ted was considered unbeatable in his odd barn, which was ferociously hot (and poorly venti-
lated) in the summer months; in the winter, because the barn was
unheated, the court was often unbearably cold—the ball would have
little more bounce than a stone.

In their one match, Ted warned Eddie of the oddities of the court,
but Eddie had played the game only once before; to him, the court in
the barn presented the same difficulties as any other squash court. Ted
had him running from corner to corner. Ted himself would take a position in the center T of the court; he never needed to stray more than
a half-step in any direction. Eddie, sweating and breathless, couldn't
score a point, but Ted wasn't even flushed.

"Eddie, you look like a boy who will sleep well tonight," Ted told
him after they'd finished five games. "Maybe you need to catch up on
your sleep, anyway." Ted gave the sixteen-year-old a pat on the butt
with the head of his racquet. He might or might not have been "snide,"
Eddie reported to Marion, who no longer knew what to make of her
husband's behavior.

A more pressing problem for Marion was Ruth. In the summer of '58,
the four-year-old's sleeping habits bordered on the bizarre. Often she
would sleep through the night, and so soundly that she could be found
in the morning in the exact same position in which she had fallen
asleep—and still perfectly tucked in. But other nights she would toss
and turn. She would lie sideways in the bottom bunk of her bunk bed
until her feet would get stuck in the guard rails; then she would wake
up crying for help. Worse, at times her trapped feet would become an
integral part of an ongoing nightmare; Ruth would wake up with the
conviction that a monster had attacked her and was holding her in its
terrifying grasp. On these occasions the child would not only cry to be
rescued from the guard rails; she would also need to be carried into the
master bedroom, where she would fall back to sleep, sobbing, in her
parents' bed—with either Marion or Ted.

When Ted tried removing the guard rails, Ruth fell out of bed.
There was a rug; it wasn't a bad fall. But, disoriented, the child once
wandered into the hall. And with or without the guard rails, Ruth had
nightmares. In short, for the uninterrupted pleasure of Eddie and Marion's sexual endeavors, Ruth could not be relied upon to sleep through

the night. The child might wake up screaming or she might silently appear at her mother's bedside, which made it risky for Eddie and Marion to make love in the master bedroom—or for Eddie, drifting heavenward in Marion's arms, to fall asleep there. But when they made love in Eddie's room, which was a considerable distance from Ruth's bedroom, Marion worried that she would not hear Ruth calling to her or crying, or that the child would wander into the master bedroom and be frightened that her mother wasn't there.

Thus, when they were in bed in Eddie's room, they would take turns running out in the hall to listen for Ruth. And when they lay in Marion's bed, the patter of the child's feet on the floor of the bathroom would send Eddie diving out of bed. He once lay naked on the floor on the far side of the bed for half an hour, until Ruth finally fell asleep next to her mother. Then Eddie crept out on all fours. Just before he opened the door to the hall and tiptoed away to his own room, Marion whispered, "Good night, Eddie." Apparently Ruth was only half asleep, for the child (in a sleepy voice) quickly echoed her mother: "Good night, Eddie."

After that, it was inevitable that one night neither Eddie nor Marion would hear the approaching patter of little feet. Therefore, on the night when Ruth appeared with a towel in her mother's bedroom—because the child was convinced that her mother (from the sound of her) was throwing up—Marion was unsurprised. And since she'd been mounted from behind, and her breasts were held in Eddie's hands, there was little that Marion could do about the matter; she *did* manage to stop moaning.

Eddie, however, reacted to Ruth's sudden appearance in an astonishingly acrobatic but inept fashion. His withdrawal from Marion was so abrupt that Marion felt both empty and abandoned, but with her hips still moving. Eddie, who flew but a short distance in reverse, was suspended only momentarily in midair; his failure to clear the bedside lamp brought both the boy and the destroyed lamp crashing to the carpet, where the sixteen-year-old's spontaneous but doomed effort to hide his private parts with an open-ended lamp shade provided Marion with at least an instant of passing comedy.

Her daughter's screams notwithstanding, Marion understood that this would be an episode of longer-lasting trauma for Eddie than it would be for Ruth. This conviction was what prompted Marion to say to her daughter, with seeming nonchalance, "Don't scream, honey. It's just Eddie and me. Go back to bed."

To Eddie's surprise, the child dutifully did as she was told. When Eddie was once again in bed beside Marion, Marion whispered, as if to herself, "Now *that* wasn't so bad, was it? Now we can stop worrying about *that.*" But then she rolled onto her side, with her back to Eddie, and although her shoulders shook slightly, she was not crying—or she was crying only inwardly. However, Marion would not respond to Eddie's touch or his endearments; he knew well enough to leave her alone.

The episode prompted the first clarifying response from Ted. With unflinching hypocrisy, Ted chose the moment when Eddie was driving him to Southampton for a visit with Mrs. Vaughn. "I presume it was *Marion's* mistake," Ted stated, "but that surely *was* a mistake for the two of you—to let Ruth see you together." Eddie said nothing.

"I'm not threatening you, Eddie," Ted added, "but I must tell you that you may be called upon to testify."

"Testify?" the sixteen-year-old said.

"In the event of a custody dispute, regarding which of us is more fit as a parent," Ted replied. "I would never let a child see me with another woman, whereas Marion really has made no effort to protect Ruth from seeing ... what she saw. And if you were called upon to testify to what happened, I trust that you wouldn't *lie*—not in a court of law." But Eddie still said nothing.

"From the sound of it, it was a rear-entry position—mind you, not that I have a personal problem with that, or with any other position," Ted was quick to say, "but for a child I imagine that doing it *doggishly* must seem especially ... animalistic." For only a second did Eddie imagine that Marion had told Ted; then Eddie realized, with a sinking feeling, that Ted had been talking to Ruth.

Marion concluded that Ted must have been asking Ruth all along, from the very beginning: Had the child seen Eddie and her mother together? And if together, *how* together? Suddenly, everything that Marion had misunderstood was clear.

"So *that's* why he hired you!" she cried. He'd known that Marion would take Eddie as a lover, and that Eddie could never have resisted her. But that Ted *thought* he knew Marion that well was contradicted by the fact that Ted *didn't* know her well enough to understand that she would never have battled him for custody of Ruth. Marion had always known that the child was lost to her. She had *never* wanted Ruth.

Now Marion was insulted that Ted didn't think well enough of her to realize that she would *never* claim—not even in passing conversation, not to mention in a court of law—that Ruth would be better off with her mother than with her deceitful, feckless father. Even Ted would do a better job with the child than Marion could do, or so Marion thought.

"I'm going to tell you what we're going to do, Eddie," Marion told the boy. "Don't worry. Ted's not going to make you *testify* to anything— there isn't going to be any court of law. I know a lot more about Ted than he knows about me."

For a seemingly endless three days, they couldn't make love because Marion had an infection—sex was painful for her. She nevertheless lay beside Eddie and held his face against her breasts while he masturbated to his heart's content. Marion teased Eddie by asking him if he didn't like masturbating next to her nearly as much (if not more) than making love to her. When Eddie denied this, Marion teased him further; she sincerely doubted that the women in his future would be as understanding of his preference as she was. She found it rather sweet, she told him.

But Eddie protested: he couldn't imagine that he would ever be interested in *other* women. "Other women will be interested in you," Marion told the boy. "They may not be secure enough about themselves to let you masturbate, instead of demanding that you make love to them. I'm just warning you, as a friend. Girls your own age are going to find it *neglectful* of you."

"I will never be interested in girls my own age," said Eddie O'Hare, with the kind of misery in his voice that Marion had grown fond of. And although Marion teased Eddie about this, too, it would turn out to be true. He never *would* be interested in a woman his own age. (This was not necessarily a disservice that Marion had done him.)

"You just have to trust me, Eddie," she told him. "You mustn't be afraid of Ted. I know exactly what we're going to do."

"Okay," Eddie said. He lay with his face pressed against her breasts, knowing that his time with her was coming to an end—for how could it *not* end? In less than a month he would be back at Exeter; not even a sixteen-year-old could imagine maintaining a thirty-nine-year-old mistress under boarding-school rules.

"Ted thinks that you're his pawn, Eddie," Marion told the boy. "But you're *my* pawn, not Ted's."

"Okay," Eddie said, but Eddie O'Hare did not yet realize the extent to which he truly *was* a pawn in the culminating discord of a twenty-two-year marital war.

Ruth's Right Eye

For a pawn, Eddie asked a lot of questions. When Marion had recovered sufficiently from her infection so that they could make love again, Eddie asked her about what sort of "infection" she'd had.

"It was a bladder infection," she told him. She was still more of a natural mother than she knew—she spared him the potentially upsetting news that the infection had been the result of his repeated sexual attentions.

They had just finished making love in the position that Marion favored. She liked sitting on Eddie—"riding" him, Marion called it—because she enjoyed seeing his face. It was not only that Eddie's expressions haunted her pleasantly because of their ceaseless associations with Thomas and Timothy. It was also that Marion had begun the process of saying good-bye to the boy, who had affected her more intimately than she'd ever thought he would.

She knew, of course, how strongly she had affected him—this worried her. But in looking at him, and in making love to him—especially in looking at him *while* making love to him—Marion imagined that she could see her sexual life, which had been so ardently (albeit briefly) rekindled, coming to an end.

She had not told Eddie that, before him, she'd never had sex with anyone except Ted. Nor had she told Eddie that she'd had sex with Ted only once since her sons had died, and that one time—entirely at Ted's initiation—had been strictly for the purpose of getting her pregnant. (She had not wanted to get pregnant, but she'd been too despondent to resist.) And since Ruth had been born, Marion had not been tempted to have sex at all. With Eddie, what had begun on Marion's part as a kindness toward a shy boy—in whom she saw so much of her sons—had blossomed into a relationship that had been deeply rewarding to her. But if Marion had been surprised by the excitement and gratification Eddie had provided, her enjoyment of the boy had nevertheless *not* persuaded her to alter her plans.

She was leaving more than Ted and Ruth. In saying good-bye to Eddie O'Hare, she was also saying good-bye to a sexual life of any kind. Here she was, saying good-bye to sex, when, for the first time, at thirty-nine, she was finding sex pleasurable!

If Marion and Eddie were the same height in the summer of '58, Marion was aware that she outweighed him; Eddie was excruciatingly thin. In the top position, bearing down on the boy, Marion felt that all her weight and strength were concentrated in her hips; with Eddie pinned beneath her, Marion sometimes felt that it was *she* who was penetrating *him*. Indeed, the motion of her hips was the only motion between them—Eddie wasn't strong enough to lift her weight off him. There was an instant when Marion not only felt as if she'd entered the boy's body; she was fairly certain she had paralyzed him.

When she could tell by how he held his breath that he was about to come, she would drop her weight on his chest and, holding tight to his shoulders, roll him on top of her, because she couldn't stand to see the look that transformed his face when he came. There was something too close to the anticipation of pain in it. Marion could hardly bear to hear him whimper—and he whimpered every time. It was the sound of a child crying out in a half-sleep before falling sound asleep again. Only this repeated split second, in her entire relationship with Eddie, ever caused Marion a half-moment of doubt. When the boy made this infantile sound, it made Marion feel guilty.

Afterward, Eddie lay on his side with his face against her breasts; Marion ran her fingers through the boy's hair. Even then, Marion could not stop herself from making a critical observation of Eddie's haircut—she made a mental note to tell the barber to take a little less off the back next time. Then she revised her mental note. The summer was running out; there would be no "next time."

That was when Eddie asked his second question of the night. "Tell me about the accident," he said. "I mean, do you know how it happened? Was it anybody's fault?"

A second before, pulsing against his temple, he had felt her heart beating through her breast. But now it seemed to Eddie that Marion's heart had stopped. When he lifted his head to look at her face, she was already turning her back to him. This time there wasn't even the slightest shaking of her shoulders; her spine was straight, her back rigid, her shoulders square. He came around the bed and knelt beside her and looked into her eyes, which were open but distant; her lips, which, when she slept, were full and parted, were thin and closed.

"I'm sorry," Eddie whispered. "I'll never ask you again." But Marion remained as she was—her face a mask, her body a stone.

"Mommy!" Ruth called, but Marion didn't hear her—she didn't even blink. Eddie froze, waiting for the patter of the four-year-old's feet across the bathroom floor. But the child was staying in her bed. "Mommy?" she cried, more tentatively now. There was a hint of worry in her voice. Eddie, naked, tiptoed to the bathroom. He wrapped a bath towel around his waist—a better choice than a lamp shade. Then, as quietly as possible, Eddie began to retreat in the direction of the hall.

"Eddie?" the child asked. Her voice was a whisper.

"Yes," Eddie answered, resigned. He tightened the towel around himself and padded barefoot through the bathroom to the child's room. Eddie thought that the sight of Marion would have frightened Ruth more than the child was already frightened—that is, if the four-year-old had seen her mother in Marion's newly acquired, seemingly catatonic state.

Ruth was sitting up in bed, not moving, when Eddie walked into her room. "Where's Mommy?" the child asked him.

"She's asleep," Eddie lied.

"Oh," the girl said. With a look, she indicated the towel knotted around Eddie's waist. "Did you take a bath?"

"Yes," he lied again.

"Oh," Ruth said. "But what did I dream about?"

"What did *you* dream about?" Eddie repeated stupidly. "Uh, I don't know. I didn't have your dream. What *did* you dream about?"

"Tell me!" the child demanded.

"But it's *your* dream," Eddie pointed out.

"Oh," the four-year-old said.

"Would you like a drink of water?" Eddie asked.

"Okay," Ruth replied. She waited while he ran the water until it was cold and brought it to her in a cup. When she handed the cup back to him, she asked: "Where are the feet?"

"In the photograph, where they always are," Eddie told her.

"But what happened to them?" Ruth asked.

"Nothing happened to them," Eddie assured her. "Do you want to see them?"

"Yes," the girl replied. She held out her arms, expecting to be carried, and he lifted her out of bed.

Together they navigated the unlit hall; both of them were aware of the infinite variety of expressions on the faces of the dead boys, whose photographs were mercifully in semidarkness. At the far end of the hall, the light from Eddie's room shone as brightly as a beacon. Eddie carried Ruth into the bathroom, where, without speaking, they looked at the picture of Marion in the Hôtel du Quai Voltaire.

Then Ruth said, "It was early in the morning. Mommy was just waking up. Thomas and Timothy had crawled under the covers. Daddy took the picture—in France."

"In Paris, yes," Eddie said. (Marion had told him that the hotel was located on the Seine. It had been Marion's first time in Paris—the boys' only time.)

Ruth pointed to the bigger of the bare feet. "Thomas," she said. Then she pointed to the smaller of the feet; she waited for Eddie to speak.

"Timothy," Eddie guessed.

"Right," the four-year-old said. "But what did you *did* to the feet?"

"*Me?* Nothing," Eddie lied.

"It looked like paper, little pieces of paper," Ruth told him. Her eyes searched the bathroom; she made Eddie put her down so that she could peer into the wastebasket. But the maid had come to clean the room many times since Eddie had removed the scraps of notepaper. Finally Ruth held out her arms to Eddie; once more he picked her up.

"I hope it doesn't happen again," the four-year-old said.

"Maybe it never happened; maybe it was a dream," Eddie told her.

"No," the child replied.

"I guess it's a mystery," Eddie said.

"No," Ruth told him. "It was paper. Two pieces." She kept scowling at the photograph, daring it to change. Years later, Eddie O'Hare would be unsurprised that, as a novelist, Ruth Cole was a realist.

At last he asked the girl: "Don't you want to go back to bed?"

"Yes," Ruth replied, "but bring the picture."

They went down the dark hall, which seemed darker now—the feeble night-light from the master bathroom cast only the dimmest glow through the open door of Ruth's room. Eddie carried the child against his chest. He found her heavy to carry with one arm; in his other hand, he carried the photograph.

He put Ruth back in her bed, and leaned the picture of Marion in Paris against a chest of drawers. The photograph faced Ruth, but the child complained that the photo was too far away from her bed for her to see it properly. Eddie ended up propping the photograph against the footstool, near the head of Ruth's bunk bed. Ruth was satisfied. The four-year-old fell back to sleep.

Before Eddie went back to his room, he took another look at Marion. Her eyes were closed, her lips were parted in her sleep, and her body had given up its terrifying rigidity. Only a sheet covered her hips; her upper body was bare. It was a warm night; Eddie nevertheless covered her breasts with the sheet. She looked a little less abandoned that way.

Eddie was so tired that he lay down on his bed and fell asleep with the towel still wrapped around his waist. In the morning, he woke to the sound of Marion calling for him—she was screaming out his name—and he could hear Ruth crying hysterically. He ran down the hall (still in the towel) and found Marion and Ruth bent over a bloodstained sink in the bathroom. There was blood everywhere. It was on the child's pajamas, on her face, in her hair. The source was a single deep cut in Ruth's right index finger. The pad of the first joint of her finger had been slashed to the bone. The cut was perfectly straight and extremely thin.

"She said it was glass," Marion told Eddie, "but there's no glass in the cut. *What* glass, honey?" Marion asked Ruth.

"The picture, the picture!" the child cried.

In an effort to conceal the photograph under her bunk, Ruth must have banged the picture frame against a part of her bed—or against the footstool. The glass covering the photo was shattered; the photograph itself was undamaged, although the mat was spotted with blood.

"What did I did?" the four-year-old kept asking. Eddie held her while her mother got dressed; then Marion held Ruth while Eddie dressed himself.

Ruth had stopped crying and was now more concerned about the photograph than about her finger. They took the photo, still in the blood-spotted mat, out of the shattered frame; they brought the picture in the car with them, because Ruth wanted the picture to come to the hospital. Marion tried to prepare Ruth for the stitches, and there would probably be at least one shot. In truth, there would be two—the lidocaine injection before the stitches, and then a tetanus shot. Despite how deep it was, the cut was so clean and so thin that Marion was sure it wouldn't require more than two or three stitches or leave a visible scar.

"What's a scar?" the child asked. "Am I going to die?"

"No, you are *not* going to die, honey," her mother assured her.

Then the conversation turned to the matter of fixing the photograph. When they were finished at the hospital, they would take the photo to a frame shop in Southampton and leave it to be reframed. Ruth began to cry again, because she didn't want the picture to be left at the shop. Eddie explained that there had to be a new mat, a new frame, and new glass.

"What's a mat?" the four-year-old asked.

When Marion showed Ruth the blood-spotted mat (but not the photograph), Ruth wanted to know why the bloodstain wasn't red; the spot of blood had dried and turned brown.

"Will I turn brown?" Ruth asked. "Am I going to die?"

"No, you *won't*, honey. No, you're *not*," Marion kept telling her.

Of course Ruth screamed at the needles, and at the stitches—there were only two. The doctor marveled at the perfect straightness of the wound; the pad of the right index finger had been precisely bisected. It would have been next to impossible for a surgeon to have cut the exact middle of such a small finger so deliberately, even with a scalpel.

After they dropped off the photograph at the frame shop, Ruth sat subdued in her mother's lap. Eddie drove back to Sagaponack, squinting into the morning sun. Marion lowered the sun visor on the passenger side, but Ruth was so short that the sunlight shone directly into her face, causing her to turn toward her mother. Suddenly Marion began to stare into her daughter's eyes—into Ruth's right eye, in particular.

"What's the matter?" Eddie asked. "Is there something in her eye?"

"It's nothing," Marion said.

The child curled against her mother, who shielded the sunlight from her daughter's face with her hand. Exhausted from all her crying, Ruth fell asleep before they reached Sagaponack.

"What did you see?" Eddie asked Marion, whose gaze was notably distant again. (It was not as distant as the night before, when Eddie had asked her about her boys' accident.) "Tell me," he said.

Marion pointed to the flaw in the iris of her right eye, that hexagon of yellow which Eddie had often admired; he had more than once remarked to her that he loved the tiny yellow speck in her eye—the way, in certain light or at unpredictable angles, it could turn her right eye from blue to green.

Although Ruth's eyes were brown, what Marion had seen in the iris of Ruth's right eye was the exact same hexagonal shape of bright yellow. When the four-year-old had blinked in the sunlight, the yellow hexagon had demonstrated its capacity to turn Ruth's right eye from brown to amber.

Marion continued to hug her sleeping daughter to her breast; with one hand, she still shielded the four-year-old's face from the sun. Eddie had never before seen Marion manifest such a degree of physical affection for Ruth.

"Your eye is very ... distinguished," the sixteen-year-old said. "It's like a birthmark, only more mysterious...."

"The poor child!" Marion interrupted him. "I don't want her to be like *me*!"

Dumping Mrs. Vaughn

For the next five or six days, before Ruth's stitches were removed, the child didn't go to the beach. The nuisance of keeping the cut dry made the nannies irritable. Eddie detected an increased sullenness in Ted's and Marion's behavior toward each other; they had always avoided each other, but now they never spoke to or even looked at each other. When one wanted to complain about the other, the complaint was made to Eddie. For example, Ted held Marion responsible for Ruth's injury, although Eddie had repeatedly told him that it was he who had let Ruth have the photograph.

"That's not the point," Ted said. "The point is, *you* shouldn't have gone into her room in the first place—that's her mother's job."

"I told you. Marion was asleep," Eddie lied.

"I doubt it," Ted told the boy. "I doubt that 'asleep' accurately describes Marion's condition. I would guess that she was *zonked.*"

Eddie wasn't sure what Ted meant. He said, "She wasn't drunk, if that's what you mean."

"I didn't say she was drunk—she's never drunk," Ted told Eddie. "I said she was *zonked.* Wasn't she?"

Eddie didn't know what to say; he reported the problem to Marion.

"Did you tell him *why?*" she asked the boy. "Did you tell him what you *asked* me?"

Eddie was shocked. "No, of course not," the sixteen-year-old said.

"*Tell* him!" Marion exclaimed.

So Eddie told Ted what happened when he asked Marion about the accident. "I guess *I* zonked her," Eddie explained. "I keep telling you—the whole thing is *my* fault."

"No, it's Marion's fault," Ted insisted.

"Oh, who cares whose *fault* it is?" Marion said to Eddie.

"*I* care," Eddie said. "*I'm* the one who let Ruth have the photograph in her room."

"This isn't about the photograph—don't be silly," Marion told the sixteen-year-old. "This has nothing to do with you, Eddie."

It was a blow to the boy to realize that she was right. Eddie O'Hare was involved in what would be the most important relationship in his life; yet what was happening between Ted and Marion had nothing to do with him.

Meanwhile, Ruth asked every day about the unreturned photograph; every day there was a phone call to the frame shop in Southampton, but the matting and framing of a single eight-by-ten photo was not a priority in the framer's busiest season of the year.

Would the new mat have a spot of blood on it? Ruth wanted to know. (No, it would not.) Would the new frame and the new glass be exactly like the old frame and the old glass? (Close enough.)

And every day and every night, Ruth would lead the nannies, or her mother or father, or Eddie, through the gallery of photographs hanging in the Coles' house. If she touched *that* photo, could the glass cut her? If she dropped *this* one, was it also glass and would it break? Why did glass break, anyway? And if glass could cut you, why would you want any glass in your house?

But before Ruth's repeated questions, the month of August had passed the midpoint; it was markedly cooler at night. Even the carriage house was comfortable for sleeping. One night when Eddie and Marion were sleeping there, Marion forgot to tack the towel over the skylight. They were awakened early in the morning by a low-flying flock of geese. Marion said: "Going south already?" She didn't speak to Eddie or Ruth for the rest of the day.

Ted radically revised *A Sound Like Someone Trying Not to Make a Sound;* for almost a week, he presented Eddie with a completely rewritten draft every morning. Eddie would retype the manuscript the same day; the next morning Ted's rewrite would come back to him. No sooner was Eddie beginning to feel like an actual writer's assistant than the rewriting process stopped. Eddie wouldn't see *A Sound Like Someone Trying Not to Make a Sound* again until it was published. Although it would be Ruth's favorite among her father's books, it would never be a favorite of Eddie's; he'd seen too many versions of it to appreciate the final draft.

And in the mail one day, just before Ruth's stitches were removed, was a fat envelope for Eddie from his father. It contained the names and addresses of every living Exonian in the Hamptons; in fact, it was the very same list of names and addresses that Eddie had thrown away on the ferry while crossing Long Island Sound. Someone had found the envelope with the embossed Phillips Exeter Academy return address and the senior O'Hare's carefully handwritten name—a janitor, or one of the ferry crew, or some meddler snooping through the trash. Whoever the idiot was, he or she had returned the list to Minty O'Hare.

"You should have told me that you lost this," Eddie's father wrote to him. "I would have copied the names and addresses and given them to you again. Thankfully someone recognized their value. A remarkable act of human kindness—and at a time in our history when acts of kindness are growing rare. Whoever it was, man or woman, didn't even ask to be repaid for the postage! It must have been the Exeter name—on the envelope, I mean. I've always said that you can never overestimate the influence of the academy's good name. ..." Minty had added one name and address, he noted to Eddie: an Exonian in nearby Wainscott had somehow been omitted from the original list.

It was an irritating time for Ted, too. Ruth claimed that her stitches gave her nightmares; she had most of her nightmares when it was Ted's turn to stay with her. One night the child cried and cried for her mother; *only* her mommy—and, to Ted's further exasperation, Eddie—could comfort her. Ted had to call them in the carriage house and tell them to come home. Then Eddie had to drive Ted back to the carriage house, where, Eddie imagined, the imprints of his and Marion's bodies were still visible (if not still warm) on the bed.

When Eddie returned to the Coles' house, all the upstairs lights were on. Ruth could be soothed only by being carried from photograph to photograph. Eddie volunteered to complete the guided tour, so Marion could go back to bed, but Marion seemed to be enjoying herself; in fact, Marion was aware that this would probably be her last journey through the photographic history of her dead boys with her daughter in her arms. Marion was actually prolonging the narrative that accompanied each picture. Eddie fell asleep in his room, but with the door to the upstairs hall open; for a while, he could hear Ruth's and Marion's voices.

Eddie knew by the child's question that they were looking at the photograph (in the middle guest bedroom) of Timothy crying and covered with mud. "But what happened to Timothy?" Ruth asked, although she knew the story as well as Marion did. By now, even Eddie knew all the stories.

"Thomas pushed him in a puddle," Marion told Ruth.

"How old is Timothy with the mud?" Ruth asked.

"He's *your* age, honey," her mother said. "He was just four. . . ."

Eddie knew the next photo, too: Thomas in his hockey uniform, after a game at the Exeter rink. He is standing with his arm around his mother, as if she'd been cold throughout the entire game—but she also looks extremely proud to be standing there with her son's arm around her. Even though he has taken off his skates and is standing, absurdly, in full hockey uniform but with a pair of unlaced basketball shoes on his feet, Thomas is taller than Marion. What Ruth liked about the photograph is that Thomas is grinning widely, a hockey puck gripped in his teeth.

Just before he fell asleep, Eddie heard Ruth ask her mother: "How old is Thomas with the thing in his mouth?"

"He's Eddie's age," Eddie heard Marion say. "He was just sixteen. . . ."

About seven A.M. the phone rang. Marion answered it when she was still in bed. She knew by the silence that it was Mrs. Vaughn. "He's at the other house," Marion said; then she hung up.

At breakfast Marion told Eddie: "I'll make you a bet. He breaks up with her before Ruth gets her stitches out."

"But don't the stitches come out on Friday?" Eddie asked. (There were only two days until Friday.)

"I'll bet he breaks up with her *today*," Marion replied. "Or at least he'll try. If she's difficult about it, it may take him another couple of days."

Indeed, Mrs. Vaughn would be difficult about it. Probably anticipating the difficulty, Ted tried to break up with Mrs. Vaughn by sending Eddie to do it for him.

"I'm going to do *what?*" Eddie asked. They were standing by the biggest table in Ted's workroom, where Ted had assembled a stack of about a hundred drawings of Mrs. Vaughn. Ted had some trouble closing the bulging portfolio; it was the largest portfolio he had, with his initials engraved in gold in the brown leather—T.T.C. (Theodore Thomas Cole).

"You're going to give her these, but *not* the portfolio. Just give her the drawings. I want the portfolio back," Ted instructed Eddie, who knew that the portfolio had been a gift from Marion. (Marion had told Eddie that.)

"But aren't you going to see Mrs. Vaughn today?" Eddie asked him. "Isn't she expecting you?"

"Tell her I'm not coming, but that I wanted her to have the drawings," Ted said.

"She's going to ask me when you *are* coming," Eddie replied.

"Tell her you don't know. Just give her the drawings. Say as little as you have to," Ted told the boy. Eddie scarcely had time to tell Marion.

"He's sending you to break up with her—what a coward!" Marion said, touching Eddie's hair in that motherly way she had. He was sure she was going to say something about her perpetual dissatisfaction with his haircut. Instead she said, "Better show up early—she'll still be getting dressed. That way she'll be less tempted to invite you in. You don't want her asking you a million questions. The best thing would be to ring the bell and just hand her the drawings. You don't want to let her get you inside the house, behind closed doors—believe me. Be careful she doesn't kill you."

With that in mind, Eddie O'Hare arrived at the Gin Lane address early. At the entrance to the expensively pebbled driveway, he stopped by the impressive barrier of privet to remove the hundred drawings of Mrs. Vaughn from the leather portfolio. He feared it might be awkward to give Mrs. Vaughn the drawings *and* take back the portfolio while the small, dark woman was standing furiously in front of him. But Eddie had miscalculated the wind. After Eddie put the portfolio in the trunk of the Chevy, he transferred the drawings to the backseat of the car, where the wind blew them into a disorderly pile; he had to close the doors and windows of the Chevy in order to sort through the drawings in the backseat. He couldn't help but look at the drawings then.

They began with the portraits of Mrs. Vaughn with her angry little boy. The small, tightly closed mouths of the mother and her son struck Eddie as an unkind genetic characteristic. Also, Mrs. Vaughn and her son both had intense, impatient eyes; seated side by side, they made fists of their hands and held them rigidly on their thighs. In his mother's lap, Mrs. Vaughn's son appeared to be on the verge of clawing and kicking free of her—unless she, who also appeared to be on the verge, impulsively decided to strangle him first. There were easily two dozen or more such portraits, each conveying chronic discontent and mounting tension.

Then Eddie came to Mrs. Vaughn alone—at first fully dressed, but deeply alone. Eddie instantly grieved for her. If what Eddie had first spotted in Mrs. Vaughn was her furtiveness, which had given way to her submissiveness, which in turn had led her to despair, what he'd missed seeing in her was her mortal unhappiness. Ted Cole had caught this trait even before the woman began to take off her clothes.

The nudes had their own sad progression. At first the fists remained balled up on the tense thighs, and Mrs. Vaughn sat in profile—often with one or the other shoulder blocking her small breasts from view. When at last she faced the artist, her destroyer, she hugged herself to hide her breasts, and her knees were tightly pinched together; her crotch was mostly concealed—her pubic hair, when visible at all, was only the thinnest of lines.

Then Eddie groaned in the closed car; the later nudes of Mrs. Vaughn were as *un*concealed as the frankest photographs of a cadaver.

Her arms hung loosely at her sides, as if her shoulders had been savagely dislocated in a violent fall. Her exposed and unsupported breasts drooped; the nipple of one breast seemed larger and darker and more down-pointed than the other. Her knees were spread apart, as if she'd lost all sensation in her legs—or else she'd broken her pelvis. For such a small woman, her navel was too large, her pubic hair too abundant. Her vagina was gaping and slack. The very last of the nudes was the first pornography that Eddie O'Hare had ever seen, not that Eddie fully understood what was pornographic about the drawings. Eddie felt sick and deeply sorry that he'd seen the drawings, which had reduced Mrs. Vaughn to the hole in her center; the nudes managed to make even less of Mrs. Vaughn than what had remained of her strong smell on the rental-house pillows.

Under the tires of the Chevy, the crunching of the perfect stones in the driveway leading to the Vaughn mansion sounded like the breaking bones of small animals. As Eddie passed a squirting fountain in the circular driveway, he saw the movement of an upstairs curtain. When he rang the doorbell, he nearly dropped the drawings, which he was able to hold only by hugging them with both his arms against his chest. He waited forever for the small, dark woman to appear.

Marion had been right. Mrs. Vaughn had not finished getting dressed, or possibly she'd not completed the exact phase of *un*dress that she might have been preparing in order to look alluring to Ted. Her hair was wet and lank, and her upper lip seemed rubbed raw; at one corner of her mouth, like a clown's unfinished smile, remained a trace of the hair-removal ointment that she'd too hastily tried to wipe away. Mrs. Vaughn had been hasty in her choice of a robe as well, for she stood in the doorway in a white terry-cloth thing that resembled a giant, ungainly towel. It was probably her husband's robe, for it hung over her thin ankles; one edge dragged on the doorsill. She was barefoot. The wet nail polish on her big right toe had been smeared across the top of her right foot in such a way that it looked as if she'd cut her foot and was bleeding.

"What do you want?" Mrs. Vaughn asked. Then she looked past Eddie at Ted's car. Before Eddie could answer, she asked him: "Where is he? Isn't he coming? What's wrong?"

"He couldn't make it," Eddie informed her, "but he wanted you to have ... these." In the wild wind, he didn't dare hold out the drawings to her; awkwardly, he still hugged them to his chest.

"He couldn't make it?" she repeated. "What does that mean?"

"I don't know," Eddie lied. "But there are all these drawings... May I put them down somewhere?" he begged.

"*What* drawings? Oh ... the *drawings*! Oh ..." said Mrs. Vaughn, as if someone had struck her in the stomach. She stepped back, tripping on the long white robe—she nearly fell. Eddie followed her inside, feeling like her executioner. The polished marble floor reflected the over-hanging chandelier; in the distance, through an open pair of double doors, a second chandelier hung above a dining-room table. The house looked like an art museum; the far-off dining room was as big as a ban-quet hall. Eddie walked (for what seemed to him to be a mile or so) to the table, and put the drawings down, not realizing until he turned to go that Mrs. Vaughn had followed as closely and silently behind him as his shadow. When she saw the topmost drawing—one of her with her son—she gasped.

"He's giving them to *me*!" she cried. "He doesn't *want* them?"

"I don't know," Eddie said miserably. Mrs. Vaughn rapidly leafed through the drawings until she got to the first nude; then she over-turned the stack, taking the last drawing off the bottom, which was now the top. Eddie began to edge away; he knew what the last drawing was.

"Oh ..." Mrs. Vaughn said, as if she'd been punched again. "But when is he coming?" she called after Eddie. "He's coming Friday, isn't he? I have the whole day to see him Friday—he knows I have the whole day. He *knows*!" Eddie tried to keep walking. He heard her bare feet on the marble floor—she was scampering after him. She caught up to him under the big chandelier. "Stop!" she shouted. "Is he coming Friday?"

"I don't know," Eddie repeated, backing out the door. The wind tried to keep him inside.

"Yes, you *do* know!" Mrs. Vaughn screamed. "Tell me!"

She followed him outside, but the wind almost knocked her down. Her robe blew open; she struggled to close it. Eddie would always re-tain this vision of her, as if to remind himself of what the worst kind of nakedness was—the utterly unwanted glimpse of Mrs. Vaughn's slack breasts and her dark triangle of matted pubic hair.

"Stop!" she cried again, but the sharp stones in the driveway pre-vented her from following him to the car. She bent down and picked up a handful of the pebbles, which she threw at Eddie. Most of them struck the Chevy.

"Did he *show* you those drawings? Did you *look* at them? Goddamn you—you looked at them, *didn't* you?" she cried.

"No," Eddie lied.

As Mrs. Vaughn bent down to pick up another handful of stones, a gust of wind blew her off balance. Like a gunshot, the front door behind her slammed shut.

"My God. I'm locked out!" she said to Eddie.

"Isn't there another door that's *un*locked?" he asked. (The mansion must have had a dozen doors!)

"I thought Ted was coming. He likes all the doors to be locked," said Mrs. Vaughn.

"You don't hide a key somewhere for emergencies?" Eddie asked.

"I sent the gardener home. Ted doesn't like the gardener to be around," said Mrs. Vaughn. "The gardener has an emergency key."

"Can't you call the gardener?"

"On what *phone?*" shouted Mrs. Vaughn. "You'll have to break in."

"Me?" the sixteen-year-old said.

"Well, you know how to do it, don't you?" the small, dark woman asked. *"I* don't know how to do it!" she wailed.

There were no open windows because of the air-conditioning; the Vaughns had air-conditioning because of their art collection, which was also why there were no open windows. By a garden in the back, there were French doors, but Mrs. Vaughn warned Eddie that the glass was of a special thickness and laced with chicken wire, which made it nearly impenetrable. By swinging a rock, which he tied up in his T-shirt, Eddie was finally able to smash the glass, but he still needed to find one of the gardener's tools in order to rip the chicken wire sufficiently for his hand to fit through the hole and unlock the door from the inside. The rock, which was a centerpiece to the birdbath in the garden, had dirtied Eddie's T-shirt, which had also been cut by the breaking glass. He decided to leave his shirt, and the rock, in the smashed glass by the now-open door.

But Mrs. Vaughn, who was barefoot, insisted that he carry her into the house through the French doors; she didn't want to risk cutting her feet on the broken glass. Bare-chested, Eddie carried her into her house—being careful, as he reached around her, not to get his hands on the wrong side of her robe. She seemed to weigh next to nothing, barely more than Ruth. But when he held her in his arms, even so briefly, her strong smell came close to overpowering him. Her scent was indescribable; Eddie couldn't say what she smelled like, only that the scent made him gag. When he put her down, she sensed his unconcealed revulsion.

"You look as if you're disgusted," she told him. "How *dare* you—how dare you detest *me*?" Eddie was standing in a room he'd never been in before. He didn't know his way to the big chandelier at the main entrance, and when he turned to look for the French doors to the garden, a maze of open doorways confronted him; he also didn't know how to find the door he'd just come in.

"How do I get out?" he asked Mrs. Vaughn.

"How dare you detest me?" she repeated. "You're not exactly living an unsordid life yourself—are you?" Mrs. Vaughn asked the boy.

"Please . . . I want to go home," Eddie told her. It wasn't until he spoke that he realized he really meant it, and that he meant Exeter, New Hampshire—not Sagaponack. Eddie meant that he *really* wanted to go home. It was a weakness he would carry with him for the rest of his life: he would always be inclined to cry in front of older women, as he'd once cried in front of Marion—as he now commenced to cry in front of Mrs. Vaughn.

Without another word she took him by his wrist and led him through the museum of her house to the chandelier at the front door. The touch of her small, cold hand was like a bird's foot, as if a diminutive parrot or a parakeet had grabbed hold of him. When she opened the door and pushed him into the wind, a number of doors slammed in the interior of her house, and as he turned to say good-bye, he saw the sudden whirlwind of Ted's terrible drawings—the wind had blown them off the dining-room table.

Eddie couldn't speak, nor could Mrs. Vaughn. When she heard the drawings fluttering behind her, she wheeled around in her big white robe, as if preparing herself for an attack. Indeed, before the front door again slammed shut in the wind, like a second gunshot, Mrs. Vaughn *was* about to be attacked. Surely she would recognize in those drawings at least a measure of the degree to which she'd allowed herself to be assaulted.

"She threw *rocks* at you?" Marion asked Eddie.

"They were little stones—most of them hit the car," Eddie admitted.

"She made you *carry* her?" Marion asked.

"She was barefoot," Eddie explained again. "There was all this broken glass!"

"And you left your shirt? *Why?*"

"It was ruined—it was just a T-shirt."

As for Ted, his conversation with Eddie was a little different.

"What did she mean—she has 'the whole day' Friday?" Ted asked. "Does she expect me to spend *the whole day* with her?"

"I don't know," the sixteen-year-old said.

"Why did she think you'd looked at the drawings?" Ted asked. "*Did* you—did you look at them?"

"No," Eddie lied.

"Christ, of course you did," Ted said.

"She exposed herself to me," Eddie told him.

"Jesus! She did *what?*"

"She didn't mean to," Eddie admitted, "but she exposed herself. It was the wind—it blew her robe open."

"Jesus Christ ..." Ted said.

"She locked herself out of her house, because of you," Eddie told him. "She said you wanted all the doors locked, and that you didn't like the gardener to be around."

"She told you that?"

"I had to break into her house—I smashed in the French doors with a part of the birdbath. I had to carry her through the broken glass," Eddie complained. "I lost my shirt."

"Who cares about your *shirt?*" Ted shouted. "I can't spend *the whole day* with her Friday! I'll have you drop me off there the first thing Friday morning, but you *must* come back to get me in forty-five minutes. Forget that—in half an hour! I couldn't possibly spend forty-five minutes with that crazy woman."

"You just have to trust me, Eddie," Marion told him. "I'm going to tell you what we're going to do."

"Okay," Eddie said. He couldn't stop thinking about the worst of the drawings. He wanted to tell Marion about Mrs. Vaughn's smell, but he couldn't describe it.

"On Friday morning you're going to leave him at Mrs. Vaughn's," Marion began.

"I know!" the boy said. "For half an hour."

"No, *not* for half an hour," Marion informed the sixteen-year-old. "You're going to leave him with her and *not* come back to pick him up. It will take him most of the day to get home by himself without a car. I'll bet you anything that Mrs. Vaughn won't offer to drive him."

"But what will he *do?*" Eddie asked.

"You mustn't be afraid of Ted," Marion reminded him. "What will he *do?* It will probably occur to him that the only person he knows in Southampton is Dr. Leonardis." (Dave Leonardis was one of Ted's regular squash opponents.) "It will take Ted half an hour or forty-five minutes just to walk to Dr. Leonardis's office," Marion continued. "And *then* what will he do? He'll have to wait all day, until all of Leonardis's patients have gone home, before he can get a ride home with the doctor—unless one of Leonardis's patients is someone Ted knows, or someone who happens to be driving in the direction of Sagaponack."

"Ted's going to be furious," Eddie warned her.

"You just have to trust me, Eddie."

"Okay."

"After you drive Ted to Mrs. Vaughn's, you're going to come back here and get Ruth," Marion went on. "Then you're going to take Ruth to her doctor to get her stitches out. Then I want you to take Ruth to the beach. Let her get wet—let her *celebrate* having her stitches out."

"Excuse me," Eddie interrupted. "Why doesn't one of the nannies take Ruth to the beach?"

"There will be no nannies on Friday," Marion informed him. "I need the day, or as much of the day as you can give me, to be alone here."

"But what are you going to do?" Eddie asked.

"I'm going to tell you," she told him again. "You just have to trust me, completely."

"Okay," he said, but for the first time Eddie knew that he *didn't* trust Marion—not completely. After all, he was her pawn; he'd already had the sort of day that a pawn might have.

"I looked at the drawings of Mrs. Vaughn," he confessed to Marion.

"Merciful heavens," she said to him. He didn't want to cry again, but he allowed her to pull his face into her breasts; he let her hold him there while he struggled to say what he felt.

"In the drawings, she was somehow *more* than naked," he began.

"I know," Marion whispered to him. She kissed the top of his head.

"It was not *just* that she was naked," Eddie insisted. "It was as if you could see everything that she must have submitted to. She looked like she'd been *tortured* or something."

"I know," Marion said again. "I'm so sorry...."

"Also, the wind blew her robe open and I *saw* her," Eddie blurted out. "She was exposed only for a second, but it was as if I already knew everything about her." Then he realized what it was about Mrs. Vaughn's smell. "And when I had to pick her up and carry her," Eddie said, "I noticed her smell—like on the pillows, only stronger. It made me gag."

"What did she smell like?" Marion asked him.

"Like something dead," Eddie told her.

"Poor Mrs. Vaughn," Marion said.

Why Panic at Ten O'Clock
in the Morning?

It was shortly before eight on Friday morning when Eddie picked Ted up at the carriage house for the drive to Southampton and what Ted thought would be a half-hour meeting with Mrs. Vaughn. Eddie's nervousness was extreme, and not only because he feared that Ted would have Mrs. Vaughn on his hands a lot longer than he assumed. Marion had more or less scripted Eddie's day. Eddie had a lot to remember.

When he and Ted stopped for coffee at the Sagaponack General Store, Eddie knew all about the moving truck that was parked there. The two sturdy movers were drinking coffee and reading their morning newspapers in the cab. When Eddie had returned from Mrs. Vaughn's—to take Ruth to have her stitches removed—Marion would know where she could find the movers. The movers, like Eddie, had been given their instructions: to wait at the store until Marion came to get them. Ted and Ruth—and the nannies, who'd been dismissed for the day—would never see the movers.

By the time Ted found his way home from Southampton, the movers (and everything Marion wanted to take with her) would be gone. Marion herself would be gone. She had forewarned Eddie of this. That would leave Eddie to explain it all to Ted; *that* was the script Eddie kept rehearsing on the way to Southampton.

"But who's going to explain it all to *Ruth?*" Eddie had asked. There then crept into Marion's expression that same aura of distance that Eddie had witnessed when he'd asked her about the accident. Clearly Marion had *not* scripted the part of the story where someone explains it all to Ruth.

"When Ted asks you where I've gone, just say you don't know," Marion told Eddie.

"But where *are* you going?" Eddie asked.

"You don't know," Marion repeated. "If Ted insists on a better answer, to *anything,* just say that he'll be hearing from my lawyer. My lawyer will tell him everything."

"Oh, great," Eddie said.

"And if he hits you, just hit him back. By the way, he won't make a fist—at worst he'll slap you. But you should use your fist," Marion advised Eddie. "Just punch him in the nose. If you punch him in the nose, he'll stop."

But what about Ruth? The plans for Ruth were vague. If Ted began to shout, how much should Ruth hear? If there was a fight, how much should the child see? If the nannies had been dismissed, Ruth would have to be either with Ted or with Eddie, or with them both. Why wouldn't she be upset?

"You can call Alice, if you need help with Ruth," Marion had suggested to Eddie. "I told Alice that you or Ted might call her. In fact, I told her to call the house about midafternoon—to see if you needed her after all." Alice was the afternoon nanny, the pretty college girl with her own car. She was the nanny Eddie liked the least, Eddie had reminded Marion.

"You better get to like her a little," Marion replied. "If Ted kicks you out—and I can't imagine that he'll want you to *stay*—you're going to need a ride to the ferry at Orient Point. Ted's not permitted to drive, you know—not that he would want to drive you, anyway."

"Ted's going to kick me out and I'm going to have to ask Alice for a ride," Eddie echoed.

Marion merely kissed him.

And then the moment was at hand. When Eddie stopped at Mrs. Vaughn's concealed driveway on Gin Lane, Ted said, "You better wait here for me. I'm not going to last a half hour with that woman. Maybe twenty minutes, tops. Maybe ten. ..."

"I'll go and come back," Eddie lied.

"Be back in fifteen minutes," Ted told him. Then he noticed the long scraps of his familiar drawing paper. The tatters of his drawings were blowing in the wind; his drawings had been ripped to shreds. The forbidding barrier of privet had kept most of the torn paper from blowing into the street, but the hedges were bedecked with waving flags and strips of paper, as if some unruly wedding guests had strewn the Vaughn estate with makeshift confetti.

As Ted walked up the noisy driveway at a slow, stricken pace, Eddie got out of the car to watch; he even followed Ted a short distance. The courtyard was littered with the remains of Ted's drawings. The spitting fountain was clogged with wet wads of paper; the water had turned a sepia shade of grayish brown.

"The squid ink ..." Ted said aloud. Eddie, walking backward, was already retreating to the car. He had spotted the gardener on a ladder, plucking paper from the privet. The gardener had scowled at both Eddie and Ted, but Ted had noticed neither the gardener nor the ladder; the squid ink, staining the water in the fountain, had entirely captured Ted's attention. "Oh boy," he muttered, as Eddie left him.

Compared to Ted, the gardener was better dressed. There was always something careless and rumpled about Ted's clothes—jeans, a tucked-in T-shirt, and (on this somewhat cool Friday morning) an unbuttoned flannel shirt that was flapping in the wind. And this morning Ted was unshaven, too; he was doing his best to make the worst possible impression on Mrs. Vaughn. (Ted *and* his drawings had already made the worst possible impression on Mrs. Vaughn's gardener.)

"Five—*five* minutes!" Ted called to Eddie. Given the long day ahead, it hardly mattered that Eddie didn't hear him.

Back in Sagaponack, Marion had packed a large beach bag for Ruth, who was already wearing her bathing suit under her shorts and T-shirt; in the bag were towels and two changes of clothes, including long pants and a sweatshirt. "You can take her anywhere you like for lunch," Marion told Eddie. "All she ever eats is a grilled-cheese sandwich with French fries."

"And ketchup," Ruth said.

Marion tried to give Eddie a ten-dollar bill for lunch.

"I have money," Eddie told her, but when he turned his back on her to help Ruth into the Chevy, Marion stuck the ten-dollar bill into the right rear pocket of his jeans, and he remembered what it had felt like the first time she'd pulled him to her by tugging the waist of his jeans—her knuckles against his bare stomach. Then she'd unsnapped his jeans and unzipped his fly, which he would remember for about five or ten years—every time he undressed himself.

"Remember, honey," Marion said to Ruth. "Don't cry when the doctor takes out your stitches. I promise—it's not going to hurt."

"Can I keep the stitches?" the four-year-old asked.

"I suppose . . ." Marion replied.

"Sure you can keep them," Eddie told the child.

"So long, Eddie," Marion said.

She was wearing tennis shorts and tennis shoes, although she didn't play tennis, and a floppy flannel shirt that was too big for her—it was Ted's. She wasn't wearing a bra. Earlier that morning, when Eddie was leaving to pick up Ted at the carriage house, Marion had taken his hand and put it under her shirt and held it against her bare breast; but when he tried to kiss her, she drew away, leaving Eddie's right hand with the feel of her breast, which he would go on feeling for about ten or fifteen years.

"Tell me all about the stitches," Ruth said to Eddie, as he made a left turn.

"You won't really feel them very much when the doctor takes them out," Eddie said.

"Why not?" the child asked him.

Before he made the next turn, a right, he had his last sight of Marion and the Mercedes in the rearview mirror. She would not be turning right, Eddie knew—the movers were waiting straight ahead of her. The left side of Marion's face was illuminated by the morning sun, which shone brightly through the driver's-side window of the Mercedes; the window was open, and Eddie could see the wind blowing Marion's hair. Just before he turned, Marion waved to him (and to her daughter), as if she were still intending to be there when Eddie and Ruth returned.

"Why *won't* it hurt to take the stitches out?" Ruth asked Eddie again.

"Because the cut is healed—the skin has grown back together," Eddie told her.

Marion was now gone from view. Is that *it*? he was wondering. "So long, Eddie." Were those her last words to him? "I suppose ..." were Marion's last words to her daughter. Eddie couldn't believe the abruptness of it: the open window of the Mercedes, Marion's hair blowing in the wind, Marion's arm waving out the window. And only half of Marion's face was in the sunlight; the rest of her was invisible. Eddie O'Hare couldn't have known that neither he nor Ruth would see Marion again for thirty-seven years. But, for all those years, Eddie would wonder at the seeming nonchalance of her departure.

How *could* she? Eddie would think—as one day Ruth would also think about her mother.

The two stitches were removed so quickly that Ruth didn't have time to cry. The four-year-old was more interested in the stitches themselves than in her almost perfect scar. The thin white line was discolored only slightly by traces of iodine, or whatever the antiseptic was—it had left a yellow-brown stain. Now that she could get her finger wet again, the doctor told her, this stain would be removed by her first good bath. But it was of greater concern to Ruth that the two stitches, which had each been cut in half, were saved in an envelope—and that the crusted scab, near the knotted end of one of the four pieces, not be damaged.

"I want to show my stitches to Mommy," Ruth said. "And my scab."

"First let's go to the beach," Eddie suggested.

"Let's show her the scab first, then the stitches," Ruth replied.

"We'll see..." Eddie began. He paused to consider that the doctor's office in Southampton was not more than a fifteen-minute walk from Mrs. Vaughn's mansion on Gin Lane. It was now a quarter to ten in the morning; if Ted was still there, he would already have been with Mrs. Vaughn for more than an hour. More likely, Ted was *not* with Mrs. Vaughn. But Ted might have remembered that Ruth was having her stitches removed this morning, and he might know where the doctor's office was.

"Let's go to the beach," Eddie said to Ruth. "Let's hurry."

"First the scab, then the stitches, *then* the beach," the child replied.

"Let's talk about it in the car," Eddie suggested. But there is no straightforward negotiation with a four-year-old; while not every negotiation needs to be difficult, there are few that don't require a considerable investment of time.

"Did we forgot the picture?" Ruth asked Eddie.

"The picture?" Eddie said. "What picture?"

"The feet!" Ruth cried.

"Oh, the photograph—it's not ready," Eddie told her.

"*That's* not very nice!" the child declared. "My stitches are ready. My cut is all fixed up."

"Yes," Eddie agreed. He thought he saw a way to distract the four-year-old from her desire to show her scab and stitches to her mother before going to the beach. "Let's go to the frame shop and *tell* them to give us the picture," Eddie suggested.

"All fixed up," Ruth added.

"Good idea!" Eddie proclaimed. Ted would never think of going to the frame shop, Eddie decided; the frame shop was almost as safe as the beach. First make a fuss about the photograph, he was thinking; then Ruth won't remember about showing her scab and stitches to Marion. (When the child was watching a dog scratching itself in the parking lot, Eddie put the envelope with the precious scab and stitches into the glove compartment.) But the frame shop was a little less safe than Eddie had supposed.

Ted had *not* remembered that Ruth was having her stitches removed this morning; Mrs. Vaughn hadn't given Ted the time to remember very much. Less than five minutes after his arrival at her door, Ted was chased into the courtyard and up Gin Lane by Mrs. Vaughn, who was brandishing a serrated bread knife while shrieking at him that he was "the epitome of diabolism." (He vaguely recalled that this was the title of a dreadful painting in the Vaughns' regrettable art collection.)

The gardener, who had watched "the artist" (as he witheringly thought of Ted) make his trepid approach to the Vaughn mansion, was also witness to Ted's intrepid retreat across the courtyard, where the artist was nearly driven into the murky fountain by the relentless slashes and stabs that Mrs. Vaughn made in the nearby air with her knife. Ted had bolted down the driveway and into the street with his former model in passionate pursuit.

The gardener, terrified that one or the other of them might run headlong into his ladder, which was a fifteen-footer, clung precariously to the top of the high privet hedge; from that height, the gardener was able to observe that Ted Cole could and did outrun Mrs.

Vaughn, who gave up the chase a few driveways short of the intersection of Gin Lane and Wyandanch. There was another high barrier of privet near the intersection, and—from the gardener's elevated but distant perspective—Ted had either disappeared into the hedges or turned northward onto Wyandanch Lane without once looking back. Mrs. Vaughn, still in a fury and still decrying the artist as "the epitome of diabolism," returned to her own driveway. Spontaneously—to the gardener it seemed *involuntarily*—she still slashed and stabbed the air with the serrated knife.

A period of intense quiet fell over the Vaughn estate and descended on Gin Lane. Ted, tangled deep in a dense mass of privet, could hardly move enough to see his watch; the privet was a maze of such density, not even a Jack Russell terrier could have penetrated the hedge, which had scratched Ted's hands and face and left him bleeding. Yet he had escaped the bread knife and, for the moment, Mrs. Vaughn. But where was Eddie? Ted waited in the privet for his familiar '57 Chevy to appear.

The gardener, who had begun his chore of retrieving the shredded drawings of his employer and her son a full hour or more before Ted made his appearance, had long ago stopped looking at what he could see of the remains of the drawings. Even piecemeal, the content of the drawings was too disturbing. The gardener already knew his employer's eyes and her small mouth, and the rest of her strained face; he already knew her hands, and the unnatural tension in her shoulders. Worse, the gardener had vastly preferred to *imagine* Mrs. Vaughn's breasts and her vagina; the *reality* of what he had seen of her nakedness in the ruined drawings was uninviting. Moreover, he had been working at a great pace—for although he well understood why Mrs. Vaughn would have wanted to dispose of the drawings, he could not conceive of what insanity had possessed her to rip up the pornographic exposure of herself in a windstorm with all the doors open. On the ocean side of the house, the scraps and shreds had stuck in the barrier of beach roses, but some partial views of Mrs. Vaughn and her son had found their way along the footpath and were now blowing up and down the beach.

The gardener did not especially like Mrs. Vaughn's son; he was a haughty boy who'd once peed in the birdbath and then denied it. But the gardener had been a faithful employee of the Vaughn family since before the brat's birth, and he felt some additional responsibility to the neighborhood. The gardener could think of no one who would enjoy even these partial views of Mrs. Vaughn's private parts; yet the pace at which he worked to clean up the mess was arrested by his fascination with what had become of the artist—namely, was the artist hiding in a neighbor's hedge or had he escaped toward town?

At half past nine in the morning, when Eddie O'Hare was already an hour late, Ted Cole crawled out of the privet on Gin Lane and cautiously walked past the driveway of the Vaughn estate—to give Eddie every opportunity to see him, should Eddie (for some reason) have been waiting for Ted at the west end of Gin Lane, which intersected South Main Street.

In the gardener's opinion, this was an unwise, even a reckless move. From the third-floor turret of the Vaughn mansion, Mrs. Vaughn could see *over* the privet. If the wronged woman was in the turret, she would have a commanding view of *all of* Gin Lane.

Indeed, Mrs. Vaughn must have had such a view, for not seconds after Ted had passed her driveway—and begun quickening his pace along Gin Lane—the gardener was alarmed to hear the roar of Mrs. Vaughn's car. It was a glistening black Lincoln and it shot out of the garage at such speed that it slid on the stones in the courtyard and nearly crashed into the darkened fountain. In a last-second effort to miss the fountain, Mrs. Vaughn veered too near the privet; the Lincoln clipped the bottom of the gardener's ladder, leaving the distraught man clinging to the top of the high hedge. "Run!" the gardener called to Ted.

That Ted would live to see another day must be credited to the regular and rigorous exercise he gained on the squash court that was designed to give him an unfair advantage. Even at forty-five, Ted Cole could run. He cleared some rosebushes without breaking stride and raced across a lawn, in full view of a gawking but silent man who was vacuuming a swimming pool. Ted was then chased by a dog, fortunately a small and cowardly dog; by grabbing a woman's bathing suit off a clothesline and lashing the dog in the face with it, Ted drove the craven animal away. Naturally Ted was hollered at by several gardeners and maids and housewives; undeterred, he climbed three fences and scaled one fairly high stone wall. (He trampled only two flower beds.) And he never saw Mrs. Vaughn's Lincoln cut the corner of Gin

Lane onto South Main Street, where she flattened a road sign in the eagerness of her pursuit; however, through the slats of a wooden fence on Toylsome Lane, Ted saw the black-as-a-hearse Lincoln rush parallel to him as he traversed two lawns, a yard full of fruit trees, and something resembling a Japanese garden—where he stepped into a shallow pool of goldfish, soaking his shoes and his jeans (to his knees).

Ted doubled back on Toylsome. Daring to cross that street, he saw the flicker of the black Lincoln's brake lights and feared that Mrs. Vaughn had spotted him in her rearview mirror and was stopping to double back on Toylsome herself. But she hadn't spotted him—he'd lost her. Ted entered the town of Southampton, looking much the worse for wear but walking boldly into the heart of the shops and the stores on South Main Street. If he hadn't been so energetically on the lookout for the black Lincoln, he might have seen his own '57 Chevy, which was parked by the frame shop on South Main; but Ted walked right past his car without recognizing it, and entered a bookstore diagonally across the street.

They knew him in the bookstore; they knew Ted Cole in *every* bookstore, of course, but Ted made periodic visits to this particular bookstore, where he routinely autographed however many copies of his backlist titles were in stock. The bookseller and his attendant staff were not used to seeing Mr. Cole look quite as bedraggled as he appeared before them on this Friday morning, but they had known him to be unshaven—and he was often dressed more in the manner of a college student, or a workingman, than in whatever fashion was customary among best-selling authors and illustrators of children's books.

It was chiefly the blood that lent a novelty to Ted's appearance. His scratched and bleeding face, and the dirtier blood on the backs of his hands, where he had clawed his way into and out of a hundred-year-old hedge, indicated mishap or mayhem to the surprised bookseller, whose name (inexplicably) was Mendelssohn. He was no relation to the German composer, and *this* Mendelssohn either overliked his last name or disliked his first so much that he never revealed it. (When Ted had once asked him his first name, Mendelssohn had said only: "Not Felix.")

On this Friday, whether it was the sight of Ted's blood that excited him, or the fact that Ted's jeans were dripping on the floor of the bookstore—Ted's shoes actually squirted water in several directions whenever Ted took a step—Mendelssohn grabbed Ted by the dirty tails of his untucked and unbuttoned flannel shirt and exclaimed in a too-loud voice: "Ted Cole!"

"Yes, it *is* Ted Cole," Ted admitted. "Good morning, Mendelssohn."

"It's Ted Cole—it *is*, it *is!*" Mendelssohn repeated.

"I'm sorry I'm bleeding," Ted told him calmly.

"Oh, don't be silly—it's nothing to be sorry about!" Mendelssohn shouted. Then he turned to a dumbstruck young woman on his staff; she was standing nearby, with a look of both awe and horror. Mendelssohn commanded her to bring Mr. Cole a chair. "Can't you see he's *bleeding?*" Mendelssohn said to her.

But Ted asked if he could use the washroom first—he'd just been in an accident, he solemnly said. Then he shut himself in a small bathroom with a sink and toilet. He assessed the damage in the mirror, while composing—as only a writer can—a story of surpassing simplicity regarding what sort of "accident" he'd just had. He saw that a branch of the evil hedge had lashed one eye and left it weepy. A deeper scratch was the source of the bleeding from his forehead; a scrape that bled less but looked harder to heal stood out on one cheek. He washed his hands; the cuts stung, but the bleeding from the backs of his hands had largely stopped. He removed his flannel shirt and tied the muddy sleeves—one had also been dipped in the goldfish pool—around his waist.

Ted took this moment to admire his waist; at forty-five, he was still a man who could wear a pair of jeans and tuck in his T-shirt and be proud of the overall effect. However, the T-shirt was white and its appearance was not improved by the pronounced grass stains on the left shoulder and the right breast—Ted had fallen on at least two lawns—and his jeans, which were soaked below the knees, continued to drip into his water-filled shoes.

As composed as he could be under the circumstances, Ted emerged from the bathroom and was once more effusively greeted by last-name-only Mendelssohn, who'd already prepared a chair for the visiting author. The chair was drawn up to a table, where a few dozen copies of Ted Cole's books were waiting to be signed.

But first Ted wanted to make a phone call, actually two. He tried the carriage house to find out if Eddie was there; there was no answer. And of course there was no answer at Ted's own house—Marion knew better than to answer the phone on this well-rehearsed Friday. Had Eddie crashed the car? The sixteen-year-old had been driving erratically earlier that morning. Doubtless Marion had fucked the boy's brains out! Ted concluded.

Regardless of how well Marion had rehearsed this Friday, she had been mistaken to think that Ted's only recourse for a ride home would be to walk all the way to his squash opponent's office and wait for Dr. Leonardis, or for one of the doctor's patients, to drive him to Sagaponack. Dave Leonardis's office was on the far side of Southampton, on the Montauk Highway; the bookstore was not only closer to Mrs. Vaughn's mansion—it was a much more obvious place for Ted to expect to be rescued. Ted Cole could have walked into almost any bookstore in the world and asked for a ride home.

He promptly did so, no sooner than he'd sat down at the autographing table to sign his books.

"To put it simply, I need a ride home," the famous author said.

"A ride!" cried Mendelssohn. "Yes, of course! No problem! You live in Sagaponack, don't you? I'll take you myself! Well ... I'll have to call my wife. She may be shopping, but not for long. You see, *my* car is in the shop."

"I hope it's not in the same shop *my* car was in," Ted told the enthusiast. "I just got mine back from the shop. They forgot to reattach the steering column. It was like that cartoon we've all seen—the steering wheel was in my hands but it was not *attached* to the wheels. I steered one way and the car went off the road in another. Fortunately, all I hit was privet—a vast hedge. Climbing out the driver's-side window of the car, I was scratched by the bushes. And then I stepped in a goldfish pool," Ted explained.

He had their attention now; Mendelssohn, poised by the phone, delayed the call to his wife. And the formerly dumbstruck young woman who worked there was smiling. Ted was not generally attracted to what he thought of as her type, but if *she* offered him a ride home, maybe something would come of it.

She was probably not long out of college; in her no-makeup, straight-hair, no-tan way, she was a precursor of the decade ahead. She was not pretty—truly, she was just plain dull—but her paleness represented a kind of sexual frankness to Ted, who recognized that a part of the young woman's no-frills appearance reflected an openness to experiences she might call "creative." She was the kind of young woman who was seduced intellectually. (Ted's particularly scruffy appearance at the moment might actually have elevated him in her eyes.) And sexual encounters, because the woman was still young enough to find them novel, were doubtless an area of experience she might call "authentic"—especially with a famous writer.

Sadly, she didn't have a car. "I use a bicycle," she told Ted, "or else I'd take you home."

Too bad, Ted thought, but he rationalized that he didn't really like the discrepancy between the thinness of her lower lip and the exaggerated puffiness of her upper.

Mendelssohn fretted because his wife was still out shopping. He would keep calling—she would be back soon, Mendelssohn assured Ted. A boy with an indescribable speech impediment—the only other staff in the bookstore on this Friday morning—offered an apology, for he had lent his car to a friend who'd wanted to go to the beach.

Ted just sat there, slowly signing books. It was only ten. If Marion had known where Ted was, and how close he could be to getting a ride home, she might have panicked. If Eddie O'Hare had known that Ted was autographing books across the street from the frame shop—where Eddie was insisting that the "feet" photograph *should* be ready for Ruth to take home today—Eddie might have panicked, too.

But there was no cause for Ted to feel any panic. He didn't know that his wife was leaving him—he still imagined that *he* was leaving *her*. And he was safely off the streets; therefore, he was out of immediate harm's way (meaning Mrs. Vaughn). And even if Mendelssohn's wife *never* came home from shopping, it was only a matter of minutes before *someone* would come into the bookstore who was a devoted Ted Cole reader. It would probably be a woman, and Ted would actually have to *buy* one of his own autographed books for her, but she would give him a ride home. And if she was good-looking, and so on, and so forth, who knew what might come of it? Why panic at ten o'clock in the morning? Ted was thinking.

He had no idea.

How the Writer's Assistant Became a Writer

Meanwhile, in the nearby frame shop, Eddie O'Hare was finding his voice. At first Eddie was unaware of the powerful change within him; he thought he was merely angry. There was reason to be angry. The saleswoman who waited on Eddie was rude to him. She was not much older than he, but she too brusquely estimated that a sixteen-year-old boy and a four-year-old girl asking about the matting and framing of a single eight-by-ten photograph were not high on the list of those well-heeled Southampton patrons of the arts whom the frame shop sought to serve.

Eddie asked to speak to the manager, but the saleswoman was rude again; she repeated that the photograph was not ready. "Next time," she told Eddie, "I suggest that you call before you come."

"Do you want to see my stitches?" Ruth asked the saleswoman. "I got a scab, too."

The saleswoman—a *girl*, really—clearly had no children of her own; she pointedly ignored Ruth, which raised Eddie's anger to a higher level.

"Show her your scar, Ruth," Eddie said to the four-year-old.

"Look …" the salesgirl began.

"No, *you* look," Eddie said, still not understanding that he was finding his voice. He'd never spoken to anyone in this manner before; now, suddenly, he was unable to stop. His newfound voice continued. "I'm willing to keep trying with someone who's rude to me, but I won't have anything to do with someone who's rude to a child," Eddie heard himself say. "If there's no manager here, there must be someone else— whoever it is who does the actual work, for example. I mean, is there a back room where the mats are cut and the pictures are framed? There must be someone here besides you. I'm not leaving without that photograph, and I'm not talking to you."

Ruth looked at Eddie. "Did you got mad at her?" the four-year-old asked him.

"Yes, I did," Eddie replied. He felt unsure of who he was, but the salesgirl would never have guessed that Eddie O'Hare was a young man who was often full of doubt. To her, he was confidence itself—he was absolutely terrifying.

Without a word, she retreated to the very same "back room" that Eddie had so confidently mentioned. Indeed, there were *two* back rooms in the frame shop—a manager's office and what Ted would have called a workroom. Both the manager, a Southampton socialite and divorcée named Penny Pierce, and the boy who cut the mats and framed (and framed and framed) all day were there.

The unpleasant salesgirl conveyed the impression that Eddie, despite his appearance to the contrary, was "scary." While Penny Pierce knew who Ted Cole was—and she vividly remembered Marion, because Marion was beautiful—Mrs. Pierce did not know who Eddie O'Hare was. The child, she presumed, was the unlucky little girl Ted and Marion had had to compensate for their dead sons. Mrs. Pierce vividly remembered the sons, too. Who could forget the frame shop's good fortune? There had been *hundreds* of photographs to mat and frame, and Marion had not chosen inexpensively. It had been an account in the *thousands* of dollars, Penny Pierce recalled; the shop really should have rematted and reframed the single photograph with the bloodstained mat promptly. We should probably have done it *gratis,* Mrs. Pierce now considered.

But just who did this teenager think he was? Who was *he* to say he wasn't leaving without the photograph?

"He's scary," the fool salesgirl repeated.

Penny Pierce's divorce lawyer had taught her one thing: don't let anyone who's angry *talk*—make them put it in writing. She'd carried this policy with her into the framing business, which her ex-husband had bought for her as a part of the divorce settlement.

Before Mrs. Pierce confronted Eddie, she instructed the boy in the workroom to stop what he was doing and immediately remat and reframe the photograph of Marion in the Hôtel du Quai Voltaire. Penny Pierce had not seen this particular photo in—what was it now?—about five years. Mrs. Pierce remembered Marion bringing in all the snapshots; some of the negatives were scratched. When the boys had been alive, the old pictures of them had been taken for granted and had not been very well cared for. After the boys had died, Penny Pierce assumed, almost every snapshot of them had struck Marion as worthy of enlarging and framing—scratched or not.

Knowing the story of the accident, Mrs. Pierce had not been able to restrain herself from looking closely at *all* the photographs. "Oh, it's *this* one," she said when she saw the picture of Marion in bed with her boys' feet. What had always struck Penny Pierce about *this* photograph was the evidence of Marion's distinct happiness—in addition to her unmatched beauty. And now Marion's beauty was unchanged while her happiness had fled. This fact about Marion was universally striking to other women. While neither beauty nor happiness had entirely abandoned Penny Pierce, she felt that she'd never known either to the extent that Marion had.

Mrs. Pierce gathered a dozen or more sheets of stationery from her desk before she approached Eddie. "I understand that you're angry. I'm very sorry about that," she said pleasantly to the handsome sixteen-year-old, who looked to her incapable of frightening anyone. (I have *got* to get better help, Penny Pierce was thinking to herself as she went on, visually underestimating Eddie. The closer she looked at him, the more she thought he was too pretty to qualify as handsome.) "When my customers are angry, I ask them to voice their complaints in writing—if you don't mind," Mrs. Pierce added, again pleasantly. The sixteen-year-old saw that the manager had presented him with paper and a pen.

"I work for Mr. Cole. I'm a writer's assistant," Eddie said.

"Then you won't mind *writing*, will you?" Penny Pierce replied.

Eddie picked up the pen. The manager smiled at him encouragingly—she was neither beautiful nor brimming with happiness, but she was nevertheless not *un*attractive and she was good-natured. No, he *wouldn't* mind writing, Eddie realized. It was exactly the invitation that Eddie needed; it was what his *voice,* long trapped inside him, wanted. He *wanted* to write. After all, that was why he had sought the job. What he'd got, instead of writing, was Marion. Now that he was losing her, he was finding what he'd wanted before the summer started.

And it wasn't Ted who'd taught him anything. What Eddie O'Hare had learned from Ted Cole, he'd learned from reading him. It was from just a few sentences that any writer learned anything from another writer. From *The Mouse Crawling Between the Walls,* Eddie had learned something from only *two* sentences. The first one was this: "Tom woke up, but Tim did not." And then there was this sentence: "It was a sound like, in the closet, if one of Mommy's dresses came alive and it tried to climb down off the hanger."

If, because of that sentence, Ruth Cole would think differently of closets and dresses for the rest of her life, Eddie O'Hare could hear the sound of that dress coming alive and climbing down off that hanger as clearly as any sound he'd ever heard; he could see the movement of that slithery dress in the half-dark of that closet in his sleep.

And from *The Door in the Floor* there was another first sentence that wasn't half bad: "There was a little boy who didn't know if he wanted to be born." After the summer of '58, Eddie O'Hare would finally understand how that little boy felt. There was this sentence, too: "His mommy didn't know if she wanted him to be born, either." It was only after he'd met Marion that Eddie understood how that mommy felt.

That Friday in the frame shop in Southampton, Eddie O'Hare had a life-changing realization: if the writer's assistant had become a writer, it was *Marion* who'd given him his voice. If when he'd been in her arms—in her bed, inside her—he'd felt, for the first time, that he was almost a man, it was losing her that had given him something to *say*. It was the thought of his life *without* Marion that provided Eddie O'Hare with the authority to write.

"Do you have a picture of Marion Cole in your mind?" Eddie wrote. "I mean, in your mind's eye, can you see exactly what she looks like?" Eddie showed his first two sentences to Penny Pierce.

"Yes, of course—she's very beautiful," the manager said.

Eddie nodded. Then he kept on writing, as follows: "Okay. Although I am Mr. Cole's assistant, I have been sleeping with *Mrs.* Cole this summer. I would estimate that Marion and I have made love about sixty times."

"*Sixty?*" Mrs. Pierce said aloud. She'd come around the countertop so that she could read what he wrote over his shoulder.

Eddie wrote: "We've been doing it for six, almost seven weeks, and we usually do it twice a day—often more than twice a day. But there was the time she had an infection, and we couldn't do it. And when you take into consideration her *period* . . ."

"I see—about sixty times, then," Penny Pierce said. "Go on."

"Okay," Eddie wrote. "While Marion and I have been lovers, *Mr.* Cole—his name is Ted—has had a mistress. She was his model, actually. Do you know Mrs. Vaughn?"

"The Vaughns on Gin Lane? They have quite a ... collection," the frame-shop manager said. (Now *there* was a framing job she would have liked!)

"Yes—that Mrs. Vaughn," Eddie wrote. "She has a son, a little boy."

"Yes, yes—I know!" said Mrs. Pierce. "Please go on."

"Okay," Eddie wrote. "This morning Ted—that is, Mr. Cole—has broken up with Mrs. Vaughn. I don't imagine that there could have been a very happy resolution to their affair. Mrs. Vaughn seemed pretty upset about it. And, meanwhile, Marion is packing up—she's leaving. Ted doesn't know she's leaving, but she is. And Ruth—this is Ruth, she's four."

"Yes, yes!" Penny Pierce interjected.

"Ruth doesn't know her mother is leaving, either," Eddie wrote. "Both Ruth and her father are going to go back home to the house in Sagaponack and realize that Marion is gone. And all the photographs, those pictures that you framed—every one of them, except the one you have here, in the shop."

"Yes, yes—my God, *what?*" Penny Pierce said. Ruth scowled at her. Mrs. Pierce tried her best to smile at the child.

Eddie wrote: "Marion is taking the pictures with her. When Ruth gets home, both her mother and all the pictures will be gone. Her dead brothers *and* her mother will be gone. And the thing about those photographs is that there's a story that goes with all of them—there are *hundreds* of stories, and Ruth knows each and every one of them by heart."

"What do you want from me?" Mrs. Pierce cried.

"Just the photograph of Ruth's mother," Eddie said aloud. "She's in bed in a hotel room, in Paris..."

"Yes, I know the picture—of course you can have it!" Penny Pierce said.

"That's it, then," Eddie said. He wrote: "I just thought that the child would probably really need to have *something* to put near her bed tonight. There won't be any other pictures—all those pictures she's been used to. I thought that if there was one of her mother, especially..."

"But it's not a good picture of the boys—only their *feet*," Mrs. Pierce interrupted.

"Yes, I know," Eddie said. "Ruth particularly likes the feet."

"Are the feet ready?" the four-year-old asked.

"Yes, they are, dear," Penny Pierce said solicitously to Ruth.

"Do you want to see my stitches?" the child asked the manager. "And ... my scab?"

"The envelope is in the car, Ruth—it's in the glove compartment," Eddie explained.

"Oh," Ruth said. "What's a glove department?"

"I'll go check to be sure that the photograph is ready," Penny Pierce announced. "It's *almost* ready, I'm sure." Nervously, she scooped up the pages of stationery from the countertop, although Eddie still held the pen. Before she could leave his side, Eddie caught her by the arm.

"Excuse me," he said, handing her the pen. "The pen is yours, but could I please have my writing back?"

"Yes, of course!" the manager replied. She handed him all the paper, even the blank sheets.

"What did you did?" Ruth asked Eddie.

"I told the lady a story," the sixteen-year-old explained.

"Tell *me* the story," the child said.

"I'll tell you another story, in the car," Eddie promised her. "After we get the picture of your mommy."

"And the *feet!*" the four-year-old insisted.

"The feet, too," Eddie promised.

"What story are you going to tell me?" Ruth asked him.

"I don't know," the boy admitted. He would have to think of one; surprisingly, he wasn't in the least bit worried about it. One would come, he was sure. Nor was he worried anymore about what he had to say to Ted. He would tell Ted everything that Marion had told him to say—and anything else that came into his mind. I can do it, he believed. He had the authority.

Penny Pierce knew he had it, too. When the manager re-emerged from the back rooms of the frame shop, she brought more than the re-matted, reframed photograph with her. Although Mrs. Pierce had not changed her clothes, she had somehow transformed herself; she brought with her a substantially revised *presence*—not merely a fresh scent (a new perfume), but a change in attitude that made her almost alluring. To Eddie, she was borderline seductive—he'd not really noticed her *as a woman* before.

Her hair, which had been up, was down. There'd been some alterations in her makeup, too. Exactly what Mrs. Pierce had done to herself was not hard for Eddie to pinpoint. Her eyes were darker and more pronounced; her lipstick was darker, too. Her face, if not more youthful, was more flushed. And she'd opened her suit jacket, and pushed up the sleeves—and the top *two* buttons of her blouse were unbuttoned. (Only the topmost button had been unbuttoned before.)

In bending down to show Ruth the photograph, Mrs. Pierce revealed a depth of cleavage that Eddie would never have guessed at; when she stood up, she whispered to Eddie: "There's no charge for the photograph, of course."

Eddie nodded and smiled, but Penny Pierce was not through with him. She showed him a page of stationery; she had a question for him—in writing, because it wasn't a question that Mrs. Pierce would ever have asked out loud in front of the child.

"Is Marion Cole leaving *you,* too?" Penny Pierce had written.

"Yes," Eddie told her. Mrs. Pierce gave his wrist a comforting little squeeze.

"I'm sorry," she whispered. Eddie didn't know what to say.

"Did the blood get all gone?" Ruth asked. It was a miracle to the four-year-old that the photograph had been so completely restored. As a result of the accident, she herself bore a scar.

"Yes, dear—it's as good as new!" Mrs. Pierce told the child. "Young man," the manager added, as Eddie took Ruth by the hand, "if you're ever interested in a *job...*" Since Eddie had the photograph in one hand, and Ruth's hand in his other hand, he had no hand free to take the business card that Penny Pierce held out to him. In a move that reminded Eddie of Marion putting the ten-dollar bill in his right rear pocket, Mrs. Pierce deftly inserted the card into the left front pocket of the boy's jeans. "Perhaps next summer, or the summer after that—I'm always looking for help in the summer," the manager said.

Again, Eddie didn't know what to say; once more, he nodded and smiled. It was a posh place, the frame shop. The display room was tasteful; there were mostly examples of customized frames. The poster art, always a favorite in the summer, featured movie posters of the thirties—Greta Garbo as Anna Karenina, Margaret Sullavan as the woman who dies and becomes a ghost at the end of *Three Comrades.* Also, liquor and wine advertisements were popular poster material: there was a dangerous-looking woman sipping a Campari and soda, and a man as handsome as Ted Cole was drinking a martini made with just the right amount and the right brand of vermouth.

Cinzano, Eddie nearly said aloud—he was trying to imagine what it might be like to work there. It would take him about a year and a half to realize that Penny Pierce had been offering him more than a job. His newfound "authority" was so new to him, Eddie O'Hare hadn't yet comprehended the extent of his power.

Something Almost Biblical

Meanwhile, back in the bookstore, Ted Cole was reaching calligraphic heights at the autographing table. His penmanship was perfect; his slow, seemingly carved signature was a thing of beauty. For someone whose books were so short—and he wrote so little—Ted's autograph was a labor of love. ("A labor of *self*-love," Marion had once described Ted's signature to Eddie.) To those booksellers who often complained that the signatures of authors were messy scrawls, as indecipherable as doctors' prescriptions, Ted Cole was the king of autographers. There was nothing dashed-off about his signature, not even on checks. The cursive script was more like italicized print than handwriting.

Ted complained about the pens. He had Mendelssohn hopping around the shop searching for the perfect pen; it had to be a fountain pen, one with just the right nib. And the ink had to be either black or the proper shade of red. ("More like blood than like a fire engine," Ted explained to the bookseller.) As for blue, any shade of blue was an abomination to Ted.

And so Eddie O'Hare was lucky. While Eddie took Ruth's hand and walked with her to the Chevy, Ted took his time. He knew that every autograph-seeker who approached him at the signing table was a potential ride home, but he was picky; he didn't want to be just anyone's passenger.

For example, Mendelssohn introduced him to a woman who lived in Wainscott. Mrs. Hickenlooper said she would be happy to drop Ted at his house in Sagaponack. It really wasn't out of her way. However, she did have some other shopping to do in Southampton. It would take her a little more than an hour, after which she didn't mind stopping back at the bookstore. But Ted told her not to trouble herself; he said he was sure another ride would come his way within the hour.

"But I really don't *mind*," Mrs. Hickenlooper said.

I mind! Ted thought to himself; amiably, he waved the woman away. She went off with an inscribed copy of *The Mouse Crawling Between the Walls*, which Ted had painstakingly dedicated to Mrs. Hickenlooper's five children. She should have bought *five* copies, Ted believed, but he dutifully signed the one, fitting all five names of the Hickenlooper progeny on a single, crowded page.

"My kids are all grown up now," Mrs. Hickenlooper told Ted, "but they sure loved you when they were little ones."

Ted just smiled. Mrs. Hickenlooper was pushing fifty. She had hips like a mule. There was a farmlike solidity to her. She was a gardener, or so it appeared; she wore a broad denim skirt, and her knees were red and stained with soil. "There's no way to be a good weeder without kneeling!" Ted had overheard her telling another man in the bookstore. He was a fellow gardener, apparently—they were comparing gardening books.

It was ungenerous of Ted to take a disparaging view of gardeners. After all, he owed his *life* to Mrs. Vaughn's gardener—for if the courageous man hadn't warned Ted to run, Ted might not have escaped the black Lincoln. Nevertheless, Mrs. Hickenlooper just wasn't the ride home that Ted Cole was looking for.

Then he spotted a more promising candidate. A standoffish young woman—she was at least of legal *driving* age—had hesitated in her approach to the autographing table; she was observing the famous author and illustrator with the characteristic combination of shyness and frolicsomeness that Ted associated with girls who stood on the threshold of attaining more womanly qualities. In a few years, what was now hesitant about her would turn calculating, even shrewd. And what was now coltish, even daring, soon would be better contained. She *had* to be at least seventeen, but not yet twenty; she was both frisky and awkward, both unsure of herself and eager to test herself. She was a little clumsy, but she was bold. Probably a virgin, Ted was thinking; at least she was *very* inexperienced—he was sure.

"Hi," he said.

The pretty girl who was almost a woman was so startled by Ted's unexpected attention that she was speechless; she also turned a prominent shade of red, midway between blood and a fire engine. Her

friend—a vastly plainer, deceptively stupid-looking girl—exploded
into snorts and giggles. Ted had failed to notice that the pretty girl was
in the company of an ugly friend. With any interesting-looking young
woman who was sexually vulnerable, wasn't there always an oafish, unappealing companion to contend with?

But Ted was undaunted by the sidekick. If anything, he saw her as an
intriguing challenge; if her presence meant it was unlikely that he
would get laid today, the potential seduction of the pretty young
woman was no less inviting to him. As Marion had pointed out to
Eddie, it was less the occurrence of sex than the anticipation of it that
titillated Ted; he seemed driven less to do it than to look forward to it.

"Hi," the pretty girl finally managed to reply.

Her pear-shaped friend couldn't contain herself. To the embarrassment of the pretty girl, the ugly one said: "She wrote her freshman English term paper on you!"

"Shut up, Effie!" the pretty girl said.

So she's a college girl, Ted Cole concluded; he guessed that she worshiped *The Door in the Floor*.

"What was the title of your term paper?" Ted asked.

" 'An Analysis of the Atavistic Symbols of Fear in *The Door in the
Floor*,' " the pretty girl, who was clearly mortified, said. "You know, like
the boy not being sure that he wants to be born—and the mother not
being sure that she wants to have him. That's very tribal. Primitive
tribes have those fears. And the myths and fairy tales of primitive
tribes are full of images like magic doors, and children disappearing,
and people being so frightened that their hair turns white overnight.
And in myths and fairy tales there are lots of animals that can suddenly
change their size, like the snake—the snake is very tribal, too, of
course...."

"Of course," Ted agreed. "How long was this paper?"

"Twelve pages," the pretty girl informed him, "not counting the
footnotes and the bibliography."

Not counting the illustrations—just manuscript pages, in ordinary
double-spaced typescript—*The Door in the Floor* was only a page and a
half long; yet it had been published as if it were a whole book, and college students were permitted to write term papers about it. What a
joke! Ted was thinking.

He liked the girl's lips; her mouth was round and small. And her
breasts were full—they were almost fat. In a few years, she would have

to struggle with her weight, but now her plumpness was appealing and she still had a waist. Ted was fond of assessing women by their body types; with most women, Ted believed he could visualize what the future would do to their bodies. This one would have one baby and lose her waist; she would also run the risk of her hips taking over her body, whereas now her voluptuousness was contained—if barely. By the time she's thirty, she'll be as pear-shaped as her friend, Ted was thinking, but all he said was, "What's your name?"

"Glorie—not with a *y* but with an *i-e,*" the pretty girl replied. "And this is Effie."

I'll show you something *atavistic,* Glorie, Ted was thinking. Weren't forty-five-year-old men and eighteen-year-old girls frequently paired together in primitive tribes? I'll show you something *tribal,* Ted Cole thought, but what he said was: "I don't suppose you girls have a car. Believe it or not, I need a ride."

Believe it or not, Mrs. Vaughn, having lost Ted, had irrationally directed her considerable anger toward her brave but defenseless gardener. She'd parked the Lincoln—facing out, motor running—in the entrance of her driveway; the black nose of the car's sleek hood and its gleaming-silver grille were poking into Gin Lane. Poised at the steering wheel, where she sat for almost half an hour (until the Lincoln ran out of gas), Mrs. Vaughn waited for the '57 black and white Chevy to make the turn onto Gin Lane from either Wyandanch Lane or South Main Street. She thought that Ted would not stray far from the vicinity, for she, along with Ted, still assumed that Marion's lover—"the pretty boy," as Mrs. Vaughn thought of Eddie—remained Ted's chauffeur. Therefore, Mrs. Vaughn turned up the tune on the radio and waited.

Inside the black Lincoln, the music throbbed; the sheer volume, and the degree to which the bass vibrated the speakers in the car, almost concealed from Mrs. Vaughn that the Lincoln had run out of gas. Had the car not shuddered so violently at that moment, Mrs. Vaughn might have gone on waiting at the steering wheel until her son was brought home from his afternoon tennis lesson.

More important, that the Lincoln finally ran out of gas may have spared Mrs. Vaughn's gardener a cruel death. The poor man, whose ladder had been knocked from under him, had all this while been trapped in the remorseless privet, where the carbon-monoxide fumes from the Lincoln's exhaust had at first made him sick and then nearly killed him. He was half asleep, but conscious of the fact that he was half dead, when the car conked out and a fresh sea breeze revived him.

In his earlier effort to climb down from the top of the hedge, the heel of his right foot had become stuck in a twisted notch of the privet. In attempting to free his boot from the notch, the gardener had lost his balance and fallen upside down in the thick hedge—thus wedging his boot heel more snugly than before in the tenacious privet. His ankle was sorely twisted in the fall, and—hanging by his heel in the tangled hedge—he had pulled an abdominal muscle while trying to untie his boot.

A small man of Hispanic descent, with an appropriately small pot-belly, Eduardo Gomez was not used to performing upside-down sit-ups in a hedge. His boots were of the above-ankle sort, and although he'd struggled to sit up long enough to untie the laces, he had not been able to bear the pain of the position long enough to *loosen* the laces. The boot would not slip off.

Meanwhile, Mrs. Vaughn couldn't hear Eduardo's calls for help above the volume and the throbbing bass of her car radio. The miser-able hanging gardener, aware of the rising fumes from the Lincoln's exhaust, which were gathering in the dense and seemingly airless hedge, was convinced that the privet would be his final resting place. Eduardo Gomez would be the victim of another man's lust, and of an-other man's proverbial "woman scorned." Nor did the dying gardener miss the irony that it was the shredded pornographic drawings of his employer that had led him to his position in the murderous privet. Had the Lincoln not run out of gas, the gardener might have become Southampton's first fatality ever ascribed to pornography—but doubt-less not the last, Eduardo was thinking, as he drifted off in the carbon-monoxide fumes. It crossed his poisoned mind that Ted Cole deserved to die this way, but not an innocent gardener.

In Mrs. Vaughn's view, her gardener was *not* innocent. Earlier, she'd heard him cry out: "Run!" By warning Ted, Eduardo had betrayed her! If the wretched dangling man had kept his mouth shut, Ted would not have been afforded those valuable extra seconds. As it turned out, Ted broke into a full sprint before the black Lincoln shot onto Gin Lane. Mrs. Vaughn was certain that she would have flattened him as incon-trovertibly as she'd flattened the road sign at the corner of South Main

Street. It was because of her own disloyal gardener that Ted Cole had got away!

Thus, when the Lincoln ran out of gas and Mrs. Vaughn got out of the car—first slamming the door shut and then opening it again, for she'd forgotten to turn off the infernal radio—she first heard Eduardo's weakened cries for help and her heart was instantly hardened against him. She tromped on the little crushed stones of the courtyard, nearly tripping on the fallen ladder, and there she beheld her betrayer, who was ridiculously suspended by his foot in the midst of the privet. Mrs. Vaughn was further incensed to see that Eduardo had not yet cleaned up those revealing drawings. In addition, there was a totally illogical aspect to her hatred of the gardener: he had doubtless seen her terrible nakedness in the drawings. (How could he *not* have seen it?) And so she hated Eduardo Gomez in the manner that she hated Eddie O'Hare, who had also seen her so ... *exposed.*

"Please, ma'am," Eduardo begged her. "If you are able to lift the ladder, if I can just hold on to it, I might be able to get down."

"You!" Mrs. Vaughn shouted at him. She picked up a handful of the little stones and threw them into the hedge. The gardener shut his eyes, but the privet was so thick that none of the stones hit him. "You *warned* him! You *vile* little man!" Mrs. Vaughn screamed. She threw another handful of stones, which were equally harmless. That she couldn't manage to hit a motionless, upside-down gardener made her even madder. "You *betrayed* me!" she cried.

"If you'd killed him, you'd have gone to jail," Eduardo said, trying to reason with her. But she was strutting away from him; even from upside down he could tell that she was returning to her house. Her purposeful little steps ... her tight little butt. He knew before she got to the door that she was going to slam it behind her. Eduardo had long ago imagined this about her: she was a woman of tantrums, a veteran door-slammer—as if the big bang that the door made offered her consolation for her diminutiveness. The gardener had a dread of small women; he'd always imagined them to have an anger disproportionate to their size. His own wife was large and comfortingly soft; she was a good-natured woman with a generous, forgiving disposition.

"Clean up this *mess*! And then *leave*! This is your *last* day!" Mrs. Vaughn was shouting to Eduardo, who hung perfectly still—as if paralyzed by disbelief. "You're *fired*!" she added.

"But I can't get down!" he called softly to her, knowing even before he spoke that the door would slam shut on his words.

Despite the pulled muscle in his abdomen, Eduardo found the strength to surmount his pain; doubtless he was helped by a sense of injustice, for he managed to perform another upside-down sit-up—he held the agonizing position long enough to sufficiently unlace his boot. His trapped foot slipped free. He plummeted headfirst through the heart of the hedge, flailing with both arms and legs, and (to his relief) landed on all fours among the roots; he crawled into the courtyard, spitting out twigs and leaves.

Eduardo was still nauseated and dizzy and intermittently lethargic from his lengthy exposure to the Lincoln's exhaust fumes, and his upper lip had been cut by a branch. He tried to walk, but he quickly returned to all fours, and in this animalistic state approached the clogged fountain. He plunged his head into the water, forgetting the squid ink. The water was foul and fishy-smelling, and when the gardener withdrew his head from the fountain and wrung the water out of his hair, his face and hands were sepia-colored. Eduardo felt like throwing up while he climbed the ladder to retrieve his boot.

Then the stunned man limped aimlessly about the courtyard—since he'd already been fired, what point was there in his completing the task of gathering the scraps of pornography (as Mrs. Vaughn had demanded)? He could see no wisdom in performing *any* task for a woman who had not only fired him but had also left him for dead; yet when he decided that he would leave, he realized that the out-of-gas Lincoln was obstructing the driveway. Eduardo's truck, which was always parked out of sight (behind the toolhouse and the garage and the potting shed), could not slip past the privet while the Lincoln was blocking the way. The gardener had to syphon gas from the lawn mower in order to start the Lincoln and return the abandoned car to the garage. Alas, this activity did not go unnoticed by Mrs. Vaughn.

She confronted Eduardo in the courtyard, where only the fountain separated them. The stained pool was now as unsightly as a shallow birdbath in which a hundred bats had drowned. Mrs. Vaughn held something in her hand—it was a check—and the wrecked gardener eyed her warily; he limped sideways, keeping the fountain between them, as Mrs. Vaughn began to circle the blackened water in his direction.

"Don't you want this? It's your *last* paycheck!" the evil little woman said.

Eduardo halted. If she was going to pay him, perhaps he would stay and clean up the last of the ripped-to-shreds pornography. After all, the maintenance of the Vaughn estate had been his principal source of income for many years. The gardener was a proud man, and the miniature bitch had humiliated him; yet he thought that even if the check she was offering him was the *last* paycheck he would ever receive from her, it would be sizable.

With his hand held out in front of him, Eduardo cautiously inched around the spoiled fountain in Mrs. Vaughn's direction. She allowed him to approach her. She was almost within his reach when she made several hasty folds in the check, and—when it was crudely shaped like a boat—she launched it into the murky water. The check sailed into the middle of the funereal pool. It was necessary for Eduardo to wade into the fountain, which he did with trepidation.

"Go *fish!*" Mrs. Vaughn shrieked at him.

Even as he plucked the check out of the water, Eduardo was aware that the ink had run; he couldn't read what the amount had been *or* Mrs. Vaughn's cramped signature. And before he could step out of the fishy-smelling fountain, he knew (without once looking at her haughty, retreating figure) that the door would slam again. The fired gardener dried the worthless check against his pants and preserved it in his wallet; he didn't know why he bothered.

Dutifully, Eduardo returned the ladder to its usual place alongside the potting shed. He saw a rake that he'd meant to repair and briefly wondered what he should do with it; he left it on the worktable in the toolhouse. He would have gone home then—he was already limping slowly toward his truck—but he suddenly saw the three large leaf bags that he'd already filled with the scraps of the shredded drawings; he had calculated that the remaining mess, when it was all cleaned up, might fill another two bags.

Eduardo Gomez picked up the first of the three full bags and emptied it onto the lawn. The wind quickly blew some of the paper all around, but the gardener was dissatisfied with the results; he ran limping through the pile of paper, kicking his feet like a child in a heap of leaves. The long tatters flew through the garden and draped the birdbath. The beach roses at the back of the yard, where the footpath led to the beach, were a magnet to the scraps and shreds of paper; the torn paper clung to everything it touched, like tinsel to a Christmas tree.

The gardener limped into the courtyard with the remaining two full bags. The first of these he upended in the fountain, where the mass of ripped drawings soaked up the blackened water like a giant, immovable sponge. The last full bag, which by coincidence included some of the best (albeit largely destroyed) views of Mrs. Vaughn's crotch, was no challenge to Eduardo's remaining creativity. The inspired man limped in circles around the courtyard, holding the open bag above his head. It was like a kite that refused to fly, but the countless snippets of pornography did indeed take flight; they rose into the privet, from which the heroic gardener had earlier plucked them, and they rose *above* the privet, too. As if to reward Eduardo Gomez for his courage, a strong sea breeze blew partial views of Mrs. Vaughn's breasts and vagina to both ends of Gin Lane.

It was later reported to the Southampton police that two boys on bicycles were treated to a questionable glimpse of Mrs. Vaughn's anatomy, which the boys found as far away as First Neck Lane—a testimony to the strength of the wind, which had blown this particular close-up of Mrs. Vaughn's nipple, and her irregularly enlarged areola, across Agawam Lake. (The boys, who were brothers, brought the scrap of the pornographic drawing home, where their parents discovered the obscenity and called the cops.)

Agawam Lake, which was no larger than a pond, separated Gin Lane from First Neck Lane, where—at the very moment Eduardo released the remains of Ted Cole's drawings—the artist himself was pursuing his seduction of a slightly overweight eighteen-year-old girl. Glorie had brought Ted home to meet her mother, largely because the girl had no car of her own and needed her mother's permission in order to borrow the family vehicle.

It had not been too long a walk from the bookstore to Glorie's house on First Neck Lane, but Ted's subtle courtship of the college girl had several times been interrupted by insulting questions from Glorie's pathetic pear-shaped friend. Effie was far less a fan of *The Door in the Floor* than Glorie was; the tragically unattractive girl had *not* written *her* term paper on the perceived atavism in Ted Cole's symbols of fear. Though she was intensely ugly, Effie was a lot less full of shit than Glorie was.

Effie was a lot less full of shit than Ted, too. In fact, the fat girl was insightful: she wisely grew to dislike the famous author in the course of their short walk; Effie also saw the efforts of Ted's seduction-in-progress for what it was. Glorie, if she saw what was progressing, offered little resistance.

That Ted took an unexpected interest (of a sexual kind) in Glorie's *mother* surprised him. If Glorie was a little *too* young and inexperienced for his usual taste—and she was borderline overweight—Glorie's mom was older than Marion and the type of woman Ted generally ignored. Mrs. Mountsier was preternaturally thin, the result of an inability to eat that had been brought on by her husband's recent and wholly unanticipated death. She was clearly a widow who'd not only deeply loved her husband; she was also—and this was obvious, even to Ted—a widow still caught in the detectable stages of grief. In short, she was not a woman who could be seduced by *anybody*; yet Ted Cole was not just anybody, and he couldn't suppress his unpredictable attraction to her.

Glorie must have inherited her penchant for curvaceousness from a grandmother or an even more distant relation. Mrs. Mountsier was a classical but wraithlike beauty, a pretender in Marion's inimitable mold. Whereas Marion's perpetual sorrow had turned Ted away from her, Mrs. Mountsier's regal sadness turned Ted on. Yet his attraction to her daughter was undiminished—it was suddenly the *two* of them he wanted! In a similar situation, most men might have thought: What a dilemma! But Ted Cole thought only in terms of possibilities. What a *possibility*! he was thinking, as he allowed Mrs. Mountsier to make him a sandwich—after all, it was almost lunchtime—*and* he yielded to Glorie's insistence that he allow her to put his wet blue jeans and his soaked-through shoes in the dryer.

"They'll be dry in fifteen or twenty minutes," the eighteen-year-old promised. (The shoes would take at least half an hour, but what was the hurry?)

While he ate his lunch, Ted wore a bathrobe belonging to the late *Mr.* Mountsier. Mrs. Mountsier had shown Ted where the bathroom was, so he could change, and she'd handed him her dead husband's bathrobe with an especially appealing sort of sadness.

Ted had never tried to seduce a widow before—not to mention a mother and her daughter. He'd spent the summer drawing Mrs.

Vaughn. The illustrations for the unfinished *A Sound Like Someone Trying Not to Make a Sound* had been long neglected; he'd barely begun to think about what those illustrations should be. Yet here, in a comfortable house on First Neck Lane, a mother-and-daughter portrait of unusual promise had presented itself to him—he knew he had to try it.

Mrs. Mountsier did not eat lunch. The thinness of her face, which looked frail and brittle in the midday light, suggested that she had at best an intermittent appetite, or that she had some difficulty keeping food down. She'd delicately powdered the dark circles under her eyes; like Marion, Mrs. Mountsier could sleep only for short periods of time, when she was utterly exhausted. Ted noticed that the thumb of Mrs. Mountsier's left hand could not leave her wedding ring alone, although she was unaware of how constantly she touched it.

When Glorie saw what her mother was doing to her wedding ring, she reached out and squeezed her hand. The look that Mrs. Mountsier gave her daughter was both thankful and apologetic; the sympathy passed between them like a letter slipped under a door. (In the first of the drawings, Ted would pose them with the daughter holding her mother's hand.)

"You know, this is quite a coincidence," he began, "but I've been looking for two suitable subjects for a mother-and-daughter portrait—it's something I've been thinking about for my next book."

"Is it another children's book?" asked Mrs. Mountsier.

"Categorically, yes," Ted answered her, "but I don't think that any of my books are truly for children. First of all, there are the mothers who must buy them, and—usually—the mothers are the first to read them aloud. Children usually *hear* them before they're able to read them. And when those children are adults, they often go back to my books and read them again."

"That's just how it happened to me!" Glorie said. Effie, who was sulking, rolled her eyes.

Everyone but Effie was pleased. Mrs. Mountsier had been assured that mothers came first. Glorie had been congratulated for no longer being a child; the famous author had recognized that she was an adult now.

"What sort of drawings do you have in mind?" Mrs. Mountsier asked.

"Well. At first I would want to draw you and your daughter together," Ted told her. "That way, when I draw each of you separately, the presence of the one who's missing is ... well, somehow, *there.*"

"Wow! Do you want to do it, Mom?" Glorie asked. (Effie was rolling her eyes again, but Ted never paid much attention to someone who wasn't attractive.)

"I don't know. How long would it take?" Mrs. Mountsier asked. "Or which of us would you want to draw first? I mean separately. I mean, after you've drawn us together." (In a rush of desire, Ted realized that the widow was a wreck.)

"When do you go back to college?" Ted asked Glorie.

"September fifth or something," Glorie said.

"September third," Effie corrected her. "And you were going to spend Labor Day weekend in Maine, with me," she added.

"I should do Glorie first, then," Ted told Mrs. Mountsier. "First the two of you together. Then Glorie alone. Then, when Glorie is back in college, *you* alone."

"Oh, I don't know," Mrs. Mountsier said.

"Come on, Mom! It'll be fun!" Glorie said.

"Well." It was Ted's famous, never-ending "Well."

"Well *what?*" Effie asked rudely.

"I mean, you don't have to decide *today*," Ted told Mrs. Mountsier. "Just think about it," he said to Glorie. Ted could tell what Glorie was already thinking about. Glorie would be the easy one. And then... what a pleasantly long fall and winter it might be! (Ted was imagining the vastly slower seduction of the grieving Mrs. Mountsier—it might take months, even a year.)

It called upon tact to permit *both* the mother and daughter to drive him back to Sagaponack. Mrs. Mountsier volunteered; then she realized that she'd hurt her daughter's feelings, that Glorie truly had her heart set on driving the famous author and illustrator home.

"Oh, please—*you* do it, then, Glorie," Mrs. Mountsier said. "I hadn't realized how much you *wanted* to do it."

It won't work if they quarrel, Ted was thinking. "Speaking selfishly," he said—he smiled charmingly at Effie—"I'd be honored if you *all* drove me home." Although his charm didn't work with Effie, mother and daughter were instantly reconciled—for now.

Ted also played the role of peacemaker when it came to deciding whether Mrs. Mountsier or Glorie should drive. "Personally," he said, smiling at Glorie, "I think people of your age are better drivers than their parents. On the other hand"—he turned his smile to Mrs. Mountsier—"people like us are unbearable backseat drivers." Ted turned back to Glorie. "Let your mother drive," he told the girl. "It's the only way to keep her from being a backseat driver."

Although Ted had seemed indifferent to Effie's rolling her eyes, this time he anticipated her; he turned to the ugly wretch and rolled *his* eyes, just to show her that he knew.

To anyone seeing them, they were seated in the car like a reasonably normal family. Mrs. Mountsier was at the wheel with the convicted DWI celebrity in the passenger seat beside her. In the back were the children. The one with the misfortune to be ugly was, naturally, sullen and withdrawn; it was probably to be expected, because her apparent "sister" was comparatively pretty. Effie sat behind Ted, glaring at the back of his head. Glorie leaned forward, filling the space between the two front seats of Mrs. Mountsier's dark-green Saab. By turning in his seat to view Mrs. Mountsier's stunning profile, Ted could also glimpse her vivacious if not exactly beautiful daughter.

Mrs. Mountsier was a good driver who never took her eyes off the road. The daughter couldn't take her eyes off Ted. For a day that had started out so badly, look what opportunities had come out of it! Ted glanced at his watch and was surprised to see that it was early in the afternoon. He would be home before two—plenty of time to show the mother and daughter his workroom while there was still good light. You can't judge a day by its beginning, Ted had decided, as Mrs. Mountsier passed Agawam Lake and turned from Dune Road onto Gin Lane. Ted had been so transfixed by the visual comparison between mother and daughter that he'd not been watching the road.

"Oh, you're going *this* way . . ." he said in a whisper.

"Why are you whispering?" Effie asked him.

On Gin Lane, Mrs. Mountsier was forced to slow the car to a crawl. The street was littered with paper; it hung from the hedges. As Mrs. Mountsier's car passed, the paper swirled around it. A piece stuck to the windshield. Mrs. Mountsier considered stopping the car.

"Don't stop!" Ted told her. "Just use your windshield wipers!"

"Talk about backseat drivers . . ." Effie remarked.

But, to Ted's relief, the windshield wipers worked. The offending scrap of paper flew on. (Ted had briefly seen what he was sure was Mrs. Vaughn's armpit; it was from one of the most compromising series, when she was on her back with her hands crossed behind her head.)

"What *is* all this stuff?" Glorie asked.

"Someone's trash, I guess," her mother replied.

"Yes," Ted said. "Someone's dog must have got into someone's trash."

"What a mess," Effie observed.

"They should fine whoever it is," Mrs. Mountsier said.

"Yes," Ted agreed. "Even if the culprit is a dog—fine the dog!" Everyone but Effie laughed.

As they neared the end of Gin Lane, a spirited gathering of shredded paper flew all around the moving car; it was as if the ripped drawings of Mrs. Vaughn's humiliation didn't want to let Ted go. But the corner was turned; the road ahead was clear. Ted felt a surge of wild happiness, but he made no attempt to express it. A rare moment of reflection overcame him; it was something almost biblical. In his undeserved escape from Mrs. Vaughn, and in the stimulating company of Mrs. Mountsier and her daughter, Ted Cole's overriding thought repeated itself in his mind like a litany. Lust begets lust, begets lust, begets lust—over and over again. That was the thrill of it.

The Authority of the Written Word

The story that Eddie told Ruth in the car was something she would always remember. When she even momentarily forgot it, she had only to look at the thin scar on her right index finger, which would always be there. (When Ruth was in her forties, the scar was so small that it was visible only to her, or to someone who already knew it was there—someone who was looking for it.)

"There was once a little girl," Eddie began.

"What was her name?" Ruth asked.

"Ruth," Eddie replied.

"Yes," Ruth agreed. "Go on."

"She cut her finger on some broken glass," Eddie continued, "and her finger bled and bled and bled. There was much more blood than Ruth thought could possibly be in her finger. She thought the blood must be coming from everywhere, from her whole body."

"Right," Ruth said.

"But when she went to the hospital, she needed only two shots and two stitches."

"Three needles," Ruth reminded him, counting the stitches.

"Oh, yes," Eddie agreed. "But Ruth was very brave, and she didn't mind that, for almost a week, she couldn't swim in the ocean or even get her finger wet when she took a bath."

"Why didn't I mind?" Ruth asked him.

"Okay, maybe you minded a *little*," Eddie admitted. "But you didn't complain about it."

"I was brave?" the four-year-old asked.

"You were—you *are* brave," Eddie told her.

"What does *brave* mean?" Ruth asked him.

"It means that you don't cry," Eddie said.

"I cried a little," Ruth pointed out.

"A little is okay," Eddie told her. "*Brave* means that you accept what happens to you—you just try to make the best of it."

"Tell me more about the cut," the child said.

"When the doctor took out the stitches, the scar was thin and white and a perfect straight line," Eddie told her. "In the whole rest of your life, if you ever need to feel brave, just look at your scar."

Ruth stared at it. "Will it always be there?" she asked Eddie.

"Always," he told her. "Your hand will grow bigger, and your finger will grow bigger, but the scar will stay the same size. When you're all grown up, the scar will *look* smaller, but that will be because the rest of you has grown bigger—the scar will always be the same. It will just not be as noticeable, which means that it will become harder and harder to see. You'll have to show it to people in good light, and you'll have to say, 'Can you see my scar?' And they'll have to look really closely; only then will they be able to see it. *You'll* always be able to see it because you'll know where to look. And, of course, it will always show up on a finger-print."

"What's a fingerprint?" Ruth asked.

"It's kind of hard to show you while we're in the car," Eddie said.

When they got to the beach, Ruth asked him again, but even in the wet sand, Ruth's fingers were too small to leave clear fingerprints—or else the sand was too coarse. As Ruth played in the shallow water, the yellow-brown antiseptic was completely washed away; but the scar remained a bright white line on her finger. Not until they went to a restaurant could she see what a fingerprint was.

There, on the same plate with her grilled-cheese sandwich and her French fries, Eddie poured out a spreading puddle of ketchup. He dipped the index finger of Ruth's right hand in the ketchup and gently pressed her finger on a paper napkin. Beside the fingerprint of her right index finger, Eddie made a second print—this time using the index finger from Ruth's left hand. Eddie told her to look at the napkin through her water glass, which magnified the fingerprints so that Ruth could see the unmatched whorls. And there it was—as it would be, forever: the perfectly vertical line on her right index finger; seen through the water glass, it was nearly twice the size of the scar itself.

"Those are your fingerprints—nobody else will ever have fingerprints like yours," Eddie told her.

"And my scar will always be there?" Ruth asked him again.

"Your scar will be a part of you forever," Eddie promised her.

After their lunch in Bridgehampton, Ruth wanted to keep the napkin with her fingerprints. Eddie put it in the envelope with her stitches and her scab. He saw that the scab had shriveled up; it was a quarter the size of a ladybug, but of a similar russet color and spotted black.

At about 2:15 on that Friday afternoon, Eddie O'Hare turned onto Parsonage Lane, Sagaponack. When he was still some distance from the Coles' house, he was relieved to see that the moving truck and Marion's Mercedes were nowhere in sight. However, an unfamiliar car—a dark-green Saab—was parked in the driveway. As Eddie slowed the Chevy to a crawl, Ted, the obdurate womanizer, was saying good-bye to the three women in the Saab.

Ted had already shown his workroom to his future models—Mrs. Mountsier and her daughter, Glorie. Effie had refused to leave the backseat of the car. Poor Effie was ahead of her time: she was a young woman of integrity and insight and intelligence, trapped in a body that most men either ignored or spurned; of the three women in the dark-green Saab on that Friday afternoon, Effie was the only one with the wisdom to see that Ted Cole was as deceitful as a damaged condom.

For a heart-stopping second Eddie thought that the driver of the dark-green Saab was Marion, but as Eddie turned into the driveway he saw that Mrs. Mountsier did not as closely resemble Marion as he'd thought. For just a second, Eddie had hoped that Marion had had a change of heart. She's *not* leaving Ruth, he thought—or *me*. But Mrs. Mountsier was not Marion; nor did Mrs. Mountsier's daughter, Glorie, resemble Alice—the pretty college-girl nanny whom Eddie despised. (Eddie had also jumped to the conclusion that Glorie was Alice.) Now Eddie realized that they were merely a bunch of women who'd given Ted a ride home. The boy wondered which one Ted had taken an interest in—certainly not the one in the backseat.

As the dark-green Saab pulled out of the driveway, Eddie could instantly tell from Ted's innocent, only mildly puzzled expression that he didn't know Marion was gone.

"Daddy! Daddy!" Ruth cried. "Do you want to see my stitches? There are four pieces. And I got a scab. Show Daddy the scab!" the four-year-old told Eddie, who handed Ted the envelope.

"Those are my fingerprints," the child explained to her father. He was staring at the paper napkin with the ketchup stains.

"Careful the scab doesn't blow away in the wind," Eddie warned Ted. The scab was so small that Ted peered at it without taking it out of the envelope.

"That's really neat, Ruthie," Ruth's father said. "So . . . you were at the doctor, getting her stitches taken out?" Ted asked Eddie.

"And we went to the beach, and we had lunch," Ruth told her father. "I had a grilled-cheese sandwich and French fries with ketchup. And Eddie showed me my fingerprints. I'm going to keep my scar forever."

"That's nice, Ruthie." Ted was watching Eddie take the beach bag out of the Chevy. On top were the pages of stationery from the frame shop in Southampton—the story of the summer of '58, which Eddie had written for Penny Pierce. Seeing the pages gave Eddie an idea. He went to the trunk of the Chevy and took out the rematted, reframed photograph of Marion in Paris. Ted was now watching Eddie's every move with increasing unease.

"I see the photograph was ready, finally," Ted observed.

"We got the *feet* back, Daddy! The picture is all fixed," Ruth said.

Ted picked up his daughter and held her, kissing her forehead. "You've got sand in your hair, and salt water to rinse out. You need a bath, Ruthie."

"But not a shampoo!" Ruth cried.

"Well, yes, Ruthie—you need a shampoo, too."

"But I *hate* shampoos—they make me cry!" Ruth exclaimed.

"Well." Ted stopped as usual. He couldn't take his eyes off Eddie. To Eddie, Ted said: "I waited quite a while for you this morning. Where were you?"

Eddie handed him the pages he'd written for Penny Pierce. "The lady in the frame shop asked me to write this," Eddie began. "She wanted me to explain to her, in writing, why I wouldn't leave the shop without the photograph."

Ted didn't take the pages, but he put Ruth down and stared at his own house. "Where's Alice?" he asked Eddie. "Isn't it Alice who's here in the afternoons? Where's the nanny? Where's *Marion*?"

"I'll give Ruth a bath," Eddie answered him. Once again the sixteen-year-old handed Ted the pages. "Better read this," Eddie told him.

"Answer me, Eddie."

"Read that first," Eddie said. He picked up Ruth and started carrying her toward the house with the beach bag slung over his shoulder. He held Ruth with one arm, carrying the photo of Marion and the feet in his free hand.

"You haven't given Ruth a bath before," Ted called after him. "You don't know *how* to give her a bath!"

"I can figure it out. Ruth can tell me," Eddie called back to him. "Read that," Eddie repeated.

"Okay, okay," Ted told him. He started reading aloud: " 'Do you have a picture of Marion Cole in your mind?' Hey! What *is* this?"

"It's the only good writing I've done all summer," Eddie answered, carrying Ruth inside the house. Once inside, Eddie wondered how he could get Ruth in a bath—in *any* of the house's several bathtubs—without her noticing that the photographs of her dead brothers were gone.

The phone was ringing. Eddie hoped it was Alice. Still carrying Ruth, he answered the phone in the kitchen. There had never been more than three or four photos of Thomas and Timothy in the kitchen; Eddie hoped that Ruth might not notice they were gone. And, because of the ringing phone, Eddie had rushed through the front hall with Ruth in his arms. Ruth might not have noticed the darker rectangles of unfaded wallpaper; the bare walls were also distinguished by the picture hooks, which Marion had left behind.

It was Alice on the phone. Eddie told her to come over right away. Then he put Ruth over his shoulder, and—holding her tight—he ran with her up the stairs. "It's a race to the bathtub!" Eddie said. "*Which* bathtub do you want? Your mommy and daddy's bathtub, *my* bathtub, *another* bathtub ..."

"*Your* bathtub!" Ruth shrieked.

He veered into the long upstairs hall, where he was surprised to see how vividly the picture hooks stood out against the walls. Some of the hooks were black; some were the color of gold or silver. All of them were somehow ugly. It was as if the house had suffered an infestation of metallic beetles.

"Did you saw that?" Ruth asked.

But Eddie, still running, carried her into his bedroom at the far end of the hall—and then into his bathroom, where he hung the photograph of Marion in the Hôtel du Quai Voltaire exactly where it had been when the summer began.

Eddie started the bath running as he helped Ruth out of her clothes, which was a struggle because Ruth kept trying to look at the bathroom walls while Eddie was pulling her T-shirt off. Except for the photo of Marion in Paris, the walls were bare. The other photographs were missing. The naked picture hooks seemed more numerous than they were. To Eddie, the beetlelike picture hooks seemed to be crawling on the walls.

"Where are the other pictures?" Ruth asked, as Eddie lifted her into the filling tub.

"Maybe your mommy moved them," Eddie told her. "Look at you—there's sand between your toes, and in your hair, and in your ears!"

"It got in my crack, too—it always does," Ruth remarked.

"Oh, yes ..." Eddie said. "It's a good time to have a bath, all right!"

"No shampoo," Ruth insisted.

"But the sand is in your hair," Eddie told her. The bathtub had a European fixture, a movable hose with which Eddie began to spray the child while she shrieked.

"No shampoo!"

"Just a little shampoo," Eddie told her. "Just close your eyes."

"It's going in my ears, too!" the four-year-old screamed.

"I thought you were brave. Aren't you brave?" Eddie asked her. As soon as the shampooing was finished, Ruth stopped crying. Eddie let her play with the hose until she sprayed him.

"Where did Mommy move the pictures?" Ruth asked.

"I don't know," Eddie admitted. (By tonight, even before it was dark, this would become a refrain.)

"Did Mommy move the pictures from the halls, too?" the child asked.

"Yes, Ruth."

"Why?" the four-year-old asked.

"I don't know," he repeated.

Pointing at the bathroom walls, Ruth said: "But Mommy didn't move *those* things. What are those things called?"

"Picture hooks," Eddie said.

"Why didn't Mommy move them?" Ruth asked.

"I don't know," Eddie repeated. The child was standing in the emptying tub, which was filled with sand. Ruth began to shiver as soon as Eddie lifted her to the bath mat.

As he was drying her off, he wondered how he was supposed to untangle the little girl's hair; it was quite long and full of knots. Eddie was distracted by trying to remember, word for word, what he'd written for Penny Pierce; he was also trying to imagine Ted's reaction to certain sentences. For example: "I would estimate that Marion and I have made love about sixty times." And following *that* sentence, there were *these* sentences, too: "When Ruth gets home, both her mother and all the pictures will be gone. Her dead brothers *and* her mother will be gone."

Remembering his conclusion, word for word, Eddie wondered if Ted would appreciate the understatement. "I just thought that the child would probably really need to have *something* to put near her bed tonight," Eddie had written. "There won't be any other pictures—all those pictures she's been used to. I thought that if there was one of her mother, especially ..."

Eddie had already wrapped Ruth up in a towel before he noticed Ted standing in the bathroom doorway. In a wordless exchange, Eddie picked up the child and handed her to her father while Ted gave Eddie back the pages he'd written.

"Daddy! Daddy!" Ruth said. "Mommy *moved* all the pictures! But not the ... what are they called?" she asked Eddie.

"The picture hooks."

"Right," Ruth said. "Why did she did that?" the four-year-old asked her father.

"I don't know, Ruthie."

"I'm going to take a quick shower," Eddie told Ted.

"Yes, make it a quick one," Ted told him. He carried his daughter into the hall.

"Look at all the ... what are they called?" Ruth asked Ted.

"Picture hooks, Ruthie."

Only after he'd showered did Eddie realize that Ted and Ruth had taken the photograph of Marion off the bathroom wall; they must have moved it to Ruth's room. It was fascinating to Eddie to realize that what he'd written was coming true. He wanted to be alone with Ted, to tell him everything that Marion had instructed him to say—and anything that Eddie could add. He wanted to hurt Ted with as many truths as he could summon. But at the same time Eddie wanted to lie to Ruth. For thirty-seven years he would want to lie to her, to tell her anything that might make her feel better.

When Eddie had dressed, he put the pages he'd written into his empty duffel bag. He would be packing soon, and he wanted to be sure to take his writing with him. But, to his surprise, the duffel bag wasn't empty. At the bottom was Marion's pink cashmere cardigan; she'd also included her lilac-colored silk camisole and matching panties, despite her observation that pink with lilac was an unwise combination. She knew it was the décolletage (and the lace) that had appealed to Eddie.

Eddie rummaged through the bag, hoping to find more; maybe Marion had written him a letter. What he found surprised him as much as the discovery of her clothing. It was the crushed, bread loaf–shaped present that Eddie's father had given him as he'd boarded the ferry for Long Island; it was Ruth's present, the wrapping much the worse for its summerlong residence in the bottom of the duffel bag. Eddie didn't think now was the right time to give Ruth the present, whatever it was.

Suddenly he thought of *another* use for the pages he'd written for Penny Pierce and shown to Ted. When Alice arrived, the pages would be useful in bringing her up to date; surely the nanny needed to know— at least if she was going to be sensitive to everything Ruth would be feeling. Eddie folded the pages and stuck them in his right rear pocket. His jeans were a little damp, because he'd worn them over his wet bathing suit when he and Ruth had left the beach. The ten-dollar bill that Marion had given him was also a little damp, as was Penny Pierce's business card, with her home phone number written in by hand. He put

them both in the duffel bag; they were already in the category of me-
mentos of the summer of '58, which Eddie was beginning to realize was
both a watershed in his life and a legacy that Ruth would carry with her
for as long as she would carry her scar.

The poor kid, Eddie was thinking, not realizing that this was also a
watershed. At sixteen, Eddie O'Hare had ceased to be a teenager, in the
sense that he was no longer as self-absorbed; he was concerned for
someone else. The rest of today and tonight, Eddie promised himself,
he would do what he did and say what he said for *Ruth*. He walked
down the hall toward Ruth's bedroom, where Ted had already hung the
photograph of Marion and the feet from one of the many exposed picture hooks on Ruth's stark walls.

"Look, Eddie!" the child said, pointing to the photo of her mother.

"I see," Eddie told her. "It looks very nice there."

From the downstairs of the house, a woman's voice called up to
them. "Hello! Hello?"

"Mommy!" Ruth cried.

"Marion?" Ted called.

"It's Alice," Eddie told them.

Eddie stopped the nanny when she was halfway up the stairs.
"There's a situation you should know about, Alice," he told the college
girl, handing her the pages. "Better read this."

Oh, the authority of the written word.

A Motherless Child

A four-year-old has a limited understanding of time. From Ruth's
point of view, it was self-evident only that her mother and the photographs of her dead brothers were missing. It would soon occur to the
child to ask when her mother and the photographs were coming back.

There was a quality to Marion's absence that, even to a four-year-
old, suggested permanence. Even the late-afternoon light, which is
long-lasting on the seacoast, seemed to linger longer than usual on that

Friday afternoon; it appeared that night would never come. And the presence of the picture hooks—not to mention those darker rectangles that stood out against the faded wallpaper—contributed to the feeling that the photographs were gone forever.

If Marion had left the walls *completely* bare, it would have been better. The picture hooks were like a map of a beloved but destroyed city. After all, the photographs of Thomas and Timothy were the principal stories in Ruth's life—up to and including her initial experience with *The Mouse Crawling Between the Walls*. Nor could Ruth be comforted by the single and most unsatisfying answer to her many questions.

"When is Mommy coming back?" would summon no better than the "I don't know" refrain, which Ruth had heard repeated by her father and Eddie and, more recently, by the shocked nanny. Alice, following her brief reading experience, could not recover her formerly confident personality. She repeated the pathetic "I don't know" refrain in a barely audible whisper.

And the four-year-old went on asking questions. "Where are the pictures *now*? Did any of the glass got broken? *When* is Mommy coming back?"

Given Ruth's limited understanding of time, which answers *could* have comforted her? Maybe "tomorrow" would have worked, but only until tomorrow came and went; Marion would still be missing. As for "next week" or "next month," to a four-year-old you might as well say "next year." As for the truth, it couldn't have comforted Ruth—nor could she have comprehended it. Ruth's mommy *wasn't* coming back—not for thirty-seven years.

"I suppose Marion thinks she isn't coming back," Ted said to Eddie, when they were at last alone together.

"She says she isn't," Eddie told him. They were in Ted's workroom, where Ted had already fixed himself a drink. Ted had also called Dr. Leonardis and canceled their squash game. ("I can't play today, Dave—my wife's left me.") Eddie felt compelled to tell Ted that Marion had been sure Ted would get a ride home from Southampton with Dr. Leonardis. When Ted replied that he'd gone to the bookstore, Eddie would suffer his first and only religious experience.

For seven, almost eight years—lasting through college but not enduring through graduate school—Eddie O'Hare would be unimpressively yet sincerely religious, because he believed that God or *some* heavenly power had to have kept Ted from seeing the Chevy, which was parked diagonally across from the bookstore the entire time that Eddie and Ruth had been negotiating for the photograph in Penny Pierce's frame shop. (If *that* wasn't a miracle, what was?)

"So where *is* she?" Ted asked him, shaking the ice cubes in his drink.

"I don't know," Eddie told him.

"Don't lie to me!" Ted shouted. Not even pausing to put down his drink, Ted slapped Eddie in the face with his free hand. Eddie did as he'd been told. He made a fist—hesitating, because he'd never hit anyone before. Then he punched Ted Cole in the nose.

"Jesus!" Ted cried. He walked in circles, spilling his drink. He held the cold glass against his nose. "Christ, I hit you with my open hand—with the *flat* of my hand—and you make a fist and punch me in the nose. Jesus!"

"Marion said it would make you stop," Eddie told him.

" 'Marion said,' " Ted repeated. "Christ, what *else* did she say?"

"I'm trying to tell you," Eddie said. "She said you don't have to remember anything I say, because her lawyer will tell you everything again."

"If she thinks she's got a rat's ass of a chance to get custody of Ruth, she's got another think coming!" Ted shouted.

"She doesn't expect to get custody of Ruth," Eddie explained. "She has no intention of trying."

"She told you that?"

"She told me everything I'm telling you," Eddie replied.

"What kind of mother doesn't even try to get custody of her child?" Ted shouted.

"She didn't tell me that," Eddie admitted.

"Jesus ..." Ted began.

"There's just one thing about the custody," Eddie interrupted him. "You've got to watch your drinking. No more DWI—if you get another drunk-driving conviction, you could lose custody of Ruth. Marion wants to know that it's safe for Ruth to drive with you...."

"Who is she to say *I* wouldn't be safe for Ruth?" Ted shouted.

"I'm sure the lawyer will explain," Eddie said. "I'm just telling you what Marion told me."

"After the summer she's had with *you*, who's going to listen to Marion?" Ted asked.

"She said you'd say that," Eddie told him. "She said she knows more than a few Mrs. Vaughns who'd be willing to testify, if it came to that. But she doesn't *expect* to get custody of Ruth. I'm just telling you that you've got to watch your drinking."

"Okay, okay," Ted said, finishing his drink. "Christ! Why did she have to take all the photographs? There are negatives. She could have taken the negatives and made her *own* pictures."

"She took all the negatives, too," Eddie told him.

"The hell she did!" Ted cried. He stormed out of his workroom, with Eddie following behind. The negatives had been with the original snapshots; they were in about a hundred envelopes, all of them in the rolltop desk in the alcove between the kitchen and the dining room. It was the desk where Marion worked when she was paying bills. Now both Ted and Eddie could see that the rolltop desk itself was gone.

"I forgot that part," Eddie admitted to Ted. "She said it was her desk—it was the only furniture she wanted."

"I don't give a shit about the goddamn desk!" Ted yelled. "But she can't have the photographs *and* the negatives. They were my sons, too!"

"She said you'd say that," Eddie told him. "She said you wanted to have Ruth, and she didn't. Now you have Ruth. She has the boys."

"I should have half the photographs, for Christ's sake," Ted said. "Jesus ... what about Ruth? Shouldn't *Ruth* have half the pictures?"

"Marion didn't say anything about that," Eddie confessed. "I'm sure the lawyer will explain."

"Marion won't get far," Ted said. "Even the car is in my name—*both* cars are in my name."

"The lawyer will be telling you where the Mercedes is," Eddie informed him. "Marion will send the keys to the lawyer, and the lawyer will tell you where the car is parked. She said she didn't need a car."

"She's going to need money," Ted said nastily. "What's she going to do for money?"

"She said the lawyer will tell you what she needs for money," Eddie told him.

"Christ!" Ted said.

"You were planning to get a divorce, anyway, weren't you?" Eddie asked him.

"Is that Marion's question or yours?" Ted asked.

"Mine," Eddie admitted.

"Just stick to what Marion told you to say, Eddie."

"She didn't tell me to get the photograph," Eddie told him. "That was Ruth's idea, and mine. Ruth thought of it first."

"That was a good idea," Ted admitted.

"I was thinking of Ruth," Eddie told him.

"I know you were—thank you," Ted said.

They were quiet for a second or two, then. They could hear Ruth harassing the nanny nonstop. At the moment, Alice seemed closer to breaking down than Ruth did.

"What about this one? Tell it!" the four-year-old demanded. Ted and Eddie knew that Ruth must have been pointing to one of the picture hooks; the child wanted the nanny to tell her the story behind the missing photograph. Naturally Alice couldn't remember which of the photographs had hung from the picture hook that Ruth was pointing to. Alice didn't know the stories behind most of the photos, anyway. "Tell it! What about this one?" Ruth asked again.

"I'm sorry, Ruth. I don't know," Alice said.

"This is the one with Thomas in the tall hat," Ruth told the nanny crossly. "Timothy is trying to reach Thomas's hat, but he can't reach it because Thomas is standing on a ball."

"Oh, you remember," Alice said.

For how long will Ruth remember? Eddie was thinking. He watched Ted fix himself another drink.

"Timothy kicked the ball and made Thomas fall down," Ruth continued. "Thomas got mad and started a fight. Thomas won all the fights because Timothy was smaller."

"Was the fight in the photograph?" Alice asked.

Wrong question, Eddie knew.

"No, silly!" Ruth screamed. "The fight was *after* the picture!"

"Oh," Alice said. "I'm sorry...."

"You want a drink?" Ted asked Eddie.

"No," Eddie told him. "We should drive over to the carriage house and see if Marion left anything there."

"Good idea," Ted said. "You're the driver."

At first they found nothing in the dismal rental house above the garage. Marion had taken what few clothes she'd kept there, although Eddie knew—and would always appreciate—what she'd done with the pink cashmere cardigan and the lilac-colored camisole and matching panties. Of the few photographs Marion had moved to the carriage house for the summer, all but one were gone. Marion had left behind the photograph of the dead boys that hung above the bed: Thomas and Timothy in the doorway of the Main Academy Building, on the threshold of manhood—their last year at Exeter.

HVC VENITE PVERI VT VIRI SITIS

"Come hither boys ..." Marion had translated, in a whisper, "... and become men."

It was the photograph that marked the site of Eddie's sexual initiation. A piece of notepaper was taped to the glass. Marion's handwriting was unmistakable.

FOR EDDIE

"For *you?*" Ted shouted. He ripped the notepaper off the glass. He picked at the remnant of Scotch tape with his fingernail. "Well, it's *not* for you, Eddie. They're my sons—it's the only picture I have of them!"

Eddie didn't argue. He could remember the Latin well enough without the photograph. He had two more years to be at Exeter; he would pass through that doorway and under that inscription often enough. Nor did he need a picture of Thomas and Timothy; it wasn't them he needed to remember. He could remember Marion without them; he'd only known her without them, although he would certainly admit to the *presence* of those dead boys.

"Of course it's your picture," Eddie said.

"You bet your ass it is," Ted told him. "How could she even *think* of giving it to you?"

"I don't know," Eddie lied. In one day, "I don't know" had become everyone's answer for everything.

Thus the photograph of Thomas and Timothy in the doorway at Exeter belonged to Ted. It was a better likeness of the dead boys than that partial view of them—namely, their feet—which now hung in Ruth's bedroom. Ted would hang the photo of the boys in the master bedroom, on one of the many available picture hooks that were exposed there.

When Ted and Eddie left the shabby apartment over the garage, Eddie took his few things with him—he wanted to pack. He was waiting for Ted to tell him to leave; obligingly, Ted told him in the car when they were driving back to the house on Parsonage Lane.

"What's tomorrow—Saturday?" he asked.

"Yes, it's Saturday," Eddie replied.

"I want you out of here tomorrow. By Sunday at the latest," Ted told him.

"Okay," Eddie said. "I just need to find a ride to the ferry."

"Alice can take you."

Eddie decided it was wise *not* to tell Ted that Marion had already thought of Alice as Eddie's best bet for a ride to Orient Point.

When they got back to the house, Ruth had cried herself to sleep—the child had also refused to eat her supper—and Alice was crying quietly in the upstairs hall. For a college girl, the nanny seemed excessively undone by the situation. Eddie couldn't muster much sympathy for Alice; she was a snob who had immediately lorded her presumed superiority over him. (Alice's only superiority to Eddie was that she was a few years older than sixteen.)

Ted helped Alice navigate the stairs, and he gave her a clean handkerchief with which to blow her nose. "I'm sorry for springing all this on you, Alice," Ted told the college girl, but the nanny wouldn't be appeased.

"My father left my mother when I was a little girl," Alice sniffed. "So I *quit.* That's all—I just *quit.* And you should have the decency to quit, too," Alice added to Eddie.

"It's too late for me to quit, Alice," Eddie said. "I just got fired."

"I never knew you were such a *superior* person, Alice," Ted told the girl.

"Alice has been *superior* to me all summer," Eddie said to Ted. Eddie didn't like this aspect of the change inside him; together with authority, with finding his own voice, he'd also developed a taste for a kind of cruelty he'd been incapable of before.

"I am *morally* superior to you, Eddie—I know that much," the nanny told him.

"*Morally* superior," Ted repeated. "Now *there's* a concept! Don't you ever feel '*morally* superior,' Eddie?"

"To *you* I do," the boy said.

"You see, Alice?" Ted asked. "Everyone feels '*morally* superior' to *someone*!" Eddie hadn't realized that Ted was already drunk.

Alice went off weeping. Eddie and Ted watched her drive away.

"There goes my ride to the ferry," Eddie pointed out.

"I still want you out of here tomorrow," Ted told him.

"Fine," Eddie said. "But I can't walk to Orient Point. And you can't drive me."

"You're a smart boy—you'll think of someone to give you a ride," Ted said.

"You're the one who's good at getting rides," Eddie replied.

They could have gone on being petty all night—and it wasn't even dark outside. It was much too early for Ruth to have fallen asleep. Ted worried aloud that he should wake her up and try to convince her to eat something for supper. But when he tiptoed into Ruth's room, the child was at work at her easel; she'd either woken up or she'd fooled Alice into thinking that she was asleep.

For a four-year-old's, Ruth's drawings were markedly advanced. Whether this was a sign of her talent or the more modest effect of her father having shown her how to draw certain things—faces, primarily—it was too soon to know. She decidedly knew how to draw a face; in fact, faces were all that Ruth ever drew. (As an adult, she wouldn't draw at all.)

Now the child was drawing unfamiliar things: they were stick figures of the clumsy, unformed kind that more normal four-year-olds (non-practicing artists) might draw. There were three such figures, not at all well drawn, and they had faceless, oval heads as plain as melons. Over them, or perhaps behind them—the perspective wasn't clear—loomed several large mounds that looked like mountains. But Ruth was a child of the potato fields and the ocean; where she'd grown up, everything was flat.

"Are those mountains, Ruthie?" Ted asked.

"No!" the child screamed. She wanted Eddie to come look at her drawing, too. Ted called for him.

"Are those mountains?" Eddie asked, when he saw the drawing.

"No! No! No!" Ruth cried.

"Ruthie, honey, don't cry." Ted pointed to the faceless stick figures. "Who are these people, Ruthie?"

"Died persons," Ruth told him.

"Do you mean dead people, Ruthie?"

"Yes, died persons," the child repeated.

"I see—they're skeletons," her father said.

"Where are their faces?" Eddie asked the four-year-old.

"Died persons don't have faces," Ruth said.

"Why not, honey?" Ted asked her.

"Because they got buried. They're under the ground," Ruth told him.

Ted pointed to the mounds that weren't mountains. "So this is the ground, right?"

"Right," Ruth said. "The died persons are under it."

"I see," Ted said.

Pointing to the middle stick figure with the melon head, Ruth said: "That one is Mommy."

"But your mommy isn't dead, sweetheart," Ted said. "Mommy isn't a died person."

"And this is Thomas, and this is Timothy," Ruth continued, pointing to the other skeletons.

"Ruthie, Mommy isn't dead—she's just gone away."

"That one is Mommy," Ruth repeated, pointing again to the skeleton in the middle.

"How about a grilled-cheese sandwich with French fries?" Eddie asked Ruth.

"And ketchup," Ruth said.

"Good idea, Eddie," Ted told the sixteen-year-old.

The French fries were frozen, the oven had to be preheated, and Ted was too drunk to find the skillet he preferred to use for grilled-cheese sandwiches; yet all three of them managed to eat this lamentable food—the ketchup helped. Eddie did the dishes while Ted tried to put Ruth to bed. Under the circumstances, it had been a civilized supper, Eddie was thinking as he listened to Ruth and her father go through the upstairs of the house, describing the missing photographs to each other. Sometimes Ted made one up—at least Ted described a photograph that Eddie couldn't recall having seen—but Ruth didn't seem to mind. Ruth also made up one or two photographs.

One day, when she couldn't remember many of the photos, she would make up nearly everything. Eddie, long after he'd forgotten almost all the photographs, would make them up, too. Only Marion would be free of inventing Thomas and Timothy. Ruth, of course, would soon learn to invent her mother as well.

All the while that Eddie was packing, Ruth and Ted were going on and on about the photographs—real and imagined. They made it difficult for Eddie to concentrate on his immediate problem. Who was going to drive him to the ferry at Orient Point? That was when he happened upon the list of every living Exonian in the Hamptons; the most recent addition to the list, a Percy S. Wilmot from the class of '46, lived in nearby Wainscott.

Eddie would have been Ruth's age when Mr. Wilmot graduated from Exeter, but possibly Mr. Wilmot would remember Eddie's father. Surely every Exonian had at least *heard* of Minty O'Hare! But was the Exeter connection worth a ride to Orient Point? Eddie doubted it. Yet he thought it would be at least educative to call Percy Wilmot—if only to spite his father. If only for the thrill of telling Minty: "Listen, I called *every* living Exonian in the Hamptons and *begged* for a ride to the ferry, and they *all* turned me down!"

But when Eddie went downstairs to the telephone in the kitchen, he glanced at the kitchen clock. It was almost midnight; it would be wiser to call Mr. Wilmot in the morning. However, as late as it was, he didn't hesitate to call his parents; Eddie could have a short conversation with his father only if his father was half asleep. Eddie wanted to keep the conversation short. Even when half asleep, Minty was excitable.

"Everything's fine, Dad. No, there's nothing wrong," Eddie said. "I just wanted you or Mom to be around the phone tomorrow, in case I call. If I can get a ride to the ferry, I'll call before I leave."

"Have you been *fired?*" Minty asked. Eddie heard his father whisper to his mom: "It's Edward—I think he's been *fired!*"

"No, I haven't been fired," Eddie lied. "I just finished the job."

Naturally Minty went on and on—on the subject of how he'd never imagined that it was the sort of job one ever, exactly, "finished." Minty also calculated that he needed thirty more minutes to drive to New London from Exeter than Eddie would need to drive to Orient Point from Sagaponack—*and* take the ferry to New London.

"Then I'll just wait for you in New London, Dad."

Knowing Minty, Eddie knew that—even on short notice—Minty would be waiting at the dock in New London. His father would take his mom along, too; she would be the "navigator."

That done, Eddie wandered into the yard. He needed to escape the murmuring from the upstairs of the house, where Ted and Ruth were still reciting the stories of the missing photographs—from both their memories *and* their imaginations. In the cool of the yard, their voices were lost to Eddie in the cacophony of crickets and tree frogs, and in the distant thumping of the surf.

The only actual argument Eddie had ever overheard between Ted and Marion had been there, in the spacious but unmanaged yard. Marion had called it a yard-in-progress, but it was more accurately a yard that had been halted by disagreement and indecision. Ted had wanted a swimming pool. Marion had said that a swimming pool would spoil Ruth, or else the child would drown in it.

"Not with all the nannies she has looking after her," Ted had argued, which Marion had interpreted as a further indictment of her as a mother.

Ted had also wanted an outdoor shower—something handy to the squash court in the barn, but near enough to the swimming pool so that children returning from the beach could rinse the sand off before going in the pool.

"*What* children?" Marion had asked him.

"Not to mention before going in the house," Ted had added. He hated sand in the house. Ted never went to the beach, except in the winter after storms. He liked to see what the storms washed up; sometimes there were things he brought home to draw. (Driftwood in peculiar shapes; the shell of a horseshoe crab; a skate with its face like a Halloween mask, and its barbed tail; a dead seagull.)

Marion went to the beach only if Ruth wanted to go, and if it was a weekend—or if, for some reason, there was no nanny to take the child. Marion didn't like too much sun; at the beach she would cover herself in a long-sleeved shirt. She wore a baseball cap and sunglasses, so that no one ever knew who she was, and she sat watching Ruth play by herself at the water's edge. "Not like a mother, more like a nanny," Marion had described herself at the beach to Eddie. "Like someone even *less* interested in a child than a *good* nanny would be," Marion had said.

Ted had wanted multiple showerheads for the outdoor shower; that way, he and his squash opponent could take a shower together—"like in a locker room," Ted had said. "Or all the children can shower together."

"*What* children?" Marion had repeated.

"Ruth and her nanny, then," Ted had replied.

The lawn in the presently unmanaged yard gave way to an untended field of tall grass and daisies. There should be *more* lawn, Ted had decided. And some sort of barrier to keep the neighbors from seeing you when you were in the pool.

"*What* neighbors?" Marion had asked.

"Oh, there will be lots more neighbors one day," Ted had told her. (He was right about that.)

But Marion had wanted a different sort of yard. She liked the field of tall grass, and the daisies; more wildflowers would have suited her. She liked the look of an untamed garden. And maybe a grape arbor, but with the vines allowed to run unchecked. And there should be *less* lawn, not more—and more flowers, but not *prissy* flowers.

" 'Prissy ...' " Ted had said scornfully.

"Swimming pools are prissy," Marion had said. "And if there's more lawn, it will look like an athletic field. What do we need an athletic field for? Is Ruth going to be throwing or kicking a ball with an entire *team?*"

"You'd want more lawn if the boys were alive," Ted had told her. "The boys liked to play ball."

That had been the end of it. The yard had stayed as it was—if not exactly a yard-in-progress, at least an unfinished yard.

In the dark, listening to the crickets and the tree frogs and the distant percussion of the surf, Eddie was imagining what would become of the yard. He heard the ice cubes rattling in Ted's glass before he saw Ted, and before Ted saw him.

There were no lights on in the downstairs of the house, only the light from the upstairs hall, and from the guest bedroom, where Eddie had left his light on, and from the feeble night-light in the master bathroom, which was always left on for Ruth. Eddie marveled how Ted had managed to make himself another drink in the dark kitchen.

"Is Ruth asleep?" Eddie asked him.

"Finally," Ted said. "The poor kid." He went on shaking the ice cubes in his glass; he kept sucking his drink. For a third time, Ted offered Eddie a drink and Eddie declined.

"At least have a beer, for Christ's sake," Ted said. "Jesus ... just look at this yard."

Eddie decided to have a beer. The sixteen-year-old had never had a beer before. His parents, on special occasions, drank wine with dinner, and Eddie had been permitted to have wine with them. Eddie had never liked the wine.

The beer was cold but bitter-tasting—Eddie wouldn't finish it. Yet going to the refrigerator to get it, and turning on (and leaving on) the kitchen light, had broken Ted's train of thought. Ted had forgotten about the yard; he was thinking more directly of Marion instead.

"I can't believe she doesn't want custody of her own daughter," Ted said.

"I don't know if that's it," Eddie replied. "It's not that she doesn't *want* Ruth. Marion just doesn't want to be a bad mother—she thinks she'll do a bad job."

"What kind of mother *leaves* her daughter?" Ted asked the boy. "Talk about 'a bad job'!"

"She said she wanted to be a writer, once," Eddie said.

"Marion *is* a writer—she just doesn't do it," Ted told him.

Marion had told Eddie that she couldn't keep turning to her inner-most thoughts when all she thought about was the death of her boys. Eddie said cautiously to Ted: "I think Marion still wants to be a writer, but the death of the boys is her only subject. I mean that it's the only subject that keeps presenting itself to her, and she can't write about it."

"Let me see if I follow you, Eddie," Ted said. "So ... Marion takes every existent photograph of the boys that she can lay her hands on—and all the negatives, too—and she goes off to be a writer, because the boys' death is the only subject that keeps presenting itself to her, although she can't write about it. Yeah ..." Ted said, "that makes a lot of sense, doesn't it?"

"I don't know," Eddie said. Whatever theory there was about Marion, the theory had a hole in it; there was a gap in what anybody knew or said about her. "I don't know her well enough to judge her," Eddie told Ted.

"Let me tell you something, Eddie," Ted said. "*I* don't know her well enough to judge her, either."

Eddie could believe that, but he wasn't about to let Ted feel virtuous. "Don't forget—it's *you* she's really leaving," Eddie told him. "I guess she knew you pretty well."

"Well enough to judge me, you mean? Oh, certainly!" Ted agreed. His drink was already more than half gone. He kept sucking on the ice cubes and spitting them back in the glass; then he'd drink a little more.

"But she's leaving you, too, isn't she, Eddie?" Ted asked the sixteen-year-old. "You don't expect her to ring you up for a rendezvous, do you?"

"No—I don't expect to hear from her," Eddie admitted.

"Well ... me neither," Ted said. He spat a few more ice cubes into his glass. "Jesus, this drink tastes terrible," he said.

"Do you have any drawings of Marion?" Eddie suddenly asked him. "Didn't you ever draw *her*?"

"It was long, long ago," Ted began. "Do you want to see?" Even in the half-dark—the only light in the yard was coming from the kitchen windows—Eddie could sense Ted's reluctance.

"Sure," Eddie said. He followed Ted into the house. Ted flicked on the light in the front hall, and then they were standing together in Ted's workroom, the overhead fluorescent lamps unnaturally bright after the dark yard.

In all, there were fewer than a dozen drawings of Marion. At first Eddie thought it was the fault of the light that the drawings looked unnatural.

"These are the only ones I kept," Ted said defensively. "Marion never liked to pose." It was apparent to Eddie that Marion hadn't wanted to undress, either—there were no nudes. (None that Ted had kept, anyway.) In the drawings where Marion was seated with Thomas and Timothy, she must have been very young—because the boys were very young—but Marion's beauty was without age to Eddie. Beyond her prettiness, all that Ted had truly caught of Marion was her aloofness. Especially when she was seated alone, she seemed remote, even cold.

Then Eddie realized what was different about the drawings of Marion from Ted's *other* drawings, most notably the drawings of Mrs. Vaughn. There was nothing of Ted's restless lust in them. As old as the drawings of Marion were, Ted had already lost his desire for her. That was why Marion didn't look like Marion—at least not to Eddie, whose desire for Marion was limitless.

"Do you want one? You can have one," Ted said.

Eddie *didn't* want one; none of them was the Marion he knew. "I think Ruth should have them," Eddie answered.

"Good idea. You're full of good ideas, Eddie."

They both noticed the color of Ted's drink. The contents of the near-empty glass were as sepia-like as the water in Mrs. Vaughn's fountain. In the dark kitchen, Ted had used the wrong ice tray; he'd made a whiskey and water with cubes of frozen squid ink, which had half-melted in his glass. Ted's lips and tongue, and even his teeth, were brownish-black.

Marion would have appreciated it: Ted on his knees before the toilet in the front-hall washroom. The sound of his vomiting reached Eddie in Ted's workroom, where the sixteen-year-old still stared at the drawings. "Jesus . . ." Ted was saying, between heaves. "This is it for me and the hard stuff—from now on, I'm sticking to wine and beer." He made no mention of the squid ink, which Eddie thought was odd; it was the ink, not the whiskey, that had made him sick.

And it hardly mattered to Eddie that Ted would keep this promise. However, ridding himself of hard liquor was either consciously or unconsciously in keeping with Marion's caveat that he watch his drinking. Ted Cole would not suffer a drunk-driving conviction again. If his driving wasn't always alcohol-free, he at least never drank and drove when he was with Ruth.

Sadly, *any* moderation in Ted's drinking served only to exacerbate his womanizing; the long-term effects of Ted's womanizing would prove more hazardous to him than his drinking.

At the time, it seemed a fitting ending to what had been a long and trying day: Ted Cole on his knees, puking into a toilet. Eddie bid Ted a superior-sounding good night. Of course Ted could not respond, because of the violence of his barfing.

Eddie also checked on Ruth, never intending that his brief glimpse of the four-year-old, who was sleeping peacefully, would be his last for more than thirty years. He couldn't have known that he would be leaving before Ruth was awake.

In the morning, Eddie assumed, he would give Ruth his parents' present and kiss her good-bye. But Eddie assumed too many things. His experience with Marion notwithstanding, he was still a sixteen-year-old who had underestimated the emotional rawness of the moment—after all, he hadn't known such moments. And, standing in the four-year-old's room watching her sleep, Eddie found it easy to speculate that everything would be all right.

There are few things as seemingly untouched by the real world as a child asleep.

The Leg

This happened on the penultimate Saturday in August, in the summer of 1958. At about three in the morning, the wind shifted from the southwest to the northeast. Eddie O'Hare, in the half-dark of his bedroom, could no longer hear the surf; only a southerly wind could carry the sound of the sea as far inland as Parsonage Lane. And Eddie knew it was a northeast wind because he was cold. While it seemed fitting that his last night on Long Island should feel like the fall, Eddie could not wake up enough to get out of bed and close his bedroom windows. Instead, he pulled the scant covers more closely around him; he drew his body into a ball, and, breathing into his cold, cupped hands, he tried to fall more deeply asleep.

Seconds, maybe minutes later, he dreamed that Marion was still sleeping beside him, but that she'd got out of bed to close the windows. He extended his arm, expecting to find the warm spot that Marion would surely have left, but the bed was cold. Then, having heard the windows being closed, Eddie heard the curtains closing, too. Eddie never closed the curtains; he'd persuaded Marion to leave them open. He had loved seeing Marion asleep in the predawn glow.

Even in the dead of night, and three in the morning is about as dead as the night ever gets, there was some faint light in Eddie's bedroom; at least the clumped-together outlines of the furniture were visible in the half-dark. The shape of the gooseneck lamp on the bedside table cast a dull shadow of itself on the headboard of the bed. And the bedroom door, which was always left ajar—so that Marion could hear Ruth calling for her, if Ruth called—was edged with a dark-gray light. This was whatever light was able to penetrate the long hall, even if it was only the distant light from the feeble night-light in the master bathroom— even *that* light found its dim way to Eddie's room, because the door to Ruth's room was always open, too.

But on *this* night someone had closed the windows *and* the curtains, and when Eddie opened his eyes to an unnatural and total darkness, someone had closed his bedroom door. When Eddie held his breath, he could hear someone breathing.

Many sixteen-year-olds see only the persistence of darkness. Everywhere they look, they see gloom. Blessed by more hopeful expectations, Eddie O'Hare tended to look for the persistence of light. In the total darkness of his bedroom, Eddie's first thought was that Marion had come back to him.

"Marion?" the boy whispered.

"Jesus ... aren't you the optimist?" Ted Cole said. "I thought you'd never wake up." His voice came from everywhere, or from nowhere in particular, in the surrounding blackness. Eddie sat up in bed and groped for the bedside lamp, but he was unaccustomed to being unable to see it—he couldn't find it. "Forget the light, Eddie," Ted told him. "This story is better in the dark."

"*What* story?" Eddie asked.

"I know you want to hear it," Ted said. "You told me that you asked Marion to tell it to you, but Marion can't handle this story. It turns her to stone, just thinking about it. You remember when you turned her to stone by just *asking* her about it—don't you, Eddie?"

"Yes, I remember," Eddie said. So it was *that* story. Ted wanted to tell him about the accident.

Eddie had wanted *Marion* to tell him the story. But what should the sixteen-year-old have said? Eddie certainly needed to hear the story, even if he didn't want to hear it from Ted.

"Go on, tell it," the boy said as casually as possible. Eddie couldn't see where in the room Ted was, or if he was standing or sitting—not that it mattered, because Ted's narrative voice, in *any* of his stories, was greatly enhanced by an overall atmosphere of darkness.

Stylistically, the story of Thomas and Timothy's accident had much in common with Ted Cole's *The Mouse Crawling Between the Walls* and *The Door in the Floor*—not to mention the many drafts that Eddie had faithfully transcribed of *A Sound Like Someone Trying Not to Make a Sound.* In other words, it was a Ted Cole kind of story; when it came to this kind of story, Marion's version could never have been a match for Ted's.

For one thing—and this was immediately clear to Eddie—Ted had worked on the story. It would have killed Marion to have paid as close attention to the details of her boys' deaths as Ted had. And for another thing, Marion would have told the story without devices; she could have told it only as plainly as possible. In contrast, the principal device in Ted's telling of the tale was extremely self-conscious, even artificial; yet without it, Ted might not have been able to tell the story at all.

As in most Ted Cole stories, the principal device was also clever. In the story of Thomas and Timothy's accident, Ted talked about himself in the third person; thus he stood at a considerable distance from himself *and* from the story. He was never "I" or "me" or "myself"; he was always only "Ted"—or "he" or "him" or "himself." He was merely a supporting character in a story about other, more important people.

If Marion had ever told the story, she would have stood so close to it that, in the telling of it, she would have descended into a final madness—a madness much greater than whatever madness had caused Marion to abandon her only living child.

"Well, here's the deal," Ted began. "Thomas had his driver's license, but Timothy did not. Tommy was seventeen—he'd been driving for a year. And Timmy was fifteen; he'd only started to take driving lessons, from his father. Ted had earlier taught Thomas how to drive; it was Ted's opinion that Timothy, who was only learning, was already a more attentive student than Thomas had ever been. Not that Thomas was a bad driver. He was alert, and confident—he had excellent reflexes. And Thomas was cynical enough to anticipate what *bad* drivers were going to do, even before the drivers themselves knew what they were going to do. That was the key, Ted had told him, and Thomas believed it: always assume that every other driver is a bad driver.

"There was one particularly important area of driving where Ted thought that his younger son, Timothy, was a better driver—or a *potentially* better driver—than Thomas was. Timothy had always been more patient than Thomas. Timmy, for example, had the patience to faithfully check the rearview mirror, whereas Tommy neglected to look in the rearview mirror as routinely as Ted thought a driver *should* look there. And it is often in the area of left turns that a driver's patience is tested in a most subtle but most specific way—namely, when you are stopped and waiting to turn left across a lane of oncoming traffic, you must never, *ever* turn your wheels to the left in anticipation of the turn you are waiting to make. Never—not *ever*!

"Anyway," Ted continued, "Thomas was one of those impatient young men who would often turn his wheels to the left while anticipating a left-hand turn, although his father *and* his mother—and even his younger brother—had repeatedly told Tommy *not* to turn his wheels until he was actually making the turn. Do you know why, Eddie?" Ted asked.

"So that, if you are rear-ended by a vehicle coming up behind you, you will *not* be pushed into the lane of oncoming traffic," Eddie answered. "You would simply be pushed straight ahead, staying in your own lane."

"Who taught you to drive, Eddie?" Ted asked.

"My dad," Eddie said.

"Good for him! Tell him for me that he did a good job," Ted said.

"Okay," Eddie answered in the dark. "Go on ..."

"Well. Where were we? We were out West, actually. It was one of those ski vacations that people from the East take in the spring, when what amounts to so-called spring skiing can't be trusted in the East. If you want to be sure there's snow in March or April, you better go west. And so ... here were the displaced easterners, who were not at home out West. And it wasn't just that it was *Exeter's* spring vacation; it was doubtless spring break for countless schools and universities, and so there were many out-of-towners who were not only unfamiliar with the mountains but unfamiliar with the roads. And many of these skiers were driving unfamiliar cars—rental cars, for example. The Cole family had rented a car."

"I get the picture," Eddie said, sure that Ted was deliberately taking his time to get to what happened—probably because Ted wanted Eddie to *anticipate* the accident almost as much as Ted wanted Eddie to *see* it.

"Well. It was after a long day of skiing, and it had snowed all day. A wet, heavy snow. A degree or two warmer," Ted said, "and this snow would have been rain. And Ted and Marion were not *quite* the diehard, nonstop skiers that their two sons were. At seventeen and fifteen, respectively, Thomas and Timothy could ski the pants off their parents, who at the time were forty and thirty-four, respectively, and who often finished a day on the slopes a trifle earlier than their boys. *That* day, in fact, Ted and Marion had retired to the bar at the ski resort, where they were waiting (what seemed to them) a rather long time for Thomas and Timothy to finish their last run—and then the last run after that. You know how boys are—the kids can't get enough of the skiing, and so the mom and the dad do the waiting. ..."

"I get the picture—you were drunk," Eddie said.

"That was one aspect of what would become trivial—in the area of the ongoing argument between Ted and Marion, I mean," Ted told

Eddie. "Marion *said* that Ted was drunk, although in Ted's view he wasn't. And Marion, while not drunk, had had more to drink at that late-afternoon time than was customary for her. When Thomas and Timothy found their parents in the bar, it was evident to both boys that neither their father *nor* their mother was in *ideal* shape to drive the rental car. Besides, Thomas had his driver's license, and Thomas hadn't been drinking. There was no question as to who among them should be the driver."

"So Thomas was driving," Eddie interrupted.

"And, brothers being brothers, Timothy sat beside him—in the passenger seat. As for the parents," Ted told Eddie, "they sat where, one day, most parents will end up: in the backseat. And, in Ted and Marion's case, they continued to do what many parents do without cease: they kept arguing, although the nature of their arguments remained trivial, *enduringly* trivial. Ted, for example, had cleared the windshield of snow, but not the rear window. Marion argued that Ted should have cleared the rear window, too. Ted countered that as soon as the car was warm and moving, the snow would slide off. And although this proved to be the case—the snow slid off the rear window as soon as they were traveling at less-than-highway speed—Marion and Ted continued to argue. Only the topic changed; the triviality endured.

"It was one of those ski towns where the town itself isn't much to speak of. The main street is actually a three-lane highway, where the middle lane is designated for left turns, although not a few morons confuse what is a *turning* lane with a *passing* lane, if you know what I mean. I *hate* three-lane highways, Eddie—don't you?"

Eddie refused to answer him. It was a Ted Cole story: you always see what you're supposed to be afraid of; you see it coming, and coming. The problem is, you never see *everything* that's coming.

"Anyway," Ted continued, "Thomas was doing a good job of driving, considering the adverse conditions. The snow was still falling. And now it was dark, too—truly everything was unfamiliar. Ted and Marion began to quarrel about the best route to the hotel where they were staying. This was foolish, because the entire town was on one or the other side of this three-lane highway, and since this highway was in actuality a *strip* of hotels and motels and gas stations and restaurants and bars, which lined both sides of the road, it was necessary to know only which side of the highway you were going to. And Thomas knew. It would be a left turn, no matter how he did it. It hardly helped him, as a driver, that his mother and father were determined to choose precisely *where* he should turn left. He could, for example, turn left at the hotel itself—Ted approved of this direct approach—or he could drive past the hotel to the next set of traffic lights. There, when the light was green, he could execute a left U-turn; then he would be approaching the hotel on his right. Marion thought the U-turn at the traffic lights was safer than the left turn from the turning lane, where there were no lights."

"Okay! Okay!" Eddie screamed in the dark. "I see it! I see it!"

"No, you don't!" Ted shouted at him. "You can't possibly see it until it's *over*! Or do you want me to stop?"

"No—please go on," Eddie answered.

"So ... Thomas moves into the center lane, the *turning* lane—it's *not* a passing lane—and Tommy puts on his blinker, not knowing that both his taillights are covered with wet, sticky snow, which his father had failed to clear off at the same time his father failed to clear the rear window. No one behind Thomas's car can see his directional signal, or even the taillights or the brake lights. The car is not visible—or it is visible only at the last second—to anyone approaching it from behind.

"Meanwhile, Marion says: 'Don't turn here, Tommy—it's safer up ahead, at the lights.'

" 'You want him to make a U-turn and get a ticket, Marion?' Ted asked his wife.

" 'I don't care if he gets a ticket, Ted—it's safer to turn at the lights,' Marion said.

" 'Break it up, you two,' Thomas said. 'I don't want to get a ticket, Mom,' the boy added.

" 'Okay—so turn here, then,' Marion told him.

" 'Better just do it, Tommy—don't sit here,' Ted said.

" 'Great backseat driving,' Timothy commented. Then Timmy noticed that his brother had cranked the wheels to the left while he was still waiting to turn. 'You cut your wheels too soon again,' Tim told him.

" 'It's because I thought I was going to turn, and then I thought I wasn't, asshole!' Thomas said.

" 'Tommy, don't call your brother an asshole, please,' Marion told her son.

" 'At least not in front of your mother,' Ted added.

" 'No—that's not what I mean, Ted,' Marion told her husband. 'I mean that he shouldn't call his brother an asshole—period.'

" 'You hear that, asshole?' Timothy asked his brother.

" 'Timmy, *please...*' Marion said.

" 'You can turn after this snowplow,' Ted told his son.

" 'Dad, I know. I'm the driver,' the seventeen-year-old said.

"But suddenly the interior of their car was flooded with light—it was the headlights of the car coming up on them from behind. It was a station wagon full of college kids from New Jersey. They'd never been in Colorado before. It's conceivable that, in New Jersey, there's no difference between turning lanes and passing lanes.

"Anyway, the college kids thought they were *passing.* They didn't see (until the last second) the car that was waiting to turn left in front of them—as soon as the snowplow, in the oncoming lane, passed by. And so Thomas's car was rear-ended, and, because Thomas had already turned his wheels, his car was pushed into the lane of oncoming traffic, which in this case consisted of a very large snowplow, moving about forty-five miles per hour. The college kids said later that they thought their station wagon was doing about fifty."

"Jesus..." Eddie said.

"The snowplow cut Thomas's car almost perfectly in half," Ted went on. "Thomas was killed by the steering column of the car he was driving—it crushed his chest. Tommy died instantly. And—for about twenty minutes—Ted was trapped in the backseat, where he was seated directly behind Thomas. Ted couldn't see Thomas, although Ted knew that Tommy was dead because Marion could see Tommy, and although she would never use the 'dead' word, she kept repeating to her husband, 'Oh, Ted—Tommy's gone. Tommy's gone. Can you see Timmy? Timmy's not gone, too—is he? Can you see if he's gone?'

"Because Marion was trapped in the backseat behind Timothy—for more than half an hour—she couldn't see Timothy, who was directly in front of her. Ted, however, had a pretty good view of his younger son, who'd been knocked unconscious when his head went through the windshield; for a while, however, Timothy was still alive. Ted could see that Timmy was breathing, but Ted *couldn't* see that the snowplow, as it had cut the car in two, had also cut off Timmy's left leg at the thigh. While an ambulance and rescue crew struggled to disengage them all from the crumpled car, which had been accordioned between the snowplow and the station wagon, Timothy Cole bled to death from a severed femoral artery.

"For what seemed like twenty minutes—maybe it was less than five—Ted watched his younger son die. Since Ted was freed from the wreckage about ten minutes before the rescue workers were able to free Marion... Ted had broken only a few ribs; he was otherwise un-hurt... Ted saw the paramedics remove Timmy's body (but *not* Timmy's left leg) from the car. The boy's severed leg was still pinned to the front seat by the snowplow when the rescue workers finally extri-cated Marion from the backseat of the car. She knew that her Thomas was dead, but only that her Timothy had been taken from the wreck-age—to the *hospital,* she hoped, for she kept asking Ted, 'Timmy's not gone, too—is he? Can you see if he's gone?'

"But Ted was a coward when it came to answering that question, which he left unanswered—and would leave unanswered. He asked one of the rescue workers to cover Timmy's leg with a tarpaulin, so Marion would not see it. And when Marion was safely outside the car... she was actually standing, and even limping around, although it would turn out that she had a broken ankle... Ted tried to tell his wife that her younger son, like her older son, was dead. He just never quite managed to *say* it. Before Ted could tell her, Marion spotted Timmy's shoe. She couldn't have known—she couldn't have *imagined*—that her boy's shoe was still attached to his leg. She thought it was just his shoe. And she said, 'Oh, Ted, look—he's going to need his shoe.' And without anyone stopping her, she limped to the wreckage and bent down to pick up the shoe.

"Ted *wanted* to stop her, of course, but—talk about 'turned to stone'—he felt at that moment absolutely paralyzed. He could not move, he couldn't even speak. And so he allowed his wife to discover that her son's shoe was still attached to a *leg*. That was when Marion began to realize that Timothy was gone, too. And *that* ..." Ted Cole said, in his fashion, "that is the end of the story."

"Get out of here," Eddie told him. "This is *my* room, at least for one more night."

"It's almost morning," Ted told the boy. He opened one curtain so that Eddie could see the faint beginning of a dead-looking light.

"Get out of here," Eddie repeated.

"Just don't think that you know me, or Marion," Ted said. "You don't know us—you don't know Marion, especially."

"Okay, okay," Eddie said. He saw that the bedroom door was open; there was the familiar dark-gray light from the long hall.

"It was after Ruth was born, before Marion said anything to me," Ted continued. "I mean, she hadn't said a *word*—not one word about the accident. But one day, after Ruth was born, Marion just walked into my workroom—you know, she never went anywhere near my workroom—and she said to me: 'How could you have let me see Timmy's leg? How *could* you?' I had to tell her that I'd been physically unable to move—that I was paralyzed, turned to stone. But all she said was: 'How *could* you?' And we never talked about it again. I tried, but she just wouldn't talk about it."

"Please get out of here," Eddie said.

As he was leaving, Ted said: "See you in the morning, Eddie."

The one curtain that Ted had opened did not admit enough of the faint, predawn light for Eddie to see what time it was; he saw only that his wristwatch and his wrist—including his whole arm and hand—were the sickly, silver-gray color of a corpse. Eddie rotated his hand, but he could discern no difference in the shade of gray. The palm and the back of his hand were the same; in fact, his skin and the pillows and the wrinkled sheets were uniformly dead-gray. He lay awake, waiting for truer light. Through the window, he watched the sky; it slowly faded. Shortly before sunrise, the sky had lightened to the color of a week-old bruise.

Eddie knew that Marion must have seen many hours of this predawn light. She was probably seeing it now—for surely she couldn't have been asleep, wherever she was. And whenever Marion was awake, Eddie now understood what she saw: the wet snow melting on the wet, black highway, which would also have been streaked with reflected light; the inviting neon of the signs, which promised food and drink and shelter (even entertainment); the constantly passing headlights, the cars inching by so slowly because everyone needed to gawk at the accident; the circulating blue of the police cars' lights, the blinking yellow lights of the wrecking truck, and the flashing red lights of the ambulance, too. Yet, even in this mayhem, Marion had spotted the *shoe*!

"Oh, Ted, look—he's going to need his shoe," she would always remember saying, as she limped to the wreck and bent down.

What kind of shoe was it? Eddie wondered. The absence of detail stopped him from seeing the leg exactly. An après-ski boot, possibly. Maybe it was an old tennis shoe—something that Timothy didn't mind getting wet. But the namelessness of the shoe or boot—whatever it was—stopped Eddie from seeing it, and not seeing the shoe prevented him from seeing the leg. He couldn't even imagine the leg.

Lucky Eddie. Marion was not so lucky. She would always remember the blood-soaked shoe; the exact detail of the shoe would always lead her to remember the leg.

Working for Mr. Cole

It was because he didn't know what kind of shoe it was that Eddie fell asleep without meaning to. He woke with the low sun shining in the one window with the open curtain; the sky was a crisp and cloudless blue. Eddie opened a window to feel how cold it was—it would be a chilly trip on the ferry, *if* he could get a ride to Orient Point—and there in the driveway he saw an unfamiliar truck. It was a pickup truck. Both a sit-down, tractor-type lawn mower and the kind of lawn mower that you walk behind were in the back of the truck, together with some rakes and spades and hoes and an assortment of sprinkler heads; there was also a long, neatly coiled hose.

Ted Cole mowed his own lawn; and Ted watered the lawn only when it looked as if it needed it, or when he got around to it. Since the yard was unfinished, a result of Ted's standoff with Marion, it was hardly a yard that merited the attention of a full-time gardener. Yet the guy in the pickup truck looked like a full-time gardener.

Eddie dressed himself and went down to the kitchen; one of the kitchen windows would offer him a better view of the man in the truck. Ted, who was surprisingly awake and had already made a pot of coffee, was peeking out a kitchen window at the mystery gardener, who was no mystery to Ted.

"It's Eduardo," Ted whispered to Eddie. "What's Eduardo doing here?"

Eddie now recognized Mrs. Vaughn's gardener, although Eddie had seen the gardener only once—and briefly—when Eduardo Gomez had scowled at Eddie from the vantage of his ladder, from which the tragically mistreated man had been plucking pieces of pornography from the Vaughns' privet.

"Maybe Mrs. Vaughn has hired him to kill you," Eddie speculated.

"No, not *Eduardo!*" Ted said. "But do you see *her* anywhere? She's not in the cab or in the back."

"Maybe she's lying down under the truck," Eddie suggested.

"I'm being serious, for Christ's sake," Ted told the boy.

"So am I," Eddie said.

They both had reason to believe that Mrs. Vaughn was capable of murder, but it appeared that Eduardo Gomez was alone; the gardener was just sitting in the cab of his truck. Ted and Eddie could see the steam escape from Eduardo's thermos when he poured himself a cup of coffee; the gardener was politely waiting for the household itself to give him some active indication that it was awake.

"Why don't you go find out what he wants?" Ted asked Eddie.

"Not *me,*" Eddie said. "I've been fired—isn't that right?"

"For Christ's sake... at least come with me, then," Ted told the sixteen-year-old.

"I better stay by the phone," Eddie said. "If he has a gun and shoots you, I'll call the police."

But Eduardo Gomez was unarmed; the gardener's only weapon was a harmless-looking piece of paper, which he removed from his wallet. He showed it to Ted; it was the smudged, illegible check that Mrs. Vaughn had sailed into the fountain.

"She said it was my *last* paycheck," Eduardo explained to Ted.

"She *fired* you?" Ted asked the gardener.

"Because I warned you that she was coming after you in her car," Eduardo said.

"Oh," Ted said; he kept staring at the worthless check. "You can't even read this," he told Eduardo. "It might as well be blank." From its adventure in the fountain, the check was coated with a patina of faded squid ink.

"It wasn't my only job," the gardener explained, "but it was my biggest. My principal income."

"Oh," Ted said; he handed Eduardo the sepia-colored check, which the gardener solemnly returned to his wallet. "Let me be sure that I understand you, Eduardo," Ted began. "You think that you saved my life, and that this cost you your job."

"I *did* save your life—it *did* cost me my job," Eduardo Gomez replied.

Ted's vanity, which was extended to his fleetness of foot, compelled him to believe that, even from a standing start, he could have outrun Mrs. Vaughn in her Lincoln. Nonetheless, Ted would never have disputed the fact that the gardener had behaved courageously.

"How much money are we talking about, exactly?" Ted asked.

"I don't want your money—I'm not here for a handout," Eduardo told him. "I was hoping that you might have some work for me."

"You want a job?" Ted asked.

"Only if you've got one for me," Eduardo replied. The gardener was looking despairingly at the scruffy yard. Not even the patchy lawn showed signs of professional care. It needed fertilizer—not to mention that it clearly didn't get enough water. And there were no flowering shrubs, no perennials, no annuals—at least none that Eduardo could see. Mrs. Vaughn had once told Eduardo that Ted Cole was rich and famous. (I guess the money doesn't go into the landscaping, Eduardo was thinking.) "It doesn't look as if you've got a job for me," the gardener told Ted.

"Just wait a minute," Ted said. "Let me show you where I want to put a swimming pool, and some other stuff."

From the kitchen window, Eddie watched them walk around the house. It did not strike Eddie that they were having a life-threatening conversation. The boy assumed that it was safe to join them in the yard.

"I want a simple, rectangular pool—it doesn't have to be Olympic size," Ted was telling Eduardo. "I just want a deep end and a shallow end—with steps. And no diving board. I think diving boards are dangerous for children. I've got a four-year-old daughter."

"I've got a four-year-old granddaughter, and I agree with you," Eduardo told Ted. "I don't build pools, but I know some guys who do. I can *maintain* a pool, of course. I can do the vacuuming and keep the chemicals in balance. You know, so the water doesn't get cloudy—or your skin doesn't turn green, or something."

"Whatever you say," Ted said. "You can be in charge. I just don't want a diving board. And there have to be some plantings around the pool—so that the neighbors and passersby aren't always staring at us."

"I would recommend a berm—actually, three berms," Eduardo said. "And on top of the berms, to hold the soil, I would suggest some Russian olives. They do well here, and the leaves are nice—a sort of silvery green. They have fragrant yellow flowers and an olivelike fruit. Oleaster is another name for them."

"Whatever you say," Ted told him. "You're in charge. And there's the matter of the perimeter of the property itself—I don't feel that there's ever been a visible border to the property."

"There's always privet," Eduardo Gomez replied. The small man seemed to shiver a little when he thought of the hedge where he'd hung dying in the exhaust fumes. Nevertheless, the gardener could work wonders with privet: in his care, Mrs. Vaughn's privet had grown an average of eighteen inches a year. "You just got to feed it and water it, and most of all *prune* it," the gardener added.

"Sure—let's do privet, then," Ted said. "I like hedges."

"Me, too," Eduardo lied.

"And I want more lawn," Ted said. "I want to get rid of the dumb daisies and the tall grass. I'll bet there are ticks in that tall grass."

"Sure there are," Eduardo told him.

"I want a lawn like an athletic field," Ted said with a vengeance.

"You want *lines* painted on it?" the gardener asked.

"No, no!" Ted cried. "I mean, I want the lawn to be the *size* of an athletic field."

"Oh," Eduardo said. "That's a lot of lawn, a lot of mowing, a lot of sprinklers..."

"What about carpentry?" Ted asked the gardener.

"What about it?" Eduardo asked.

"I mean, can you do carpentry? I was thinking about an outdoor shower—multiple showerheads," Ted explained. "Not a *lot* of carpentry."

"Sure, I can do that," Eduardo told him. "I don't do plumbing, but I know a guy ..."

"Whatever you say," Ted said again. "I'm putting you in charge. And what about your wife?" he added.

"What about her?" Eduardo asked.

"Well, I mean, does she work? What does she do?" Ted asked him.

"She cooks," Eduardo told him. "She looks after our grandchild sometimes—and some other people's children, too. She cleans some people's houses...."

"Maybe she'd like to clean *this* house," Ted said. "Maybe she'd like to cook for me, and look after my four-year-old girl. She's a nice little girl. Her name is Ruth."

"Sure, I'll ask my wife. I'll bet she'll want to do it," Eduardo replied.

Eddie felt certain that Marion would have been devastated if she'd been a witness to these transactions. Marion had been gone less than twenty-four hours, but her husband—at least in his mind—had already replaced her. Ted had hired a gardener and a carpenter, a virtual caretaker and handyman—and Eduardo's wife would soon be doing the cooking, *and* looking after Ruth!

"What's your wife's name?" Ted asked Eduardo.

"Conchita—not like the banana," Eduardo told him.

Conchita would end up cooking for Ted and Ruth; she would not only become Ruth's principal nanny, but when Ted took a trip, Conchita and Eduardo would move into the house on Parsonage Lane and look after Ruth as if they were her mother and father. And the Gomez's granddaughter, Maria, who was Ruth's age, would be her frequent playmate in the years that Ruth was growing up.

Getting fired by Mrs. Vaughn would have only happy and prosperous results for Eduardo; soon his principal income would be from Ted Cole, who would also provide for Conchita's principal income. As an *employer*, Ted would prove to be a lot more likable and reliable than he was as a *man*. (If not to Eddie O'Hare.)

"So when can you start?" Ted asked Eduardo on that early Saturday morning in August 1958.

"Whenever you want," Eduardo answered.

"Well. You can start today, Eduardo," Ted told him. Without looking at Eddie, who was standing there beside them in the yard, Ted said: "You can begin by driving this boy to the ferry at Orient Point."

"Sure, I can do that," Eduardo said. He nodded politely to Eddie, who nodded back.

"You can leave immediately, Eddie," Ted told the sixteen-year-old. "I mean, before breakfast."

"That's fine with me," Eddie replied. "I'll go get my things."

And that was how it happened that Eddie O'Hare left without saying good-bye to Ruth; he had to leave when the child was still asleep. Eddie barely took the time to call home. He'd awakened his father and mother after midnight; now he woke them again, before seven in the morning.

"If I get to New London first, I'll just wait for you at the docks," Eddie told his dad. "Drive safely."

"I'll be there! I'll meet your ferry! We'll *both* be there, Edward!" Minty breathlessly told his son.

As for the list of every living Exonian in the Hamptons, Eddie almost packed it. Instead he ripped each of the pages into long, thin strips and wadded them into a ball, which he left in his guest-bedroom wastebasket. After Eddie had gone, Ted would snoop through the room, discovering the list, which Ted would mistake for love letters. Ted would painstakingly reassemble the list, until he realized that neither Eddie nor Marion could have composed such "love letters" as these.

At the top of his small suitcase, Eddie had already packed the O'Hare family's copy of *The Mouse Crawling Between the Walls;* it was the copy that Minty had wanted Mr. Cole to autograph, but Eddie could not (under the circumstances) bring himself to ask the famous author and illustrator for his signature. Instead, Eddie stole one of Ted's pens; it was a fountain pen with the kind of nib Ted liked best for autographs. On the ferry, Eddie assumed, he would have time to try his best imitation of Ted Cole's careful calligraphy. Eddie hoped that his mom and dad would never know the difference.

In the driveway, there was little to say in the way of good-byes—formal or informal.

"Well." Ted stopped. "You're a good driver, Eddie," Ted managed to say; he held out his hand. Eddie accepted the handshake. He cautiously extended the mangled, bread loaf–shaped present for Ruth in his left hand. There was nothing to do but give it to Ted, which Eddie did.

"It's for Ruth, but I don't know what it is," Eddie said. "It's from my parents. It was in my duffel bag all summer," he explained. He could see the distaste with which Ted examined the crushed wrapping paper, which was virtually undone. The present begged to be opened, if only to be free of its dreadful wrapping. Certainly Eddie was curious to see what it was; he also suspected he would be *embarrassed* to see what it was. Eddie could tell that Ted wanted to open it, too.

"Should I open it, or let Ruth open it?" Ted asked Eddie.

"Why don't *you* open it?" Eddie said.

When Ted opened the present, it was clothing—a little T-shirt. What four-year-old is interested in clothing? If Ruth had opened the present, she would have been disappointed that it wasn't a toy or a book. Besides, the little T-shirt was already too small for Ruth; by next summer, when it was T-shirt weather again, the child would have completely outgrown it.

Ted fully unfolded the T-shirt and held it up for Eddie to see. The Exeter theme should not have surprised Eddie, but the boy—for the first time in sixteen years—had just spent almost three months in a world where the academy was *not* the day-in, day-out topic of discussion. Across the chest of the little shirt, Eddie could read the maroon lettering on a field of gray:

EXETER 197__

Ted also showed Eddie the enclosed note from Minty. His father had written: "Not that it's likely—at least not in *our* lifetimes—that the academy will ever admit girls, but I thought that, as a fellow Exonian, you would appreciate the possibility of your daughter attending Exeter. With my thanks for giving my boy his first job!" The note was signed *Joe O'Hare, '36*. It was ironic, Eddie thought, that 1936, which was the year that his father had graduated from Exeter, was also the year Ted had married Marion.

It was more ironic that Ruth Cole *would* go to Exeter, despite Minty's (and many of the Exeter faculty's) belief that coeducation at the old academy was unlikely. In fact, on February 27, 1970, the trustees announced that Exeter would admit girls in the fall of that year. Ruth would then leave her life on Long Island for the venerable boarding school in New Hampshire; she was sixteen. At the age of nineteen, she would graduate from Exeter, in the class of '73.

That year, Eddie's mother, Dot O'Hare, would send her son a letter, telling him that his former employer's daughter had graduated from the academy—along with 46 other girls, who were the female classmates of 239 boys. Dot admitted to Eddie that the numbers might be even more one-sided, because she had counted several of the boys as girls—so many of the boys had such long hair.

It's true: the Exeter class of '73 demonstrated that long hair for boys was in fashion; long, straight hair that was parted in the middle was also fashionable for girls. At the time, Ruth was no exception. She would go through college with long, straight hair parted in the middle, before she finally became the master of her own hair and cut it short—the way (she would say) she'd always wanted it, and not *only* to spite her father.

In the summer of '73, when Eddie O'Hare was briefly at home, visiting his parents, he would pay no more than passing attention to the yearbook of Ruth's graduating class. (Minty had foisted the '73 *PEAN* on him.)

"I think she's got her mother's looks," Minty told Eddie, not that Minty would know. He'd never met Marion. Minty may have seen a photograph of her in a newspaper or magazine, around the time the boys died, but what he said nonetheless got Eddie's attention.

When Eddie saw Ruth's senior portrait, his opinion was that Ruth looked more like Ted. It wasn't just the dark hair—it was her square face, the wide-apart eyes, her small mouth, her big jaw. Ruth was certainly attractive, but she was more handsome than she was beautiful; she was good-looking in an almost masculine way.

And this impression of Ruth at nineteen was enhanced by her jockish appearance in the team photograph for Varsity Squash. There would not be a *girls'* squash team at Exeter until the following year; in '73, Ruth was permitted to play on the boys' varsity, where she was the third-ranked player. In the team photo, Ruth could easily have been mistaken for one of the boys.

The only other photograph of Ruth Cole in the '73 Exeter yearbook was a group portrait of the girls in her dormitory, Bancroft Hall. Ruth is smiling serenely in the center of a group of girls; she looks content, but alone.

And so his dismissive glimpse of Ruth in her Exeter yearbook photographs would permit Eddie to continue to think of her as "the poor kid" he had last seen asleep in the summer of 1958. It would be twenty-two years from that date before Ruth Cole would publish her first novel—when she was twenty-six. Eddie O'Hare would be thirty-eight when he read it; only then would he acknowledge that there was arguably more of Marion in Ruth than there was of Ted. And Ruth herself would be forty-one before Eddie realized that there was more of *Ruth* in Ruth than there was of either Ted or Marion.

But how could Eddie O'Hare have predicted this from a T-shirt that, in the summer of '58, was already too small for Ruth to wear? At that moment, Eddie—like Marion—wanted only to leave, and his ride was waiting. The sixteen-year-old got into the cab of the pickup truck beside Eduardo Gomez; as the gardener was backing out the driveway, Eddie was debating whether or not he would wave good-bye to Ted, who was still standing in the driveway. If he waves first, I'll wave back, Eddie decided; it seemed to him that Ted was on the verge of waving the little T-shirt, but Ted had something more emphatic than waving on his mind.

Before Eduardo could exit the driveway, Ted ran forward and stopped the truck. Although the morning air was cool, Eddie—wearing his inside-out Exeter sweatshirt—had his elbow resting on the open passenger-side window of the cab. Ted squeezed Eddie's elbow as he spoke. "About Marion—there's another thing you should know," he told the boy. "Even before the accident, she was a difficult woman. I mean, if there had never been an accident, Marion would still be difficult. Do you understand what I'm saying, Eddie?"

Ted's grip on Eddie's elbow exerted a steady pressure, but Eddie could neither move his arm nor speak. He stops the truck to tell me that Marion is "a difficult woman," Eddie was thinking. Even to a six-teen-year-old, the phrase did not ring true; in fact, it rang utterly false. It was strictly a male expression. It was what men who thought they were being polite said of their ex-wives. It was what a man said about a woman who was unavailable to him—or who had made herself in some way inaccessible. It was what a man said about a woman when he meant something else, when he meant *anything* else. And when a man said it, it was always derogatory, wasn't it? But Eddie could think of nothing to say.

"I forgot something—there's just one last thing," Ted told the sixteen-year-old. "About the shoe . . ." If Eddie could have moved, he would have covered his ears, but the boy was paralyzed—a pillar of salt. Eddie could appreciate how Marion had turned to stone at the mere mention of the accident. "It was a basketball shoe," Ted went on. "Timmy called them his high-tops."

That was all Ted had to say.

As the pickup truck passed through Sag Harbor, Eduardo said: "This is where I live. I could sell my house for a lot of money. But the way things are going, I couldn't afford to buy another house—at least not around here."

Eddie nodded and smiled to the gardener. But the boy couldn't talk; his elbow, which was still sticking out the passenger-side window, was numb from the cold air, but Eddie couldn't move his arm.

They took the first small ferry to Shelter Island, and drove across the island, and took the other small ferry from the north end of the island to Greenport. (Years later, Ruth would always think of these little ferries as her preparation for leaving home—for going back to Exeter.)

In Greenport, Eduardo Gomez said to Eddie O'Hare: "With what I could get for my house in Sag Harbor, I could buy a really nice house here. But you can't make much of a living as a gardener in Greenport."

"No, I wouldn't suppose so," Eddie was able to say, although his tongue felt funny and his own speech sounded foreign to him.

At Orient Point, the ferry was not yet in sight; the dark-blue water was flecked with whitecaps. Since it was a Saturday, a lot of day-trippers were waiting for the ferry; most of them were foot passengers who were going shopping in New London. It was a different crowd from that day in June when Eddie had landed at Orient Point and Marion had met him. ("Hello, Eddie," Marion had said. "I thought you'd never see me." As if he *hadn't* seen her! As if he could have *missed* seeing her!)

"Well, so long," Eddie said to the gardener. "Thanks for the ride."

"If you don't mind my asking," Eduardo said sincerely, "what's it like working for Mr. Cole?"

Leaving Long Island

It was so cold and windy on the upper deck of the Cross Sound Ferry that Eddie sought refuge in the lee of the pilothouse; there, out of the wind, he practiced Ted Cole's signature in one of his writing notebooks. The block letters of the capitals, T and C, were easy; here Ted's handwriting resembled a sans-serif typeface. But the lowercase letters were a challenge; Ted's lowercase letters were small and perfectly slanted, the handwritten equivalent of Baskerville italics. After twenty-odd attempts in his notebook, Eddie could still see signs of his own, more spontaneous handwriting in his imitations of Ted's signature. Eddie feared that his parents, who knew their son's handwriting very well, would suspect the forgery.

He was concentrating so fiercely that he failed to notice the very same clam-truck driver who had crossed the sound with him on that fateful June day. The clam-truck driver, who took the ferry from Orient Point to New London (and back again) every day except Sunday, recognized Eddie and sat down on the bench beside him. The driver couldn't help observing that Eddie was caught up in the act of perfecting an apparent signature; remembering that Eddie had been hired to do something strange—there had been a brief discussion of exactly what a so-called writer's assistant might *do*—the clam-truck driver assumed that Eddie's chore of rewriting the same short name must be part of the boy's peculiar job.

"How's it going, kid?" the clam-truck driver asked. "Looks like you're working hard."

A future novelist, if never a hugely successful one, Eddie O'Hare was a young man with an instinct for spotting closure; as such, he was happy to see the clam-truck driver again. Eddie explained to the driver the task at hand: having "forgotten" to ask Ted Cole for his autograph, the boy didn't want to disappoint his mom and dad.

"Let *me* try," the clam-truck driver said.

Thus, in the lee of the pilothouse on the wind-blown upper deck, the driver of a clam truck rendered a flawless imitation of the best-selling author's signature. After only a half-dozen attempts in the notebook, the clam-truck driver was ready for the real thing; Eddie allowed the excited man to autograph the O'Hare family's copy of *The Mouse Crawling Between the Walls*. Snugly out of the wind, both man and boy admired the results. In gratitude, Eddie offered the clam-truck driver Ted Cole's fountain pen.

"You gotta be kidding," the clam-truck driver said.

"Take it—it's yours," Eddie told him. "I really don't want it." He really *didn't* want the pen, which the clam-truck driver happily clipped to the inside pocket of his dirty windbreaker. The man smelled of hot dogs and beer, but also—especially out of the wind—of clams. He offered Eddie a beer, which Eddie declined, and then he asked Eddie if "the writer's assistant" would be returning to Long Island the following summer.

Eddie didn't think so. But, in truth, Eddie O'Hare would never quite leave Long Island—least of all, in his mind—and although he would spend the following summer at home in Exeter, where he worked for the academy as a guide in the admissions office, giving tours of the school to prospective Exonians and their parents, Eddie would return to Long Island as soon as the summer after that.

In the year of his graduation from Exeter (1960), Eddie was prompted to seek a summer job away from home; this desire, in combination with Eddie's developing awareness that he was attracted to older women—and that they were attracted to him—would lead Eddie to remember Penny Pierce's business card, which he had saved. Only when Eddie was anticipating his graduation from the academy—about a year and half *after* Penny Pierce had offered him a job in her Southampton frame shop—did he realize that Mrs. Pierce *might* have been offering him more than a job.

The Exeter senior would write to the Southampton divorcée with disarming candor. ("Hi! You may not remember me. I was formerly a writer's assistant to Ted Cole. I was in your shop one day and you offered me a job. You *may* remember that I was, albeit briefly, Marion Cole's lover?")

Penny Pierce would not mince words in her reply. ("Hi yourself. *Remember* you? Who could forget sixty times in—what was it?—six or seven weeks? If it's a summer job you want, it's yours.")

In addition to the frame-shop job, Eddie would, of course, be Mrs. Pierce's lover. The summer of '60 would start out with Eddie staying in a guest bedroom of Mrs. Pierce's newly acquired property on First Neck Lane, until such a time as he found suitable lodging of his own. But they became lovers before he found such a place—truly, before he'd begun to look. Penny Pierce would be glad to have Eddie's company in the big, empty house, which was in need of some enlivening interior decoration.

However, it would take more than new wallpaper and upholstery to banish from the house an aura of tragedy. A widow, a certain Mrs. Mountsier, had not long ago committed suicide on the grounds of the property, which was summarily sold by her only child—a daughter who was still in college, and who was said to have been estranged from her mother at the time of her mother's death.

Eddie would never know that Mrs. Mountsier was the same woman he'd mistaken for Marion in the Coles' driveway—not to mention the role that Ted had played in the unhappy mother-and-daughter story.

In the summer of '60, Eddie would have no contact with Ted—nor would he see Ruth. He would, however, see some photographs of her, which Eduardo Gomez brought to Penny Pierce's shop to have framed. Penny told Eddie that, in the two years since Marion had taken away the photos of Ruth's dead brothers, only a small number of replacement photographs had been brought to her shop for framing.

They were all of Ruth, and—like the half-dozen photos Eddie saw in the summer of '60—were all unnaturally posed. They possessed none of the candid magic of those hundreds of photographs of Thomas and Timothy. Ruth was a sober, frowning child who viewed the camera with a suspicious eye; when a smile was occasionally coaxed out of her, it lacked spontaneity.

In two years, Ruth had grown taller; her hair, which was darker and longer, was often in pigtails. Penny Pierce would point out to Eddie that the pigtails were expertly braided, and some care had been given to the ribbons at the end of each pigtail, too. This couldn't be Ted's work, Penny told Eddie—nor could the six-year-old have managed it herself. (Conchita Gomez was responsible for the pigtails and the ribbons.)

"She's a cute little girl," Mrs. Pierce said of Ruth, "but I'm afraid she's going to miss getting her mother's looks—by about a mile."

After making love to Marion an estimated sixty times in the summer of 1958, Eddie O'Hare would not have sex for almost two years. In his senior year at Exeter, he would qualify for English 4W—the *W* stood for writing of the creative kind—and it was in this class, under the guidance of Mr. Havelock, that Eddie would begin to write about a young man's sexual initiation in the arms of an older woman. Before this, his only efforts to fictionalize his experiences in the summer of '58 had entailed an overlong short story that was based on his disastrous delivery of Ted Cole's drawings to Mrs. Vaughn.

In Eddie's story, they are *not* drawings; they are pornographic poems. The character of the writer's assistant is very Eddie-like, a hapless victim of Mrs. Vaughn's rage, and Mrs. Vaughn herself is unchanged—except for her name, which is Mrs. Wilmot (after the only name Eddie could remember from the list of every living Exonian in the Hamptons). Naturally Mrs. Wilmot has a sympathetic gardener of Hispanic descent, and it falls to the noble gardener to retrieve the shredded pornographic poems from the surrounding hedges—*and* from the small fountain in the circular driveway.

The character of the poet is only distantly based on Ted. The poet is blind, which is why he needs a writer's assistant in the first place—

not to mention why the poet also needs a *driver*. In Eddie's story, the poet is unmarried, and the end of his affair with the character named Mrs. Wilmot—to whom, and about whom, he has written his shocking poems—is described as the *woman's* fault. The blind poet is an entirely sympathetic character, whose plight it is to be repeatedly seduced and abandoned by ugly women.

As the go-between for the poet, whose love for the wicked Mrs. Wilmot shows signs of being tragically unswerving, the much-abused writer's assistant makes a heroic effort that costs him his job. He describes to the blind poet what the hideous Mrs. Wilmot truly looks like; while the description so enrages the poet that he fires the young man, the truth of the description finally frees the poet from his self-destructive attraction to women of Mrs. Wilmot's kind. (The ugliness theme is a little unpolished, even amateurish, for while Eddie meant by this an *inner* ugliness, it is largely the *outer* ugliness of Mrs. Wilmot that is apparent—and unseemly—to the reader.)

Frankly, it was an awful story. But as a sample of young Eddie's *promise* as a writer of fiction, it made enough of an impression on Mr. Havelock that he admitted Eddie to English 4W, and it was there, in that class of aspiring young writers, that Eddie's more beguiling theme—the younger man with the older woman—began to flow.

Naturally, Eddie was too shy to show his earliest efforts to the class. These stories he presented in confidentiality to Mr. Havelock, who showed them only to his wife; *yes,* she was that selfsame woman whose bralessness and furry armpits had once provided Eddie with his beginner phase of masturbatory bliss. Mrs. Havelock would take an active interest in Eddie's development of the younger-man-with-the-older-woman theme.

It is understandable that this subject was more interesting to Mrs. Havelock than Eddie's prose was. After all, Mrs. Havelock was a childless woman in her thirties who was the only visible object of desire in a closed community of almost eight hundred teenaged boys. While she had never been sexually tempted by a single one of them, it had not escaped her notice that they lusted after her. The sheer possibility of such a relationship appalled her. She was happily married and unstintingly thought that boys were . . . well, just boys. Therefore, the very nature of a sexual relationship between a sixteen-year-old boy and a thirty-nine-year-old woman, which Eddie's stories repeatedly described, attracted Mrs. Havelock's grim curiosity. She was German-born; she had met her husband when she was a foreign-exchange student in Scotland—Mr. Havelock was English—and her entrapment in one of America's elite, all-boys' boarding schools continually bewildered and depressed her.

Notwithstanding Eddie's mother's opinion of Mrs. Havelock's "bohemianism," Mrs. Havelock did nothing to deliberately make herself sexually attractive to the boys. Like a good wife, she made herself as attractive as she could to her husband; it was *Mr.* Havelock who favored bralessness and who begged his wife to leave her armpits unshaven—naturalness appealed to him above all things. Mrs. Havelock regarded herself as somewhat frumpy; she was dismayed at her obvious effect on these horny boys, who she knew beat off with abandon to her image.

Anna Havelock, née Rainer, could not emerge from her dormitory apartment without causing several stray boys in the dormitory hall to blush, or to walk into doors or walls because they couldn't take their eyes off her; she could not serve coffee and doughnuts in her apartment to her husband's advisees, or to his students in English 4W, without rendering them tongue-tied—they were so smitten by her. Quite sensibly, she hated it. She begged her husband to take her back to Great Britain, or to Germany, where she knew from experience she could live her life unnoticed. But her husband, Arthur Havelock, adored the life at Exeter, where he was an energetic teacher who was well liked by the students and his fellow members of the faculty.

It was into this basically good marriage, with its single subject of contention, that Eddie O'Hare brought his disturbing stories of his sexual entanglement with Marion Cole. Naturally, Eddie had shielded himself—not to mention Marion. The Eddie character, in Eddie's stories, was *not* a writer's assistant to a famous author and illustrator of children's books. (Because Minty O'Hare had glamorized his son's first summer job beyond boredom, *everyone* in the Exeter English Department knew that Eddie had once worked for Ted Cole.)

In Eddie's stories, the sixteen-year-old had a summer job in a frame shop in Southampton, and the Marion character was modeled on Eddie's imperfect memory of Penny Pierce; because Eddie could not recall what Mrs. Pierce looked like, her physical description was an inaccurate combination of Marion's beautiful face and Penny Pierce's matronly body, which was no match for Marion's.

Like Mrs. Pierce, the Marion character in Eddie's stories was comfortably divorced. The Eddie character certainly enjoyed the wild fruits of his sexual initiation; *sixty* times in less than one summer was a shocking concept to both Mr. and Mrs. Havelock. The Eddie character also enjoyed the benefits of Penny Pierce's generous alimony settlement—for in Eddie's stories the sixteen-year-old lived in the frameshop owner's splendid house in Southampton, a lavish estate that bore a striking resemblance to Mrs. Vaughn's mansion on Gin Lane.

While Mrs. Havelock was riveted and greatly upset by the sexual authenticity of Eddie's stories, Mr. Havelock—good teacher that he was—concerned himself more with the quality of Eddie's writing. He would point out to Eddie what Eddie already suspected: there were areas of the young man's writing that seemed more authentic than others. The sexual detail, the boy's gloomy foreknowledge that the summer will end—and with it his love affair with a woman who means everything to him (while he believes he means much less to her)—and the relentless *anticipation* of sex, which is almost as thrilling as the act itself ... well, these elements in Eddie's stories rang true. (They *were* true, Eddie knew.)

But other details were less convincing. Going back to Eddie's description of the blind poet with the writer's assistant, for example: the poet himself was an undeveloped character; the pornographic poems were neither believable as poems nor sufficiently graphic for pornography—whereas the description of the Mrs. Vaughn character's anger, of her reaction to the pornography *and* to the hapless writer's assistant who delivers the poems to her ... ah, this was good stuff. It rang true, too. (Because it *was* true, Eddie knew.)

Eddie had *made up* the blind poet and the pornographic poems; he had *made up* the physical description of the Marion character, who was this unconvincing mixture of Marion and Penny Pierce. Both Mr. and Mrs. Havelock said that the Marion character herself was unclear; they couldn't "see" her, they told Eddie.

When the source of his fiction was autobiographical, Eddie could write with authority and authenticity. But when he tried to imagine—to invent, to create—he simply could not succeed as well as when he remembered. This is a serious limitation for a fiction writer! (At the time, when he was still a student at Exeter, Eddie didn't know *how* serious.)

Eventually, Eddie would be afforded a small but literary reputation; he would play a little-known but respected role. He would never have the impact on the American psyche that Ruth Cole would; he would not have *her* command of the language, or ever approach the magnitude and complexity of *her* characters and plots—not to mention her narrative momentum.

But Eddie would make a living as a novelist, nonetheless. One can't deny him his *existence* as a writer simply because he would never be, as Chesterton once wrote of Dickens, "a naked flame of mere genius, breaking out in a man without culture, without tradition, without help from historic religions and philosophies or from the great foreign schools."

No, that wouldn't be Eddie O'Hare. (It would be overly generous to extend Chesterton's praise to Ruth Cole, too.) But at least Eddie would be published.

The point is: Eddie wrote familiar, autobiographical novels—all of them variations on an overworked theme—and despite the carefulness with which he wrote (he had a lucid prose style), and a faithfulness to time and place (and to characters who were credible, and who stayed in character), his novels lacked imagination; or else, when he made an effort to allow his imagination looser rein, his novels lacked believability.

His first novel, while generally well received, would not escape those pitfalls that his good teacher Mr. Havelock had pointed out to Eddie at the earliest opportunity. Titled *Summer Job*, the novel was basically another version of the stories Eddie wrote at Exeter. (Its publication, in 1973, coincided almost exactly with Ruth Cole's graduation from the former all-boys' school.)

In *Summer Job*, the poet is deaf rather than blind, and his need of a writer's assistant comes closer to the truth of Ted's need for hiring Eddie: namely, the deaf poet is a drunk. But while the relationship between the younger and older man is convincing, the poems are not credible poems—Eddie could never write poetry—and what is allegedly pornographic about them is neither raw nor invasive enough to qualify as pornography. The deaf, drunk poet's angry lover, the Mrs. Vaughn character (who is still called Mrs. Wilmot), is a skillful portrait of heightened ugliness, but the poet's long-suffering wife, the Marion character, is *not* convincing; she is neither Marion nor Penny Pierce.

Eddie tried to make her a most ethereal but universal older woman; as such, she is entirely too vague to be believable as the love object of the writer's assistant. Nor is her motivation sufficiently established; the reader can't understand what she sees in the sixteen-year-old. What

Eddie left out of *Summer Job* were the lost sons; those dead boys make no appearance in Eddie's novel, nor is there a Ruth character.

Ted Cole, who would be amused to read *Summer Job*, which he smugly recognized as a minor work of fiction, would also be grateful to Eddie for the altered reality of the thirty-one-year-old author's first novel. Ruth, who, when she was old enough, had been told by her father that Eddie O'Hare and her mother were lovers, was no less grateful to Eddie for excluding her from the story. Nor did it occur to Ruth that the Marion character even remotely resembled her mother; Ruth would know only that her mother was still missing.

On that August Saturday in 1958, when he crossed Long Island Sound with the clam-truck driver, Eddie O'Hare had no telescope trained on the future. He could never have foreseen his career as a faintly praised, little-known novelist. Yet Eddie would never be without a small but loyal following of readers; it would depress him, at times, that his fans were chiefly older women and, albeit less frequently, younger men. Nevertheless, there was evidence of literary *effort* in his writing— Eddie would never be out of a job. He would eke out a living by teaching at the university level—a job he did honorably, if without much flair or distinction. He would be respected by his students and his fellow faculty members, if never adored.

When the clam-truck driver asked him, "If you're not gonna be a writer's assistant, what are you gonna be?" Eddie didn't hesitate in replying to the forthright but smelly man.

"I'm going to be a writer," Eddie replied.

Surely the sixteen-year-old couldn't have imagined the grief he would occasionally cause. He would hurt the Havelocks, without ever meaning to—not to mention Penny Pierce, whom he had meant to hurt only a little. And the Havelocks had been so kind to him! Mrs. Havelock liked Eddie—in part because she sensed that he was beyond whatever lust he'd once felt for her. She could tell he was in love with someone else, and it didn't take her long to come out and ask him. Both Mr. and Mrs. Havelock knew that Eddie was not a good enough writer to have *imagined* those scenes of sexual explicitness between a younger man and an older woman. Too many of the details were just right.

And so it was to Mr. and Mrs. Havelock that Eddie would confess his six- or seven-week affair with Marion; he told them the awful things, too—the parts he'd been unable to write about. At first Mrs. Havelock responded by saying that Marion had virtually *raped* him; that Marion was guilty of taking criminal advantage of what Mrs. Havelock called "an underage boy." But Eddie persuaded Mrs. Havelock that it hadn't really been like that.

As was his habit with older women, Eddie found it easy and comforting to cry in front of Mrs. Havelock, whose hairy armpits and mobile, uncontained breasts could still remind him of his *former* lust for her. Like an ex-girlfriend, Mrs. Havelock would only occasionally and halfheartedly arouse him—yet he was not above feeling a *flicker* of arousal in her warm, maternal presence.

What a pity, then, that he would write about her as he did. It could be described as a worse-than-usual case of "second novelitis," for Eddie's second novel was his worst; indeed, following (as it did) upon the relative success of *Summer Job*, Eddie's second novel would be the low point of his career. After it, his literary reputation would slightly improve and thereafter hold to its steady, undistinguished course.

It seems certain that Eddie must have been thinking too much about Robert Anderson's play *Tea and Sympathy;* it was later a movie, starring Deborah Kerr as the older woman, and it doubtless made a lasting impression on Eddie O'Hare. *Tea and Sympathy* was especially well known in the Exeter community because Robert Anderson, '35, was an Exonian; this made it all the more embarrassing for Mrs. Havelock when Eddie's second novel, *Coffee and Doughnuts*, was published.

In *Coffee and Doughnuts*, an Exeter student is frequently overcome by fainting fits in the presence of the wife of his favorite English teacher. The wife—whose braless, pendulous breasts and furry, unshaven armpits forever identify her as Mrs. Havelock—begs her husband to take her away from the confines of the school. She feels humiliated to be the object of desire of so *many* boys—in addition to how sorry she feels for the particular boy whom her unintentional sexuality has completely undone.

This was "much too close to home," as Minty O'Hare would later tell his son. Even Dot O'Hare would look pityingly upon the stricken countenance of Anna Havelock after *Coffee and Doughnuts* was published. In his naïveté, Eddie had thought of the book as a kind of homage to *Tea and Sympathy*—and to the Havelocks, who had been such a help to him. But in the novel, the Mrs. Havelock character sleeps with the infatuated teenager; this is the only means she has to convince her insensitive husband to remove her from the school's masturbatory atmosphere. (How Eddie O'Hare could have thought of his book as *homage* to the Havelocks is anybody's guess.)

For Mrs. Havelock, the publication of *Coffee and Doughnuts* did have at least one desired effect. Her husband took her back to Great Britain, just as she'd asked him to. Arthur Havelock ended up teaching somewhere in Scotland, the country where he and Anna had first met. But if the *result* of Eddie's writing *Coffee and Doughnuts* was, unwittingly, a happy ending for the Havelocks, they never thanked Eddie for his embarrassing book; indeed, they never spoke to him again.

About the only person who ever liked *Coffee and Doughnuts* was someone pretending to be Robert Anderson, '35; the alleged author of *Tea and Sympathy* sent Eddie an elegant letter, expressing his understanding of both the intended homage *and* the intended comedy. (It was devastating to Eddie that, in the parentheses following Robert Anderson's name, the imposter had written, "Just kidding!")

On that Saturday when he was sharing the upper deck of the Cross Sound Ferry with the clam-truck driver, Eddie's mood was morose. It was almost as if he could foresee not only his summerlong affair with Penny Pierce but her bitter letter to him after she'd read *Summer Job*. Penny would not like the Marion character in that novel—Penny would see her as the *Penny* character, of course.

To be fair, Mrs. Pierce would be disappointed in Eddie O'Hare long before she read *Summer Job*. In the summer of '60, she would sleep with Eddie for three months; she would have almost twice as much time to sleep with him as Marion had had, yet Eddie wouldn't come close to making love to Mrs. Pierce sixty times.

"You know what I remember, kid?" the clam-truck driver was saying. To be sure he had the boy's attention, the driver extended his beer bottle beyond the protecting wall of the pilothouse; the wind made the bottle *toot*.

"No, what do you remember?" Eddie asked the driver.

"That *broad* you was with," the clam-truck driver said. "The one in the pink sweater. She picked you up in that sweet little Mercedes. You wasn't *her* assistant, were you?"

Eddie paused. "No, her husband's," Eddie said. "Her husband was the writer."

"Now *there's* a lucky guy!" the clam-truck driver said. "But don't get me wrong. I just *look* at other women, I don't mess around. I been married for almost thirty-five years—my high-school sweetheart. We're pretty happy, I guess. She's not great-looking but she's my wife. It's like the clams."

"Excuse me?" Eddie said.

"The wife, the clams...I mean, maybe it's not the most exciting choice, but it works," the clam-truck driver explained. "I wanted my own trucking business, at least my own truck. I didn't want to drive for nobody else. I used to haul lots of things—other stuff. But it was complicated. When I saw I could make it with just the clams, it was easier. I kind of *lapsed* into the clams, you might say."

"I see," Eddie said. The wife, the clams ... it was a tortured analogy, no matter how you expressed it, the future novelist thought. And it would be unfair to say that Eddie O'Hare, as a writer, would become the literary equivalent of *lapsing* into clams. He wasn't *that* bad.

The clam-truck driver once more extended his beer bottle beyond the pilothouse wall; the bottle, which was now empty, tooted at a lower pitch than before. The ferry slowed as it approached the slip.

Eddie and the driver walked to the bow of the upper deck, where they faced into the wind. Eddie's mother and father were waving madly from the docks; their dutiful son waved back. Both Minty and Dot were weeping; they hugged each other and wiped each other's wet faces, as if Eddie were returning safely from a war. Rather than feel his usual embarrassment, or even the slightest shame at his parents' hysterical behavior, Eddie realized how much he loved them and how fortunate he was to have the kind of parents Ruth Cole would never know.

Then the gangplank chains, lowering the ferry's ramp, commenced their usual loud grinding; the stevedores were shouting to one another above the clamor. "Nice talking to you, kid!" the clam-truck driver was calling.

Eddie took what he imagined was a last look out of the harbor at the choppy water of Long Island Sound. He had no idea that the trip on the Cross Sound Ferry would one day be as familiar to him as passing through the doorway of the Main Academy Building, under that Latin inscription which bid him to come hither and become a man.

"Edward! My Edward!" his father was bawling. Eddie's mom was weeping too copiously to speak. One look at them and Eddie knew that he could never tell them what had happened to him. With more pow-

ers of premonition than he possessed, Eddie might—at this very moment—have recognized his limitations as a fiction writer: he would always be an unreliable liar. Not only could he never tell his parents the
truth about his relationship with Ted and Marion and Ruth; neither
could he make up a satisfying lie.

Eddie would lie largely by omission, saying simply that it had been
a sad summer for him because Mr. and Mrs. Cole were caught up in the
prelude to a divorce; now Marion had left Ted with the little girl, and
that was that. A more challenging opportunity to lie would present itself to Eddie when his mother discovered Marion's pink cashmere
cardigan hanging in her son's closet.

Eddie's lie was more spontaneous and more convincing than most of
what was imperfectly imagined in his fiction. He told his mom that
once when he'd been shopping with Mrs. Cole, she'd pointed out the
sweater in an East Hampton boutique and had told him that she'd always liked the particular garment and had hoped her husband would
buy it for her; now that they were divorcing, Mrs. Cole had implied to
Eddie, there was good reason for her husband to save his money.

Eddie had returned to the store and bought the expensive sweater.
But Mrs. Cole had left—the marriage, the house, her child, *everything*—
before Eddie had had the chance to give the sweater to her! Eddie told
his mother that he wanted to keep the sweater in case he ever ran into
Marion again.

Dot O'Hare had been proud of her son for his kind gesture. To
Eddie's embarrassment, Dot would occasionally display the pink cashmere cardigan to their faculty friends—the tale of Eddie's thoughtfulness toward the unhappy Mrs. Cole was Dot's idea of good dinner-party
conversation. And Eddie's lie would further backfire. In the summer of
'60, when Eddie was falling short of making love to Penny Pierce the
requisite sixty times, Dot O'Hare would meet a woman among the Exeter faculty wives who was just the right size for Marion's sweater. When
Eddie came home from Long Island that second time, his mom had
given Marion's pink cashmere cardigan away.

It was lucky for Eddie that his mother never found Marion's lilac-
colored camisole and matching panties, which Eddie kept buried in the
drawer containing his athletic supporters and his squash shorts. It is
doubtful that Dot O'Hare would have congratulated her son for his
"thoughtfulness" in buying Mrs. Cole such suggestive underwear.

At the docks in New London, on that Saturday in August '58, there was something in the firmness of Eddie's embrace that persuaded Minty to give his son the keys to the car. There was not a word about the traffic that lay ahead of them being "different from Exeter traffic." Minty wasn't worried; he saw that Eddie had matured. ("Joe—he's all grown up!" Dot whispered to her husband.)

Minty had parked the car at some distance from the docks, near the station platform for the New London railroad depot. After a small fuss between them concerning whether Dot or Minty would ride in the passenger seat and be Eddie's "navigator" for the long ride home, Eddie's parents settled into the car as trustingly as children. There was no question that Eddie was in charge.

Only when he was leaving the railroad-depot parking lot did Eddie spot Marion's tomato-red Mercedes; it was parked within easy walking distance of the station platform. Probably the keys were already in the mail to her lawyer, who would repeat to Ted the list of Marion's demands.

So she had probably *not* gone to New York. This awareness came as no more than a mild surprise to Eddie. And if Marion had left her car at the train station in New London, this didn't necessarily mean she had gone back to New England—she might have been heading farther north. (Montreal, maybe. Eddie knew she could speak French.)

But what was she thinking? Eddie wondered, as he would wonder about Marion for thirty-seven years. What was she doing? Where had she gone?

II

FALL
1990

Eddie at Forty-Eight

It was early on a rainy Monday evening in September. Eddie O'Hare stood stiffly at the bar in the tap room of the New York Athletic Club. He was forty-eight, his formerly dark-brown hair was heavily streaked with silver-gray, and—because he was trying to read while standing at the bar—a thick lock of his hair kept flopping over one of his eyes. He kept brushing his hair back, his long fingers like a comb. He never carried a comb, and his hair had a fluffy, just-washed wildness to it; it was the only wild thing about him, really.

Eddie was tall and thin. Sitting or standing, he squared his shoulders in an unnatural way; his body maintained a tense, almost military overerectness. He suffered from chronic lower back pain. He had just lost three straight games of squash to a little bald man named Jimmy. Eddie could never remember Jimmy's last name. Jimmy was retired— he was rumored to be in his seventies—and he spent every afternoon at the New York Athletic Club, waiting for pickup squash games with younger players whose would-be opponents had stood them up.

Eddie, who was drinking a Diet Coke—it was all he ever drank— had lost to Jimmy before; naturally he'd been stood up before, too. Eddie had a few close friends in New York, but none of them played squash. He'd become a member of the club only three years earlier, in 1987, upon the publication of his fourth novel, *Sixty Times*. Despite favorable (if tepid) reviews, the novel's subject matter had not appealed to the only member of the Membership Committee who'd read it. Another member on the committee had confided to Eddie that Eddie's membership had finally been approved because of his name, not because of his novels. (There had been a long history of O'Hares at the New York Athletic Club, although none of them were related to Eddie.)

Still, despite what Eddie perceived as the selective, grudging friend-liness of the club, he enjoyed being a member. It was an inexpensive place to stay whenever he came into the city. For almost ten years now, since the publication of his third novel, *Leaving Long Island,* Eddie came into the city fairly frequently—if only for a night or two. In '81, he had bought his first and only house—in Bridgehampton, about a five-minute drive from Ted Cole's house in Sagaponack. In his nine years as a taxpaying resident of Suffolk County, Eddie had not once driven by Ted's house on Parsonage Lane.

Eddie's house was on Maple Lane—so close to the Bridgehampton railroad station that Eddie could walk to the train, which he rarely did. Eddie hated trains. The trains passed so close to his house that Eddie sometimes felt he *lived* on a train. And although the real estate agent herself had admitted to Eddie that his Maple Lane location left some-thing to be desired, the house had been affordable and was not *so* innocuous that Eddie had ever failed to rent it. Eddie hated the Hamp-tons in July and August; he made an exorbitant amount of money by renting his thoroughly modest house in those lunatic months.

With what he made from his writing and from the summer rentals, Eddie needed to teach only one semester every academic year. At one college or university or another, he was a perpetual visiting writer-in-residence. Eddie was also doomed to travel to various writers' confer-ences, and every summer he needed to find a cheaper summer rental than what he charged for his house in the Hamptons. Yet Eddie would never have complained about his circumstances; he was well liked on the teaching-writing circuit, where he could be relied upon *not* to sleep with the students. Not with the *younger* students, anyway.

True to his declaration to Marion thirty-two years ago, Eddie O'Hare had never slept with a woman his own age—or younger. Al-though many of the writing students who attended the writers' confer-ences were older women—divorcées and widows who had turned to writing as a form of therapy—no one thought of these women as inno-cent or in need of protection from the sexual inclinations of the teaching-writing faculty. Besides, in Eddie's case, it was always the older women who made the first advances; his reputation preceded him.

All things considered, Eddie was a man who'd made very few ene-mies; there were only those older women who took offense that he'd written about them. But they were wrong to take Eddie's older-women characters so personally. He had merely used their bodies and their hair, their gestures and their favorite expressions. And the undying love that each of Eddie's younger men felt for each of Eddie's older women was always a version of what Eddie felt for Marion; he had not felt such a love for any of the older women since.

As a novelist, he'd merely borrowed the locations of their apartments and the feel of their clothes; sometimes he used the upholstery of their living-room couches—once the rosebush pattern of a lonely librarian's sheets and pillowcases, but *not* the librarian herself. (Not exactly, although he *had* borrowed the mole on her left breast.)

And if Eddie had made enemies of these *few* older women who saw versions of themselves in one or another of his four novels, he'd also made lasting friends among *many* older women—including several he had once slept with. A woman once told Eddie that she was suspicious of any man who remained a friend of former lovers; it must mean that he was never much of a lover, or nothing more than a nice guy. But Eddie O'Hare had long ago made peace with himself on the subject of his being "nothing more than a nice guy"; countless women had told Eddie that he could hang his hat on being a nice guy. (There were so few of them, the women said.)

Eddie once more brushed his hair away from his right eye. He looked up at the tap-room mirror in the gloom of the rainy evening and recognized in his reflected countenance a tall, tired-looking man who was, at that moment, extremely short on confidence. He returned his attention to the manuscript pages on the bar; he sipped his Diet Coke. It was a manuscript of almost twenty typed pages that had been much revised by Eddie's red pen; he called the pen his "teacher's favorite." He had also written the squash scores of his games with Jimmy at the top of the first manuscript page: 15–9, 15–5, 15–3. Whenever Eddie had been run ragged by Jimmy, Eddie always imagined that he'd lost again to Ted Cole. Eddie calculated that Ted was now in his late seventies, about Jimmy's age.

In his nine years in Bridgehampton, it had been no accident that Eddie had not driven past Ted's house; to live on Maple Lane in Bridgehampton and never once find yourself turning onto Parsonage Lane in Sagaponack required fairly constant forethought. But Eddie was surprised not to have run into Ted at a cocktail party, or at the

Bridgehampton I.G.A.—Eddie should have guessed that Conchita Gomez (now also in her late seventies) did all of Ted's shopping. Ted never shopped.

Regarding the cocktail parties: Eddie and Ted were of different generations; they attended different parties. Also, although Ted Cole's books for children were still widely read, Ted himself (at seventy-seven) was decreasingly famous—at least in the Hamptons. It pleased Eddie to think that Ted was not nearly the celebrity that his *daughter* was.

But if Ted Cole's fame was slipping away, Ted's squash game—especially in his tricky barn—was every bit as tough as Jimmy's. At seventy-seven, Ted would have whipped Eddie as easily in the fall of 1990 as he'd whipped him in the summer of 1958. Eddie was a terrible player, really. Ungainly and slow, he never anticipated where his opponent's shot was going; he got to the ball late, if he got to it at all, and he rushed his shot accordingly. Nor would Eddie's lob serve, which was his best serve, have worked in Ted's barn, where the ceiling was less than fifteen feet from the floor.

Ruth, who was a good enough player to have been third-best on the *boys'* varsity at Exeter, had not yet beaten her father on his infuriating home court; her lob serve was her best, too. Ruth was thirty-six in the fall of 1990, and the *only* reason she ever went home to Sagaponack was that she wanted to beat her father in his barn before he died. But, even at seventy-seven, Ted Cole showed no signs of dying.

Outside the New York Athletic Club, at the corner of Central Park South and Seventh Avenue, the rain beat down on the club's cream-colored awning; if Eddie had known how many members were already lined up under the awning waiting in turn for a cab, he would long ago have left the tap room and taken his place at the rear of the line. But he went on rereading and revising his overlong, messy manuscript, unaware that he should have been less worried about preparing his speech than he should have been about arriving too late to deliver it.

At Fifty-ninth Street and Seventh Avenue, he was too far away from the 92nd Street Y (on Lexington) to walk—especially in the rain, for he had no raincoat or umbrella. And he should have known the effect of rain on the availability of taxis in New York, especially in the early-evening hours. But Eddie was too preoccupied with the flaws in his speech; he had always suffered from defeatist tendencies, and now he wished that he'd never agreed to give such a speech in the first place.

Who am I, he thought miserably, *to introduce Ruth Cole?*

It was the bartender who saved Eddie from missing the dreaded event altogether. "You want another Diet Coke, Mr. O'Hare?" the bartender asked. Eddie looked at his watch. If, at that moment, Marion had been in the tap room observing Eddie's expression, she would have seen something of a sixteen-year-old's haplessness in her former lover's face.

It was 7:20; Eddie was expected at the Y in ten minutes. It was at least a ten-minute cab ride to Lexington and Ninety-second, provided Eddie caught a cab the second he stepped out the door of the club. Instead, he stepped into a lineup of disgruntled members. On the cream-colored awning, the blood-red emblem of the N.Y.A.C.—a winged foot—was dripping rain.

Eddie shifted the books and the manuscript of his speech in his bulky brown briefcase. He would be late if he waited for a cab. He was about to get very wet, but even before Eddie's encounter with the rain there was an aspect of professorial disarray about his clothes. Notwithstanding the coat-and-tie dress code of the New York Athletic Club, and despite the fact that Eddie was of an age and background that felt comfortable in coats and ties—after all, he was an Exonian—the club doorman always looked at Eddie's clothes as if they were in violation of the code.

Without a plan, Eddie jogged along Central Park South in what had become a downpour. He wished vaguely, as he approached first the St. Moritz and then the Plaza, that he would discover a string of taxis waiting for the hotel guests at the curb. What he found instead were two lines of determined hotel guests waiting for taxis.

Eddie darted into the Plaza and presented himself at the registration desk, where he asked for change—*lots* of change—for a ten-dollar bill. He could take a bus up Madison Avenue if he had the exact fare. But before he could mumble what he wanted, the woman at the registration desk asked him if he was a guest at the hotel. Sometimes, spontaneously, Eddie was capable of lying, but almost never when he *wanted* to.

"No, I'm not a guest—I just need bus money," he admitted. The woman shook her head.

"I'd get in trouble if you're not a guest," she said.

He had to run up Fifth Avenue before he could cross at Sixty-second. Then he ran up Madison until he found a coffee shop where he could buy a Diet Coke, solely because he wanted some change. He left the Diet Coke at the cash register, together with a tip of disproportionate generosity, but the woman at the cash register judged the tip to be insufficient. The way she saw it, Eddie had left her with a Diet Coke to dispose of—a task unworthy of her or insurmountable, or both.

"Like I *need* this trouble!" she shouted after him. She must have hated making extra change.

Eddie waited in the rain for the Madison Avenue bus. He was already soaked, and five minutes late. It was now 7:35. The event began at 8:00. The organizers of Ruth Cole's reading at the Y had wanted Eddie and Ruth to meet backstage, to have a little time to relax—"to get to know each other." No one, least of all Eddie or Ruth, had said "to get *reacquainted*." (How does one get *reacquainted* with a four-year-old when she's thirty-six?)

The other people waiting for the bus knew enough to step back from the curb, but Eddie stood where he was. The bus, before it stopped, splashed dirty water from the flooded gutter onto Eddie's chest and midsection. Now he was not only wet, but also filthy, and a part of the dirty puddle was sloshing in the bottom of his briefcase.

He'd inscribed a copy of *Sixty Times* for Ruth, although it had been published three years before and if Ruth had been inclined to read it, she would already have done so. Eddie had often imagined Ted Cole's remarks to his daughter on the subject of *Sixty Times*. "Wishful thinking," Ted would have said. Or: "Sheer exaggeration—your mother hardly knew the guy." What Ted had actually said to Ruth is more interesting, and totally true of Eddie. What Ted had told his daughter was: "This poor kid never got over fucking your mother."

"He's not a kid anymore, Daddy," Ruth had replied. "If I'm in my thirties, Eddie O'Hare is in his forties—right?"

"He's still a kid, Ruthie," Ted had told her. "Eddie will always be a kid."

Indeed, as he struggled onto the Madison Avenue bus, Eddie's accumulated distress and anxiety made him resemble a forty-eight-year-old adolescent. The driver was angry with him for not knowing what the exact fare was, and although Eddie had a bulging fistful of change in his pocket, his pants were so wet that he could retrieve the coins only one at a time. The people standing behind him—most of them still in the rain—were angry with Eddie, too.

Then, in attempting to empty his briefcase of the water from the gutter, Eddie poured a brownish puddle on the shoe of an elderly man who did not speak English. Eddie could not understand the language the man spoke to him; Eddie didn't even know which language it was. It was also hard to hear on the bus, and impossible to make out the driver's occasional utterances—the names of the cross streets, the stops or the *potential* stops they were passing?

The reason Eddie couldn't hear was that a young black man sat in an aisle seat of the bus with a large portable radio and cassette player in his lap. A loud, lewd song throbbed throughout the bus, the only discernible lyrics being a repeated phrase; it was something like, "Ya wouldn't know da truth, mon, if she sat on ya face!"

"Excuse me," Eddie said to the young man. "Would you mind turning that down a little? I can't hear what the driver is saying."

The young man smiled charmingly and said, "I can't hear what you sayin', man, 'cause the *box* is too fuckin' loud!"

Some of the surrounding passengers, whether out of nervousness or genuine appreciation, laughed. Eddie leaned over a matronly black woman in a nearby seat; he rubbed the fogged-up window with the heel of his hand. Possibly he could *see* the upcoming cross streets. But his bulky brown briefcase slipped off his shoulder—the shoulder strap was as wet as Eddie's clothes—and the briefcase struck the woman in her face.

The wet briefcase knocked the woman's glasses off; she was fortunate to catch them in her lap, but she caught them too hard. She popped one of the lenses out of the frame. She looked blindly up at Eddie with a lunacy born of many disappointments and sorrows. "What you wanna be makin' trouble for *me* for?" she asked.

The throbbing song about the truth sitting on someone's face instantly stopped. The young black man seated across the aisle stood up, the silent boom box hugged to his chest like a boulder.

"That my mom," the boy said. He was short—the top of his head came only to the knot in Eddie's tie—but the boy's neck was as big around as Eddie's thigh, and the boy's shoulders were twice as broad and thick as Eddie's. "Why you makin' trouble for my *mom?*" the powerful-looking young man asked.

Since Eddie had left the New York Athletic Club, it was the fourth mention of "trouble" that he had heard. It was why he'd never wanted to live in New York.

"I was just trying to see my stop—where I get out," Eddie said.

"This here your stop," the brutish boy told him, pushing the signal cord. The bus braked, throwing Eddie off balance. Again his heavy briefcase slipped off his shoulder; this time it hit no one, because Eddie clutched it in both his hands. "This here where you get out," the squat young man said. His mother, and several surrounding passengers, agreed.

Oh, well, Eddie thought as he got off the bus—maybe it was *almost* Ninety-second Street. (It was Eighty-first.) He heard someone say "Good riddance!" just before the bus moved on.

Minutes later, Eddie ran along Eighty-ninth Street, crossing to the east side of Park Avenue, where he spotted an available taxi. Without thinking that he was now only three uptown blocks and one crosstown block from his destination, Eddie hailed the cab; he got into the taxi and told the cabbie where to go.

"Ninety-second and *Lex?*" the taxi driver said. "Christ, you shoulda *walked*—you're already wet!"

"But I'm late," Eddie lamely replied.

"Everyone's late," the cabbie told him. The fare was so small, Eddie tried to compensate the taxi driver by giving him his entire ball of change.

"Christ!" the cabbie shouted. "What do I want with all that?"

At least he didn't say "trouble," Eddie thought, stuffing the coins into his jacket pocket. All the bills in Eddie's wallet were wet; the taxi driver disapproved of them, too.

"You're worse than late, *and* wet," the driver told Eddie. "You're fuckin' *trouble*."

"Thank you," Eddie said. (In one of his more philosophical moments, Minty O'Hare had told his son to never look down his nose at a compliment—there might not be all that many.)

Thus did a muddied and dripping Eddie O'Hare present himself to a young woman taking tickets in the crowded lobby of the 92nd Street Y. "I'm here for the reading. I know I'm a little late...." Eddie began.

"Where's your ticket?" the girl asked him. "We're sold out. We've been sold out for weeks."

Sold out! Eddie had rarely seen a sell-out crowd at the Kaufman Concert Hall. He'd heard several famous authors read there; he'd even introduced a couple of them. When Eddie had given a reading in the concert hall, of course, he had never read alone; only well-known writers, like Ruth Cole, read alone. The last time Eddie had read there, it had been billed as An Evening of Novels of Manners—or maybe it was An Evening of *Comic* Novels of Manners. Or Comic Manners? All Eddie could remember was that the other two novelists who read with him had been funnier than *he* had been.

"Uh…" Eddie said to the girl taking tickets, "I don't need a ticket because I'm the introducer." He was fishing through his drenched briefcase for the copy of *Sixty Times* that he'd inscribed to Ruth. He wanted to show the girl his jacket photo, to prove he was really who he said he was.

"You're the *what?*" the girl said. Then she saw the sodden book that he held out to her.

Sixty Times

A NOVEL

Ed O'Hare

(It was only on his books that Eddie finally got to be called Ed. His father still called him Edward, and everyone else called him Eddie. Even in his not-so-good reviews, Eddie was pleased when he was referred to as just plain Ed O'Hare.)

"I'm the *introducer*," Eddie repeated to the girl taking tickets. "I'm Ed O'Hare."

"Oh, my *Gawd!*" the girl cried. "You're Eddie O'Hare! They've been waiting and *waiting* for you. You're very late."

"I'm sorry…" he began, but the girl was already pulling him through the crowd.

Sold out! Eddie was thinking. What a mob it was. And how *young* they were. Most of them looked as if they were still in college. It wasn't the typical audience at the Y, although Eddie began to see that the usual people were also there. In Eddie's estimation, the "usual people" were a grave-looking literary crowd, frowning in advance of what they were about to hear. It was not Eddie O'Hare's kind of audience: absent were those fragile-looking older women who were always alone, or with a deeply troubled woman friend; and those traumatized, self-conscious younger men who always struck Eddie as too pretty, in an unmanly sort of way. (It was the way Eddie saw himself: too pretty, in an unmanly sort of way.)

Jesus God, what am I *doing* here? Eddie thought. *Why* had he agreed to introduce Ruth Cole? Why had they *asked* him? he wondered desperately. Had it been *Ruth's* idea?

The backstage of the concert hall was so muggy that Eddie couldn't tell the difference between his sweat and the rain damage to his clothes—not to mention the remains of the giant mud puddle. "There's a washroom just off the greenroom," the girl was saying, "in case you want to ... uh, clean up."

I'm a mess and I have nothing interesting to say, Eddie concluded. For *years* he had imagined meeting Ruth again. But he had pictured a meeting vastly different from this—something more private, maybe lunch or dinner. And Ruth must have at least *occasionally* imagined meeting him. After all, Ted would have *had* to tell his daughter about her mother and the circumstances of that summer of '58; Ted could never have restrained himself. Naturally Eddie would have been a part of the story, if not the principal villain.

And wasn't it fair to anticipate that Eddie and Ruth would have much to talk about, even if their chief interest in common was Marion? After all, they both wrote novels, although their novels were worlds apart—Ruth was a superstar and Eddie was ... God, what *am* I? Eddie considered. Compared to Ruth Cole, I'm a nobody, he concluded. Maybe *that* was the way to begin his introduction.

Yet, when he'd been invited to introduce her, Eddie had fervently believed he had the best of all reasons to accept the invitation. For six years, he'd harbored a secret that he wanted to share with Ruth. For six years, he'd kept the evidence to himself. Now, on this miserable night, he carried the evidence with him in his bulky brown briefcase. What did it matter that the evidence had got a little *wet*?

In his briefcase there was a second book, a book of much more importance to Ruth, Eddie believed, than his personally inscribed copy of *Sixty Times*. Six years ago, when Eddie had first read this *other* book, he'd been tempted to tell Ruth *then*; he'd even considered bringing the book to Ruth's attention by some anonymous means. But then he'd seen a TV interview with Ruth, and something she'd said had prevented Eddie from pressing the matter.

Ruth never talked in depth about her father—or about whether or not she ever intended to write a book for children. When interviewers asked if her father had taught her to write, she said: "He taught me something about storytelling, and squash. But about writing ... no, he taught me nothing about writing, really." And when they would ask her about her mother—if her mother was still "missing," or if being "abandoned" as a child had had any great effect on her (either as a writer *or* as a woman)—Ruth would seem fairly indifferent to the question.

"Yes, you might say that my mother is still 'missing,' although I'm not looking for her. If she were looking for me, she would have found me. Since she's the one who left, I would never press myself on her. If she wants to find me, I'm the one who's easy to find," Ruth had said.

And in the particular TV interview that had stopped Eddie from making contact with Ruth six years ago, the interviewer had pursued a personal interpretation of Ruth Cole's novels. "But, in your books—in *all* your books—there are no mothers." ("There are no fathers, either," Ruth had replied.) "Yes, *but* ..." the interviewer had gone on, "your women characters have women friends, and they have boyfriends—you know, *lovers*—but they are *women* characters who have *no* relationship with their mothers. We rarely even *meet* their mothers. Don't you think that's ... um, *unusual?*" the interviewer had asked. ("Not if you don't have a mother," Ruth had answered.)

Ruth didn't *want* to know about her mother, Eddie had surmised. And so he had kept his "evidence" to himself. But then, when he'd received the invitation to introduce Ruth Cole at the 92nd Street Y, Eddie had decided that *of course* Ruth wanted to know about her mother! And so he'd agreed to introduce her. And in his soggy briefcase he now carried this mysterious book, which, six years ago, he had come close to forcing on Ruth.

Eddie O'Hare was convinced that the book had been written by Marion.

It was already past eight o'clock. Like a large, restless animal in a cage, the enormous audience in the concert hall made their impatient presence felt, although Eddie could no longer see them. The girl led him by his wet arm through a dark, mildewy hall, up a spiral staircase, past the towering curtains behind the dim stage. There Eddie saw a stagehand seated on a stool. The sinister-looking young man was transfixed by the TV monitor; the camera was trained on the podium on the stage. Eddie singled out the waiting water glass and the microphone. He made a mental note not to drink from the water glass. The water was for Ruth, *not* for her lowly introducer.

Then Eddie was shoved into the greenroom, which was overbright with dazzling mirrors and the glare of makeup lights. Eddie had long rehearsed what he would say to Ruth when they met—"My goodness, how you've grown!" For a comic novelist, he was bad at jokes. Nevertheless, the line was on his lips—he freed his soaking right hand from the shoulder strap of his briefcase—but the woman who stepped forward to greet him was not Ruth, nor did she shake Eddie's outstretched hand. It was that awfully nice woman who was one of the organizers at the Y. Eddie had met her several times. She was always friendly and sincere, and she did her best to put Eddie at ease, which was impossible. *Melissa*—that was her name. She kissed Eddie's wet cheek and said to him, "We were so worried about you!"

Eddie said: "My goodness, how you've grown!"

Melissa, who had *not* grown—she was not pregnant at the time, either—was somewhat taken aback. But Melissa was such a nice person that she seemed more concerned for Eddie's well-being than offended, although Eddie felt ready to burst into tears on Melissa's behalf.

Then someone shook Eddie's outstretched hand; it was too large and vigorous a handshake to have been Ruth's, and so Eddie managed to restrain himself from saying, "My goodness, how you've grown!" *again*. It was Karl, another of the good people who directed the activities at the Unterberg Poetry Center. Karl was a poet; he was also smart, and as tall as Eddie, and he'd always been immensely kind to Eddie. (It was Karl who was kind enough to include Eddie in many events at the 92nd Street Y, even those that Eddie felt unworthy of—like this one.)

"It's . . . raining," Eddie told Karl. There must have been a half-dozen people crammed into the greenroom. At Eddie's remark, they roared with laughter. This was vintage deadpan humor of the kind they would expect to encounter in a novel by Ed O'Hare! But Eddie simply hadn't known what else to say. He just went on shaking hands, shedding water like a wet dog.

That Very Important Person at Random House, Ruth's editor, was there. (The editor of Ruth's first two novels, a woman, had died recently, and now this man had succeeded her.) Eddie had met him three or four times, but could never recall his name. Whatever his name was, he never remembered that he'd met Eddie before. Not once had Eddie taken it personally, until now.

The walls of the greenroom were studded with photographs of the world's most important authors; Eddie was surrounded by writers of international stature and renown. He recognized Ruth's photograph before he noticed Ruth; her picture was not out of place on a wall with several Nobel Prize winners. (It would never have occurred to Eddie to look for his own photograph there; indeed, he would not have found it.)

It was her new editor who literally pushed Ruth forward to meet Eddie. The man from Random House had a hearty, aggressive air—an avuncular style. He placed a large, familiar hand squarely between Ruth's shoulders and shoved her out of the corner of the room, where she appeared to have been holding herself back. Ruth was not shy; Eddie knew this about her from her many interviews. But seeing her, in person—for the first time as an adult—Eddie realized that there was something *deliberately* small about Ruth Cole. It was as if she had *willed* herself to be small.

In fact, she was no shorter than the thug on the Madison Avenue bus. Although Ruth was her father's height, which was not notably short for a woman, she wasn't as tall as Marion. Yet her smallness was distinct from her height; like Ted, she was athletically compact. She was wearing her signature black T-shirt, in which Eddie could instantly discern the greater muscular development in Ruth's right arm; both its forearm and biceps were noticeably bigger and stronger than their counterparts on her thin left arm. Squash, like tennis, did that to you.

Eddie took one look at her and assumed that she could beat the shit out of Ted. Indeed, on any squash court of regulation size, she could have. Eddie could never have imagined how badly Ruth *wanted* to beat the shit out of her father, nor could Eddie have guessed that the old man still got the better of his hard-looking daughter in his barn of unfair advantages.

"Hello, Ruth—I've been looking forward to seeing you," Eddie said.

"Hello ... again," Ruth said, shaking his hand. She had her father's short, square fingers.

"Oh," said the Random House editor. "I didn't know you two had met." Ruth had her father's wry smile, too; her smile arrested Eddie's speech.

"Do you want to use the bathroom first?" she asked Eddie. And there again came the avuncular editor's large hand, this time a little too familiarly between Eddie's shoulders.

"Yes, yes—let's allow Mr. O'Hare a minute for some hasty repairs," Ruth's new editor said.

It was not until he was alone in the bathroom that Eddie realized the degree to which "repairs" were in order. He was not just wet and dirty:

a cellophane package, like something from a pack of cigarettes, clung to his tie; a gum wrapper, which upon closer inspection revealed a well-chewed piece of gum, had adhered to his fly. His shirt was soaked through. In the mirror, Eddie at first failed to recognize his nipples; he tried to brush them off, as if they were more chewing gum.

He decided that his best recourse was to remove his jacket and his shirt and wring them out in his hands; he wrung the excess water from his tie, too. But when he redressed himself, he saw that he'd created the most extraordinary wrinkles in both his tie and his shirt, and that his shirt, which had formerly been dress-white, was now a streaked and faded *pink*. He looked at his hands, which were stained from the familiar red ink of his correcting pen (his so-called teacher's favorite), and—even before he peered in his briefcase—he knew that the revisions in red on the manuscript of his speech would have first run red and then turned to pink on the wet pages.

When he looked at his introductory speech, he saw that *all* his handwritten revisions were erased or blurred beyond recognition, and that the original typescript, which was now offset against a *pink* background, was notably less clear than it had been. After all, it had once stood out against a clean, *white* page.

The ball of coins pulled his jacket askew. Eddie could find no wastebasket in the bathroom; at what he hoped was the height of his ill-advised behavior for the day, he dumped all his change into the toilet. After he flushed, and the water cleared, he saw with his usual resignation that the quarters had remained in the bottom of the toilet bowl.

Ruth used the bathroom after Eddie. When he was following her backstage—while most of the others found their way into the audience and to their seats—she looked over her shoulder and said to him, "An odd place for a wishing well, wasn't it?" It took him a second or two to realize that she was referring to the coins in the toilet bowl; he couldn't tell, of course, if she knew it was *his* money.

Then, more straightforwardly—without mischief—she said, "We'll have dinner after this, I hope—a chance to talk."

Eddie's heart jumped. Had she meant that they would have dinner *alone*? Even Eddie knew better than to hope so. She'd meant with Karl, and with Melissa, and doubtless with her avuncular new editor from Random House—not to mention with his large, too-familiar hands. Yet maybe Eddie could steal a moment alone with her; if not, he might be able to suggest a later, more private meeting.

He was smiling idiotically, transfixed as he was by her handsome, some would say pretty, face. Ruth's thin upper lip was Marion's upper lip; her full breasts, which were slightly pendulous, were her mother's, too. However, without Marion's long waist, Ruth's breasts appeared too big for the rest of her. And she had her father's short, sturdy legs.

Ruth's black T-shirt was an expensive one. It fit her very nicely. It was made of some silky material—something finer than cotton, Eddie supposed. Her jeans were something better than jeans, too. They were also black; they also fit her nicely. And Eddie had seen her give her jacket to her editor; it was a tailored black cashmere jacket that dressed up the T-shirt and the jeans. For her reading, Ruth hadn't wanted the jacket; her fans expected the T-shirt, Eddie concluded. And she was definitely a writer with more than mere readers. Ruth Cole had *fans*. Eddie was frankly frightened to be speaking to them.

When Eddie noticed that Karl was at that moment engaged in introducing *him*, he chose not to listen. The sinister-looking stagehand had offered Ruth his stool, but she chose to stand, shifting her weight from foot to foot—as if she were about to play squash rather than give a reading.

"My speech ..." Eddie said to Ruth. "I'm not very pleased with it. All the ink ran."

She put one of her short, square index fingers to her lips. When he stopped talking, she leaned forward and whispered in his ear. "Thank you for not writing about me," she whispered. "I know you could have." Eddie couldn't speak. Until he heard her whisper, he'd not realized that Ruth had her mother's voice.

Then Ruth was pushing him toward the stage. Since he hadn't been listening to Karl's introduction, Eddie didn't know that Karl and the audience, which was Ruth Cole's audience, were waiting for him.

Ruth had been waiting her whole life to meet Eddie O'Hare; from the first time she'd been told about Eddie and her mother, Ruth had wanted to meet him. Now she couldn't bear to watch him walk out on the stage, because he was walking away from her. Instead she watched him on the TV monitor. From the camera's perspective, which was the view from the audience, Eddie wasn't walking away—he was walking toward the audience; he was facing the audience and the crowd. He is coming to meet me, at last! Ruth was imagining.

But what on earth could my mother ever have seen in him? Ruth wondered. What a pathetic, unfortunate man! On the small screen of the TV monitor, she studied Eddie in black and white. The primitive image made Eddie appear youthful; she could see what a beautiful boy he must have been. But, in a man, prettiness had only a temporary appeal.

As Eddie O'Hare began to speak about her and her writing, Ruth distracted herself with a familiar and troublesome question: What *permanently* appealed to her in a man?

Ruth at Thirty-Six

A man should be confident, Ruth thought; after all, men were designed to be aggressive. Yet her attraction to confident, aggressive men had led her into some questionable relationships. She would never tolerate *physical* aggression; so far she'd been spared any violent episodes, some of which had befallen her friends. Ruth held her friends at least partially responsible for these abusive relationships. Given how little she liked or trusted her instincts with men, Ruth surprisingly believed that she could detect a man's capacity for violence against women on the very first date.

In the confounding world of sex, it was one of the few things Ruth was proud of about herself, although Hannah Grant, who was Ruth's best friend, had repeatedly told Ruth that she'd simply been lucky. ("You just haven't met the right guy—I mean the *wrong* guy," Hannah had told her. "You just haven't had *that* date.")

A man should respect my independence, Ruth believed. She never concealed the fact that she was uncertain about marriage, and more uncertain about motherhood. Yet those men who acknowledged her so-called independence often exhibited the most unacceptable form of lack of commitment. Ruth wouldn't tolerate infidelity; indeed, she demanded faithfulness from even the newest boyfriend. Was she merely old-fashioned?

Hannah had often ridiculed Ruth for what Hannah called "contradictory behavior." At thirty-six, Ruth had never lived with a man; yet

Ruth expected any boyfriend-of-the-moment to be faithful to her while *not* living with her. "I fail to see anything 'contradictory' in that," Ruth had told Hannah, but Hannah presumed a superiority to Ruth in matters of male-female relationships. (On the basis of having had more of them, Ruth supposed.)

By Ruth's standards—even by more liberal sexual standards than Ruth's—Hannah Grant was promiscuous. At the moment, as Ruth waited to read from her new novel at the 92nd Street Y, Hannah was also late. Ruth had expected Hannah to meet her in the greenroom before the event; now Ruth worried that Hannah would arrive too late to be admitted, although a seat had been reserved for her. It was just like Hannah—she'd probably met a guy and got to talking. (Hannah would have got to more than talking.)

Returning her attention to the small black-and-white screen of the TV monitor, Ruth tried to concentrate on what Eddie O'Hare was saying. She had been introduced on many occasions, but never by her mother's former lover; while this certainly distinguished Eddie, there was nothing distinguished about Eddie's introduction.

"Ten years ago," Eddie had begun, and Ruth lowered her chin to her chest. This time, when the young stagehand offered her his stool, she accepted; if Eddie was going to begin at the beginning, Ruth knew she had better sit down.

"Published in 1980, when she was only twenty-six," Eddie intoned, "Ruth Cole's first novel, *The Same Orphanage*, was set in a rural New England village that was renowned for its history of supporting alternative lifestyles. Both a socialist and a lesbian commune had prospered there, but they eventually disbanded. A college with questionable admissions standards had briefly flourished; it existed solely to provide a four-year student deferment for those young men seeking *not* to be drafted into the war in Vietnam. When the war was over, the college folded. And, throughout the sixties and the early seventies—prior to the *Roe* v. *Wade* Supreme Court decision, which legalized abortion in 1973—the village also supported a small orphanage. In those years when the procedure was still illegal, it was well known—at least locally—that the orphanage physician would provide abortions."

Here Eddie paused. The houselights were so low that he couldn't see a single face in the vast audience. Without thinking, he took a sip from Ruth's water glass.

In fact, Ruth had graduated from Exeter in the same year as the *Roe v. Wade* decision. In her novel, two Exeter girls get pregnant; they are expelled from school without ever identifying the would-be father—it turns out that they had the same boyfriend. The twenty-six-year-old author once joked in an interview that "the working title" for *The Same Orphanage* was *The Same Boyfriend*.

Eddie O'Hare, who was doomed to be *only* autobiographical in his novels, knew better than to presume that Ruth Cole was writing about herself. He understood from the first time he read her that she was better than that. But, in several interviews, Ruth had admitted to having had a close friendship at Exeter—namely, a girlfriend with whom she'd shared a crush on the same boy. Eddie didn't know that Ruth's roommate and best friend at Exeter had been Hannah Grant—nor did he know that Hannah was expected to attend Ruth's reading. Hannah had heard Ruth read before, many times; what made this reading special to her, and to Ruth, was that the two friends had spent much of their time together talking about Eddie O'Hare. Hannah had been dying to meet Eddie.

As for the two friends having once had a "crush" on the same boy at Exeter, Eddie couldn't have known, but he guessed—correctly—that Ruth had never had sex at Exeter. In fact—and this was no easy accomplishment in the seventies—Ruth managed to get through her college years without having had sex, either. (Hannah, of course, hadn't waited. She'd had sex several times at Exeter, and her first abortion before she graduated.)

In Ruth's novel, the expelled Exeter girls with a boyfriend in common are taken by one of the girls' parents to the same orphanage of the title. One of these young women has her baby delivered in the orphanage, but she elects to keep the baby; she can't bear to let it be adopted. The other young woman has an illegal abortion. The Exeter boy, twice a would-be father—and now graduated from the academy—marries the girl with the baby. The young couple make an effort to stay married for the sake of the child, but the marriage fails—after a mere eighteen years! The girl who chose the abortion, now an unmarried woman in her late thirties, is reunited with her ex-boyfriend; she marries him.

Throughout the novel, the friendship between the Exeter women is tested. The abortion-or-adoption decision, and the changing moral climate of the times, will haunt them as they grow older. While Ruth portrays both women sympathetically, her personal views on abortion (she supported the pro-choice position) were heralded by feminists. And, notwithstanding that it was a didactic novel, *The Same Orphanage* was critically acclaimed—in more than twenty-five languages.

It had its dissenters, too. That the novel concludes with the bitter dissolution of the two women's friendship did not make *every* feminist happy. That the woman who chooses to have the abortion is unable to get pregnant with her ex-boyfriend was denounced by some pro-choice feminists as "anti-abortion mythology," although Ruth never implies that the woman can't get pregnant *because of* her previous abortion. "Maybe she can't get pregnant because she's thirty-eight," Ruth said in an interview, which was denounced by several women who said they were speaking on behalf of all those women over forty who are able to get pregnant.

It was that kind of novel—it wasn't going to escape scot-free. The divorced woman in *The Same Orphanage*—the one who has the baby soon after she's expelled from Exeter—offers to have *another* baby and give it to her friend. She'll be a surrogate mom—with her ex-husband's sperm! But the woman who can't conceive declines the offer; she settles for childlessness instead. In the novel, the motivation of the ex-wife to play the role of "surrogate mom" is suspect; yet, unsurprisingly, a few pioneer surrogate mothers attacked the book for misrepresenting *them*.

Ruth Cole, even at twenty-six, never went to great lengths to defend herself from her critics. "Look—it's a novel," she said. "They're my characters—they do what I want them to do." She was similarly dismissive of the most common description of *The Same Orphanage*: namely, that it was "about" abortion. "It's a *novel*," Ruth repeated. "It's not 'about' anything. It's a good story. It's a demonstration of how the choices two women make will affect the rest of their lives. The choices we make *do* affect us, don't they?"

And Ruth distanced herself from not a few of her more avid readers by admitting that she'd never had an abortion. It was insulting to some of her readers who'd had abortions that Ruth had "just imagined" having one. "I'm certainly not opposed to having an abortion, or to anyone else having one," Ruth said. "In my case, it just never came up."

As Ruth well knew, an abortion "came up" on two more occasions for Hannah Grant. They had applied to the same colleges—only the best ones. When Hannah didn't get into most of them, they'd attended Middlebury. What mattered to both of them, or so they said, was staying together, even if it meant spending four years in Vermont.

In retrospect, Ruth wondered why "staying together" had mattered to Hannah, who had spent most of her time at Middlebury with a hockey player with a removable false tooth; he got her pregnant twice, and when they broke up, he tried to date Ruth. It had prompted Ruth's now-notorious remark to Hannah on the subject of "rules for relationships."

"*What* rules?" Hannah had asked. "There are no rules among friends, surely."

"Rules among friends are *especially* necessary," Ruth had told her friend. "For example, I don't go out with anyone who ever went out with you—or who asked you first."

"And vice versa?" Hannah had asked.

"Well." (It was a habit Ruth had picked up from her father.) "That's your choice," she'd told Hannah, who had never tested the rule—at least not that Ruth knew. For Ruth's part, she'd stuck to her own rule absolutely.

And now Hannah was late! While Ruth tried to watch the TV monitor, where Eddie O'Hare was struggling on and on, she was aware that the sneaky-looking stagehand was watching her. He was the kind of guy Hannah would have called "cute"; doubtless Hannah would have flirted with him, but Ruth rarely flirted. Besides, he was not her type—if she had a type. (She *did* have a type, and the type bothered her about herself more than she could say.)

Ruth looked at her watch. Eddie was still talking about her *first* novel. With two more novels to go, we'll be here all night! Ruth was thinking, as she again watched Eddie drink her water. And if he's got a cold, I'll catch it, she thought to herself.

Ruth considered trying to get Eddie's attention. Instead she looked up at the stagehand, who was ogling her breasts. If Ruth had to pick one thing that most men were utterly stupid about, it was that they didn't seem to know that it was *obvious* to a woman when a man was staring at her breasts.

"I wouldn't say that was *my* pet peeve with men," Hannah had told Ruth. Hannah's breasts were rather small—at least in Hannah's estimation. "With boobs like yours, what *else* are men going to stare at?" Hannah had asked Ruth.

Yet, whenever Ruth and Hannah were together, men generally looked at Hannah first. She was tall and blond; she had a slinky figure. She was sexier than Ruth, Ruth thought.

"It's just my clothes—my *clothes* are sexier," Hannah had told her. "If you'd try dressing like a woman, men might notice you more."

"It's enough that they notice my boobs," Ruth had replied.

Maybe they'd managed so well as roommates, and had on numerous occasions traveled together, which is even harder than being roommates, because they wouldn't—indeed, *couldn't*—wear the same clothes.

It was not because she had grown up without a mother that Ruth Cole preferred to wear men's clothes; as a child, she'd been dressed in an exceedingly girlish fashion by Conchita Gomez, who had sent Ruth off to Exeter with a trunk full of little-girl skirts and dresses, which Ruth hated.

She liked jeans, or pants that fit her as snugly as jeans. She liked T-shirts, and boys' or men's dress shirts—not turtlenecks, because she was short and had no neck to begin with, and not sweaters, which were too bulky and made her look fat. She was not fat and she only *seemed* short. Regardless, Ruth had tested the dress code at Exeter by conforming to the dress code for *boys;* since then, it had become her style.

Now, of course, her jackets—even if they were men's jackets—were tailored to fit her figure. For black-tie occasions, Ruth wore a *woman's* tuxedo, which was tailored to her figure, too. She did own the so-called standard little black dress, but Ruth never (except on the hottest summer days) wore a dress. Her most frequent substitute for a dress was a navy-blue pinstriped pantsuit, which she preferred for cocktail parties and fancy restaurants; it was her uniform for funerals, too.

Ruth spent a fair amount of money on clothes, but they were always the same clothes. She spent more money on shoes. Because she liked a low, sturdy heel—something that made her ankles feel almost as secure as they did in her squash shoes—her shoes tended to have a sameness about them, too.

Ruth let Hannah tell her where to get her hair cut, but she wouldn't listen to Hannah's advice that she should grow her hair longer. And aside from lip gloss and a certain kind of colorless lipstick, Ruth didn't wear makeup. A good moisturizer, the right shampoo, and the right deodorant—these would do. She let Hannah buy her underwear, too. "Jesus, it kills me to buy you your goddamn thirty-four D!" Hannah would complain. "Both of my boobs could fit in one of your fucking cups!"

Ruth thought that she was too old to consider breast-reduction surgery. But as a teenager she'd begged her father to allow her to have the operation. Not just the size but the weight of her breasts had bothered her; Ruth despaired that her nipples (and the surrounding areolae) were too low and too large. Her father would hear none of it; he said it was nonsense to "mutilate" her "God-given good figure." (Breasts could never be too large for Ted Cole.)

Oh, Daddy, Daddy, Daddy! Ruth thought angrily, as the gaze of the single-minded stagehand remained riveted to her breasts.

She sensed that Eddie O'Hare overpraised her; he said something about her well-publicized claim that she did not write autobiographical fiction. But Eddie was still mired in Ruth Cole's *first* novel. This was the longest introduction in the world! By the time it was her turn, the audience would be fast asleep.

Hannah Grant had told Ruth that she should get off her high horse about not writing autobiographical fiction. "For Christ's sake, aren't *I* autobiographical?" Hannah had asked her. "You *always* write about *me!*"

"I may borrow from your experiences, Hannah," Ruth had replied. "After all, you've had many more experiences than I've had. But I assure you, I do not write 'about' you. I make up my characters *and* their stories."

"You make *me* up again and again," Hannah had argued. "It may be your version of me, but it's me—always me. You're more autobiographical than you think you are, baby." (Ruth hated Hannah's usage of "baby.")

Hannah was a journalist. She presumed that all novels were substantially autobiographical. Ruth was a novelist; she looked at her books and saw what she had invented. Hannah looked at them and saw what was real—namely, variations of Hannah herself. (The truth, of course, lay somewhere in between.)

In Ruth's novels, there was usually a woman character who was an adventurer—the *Hannah* character, Hannah called her. And there was always another woman character who held herself back; the less-bold character, Ruth called her—the *Ruth* character, Hannah said.

Ruth both admired and was appalled by Hannah's boldness. For her part, Hannah both looked up to Ruth and constantly criticized her. Hannah respected Ruth's success while at the same time she reduced

Ruth's novels to a form of nonfiction. Ruth was extremely sensitive to her friend's Ruth-character, Hannah-character interpretations.

In Ruth's second novel, *Before the Fall of Saigon* (1985), the so-called Ruth and Hannah characters are roommates at Middlebury during the Vietnam War. The Hannah character, who is boldness personified, makes a deal with her boyfriend: she'll marry him and have his baby, so that when he graduates and his student draft deferment expires, he will be protected from the draft under his new draft status—3A, married with child. She makes him promise that, if the marriage doesn't work out, he'll divorce her—on her terms. (She gets custody of the child; he pays child support.) The problem is, she can't get pregnant.

"How dare you call her 'the Hannah character'?" Ruth demanded of Hannah repeatedly. "You went through college trying *not* to get pregnant while managing to get pregnant every minute!" But Hannah said that the character's "capacity for risk-taking" was entirely hers.

In the novel, the woman who can't get pregnant (the Hannah character) makes a new deal—this time with her roommate (the Ruth character). The Hannah character convinces the Ruth character to sleep with the Hannah character's boyfriend and get pregnant with the boyfriend's baby; the deal is that the *roommate* (the Ruth character) will then marry the Hannah character's boyfriend, thus keeping him out of Vietnam. When the war (or the draft) is over, the dutiful roommate, who is a virgin before this dreadful experience, will divorce the boyfriend; he will immediately marry the Hannah character, and together they will raise the roommate's baby.

How Hannah dared to call the virgin roommate "the Ruth character" was vexing to Ruth, who had *not* lost her virginity at college—much less got herself pregnant by means of Hannah's boyfriend! (And Hannah Grant was the only one of Ruth's friends who knew how and when Ruth *had* lost her virginity, which was another story.) But Hannah said that the roommate's "*anxiety* about losing her virginity" was entirely Ruth's.

In the novel, naturally, the Ruth character despises her roommate's boyfriend and is traumatized by their single sexual encounter; the boyfriend, on the other hand, falls in love with his girlfriend's roommate and balks at divorcing her when the Vietnam War is over.

The fall of Saigon, in April '75, is the background to the end of the novel, when the roommate (who agrees to have her roommate's boyfriend's baby) realizes that she can't give the baby up. Her loathing of her baby's father notwithstanding, she accepts joint custody of their child upon their divorce. The Hannah character, who has instigated the match between her boyfriend and her best friend, loses both the boyfriend and the baby—not to mention the friendship with her former roommate.

It is a sexual farce, but with bitter consequences, and its comic touches are offset by the darker rifts between the characters—which is a microcosm of how the country itself was divided by the war in Vietnam, and (for Ruth's generation of young men) by what to *do* about the draft. "A woman's quaint perspective on dodging the draft," one male reviewer wrote of the novel.

Hannah had told Ruth that she had slept with this particular reviewer at one time or another; she also happened to know *his* draft-dodging story. The man had claimed psychological damage from having sex with his mother. His mother had substantiated the claim; the telling of the lie had been the mother's idea in the first place. And as a result of successfully evading the draft in this fashion, the man eventually *had* had sex with his mother.

"I guess he knows a 'quaint perspective' when he encounters one," Ruth had said. It irritated Hannah that Ruth didn't rail against her negative reviews as vociferously as Hannah railed against them. "Reviews are free publicity," Ruth liked to say. "Even the bad ones."

It was a measure of Ruth Cole's international stature and renown that the anticipation of her third and most recent novel was so keen in those European countries where she was translated that two translations were being published simultaneously with the British and American editions.

Following her reading at the Y, Ruth was spending a day in New York; she'd agreed to several interviews and to some related publicity. Then she was spending a day and a night in Sagaponack with her father, before leaving for Germany and the Frankfurt Book Fair. (After Frankfurt, and the promotion of the German translation, she was expected in Amsterdam, where the Dutch translation had just been published.)

Ruth's visits with her father in Sagaponack were few, yet she was frankly looking forward to this one. Doubtless there would be a little squash in the barn, and much arguing—about nearly everything—and even some rest. Hannah had promised to come to Sagaponack with her. It was always better for Ruth if she avoided spending time with her father alone; with a friend—even if it was one of Ruth's infrequent but consistently ill-chosen boyfriends—there was someone to run interference.

But Hannah flirted with Ruth's father, which made Ruth cross. Ruth suspected Hannah of flirting with him *because* it made Ruth cross. And Ruth's father, who knew of no other way to behave with women, flirted back.

It had been Hannah to whom Ruth had made her vulgar remark about her father's attractiveness to women—in which Ruth had said: "You could hear the women's panties sliding to the floor."

When Hannah had first met Ted Cole, she'd said to Ruth: "What *is* that sound? Do you hear it?" Ruth rarely saw a joke coming; her first thought, always, was that everyone was totally serious.

"*What* sound? No, I don't hear it," Ruth had replied, looking around.

"Oh, it's just my panties sliding to the floor," Hannah had told her. It had become a code between them.

Whenever Ruth was introduced to one of Hannah's many boyfriends, *if* Ruth liked him, she would ask Hannah: "Did you hear that sound?" If Ruth didn't care for the boyfriend, which was often the case, Ruth would say: "I didn't hear a thing. Did *you?*"

Ruth was reluctant to introduce her boyfriends to Hannah because Hannah *always* said: "What a racket! Boy, did something *wet* just hit the ground, or am I imagining things?" (Wetness was a carryover in Hannah's sexual vocabulary; it went all the way back to their Exeter days.) And Ruth was generally not proud of her boyfriends; she rarely wanted *anyone* to meet them. Nor were Ruth's boyfriends usually in her life long enough for Hannah to *have* to meet them.

Yet now, as Ruth sat on a stool, enduring the stares of the stagehand who was enamored of her breasts—*and* enduring Eddie's laborious introduction to her life's work (poor Eddie was now bogged down in her *second* novel)—she thought again of her exasperation with Hannah for being late to her reading, or for not showing up at all.

Not only had they talked with such excitement about the prospect of meeting Eddie O'Hare, but in the case of Ruth's *present* boyfriend, Ruth had very much wanted Hannah to meet him. Ruth felt, for once, that she actually *needed* to hear Hannah's opinion. There'd been so many times when Ruth wished that Hannah had *withheld* her opinion. Now, when I need her, where *is* she? Ruth wondered. Doubtless fucking her brains out, as Hannah would say—or so Ruth imagined.

She sighed deeply; she was aware of the rise and fall of her breasts, and of the idiot stagehand's rapt attention to this detail. She could have heard the lecherous young man sigh in response, if Eddie hadn't been droning on and on. Out of boredom, Ruth met the young stagehand's stare and held it until he looked away. He had one of those wispy half-beards, a goatee-in-progress and a mustache as insubstantial as soot. If I neglected my regular wax job, Ruth thought, *I* could grow a better mustache than that.

She sighed again, daring the letch to take another look at her breasts, but the scruffy young man had suddenly grown self-conscious about staring at her. Therefore, Ruth made a concentrated effort to stare at him. She soon lost interest. His jeans were ripped open at one knee—probably the pair he preferred for public appearances. What was likely a food spill had left an oily stain on the chest of his dark-brown turtleneck, which was stretched out of shape; bulges the size of tennis balls hung at the elbows.

But as soon as Ruth turned her attention to her pending reading—indeed, the second she opened her new novel to the passage she'd chosen to read—the stagehand's feral gaze once more fell upon her heralded breasts. Ruth thought that he had confused eyes; they were alert but puzzled, a little like a dog's—given to a slavish loyalty, bordering on fawning.

Then Ruth changed her mind about the passage she'd selected to read; she would read the first chapter instead. She hunched forward on the stagehand's stool and held her open book in front of her, as she might have held a hymnal from which she was about to sing; thus she obscured her breasts from the stagehand's view.

It was a relief to Ruth that Eddie was finally addressing the subject of her third and most recent novel—"a variation on Ms. Cole's familiar theme of female friendships gone awry," Eddie was saying.

More unmitigated sophistries! Ruth thought to herself. But there was a grain of truth to Eddie's thesis; Ruth had already heard a similar analysis from Hannah. "So ... *this* time," Hannah had told her, "the Ruth character and the Hannah character start out as enemies. In the end, we become friends. I agree it's different, but not *very* different."

In Ruth's new novel, the Ruth character was a recent widow—a novelist named Jane Dash. It was the first time that Ruth had written about a writer; she was letting herself in for more autobiographical interpretations, of the very kind she loathed.

The Hannah character, who begins the novel as Mrs. Dash's enemy and ends the book as the widow's best friend, is named Eleanor Holt. The women, who have long antagonized each other, are brought together much against their wills by their grown children; their son and daughter, respectively, fall in love and marry each other.

Jane Dash, the mother of the groom, and Eleanor Holt, the mother of the bride, must share the responsibility of raising their grandchildren when the children's parents are killed in a plane crash. (The trip was to be a second honeymoon for the young couple, who were celebrating their tenth anniversary.) At the time of the plane crash, Mrs. Dash is already a widow—she never remarries—and Eleanor Holt is divorced for the second time.

It was Ruth Cole's first novel to have an optimistic (if not altogether happy) ending, although Jane Dash remains uneasy about her friendship with Eleanor Holt—on the basis of "the sea changes in Eleanor's character, which had so distinguished Eleanor's past." Hannah, fully recognizing Eleanor as "the Hannah character," had taken offense at this line.

"What 'sea changes' have you observed in *my* character?" Hannah demanded to know. "You may not always approve of my behavior, but exactly what about my character is inconsistent or contradictory?"

"There's nothing about you that's 'contradictory,' Hannah," Ruth had told her friend. "And you're much more consistent than *I* am. I haven't noticed a single change in your character—not even a little change, or a *welcome* change, much less a 'sea change.' "

Hannah found this a confounding answer, and she said so, but Ruth merely suggested that this was evidence—if Hannah needed any—that Eleanor Holt was *not* the Hannah character that Hannah thought she was. It was there that an uneasy standoff between Ruth and Hannah had ended—at least until Ruth had invited Hannah to come hear her read from the novel, and that invitation had had less to do with the novel, which Hannah had already read, than with the exciting prospect of meeting Eddie O'Hare.

The *other* person whom Hannah had expressed an almost equal excitement about meeting was the man Ruth had described to her as her "present" boyfriend. In truth, he was more in the category of a *would-be* boyfriend—"a boyfriend candidate," as Hannah would say. This boyfriend-in-waiting also happened to be Ruth's new editor—that same Very Important Person at Random House whom Eddie O'Hare had taken a dislike to on the basis of his avuncular heartiness, and of his never remembering that he'd met Eddie before.

Yes, Ruth had already told Hannah, he was the best editor she'd ever worked with. Yes, she had never—not to this degree—met a man she could talk to *and* listen to. Ruth felt there was no one, with the possible exception of Hannah, who knew her so well. Not only was he forthright and strong, but he challenged her "in all the good ways."

"What are the 'good ways'?" Hannah had asked.

"Oh, you'll meet him—you'll see," Ruth had told her. "He's also a gentleman."

"He's *old* enough to be," Hannah had replied. "I mean, he's the right generation for gentlemanly behavior. What is he, anyway—twelve, *fifteen* years older than you are?" (She'd seen a photograph.)

"Eighteen," Ruth had said quietly.

"That's a gentleman, all right," Hannah had said. "And doesn't he have children? My God, how old are *they*? They could be as old as *you* are!"

"He has no children," Ruth replied.

"But I thought he was married for years and years," Hannah said. "Why *doesn't* he have children?"

"His wife didn't want children—she was afraid of having children," Ruth said.

"Sounds like you, sort of," Hannah said.

"Allan wanted a child, his wife didn't," Ruth admitted.

"So he still wants a child," Hannah concluded.

"It's something we're talking about," Ruth confessed.

"And I suppose he still talks to the ex-wife. Let's hope that his will be the last generation of men who feel it's necessary to keep talking to their ex-wives," Hannah dismissively said. It was her journalist's sensibility: everyone's statistics are presumed to comply to age, to education, to *type*. It was an infuriating way to think, but Ruth bit her tongue. "So," Hannah had added philosophically, "I suppose the sex is…all you expected?"

"We haven't had sex yet," Ruth admitted.

"Who's waiting?" Hannah asked.

"We both are," Ruth had lied. Allan was being patient; it was Ruth who was "waiting." She was so afraid that she wouldn't like sex with him that she had procrastinated. She didn't want to have to stop thinking of him as the man in her life.

"But you said he asked you to *marry* him!" Hannah had cried. "He wants to marry you and he hasn't had sex with you yet? That's not even generational behavior—that's his *father's* generation, or his *grandfather's!*"

"He wants me to know that I'm not just another girlfriend to him," Ruth told Hannah.

"You're not yet a girlfriend at all!" Hannah said.

"I think it's sweet," Ruth said. "He's in love with me *before* he's slept with me. I think it's nice."

"It's *different,*" Hannah allowed. "So what are you afraid of?"

"I'm not afraid of anything," Ruth lied.

"You don't usually want me to meet your boyfriends," Hannah reminded her.

"This one's special," Ruth said.

"So special that you haven't slept with him."

"He can beat me at squash," Ruth added feebly.

"So can your father, and how old is he?"

"Seventy-seven," Ruth said. "You know how old my father is."

"Jesus, is he really? He doesn't look it," Hannah said.

"I am talking about Allan Albright, *not* my father," Ruth said angrily. "Allan Albright is only fifty-four. He loves me, he wants to marry me, and I think I would be happy living with him."

"Did you say you loved him?" Hannah asked. "I didn't hear you say that."

"I didn't say that," Ruth admitted. "I don't know that. I don't know how to tell," she added.

"If you can't tell, you don't love him," Hannah said. "And I thought he had the reputation of ... uh, he was quite a ladies' man, wasn't he?"

"Yes, he *was,*" Ruth said slowly. "He told me that himself, and that he's changed."

"Uh-oh," Hannah said. "Do men change?"

"Do *we?*" Ruth asked.

"You want to, don't you?" Hannah said.

"I'm tired of bad boyfriends," Ruth confessed.

"You sure can pick them," Hannah told her. "But I thought you picked them because you *knew* they were bad. I thought you picked them because you knew they'd go away. Sometimes even before you told them to."

"You've picked some bad boyfriends, too," Ruth said.

"Sure, all the time," Hannah admitted. "But I've also picked some good ones—they just don't stay around."

"I think Allan will stay around," Ruth said.

"Sure he will," Hannah told her. "So you're worried if *you'll* stay around—is that it?"

"Yes," Ruth finally confessed. "That's it."

"I want to meet him," Hannah said. "I'll tell you if you'll stay around. I'll know the minute I meet him."

And now she's stood me up! Ruth thought. She thumped her copy of the novel shut; she held the book against her breasts. She felt like bursting into tears, she was so angry with Hannah, but she saw how she had startled the horny stagehand by her sudden gesture; she enjoyed his look of alarm.

"The audience can hear you backstage," the sly boy whispered to her. He had a supercilious smile.

Ruth's response was not spontaneous; almost everything she said was deliberate. "In case you've been wondering," Ruth whispered to the stagehand, "they're thirty-four D."

"What?" the boy whispered.

He's too dumb to get it, Ruth decided. Besides, the audience had broken into a resounding applause. Without hearing what Eddie had said, Ruth understood that Eddie had finally finished.

She paused onstage, to shake his hand, before approaching the podium. Eddie, confused, walked backstage instead of to his reserved seat in the audience; once backstage, he was too embarrassed to go to his seat. He looked helplessly at the unfriendly stagehand, who was not about to offer Eddie his stool.

Ruth waited out the applause. She picked up her empty water glass and immediately put it down. Oh, God, I drank her water! Eddie realized.

"What a set of hooters, huh?" the stagehand whispered to Eddie, who said nothing but looked guilty. (He hadn't heard what the stagehand said; Eddie assumed it was something about the glass of water.)

For his small part in the evening's proceedings, the stagehand suddenly felt smaller than usual; no sooner had the word "hooters" died on his lips than the shallow young man grasped what the famous novelist had whispered to him. She's a 34D! the slow-witted fool realized. But why had she told him? Was she coming on to me or *what?* the moron wondered.

When the applause had at last died down, Ruth said: "Would you turn up the houselights a little, please? I want to be able to see my editor's face. If I see him cringe, I'll know there's something I missed—or something he missed."

It got a laugh, as it was intended to do, but that wasn't entirely why she had said it. She didn't need to see Allan Albright's face; he was enough on her mind already. What Ruth wanted to see was the empty seat beside Allan, the seat that had been reserved for Hannah Grant. Actually, there were *two* empty seats beside Allan, because Eddie had become trapped backstage, but Ruth noticed only Hannah's absence.

Goddamn you, Hannah! Ruth thought, but she was onstage now. All she needed to do was cast her eyes on the page; her writing completely absorbed her. Outwardly, she was what Ruth Cole always was: composed. And as soon as she began to read, she would feel inwardly composed, too.

She might not know what to do about boyfriends—especially one who wanted to marry her—and she might not know how to deal with her father, about whom her feelings were sorely mixed. She might not know whether to hate her best friend, Hannah, or to forgive her. But when it came to her writing, Ruth Cole was the picture of confidence and concentration.

In fact, she was concentrating so completely on reading the first chapter, which was called "The Red and Blue Air Mattress," that she forgot to tell the audience the title of her new novel. No matter; most of them already knew the title. (More than half the people in the audience had read the whole book.)

The first chapter's origins were peculiar. The magazine section of a German newspaper, the *Süddeutsche Zeitung,* had asked Ruth to submit a short story for the annual fiction issue. Ruth rarely wrote short stories; there was always a novel on her mind, even if she hadn't begun to write it. But the rules regarding the submission to the *Süddeutsche Zeitung* intrigued her: every short story published in the magazine was called "The Red and Blue Air Mattress"; and, at least once in every story, an actual red and blue air mattress had to make an appearance. (It was further suggested that the air mattress had to be of sufficient significance to the story to merit its existence as a title.)

Ruth liked rules. For most writers, rules were laughable, but Ruth was also a squash player; she had a fondness for games. The fun for Ruth was where and how to bring the air mattress into the story. She already knew who her characters were: they would be Jane Dash, newly a widow, and Mrs. Dash's then-enemy Eleanor Holt.

"And so," Ruth told the audience at the 92nd Street Y, "I owe my first chapter to an air mattress." The audience laughed. It was now a game for the audience, too.

It was Eddie O'Hare's impression that even the boorish stagehand was full of anticipation for the red and blue air mattress. It was further testimony to how international a writer Ruth Cole had become: the first chapter of her new novel had been published in German under the title "Die blaurote Luftmatratze," before any of Ruth's many readers could read it in English!

Ruth told the audience: "I want to dedicate this reading to my best friend, Hannah Grant." One day Hannah would hear of the dedication she had missed; someone in the audience would be sure to mention it to her.

You could have heard a pin drop, as they say, when Ruth began to read her first chapter.

The Red and Blue Air Mattress

She'd been a widow for one year, yet Jane Dash was as prone to being swept away by a so-called flood of memories as she was on that morning when she'd awakened with her husband dead beside her. She was a novelist. She had no intentions of writing a memoir; autobiography didn't interest her, her own, especially. But she did want to keep her memories of the past under control, as any widow must.

A most unwelcome intrusion from Mrs. Dash's past was the former hippie Eleanor Holt. Eleanor was drawn to the misfortunes of others;

truly, she seemed uplifted by them. Widows in particular appealed to her. Eleanor was living evidence of Mrs. Dash's conviction that poetic justice is not forthcoming on a regular basis. Not even Plutarch could convince Jane Dash that Eleanor Holt would ever receive her just rewards.

What was it called—what Plutarch had written? Jane thought it was "Why the Gods Are So Slow to Punish the Wicked," but she couldn't exactly remember. Anyway, despite the centuries that separated them, Plutarch must have had Eleanor Holt in mind.

Mrs. Dash's late husband had once referred to Eleanor as a woman under the constant pressure of revising herself. (Jane thought this assessment was overly kind.) When she was first married, Eleanor Holt was one of those women who flaunted the happiness of her marriage to such a degree that anyone who'd ever been divorced cordially loathed her. When she was newly divorced, Eleanor became such an advocate of divorce that anyone who was happily married wanted to kill her.

In the sixties, to no one's surprise, she was a socialist, in the seventies a feminist. When she lived in New York, she thought that life in the Hamptons, which she called "the country," was suitable only for fair-weather weekends; to live in the Hamptons year-round, or in bad weather, was strictly for bumpkins and other dullards.

When she left Manhattan for a year-round residence in the Hamptons—and for her second marriage—she pronounced that city life was fit only for sexual predators and thrill-seekers who were without her capacity for self-knowledge. (After many years in Bridgehampton, Eleanor continued to think of the south fork of Long Island as rural, for she had no experience with genuine country living. She had attended an all-women's college in Massachusetts, and while she looked back on her experience there as decidedly unnatural, she did not categorize it as either rural *or* urban.)

Eleanor had once burned her bra in public, before a small gathering in a Grand Union parking lot, but throughout the eighties she was a politically active Republican—the alleged influence of her second husband. Having tried unsuccessfully, for years, to get pregnant, she finally conceived her only child with the aid of an anonymous sperm donor; thereupon she became adamantly opposed to abortion. Possibly this was the alleged influence of what Mrs. Dash's late husband called "the mystery sperm."

During two decades, Eleanor Holt went from eating everything to strict vegetarianism to eating everything again. The changes in her diet were confusingly imposed upon her sperm-donated child, a haunted girl, whose birthday party—she was only six at the time—was spoiled for her, and for the other children in attendance, by Eleanor's decision to show the home movie of her daughter's birth.

Jane Dash's only son had been one of the traumatized children at the birthday party. The episode had troubled Mrs. Dash, for she had always been physically modest in the presence of her son. Her late husband had frequently been naked around the house—he slept in the nude, and so forth—but this hadn't troubled Jane, at least not for her son's sake. After all, they were both boys. Jane, however, had made every effort to cover herself. Then her son had come home from the Holt girl's birthday party, having seen an apparently vivid film of a live birth—having seen Eleanor Holt, displayed like an open book!

And over the years, Eleanor would again from time to time impose the obstetrical film on her poor daughter—and not necessarily for educational reasons. Rather it was for Eleanor Holt's unstoppable self-importance: the woman needed to demonstrate to her own daughter how, at least at the moment of giving birth, she had suffered.

As for the daughter, she either developed or had been born with a contrary personality; whether this was the result of her overexposure to the gore of her own delivery or something in the secret genes of "the mystery sperm," the daughter seemed intent on embarrassing her mother. And the poor girl's contrariness encouraged Eleanor to attack other possible sources that might be disturbing her daughter—for Eleanor Holt never faulted herself, not for anything.

What Mrs. Dash would always remember was Eleanor Holt's emergence as an anti-pornography picketer. The porn shop, which was on the outskirts of Riverhead, Long Island, a far cry from the Hamptons, was not a place that lured young or unsuspecting or otherwise innocent readers to its door. It was a low, shingled building with small windows and a shed roof. The sign outside was not ambiguous.

X-RATED BOOKS & MAGAZINES
ADULTS ONLY!

Eleanor and a small band of outraged matronly women only once entered the building. They abruptly withdrew, agitated and flushed. ("The strong victimizing the weak!" Eleanor told a local reporter.) The couple who ran the pornography shop were elderly; they had been longing to escape the dreary Long Island winters. In the ensuing fuss, they conned a concerned-citizens' group (of Eleanor's initiation) into buying the building. But the concerned citizens not only paid too much for the old shed, they were left with ... ah, the inventory, as Mrs. Dash thought of it.

As a novelist, and as an interested party, Jane Dash volunteered to estimate the value of the stock. She had previously but politely declined an invitation to join Eleanor's crusade against pornography, on the grounds that she was a writer; she was basically opposed to censorship. When Eleanor pressed her case—that she was appealing to Jane "as a woman first and a writer second"—Jane had surprised both Eleanor and herself by her response.

"I'm a writer first," Mrs. Dash had said.

Jane was allowed to investigate the pornography at her leisure. Its "value" aside, Mrs. Dash found it disappointing. The coarseness of it was to be expected—apparently not by Eleanor Holt! But grossness was the norm for many people. Crudeness and prurient interests were the motivating humors for all sorts of individuals; Mrs. Dash happily did not associate with them. Whereas she wished more of the population were better educated, she also believed that education was largely wasted on the majority of people she had met.

In the unseemly collection from the porn shop, now closed for good, there were no depictions of sexual acts with animals or with underage children. Mrs. Dash considered it mildly reassuring that these depravities had not made their way as far east of Manhattan as Suffolk County—at least not in magazine or book form. What she found in ample evidence was the commonplace exaggeration of female orgasms, and men (always with penises of unlikely size) who displayed an unconvincing interest in the labors they were performing. Bad acting on the part of both sexes, Jane Dash concluded. She thought the close-up views of the countless and various female genitalia were ... well, clinically interesting. She'd never before looked at other women in such uninviting detail.

Pressed for her evaluation, Jane declared the contents of the shop to be worthless trash—unless the concerned citizens wanted to reduce their expenses by selling off the remaining stock to certain curious locals. But such a sidewalk sale in Riverhead would have amounted to the concerned citizens playing the role of pornographers. Therefore, the books and magazines were burned—a total loss.

Again defining herself as "a writer first," Mrs. Dash said she wanted no part of the burning ceremony; she wouldn't even watch it. The local newspapers captured a small but triumphant band of women tending to a fire. Real firemen stood anxiously nearby, in case the burning photographs of strenuous sexual endeavors and stray genitals should suddenly develop into a spreading flame.

In Suffolk County, six years passed without further public demonstrations in the field of sexual morality. The sperm-donated daughter was twelve when she took Eleanor Holt's dildo—a battery-powered vibrator—to the Bridgehampton alternative middle school for that ill-considered part of American education known as Show and Tell. Once again, Jane Dash's son, who'd been witness to the film of the live birth at the six-year-old's birthday party, was privileged to see this brief glimpse of Eleanor's formerly private experience.

The twelve-year-old daughter was fortunately inexpert at demonstrating the tool, which the astonished teacher quickly took away from her. There was little more to observe than the shocking size of the thing. Mrs. Dash, who never saw it, gathered from her son's description that the dildo was modeled on nothing resembling an actual male member. The boy compared the vibrator to "some kind of missile." Also fixed in the lad's memory was the sound that the missile made when it was turned on. The vibrator, of course, vibrated. While this was not highly detectable, before the teacher grabbed the dildo from the twelve-year-old and turned it off, the particular sound was a surprise to all who heard it.

"Exactly what did it sound like?" Jane asked her son.

"Zzzt! Zzzt! Zzzt!" the boy reported. There was a hint of warning in this sound, Mrs. Dash thought—a buzzing sound, with a *t* on the end. The novelist couldn't get this sound out of her head.

And here the playfulness of Mrs. Dash's late husband would return to haunt her. Whenever they had spotted Eleanor Holt—at a dinner party, in the supermarket, or dropping off her daughter at the alternative middle school—Jane's husband would whisper in the novelist's ear,

"*Zzzt!*" It seemed to Jane that, in his clever way, he was telling her to be careful.

Repeatedly, it was the sheer good fun of him that Mrs. Dash missed most of all. Even the sight of Eleanor Holt would forcefully remind Jane of her widowhood and what she'd lost.

Five more years passed, yet Jane remembered the dildo episode as if it had happened only yesterday. What possessed Mrs. Dash to confront Eleanor Holt with an almost perfect imitation of the sound made by her vibrator was twofold: Jane keenly desired to bring back to her life her late husband's sense of humor, and Jane knew that if she didn't do something to Eleanor directly, she would be driven to write about her, which would be worse. As a novelist, Mrs. Dash despised writing about real people; she found it a failure of the imagination—for any novelist worthy of the name ought to be able to invent a more interesting character than any real person. To turn Eleanor Holt into fiction, even for the purpose of derision, would be a kind of flattery.

Besides, the moment of Mrs. Dash's decision to imitate the sound of Eleanor's vibrator was no "decision" at all. It was completely accidental. It was not, quite unlike a Jane Dash novel, a planned act. The situation was the annual picnic for the alternative middle school, which was an alternative kind of school picnic, coming as it did well after the close of the school year; it was intended to coincide with the first good swimming weather of the early summer. The Atlantic Ocean was exceedingly cold until the end of June. But if the school waited for its picnic as late as July, the public beach would be overcrowded with "the summer renters."

Mrs. Dash had no intentions of swimming before August; she never swam at the school picnics, not even when her husband had been alive. And since her son had graduated from the alternative middle school, his attendance (and Jane's) at this year's picnic was more in the spirit of an alumni gathering, a reunion of sorts, which also marked Mrs. Dash's most public outing in Bridgehampton since she'd become a widow. Some were surprised to see her. Not Eleanor Holt.

"Good for you," Eleanor said to Jane. "It's about time you went out in the world again." That was probably what set Mrs. Dash to thinking. She hardly considered the alternative middle school's picnic as "the world," nor did she care to be congratulated by Eleanor Holt.

Jane distracted herself with pleasant observations of her son: how he had grown! And his former schoolmates... well, they had grown up, too. Even Eleanor's troubled daughter was quite a pretty girl, relaxed and outgoing—now that she was in a boarding school and wasn't living in the same house with the lurid movie of her own birth and her mother's nuclear missile of pleasure.

Jane also distracted herself by observing the smaller children. She didn't know many of them, and some of the younger parents were strangers to her as well. The teacher who'd taken away the vibrating dildo came to sit beside Mrs. Dash. Jane didn't hear what she was saying; the novelist was trying to imagine how to frame her question, and if she dared to ask it. ("When you grabbed hold of the thing, how hard was it shaking? I mean, like a blender, maybe, or a food processor, or was it... ah, gentler than that?") But of course Mrs. Dash would never ask such a question; she just smiled. Eventually the teacher wandered away.

As the afternoon darkened, the younger children shivered with cold. The beach turned an eggshell-brown color, the ocean gray. There were shivering children in the parking lot, too, as Mrs. Dash and her son put their picnic basket and their towels and beach blankets into the trunk of their car. They were parked beside Eleanor Holt and her daughter. Jane was surprised to see Eleanor's second husband. He was an excessively litigious divorce lawyer who rarely appeared at social events.

A wind came up. The younger children moaned. Something colorful—it looked like a raft—was lifted by the wind. It flew out of the hands of a small boy and landed on the roof of Eleanor Holt's car. The divorce lawyer reached for the colorful thing, but it flew on. Jane Dash caught it in the air.

It was a partially deflated air mattress, red and blue, and the little boy who'd lost control of it came running up to Mrs. Dash. "I was trying to let the air out of it," the little boy said. "It won't fit in the car. Then it got away, in the wind."

"Well now, let me show you—there's a trick to this," Mrs. Dash told the boy. Jane was watching Eleanor Holt bend over. Eleanor knelt down on one knee; she was tying her shoe. Her litigious husband had aggressively positioned himself at the steering wheel. Her mystery-sperm daughter was sitting sullenly alone in the backseat—doubtless returned to her childhood horrors by this reunion.

Jane found a pebble of the right size in the parking lot. She unscrewed the cap that covered the air valve for the red and blue air mattress, and she stuck the pebble into the valve. The pebble pressed the valve needle down. The air hissed out.

"Just push down on the pebble," Mrs. Dash said. She demonstrated for the small boy. "Like this." The air escaped the mattress in sudden blasts. "And ... if you hug the mattress hard, like this, it will deflate faster."

But when Jane did this, the air rattled the pebble against the valve. Eleanor heard the sound just as she was standing up.

"*Zzzt! Zzzt! Zzzt!*" said the red and blue air mattress. The delight in the little boy's face was apparent. It was quite a wonderful sound, to him. But in Eleanor Holt's expression was the sudden recognition that she had been exposed. At the steering wheel, her husband turned his face (like a lawsuit) to the sound. Then Eleanor's daughter turned to face the sound, too. Even Jane Dash's son, twice introduced to the intimate life of Eleanor Holt, turned in recognition of the thrilling sound.

Eleanor stared at Mrs. Dash, and at the rapidly deflating air mattress, like a woman who'd been undressed before a mob.

"It *is* about time I went out in the world again," Jane admitted to Eleanor.

Yet, on the subject of "the world"—and what it was, and when it was time for a widow to re-enter it safely—the red and blue air mattress offered only a cautionary word: "*Zzzt!*"

Allan at Fifty-Four

Ruth had read aloud in a deadpan voice. Some of the audience seemed disconcerted by her final "*Zzzt!*" Eddie, who'd read the whole book twice, loved the ending of the first chapter, but a portion of the audience briefly withheld their applause; they weren't sure the chapter had ended. The stupid stagehand stared open-mouthed at the TV monitor, as if he were preparing himself to deliver an epilogue. Not a single word was forthcoming—not even another charmless comment regarding his tireless appreciation of the famous novelist's "hooters."

It was Allan Albright who clapped first, even before Eddie. As Ruth Cole's editor, Allan well knew the *"Zzzt!"* with which the first chapter concluded. The applause that eventually followed was generous, and it was sufficiently sustained for Ruth to appraise the solitary ice cube in the bottom of her water glass. The ice had melted enough to provide her with a single swallow.

The questions and answers that followed the reading were a disappointment; Eddie felt bad for Ruth that, after an entertaining performance, she had to suffer through the anticlimax that questions from the audience always engendered. And throughout the entire Q and A, Allan Albright had frowned at Ruth—as if she could have done something to elevate the intelligence of the questions! During her reading, Allan's animated expressions in the audience had irritated her—as if it were his role to entertain Ruth at her own reading!

The first question was openly hostile; it set a tone that the subsequent questions and answers could not break free of.

"Why do you repeat yourself?" a young man asked the author. "Or is it unintentional?"

Ruth judged him to be in his late twenties. Admittedly, the houselights were not bright enough for her to see his exact expression—he was seated near the back of the concert hall—but from his tone of voice Ruth had no doubt that he was sneering at her.

After three novels, Ruth was familiar with the charge that her characters were "recycled" from one book to the next, and that there were also "signature eccentricities" that she repeated in novel after novel. I suppose I *do* develop a fairly limited cast of characters, Ruth considered. But, in her experience, people who accused an author of repetition were usually referring to a detail that they hadn't liked the *first* time. After all, even in literature, if one *likes* something, what is the objection to repeating it?

"I assume you mean the dildo," Ruth said to the accusing young man. There had been a dildo in her second novel, too. But no dildo had reared its head (so to speak) in her first novel—doubtless an oversight, Ruth thought to herself. What she said was: "I know that many of you young men feel threatened by dildos, but you really needn't worry that you'll ever be *entirely* replaced." She paused for the laughter. Then she added: "And *this* dildo is really not at all the same *type* of dildo as the dildo in my previous novel. Not every dildo is the same, you know."

"You repeat more than dildos," the young man commented.

"Yes, I know—'female friendships gone awry,' or lost and found again," Ruth remarked, realizing (only after she spoke) that she was quoting from Eddie O'Hare's tedious introduction. Backstage, Eddie at first felt awfully pleased; then he wondered if she'd been mocking him.

"Bad boyfriends," the persistent young man added. (Now *there* was a theme!)

"The boyfriend in *The Same Orphanage* was a decent guy," Ruth reminded her antagonistic reader.

"No mothers!" shouted an older woman in the audience.

"No fathers, either," Ruth snapped.

Allan Albright was holding his head in his hands. He had advised her against Q and A. He'd told her that if she couldn't let a hostile or a baiting remark go—if she couldn't just "let it lie"—she should not do Q and A. And she shouldn't be "so ready to bite back."

"But I *like* to bite back," Ruth had told him.

"But you shouldn't bite back the first time, or even the second," Allan had warned her. His motto was: "Be nice twice." On principle, Ruth approved of the idea, but she found it hard advice to follow.

Allan's notion was that you ignored the first *and* the second rudeness. If someone baited you or was plainly hostile to you a *third* time, then you let him have it. Maybe this was too *gentlemanly* a principle for Ruth to adhere to.

The sight of Allan with his head in his hands caused Ruth to resent his demonstrable disapproval. Why was she so frequently in a mood to find fault with him? For the most part, she admired Allan's habits—at least his *work* habits—and she had no doubt that he was a good influence on her.

What Ruth Cole needed was an editor for her *life* more than for her novels. (Even Hannah Grant would have agreed with her.)

"Next question?" Ruth asked. She had tried to sound cheerful, even inviting, but there was no hiding the animosity in her voice. She'd *not* extended an invitation to her audience; she'd issued a challenge.

"Where do you get your ideas?" some innocent soul asked the author; it was someone unseen, a strangely sexless voice in the vast hall. Allan rolled his eyes. It was what Allan called "the shopping question": the homey speculation that one *shopped* for the ingredients in a novel.

"My novels aren't ideas—I don't have any ideas," Ruth replied. "I begin with the characters, which leads me to the problems that the characters are prone to have, which yields a story—every time." (Backstage, Eddie felt as if he should be taking notes.)

"Is it true that you never had a job, a real job?" It was the impertinent young man again, the one who'd asked her why she repeated herself. She hadn't called on him; he was at her again, uninvited.

It *was* true that Ruth had never had a "real" job, but before Ruth could respond to the insinuating question, Allan Albright stood up and turned around, doubtless in order to address the uncivil young man in the back of the concert hall.

"Being a writer *is* a real job, you asshole!" Allan said. Ruth knew he'd been counting. By his count, he'd been nice twice.

Medium applause followed Allan's outburst. When Allan turned toward the stage, to face Ruth, he gave her his characteristic cue—the thumb of his right hand drawn across his throat like a knife. This meant: Get off the stage.

"Thank you, thank you again," Ruth told the audience. On her way backstage, she stopped once. She turned and waved to the audience; their applause was still warm.

"How come you don't autograph books? Every other writer signs books!" her persecutor called.

Before she continued on her way backstage, Allan stood and turned again. Ruth didn't have to watch him; she already knew that Allan would give her tormentor the finger. Allan was extraordinarily fond of giving people the finger.

I really *do* like him—and he really *will* take care of me, she thought. Yet Ruth couldn't deny that Allan also irritated her.

Back in the greenroom, Allan irritated her again. The first thing he said to her was: "You never mentioned the title of the book!"

"I just forgot," Ruth said. What was he—*always* an editor?

"I didn't think you were going to read the first chapter," Allan added. "You told me you thought it was too comic, and that it didn't represent the novel as a whole."

"I changed my mind," Ruth told him. "I decided I *wanted* to be comic."

"You were no barrel of laughs in the Q and A," he reminded her.

"At least I didn't call anyone an 'asshole,' " Ruth said.

"I gave the guy his two times," Allan replied.

An elderly lady with a shopping bag of books had negotiated her way backstage. She'd lied to someone who had tried to stop her—she'd said she was Ruth's mother. She tried to lie to Eddie, too. She found Eddie standing in the doorway of the greenroom; indecisive as always, Eddie was half in, half out. The old woman with the shopping bag mistook him for someone in charge.

"I've got to see Ruth Cole," the elderly lady told Eddie. Eddie saw the books in the shopping bag.

"Ruth Cole doesn't autograph books," Eddie warned the old woman. "She never signs."

"Let me in. I'm her mother," the old lady lied.

Eddie, of all people, didn't need to look very closely at the elderly woman—only enough to realize that she was about the same age as Marion would be now. (Marion would be seventy-one.)

"Madam," Eddie said to the old woman, "you are *not* Ruth Cole's mother."

But Ruth had heard someone say she was her mother. She pushed past Allan to the doorway of the greenroom, where the elderly lady seized her hand.

"I brought these books all the way from Litchfield for you to sign," the old woman said. "That's in Connecticut."

"You shouldn't lie about being someone's mother," Ruth told her.

"There's one for each of my grandchildren," the old lady said. There were a half-dozen copies of Ruth's novels in the shopping bag, but before the elderly woman could begin removing the books from the bag, Allan was there—his big hand on the old lady's shoulder. He was gently pushing her out the door.

"It was announced: Ruth Cole doesn't autograph books—she simply does not do it," Allan said. "I'm sorry, but if she signed your books, it wouldn't be fair to all the other people who also want her signature, would it?"

The old woman ignored him. She had not let go of Ruth's hand. "My grandchildren adore everything you've written," she told Ruth. "It will take you just two minutes."

Ruth stood as if frozen.

"Please," Allan said to the lady with the shopping bag, but the old lady, with surprising quickness, put down her bag of books and knocked Allan's hand off her shoulder.

"Don't you dare push me," the old woman said.

"She's not my mother, is she?" Ruth asked Eddie.

"No, of course not," Eddie told her.

"Look—I'm asking you to sign these books for my *grandchildren*! Your own books!" the elderly lady said to Ruth. "I *bought* these books ..."

"Madam, *please* ..." Allan said to the old woman.

"What on earth is the matter with you, anyway?" the old woman asked Ruth.

"Fuck you *and* your grandchildren," Ruth said to her. The old lady looked as if she'd been slapped.

"*What* did you say to me?" she asked. She had an imperiousness that Hannah would have called "generational," but which Ruth thought was more a matter of the obnoxious old woman's wealth and privilege; surely the woman's pushiness wasn't strictly a matter of her age.

Ruth reached into the shopping bag and took out one of her own novels. "Do you have a pen?" she asked Eddie, who fumbled inside his damp jacket and produced a red pen—his teacher's favorite.

As Ruth inscribed the old woman's book, she repeated aloud the words as she wrote them: "Fuck you *and* your grandchildren." She put the book back in the bag and would have withdrawn another—she would have inscribed them all in that fashion, *and* left them all un-signed—but the old woman grabbed the shopping bag away from her.

"How *dare* you?" the elderly lady cried.

"Fuck you *and* your grandchildren," Ruth repeated flatly. It was her voice for reading aloud. She went back inside the greenroom, saying to Allan, in passing, "*Fuck* being nice twice. Fuck being nice *once*."

Eddie, who knew that his introduction had been too long and too academic, saw a way to atone. Whoever the old woman was, she was about Marion's age; Eddie did not look upon women of Marion's age as "old." They *were* older women, of course, but they were *not* el-derly—not in Eddie's opinion.

Eddie had seen a printed bookplate on the inside title page that Ruth had inscribed for the aggressive grandmother.

ELIZABETH J. BENTON

"Mrs. Benton?" Eddie asked the older woman.

"What?" Mrs. Benton said. "Who are you?"

"Ed O'Hare," Eddie said, offering the older woman his hand. "That's an admirable brooch you have."

Mrs. Benton stared at the lapel of her plum-colored suit jacket; her brooch was a scallop shell of silver, studded with pearls. "It was my mother's," the older woman told Eddie.

"Isn't that interesting?" Eddie said. "*My* mother had one just like it—in fact, she was *buried* with it," Eddie lied. (Eddie's mom, Dot O'Hare, was still very much alive.)

"Oh..." Mrs. Benton said. "I'm sorry."

Eddie's long fingers seemed suspended above the older woman's intensely ugly brooch. Mrs. Benton, swelling her breast in the direction of Eddie's hovering hand, allowed him to touch the scallop shell of silver; she let him finger her pearls.

"I never thought I'd see a brooch like this again," Eddie said.

"Oh..." Mrs. Benton said. "Were you very close to your mother? You must have been very close."

"Yes," Eddie lied. (Why can't I do this in my *books?* he wondered. It was a mystery where the lies came from, and why he couldn't summon them when he *wanted* them; it was as if he could only wait and hope for a good enough lie to appear at the opportune moment.)

Minutes later, Eddie had walked the older woman to the stage-entrance door. Outside, in the steady rain, a small but determined gathering of young people were waiting for a glimpse of Ruth Cole—and to ask her to sign *their* books.

"The author has already left. She went out the front door," Eddie lied. It amazed him that he'd been incapable of lying to the woman at the registration desk in the Plaza. If only he'd been able to lie to her, he'd have got change for the bus a little sooner; he might even have had the good luck to catch an earlier bus.

Mrs. Benton, who was more in command of her capabilities as a liar than Eddie O'Hare, basked for a moment longer in Eddie's company before she bid him a lilting good night; she made a point of thanking him for his "gentlemanly behavior."

Eddie had volunteered to get Ruth Cole's autograph for Mrs. Benton's grandchildren. He'd persuaded the older woman to leave her shopping bag of books with him, including the book that Ruth had "spoiled." (That was how Mrs. Benton thought of it.) Eddie knew that if he couldn't get Ruth's signature, he could at least provide Mrs. Benton with a reasonably convincing forgery.

Eddie would have confessed to a fondness for Mrs. Benton's boldness: her assertion that she was Ruth's mother notwithstanding, Eddie had admired the way she'd stood up to Allan Albright. There was also something bold about Mrs. Benton's amethyst earrings—something *too* bold, perhaps. They were not quite right with the more muted plum color of her suit. And the big ring that hung a little too loosely from her right middle finger ... perhaps it had once fit the ring finger of that hand.

Eddie had a soft spot for the thinning and caving-in of Mrs. Benton's body, too—for he could tell that Mrs. Benton still thought of herself as a younger woman. How could she *not* think of herself as younger, sometimes? How could Eddie *not* be moved by her? And, like most writers (Ted Cole excluded), Eddie O'Hare believed that a writer's autograph was intrinsically unimportant. Why not do for Mrs. Benton what he could?

What did it matter to Mrs. Benton that Ruth Cole's reasons for avoiding public book-signings were well founded? Ruth hated how exposed she felt when she was signing books for a mob. There was always someone who just stared at her; often it was someone standing to one side of the line, usually without a book.

Publicly, Ruth had said that when she was in Helsinki, for example, she would sign books—her Finnish translations—because she couldn't speak Finnish. In Finland, or in many other foreign countries, there was nothing she could do but autograph her books. But in her own country, she would rather read to an audience, or just talk to her readers—*anything* rather than sign books. Yet, in truth, she didn't like talking to her readers, either, as had been painfully apparent to anyone observing her agitation during the disastrous Q and A at the Y. Ruth Cole was afraid of her readers.

She'd had her share of stalkers. Usually Ruth's stalkers were creepy young men. They presumed they already knew her, because of how obsessively they'd read her novels. They presumed they would be *good* for her, in some way—as lovers, they often implied, or merely as like-minded literary correspondents. (Many of them were would-be writers, of course.)

Yet the few *women* who'd stalked her had upset Ruth more than the creepy young men. They were often women who wanted Ruth to write *their* stories; they thought they belonged in a Ruth Cole novel.

Ruth wanted her privacy. She traveled frequently; she could happily write in hotels, or in a variety of rented houses and apartments, surrounded by other people's photographs and furniture and clothes, or even caring for other people's pets. Ruth owned only one home—an old farmhouse in Vermont, which she was halfheartedly restoring. She'd bought the farmhouse only because she needed to have a place to keep coming back to, and because a caretaker had virtually come with the property. A tireless man and his wife and family lived nearby on a working farm. They were a couple with a seemingly uncountable number of children; Ruth tried to keep them busy with odd jobs, and with the larger task of "restoring" her farmhouse—one room at a time, and always when Ruth was traveling.

For four years at Middlebury, Ruth and Hannah had complained about the isolation of Vermont—not to mention the winters, because neither of them was a skier. Now Ruth loved Vermont, even the winters, and she enjoyed having a house in the country. But she liked going away, too. Her traveling was the simple answer she gave to the question of why she hadn't married, and why she didn't want children.

Allan Albright was too smart to accept the simple answer. They had talked and talked about Ruth's more complex reasons for saying no to marriage, and to children; except with Hannah, Ruth had never before discussed the more complex reasons. She particularly regretted that she'd never discussed them with her father.

Back in the greenroom, Ruth thanked Eddie for his welcome and timely interference with Mrs. Benton.

"It seems I have a way with her age group," Eddie admitted—without irony, Ruth observed. (She'd also observed that Eddie had returned with Mrs. Benton's bag of books.)

Even Allan managed some gruff congratulations, which amounted to his overmanly approval of Eddie's heroics with the relentless autograph-seeker.

"Well done, O'Hare," Allan heartily exclaimed. He was one of those bluff men who called other men by their last names. (Hannah would have cited the last-name usage as a distinguishing habit of Allan's "generation.")

Finally it had stopped raining. As they left by the stage-entrance door, Ruth told Allan and Eddie how grateful she was to them.

"I know that you both did your best to save me from myself," she told them.

"It's not yourself you need saving from," Allan said to Ruth. "It's the assholes."

No, it's *myself* I need saving from, Ruth thought, but she just smiled at Allan and squeezed his arm. Eddie, who was silent, was thinking that Ruth needed saving from herself *and* from the assholes—and possibly from Allan Albright.

Speaking of assholes, there was one waiting for Ruth on Second Avenue between Eighty-fourth and Eighty-fifth; he must have guessed the restaurant they were going to, or he'd been clever enough to follow Karl and Melissa there. It was the impudent young man from the rear of the concert hall, the one with the needling questions.

"I want to apologize," he said to Ruth. "It wasn't my intention to make you angry." He didn't *sound* very apologetic.

"You didn't make me angry at *you*," Ruth told him, not entirely truthfully. "I get angry with myself every time I go out in public. I shouldn't let myself go out in public."

"But why is that?" the young man asked.

"You've asked enough questions, fella," Allan told him. When Allan called someone "fella," he was willing to pick a fight.

"I get angry with myself when I *expose* myself in public," Ruth said. Suddenly she added: "Oh, God—you're a *journalist*, aren't you?"

"You don't like journalists, do you?" the young journalist asked.

Ruth left him outside the restaurant, where he went on arguing with Allan for an interminable amount of time. Eddie stayed with Allan and the journalist, but only briefly. He then came into the restaurant and joined Ruth, who was sitting with Karl and Melissa.

"They're not going to get into a fight," Eddie assured Ruth. "If they were going to have a fight, they already would have."

It turned out that the journalist was someone who'd not been granted an interview with Ruth the following day. Apparently the publicist at Random House hadn't thought he was important enough, and Ruth always put a limit on how many interviews she would do.

"You don't have to do *any*," Allan had told her, but she'd yielded to the publicity people.

Allan was notorious at Random House for undermining the efforts of the publicity people. His idea of a novelist—even of a best-selling novelist, like Ruth Cole—was that he or she should stay home and write. What his authors appreciated about Allan Albright was that he didn't burden them with all the other expectations publishers have. He was devoted to his authors; sometimes Allan was more devoted to his authors' actual writing than the authors themselves were. Ruth never doubted that she loved *that* aspect of Allan. But that he was unafraid to criticize her, about *anything,* was an aspect of Allan that Ruth did not so wholeheartedly adore.

While Allan was still out on the sidewalk, arguing with the aggressive young journalist, Ruth quickly signed the books in Mrs. Benton's shopping bag, including the one she had "spoiled." (On that one she wrote "Sorry!" in parentheses.) Then Eddie hid the shopping bag under the table, because Ruth told him that Allan would be disappointed in her for signing the self-assertive grandmother's books. The way Ruth said it, Eddie surmised that Allan took more than an editorial interest in his renowned author.

When Allan at last joined them at the table, Eddie was alert to Allan's *other* interest in Ruth. Ruth was alert to Allan's other interest in her, too.

During the editing of her novel, including their bitter argument about the title, she'd not sensed Allan's romantic inclination toward her; he'd been strictly business, an absolute professional. Nor had she seen, at the time, that his dislike of her chosen title had grown curiously personal; that she wouldn't yield to him—she wouldn't even consider his suggested alternative—had affected him oddly. He bore the title like a grudge. He referred to it obdurately, in the manner that a vexed husband might repeatedly mention an enduring disagreement in a long and otherwise successful marriage.

She'd called her third novel *Not for Children.* (Indeed, it was not.) In the novel, it is a slogan favored by the anti-pornography picketers; the slogan is the invention of Mrs. Dash's enemy (who would eventually become her friend) Eleanor Holt. However, in the course of the novel, the phrase comes to mean something quite different from its original intent. In their mutual need to love and raise their orphaned grandchildren, Eleanor Holt and Jane Dash realize that their expressed disapproval of each other must be set aside; their old antagonisms are also "not for children."

Allan had wanted to call the novel *For the Children's Sake.* (He'd said that the two adversaries make friends in the manner of a couple who endure a bad marriage "for the children's sake.") But Ruth wanted to keep the anti-pornography connection that was both explicit and implicit in *Not for Children*. It mattered to her that her own political opinion about pornography was strongly voiced in the title—her political opinion being that she feared censorship more than she disliked pornography, which she disliked a great deal.

As for protecting *children* from pornography, that was everyone's responsibility; it was a matter of common sense, not censorship, to protect children from *everything* that was unsuitable for them. ("Including," Ruth had said in several interviews, "any novel by Ruth Cole.")

Ruth basically hated arguing with men. It reminded her of arguing with her father. If she let her father win, he had a puerile way of reminding her that he'd been right. But if Ruth clearly won, either Ted wouldn't admit it or he'd be petulant.

"You always order the arugula," Allan said to her now.

"I *like* arugula," Ruth told him. "It's not *always* available."

To Eddie, they sounded as if they'd been married for years. Eddie wanted to talk to Ruth about Marion, but he would have to wait. When he excused himself from the table—to go to the men's room, when he didn't really need to go—he hoped that Ruth would take this as an opportunity to visit the *women's;* they could at least have a few words together, if only in a corridor. But Ruth stayed at the table.

"My God," Allan said, when Eddie was gone. "Why was O'Hare the introducer?"

"I thought he was fine," Ruth lied.

Karl explained that he and Melissa often asked Eddie O'Hare to be the introducer. Because he was reliable, Karl said. And he'd never refused to introduce *anybody*, Melissa added.

Ruth smiled to hear this about Eddie, but Allan said, "My God—'reliable'? He was *late*! He looked like he'd been run over by a *bus!*"

He *had* gone on a little too long, Karl and Melissa agreed; they'd never heard him go on too long before.

"But why did *you* want him to introduce you?" Allan asked Ruth. "You told me you liked the idea." (In fact, Eddie had been *her* idea.)

Who was it who said that there was no better company for an especially *personal* revelation than the company of virtual strangers? (Ruth herself had written that—in *The Same Orphanage*.)

"Well." Ruth was aware that Karl and Melissa were the "virtual strangers" in this case. "Eddie O'Hare was my mother's lover," she announced. "It was when he was sixteen and my mother was thirty-nine.

I haven't seen him since I was four, but I've always *wanted* to see him again. As you might imagine..." She waited.

No one said a word. Ruth knew how hurt Allan would be—that she'd not told him before, *and* that when she'd finally told him, it was in front of Karl and Melissa.

"May I ask," Allan began—formally, for him, "if the older woman in *all* of O'Hare's novels is your mother?"

"No, not according to my father," Ruth replied. "But I believe that Eddie truly loved my mother, and that his love for her, as an older woman, *is* in all of his novels."

"I see," Allan said. He'd already picked some of Ruth's arugula off her salad plate with his fingers. For a gentleman, which he was—and a lifelong New Yorker, a sophisticated man—Allan's table manners were atrocious. He ate off everybody's plate—he was not above expressing his dislike of your food after he'd eaten it, either—and food had a way of getting caught between his teeth.

Ruth glanced at him now, expecting to see a telltale flag of arugula in the vicinity of one of his overlong canines. He had a long nose and a long chin, too, but they conveyed a remote elegance, which was offset by a broad, flat forehead and a closely cropped head of dark-brown hair. At fifty-four, Allan Albright showed no signs of baldness; he had not a single gray hair, either.

He was almost handsome except for his long teeth, which lent him a lupine appearance. And although he was quite lean and fit, he ate with gusto. He occasionally drank with a little too much gusto, Ruth worried, assessing him. Now, *always,* it seemed, she was assessing him—and too often unkindly. I should sleep with him and make up my mind, she thought.

Then Ruth remembered that Hannah Grant had stood her up. Ruth had intended to use Hannah as her excuse for *not* sleeping with Allan—that is, Hannah would be Ruth's excuse *this* time. She was going to tell Allan that she and Hannah were such old friends that they always stayed up all night and talked and talked.

When Ruth's publisher wasn't paying for her accommodations in New York, Ruth usually stayed with Hannah; Ruth even had her own set of keys to Hannah's apartment.

Now, without Hannah there, Allan would suggest that Ruth come back to his apartment, or he would ask to see her suite at the Stanhope, which Random House had provided for her. Allan had been very patient with her reluctance to sleep with him; he'd even construed her reluctance to mean that she was taking his affection for her with the utmost seriousness, which she *was*. It just hadn't occurred to Allan that Ruth was reluctant because she thought she might *hate* sleeping with him. It had something to do with his habit of taking food off other people's plates, and the haste with which he ate.

It *wasn't* because of his reputation as a former ladies' man. He'd told her frankly that "the right woman," which she apparently was, had changed all that; she had no reason not to believe him. It wasn't his age, either. He was in better shape than many younger men; he didn't *look* fifty-four, and he was intellectually stimulating. They had once stayed up all night—much more recently than Ruth and Hannah had stayed up all night—reading their favorite passages of Graham Greene to each other.

Allan's first present to Ruth had been volume one of the Norman Sherry biography of Graham Greene. Ruth had been reading it with a deliberate slowness, both savoring it and afraid of what she might learn about Greene that she wouldn't like. It disturbed her to read biographies of writers she loved; she preferred not to know anything unlovable about them. Thus far, the Sherry biography had treated Greene with the honor Ruth thought Greene deserved. But Allan was more impatient with her for reading Norman Sherry slowly than he was impatient with her for her sexual reticence. (Allan had observed that Norman Sherry was sure to publish the second volume of *The Life of Graham Greene* before Ruth finished reading the first.)

Now, with Hannah not present, Ruth realized that she could use Eddie O'Hare as her reason for not sleeping with Allan tonight. Before Eddie returned from the men's room, Ruth said: "After dinner—I hope none of you will mind—I want to have Eddie all to myself." Karl and Melissa waited for Allan to respond, but Ruth pressed ahead. "I can't imagine what my mother saw in him," Ruth said, "except that, at sixteen, I'm sure he must have been awfully pretty."

"O'Hare is still 'awfully pretty,' " Allan growled. Ruth thought: Oh, God—don't tell me he's going to be *jealous*!

Ruth said: "My mother may not have cared for him as much as he cared for her. Even my father can't read Eddie O'Hare's books without commenting that Eddie must have *worshiped* my mother."

"Ad nauseam," said Allan Albright, who couldn't read a book by Eddie O'Hare without failing to make comments of that kind.

"Please don't be jealous, Allan," Ruth said. It was her reading-aloud voice, her inimitable deadpan, which they all knew. Allan looked stung. Ruth hated herself. In one evening she'd said "Fuck you" to a grandmother, *and* to the old lady's grandchildren, and now she'd wounded the only man she'd ever *considered* marrying.

"Anyway," Ruth told them at the table, "a chance to be alone with Eddie O'Hare is exciting for me."

Poor Karl and Melissa! Ruth thought. But they were used to writers and had doubtless been exposed to more inappropriate behavior than hers.

"Your mother clearly didn't leave your father for O'Hare," Allan said; he spoke more carefully than he usually did. He was trying to behave himself. He was a good man. Ruth saw that she'd made him afraid of her temper, for which she hated herself anew.

"That must be true," Ruth replied, with equal care. "But *any* woman would have had just cause to leave my father."

"Your mother left *you*, too," Allan interjected. (Of course they had talked and talked about that.)

"That's also true," Ruth replied. "That's precisely what I want to talk to Eddie about. I've heard what my father has to say about my mother, but my father doesn't love her. I want to hear what someone who loves her has to say about that."

"You think O'Hare *still* loves your mother?" Allan asked.

"You've read his books," Ruth answered.

"Ad nauseam," Allan said again. He's an awful snob, Ruth thought. But she liked snobs.

Then Eddie came back to the table.

"We've been talking about you, O'Hare," Allan said in a cavalier fashion. Eddie looked nervous.

"I told them about you and Mother," Ruth said to Eddie.

Eddie tried to look composed, although the wet wool of his jacket clung to him like a shroud. In the candlelight he saw the bright yellow hexagon shining in the iris of Ruth's right eye; when the light flickered, or when she turned her face toward the light, her eye changed color— from brown to amber—in the same way that the same hexagon of yellow could turn Marion's right eye from blue to green.

"I love your mother," Eddie began, without embarrassment. He'd needed only to think of Marion and he at once regained his composure, which he'd lost on the squash court while losing three games to Jimmy; Eddie's composure had not seemed to him recoverable until now.

Allan looked astonished when Eddie asked the waiter for some ketchup and a paper napkin. It was not the kind of restaurant where ketchup was served, nor was there a paper napkin in the place. Allan took charge; it was one of his likable qualities. He went out on Second Avenue and quickly located a cheaper sort of restaurant; he was back at the table in five minutes with a half-dozen paper napkins and a ketchup bottle that was less than a quarter full.

"I hope it's enough," he said. He'd paid five dollars for the nearly empty ketchup bottle.

"It's plenty, for my purposes," Eddie told him.

"Thank you, Allan," Ruth said warmly. Gallantly, he blew her a kiss.

Eddie poured a spreading puddle of the ketchup on his butter plate. The waiter looked on with grave distaste.

"Stick your right index finger in the ketchup," Eddie said to Ruth.

"*My* finger?" Ruth asked him.

"Please," Eddie said to her. "I just want to see how much you remember."

"How much I remember ..." Ruth said. She dabbed her finger in the ketchup, wrinkling her nose—like a child.

"Now touch the napkin," Eddie told her, sliding the paper napkin toward her. Ruth hesitated, but Eddie took her hand and gently pressed her right index finger on the napkin.

Ruth licked the rest of the ketchup off her finger while Eddie positioned the napkin exactly where he wanted it: on the far side of Ruth's water glass, so that the glass magnified the fingerprint. And there it was—as it would be, forever: the perfectly vertical line on her right index finger; seen through the water glass, it was nearly twice the size of the scar itself.

"Do you remember?" Eddie asked her. The yellow hexagon in Ruth's right eye was dulled with tears. She couldn't speak. "Nobody else will ever have fingerprints like yours," Eddie told her, as he'd told her on the day her mother left.

"And my scar will always be there?" Ruth asked him, as she had asked him thirty-two years ago, when she was four.

"Your scar will be part of you forever," Eddie promised her, as he had promised her then.

"Yes," Ruth whispered, "I remember. I remember almost everything," she told him through her tears.

Later, alone in her suite at the Stanhope, Ruth remembered that Eddie had held her hand while she cried. She also recalled how wonderfully understanding Allan had been. Without a word, which was so uncharacteristic of him, Allan had ushered Karl and Melissa—and, most remarkably, *himself*—to another table in the restaurant. And Allan had insisted to the maître d' that it be a *faraway* table, not within hearing distance of Ruth and Eddie. Ruth was unaware of when Allan and Karl and Melissa left the restaurant. Finally, while she and Eddie were debating the subject of which of them would pay for their dinner—Ruth had drunk an entire bottle of wine, and Eddie didn't drink—the waiter interrupted their debate by telling them that Allan had already paid for everything.

Now, in the bedroom of her hotel, Ruth considered calling Allan and thanking him, but he would probably be asleep. It was almost one A.M. And she had been so stimulated to talk and listen to Eddie that she didn't want to feel let down—as she might, if she talked to Allan.

Allan's sensitivity had impressed her, but the subject of her mother, which Eddie had instantly taken up, was too much on her mind. Although she hardly needed more to drink, Ruth opened one of those lethal little bottles of cognac that always lurk in minibars. She lay in her bed, sipping the strong drink and wondering what to write in her diary; there was so much she wanted to say.

Most of all, Eddie had assured her that her mother had loved her. (One might write a whole book about that!) Ruth's father had *tried* to reassure her of that—for thirty-two years—but her father, given his cynicism about her mother, had failed to convince her.

Naturally Ruth had heard the theory of how her dead brothers had robbed her mother of her capacity to love another child; there was also the theory that Marion had been afraid to love Ruth, out of fear of losing her only daughter to some calamity of the kind that had claimed her sons.

But Eddie had told Ruth the story of the moment when Marion recognized that Ruth had a flawed eye—that hexagon of bright yellow, which her mother also had in *her* eye. Eddie told Ruth how Marion had cried in fear—for this yellow flaw meant to her that Ruth might be *like* her, and her mother hadn't wanted Ruth to be like her.

For Ruth, there was suddenly more love in her mother—for *not* wishing anything of herself on her daughter—than Ruth could bear.

Ruth and Eddie had talked about whether Ruth was more like her mother or her father. (The more he listened to Ruth, the more Eddie saw of Marion in her.) The subject mattered greatly to Ruth, because she didn't want to be a mother if she was going to be a bad one.

"That's just what your mother said," Eddie told her.

"But what *worse* thing could a mother do than leave her child?" Ruth had asked him.

"That's what your father says, isn't it?" Eddie asked her.

Her father was a "sexual predator," Ruth told Eddie, but he'd been "halfway decent" as a father. He'd never neglected her. It was as a woman that she loathed him. As a child, she had doted on him—at least he was *there*.

"He would have been a terrible influence on those boys, had they lived," Eddie told her. Ruth instantly agreed. "That's why your mother had already thought of leaving him—I mean, *before* the boys were killed," Eddie added.

Ruth hadn't known that. She expressed considerable bitterness toward her father for withholding that information from her, but Eddie explained that Ted *couldn't* have told her because Ted hadn't *known* that Marion might leave him.

Ruth and Eddie had talked about so much that Ruth couldn't begin to describe it in her diary. Eddie had even called Marion "the sexual beginning *and* the sexual peak" of his life. (Ruth *did* manage to write that down.)

And in the taxi ride to the Stanhope, with that awful old woman's shopping bag of books between his knees, Eddie had said to Ruth: "That 'awful old woman,' as you call her, is about your mother's age. Therefore, she's not an 'awful old woman' to *me*."

It was staggering to Ruth that a forty-eight-year-old man was *still* carrying a torch for a woman who was now seventy-one!

"Supposing that my mother lives into her nineties, will you be a lovestruck *sixty*-eight-year-old?" Ruth had asked Eddie.

"I'm absolutely certain of it," Eddie had told her.

What Ruth Cole also wrote in her diary was that Eddie O'Hare was the antithesis of her father. At seventy-seven, Ted Cole was now chasing women who were Ruth's age, although he was less and less successful at it. His more common successes were with women in their late forties—women who were Eddie's age!

If Ruth's father lived into his nineties, he might finally be pursuing women who at least *looked* closer to his age—namely, women who were "merely" in their seventies!

The phone rang. Ruth couldn't help being disappointed that it was Allan. She'd picked up the phone with the hope that it might be Eddie. Maybe he's remembered something else to tell me! Ruth had wished.

"Not asleep, I hope," Allan said. "And you're *alone*, I trust."

"Not asleep, definitely alone," Ruth answered him. Why did he have to spoil what a favorable impression he'd made by sounding the jealousy note?

"How'd it go?" Allan asked her.

She felt suddenly too tired to tell him the details, which, only moments before he called, had so excited her.

"It was a very special evening," Ruth said. "It's given me so much more of a picture of my mother—actually, both of her *and* of myself," she added. "Maybe I *shouldn't* be afraid that I'd be a rotten wife. Maybe I *wouldn't* make a bad mother."

"*I've* told you that," Allan reminded her. Why couldn't he just be grateful that she was possibly coming around to the idea of what he wanted?

That was when Ruth knew that she would not have sex with Allan the next night, either. What sense did it make to sleep with someone and then go off to Europe for two, almost three weeks? (As much sense as it made to keep putting off sleeping with him, Ruth reconsidered. She wouldn't agree to marry Allan without sleeping with him first—at least once.)

"Allan, I'm awfully tired—and there's too much that's too new on my mind," Ruth began.

"I'm listening," he said.

"I don't want to have dinner with you tomorrow night—I don't want to see you until I'm back from Europe," she told him. She half-hoped that he would try to dissuade her, but he was silent. Even his patience with her was irritating.

"I'm still listening," he said, because she had paused.

"I *want* to sleep with you—I *must* sleep with you," Ruth assured him. "But not just before I go away. And not just before I see my father," Ruth added, which she knew was apropos of nothing. "I want the time away to think about us." That was finally how she put it.

"I understand," Allan said. It broke her heart to know he was a good man, but not to know if he was the *right* one. And how would "time away" help her to determine *that?* What she needed, in order to know, was more time *with* Allan.

But what she said was: "I knew you'd understand."

"I love you very much," Allan told her.

"I know you do," Ruth said.

Later, as she struggled to fall asleep, she tried not to think of her father. Although Ted Cole had told his daughter about her mother's affair with Eddie O'Hare, Ted had neglected to tell Ruth that their affair had been *his* idea. When Eddie had told her that her father had *purposely* brought him and Marion together, Ruth had been shocked. That her father had connived to make her mother feel that she was unfit to be a mother was *not* what shocked Ruth; she already knew that her father was a conniver. What shocked Ruth was that her father had wanted her all to himself, that he'd *wanted* to be her father so badly!

At thirty-six, both loving and hating her father as she now did, it tormented Ruth to know how much her father loved her.

Hannah at Thirty-Five

Ruth couldn't sleep. The cause of her insomnia was the cognac—in combination with what she had confessed to Eddie O'Hare, which was something she'd not told even Hannah Grant. At every important passage in her life, Ruth had anticipated that she would hear from her mother. Upon her graduation from Exeter, for example, but it didn't happen. And there came and went her graduation from Middlebury, without a word.

Nevertheless, Ruth had gone on expecting to hear from Marion—especially in 1980, upon the publication of her first novel. And there were then the publications of two more novels, the second in '85 and the third right now—in the fall of 1990. That was why, when the presumptuous Mrs. Benton had attempted to pass herself off as Ruth's mother, Ruth had been so angry. For years she'd imagined that Marion might suddenly announce herself in exactly that way.

"Do you think she ever *will* make an appearance?" Ruth had asked Eddie in the taxi.

Eddie had disappointed her. In the course of her thrilling evening with him, Eddie had done much to contradict Ruth's first, unfair impression of him, but in the taxi he'd fumbled badly.

"Uh ..." he began, "I imagine that your mother must make peace with herself before she can...uh, well, re-enter your life." Eddie paused—as if he hoped that the taxi had already arrived at the Stanhope. "Uh ..." he said again, "Marion has her demons—her *ghosts*, I suppose—and she must somehow try to deal with them before she can make herself available to you."

"She's my *mother*, for Christ's sake!" Ruth had cried in the cab. "*I'm* the demon she should be trying to deal with!"

But all that Eddie had managed to say was: "I almost forgot! There was a book—actually, *two* books—that I wanted to give you."

Here she'd asked him the most important question in her life: Was it reasonable for her to hope that her mother would *ever* contact her? And Eddie had pawed around in his wet briefcase, producing two water-damaged books.

One of them was the inscribed copy of his litany of sexual bliss to Marion, *Sixty Times*. And the other? He'd been at a loss to say what the other book was. He'd simply thrust it into her lap in the taxi.

"You said you were going to Europe," Eddie told her. "This is good airplane reading."

At such a time, and in answer to Ruth's all-important question, he'd offered her "airplane reading." Then the taxi had stopped at the Stanhope. Eddie had given Ruth the clumsiest of handshakes. She'd kissed him, of course, and he'd blushed—like a sixteen-year-old boy!

"We must get together when you're back from Europe!" Eddie had called from the departing cab.

Maybe he was bad at good-byes. In all honesty, "pathetic" and "unfortunate" did not do him justice. He'd made an art form of his modesty. "He wore his self-deprecation like a badge of honor," Ruth wrote in her diary. "And there was nothing of the weasel about him." (Ruth had heard her father call Eddie a weasel on more than one occasion.)

Also, when it was still early in their evening together, Ruth had understood something about Eddie: he never complained. In addition to his prettiness, his frail-looking beauty, what her mother might have seen in him was something that extended beyond his loyalty to her. Despite his appearance to the contrary, Eddie O'Hare was remarkably brave; he had accepted Marion as she was. And in the summer of '58, Ruth imagined, her mother had not necessarily been at her psychological best.

Half naked, Ruth went looking through her suite at the Stanhope for the alleged "airplane reading" that Eddie had given her. She was too drunk to waste a word of *The Life of Graham Greene,* and she had already read *Sixty Times;* in truth, she'd read it twice.

To her dismay, the "airplane reading" appeared to be some kind of crime fiction. Ruth was immediately put off by the title, *Followed Home from the Flying Food Circus.* Both the author and the publisher were unknown to her. Upon closer inspection, Ruth saw that the publisher was Canadian.

Even the author photo was a mystery, for the woman—the unknown writer was a woman—was in profile to the camera, and what little could be seen of her face was backlit. The woman also wore a hat, which shaded the only eye that was exposed to the camera. All that could be seen of her face was a fine nose, a strong chin, a sharp cheekbone. Her hair—what of it that fell free of the hat—might have been blond or gray, or almost white. Her age was indeterminable.

It was an exasperating photograph, and Ruth was not surprised to read that the unknown author's name was a nom de plume; a woman who hid her face *would* choose a pen name. So *this* was what Eddie called "airplane reading." Even before she began the book, Ruth was unimpressed. And the beginning of the novel was not much better than Ruth's initial judgment of the book (by its cover).

Ruth read: "A salesgirl who was also a waitress had been found dead in her apartment on Jarvis, south of Gerrard. It was an apartment within her means, but only because she had shared it with two other salesgirls. The three of them sold bras at Eaton's."

A detective novel! Ruth snapped the book shut. Where was there a Jarvis Street, or a Gerrard? What was Eaton's? What did Ruth Cole care about girls who sold bras?

She'd finally fallen asleep—it was after two—when the telephone woke her.

"Are you alone? Can you talk?" Hannah asked her in a whisper.

"Definitely alone," Ruth said. "But why would I want to talk to you? You traitor."

"I knew you'd be angry," Hannah said. "I almost didn't call."

"Is that an apology?" Ruth asked her best friend. She had never heard Hannah apologize.

"Something came up," Hannah whispered.

"Something or some*one*?" Ruth asked.

"Same difference," Hannah replied. "I was suddenly called out of town."

"Why are you whispering?" Ruth asked her.

"I'd rather not wake him up," Hannah said.

"You mean you're with someone *now*?" Ruth asked. "Is he *there*?"

"Not exactly," Hannah whispered. "I had to move to another bedroom because he snores. I never imagined that he would *snore*."

Ruth refrained from comment. Hannah never failed to mention some intimacy involving her sexual partners.

"I was disappointed that you weren't with me," Ruth finally said. But, even as she spoke, it occurred to Ruth that if Hannah *had* been there, Hannah would never have let Ruth be alone with Eddie. Hannah would have been too curious about Eddie—she would have wanted Eddie all to herself! "On second thought," Ruth told her friend, "I'm glad you *weren't* with me. I got to be alone with Eddie O'Hare."

"So you still haven't done it with Allan," Hannah whispered.

"The main thing about this evening was *Eddie,*" Ruth replied. "I never saw my mother as clearly as I can see her now."

"But when are you *gonna* do it with Allan?" Hannah asked.

"When I get back from Europe, probably," Ruth said. "Don't you want to hear about my mother?"

"When you get back from *Europe!*" Hannah whispered. "That's what? In two or three *weeks*? God, he might meet someone else before you get back! And what about you? Even *you* might meet someone else!"

"If either Allan or I meet someone else," Ruth replied, "then it will be an especially good thing that we *haven't* slept together." It wasn't until she put it that way that Ruth feared she cared more about losing Allan as an *editor* than about losing him as a *husband*.

"So tell me everything about Eddie O'Hare," Hannah whispered.

"He's very sweet," Ruth began. "He's quite odd, but mainly sweet."

"But is he *sexy*?" Hannah asked. "I mean, could you *imagine* him with your mother? Your mother was so beautiful ..."

"Eddie O'Hare is a *little* beautiful," Ruth replied.

"Do you mean he's effeminate?" Hannah asked. "My God—he's not *gay*, is he?"

"No, no—he's not gay. He's not effeminate, either," Ruth told Hannah. "He's just very gentle. Surprisingly delicate-looking."

"I thought he was tall," Hannah said.

"Tall and delicate," Ruth replied.

"I can't see it—he sounds odd," Hannah said.

"I *said* he was odd," Ruth told her. "Odd and sweet, and delicate. And he's *devoted* to my mother. I mean, he would marry her *tomorrow*!"

"He *would*?" Hannah whispered. "But how old would your mother be? *Seventy*-something?"

"Seventy-one," Ruth said. "And Eddie is only forty-eight."

"That *is* odd," Hannah whispered.

"Don't you want to hear about my *mother*?" Ruth repeated.

"Just a minute," Hannah told her. She went away from the phone; then she was back. "I thought he said something, but it was just more snoring."

"I can tell you another time, if you're not interested," Ruth said coldly. (It was almost her reading-aloud voice.)

"Of course I'm *interested*!" Hannah whispered. "I suppose you and Eddie talked about your dead brothers."

"We talked about the *photographs* of my dead brothers," Ruth told her.

"I should *hope* so!" Hannah answered.

"It was strange because there were some that he remembered that I didn't. And there were others that *I* remembered, but he didn't. We agreed that we must have *invented* these particular photographs. Then there were others that we *both* remembered, and we thought that these must be the real ones. I think we each had more invented photographs than we had real ones."

"You and what's 'real' and what's 'invented,'" Hannah remarked. "Your favorite subject ..."

Ruth resented Hannah's obvious lack of interest, but she went on. "The photo of Thomas playing doctor to Timothy's knee—that one is definitely real," Ruth said. "And the one where Thomas is taller than my mother, and he's holding a hockey puck in his teeth—we both remember that one, too."

"I remember the one of your mother in bed, with your brothers' feet," Hannah said.

It was hardly surprising that Hannah would remember that one. Ruth had taken it to Exeter with her, and to Middlebury, too; presently, it was in the bedroom of her house in Vermont. (Eddie had *not* told Ruth that he'd masturbated to this particular picture of Marion, after he'd hidden the feet. When Ruth had raised the memory of those feet being covered with "what looked like little pieces of paper," Eddie had told her that he didn't remember anything covering the feet. "Then I must have invented that, too," Ruth had said.)

"And I remember the one of your brothers at Exeter, under the good old 'Come hither boys and be men' bullshit," Hannah said. "God, they were good-looking guys."

Ruth had shown Hannah that photo of her brothers the first time Hannah had come home with her to Sagaponack. They'd been students at Middlebury at the time. The photo was always in her father's bedroom, and Ruth had brought Hannah into his bedroom when her father was playing squash in his devious barn. Hannah had said the same thing then—that they were good-looking guys. That *would* be what Hannah would remember, Ruth thought.

"Eddie and I remembered the featured photograph in the kitchen— the one of both boys eating lobster," Ruth went on. "Thomas is dismantling his lobster with the ease and dispassion of a scientist—there's not the slightest strain on his face. Whereas it's as if Timothy is *fighting* his lobster, and the lobster's winning! I think that's the picture I remember best. And all these years I wondered if I invented it or if it was real. Eddie said it was the one *he* remembered best, so it must be real."

"Didn't you ever ask your father about the photographs?" Hannah asked. "Surely he would remember them better than you or Eddie."

"He was so angry at my mother for taking them with her that he refused to talk about them," Ruth answered.

"You're too hard on him," Hannah told her. "I think he's charming."

"I've seen him be 'charming' a few too many times," Ruth told Hannah. "Besides, all he ever *is* is charming—especially when he's around *you*." Uncharacteristically, Hannah let Ruth's remark pass.

It was Hannah's theory that many women who had known Marion (even if only by a photograph) must have been flattered by Ted Cole's attentions to them—simply because of how beautiful Marion had been. Ruth's response to Hannah's theory was: "I'm sure that must have made my mother feel *terrific.*"

Now Ruth felt frankly tired of trying to explain the importance of her evening with Eddie to Hannah. Hannah just wasn't getting it.

"But what did Eddie say about the *sex?* Or *did* he say anything about it?" Hannah asked.

It's absolutely all she's interested in! Ruth thought. Ruth despaired of talking about sex, because that subject would soon lead Hannah back to her questions regarding when Ruth was going to "do it" with Allan.

"That photograph you remember so well," Ruth began. "My good-looking brothers in the doorway of the Main Academy Building ..."

"What about it?" Hannah asked.

"Eddie told me that my mother made love to him under that photograph," Ruth reported. "It was the first time they did it. My mother left the photo for Eddie, but my father took it."

"And he hung it in his *bedroom!*" Hannah whispered harshly. "*That's* interesting!"

"What a remarkable memory you have, Hannah," Ruth said. "You even remember that the photograph of my brothers is in my father's bedroom!" But Hannah made no response, and Ruth thought again: I'm tired of this conversation. (She was most of all tired of Hannah never saying she was sorry.)

Ruth sometimes wondered if Hannah would still be her friend if Ruth hadn't become famous. In her own way—in the smaller world of magazines—Hannah was famous, too. She'd first made a name for herself writing personal essays. She'd kept a comedic diary; for the most part, it was a journal of her sexual exploits. But she'd soon tired of autobiography. Hannah had "graduated" to death and devastation.

In her morbid phase, Hannah had interviewed people who were dying; she'd devoted herself to terminal cases. Terminal *children* had captured her attention for about eighteen months. Later there'd been a piece on a burn ward, and one on a leper colony, too. She'd traveled to war zones, and to countries with widespread famine.

Then Hannah had "graduated" once again; she'd left death and devastation for the world of the perverse and the bizarre. She once wrote about a male porn star who was reputed to have a perpetual hard-on—

his name, in the business, was "Mr. Metal." Hannah had also interviewed a Belgian woman in her seventies who'd performed in over three thousand live-sex shows; her only partner had been her husband, who'd died following a sex performance. The grieving widow had not had sex since. Not only had she been faithful to her husband for forty years; for the last twenty years of their marriage, they'd had sex *only* in front of an audience.

Now Hannah had transformed herself yet again. Her current interest was famous people, which in the United States meant mainly movie stars and sports heroes and the occasional eccentric who was disturbingly rich. Hannah had never interviewed a writer, although she'd raised the subject of an "extensive"—or had Hannah said "exhaustive"?—interview with Ruth.

Ruth had long believed that the *only* interesting thing about herself was her writing. She was deeply leery of the idea of Hannah interviewing her, because Hannah was more interested in Ruth's personal life than she was in Ruth's novels. And what *did* interest Hannah in Ruth's writing was what was personal—what Hannah would have called "real"—about it.

Hannah will probably *hate* Allan, Ruth suddenly thought. Allan had already admitted that Ruth's fame was, if not a burden, a nuisance to him. He had edited a number of famous authors, but he would submit to an interview only on the grounds that his remarks were "not for attribution." Allan was so private that he didn't even permit his writers to dedicate their books to him; when one writer had insisted, Allan said, "Only if you use my initials, *just* my initials." Thus the book was dedicated: TO A.F.A. It struck Ruth as disloyal that she couldn't recall what the *F.* stood for.

"I gotta go—I think I hear him," Hannah was whispering.

"You're not going to stand me up in Sagaponack, are you?" Ruth asked. "I'm counting on you to save me from my father."

"I'll be there. I'll get myself there somehow," Hannah whispered. "I think it's your father who needs saving from *you*—the poor man."

Since when had her father become "the poor man"? But Ruth was tired; she let Hannah's remark pass.

After she'd hung up the phone, Ruth reconsidered her plans. Since she was not seeing Allan for dinner the next night, she could leave for Sagaponack after her last interview, a day earlier than she'd planned; then she would have one night alone with her father. *One* night alone with him might be tolerable. Hannah would arrive the next day, and they would have a night together—just the three of them.

Ruth couldn't wait to tell her father how much she had liked Eddie O'Hare—not to mention some of the things that Eddie had told her about her mother. It would be best if Hannah was *not* there when Ruth told her father that her mother had thought of leaving him *before* the boys had been killed. Ruth didn't want Hannah around for that conversation, because Hannah always stood up for Ruth's father—maybe just to provoke her.

Ruth was still so irritated with Hannah that she had some difficulty falling back to sleep. Lying awake, she found herself remembering the time she lost her virginity. It was impossible for her to recall the event without considering Hannah's contribution to the minor disaster.

Although she was a year younger than Ruth, Hannah had always seemed older, not only because Hannah had had three abortions before Ruth managed to lose her virginity but also because Hannah's greater sexual experience lent her an air of maturity and sophistication.

Ruth had been sixteen, Hannah fifteen when they'd met—yet Hannah had demonstrated greater sexual confidence. (And this was before Hannah had had sex!) In her diary, Ruth once wrote of Hannah: "She projected an aura of worldliness long before she'd been in the world."

Hannah's parents, who were happily married—she called them "boring" and "staid"—had brought up their only child in a fine old house on Brattle Street in Cambridge, Massachusetts. Hannah's father, a professor at Harvard Law School, had a patrician demeanor; his deportment bespoke a steadfast inclination to remain *uninvolved,* which Hannah said suited a man who'd married a wealthy and utterly unambitious woman.

Ruth had always liked Hannah's mother, who was good-natured and gracious to the point of being utterly benign. She also read a great deal—one never saw her without a book. Mrs. Grant had once told Ruth that she'd had only one child because, after Hannah was born, she missed all the time she'd once had to read. Hannah told Ruth that her mother couldn't wait for Hannah to be old enough to amuse herself so that Mrs. Grant could get back to her books. And "amuse herself," Hannah did. (Perhaps it was her mother who'd made Hannah the superficial and impatient reader that she was.)

While Ruth thought Hannah was fortunate to have a father who was faithful to his wife, Hannah said that a little womanizing might have made her father less predictable; to Hannah, "less predictable" meant "more interesting." She claimed that her father's remoteness was the result of his years in the law school, where his abstract ruminations on the *theoretical* levels of the law appeared to have distanced him from any appreciation of the *practice* of law itself. He had a great disdain for lawyers.

Professor Grant had urged the study of foreign languages on his daughter; his highest hope for Hannah was for her to pursue a career in international banking. (International banking had been where the best and the brightest of his students at Harvard Law School had ended up.)

Her father had a great disdain for journalists, too. Hannah was at Middlebury, where she was majoring in French and German, when she decided that journalism was the career for her. She knew this with the same certainty that Ruth had known, at an earlier age, that she wanted to be a novelist. Hannah announced with a most matter-of-fact surety that she would go to New York and make her way in the world of magazines. To that end, upon her graduation from college, she asked her parents to send her to Europe for a year. There she could practice her French and German, and she would keep a journal; her "powers of observation," as Hannah put it, "would be honed."

Ruth, who'd applied (and been accepted) to the graduate program in creative writing at the University of Iowa, had been caught off guard by Hannah's suggestion that Ruth come to Europe with her. "If you're going to be a writer, you need something to write *about*," Hannah had told her friend.

Ruth already knew that it didn't work that way—at least not for her. She needed only *time* to write; what she would write about already awaited her in her imagination. But she deferred her acceptance to Iowa. After all, her father could afford it. And a year in Europe with Hannah would be *fun*.

"Besides," Hannah told her, "it's high time you got laid. If you stick with me, it's bound to happen."

It had not happened in London, the first city on their tour, but Ruth was groped by a boy in the bar of the Royal Court Hotel. She'd met him at the National Portrait Gallery, where Ruth had gone to see the portraits of several of her favorite writers. The young man took her to the theater, and to an expensive Italian restaurant off Sloane Square. He was an American who lived in London; his father was a diplomat of some kind. He was the first boy she'd gone out with who'd had credit cards, although Ruth suspected that the cards belonged to his father.

They'd got drunk in the bar of the Royal Court, *instead of* getting laid, because Hannah was already "using" Ruth and Hannah's room at the Royal Court by the time Ruth got up the nerve to bring the young man to her hotel. Hannah was noisily making love to a Lebanese she'd picked up in a bank; she'd met him when she was cashing a traveler's check. ("My first experience in the field of international banking," she'd written in her journal. "My father would finally have been proud of me.")

The second city on their European tour was Stockholm. Contrary to Hannah's prediction, not all Swedes were blond. The two young men who picked up Hannah and Ruth were dark-haired and handsome; they were still at the university, yet they were very sure of themselves, and one of them—the one who ended up with Ruth—spoke excellent English. The slightly better-looking one, who spoke hardly a word of English, had immediately latched on to Hannah.

Ruth's designated young man drove the four of them to his parents' house, which was three quarters of an hour from Stockholm. His parents were away for the weekend.

It was a modern house with lots of light-colored wood. Ruth's young man, whose name was Per, poached a salmon with some dill, which they ate with new potatoes and a salad of watercress and hard-boiled eggs with chives. Hannah and Ruth drank two bottles of white wine while the boys drank beer, and then the slightly better-looking boy took Hannah off to one of the guest bedrooms.

It was not the first time that Ruth had overheard Hannah making love, but it was somehow different, knowing that the young man with Hannah couldn't speak English—and because, the entire time that Hannah was grunting away, Ruth and Per were washing the dishes.

Per kept saying, "I'm awfully glad your friend is having *such* a grand time."

And Ruth kept saying, "Hannah *always* has a grand time."

Ruth wished there were more dishes to wash, but she knew she had stalled long enough. Finally she said: "I'm a virgin."

"Do you still want to be?" Per asked her.

"No, but I'm very nervous," she warned him.

She also thrust a condom at him before he had even begun to take off his clothes. Hannah's three pregnancies had taught Ruth a thing or two; albeit belatedly, they had even taught a thing or two to Hannah.

But when Ruth thrust a condom at Per, the young Swede looked surprised. "Are you sure you're a virgin?" he asked her. "I've never been with a virgin."

Per was nearly as nervous as Ruth was, which Ruth appreciated. He'd also had too much beer, which he remarked on, mid-coitus. *"Öl,"* he said in her ear, which Ruth mistook as an announcement that he was coming. On the contrary, he was apologizing for why it was taking him so long to come. (*Öl* is Swedish for *beer.*)

But Ruth had no experience to compare this to; their lovemaking was neither too long nor too short for her. Her principal motivation was to have the experience behind her, to simply (at last) have *done* it. She felt nothing.

So, thinking it proper sex etiquette in Sweden, Ruth said *"Öl,"* too, although she wasn't coming.

When Per withdrew from her, he seemed disappointed that there was not more blood. He'd expected a virgin to bleed *a lot.* Ruth assumed this meant that the whole experience had been less than he'd expected.

It was definitely less than *she'd* expected. Less fun, less passion, even less pain. It had *all* been less. It made it hard to imagine what Hannah Grant had been so fiercely *grunting* about for all these years.

But what Ruth Cole learned from her very first experience in Sweden was that the *consequences* of sex are often more memorable than the act itself. For Hannah, there were no consequences that she considered worth remembering; not even her three abortions had deterred her from repeating and repeating the act, which she apparently found to be of far greater importance than whatever its consequences were.

But on the morning when Per's parents returned home, greatly ahead of schedule, Ruth was alone and naked in Per's parents' bed. Per was taking a shower when his mother walked into her bedroom and began speaking Swedish to Ruth.

In addition to not understanding the woman, Ruth could not find her clothes—nor could Per hear his mother's sharply rising voice over the sound of his shower.

Then Per's father walked into the bedroom. While Per may have been disappointed in how little Ruth had bled, Ruth saw that she had bled on the towel she'd spread on the bed. (She had conscientiously taken pains, in advance, not to stain Per's parents' sheets.) Now, as she hastily tried to cover herself with the bloodstained towel, she was aware that Per's mother and father had seen all of her *and* her blood.

Per's father, a dour-looking man, was speechless; yet his staring at Ruth was as unremitting as his wife's mounting hysteria.

It was Hannah who helped Ruth find her clothes. Hannah also had the presence of mind to open the bathroom door and yell at Per to get out of the shower. "Tell your mother to stop shouting at my friend!" Hannah had yelled at him. Then she'd yelled at Per's mother, too. "Shout at your *son*, not at *her*—you dumb cunt!"

But Per's mother could not stop herself from shouting at Ruth, and Per was too cowardly—or too easily convinced that he and Ruth were in the wrong—to oppose his mother.

As for Ruth, she was as incapable of decisive movement as she was of coherent speech. She mutely let Hannah dress her, like a child.

"Poor baby," Hannah said to her. "What lousy luck for your first time. It usually ends up better than this."

"The sex was okay," Ruth mumbled.

"Just 'okay'?" Hannah asked her. "Did you hear that, you limp dick?" Hannah shouted at Per. "She says you were just 'okay.' "

Then Hannah noticed that Per's father was still staring at Ruth, and she shouted at him. "Hey, you—fuckface!" she called him. "Do you get off on *gawking*, or what?"

"Shall I call you and your companion a cab?" Per's father asked Hannah, in English even better than his son's.

"If you can understand me," Hannah said to him, "tell your abusive bitch of a wife to stop shouting at my friend—tell her to shout at your jerk-off son instead!"

"Young lady," Per's father said, "my words have had no discernible effect on my wife for years."

Ruth would remember the elder Swede's stately sadness better than she would ever remember the craven Per. And when Per's father had stared at her nakedness, it was not lust that Ruth saw in his eyes—only his crippling envy of his lucky son.

In the taxi riding back to Stockholm, Hannah had asked Ruth: "Wasn't Hamlet's father a Swede? And his bitch of a mother, too—*and* the bad uncle, I suppose. Not to mention the dumb girl who drowns herself. Weren't they all Swedes?"

"No, they were Danes," Ruth replied. She took a grim satisfaction from the fact that she was still bleeding, if only a little.

"Swedes, Danes—same difference," Hannah said. "They're all assholes."

Later Hannah had announced: "I'm sorry your sex was just 'okay'—mine was terrific. He had the biggest schlong I've ever seen, so far," she added.

"Why is bigger better?" Ruth had asked. "I didn't look at Per's," she'd admitted. "Was I supposed to?"

"Poor baby. Don't worry," Hannah had told her. "Remember to look at it the next time. Anyway, it's how it *feels* that matters."

"It felt okay, I guess," Ruth had said. "It just wasn't what I expected."

"Did you expect worse or better?" Hannah had asked her.

"I think I expected worse *and* better," Ruth had replied.

"That'll happen," Hannah had told her. "You can count on it: you'll definitely have worse and better."

At least Hannah had been right about that. At last Ruth fell back to sleep.

Ted at Seventy-Seven

He didn't look a day over *fifty*-seven, of course. It was not merely a matter of the squash keeping him fit, although it troubled Ruth that her father's trim, compact body, which was the prototype of her own body, had established itself in her mind's eye as the model of the male form. Ted had kept himself small. (In addition to Allan Albright's habit of eating off other people's plates, there was the problem of Allan's size: he was much taller and a little heavier than the men Ruth generally preferred.)

But Ruth's theory, in regard to how her father had failed to age, was separate from her father's physical fitness or his size. Ted's forehead was unlined; there were no pouches under his eyes. Ruth's crow's-feet were almost as pronounced as his. The skin of her father's face was so smooth and clean that it might have been the face of a boy who'd only begun to shave, or who needed to shave only twice a week.

Since Marion had left him, and—retching squid ink into a toilet—he'd sworn off hard liquor (he drank only beer and wine), Ted slept as soundly as a child. And however much he'd suffered from the loss of his sons—and, later, from losing their photographs—he appeared to have put his suffering to rest. Maybe the man's most infuriating gift was how soundly, and for how long, he could *sleep*!

In Ruth's view, her father was a man without a conscience *or* the usual anxieties; he felt no stress. As Marion had observed, Ted did almost nothing; as an author and illustrator of children's books, he had already succeeded (as long ago as 1942) in excess of his small ambitions. He hadn't written anything in years, but he didn't have to; Ruth wondered if he had ever really *wanted* to.

The Mouse Crawling Between the Walls, The Door in the Floor, A Sound Like Someone Trying Not to Make a Sound ... there wasn't a bookstore anywhere in the world (with a decent children's section) that didn't carry Ted Cole's backlist. There were videocassettes, too; Ted had provided the drawings for the animation. About all Ted did now was draw.

And if his celebrity status had dimmed in the Hamptons, Ted was in demand elsewhere. Every summer he seduced at least one mother at a fair-weather writers' conference in California, and another at a conference in Colorado, and another in Vermont. He was also popular on college campuses—especially at state universities in out-of-the-way states. With occasional exceptions, today's college students were too young to be seduced by even as ageless a man as Ted was, but the neglected loneliness among faculty wives whose children had grown up and left home was unabated; those women were still younger women to Ted.

Between the writers' conferences and the college campuses, it was surprising that, in thirty-two years, Ted Cole had never crossed paths with Eddie O'Hare, but Eddie had taken pains to avoid such an encounter. For him, it was merely a matter of inquiring who comprised the guest faculty and the visiting lecturers; whenever Eddie had heard Ted's name, he'd declined the invitation.

And, if her crow's-feet were any indication, Ruth despaired that she was showing her age more than her father showed his. Worse, she was deeply concerned that her father's low opinion of marriage might have made a lasting impression on her.

On the occasion of her thirtieth birthday, which she'd celebrated with her father and Hannah in New York, Ruth had made an uncharacteristically lighthearted remark on the subject of her few and fast-failing relationships with men.

"Well, Daddy," she'd said to him, "you probably thought I'd be married by now, and that you could stop worrying about me."

"No, Ruthie," he'd told her. "It's when you *are* married that I'll *start* worrying about you."

"Yeah, why get married?" Hannah had said. "You can have all the guys you want."

"All men are basically unfaithful, Ruthie," her father had said. He'd already told her that—even before she went to Exeter, when she'd been fifteen!—but he found a way to repeat it, at least semiannually.

"However, if I want a child ..." Ruth had said. She knew Hannah's opinion of having a child; Hannah didn't want one. And Ruth was well aware of her father's point of view: that to have a child was to live in constant fear that something would happen to your child—not to mention the evidence that Ruth's mother had (in her father's words) "failed the mother test."

"*Do* you want to have a child, Ruthie?" her father had asked her.

"I don't know," Ruth had admitted.

"There's a lot of time to stay single, then," Hannah had told her.

But now she was thirty-six; if Ruth wanted a child, there was not a lot of time left. And when she'd merely *mentioned* Allan Albright to her father, Ted Cole had said: "What is he? Twelve, fifteen years older than you are, isn't he?" (Because her father knew everything about everyone in publishing. Ted may have stopped writing, but he kept up with the *business* of writing.)

"Allan is eighteen years older than I am, Daddy," Ruth had acknowledged. "But he's like you. He's very healthy."

"I don't care how healthy he is," Ted had said. "If he's eighteen years older than you are, he's going to die on you, Ruthie. And what if he leaves you with a young child to raise? All by yourself ..."

The specter of raising a young child by herself had haunted her. She knew how lucky both she and her father had been; Conchita Gomez had virtually raised Ruth. But Eduardo and Conchita were her father's age, the difference being that they *looked* it. If Ruth didn't have a baby sometime soon, Conchita would be too old to help her raise it. And how could Conchita help Ruth raise a baby, anyway? The Gomezes still worked for her father.

As usual, when it came to the subject of marriage and children, Ruth had put the cart before the horse; she was jumping ahead to the question of having a child before she'd answered the question of whom, or whether, to marry. And Ruth had no one she could talk to about this, except Allan. Her best friend didn't want a child—Hannah was Hannah—and her father was . . . well, her father. Now, even more than when she'd been a child, Ruth wanted to talk to her mother.

Damn her, anyway! Ruth thought. Ruth had long ago resolved that she would not go looking for her mother. Marion was the one who'd left. Either Marion would come back or she wouldn't.

And what sort of man had no male friends? Ruth reflected. She'd once put the accusation to her father directly.

"I *have* male friends!" her father had protested.

"Name two, name just *one!*" Ruth had challenged him.

To her surprise, he'd named four. They were unfamiliar names to her. He'd boldly listed his current squash opponents; their names changed every few years because Ted's opponents invariably grew too old to keep up with him. His present opponents were Eddie's age or younger. Ruth had met the youngest of them.

Her father had the swimming pool he'd always wanted, and the outdoor shower—much as he'd described his image of them to Eduardo and Eddie in the summer of '58, on the morning after Marion had left. There were two showers in a single wooden stall, side by side—"locker room–style," Ted called it.

Ruth had grown up watching naked men, and her naked father, running out of the outdoor shower and jumping into the pool. As sexually inexperienced as she was, Ruth had *seen* a lot of penises. It was perhaps this image, of unknown men showering and swimming naked with her father, that had caused Ruth to question Hannah's assumption that *bigger* was necessarily *better*.

It had been a year ago last summer when she'd "met" her father's youngest squash opponent of the moment, a lawyer in his late thirties—Scott Somebody. She'd come out on the deck of the swimming pool to dry her beach towel and her swimming suit on the line, and there were her father and his young opponent in their après-squash or après-shower nakedness.

"Ruthie, this is Scott. My daughter, Ruth ..." Ted had started to say, but Scott saw her and dove into the pool. "He's a lawyer," her father had added, while Scott was still underwater. Then Scott Somebody had surfaced in the deep end, where he began to tread water. He was a strawberry blond and built like her father. He had a medium-size schlong, she thought.

"Nice to meet you, Ruth," the young lawyer had said. He had short, curly hair and freckles.

"Nice to meet *you*, Scott," Ruth had replied, going back inside the house.

Her father, still standing naked on the deck, had remarked to Scott: "I can't decide whether to go in or not. Is it cold? It was quite cold yesterday."

"It's pretty cold," Ruth had heard Scott say. "But it's okay, once you're in."

And these ever-changing squash opponents were what passed for Ted's only male friends! Nor were her father's opponents very good squash players; her father didn't like to lose. His most frequent opponents were good athletes who were relatively new to the game. In the winter months, Ted found a lot of tennis players who wanted the exercise; they had a feeling for racquet sports, but squash strokes are not tennis strokes—squash is a game you play with your wrist. In the summer, when the tennis players would return to their tennis, they would discover that their game had deteriorated—you can't play tennis with your wrist. Then Ted might have a convert to squash on his hands.

Her father chose his squash opponents as selfishly, and with as great a degree of calculation, as he chose his lovers. Maybe they *were* his only friends. Was her father invited to their homes for dinner? Did he hit on their wives? Did her father have *any* rules? Ruth wanted to know.

She was standing on the south side of Forty-first Street, between Lexington and Third, waiting for the jitney that would take her to the Hamptons. Once she arrived in Bridgehampton, she would call her father to pick her up.

Ruth had already tried to call him, but her father was out, or not answering the phone, and he'd left his answering machine off. Ruth had a lot of luggage—all the clothes she would need in Europe. She was thinking that she should have called Eduardo or Conchita Gomez. If they weren't doing something for her father, or actually working at her father's house, the Gomezes were always home. Thus her mind was beset with the trivia of last-minute travel when her father's youngest squash opponent approached her on the sidewalk of Forty-first Street.

"Going home?" Scott Somebody asked her. "You're Ruth Cole, aren't you?"

Ruth was used to being recognized. At first she mistook him for one of her readers. Then she noted his boyish freckles and his short, curly hair; she'd not known many strawberry blonds. Besides, he was carrying nothing but a slim briefcase and a gym bag; two squash racquets protruded from the half-open zipper of the bag.

"Oh, it's the *swimmer*," Ruth said. It was strangely satisfying to see him blush.

It was a warm, sunny Indian Summer day. Scott Somebody had removed his suit jacket and looped it through the shoulder strap of his gym bag; his tie was loosened, and the sleeves of his white shirt were rolled up above his elbows. Ruth was aware of the greater size and muscularity of his left forearm, even as he held his right hand out to her.

"It's Scott, Scott Saunders," he reminded her, shaking her hand.

"You're left-handed, aren't you?" Ruth asked him. Her father was a lefty. Ruth didn't like to play left-handers. Her best serve was to the left-hand court; a lefty could return that serve with his forehand.

"Got your racquet with you?" Scott Saunders asked her, after admitting he was left-handed. He'd noticed all her luggage.

"I've got three racquets with me," Ruth replied. "They're packed."

"Staying with your dad for a while?" the lawyer asked.

"Only two nights," Ruth said. "Then I'm going to Europe."

"Oh," Scott said. "Business?"

"Translations—yes."

She already knew they were going to sit together on the bus. Maybe he had a car parked in Bridgehampton; then *he* could drive her (*and* all her luggage) to Sagaponack. Maybe his wife was meeting him and they wouldn't mind dropping her off. In the pool, his wedding ring had reflected the late-afternoon sunlight as he'd treaded water. But when they were seated beside each other on the jitney, his wedding ring was gone. Among Ruth's rules for relationships, one of the inviolable ones was this: no married men.

There was the shattering sound of an airplane overhead—the bus was passing LaGuardia—when Ruth said, "Let me guess. My father has converted you from tennis to squash. And with your complexion... you're very fair, you must burn easily ... squash is better for your skin, anyway. It keeps you out of the sun."

He had a wicked, secretive sort of smile; it suggested his suspicion that nearly everything could lead to litigation. Scott Saunders was *not* a nice guy. Ruth felt pretty sure of that.

"Actually," he began, "I gave up tennis for squash when I got divorced. As part of the settlement, my ex-wife got to keep the country-club membership. It meant a lot to her," he added generously. "And besides, there were the children's swimming lessons."

"How old are your children?" Ruth asked him dutifully.

Hannah had told her long ago that it was the first question you should ask a guy who's divorced. "It makes divorced men feel like good fathers to *talk* about their kids," Hannah had said. "And, if you're gonna get involved with the guy, you want to know if it's a three-year-old or a teenager you might have to deal with—it makes a difference."

As the jitney moved eastward, Ruth had already forgotten the ages of Scott Saunders's children; she was more interested in how his squash game compared to her father's.

"Oh, he usually wins," the lawyer admitted. "After he wins the first three or four games, he sometimes lets me win one or two."

"You play that many games?" Ruth asked. "Five or six?"

"We play for at least an hour, often an hour and a half," Scott said. "We don't really count the number of games."

You wouldn't last an hour and a half with *me,* Ruth decided. The old man must be slipping. But all she said was: "You must like to run."

"I'm in pretty good shape," Scott Saunders said. He looked in *very* good shape, but Ruth let his remark pass; she gazed out the window, knowing that he was taking this moment to evaluate her breasts. (She could see his reflection in the bus window.) "Your father says you're a very good player, better than most men," the lawyer added. "But he says he's still better than you—for a few more years."

"He's wrong," Ruth said. "He's *not* better than I am. He's just smart enough to never play me on a court of regulation size. And he knows his barn—he never plays me anywhere else."

"There's probably something psychological about his advantage," the lawyer said.

"I'll beat him," Ruth said. "Then maybe I'll stop playing."

"Maybe we could play sometime," Scott Saunders said. "My kids are only around on the weekends. Today is Tuesday ..."

"You don't work Tuesdays?" Ruth asked.

She watched the bright flicker in his smile again—like a secret he wanted you to know existed, but which he would never tell. "I'm enjoying divorce leave," he told her. "I take as much time out of the office as I need."

"Do they really call it 'divorce leave'?" Ruth asked.

"That's what *I* call it," the lawyer said. "When it comes to the office, I'm pretty independent." He said it in the way he'd said he was in pretty good shape. It could mean that he'd just been fired, or that he was some killer lawyer with uncounted successes.

Here I go again, Ruth knew. She considered that the wrong guys always attracted her because they were so transparently short-term.

"Maybe we could play a little round-robin," Scott suggested. "You know, the three of us. You play your father, your father plays me, then I play you ..."

"I don't play round-robin," Ruth said. "I just play one-on-one, for a long time. About two hours," she added, purposely staring out the window so he was left looking at her breasts.

"Two hours ..." he repeated.

"Just kidding," she told him. Turning to face him, she smiled.

"Oh ..." Scott Saunders said. "Maybe we could play tomorrow, just the two of us."

"I want to beat my father first," Ruth said.

She knew that Allan Albright was the next person she should sleep with, but it troubled her that she'd needed to remind herself of Allan—and of what she *should* do. Historically, Scott Saunders was more her kind of guy.

The strawberry-blond lawyer had parked his car near the Little League field in Bridgehampton; he and Ruth, burdened by her luggage, had to walk about two hundred yards. Scott drove with the windows open. As they turned onto Parsonage Lane in Sagaponack, they were moving due east with the elongated shadow of the car running ahead of them. To the south, the slanting light turned the potato fields a jade-green color; the ocean, offset against the faded blue of the sky, was as brilliant and as deep a blue as a sapphire.

For everything that was overesteemed and corrupted about the Hamptons, the end of an early-fall day could still be dazzling; Ruth permitted herself to feel that the place was redeemed, if only at this time of year and at this forgiving hour of the late afternoon. Her father would have just finished his squash; he and his defeated opponent might now be showering or swimming naked in the pool.

The towering horseshoe-shaped barrier of privet that Eduardo had planted in the fall of '58 completely shaded the pool from the late-afternoon light. The hedges were so thick, only the thinnest rays of the sun could penetrate; these small diamonds of light dappled the dark water of the pool, like phosphorescence—or gold coins that floated on the surface instead of sinking. And the wooden deck overhung the water; when someone was swimming in the pool, the water sounded like the water of a lake slapping against a dock.

When they arrived at the house, Scott helped Ruth carry her bags into the front hall. The navy-blue Volvo, which was her father's only car, was in the driveway, but her father didn't answer when Ruth called.

"Daddy?"

As he was leaving, Scott said, "He's probably in the pool—it's that time of day."

"Yes," Ruth said. "Thank you!" she called after him. Oh, Allan, save me! she thought. Ruth was hoping she'd never see Scott Saunders, or another man like him, again.

She had three bags: a big suitcase, a garment bag, and a smaller suitcase that was her carry-on bag for the plane. She started by taking the garment bag and the smaller suitcase upstairs. Some years ago, when she was nine or ten, she'd moved her room from the nursery that shared her father's master bathroom to the biggest and farthest-away of the guest bedrooms; it was the room that Eddie O'Hare had occupied in the summer of '58. Ruth liked it because of its distance from her father's room, and because it had its own bathroom.

The door to the master bedroom was ajar, but her father wasn't in his bedroom—Ruth called "Daddy?" again as she passed the slightly open door. As always, the photographs in the long upstairs hall commanded her attention.

All the bare picture hooks, which she remembered better than the photos of her dead brothers, were covered now; there were hundreds of uninspired photographs of Ruth, at every phase of her childhood and throughout her young womanhood. Sometimes her father was in the photo, but usually he was the photographer. Frequently, Conchita Gomez was in the picture with Ruth. And there were the endless privet pictures. These measured her growth, summer by summer: Ruth and Eduardo, solemnly posed before the implacable privet. No matter how much Ruth grew, the unstoppable hedge grew faster, until—one day—it had more than doubled Eduardo's height. (In several of the photographs, Eduardo looked a little afraid of the privet.) And of course there were some recent photographs of Ruth with Hannah.

Ruth was walking barefoot down the carpeted stairs when she heard the splashing from the swimming pool, which was behind the house. She couldn't see the pool from the staircase, or from any of the bedrooms upstairs. All the bedrooms faced south; they were designed to have an ocean view.

Ruth hadn't noticed another car in the driveway—only her father's navy-blue Volvo—but she assumed that his present squash opponent lived near enough to have ridden a bicycle; she wouldn't have noticed a bicycle.

The degree to which Scott Saunders had tempted her left Ruth feeling familiarly unsure of herself. She didn't want to see another man today, although she seriously doubted that any of her father's *other* squash opponents could possibly have attracted her as strongly as the strawberry-blond lawyer.

In the front hall, she got a good grip on her remaining suitcase—the big one—and started upstairs with it, purposely avoiding that view of the swimming pool which was available to her as she passed the dining room. The sound of splashing followed her only halfway up the stairs. By the time she unpacked, the guy, whoever he was, would be gone. But Ruth was a veteran traveler; it took her very little time to unpack. When she'd finished, she put on her swimsuit. After her father's squash opponent was gone, Ruth thought she would jump in the pool. That always felt good, after being in the city. Then she would see about dinner. She would make her daddy a good dinner. Then they would talk.

She was still barefoot, padding down the upstairs hall, past the partially open door to her father's bedroom, when a sea breeze blew the door shut. Thinking she would find a book or a shoe, something to hold the door ajar, Ruth opened the door to the master bedroom. The first thing that caught her eye was a woman's high-heeled shoe of a beautiful salmon-pink color. Ruth picked it up. It was very good leather; the shoe had been made in Milan. Ruth saw that the bed was unmade—a small black bra lay on top of the tangled sheets.

So . . . her father was *not* in the pool with one of his squash opponents. Ruth took a closer, more critical look at the bra. It was a push-up bra, an expensive one; it would have been utterly gratuitous for Ruth to wear a push-up bra, but the woman in the pool with her father must have thought she needed one. The woman had small breasts—the bra was a 32B.

That was when Ruth recognized the open suitcase on the floor of her father's bedroom. It was a well-worn brown leather suitcase distinguished by its much-traveled appearance and its practical compartments and its useful, efficient straps. It had been Hannah's carry-on bag for as long as Ruth had known Hannah. ("The bag made Hannah look like a journalist before she was a journalist," Ruth had written in her diary—she couldn't remember how many years ago.)

Ruth stood as still in her father's bedroom as she would have stood if Hannah and her father had been naked in bed in front of her. The sea breeze blew through the bedroom window again; it blew shut the door behind her. Ruth felt as if she'd been locked in a closet. If something had brushed against her (a dress on a hanger), she would have fainted or screamed.

She struggled to summon that state of calm in which she composed her novels. Ruth thought of a novel as a great, untidy house, a disorderly mansion; her job was to make the place fit to live in, to give it at least the semblance of order. Only when she wrote was she unafraid.

When Ruth was afraid, she had difficulty breathing. Fear paralyzed her; as a child, the sudden proximity of a spider would freeze her on the spot. Once, behind a closed door, an unseen dog had barked at her; she'd not been able to remove her hand from the doorknob.

Now the thought of Hannah with her father took her breath away. Ruth had to make an enormous effort just to move. At first she moved very slowly. She folded the small black bra and put it in Hannah's open suitcase. She found Hannah's other shoe—it was under the bed—and she put the pair of salmon-pink shoes alongside the suitcase, where they could not be missed. In what Ruth knew would be the haste of things to come, she wanted Hannah not to leave any of her sexy little items behind.

Before Ruth left her father's bedroom, she looked at the photograph of her dead brothers in the doorway of the Main Academy Building. She considered that Hannah's memory was not as remarkable as she'd supposed when they'd talked on the phone.

So ... Hannah stood me up because she was fucking my father, Ruth thought. She walked into the upstairs hall, taking off her swimsuit as she went. She looked in the two smaller guest bedrooms. Both beds were made, but one was dented with the shape of a slender body, and the pillows were bunched up against the headboard of the bed. The phone, normally on the night table, sat on the side of the bed. It had been from this guest bedroom that Hannah had phoned her, whispering, so as not to wake Ruth's father—after she had fucked him.

Ruth was naked now; she trailed the swimsuit behind her as she continued down the hall to her room. There she dressed herself in more characteristic clothes: jeans, one of the good bras Hannah had bought for her, a black T-shirt. For what she was about to do, she wanted to be in her uniform.

Then Ruth went downstairs into the kitchen. Hannah, a lazy cook but an adequate one, had been planning to stir-fry some vegetables; she'd cut up a red and a yellow pepper and had tossed them in a bowl with some broccoli florets. The vegetables were sweating slightly. Ruth tasted one of the pieces of the yellow pepper. Hannah had sprinkled the vegetables with salt and sugar to make them bleed a little. Ruth recalled showing Hannah how to do that on one of the weekends they'd spent together at Ruth's house in Vermont—complaining about bad boyfriends, as Ruth now remembered it.

Hannah had also peeled a gingerroot, and mashed it; she'd set out the wok and the peanut oil, too. Ruth looked in the refrigerator and saw the shrimp marinating in a bowl. She was familiar with the dinner Hannah was preparing; Ruth had made this same dinner for Hannah, and for various boyfriends, many times. The only thing that wasn't ready to cook was the rice.

There were two bottles of white wine on the door of the refrigerator. Ruth took one out, opened it, and poured herself a glass. She walked into the dining room and out the screen door onto the terrace. When Hannah and her father heard the door close, they quickly swam away from each other, but both of them ended up in the deep end of the pool. They'd been squatting together in the shallow end—or else

Ruth's father had been squatting while Hannah bobbed in the water, in his lap.

Now, in the deep end, their heads were small against the sparkling field of blue. Hannah looked less blond than usual; her wet hair was dark. Ruth's father's hair was dark, too. His thick, wavy hair had turned a metallic shade of gray, generously streaked with white. But in the dark-blue pool, Ted's wet hair was almost black.

Hannah's head seemed as sleek as her body. She looks like a rat, Ruth thought. And Hannah's small breasts bounced as she treaded water. The image that came to Ruth's mind was that Hannah's little tits could have been darting, one-eyed fish.

"I got out here early," Hannah began, but Ruth cut her off.

"You were here last night. You called me after you fucked my father. I could have told you that he snored," Ruth said.

"Ruthie, don't ..." her father said.

"*You're* the one who has a problem with fucking, baby," Hannah told her.

"Hannah, don't ..." Ted said.

"Most civilized countries have laws," Ruth told them. "Most societies have rules ..."

"I've heard this!" Hannah called to her. Hannah's tiny face looked less confident than usual. But maybe it was only because Hannah wasn't a strong swimmer; treading water didn't come naturally to her.

"Most *families* have rules, Daddy," Ruth told her father. "Most *friends*, too," Ruth said to Hannah.

"Okay, okay—I'm lawlessness personified," Hannah told her friend.

"You never apologize, do you?" Ruth asked her.

"Okay, I'm *sorry*," Hannah said. "Does that make it better?"

"It was an accident—it was nothing planned," Ted told his daughter.

"That must have been a novelty for you, Daddy," Ruth said.

"We ran into each other in the city," Hannah began. "I saw him standing on the corner of Fifth and Fifty-ninth, by the Sherry-Netherland. He was waiting for the light to change."

"I'm sure I don't need to know the details," Ruth told them.

"You're always so superior!" Hannah cried. Then she started coughing. "I've gotta get out of this fucking pool before I drown!"

"You can get out of my house, too," Ruth told her. "Just get your things and go."

There was no ladder in Ted Cole's pool—ladders were not aesthetically pleasing to Ted. Hannah had to swim to the shallow end and walk up the steps, near Ruth.

"Since when is it *your* house," Hannah said. "I thought it was your father's."

"Hannah, *don't*..." Ted said again.

"I want you to get out of here, too, Daddy," Ruth told her father. "I want to be alone. I came home to be with you, and with my best friend," she added. "But now I want you both gone."

"I'm still your best friend, for Christ's sake," Hannah said to Ruth. She was wrapping herself in a towel—the scrawny little rat, Ruth thought.

"And I'm still your father, Ruthie. Nothing's changed," Ted said.

"What's *changed* is that I don't want to see you. I don't want to sleep in the same house with either of you," Ruth said.

"Ruthie, Ruthie..." her father said.

"I told you—she's a fucking princess, a prima donna," Hannah told Ted. "First you spoiled her—now the whole *world* is spoiling her." So they had talked about her, too.

"Hannah, don't..." Ruth's father said, but Hannah walked into the house, letting the screen door slam. Ted kept treading water in the deep end of the pool; he could tread water all day.

"I had a lot to talk to you about, Daddy," she told him.

"We can still talk, Ruthie. Nothing's changed," he repeated.

Ruth had finished her wine. She looked at her empty glass; then she threw it at her father's bobbing head. She missed him by a safe margin. The wineglass plunked into the water and sank, unbroken and dancing, like a ballet slipper, to the bottom of the deep end of the pool.

"I want to be alone," Ruth told her father again. "You wanted to fuck Hannah—now you can leave with her. Go on—just go with Hannah!"

"I'm sorry, Ruthie," her father said, but Ruth went into the house, leaving him to tread water.

Ruth stood in the kitchen; her knees shook a little when she washed the rice and let it drain in a sieve. She was sure she'd lost her appetite. To her relief, her father and Hannah didn't try to talk to her again.

Ruth heard Hannah's high-heeled shoes in the front hall; she could imagine how perfect those salmon-pink shoes looked on a slinky blonde. Then she heard the navy-blue Volvo—its wide tires crushing the stones in the driveway. (In the summer of '58, the driveway of the Coles' house in Sagaponack had been a dirt driveway, but Eduardo Gomez had convinced Ted to try crushed stones. Eduardo had got the idea for a driveway of crushed stones from the infamous driveway at Mrs. Vaughn's.)

Ruth stood in the kitchen, listening to the Volvo moving west on Parsonage Lane. Maybe her father would take Hannah back to New York. Maybe they would stay in Hannah's apartment. They should be too embarrassed to spend another night together, Ruth thought. But her father, although he could be sheepish, was never embarrassed—and Hannah wasn't even sorry! They would probably go to the American Hotel in Sag Harbor. And they would call later—both of them, but at different times. Ruth remembered that her father's answering machine was off; she resolved that she would not answer the phone.

But when the phone rang only an hour later, Ruth thought it might be Allan. She answered it.

"I'm still thinking about playing squash with you," Scott Saunders said.

"I'm not in the mood for squash," Ruth lied. There was a golden quality to his skin, she remembered; his freckles were the color of the beach.

"If I can steal you away from your father," Scott said, "how about dinner tomorrow night?"

Ruth had not been able to cook the dinner that Hannah had largely prepared; she knew she couldn't eat. "I'm sorry—I'm not in the mood for dinner," Ruth told the lawyer.

"Maybe you'll change your mind tomorrow," Scott said. Ruth could imagine his smile—the self-importance of it.

"Maybe . . ." Ruth confessed to him. Somehow she found the strength to hang up the phone.

She wouldn't answer it again, although it rang and rang for half the night. Each time it rang, she hoped it wasn't Allan and she wished she could bring herself to turn her father's answering machine on. Most of the calls, she was sure, were from Hannah or her father.

And although she'd not found the energy to eat, she'd succeeded in drinking both bottles of the white wine. She'd covered the cut vegetables with some plastic wrapping, and she'd covered and refrigerated the washed rice. The shrimp, which were still in the refrigerator, would keep well for a night in their marinade, but to be sure Ruth had added the juice of another lemon. Maybe she'd feel like eating something tomorrow night. (Maybe with Scott Saunders.)

She was sure her father would come back. She half-expected to see his car in the driveway in the morning. Ted enjoyed the martyr role; he would have loved to give Ruth the impression that he'd slept in the Volvo all night.

But in the morning the car wasn't there. The phone started ringing at seven A.M., and Ruth still wouldn't answer it. Now she tried to find her father's answering machine, but it was not in his workroom, where it usually was. Perhaps it had broken and he'd taken it somewhere to have it repaired.

Ruth regretted being in her father's workroom. Above his writing desk, where he wrote only letters nowadays, was the tacked-up list of names and phone numbers of his current squash opponents. Scott Saunders was at the top of the list. Oh, God—here I go again, she thought. There were two numbers for Saunders: his number in New York and a Bridgehampton number. She dialed the Bridgehampton number, of course. It was not yet seven-thirty; Ruth could tell by the sound of his voice that she'd awakened him.

"Are you still thinking about playing squash with me?" Ruth asked him.

"It's early," Scott said. "Have you beaten your father already?"

"I want to beat you first," Ruth told him.

"You can *try*," the lawyer said. "How about dinner after we play?"

"Let's see how the game goes," Ruth said.

"What time?" he asked her.

"The usual time—the same time you play with my father."

"I'll see you at five, then," Scott told her.

That would give Ruth the whole day to get ready for him. There were specific shots and serves she liked to practice before she played a left-hander. But her father was the lefty of all lefties; in the past, she had never been able to adequately prepare herself for him. Now she believed that playing Scott Saunders would be the perfect warm-up for playing her father.

Ruth began by calling Eduardo and Conchita. She didn't want them around the house. She told Conchita she was sorry that she wouldn't see her this visit, and Conchita did what she always did when she talked to Ruth—she cried. Ruth promised she would see Conchita when she was back from Europe, although Ruth doubted she would be visiting her father in Sagaponack then.

Ruth told Eduardo that she was going to write all day; she didn't want him mowing the lawn or clipping the hedges or doing whatever he did to the swimming pool. She needed to have a quiet day. On the outside chance that her father wouldn't come back in time to drive her to the airport tomorrow, Ruth told Eduardo that she would call him. Her flight to Munich left early Thursday evening; she wouldn't need to leave Sagaponack before two or three tomorrow afternoon.

It was like Ruth Cole to try to organize everything, to try to give her life the structure of her novels. ("You always think you can cover any contingency," Hannah had told her once. Ruth thought she could, or that she *should*.)

The one thing she should have done, but didn't, was call Allan. Instead she let the phone keep ringing, unanswered.

The two bottles of white wine had not given her a hangover, but they had left a sour taste in her mouth, and her stomach did not welcome the idea of any solid food for breakfast. Ruth found some strawberries, a peach, a banana. She put these in the blender with orange juice and three heaping tablespoons of her father's favorite protein powder; the drink tasted like cold, liquid oatmeal, but it made her feel as if she were bouncing off the walls, which was how she wanted to feel.

There were only four good shots in squash, she dogmatically believed.

In the morning, she'd practice her rail and her cross-court—good and deep, both of them. Also, there was a dead spot on the front wall of the barn; it was about thigh-high and a little to the left of center, well below the service line. Her father had sneakily marked the spot with a smudge of colored chalk. She would practice her aim at that spot. You could hit the ball as hard as you wanted, but if you hit that spot, the ball just died; it came off the wall like a drop shot. She would work on her hard serve in the morning, too. She wanted to hit all her hard shots in the morning. Afterward, she could ice her shoulder—maybe while sitting in the shallow end of the pool, both before *and* after she made herself a little lunch.

In the afternoon, she'd practice her drop shot. Ruth also had two good corner shots—one from midcourt and the other when she was close to one of the side walls. She rarely played a reverse corner; she thought of it as a low-percentage or a trick shot, and she didn't like trick shots.

She'd work on her soft serve in the afternoon, too. In the low-ceilinged barn, she wouldn't even try her lob serve, but her chip serve had lately been improving. When she sliced through the serve, which she hit low to the front wall—barely above the service line—the ball caught the side wall very low and its bounce off the floor was very flat.

It was still early in the morning when Ruth climbed the ladder from the floor area of the barn—where her father parked his car in the cold-weather months—and pushed open the trap door above her head. (The trap door was usually kept closed so that wasps and other insects would not rise to the top of the barn and end up in the squash court.) Outside the squash court, on the second floor of the barn—it had once been a hayloft—were a collection of racquets and balls and wristbands and protective eyewear. Tacked to the outside door of the court was a gray photocopy of Ruth's Exeter team; it had been copied from the pages of the '73 *PEAN*, her yearbook. Ruth was in the front row, far right, with the boys' varsity. Her father had copied the yearbook picture and proudly tacked the photocopy on the door.

Ruth crumpled up the photocopy after she'd ripped it off the squash-court door. She entered the court and stretched for a while—first her hamstrings, then her calves, last, her right shoulder. She always started by facing the side wall in the left-hand court; she liked to begin with her backhand. She hit her volleys and her cross-courts before she went to work on her hard serves. She hit nothing but hard serves for the last half hour; she hit them until they were all landing where she wanted them to.

Fuck you, Hannah! Ruth thought. The ball flew off the front wall like something alive. Goddamn you, Daddy! she said to herself—the ball flying like a wasp or a bee, only much faster. Her imaginary opponent could never return that ball on the fly. It would be all he could do just to get out of the way.

She stopped only because she thought her right arm was going to fall off. Then Ruth took off all her clothes and sat on the bottom step in the shallow end of the pool, enjoying the ice pack that perfectly conformed to her right shoulder. In the glorious Indian Summer weather, the sun at midday was warm on her face. The cool water of the pool covered her body, except for her shoulders; the right one was excruciatingly cold from the ice, but in a few minutes it would be wonderfully numb.

The terrific thing about hitting a ball that hard, and for that long, was that when she was done, she had absolutely nothing on her mind. Not Scott Saunders, and what she was going to do with him *after* they had played squash. Not her father, and what was possible or not possible to do about him. Ruth had not even thought about Allan Albright, whom she should have called. She hadn't thought about Hannah, either—not a single thought.

In the pool, in the sun—at first feeling but now not feeling the ice— Ruth's life vanished around her. (The way night falls, or the way the night gives way to the dawn.) When the phone rang, which it did repeatedly, she didn't think about that, either.

If Scott Saunders had seen Ruth's morning workout, he would have suggested that they play tennis instead—or maybe just have dinner. If Ruth's father had seen the last twenty balls she'd served, he would have known enough not to come home. If Allan Albright had even imagined how far Ruth had removed herself from *thought*, he would have been very, very worried. And if Hannah Grant, who was still Ruth Cole's best friend—Hannah, at least, knew Ruth better than anyone else knew her—had witnessed her friend's mental and physical preparations, Hannah would have known that Scott Saunders, the strawberry-blond lawyer, was facing a day (and a night) of far more demanding *performances* than he would be called upon to display in a few fast-paced games of squash.

Ruth Remembers Learning to Drive

That afternoon, after she hit her soft shots, she sat in the shallow end of the pool, icing her shoulder and reading *The Life of Graham Greene.*

Ruth was fond of the story of young Graham's first words, which allegedly were "Poor dog," a reference to his sister's dog, which had been run over in the street. Greene's nanny had put the dead dog in the baby carriage with Greene.

Of Greene as a child, his biographer wrote: "However young he was he must have had an instinctive awareness of death from the carcass, the smell, perhaps blood, perhaps the mouth pulled back over the teeth in the snarl of death. Wouldn't there be a growing sense of panic, even nausea on finding himself shut in, irrevocably committed to sharing the limited confines of a pram with a dead dog?"

There are worse things, Ruth Cole thought. "In childhood," Greene himself had written (in *The Ministry of Fear*), "we live under the brightness of immortality—heaven is as near and actual as the seaside. Beside the complicated details of the world stand the simplicities: God is good, the grown-up man or woman knows the answer to every question, there is such a thing as truth, and justice is as measured and faultless as a clock."

That hadn't been *her* childhood. Ruth's mother had left her when she was four; there was no God; her father didn't tell the truth, or he wouldn't answer her questions—or both. And as for justice, her father had slept with so many women that Ruth couldn't keep count.

On the subject of childhood, Ruth preferred what Greene had written in *The Power and the Glory:* "There is always one moment in childhood when the door opens and lets the future in." Oh, yes—Ruth agreed. But sometimes, she would have argued, there is more than *one* moment, because there is more than one future. For example, there was the summer of '58, the most obvious moment when the alleged "door" had opened and the alleged "future" had been let in. But there was also the spring of '69, when Ruth turned fifteen and her father had taught her to drive.

For more than ten years, she'd been asking her father to tell her about the accident that killed Thomas and Timothy; her father had refused. "When you're old enough to hear it, Ruthie—when you know how to drive," he'd always said.

They drove every day, usually first thing in the morning—even on the summer weekends, when the Hamptons were overcrowded. Her father wanted her to get used to bad drivers. That summer, on Sunday nights—when the traffic would be backed up in the westbound lane of the Montauk Highway, and the weekend people would already be behaving impatiently, some of them (literally) dying to get back to New York—Ted would take Ruth out in the old white Volvo. He would drive around until he found what he called "a pretty good mess." The traffic would be at a standstill, and some idiots would already have begun passing on the right, in the soft shoulder of the road, and others would be trying to break out of the line of cars, to turn around and go back to their summer homes—just to wait for an hour or two, or to have a really stiff drink before starting out again.

"This looks like a pretty good mess, Ruthie," her father would say.

And Ruth would change seats with him—sometimes while the furious driver behind them honked and honked his horn. There were side roads, of course; she knew them all. She could inch ahead on the Montauk Highway, and then break free of the traffic and race parallel to the highway on the connecting back roads, always finding a way to break back into the lineup of cars again. Her father would look behind them, then, saying, "It appears that you gained on about seven cars, if that's the same dumb Buick back there that I think it is."

Sometimes she'd drive all the way to the Long Island Expressway before her father would say, "Let's call it a night, Ruthie, or the next thing we know, we'll be in Manhattan!"

On other Sunday nights, the traffic might be so bad that her father considered it a sufficient demonstration of her driving skills if Ruth merely executed a U-turn and drove them home.

He emphasized her constant awareness of the rearview mirror, and of course she knew that when she was stopped and waiting to turn left, across a lane of oncoming traffic, she must never, *ever* turn her wheels to the left in anticipation of the turn she was waiting to make. "Never—not *ever*!" her father had told her, from her very first driving lesson. But he still hadn't told her the story of what had actually happened to Thomas and Timothy. Ruth knew only that Thomas had been driving.

"Patience, Ruthie, patience," her father would repeat and repeat to her.

"I *am* patient, Daddy," Ruth would tell him. "I'm still waiting for you to tell me the story, aren't I?"

"I mean, be a patient driver, Ruthie—always be a patient driver."

The Volvo—like all of Ted's Volvos, which he began buying in the sixties—was a stick shift. (Ted told Ruth to never trust a boy who drove an automatic transmission.) "And if you're in the passenger seat and

I'm the driver, I never look at you—I don't care what you say, or what kind of fit you're having. Even if you're choking," Ted said. "If I'm driving the car, I can talk to you, but I don't look at you—not ever. And when you're the driver, you don't look at me, or at anyone who might be in the passenger seat. Not until you get off the road and stop the car. You got it?"

"Got it," Ruth said.

"And if you're out on a date and the boy is driving, if *he* looks at you, for whatever reason, you tell him not to look at you or else you'll get out and walk. Or you tell him to let *you* drive the car. You got that, too?" her father asked.

"I got it," Ruth said. "Tell me what happened to Thomas and Timothy."

But all her father said was: "And if you're upset—like something you're thinking about suddenly upsets you, and you start to cry—and you can't see the road clearly, because of your tears . . . just suppose you're bawling your eyes out, for whatever reason . . ."

"Okay, okay—I got it!" Ruth told him.

"Well. If you ever get like that, crying so hard that you can't see the road, you just pull over to the side of the road and *stop*."

"What about the accident?" Ruth asked. "Were you there? Were you and Mommy in the car?"

In the shallow end of the swimming pool, Ruth felt the ice melting on her shoulder; the cold trickle followed the line of her collarbone and made its way across her chest into the warmer water of the pool. The sun had dropped below the towering privet.

She thought of Graham Greene's father, the schoolmaster, whose advice to his former pupils (who adored him) was odd, but in its own way charming. "Remember to be faithful to your future wife," he'd said to a boy who was leaving school to join the army in 1918. And to another, just prior to his confirmation, Charles Greene had said: "An army of women live on the lust of men."

Where had this "army of women" gone? Ruth guessed that Hannah was one of the alleged army's lost soldiers.

Since Ruth's earliest memories—not only since she'd begun to read, but from the first time her father had told her a story—books, and the characters in them, had entered her life and remained fixed there. Books, and the characters in them, were more "fixed" in Ruth's life than were her father and her best friend—not to mention the *men* in her life, who for the most part had proven themselves to be almost as unreliable as Ted and Hannah had.

"All life long," Graham Greene had written in his autobiography, *A Sort of Life*, "my instinct has been to abandon anything for which I have no talent." A good instinct, but were Ruth to put it into action, she would perforce have nothing further to do with *men*. Among the men she'd known, only Allan seemed admirable and constant; yet, as she sat in the pool, readying herself for her test with Scott Saunders, Allan's lupine teeth were foremost on her mind. And the hair on the back of his hands . . . he had too much hair there.

She'd not enjoyed playing squash with Allan. He was a good athlete and a well-coached squash player, but Allan was too large for the court—too dangerous in his lunging, looping movements. Yet Allan would never try to hurt or intimidate her. And although she'd lost to him twice, Ruth didn't doubt that she would eventually beat him. It was merely a matter of learning to keep out of his way—while at the same time not being afraid of his backswing. The two times she'd lost to him, Ruth had yielded the T. Next time, if there was a next time, Ruth was determined not to give up the preferred position on the court to him.

As she enjoyed the last of the melting ice, she thought: At worst, it might mean some stitches in an eyebrow or a broken nose. Besides, if Allan hit her with his racquet, he would feel terrible about it. Thereafter, Allan would yield the preferred position on the court to *her*. In no time, whether he hit her or not, she would be beating him easily. Then Ruth thought: Why *bother* to beat him?

How could she ever consider giving up *men*? To an even greater extent, it was *women* she didn't trust.

She'd been sitting for too long in the swimming pool, in the chill of the late-afternoon shade—not to mention the clammy cold of the ice pack, which had melted on her shoulder. The chill gave her a touch of November in the Indian Summer weather; it reminded Ruth of that November night in 1969, when her father had given her what he called "the ultimate driving lesson" and "the penultimate driving test."

She wouldn't be sixteen until the spring of the following year, when she would get her learner's permit—thereafter, she would pass her driver's test without the slightest difficulty—but that November night

her father, who didn't give a damn about learner's permits, had forewarned her: "For your sake, Ruthie, I hope you never have a tougher
driving test than *this* one. Let's go."

"Go *where?*" she'd asked. It was the Sunday night of the long Thanksgiving weekend.

The pool was already covered for winter, the fruit trees denuded of
fruit and leaves; even the privet was bare, standing skeletally, stiffly
moving in the wind. On the northern horizon was a glow: the headlights of the cars that were already at a standstill in the westbound lane
of the Montauk Highway; the weekenders on their way back to New
York. (Normally the drive took two hours—at the most, three.)

"I feel like the lights of Manhattan tonight," Ted told his daughter.
"I want to see if the Christmas decorations are already in place on Park
Avenue. I want to have a drink at the Stanhope bar. I had a 1910 Armagnac there once. Of course I don't drink Armagnac anymore, but I'd
like to have something as good as that again. A really good glass of port,
maybe. Let's go."

"You want to drive to New York *tonight*, Daddy?" Ruth asked. Short of
the end of the Labor Day weekend, or immediately following the
Fourth of July (and maybe Memorial Day weekend), it was arguably
the worst night of the year to drive to New York.

"No, *I* don't want to drive to New York, Ruthie—I *can't* drive to New
York, because I've been drinking. I've had three beers and a whole bottle of red wine. The one thing I promised your mother was that I'd
never drink and drive, at least not with you in the car. *You're* the driver,
Ruthie."

"I've never driven to New York," Ruth said. It wouldn't have been
much of a test if she *had*.

When they finally got on the Long Island Expressway at Manorville,
Ted said, "Get in the passing lane, Ruthie. Maintain the speed limit.
Remember your rearview mirror. If someone's coming up behind you
and you have enough time to move to the center lane, *and* if you have
enough room, then move over. But if someone's coming up on you,
hog-wild to pass, let him pass you on the right."

"Isn't this illegal, Daddy?" she asked him. She thought that learning
to drive had some restrictions—like maybe she wasn't supposed to
drive at night, or not beyond a fifteen-mile radius of where she lived.
She didn't know she'd already been driving illegally because she didn't
have a learner's permit.

"You can't learn everything you need to know legally," her father told her.

She had to concentrate hard on the driving; it was one of the few times they'd been out in the old white Volvo together when she *didn't* ask him to tell her about what had happened to Thomas and Timothy. Ted waited until they were approaching Flushing Meadows; then, without any warning, he began to tell her the story in exactly the same way that he'd told it to Eddie O'Hare, with Ted Cole in the third person—as if Ted were just another character in the story, and a minor character at that.

Ted interrupted the part about how much he and Marion had had to drink, and why Thomas had been the obvious choice—the only sober driver—to tell Ruth to get out of the passing lane and into the far-right lane instead. "You get on the Grand Central Parkway here, Ruthie," her father casually said. She had to change lanes a little too fast, but she managed it. Soon she saw Shea Stadium, off to her right.

At the part in the story where he and Marion were arguing about the best place to make a left turn, Ted interrupted himself again—this time to tell Ruth to take Northern Boulevard, through Queens.

She knew that the old white Volvo tended to overheat in stop-and-go traffic, but when she mentioned it, her father said, "Just don't ride the clutch, Ruthie. If you're stopped for a while, take it out of gear, put it in neutral, and step on your brake. Keep your foot off your clutch as much as you can. And remember your rearview mirror."

By then, she was crying. It was after the snowplow scene, when her mother knew that Thomas was dead, but she didn't yet know about Timothy. Marion kept asking Ted if Timmy was all right, and Ted wouldn't tell her—he'd just watched Timmy die, but he couldn't speak.

They came over the Queensboro Bridge, into Manhattan, at the moment in the story when her father was explaining about Timothy's left leg—how the snowplow had severed it at midthigh, and that when they tried to take the body away, they had to leave the leg behind.

"I can't see the road, Daddy," Ruth told him.

"Well. There's no place to pull over, is there?" her father asked her. "You'll just have to keep going, won't you?" Then he told her the part where her mother had noticed her brother's shoe. ("Oh, Ted, look— he's going to need his shoe," Marion had said, not realizing that Timmy's shoe was still attached to Timmy's leg. And so on . . .)

Ruth headed uptown on Third Avenue.

"I'll tell you when to cut over to Park," her father told her. "There's a place on Park Avenue where the Christmas decorations are especially worth seeing."

"I'm crying too much—I can't see where I'm going, Daddy," Ruth told him again.

"But that's the test, Ruthie. The test is, sometimes there's no place to pull over—sometimes you *can't* stop, and you have to find a way to keep going. You got it?"

"Got it," she said.

"So," her father said, "now you know everything."

Ruth realized later that she'd also passed that part of the test which had not been mentioned. She'd never looked at him; he'd sat unseen in the passenger seat. All the while that her father was telling the story, Ruth had never taken her eyes from the road, or from the rearview mirror. That had been part of the test, too.

That November night in '69, her father had made her drive up Park Avenue, all the while commenting on the Christmas decorations. Somewhere in the upper eighties, he'd told her to cut over to Fifth. Then they'd come down Fifth Avenue to the Stanhope, which was opposite the Met. It was the first time she'd heard the flags at the Met snapping in the wind. Her father had told her to give the keys of the old white Volvo to the doorman; his name was Manny. Ruth had been impressed that the doorman knew her father.

But they *all* knew her father at the Stanhope. He must have been a frequent guest. It's where he brings *women*! Ruth realized. "Always stay here—when you can afford it, Ruthie," her father had told her. "It's a good hotel." (Since 1980, she'd been able to afford it.)

That night they'd gone into the bar and her father changed his mind about the port. He'd ordered a bottle of an excellent Pommard instead; Ted finished the wine while Ruth drank a double espresso, knowing that she had to drive back to Sagaponack. All the time they sat in the bar, Ruth felt that she was still gripping the steering wheel. And although it would have been permissible to look at her father in the bar—before they got back in the old white Volvo—she couldn't look at him. It was as if he were still telling her the terrible story.

It was after midnight when her father directed her up Madison Avenue; somewhere in the upper nineties, he told her to turn east. They took the F.D.R. Drive to the Triborough; then the Grand Central Parkway to the L.I.E., where her father fell asleep. Ruth remembered that Manorville was the exit she wanted; she didn't have to wake her father to ask him how to get home.

She was driving against the holiday traffic—the headlights of the horde returning to the city were constantly in her eyes—but there was almost no one headed in her direction. A couple of times, she opened up the old white Volvo, just to see how fast it could go. She reached eighty-five twice, and ninety once, but at those speeds a shimmy in the front end frightened her. Most of the way, she stuck to the speed limit and thought about the story of how her brothers had died—especially the part about her mother trying to save Timmy's shoe.

Her father didn't wake up until she was driving through Bridgehampton. "How come you didn't take the back roads?" he asked.

"I felt like having all the town lights around me, and the headlights of the other cars," Ruth said.

"Oh," her father said, as if he were falling back to sleep.

"What kind of shoe was it?" Ruth asked.

"It was a basketball shoe, Timmy's favorite."

"High-tops?" she guessed.

"Right."

"Got it," Ruth said, turning onto Sagg Main. Although, at that moment, there were no other cars in sight of the Volvo, Ruth put her directional signal on; a full fifty yards before she turned, she put on her blinker.

"Good driving, Ruthie," her father told her. "If you ever have a tougher drive than this, I trust you to remember what you've learned."

Ruth was shivering when she finally got out of the pool. She knew she should warm up before she started playing squash with Scott Saunders, but both her memories of learning to drive and the Graham Greene biography had depressed her. It wasn't Norman Sherry's fault, but the Greene biography had taken a turn that Ruth opposed. Mr. Sherry was convinced that, for every major character in a Graham Greene novel, there existed a real-life counterpart. In an interview in *The Times,* Greene himself had told V. S. Pritchett: "I cannot invent." Yet, in the same interview, while admitting that his characters were "an amalgam of bits of real people," Greene also denied taking his characters from real life. "Real people are crowded out by imaginary ones. ..." he'd said. "Real people are too limiting." But, for too many pages of the biography, Mr. Sherry went on and on about the "real people."

Ruth was particularly saddened by Greene's early love life. What his biographer called "his obsessional love" for the "ardent Catholic" who would eventually become Greene's wife was precisely the kind of thing Ruth didn't want to know about a writer whose writing she loved. "There is a splinter of ice in the heart of a writer," Greene had written in *A Sort of Life*. But in the daily letters that young Graham wrote to Vivien, his wife-to-be, Ruth saw only the familiar pathos of a man who was smitten.

Ruth had never been smitten. Possibly what contributed to her reluctance to welcome Allan's proposal of marriage was her awareness of how smitten Allan was with her.

She'd stopped reading *The Life of Graham Greene* on page 338, the beginning of the twenty-fourth chapter, which was called "Marriage at Last." It was a pity that Ruth stopped reading there, for near the end of that chapter she would have found something that might have made her like Graham Greene and his bride-to-be a little better. When the couple had finally married and were on their honeymoon, Vivien presented Graham with a sealed letter that Vivien's intrusive mother had given her—"a letter on sex instruction"—but Vivien handed it to Greene unopened. He read it and immediately tore it up. Vivien never got to read the letter. Ruth would have appreciated that the new Mrs. Greene decided she could manage well enough without her mother's advice.

As for "Marriage at Last," why did the chapter title—the phrase itself—depress her? Was it the way *she* would get married, too? It sounded like the title of a novel Ruth Cole would never write, or even want to read.

Ruth thought she should stick to rereading Graham Greene; she was sure that she didn't want to know anything more about his *life*. Here she was, brooding about what Hannah called her "favorite subject," which was her tireless scrutiny of the relationship between what was "real" and what was "invented." But the mere thought of Hannah returned Ruth to the present.

She didn't want Scott Saunders to see her naked in the pool, not yet.

She went into the house and dressed in some clean, dry clothes for squash. She put some talcum powder in the right front pocket of her shorts; it would keep her racquet hand dry and smooth—no blisters. She'd already chilled the white wine, but now she arranged the rice in the electric steamer. All she would have to do later was push a button to turn it on. She'd already set the dining-room table—two place settings.

At last she climbed the ladder to the second floor of the barn, and— after she'd stretched—she began to warm up the ball.

She fell into an easy rhythm: four forehands down the wall, then she would hit the telltale tin; four backhand rails, and then the tin again. Each time she hit the tin, aiming deliberately low, she hit the ball hard enough so that the resounding tin was loud. In an actual game, Ruth almost never hit the tin; in a tough match, maybe she would hit it twice. But she wanted to be sure that when Scott Saunders arrived, he would hear her hitting the tin. And as he climbed the ladder to come play with her, he would be thinking: For a so-called pretty good player, she sure hits the tin a lot. Then, when they started to play, it would come as quite a surprise to him that Ruth rarely hit the tin at all.

You could feel a little shiver in the squash court whenever someone climbed the ladder to the second floor of the barn. When Ruth felt that shiver, she counted five more shots—hitting the tin the fifth time. She could easily hit all five shots in the time it took her to say, under her breath, "Daddy with Hannah Grant!"

Scott tapped twice on the door of the squash court with his racquet; then he cautiously opened the door. "Hi," he said. "I hope you haven't been practicing for me."

"Oh, just a little bit," Ruth said.

Two Drawers

She spotted him the first five points. Ruth wanted to see how he moved. He was reasonably quick, but he swung his racquet like a tennis player; he didn't snap his wrist. And he had only one serve: a hard one, right at her. It was usually too high; she could step out of its way and return it off the back wall. And Scott's return of serve was weak; the ball fell to the floor at midcourt. Ruth could usually kill it with a corner shot. She had him running either from the back wall to the front, or from one back corner to the other.

Ruth took the first game 15–8 before Scott had figured out how good she really was. Scott was one of those players who overestimated their abilities. When he was losing, his first thought was that his game was a little off; it wouldn't occur to him, until the third or fourth game, that he was being outplayed. Ruth tried to keep the score close in the next two games, because she enjoyed seeing Scott run.

She won the second game 15–6 and the third 15–9. Scott Saunders was in very good shape, but after the third game, he needed the water bottle. Ruth didn't drink any water. Scott was doing all the running.

He hadn't quite got his wind back when he faulted the first serve of the fourth game. Ruth could detect his frustration, like a sudden odor. "I can't believe that your father still beats you," he said between breaths.

"Oh, I'll beat him one day," Ruth said. "Maybe next time."

She won the fourth game 15–5. While he was chasing a drop shot into the front corner, Scott slipped in a puddle of his own sweat; he slid on his hip and hit his head against the tin.

"Are you okay?" Ruth asked him. "Do you want to stop?"

"Let's play one more game," he snapped at her.

Ruth didn't like his attitude. She beat him 15–1 in their last game, his only point coming when she tried (against her better judgment) a reverse corner that hit the tin. It was the one time she hit the tin in five games. Ruth was mad at herself for attempting the reverse corner; it confirmed her opinion of low-percentage shots. If she'd just kept the ball in play, she was sure she would have taken the last game 15–0.

But losing 15–1 had been bad enough for Scott Saunders. Ruth couldn't be sure if he was pouting or just making an unusually. contorted facial expression until he got his wind back. They were leaving the court when a wasp flew in the open door and Scott took an awkward swipe at it with his racquet. He missed. The wasp zigged and zagged. Its erratic, darting flight was on course to the ceiling, where it would safely be out of reach, when Ruth caught the wasp in midair with her backhand. Some say it's the toughest shot in squash: an overhead backhand volley. The strings of her racquet cut the wasp's segmented body in two.

"Good get," Scott said, as if he were about to be sick.

Ruth sat on the edge of the deck beside the swimming pool; she took off her shoes and socks, cooling her feet in the water. Scott didn't seem to know what to do. He was used to taking off all his clothes and stepping into the outdoor shower with Ted. Ruth would have to do it first.

She stood up and took off her shorts. She pulled her T-shirt off, dreading the potential awkwardness—the usual, unwanted acrobatics—of wriggling out of her sweaty sports bra. But she was able to take the spandex bra off without an embarrassing struggle. She took her underpants off last, and walked into the shower stall without looking at Scott. She'd already soaped herself, and was standing under the running water, when he stepped into the shower stall with her and turned on his showerhead. She had shampooed her hair and was rinsing the shampoo out, when she asked him if he was allergic to shrimp.

"No, I like shrimp," he told her. With her eyes closed, rinsing off the shampoo, she guessed that he *had* to be looking at her breasts.

"Good, because that's what we're having for dinner," Ruth told him. She shut off her shower and stepped out on the deck; then she dove into the deep end of the pool. When she surfaced, Scott was still standing on the deck; he was looking beyond her.

"Isn't that a wineglass at the bottom of the pool?" he asked. "Did you recently have a party?"

"No, my *father* recently had a party," Ruth answered, treading water. Scott Saunders had a bigger cock than she'd first thought. The lawyer dove to the bottom of the deep end and brought up the wineglass.

"It must have been a moderately wild party," Scott said.

"My father is more than moderately wild," Ruth replied. She floated on her back; when Hannah tried it, she could scarcely manage to make her nipples rise above the surface.

"You have beautiful breasts," Scott told Ruth. He treaded water next to her. He filled the wineglass with water, then poured the water on her breasts.

"My mother probably had better ones," Ruth said. "What do you know about my mother?" she asked him.

"Nothing—I've just heard some rumors," Scott admitted.

"They're probably true," Ruth said. "You may know almost as much about her as I do."

She swam to the shallow end, and he followed—still holding the wineglass. If he hadn't been carrying the stupid glass, he would have already touched her. Ruth got out of the pool and wrapped herself in a towel. She saw Scott drying himself, meticulously, before she walked into the house—her towel around her waist, her breasts still bare.

"If you put your clothes in the dryer, they'll be dry after dinner," she called to him. He followed her inside—his towel was around his waist. "Tell me if you're cold," she said. "You can wear something of my father's."

"I feel fine in the towel," he told her.

Ruth started the rice steamer and opened a bottle of white wine; she poured a glass for Scott and one for herself. She looked pretty good with just the towel around her waist and her breasts bare. "I feel fine in the towel, too," she told him. She let him kiss her then; he cupped one of her breasts in his hand.

"I didn't expect this," he said to her.

No kidding! Ruth thought. When she'd made up her mind about somebody, it was the height of boredom to wait for the man to seduce her. She hadn't been with anybody for four, almost five months; she didn't feel like waiting.

"Let me show you something," Ruth said to Scott. She led him into her father's workroom, where she opened the bottommost drawer of Ted's so-called writing desk. The drawer was full of black-and-white Polaroid prints—there were hundreds of them—and about a dozen tubular containers of Polaroid print coater. The print coater gave the whole drawer and all the photographs a bad smell.

Ruth handed Scott a stack of the Polaroids, without comment. They were the pictures Ted had taken of his models, both before and after he drew them. Ted told his models that the photos were necessary so that he could continue to work on the drawings when the models weren't there; he needed the photos "for reference." In fact, he never continued to work on the drawings. He just wanted the photographs.

When Scott finished looking at one stack of photos, Ruth showed him another. The pictures had that amateur quality which most really bad pornography has; that the models themselves were not professional models was only part of it. There was an awkwardness to their poses that suggested sexual shame, but there was also a sense of haste and carelessness about the photographs themselves.

"Why are you showing me these?" Scott asked Ruth.

"Do they turn you on?" she asked him.

"*You* turn me on," he told her.

"I guess they turn my father on," Ruth said. "They're all his models—he's fucked every single one of them."

Scott was leafing quickly through the photographs without really looking at them; it was hard to look at the photos if you weren't alone. "There are a lot of women here," he said.

"Yesterday, and the day before, my father fucked my best friend," Ruth told him.

"Your father fucked your best friend..." Scott repeated thoughtfully.

"We're what an idiot sociology major would call a dysfunctional family," Ruth said.

"*I* was a sociology major," Scott Saunders admitted.

"What did you learn?" Ruth asked him. She was putting the Polaroids back in the bottommost drawer. The smell from the print coater was strong enough to make her gag. In a way, it was a worse smell than the squid ink. (Ruth had first found the photographs in her father's bottommost drawer when she was twelve years old.)

"I decided to go to law school—that's what I learned from sociology," the strawberry-blond lawyer said.

"Have you heard some rumors about my brothers, too?" Ruth asked him. "They're dead," she added.

"I think I heard something," Scott answered. "Wasn't it a long time ago?"

"I'll show you a picture of them—they were good-looking guys," Ruth said, taking Scott's hand.

She led him up the carpeted stairs. Their bare feet didn't make a sound. The lid of the rice steamer was rattling; the dryer was running, too—chiefly the sound of something clicking or tapping against the revolving drum of the dryer.

Ruth took Scott into the master bedroom, where the big bed was in unmade disarray; Ruth could almost see the body imprints of her father and Hannah in the tangled sheets.

"There they are," Ruth said to Scott, pointing to the picture of her brothers.

Squinting at the photograph, Scott tried to read the Latin inscription above the doorway.

"I guess you didn't learn Latin as a sociology major," Ruth said.

"There's a lot of Latin in the law," he told her.

"My brothers were good-looking guys, weren't they?" Ruth asked him.

"Yes, they were," Scott said. "Doesn't *venite* mean *come?*" he asked her.

" 'Come hither boys and become men,' " Ruth translated for him.

"Now *there's* a challenge!" Scott Saunders said. "I liked being a boy better."

"My father never stopped being a boy," Ruth said.

"Is this your father's bedroom?" Scott asked her.

"Check out the top drawer, the drawer under the night table," Ruth told him. "Go on—open it."

Scott hesitated; he was probably thinking that there were more Polaroids in the drawer.

"Don't worry. There are no photographs in there," Ruth said. Scott opened the drawer. It was full of condoms in brightly colored foil wrappers, and there was a large tube of lubricating jelly.

"So... I guess this *is* your father's bedroom," Scott said, looking around nervously.

"That's a drawer full of a *boy's* stuff, if I ever saw one," Ruth said. (She'd first discovered the condoms and the lubricating jelly in her father's night-table drawer when she was about nine or ten.)

"Where *is* your father?" Scott asked her.

"I don't know," she said.

"You're not expecting him?" Scott asked.

"If I had to guess, I'd say I was expecting him about midmorning tomorrow," Ruth said.

Scott Saunders looked at all the condoms in the open drawer. "God, I haven't worn a condom since I was in college," he said.

"You're going to have to wear one now," Ruth told him. She took the towel off from around her waist; then she sat naked on the unmade bed. "If you've forgotten how a condom works, I can remind you," she added.

Scott picked a condom in a blue wrapper. He kissed her for a long time, and he licked her for an even longer time; she didn't need any of the jelly in her father's night-table drawer. She came just a few seconds after he was inside her, and she felt him come only a moment later. Nearly the whole time, but especially when Scott was licking her, Ruth watched the open door of her father's bedroom; she listened for her father's footsteps on the stairs, or in the upstairs hall, but all she could hear was the clicking or tapping noise in the dryer. (The lid of the rice steamer wasn't rattling anymore; the rice was cooked.) And when Scott entered her and she knew she was going to come, almost instantly—the rest of it would be over very quickly, too—Ruth thought: Come home now, Daddy! Come upstairs and see me *now*!

But Ted didn't come home in time to see his daughter as she would have liked him to see her.

Pain in an Unfamiliar Place

Hannah had used too much soy sauce in the marinade. Also, the shrimp had languished in the marinade for more than twenty-four hours; they didn't taste like shrimp anymore. But this hardly stopped Ruth and Scott from eating them all, and all the rice and the stir-fried vegetables—and all of some kind of cucumber chutney that had seen better days. They also drank a second bottle of white wine, and Ruth opened a bottle of red wine to have with the cheese and fruit. They finished the bottle of red wine, too.

They ate and drank, wearing just the towels around their waists— Ruth with her breasts defiantly bare. She hoped that her father would walk into the dining room, but he did not. And despite the conviviality of her wining and dining with Scott Saunders, not to mention the seeming success of their highly charged sexual encounter, their dinner-table conversation was strained. Scott told Ruth that his divorce had been "amicable," and that he enjoyed "an amiable relationship" with his ex-wife. Recently divorced men talked entirely too much about their ex-wives. If the divorce had been truly "amicable," why talk about it?

Ruth asked Scott to tell her what kind of law he practiced, but he said that it wasn't interesting; it had something to do with real estate. Scott also confessed to not having read her novels. He'd tried the second one, *Before the Fall of Saigon*—he thought it might be a war novel. He'd gone to considerable trouble, as a young man, not to be drafted during the Vietnam War—but the book had struck him as what he called a "women's novel." The phrase never failed to make Ruth think of a wide array of feminine-hygiene products. "About female friendship, wasn't it?" he asked. But his ex-wife had read everything Ruth Cole had written. "She's your biggest fan," Scott Saunders said. (The ex-wife *again!*)

Then he asked Ruth if she was "seeing anyone." She tried to tell him about Allan, without mentioning any names. The issue of marriage existed for her as a subject separate from Allan. Her attraction to marriage was deep, Ruth told Scott, while at the same time her fear of it was stultifying.

"You mean you're more attracted to it than you are afraid of it?" the lawyer asked.

"How does that passage from George Eliot go? I once liked it so much that I wrote it down," Ruth told him. " 'What greater thing is there for two human souls, than to feel that they are joined for life ...' *But* ..."

"Did he stay married?" Scott asked her.

"Who?" Ruth said.

"George Eliot. Did he stay married?"

Maybe if I just get up and start doing the dishes, he'll get bored and go home, Ruth thought.

But when she was loading the dishwasher, Scott stood behind her and fondled her breasts; she felt his hard-on poking against her, through both their towels. "I want to do it to you this way, from behind," he said.

"I don't like it that way," she said.

"I don't mean in the wrong hole," he told her crudely. "I mean the right hole, but from behind."

"I know what you mean," Ruth told him. He was fondling her breasts so persistently that she had some difficulty getting the wineglasses to fit properly in the top rack of the dishwasher. "I don't like it from behind—period," Ruth added.

"How do you like it, then?" he asked her.

It was clear to her that he expected to do it again. "I'll show you," she said, "as soon as I finish loading the dishwasher."

It was no accident that Ruth had left the front door unlocked—or the lights on, in both the downstairs and the upstairs hall. She'd also left the door to her father's bedroom open, in the receding hope that her father would return and find her in the act of making love to Scott. But this was not to be.

Ruth straddled Scott; she sat on him for the longest time. She nearly rocked herself to sleep in this position. (They'd both had too much to drink.) When she could tell by how he held his breath that he was about to come, she dropped her weight on his chest and, holding tight to his shoulders, rolled him on top of her, because she couldn't stand to see the look that transformed most men's faces when they came. (Ruth didn't know, of course—she would never know—that this had been a manner of making love that her mother had also preferred with Eddie O'Hare.)

Ruth lay in bed, listening to Scott flushing the condom down the toilet in the master bathroom. After Scott had come back to bed—he'd almost instantly fallen asleep—Ruth lay awake listening to the dishwasher. It was in the final rinse cycle, and it sounded to her as if two wineglasses were rubbing against each other.

Scott Saunders had fallen asleep with his left hand holding her right breast. Ruth was not terribly comfortable, but now that Scott was sound asleep and snoring, his hand no longer held her breast; rather, the hand pressed its dead weight against her like a sleeping dog's paw.

Ruth tried to remember the rest of the George Eliot passage about marriage. She didn't even know which George Eliot novel the quotation was from, although Ruth distinctly recalled copying the passage into one of her diaries long ago.

Now, as she was falling asleep, it occurred to Ruth that Eddie O'Hare might know which novel the passage was from. At least it would give her an excuse to call him. (In fact, if she'd called Eddie, he wouldn't have known the passage—Eddie wasn't a George Eliot fan. Eddie would have called his father. Minty O'Hare, even in his retirement, would have known which George Eliot novel the passage came from.)

" '... to strengthen each other in all labor...' " Ruth whispered to herself, reciting the passage from memory. She had no fear of waking up Scott, not the way he was snoring. And the wineglasses went on grinding together in the dishwasher. It had been so long since the telephone had rung that Ruth felt the world had fallen sound asleep; whoever had been calling (and calling) had given up. "... to rest on each other in all sorrow..." George Eliot had written about marriage. " '...to minister to each other in all pain,' " Ruth recited, " 'to be one with each other in silent unspeakable memories at the moment of the last parting...' " It sounded like a pretty good idea to Ruth Cole, who finally fell asleep beside an unknown man, whose breathing was as loud as a brass band.

The phone rang almost a dozen times before Ruth heard it. Scott Saunders didn't wake up until Ruth answered the phone. She felt his paw revive against her breast.

"Hello," Ruth said. When she opened her eyes, it took her a second to recognize her father's digital clock. It took a second, too, before the paw on her breast reminded her of where she was, and in what circumstances—and why she hadn't wanted to answer the phone.

"I've been so worried about you," Allan Albright said. "I've been calling and calling."

"Oh, Allan ..." Ruth said. It was a little after two in the morning. The dishwasher had stopped. The dryer had stopped long before the dishwasher. The paw against her breast had become a hand again; it cupped her breast firmly. "I was asleep," Ruth said.

"I thought you might be *dead!*" Allan told her.

"I had a fight with my father—I haven't been answering the phone," Ruth explained. The hand had let go of her breast. She saw the same hand reach across her body and open the top drawer under the night table. The hand chose a condom, another blue one; the hand also removed the tube of jelly from the drawer.

"I tried to call your friend Hannah. Wasn't she going to be out there with you?" Allan asked. "But I kept getting her answering machine—I don't even know if she got my message."

"*Don't* talk to Hannah—I had a fight with her, too," Ruth told him.

"So you're all alone out there?" Allan asked her.

"Yes, I'm alone," Ruth answered. She tried to lie on her side with her legs tight together, but Scott Saunders was strong; he was able to pull her up on her knees. He'd put enough lubricating jelly on the condom so that he slipped inside her with surprising ease; it momentarily took her breath away.

"What?" Allan said.

"I feel terrible," Ruth told him. "Let me call you in the morning."

"I could come out there," Allan said.

"No!" Ruth said—to Allan *and* to Scott.

She rested her weight on her elbows and her forehead; she kept trying to lie flat on her stomach, but Scott pulled her hips into him so forcefully that it was more comfortable for her to stay on her knees. The top of her head kept bumping the headboard of the bed. She wanted to say good night to Allan but her breathing was jerky. Besides,

Scott had jammed her so far forward that she couldn't reach the night table to return the telephone to its cradle.

"I love you," Allan told her. "I'm sorry."

"No, *I'm* sorry," Ruth managed to say, before Scott Saunders took the phone from her and hung it up. Then he cupped both her breasts in his hands, squeezing them until they ached, and he humped her from behind, like a dog—the way Eddie O'Hare had humped her mother.

Fortunately Ruth did not remember the episode of the inadequate lamp shade in great detail, but her memory was sufficient for her to never want to be in the same position herself. Now she was in it. She had to push back against Scott with all her strength or her head would have kept bumping against the headboard.

She'd been sleeping on her right shoulder, which was sore from all the squash, but her right shoulder didn't hurt her as much as Scott Saunders hurt her. There was something about the position itself that hurt her—it wasn't only a matter of her memory of it. And Scott's grip on her breasts was much rougher than she liked.

"Please stop," she asked him, but he could feel her pushing her hips back against him and he humped her all the harder.

When he was finished with her, Ruth lay on her left side, facing the empty bed; she listened to Scott flushing away another condom. At first she felt she was bleeding, but it was only an excess of the lubricating jelly. When Scott came back to bed, he tried to touch her breasts again. Ruth pushed his hand away.

"I told you I didn't like it that way," she said to him.

"I got the right hole, didn't I?" he asked her.

"I told you I didn't like it from behind—period," she said.

"Come on, your hips were moving. You liked it," Scott told her.

She knew that she'd had to move her hips against him so that she wouldn't keep bumping her head on the headboard. Maybe he knew it, too. But all Ruth said was: "You hurt me."

"Come on," Scott said. He reached for her breasts again, but she pushed his hand away.

"When a woman says 'No'—when she says 'Please stop'—well ... what's it mean when a man *won't* stop?" Ruth asked. "Isn't that a little like rape?"

He rolled over on the bed, turning his back to her. "Come on. You're talking to a lawyer," he told her.

"No, I'm talking to an asshole," she said.

"So ... who was the phone call?" Scott asked. "Someone important?"

"More important than you are," Ruth told him.

"Given the circumstances," the lawyer said, "I presume he isn't *that* important."

"Please get out of here," Ruth said. "Please just go."

"Okay, okay," he told her. But when she returned from the bathroom, he'd fallen back to sleep. He was lying on his side, his arms reaching out to what had been her side of the bed; he was taking up the whole bed.

"Get up! Get out of here!" she shouted, but either he was sound asleep again or he was pretending to be.

In retrospect, Ruth might have deliberated a little longer on her next decision. She opened the condom drawer and took out the tube of lubricating jelly, which she squirted into Scott's exposed left ear. The stuff came out of the tube a lot faster than she expected; it had a more liquid consistency than normal jelly, and it woke up Scott Saunders in a hurry.

"Time to go," Ruth reminded him. She was completely unprepared for him to hit her. With left-handers, there's always something you don't see coming.

Scott hit her only once, but it was a solid shot. One second he was holding his left ear with his left hand; then he was out of the bed, facing her. He caught Ruth on her right cheekbone with a straight left that she never saw. As she lay on the rug, approximately where she'd seen Hannah's open suitcase, Ruth realized that Hannah had been right again: Ruth's alleged instincts for detecting a man's capacity for violence against women, even on the very first date, were not the instincts she'd thought she had. Hannah had told her she'd just been lucky. ("You just haven't had *that* date," Hannah had warned her.) Now she had.

Ruth let the room stop spinning before she tried to move. Again she thought she was bleeding, but it was only the jelly that Scott had got on his left hand when he'd touched his left ear.

She lay in a fetal position, her knees pulled up to her chest. The skin over her right cheekbone felt stretched too tightly, and she sensed an unnatural warmth on her face. When she blinked her eyes, she saw stars, but when she held her eyes open, the stars disappeared after a few seconds.

She was locked in a closet again. Not since childhood had she been this afraid. She couldn't see Scott Saunders, but she called to him. "I'll get you your clothes," she told him. "They're still in the dryer."

"I know where the dryer is," he said sullenly. As if she were not part of her body, she saw him step over the spot where she lay on the rug. She heard the stairs creak as he went down them.

When she got up, she was momentarily dizzy; the feeling that she might throw up lasted longer. She carried the sick-to-her-stomach feeling downstairs, where she walked directly through the dining room to the darkened terrace. The cool night air instantly revived her. Indian Summer is over, she thought, dipping the toes of one foot in the pool; the silky-smooth water was warmer than the air.

Later she would go in the pool, but right now she didn't want to be naked. She found her old squash clothes on the deck near the outdoor shower; they were damp with cold sweat and dew—the T-shirt made her shiver. She didn't bother with her underpants, her bra, or her socks. Just the T-shirt, her shorts, and her shoes would suffice. She stretched her sore right shoulder. Her shoulder would suffice, too.

Scott Saunders's squash racquet was leaning—handle up, racquet head down—against the outdoor shower stall. It was too heavy a racquet for her, and the grip was too big for her hand. But it wasn't as if she intended to play a whole match with it. It'll be fine, Ruth thought, going back inside the house.

She found Scott in the laundry room. He'd not bothered to put on his jock. He'd pulled on his shorts and stuck the jock in his right front pocket; he'd put his socks in the left front pocket. He'd put on his shoes, but he'd left them unlaced. He was pulling his T-shirt over his head when Ruth caught him with a low backhand that crumpled his right knee. Scott managed to pop his head through the head hole in his T-shirt, maybe a half-second before Ruth struck him full in the face with a rising forehand. He covered his face with his hands, but Ruth had turned the racquet head sideways. She slashed at his elbows—one backhand, one forehand, both elbows. His arms were numb; he couldn't raise his arms to protect his face. He was already bleeding over one eyebrow. She took two overhead shots, at both his collarbones—snapping several strings on the racquet face with the first blow, and completely separating the racquet head from the handle with the second.

The handle was still a pretty effective weapon. She kept slashing at him, hitting him wherever he exposed himself. He tried to crawl out of the laundry room on all fours, but his right knee wouldn't support his weight and his left collarbone was broken. Therefore, Scott couldn't crawl. All the time she was hitting him, Ruth repeated the scores of their squash games—a fairly humiliating litany: "Fifteen–eight, fifteen–six, fifteen–nine, fifteen–five, fifteen–*one!*"

When Scott lay in a collapsed position of lopsided prayer, with his hands hiding his face, Ruth stopped hitting him. Although she didn't help him, she let him get to his feet. His damaged right knee gave him a jolting limp, which doubtless caused him considerable pain in his broken left collarbone. The cut over his eyebrow was a real bleeder. At a safe distance, Ruth followed Scott to his car. She still held his racquet handle; it felt about the right weight for her, now that the racquet head was gone.

She had a passing concern for Scott's right knee, but only if it might affect his driving. Then she saw that he drove a car with automatic transmission; he could operate the accelerator and the brake with his left foot, if he had to. It depressed her that she had almost as much contempt for a man who drove a car with automatic transmission as she did for a man who hit women.

God, look at me—I'm my father's child! Ruth thought.

After Scott had gone, Ruth found the head of his racquet in the laundry room; she threw it in the trash, together with what was left of the racquet handle. Then she started a load of laundry—just her squash gear and some underwear, and the towels that she and Scott had used. She mainly wanted to hear the washing machine; the sound of it running was reassuring to her. The empty house was too quiet.

Next she drank nearly a quart of water, and—naked again—carried a clean towel and two ice packs out to the pool. She took a long, hot shower in the outdoor stall, soaping herself twice and washing her hair twice, too, and then she sat on the bottom step in the shallow end. She put one ice pack on her right shoulder and held the other ice pack against her face, covering her cheekbone and right eye. Ruth had avoided looking in a mirror, but she could tell that her cheekbone and her eye were swollen; her right eye wouldn't open wider than a slit. In the morning, the eye would be completely closed.

After the hot shower, the pool felt cold at first, but the water was silky-smooth and much warmer than the night air. It was a clear night; there must have been a million stars. Ruth hoped it would be as clear the next night, when she had to fly to Europe. But she was too tired to think more about her trip than that; she let the ice numb her.

She was sitting so still that a small frog swam right up to her; she cupped it in her hand. She reached out and let the frog go on the deck, where it hopped away. Eventually, the chlorine would have killed it. Then Ruth rubbed her hand under the water until the sensation of the frog's slipperiness was gone; the slime had reminded her of her too-recent experiences with the lubricating jelly.

When she heard the washing machine stop, she got out of the pool and transferred her wet laundry to the dryer. She went to bed in her own room, and lay in her clean sheets, listening to the comfortingly familiar tap or click of something spinning around and around in the dryer.

But later, when she had to get out of bed to go to the bathroom, it hurt her to pee, and she thought about the unfamiliar place—far inside her—where Scott Saunders had poked her. It also hurt there. The latter pain was not sharp. It was an ache, like the onset of her cramps—only it wasn't time for her cramps, and it wasn't a place where she'd ever felt pain before.

In the morning, she called Allan before he left for the office.

"Would you love me any less if I gave up squash?" Ruth asked him. "I don't think I've got many more games in me—that is, not after I beat my father."

"Of course I wouldn't love you any less," Allan told her.

"You're too good for me," she warned him.

"I told you I loved you," he said.

God, he really *must* love me! Ruth thought. But all she said was: "I'll call you again, from the airport."

Ruth had examined the fingerprint bruises on her breasts; there were fingerprint and thumbprint bruises on her hips and buttocks, too, but Ruth couldn't see all of them because she could see only out of her left eye. She still refused to look at her face in a mirror. She knew without looking that she should continue to put ice on her right eye, which she did. Her right shoulder was stiff and sore, but she was tired of icing her shoulder. Besides, she had things to do. She'd just finished packing when her father came home.

"My God, Ruthie—who hit you?"

"It's just a squash injury," she lied.

"Who were you playing?" her father asked.

"Mostly myself," she told him.

"Ruthie, Ruthie ..." her father said. He looked tired. He didn't look seventy-seven, but Ruth decided that he looked like someone in his sixties. She loved the smooth backs of his small, square hands. Ruth found herself staring at the backs of his hands, because she couldn't look him in the eye—not with her swollen-shut right eye, anyway. "Ruthie, I'm sorry," her father began. "About Hannah ..."

"I don't want to hear about it, Daddy," Ruth told him. "You can't keep your pecker in your pants, as they say—it's the same old story."

"But *Hannah*, Ruthie ..." her father tried to say.

"I don't even want to hear her name," Ruth told him.

"Okay, Ruthie."

She couldn't stand to see how sheepish he was; she already knew he loved her more than he loved anyone else. Worse, Ruth knew that she loved him, too; she loved him more than she loved Allan, and *certainly* more than she loved Hannah. There was nobody Ruth Cole loved or hated as much as she loved and hated her father, but all she said to him was: "Get your racquet."

"Can you see out of that eye?" her father asked her.

"I can see out of the other one," Ruth told him.

Ruth Gives Her Father a Driving Lesson

It still hurt her to pee, but Ruth tried not to think about it. She quickly got into her squash clothes; she wanted to be in the court, warming up the ball, before her father was ready to play. She also wanted to erase the blue smudge of chalk that marked the dead spot on the front wall. Ruth didn't need the chalk mark to know where the dead spot was.

The ball was already warm, and very lively, when Ruth felt that almost imperceptible shudder in the floor—her father was climbing up the ladder in the barn. She sprinted once to the front wall, then turned and sprinted to the back—all before she heard her father tap his racquet twice and open the squash-court door. Ruth felt only a twinge of pain in that unfamiliar place where Scott Saunders had poked her the wrong way. If she didn't have to run too hard, she would be okay.

That she couldn't see out of her right eye was a bigger problem. There were going to be moments when she wouldn't be able to see where her father was. Ted didn't crash around the court; he moved as little as he had to, but when he moved, he glided. If you couldn't see him, you didn't know where he was.

Ruth knew it was crucial to win the first game. Ted was toughest in the middle of a match. If I'm lucky, Ruth thought, it will take him a game to locate the dead spot. When they were still warming up, she caught her father squinting at the front wall of the court, looking for that missing smudge of blue.

She took the first game 18–16, but by then her father had pinpointed the dead spot and Ruth was picking the ball up late on his hard serve— especially when she received his serve in the left-hand court. With no vision in her right eye, she practically had to turn to face him when he served. Ruth lost the next two games, 12–15 and 16–18, but—although he was leading 2–1 in games—it was her father who needed the water bottle after their third game.

Ruth won the fourth game 15–9. Her father hit the tin in losing the last point; it was the first time that either of them had hit the tin. They were tied 2–2 in games. She'd been tied with her father before—she'd always lost. Many times, just before the fifth game, her father would tell her: "I think you're going to beat me, Ruthie." Then he would beat her. This time he didn't say anything. Ruth drank a little water and took a long look at him with her one good eye.

"I think I'm going to beat you, Daddy," she told him. She won the fifth game 15–4. Once again, her father hit the tin in losing the last point. The telltale sound of the tin would ring in her ears for the next four or five years.

"Good job, Ruthie," Ted said. He had to leave the court to get the water bottle. Ruth had to be fast; she was able to pat him on the ass with her racquet as he was going out the door. What she wanted to do was give him a hug, but he wouldn't even look her in her one good eye. What an odd man he is! she thought. Then she remembered the oddness of Eddie O'Hare trying to flush his change down the toilet. Maybe all men were odd.

She'd always thought it strange that her father found it so natural to be naked in front of her. From the moment that her breasts began to develop, and they had developed most noticeably, Ruth had not felt comfortable being naked in front of him. Yet showering together in the outdoor shower, and swimming naked together in the pool...well, weren't these activities merely family rituals? In the warm weather, anyway, they seemed to be the *expected* rituals, inseparable from playing squash.

But, upon his defeat, her father looked old and tired; Ruth couldn't bear the thought of seeing him naked. Nor did she want him to see the fingerprint bruises on her breasts, and the thumbprint and fingerprint bruises on her hips and buttocks. Her father *might* have believed that her black eye was a squash injury, but he knew more than enough about sex to know that she couldn't have got her *other* bruises playing squash. She thought she would spare him those other bruises.

Of course he didn't know he was being spared. When Ruth told him that she wanted a hot bath instead of a shower and a swim, her father felt he'd been rebuffed.

"Ruthie, how are we ever going to put the Hannah episode behind us if we don't *talk* about it?"

"We'll talk about Hannah later, Daddy. Maybe after I'm back from Europe."

For twenty years, she'd been trying to beat her father at squash. Now that she'd finally defeated him, Ruth found herself weeping in the bathtub. She wished she could feel even the slightest elation at her moment of victory; instead Ruth wept because her father had reduced her best friend to an "episode." Or was it Hannah who'd reduced their friendship to something less than a fling with her father?

Oh, don't pick it apart—just get over it! Ruth told herself. So they had both betrayed her—so what?

When she got out of her bath, she made herself look in the mirror. Her right eye was a horror—a great way to begin a book tour! The eye was puffy and closed, the cheekbone swollen, but the discoloration of the skin was the most striking aspect of her injury. For an area roughly the size of a fist, her skin was a dark reddish-purple—like a sunset before a storm, the vivid colors tinged with black. It was such a lurid bruise, it was half comical. She would wear the bruise for the duration of her ten-day tour in Germany; the swelling would go down and the bruise would finally fade to a sallow yellow color, but the injury might still be discernible on her face the following week in Amsterdam, too.

She intentionally hadn't packed her squash clothes, not even her shoes. She'd purposely left her racquets in the barn. It was a good time to give up squash. Her German and Dutch publishers had arranged matches for her; they would have to cancel them. She had an obvious (even a visible) excuse. She could tell them her cheekbone was broken, and that she'd been advised by a doctor to let it heal. (Scott Saunders might very well have broken her cheekbone.)

Her black eye didn't look like a squash injury; if she'd been hit that hard by her opponent's *racquet,* she would have had a cut—and stitches— in addition to the bruise. The story should be that she was struck by her opponent's *elbow.* In order for that to happen, Ruth would have had to have been standing too close to her opponent—crowding him from be-hind. In such a circumstance, Ruth's imaginary opponent would have to have been a left-hander—in order to hit her in her right eye. (To tell a believable story, the novelist knew, you just have to get the details right.)

She could imagine it being funny in the interviews that lay ahead of her: "Traditionally, I've had a hard time with left-handers." Or: "There's always something with lefties that you don't see coming." (For example, they fuck you from behind, after you tell them you don't like it that way, and they slug you when you tell them it's time to leave—or they fuck your best friend.)

Ruth felt familiar enough with left-handed behavior to make up a pretty good story.

They were in heavy traffic on the Southern State Parkway, not far from the turnoff to the airport, when Ruth decided that she'd not defeated her father to her satisfaction. For fifteen years or more, whenever they drove anywhere together, Ruth usually drove. But not today. Back in Sagaponack, as he was putting her three bags in the trunk, her father had said to her: "Better let me drive, Ruthie. I can see out of both eyes."

Ruth hadn't argued. If her father drove, she could say *anything* to him, and he wouldn't be permitted to look at her—not while he was driving.

Ruth had begun by telling him how much she'd liked Eddie O'Hare. She'd gone on to say that her mother had already thought of leaving *be-fore* the boys were killed; it had not been Eddie who'd given Marion the idea. And Ruth told her father that she knew he had *planned* her mother's affair with Eddie; he had set them up, realizing how vulnerable Marion might be to a boy who reminded her of Thomas and Timothy. And of course it had been an even easier assumption, on her father's part, that Eddie would fall hopelessly in love with Marion.

"Ruthie, Ruthie..." her father started to say.

"Keep your eyes on the road, *and* in the rearview mirror," she told him. "If you even *think* about looking at me, you better pull over and let me drive."

"Your mother was terminally depressed, and she knew it," her father told her. "She knew she would have a terrible effect on you. It's an awful thing for a child to have a parent who's always depressed."

Talking to Eddie had meant so much to Ruth, but everything Eddie had told her meant nothing to her father. Ted had a fixed idea of who Marion was, and why she'd left him. Indeed, Ruth's meeting with Eddie had failed to make *any* impression on her father. That was probably the reason that the desire to devastate her father had never been as strong in Ruth as it was when she began to tell him about Scott Saunders.

Clever novelist that she was, Ruth first led her father into the story by *mis*leading him. She began with meeting Scott on the jitney, and their subsequent squash match.

"So *that's* who gave you the black eye!" her father said. "I'm not surprised. He charges all over the court, and he takes too big a backswing—he's a typical tennis player."

Ruth just told the story, step by step. When she got to the part about showing Scott the Polaroids in her father's bottommost drawer, Ruth began to speak of herself in the third person. Her father hadn't known that Ruth knew about those photographs—not to mention his nighttable drawer full of condoms and the lubricating jelly.

When Ruth got to the part about her *first* sexual experience with Scott—and how she'd hoped, when Scott had been licking her, that her father would come home and see them through the open door of the master bedroom—her father took his eyes off the road, if only for a half-second, and looked at her.

"You better pull over and let me drive, Daddy," Ruth told him. "One eye on the road is better than no eyes."

He watched the road, and the rearview mirror, while she went ahead with her story. The shrimp hadn't tasted much like shrimp, and she hadn't wanted to have sex a second time. Her first big mistake was to straddle Scott for so long. "Ruth fucked his brains out" was how she put it.

When she got to the part about the phone ringing, and Scott Saunders entering her from behind—even though she'd told him that she didn't like it that way—her father took his eyes off the road again. Ruth got angry with him. "Look, Daddy, if you can't concentrate on the driving, you're not fit to drive. Get off the road. I'll take over."

"Ruthie, Ruthie . . ." was all he could say. He was crying.

"If you're upset and you can't see the road, that's another reason to pull over, Daddy."

She described her head banging against the headboard of the bed, how she'd had no other choice but to push her hips back against him. And, later, how he'd hit her—*not* with a squash racquet. ("Ruth thought it was a straight left—she never saw it coming.")

She'd just curled up and hoped that he wouldn't keep hitting her. Then, when her head had cleared, she'd gone downstairs and found Scott's squash racquet. Her first shot took out his right knee. "It was a low backhand," she explained. "Naturally with the racquet face sideways."

"You took his knee out first?" her father interrupted her.

"Knee, face, both elbows, both collarbones—in that order," Ruth told him.

"He couldn't *walk?*" her father asked.

"He couldn't *crawl,*" Ruth said. "He *could* walk, with a limp."

"Jesus, Ruthie . . ."

"Did you see the sign for Kennedy?" she asked him.

"Yes, I saw it," he said.

"You didn't look like you saw it," Ruth told him.

Then she told him how it still hurt her to pee, and that there was a pain in an unfamiliar place—inside her. "I'm sure it will go away," she added, dropping the third person. "I've just got to remember to stay out of that position."

"I'll kill the bastard!" her father told her.

"Why bother?" Ruth asked. "You can still play squash with him—when he's able to run around again. He's not very good but you can get a halfway decent workout with him—he's not bad exercise."

"He virtually *raped* you! He *hit* you!" her father shouted.

"But nothing's changed," Ruth insisted. "Hannah's still my best friend. You're still my father."

"Okay, okay—I get it," her father told her. He tried to wipe the tears off his face with the sleeve of his old flannel shirt. Ruth loved this particular shirt because her father had worn it when she was a little girl. Still, she was tempted to tell him to keep both his hands on the wheel.

Instead she reminded him of what airline she was taking, and the terminal he should be looking for. "You can see, can't you?" she asked. "It's Delta."

"I can see, I can see. I *know* it's Delta," he told her. "And I get your point—I get it, I get it."

"I don't think you'll ever get it," Ruth said. "Don't look at me—we're not stopped yet!" she had to tell him.

"Ruthie, Ruthie. I'm sorry, I'm sorry . . ."

"Do you see where it says 'Departures'?" she asked him.

"Yes, I see it," he said. It was the way he'd said, "Good job, Ruthie," after she'd beaten him in his goddamn barn.

When her father finally stopped the car, Ruth said, "Good driving, Daddy." If she'd known then that it would be their last conversation, she might have tried to patch things up with him. But she could see that, for once, she'd truly defeated him. Her father was too badly beaten to be uplifted by a simple turn in their conversation. And besides, the pain in that unfamiliar place inside her was still bothering her.

In retrospect, it would have to suffice that Ruth remembered to kiss her father good-bye.

In the Delta Crown Room, before she boarded the plane, Ruth called Allan. He sounded worried on the phone, or as if he were being less than candid with her. It gave her a pang to imagine what he might think of her if he ever knew about Scott Saunders. (Allan would never know about Scott.)

Hannah had got Allan's message; she'd returned his call, but he'd been brief with her. He'd told Hannah that there was nothing wrong, that he'd spoken to Ruth and that Ruth was "fine." Hannah had suggested that they meet for lunch, or for a drink—"just to talk about Ruth"—but Allan had told Hannah that he was looking forward to meeting her, with Ruth, when Ruth was back from Europe.

"I never talk *about* Ruth," he'd told her.

It was the closest Ruth had come to telling Allan that she loved him, but she could still hear something worried in his voice and it troubled her; as her editor, he'd withheld nothing.

"What's wrong, Allan?" Ruth asked.

"Well ..." he began, sounding like her father, "nothing, really. It can wait."

"Tell me," Ruth said.

"There was something in your fan mail," Allan told her. "Normally no one reads it—we just forward it to Vermont. But this was a letter addressed to me—to your editor, that is. And so I read it. It's really a letter to you."

"Is it *hate* mail?" Ruth asked. "I get my share of it. Is that all it is?"

"I suppose that's all it is," Allan said. "But it's upsetting. I think you ought to see it."

"I *will* see it—when I get back," Ruth told him.

"Maybe I could fax it to your hotel," Allan suggested.

"Is it threatening? Is it a stalker?" she asked. The word "stalker" always gave her a chill.

"No, it's a widow—an angry widow," Allan told her.

"Oh, *that*," Ruth said. She'd expected *that*. When she wrote about abortion, not having had an abortion, she got angry letters from people who *had* had abortions; when she wrote about childbirth, not having had a child—or when she wrote about divorce, not having been divorced (*or* married)... well, there were always *those* letters. People denying that imagination was real, or insisting that imagination wasn't *as* real as personal experience; it was the same old thing. "For God's sake, Allan," Ruth said, "you're not worried about another reader telling me to write about what I *know*, are you?"

"This one is a little different," Allan replied.

"All right—fax it to me," she told him.

"I don't want to worry you," he said.

"Then *don't* fax it to me!" Ruth said. Then she added, because the thought suddenly occurred to her: "Is this a *stalking* widow or just an angry one?"

"Look, I'll fax it to you," he told her.

"Is this something you should show to the FBI—is it like *that*?" Ruth asked him.

"No, no—not really. I don't think so," he said.

"Just fax it," she told him.

"It'll be there when you arrive," Allan promised her. "Bon voyage!"

Why was it that women were absolutely the *worst* readers when it came to something that touched upon their personal lives? Ruth thought. What made a woman presume that *her* rape (her miscarriage, her marriage, her divorce, her loss of a child or a husband) was the *only* universal experience that there was? Or was it merely the case that most of Ruth's readers were women—and that women who wrote to novelists, and told them their personal disaster stories, were the most fucked-up women of all?

Ruth sat in the Delta Crown Room, holding a glass of ice water against her black eye. It must have been her faraway expression, in addition to her obvious injury, that prompted a fellow traveler—a drunken woman—to speak to her. The woman, who was about Ruth's age, had a hardened expression on her pale, drawn face. She was too thin—a chain-smoker with a raspy voice and a southern accent, thickened by booze.

"Whoever he was, sweetie, you're better off without him," the woman told Ruth.

"It was a squash injury," Ruth replied.

"He hit you with a *squash?*" the woman slurred. "Shit, it must have been a hard one!"

"It was pretty hard," Ruth admitted, smiling.

On the plane, Ruth quickly drank two beers. When she had to pee, she was relieved that it hurt a little less. There were only three other passengers in first class, and no one in the seat beside her. She told the flight attendant not to serve her any dinner, but she asked to be awakened for breakfast.

Ruth reclined in her seat; she covered herself with the thin blanket and tried to make her head comfortable on the small pillow. She would have to sleep on her back, or on her left side; the right side of her face was too sore to sleep on. Her last thought, before she fell asleep, was that Hannah had been right again: I *am* too hard on my father. (After all, as the song goes, he's just a man.)

Then Ruth was asleep. She would sleep all the way to Germany, trying in vain not to dream.

A Widow for the Rest of Her Life

It was Allan's fault. Ruth would never have dreamt all night about her *other* hate mail, or her occasional stalkers, if Allan hadn't told her about the angry widow.

There'd been a time when she'd answered all her fan mail. There was so much of it—after her first novel, especially—but she'd made the effort. Oh, she'd never bothered with the bitchy letters; if the tone of any letter was even partially pissy, Ruth threw it away without answering it. ("For the most part—your incomplete sentences notwithstanding—I was mildly enjoying your book, but the repeated inconsistencies with serial commas and your misuse of the word 'hopefully' eventually wore down my tolerance. I stopped on page 385, where the most egregious example of your grocery-list style stopped me and sent me looking for better prose than yours.") Who would bother to answer a letter like that?

But the objections to Ruth's writing were more often complaints about the content of her novels. ("What I detest in your books is that you sensationalize everything. In particular, you exaggerate the unseemly.")

As for the so-called unseemly, Ruth knew that it was of sufficient offense to some of her readers that she even *contemplated* it—not to mention that she exaggerated it. Nor was Ruth Cole entirely sure that she *did* exaggerate the unseemly. Her worst fear was that the unseemly had become so commonplace that one *couldn't* exaggerate it.

What got Ruth in trouble was that she used to answer her *good* mail; but it was the good mail that you had to be most careful about *not* answering. Particularly dangerous were those letters in which the letter writer claimed not only that he or she had loved a book by Ruth Cole but that the book had changed his or her life.

There was a pattern. The letter writer always professed an undying love for one or more of Ruth's books; usually there was some personal identification with one or more of Ruth's characters, too. Ruth would write, thanking the person for his or her letter. The second time the person wrote to Ruth, the letter writer was much more needy; often the second letter was accompanied by a manuscript. ("I loved your book; I know you're going to love mine"—that kind of thing.) Commonly, the letter writer would suggest a meeting. The third letter would express how hurt the letter writer felt, because Ruth hadn't responded to the second letter. Whether Ruth responded to the third letter or not, the fourth letter would be the angry one—or the first of many angry ones. That was the pattern.

In a way, Ruth thought, her *former* fans—those fans who were disappointed that they couldn't get to know her personally—were more frightening than the creeps who hated her from the beginning. The writing of a novel demanded privacy; it called for a virtually isolated existence. In contrast, the publication of a book was an alarmingly public experience. Ruth had never been good at the *public* part of the process.

"Guten Morgen," the flight attendant whispered in her ear. *"Frühstück..."* Ruth was wrecked by her dreams, but she was hungry and the coffee smelled good.

Across the aisle, a gentleman was shaving. He sat leaning over his breakfast, peering into a small hand-held mirror; the sound of his electric razor droned like an insect against a screen. Below the breakfast eaters lay Bavaria, growing greener as the clouds lifted; the fog was burned away by the first rays of the morning sun. It had rained overnight; the tarmac would still be wet when the plane landed in Munich.

Ruth liked Germany, and her German publishers. It was her third trip; as always, everything on her itinerary had been explained to her beforehand. And her interviewers would actually have read her book.

At the registration desk in her hotel, they were expecting her early arrival; her room was ready. The publisher had sent flowers—and photocopies of her early reviews, which were good. Ruth's German was *not* good, but she could at least understand her reviews. At Exeter, and at Middlebury, it had been her only foreign language. The Germans seemed to like her for trying to speak their language, even though she spoke it badly.

This first day, she would force herself to stay awake until noon. Then she would take a nap; two or three hours were about right for the jet lag. Her first reading was that evening—it was out in Freising. Later that weekend, after her interviews, she would be driven from Munich to Stuttgart. Everything was clear.

Clearer than it ever is at home! Ruth was thinking, when the woman at the reception desk said, "Oh—and there's a fax for you." The hate mail from the angry widow—for a moment, Ruth had forgotten all about it.

"Willkommen in Deutschland!" the woman at the desk called to her, as Ruth turned and followed the bellman to the elevator. ("Welcome to Germany!")

"My dear," the widow's letter began, "this time you have gone too far. It may be true, as I have read in one of your reviews, that you have 'a satirical gift for choreographing an unusual number of society's ills and human foibles in one book,' or 'for gathering the innumerable moral calamities of our time into the life of a single character.' But not everything in our lives is *comic* material; there are certain tragedies that resist a *humorous* interpretation. You have gone too far.

"I was married for fifty-five years," the widow continued. (Her late husband was a mortician, Ruth decided.) "When my husband died, my life stopped. He meant the world to me. When I lost him, I lost everything. And what about your own mother? Do you imagine that she found a way to put a comic spin on the death of your brothers? Do you think you were abandoned by a woman who left you and your father to pursue a life in *satire?*" (How dare she? thought Ruth Cole.)

"You write about abortion and childbirth and adoption, but you've never even been pregnant. You write about being a divorcée and a widow, but you've never even been married. You write about when it's safe for a widow to re-enter the world, but there is no such thing as a widow for one year. I will be a widow for the rest of my life!

"Horace Walpole once wrote: 'The world is a comedy to those who think, a tragedy to those who feel.' But the *real* world is tragic to those who think *and* feel; it is only comic to those who've been lucky."

Ruth flipped to the end of the letter, and then back to the beginning, but there was no return address; the angry widow hadn't even signed her name.

Her letter ended as follows: "All I have left is prayer. I will include you in my prayers. What does it say about you that, at your age, you have never been married? Not even once. I will pray for you that you get married. Maybe you will have a child, maybe not. My husband and

I loved each other so much that we never wanted children; children might have spoiled it. More important, I will pray that you will truly love your husband—and that you will lose him. What I will pray for you is that *you* become a widow for the rest of your life. Then you will know how untruthfully you have written about the real world."

In lieu of a signature, the woman had written: *A Widow for the Rest of Her Life.* And there was a P.S., which gave Ruth the shivers: "I have a lot of time for prayers."

Ruth would fax Allan in New York and ask him if the angry widow's name or address had appeared on the envelope—or, failing that, from what city or town had the letter been mailed? But the answer would be as disturbing as the letter. The letter had been hand-delivered to the Random House building on East Fiftieth Street. The receptionist could not remember the woman, or if it even was a woman, who'd brought the letter to the editorial floor.

If the praying widow had been married for fifty-five years, she had to be in her seventies—if not in her eighties or her nineties! Maybe the angry old woman *did* have a lot of time for prayers, but she didn't have a lot of time left to *live.*

Ruth slept for most of the afternoon. The ranting widow's letter was not *that* upsetting. And maybe it was fair; if a book was any good, it was a slap in the face to *someone.* An angry old woman's letter is not going to ruin my trip, Ruth decided.

She would walk, she would send postcards, she would write in her diary. Except for in Frankfurt at the book fair, where it was impossible to relax, Ruth was determined to restore herself in Germany. Her diary entries and her postcards suggest that, to some degree, she did. Even in Frankfurt!

Ruth's Diary, and Selected Postcards

Not a bad reading in Freising, but either I or the audience was duller than I expected. Dinner afterward in a former monastery with vaulted ceilings—I drank too much.

Each time I'm in Germany I'm reminded of the contrast, in a place like the lobby of the Vier Jahreszeiten, between the expensively dressed hotel guests—the business class, who are so formal—and the deliberately disreputable appearance of the journalists, who appear to revel in their grubbiness like teenagers intent on offending their parents. A society in ugly confrontation with itself—so much like ours, but at the same time in advance of ours and even more deteriorated.

Either I'm not over the jet lag or a new novel is beginning in the back of my mind—I absolutely cannot read anything without skipping ahead. The room-service menu; the list of the hotel's amenities; Norman Sherry's *The Life of Graham Greene,* volume one, which I did not intend to bring with me—I must have put it in my carry-on without thinking. All I can read are the last lines of paragraphs that seem important, those final sentences before space breaks on the page. Only occasionally will there be a sentence in the heart of a paragraph that stands out. And I'm incapable of reading anything consecutively; my mind keeps jumping ahead.

Sherry writes of Greene: "His seeking out of the seedy, the sordid, the sexual and the deviant took him in many directions, as his diary shows." I wonder if my diary shows it, too. I hope so. It galls me that seeking out the seedy, the sordid, the sexual, and the deviant is the expected (if not altogether acceptable) behavior of male writers; it would surely benefit me, as a writer, if I had the courage to seek out more of the seedy, the sordid, the sexual, and the deviant myself. But women who seek out such things are made to feel ashamed, or else they sound stridently ridiculous in defending themselves—as if they're bragging.

Suppose I paid a prostitute to let me watch her with a customer, to absorb every detail of the most furtive encounters ... isn't this, in a way, what a writer should do? Yet there are subjects that remain off-limits for women writers. It's not unlike that dichotomy which exists regarding one's sexual past: it is permissible, even attractive, for a man to have had one, but if a *woman* has had a sexual past, she'd better keep quiet about it.

I *must* be beginning a new novel; my distraction is too focused for jet lag. I'm thinking about a woman writer, someone more extreme than I am—more extreme as a writer *and* as a woman. She makes every effort to observe everything, to absorb every detail; she doesn't necessarily want to be single, but she believes that marriage will impose restraints on her. It's not that she needs to experience everything—she's not a sexual adventurer—but she does want to *see* everything.

Suppose *she* pays a prostitute to let her watch her with a customer. Suppose she doesn't dare do that alone—let's say she does it with a boyfriend. (A bad boyfriend, of course.) And what transpires with the boyfriend, as a result of observing the prostitute, is so degrading (so shameful) that it's enough to make the woman writer change her life.

Something happens that's more than seedy—something *too* sordid, *too* deviant. This novel is a demonstration of one kind of sexual inequality: the woman writer, in her need to observe, goes too far. As for exactly what happens—the specific experience with the prostitute—if the writer were a *man*, there would be no guilt, no degradation.

Norman Sherry, Greene's biographer, writes of "the novelist's right—and need—to use his own and others' experience." Mr. Sherry thinks there is a ruthlessness to this "right" of the novelist, to this terrible "need." But the relationship between observation and imagination is more complicated than mere ruthlessness. One must imagine a good story; then one must make the details seem real. It helps, when making the details *seem* real, if some of the details *are* real. Personal experience is overrated, but observation is essential.

It's definitely not jet lag; it's a novel. It begins with paying a prostitute, an act traditionally contaminated with shame. No, stupid—it begins with the bad boyfriend! No doubt I'll make him left-handed. A strawberry-blond boyfriend . . .

I'm so sick of Hannah telling me that I should shut off my biological clock and get married (or not) for the "right" reasons, not "merely" because my body thinks it wants to have a baby. Hannah may have been born without a biological clock, but she certainly responds to all the other things her body thinks it wants—if not a baby.

[In a postcard to Hannah, which was a display of sausages in Munich's Viktualienmarkt.]
I FORGIVE YOU, BUT YOU FORGIVE YOURSELF A LITTLE TOO EASILY. YOU ALWAYS HAVE.

LOVE,
RUTH

The drive from Munich to Stuttgart; the pronunciation of *Schwäbische Alb;* the farmland with red and blue and green cabbages. In Stuttgart, the hotel is on the Schillerstrasse—a modern hotel with lots of glass. The pronunciation of *Schlossgarten.*

The questions from the young people in the audience, after my reading, are all about the social problems in the United States. Because they see my books as critical of American society, they invite me to express my perceived anti-Americanism. (The interviewers extend the same invitation.) And now—given their pending reunification—the Germans also want to know what I think of *them.* What do Americans, in general, think of Germans? Are we happy about German reunification?

I would rather talk about storytelling, I tell them. They wouldn't. All I can say is that my lack of interest in what interests them is genuine. They don't like my answer.

In the new novel, the prostitute should be an older woman—someone not too intimidating to the woman writer. Her bad boyfriend wants a younger, better-looking prostitute than the one the woman writer eventually chooses. The reader should anticipate the boyfriend's awfulness, but the woman writer doesn't see it coming. She's concentrating on her observations of the prostitute—not just on the prostitute's customer, or least of all on the mechanically familiar act, but on all the surrounding details of the prostitute's room.

There should be something concerning what the woman writer likes and dislikes about men; possibly she asks the prostitute how she is able to overcome her physical abhorrence of certain types of men. Are there men the prostitute says no to? There *must* be! Prostitutes can't be totally indifferent to ... well, the *details* of men.

It should happen in Amsterdam. A.) Because prostitutes are so available there. B.) Because I'm going there. C.) Because my Dutch publisher is a nice guy; I can persuade him to see and talk to a prostitute with me.

No, stupid—you should see the prostitute alone.

What I like: Allan's aggressiveness, most of the time. (I like the limits of his aggressiveness, too.) And his criticism, at least of my writing. I can be myself with him. He tolerates me, he forgives me. (Maybe too much.) I feel safe with him; I would do more, read more, go out more with him. He wouldn't force himself on me. (He *hasn't* forced himself on me.) He would be a good father.

What I don't like: he interrupts me, but he interrupts everybody. It's not that his eating habits, I mean his table manners, embarrass me; it's more that I find the way he eats repellent. There is the fear that I would find him sexually repellent, too. And there's the matter of the hair on the backs of his hands.... Oh, get over it!

[In a postcard to Allan, which was of an 1885 Daimler in the Mercedes-Benz Museum in Stuttgart.]

DO YOU NEED A NEW CAR? I'D LIKE TO TAKE A LONG DRIVE WITH YOU.

LOVE,
RUTH

On the flight from Stuttgart to Hamburg, then in a car from Hamburg to Kiel. There are a lot of cows. We are in the state of Schleswig-Holstein—where the cows of that name come from. My driver is a sales rep for my publisher. I always learn something from sales reps. This one explains that my German readers expect me to be more "political" than I am. The sales rep tells me that my novels are political in the sense that all social commentary is political. The sales rep says: "Your books are political but you aren't!"

I'm not sure if this is offered as criticism or simply stated as a fact, but I believe it. And the subject comes up in the questions from the audience, after the reading in the Kunsthalle in Kiel—a good crowd.

Instead, I try to talk about storytelling. "I'm like someone who makes furniture," I tell them, "so let's talk about a few things that have to do with chairs or tables." I can see by their faces that they want this to be more complicated, more symbolic than it is. "I am thinking of a new novel," I explain. "It's about that point in a woman's life when she decides she wants to be married—*not* because there's a man in her life whom she truly wants to marry, but because she's sick and tired of bad boyfriends." The laughter is sporadic and discouraging. I try it in German. There's more laughter, but I suspect the laughter is because of my German.

"It could be my first book with a first-person narrator," I tell them. Now I see that they have lost all interest, in English *and* in German. "Then it would be called *My Last Bad Boyfriend.*" (The title is terrible in German; it is greeted with more dismay than laughter: *Mein letzter schlimmer Freund.* It sounds like a novel about an adolescent disease.)

I pause for a drink of water and see the audience slipping away, especially from the seats in the rear of the hall. And those who have stayed are painfully waiting for me to finish. I don't have the heart to tell them that the woman I'm going to write about is a *writer.* That would *really* kill their interest. So much for the craft of storytelling or the concrete concerns of the storyteller! Even I am bored with trying to entertain people on the subject of what it is I really do.

From my hotel room in Kiel, I can see the ferries in the bay. They are en route to and from Sweden and Denmark. Maybe one day I could go there with Allan. Maybe one day I could travel with a husband and a child, and with a nanny for the child.

The woman writer I'm thinking about: does she truly believe that marriage will be the death of her freedom to observe the world? If she were already married, she could have gone with her husband to see and talk to a prostitute! For a woman writer, having a husband could give her *more* freedom of observation. Maybe the woman I'm writing about doesn't know that.

I wonder if Allan would object to observing a prostitute with her customer with me. Of course he wouldn't!

But the person I should really ask to do this with me is my father.

[In a postcard to her father, which was of the prostitutes in their windows on the Herbertstrasse, the red-light district in the St. Pauli quarter of Hamburg.]

THINKING OF YOU, DADDY. I'M SORRY ABOUT WHAT I SAID. IT WAS MEAN. I LOVE YOU!

RUTHIE

The flight from Hamburg to Köln; the drive from Köln to Bonn; the grandeur of the university.

For the first time, someone in the audience asked about my eye. (In my interviews, *all* the journalists have asked.) This was a young woman; she looked like a student, and her English was almost perfect.

"Who hit you?" she asked.

"My father," I told her. The audience was suddenly hushed. "With his elbow. We were playing squash."

"Your father is young enough to play squash with you?" the young woman asked.

"No, he is *not* young enough," I told her, "but he's in pretty good shape for a man his age."

"I suppose you beat him, then," the student said.

"Yes, I beat him," I answered.

But after the reading, the same young woman handed me a note. *I don't believe you. Someone hit you,* the note said.

This I also like about the Germans: they come to their own conclusions.

Of course, if I write a first-person novel about a woman writer, I am inviting every book reviewer to apply the autobiographical label—to conclude that I am writing about myself. But one must never not write a certain kind of novel out of fear of what the reaction to it will be.

And I can just hear Allan on the subject of my writing two novels in a row about women writers; yet I've heard him say that editorial advice should *not* include recommendations or caveats about what to write or not write about. Doubtless I shall have to remind him of that.

But more important to this new novel: what does the bad boyfriend *do,* as a result of observing a prostitute with her customer, that is so degrading to the woman novelist? What *happens* to make her feel so ashamed that it's enough to make her change her life?

After watching the prostitute with her customer, the boyfriend could be so aroused that the way he makes love to the woman writer makes her feel that he is thinking about someone else. But that's just another version of bad sex. It must be something more awful, more humiliating than that.

In a way, I like this phase of a novel better than the actual writing of it. In the beginning, there are so many possibilities. With each detail you choose, with every word you commit yourself to, your options close down.

The matter of searching for my mother, or not; the hope that, one day, she will come looking for me. What are the remaining major events in my life? I mean the events that might make my mother come to me. My father's death; my wedding, if I have one; the birth of my child, if I have one. (If I ever get up the nerve to have children, I would want only one.) Maybe I should announce my forthcoming marriage to Eddie O'Hare. *That* might get my mother's attention. I wonder if Eddie would go along with it—after all, he wants to see her, too!

[In a postcard to Eddie O'Hare, which was of the great Cologne cathedral, the splendid Dom—the largest Gothic cathedral in Germany.]

BEING WITH YOU, TALKING WITH YOU ... IT WAS THE MOST IM-PORTANT EVENING IN MY LIFE, SO FAR. I HOPE I SEE YOU AGAIN SOON.

SINCERELY,
RUTH COLE

[In a postcard to Allan, which was of a magnificent castle on the Rhein.]

BE AN EDITOR. CHOOSE BETWEEN THESE TWO TITLES: *HER LAST BAD BOYFRIEND* OR *MY LAST BAD BOYFRIEND*. IN EITHER CASE, I LIKE THE IDEA.

LOVE,
RUTH

P.S. BUY ME THIS HOUSE AND I'LL MARRY YOU. I THINK I MIGHT MARRY YOU, ANYWAY!

On the train from Bonn to Frankfurt, another title for the new novel occurs to me; maybe it is more appealing than *My Last Bad Boyfriend*, but only because it would permit me to write another book in the third person. *What She Saw, What She Didn't Know*. I suppose it's too long and too literal. It would be even more exact with a semicolon. *What She Saw; What She Didn't Know*. I can imagine Allan's opinion of a semicolon in a title; he takes a dim view of my semicolons, anyway. "No one knows what they are anymore," he says. "If you're not in the habit of reading nineteenth-century novels, you think that the author has killed a fruit fly directly above a comma—semicolons have become nothing but a distraction." Yet I think I want to marry him!

It's a two-hour trip from Bonn to Frankfurt. My Frankfurt itinerary is my longest and busiest. Only two readings, but back-to-back interviews; and at the book fair itself there is a panel discussion, which I am dreading. The topic is German reunification.

"I'm a novelist," I will doubtless say at some point. "I'm just a storyteller."

Looking over the list of my fellow panelists—other authors, all promoting their books at the book fair—there is an atrocious American male of the Unbearable Intellectual species. And there is another American writer, female, less well known but no less atrocious; she is of the Pornography Violates My Civil Rights school. (If she hasn't already reviewed *Not for Children*, she will—and not kindly.)

There is also a young German novelist whose work has been banned in Canada. There was some charge of obscenity—in all probability, not unmerited. It's hard to forget the specific obscenity charge. A character in the young German's novel is having sex with chickens; he is caught in a posh hotel with a chicken. A terrible squawking leads the hotel staff to make the discovery—that, and the hotel maid had complained of feathers.

But the German novelist is interesting in comparison to the other panelists.

"I'm a *comic* novelist," I will doubtless say at some point; I always do. Half the audience (and more than half of my fellow panelists) will take this to mean that I am not a *serious* novelist. But comedy is ingrained. A writer doesn't choose to be comic. You can *choose* a plot, or not to have one. You can *choose* your characters. But comedy is not a choice; it just comes out that way.

Another panelist is an Englishwoman who's written a book about so-called recovered memory—in her case, *hers*. She woke up one morning and "remembered" that her father had raped her, and her brothers had raped her—and all her uncles. Her grandfather, too! Every morning she wakes up and "remembers" someone else who raped her. She must be exhausted!

Regardless of how heated the debate on the panel is, the young German novelist will have a faraway expression on his face—as if something serenely romantic has just crossed his mind. Probably a chicken.

"I'm just a storyteller," I will say again (and again). "I'm not good at generalizations."

Only the chicken-lover will understand me. He will give me a kindly look, maybe mildly desirous. His eyes will tell me: You might look a lot better with some reddish-brown feathers.

In Frankfurt, in my small room at the Hessischer Hof, drinking a beer that isn't very cold. At midnight it becomes October 3—Germany is reunited. On the TV, I watch the celebrations in Bonn and Berlin. A moment of history, alone in a hotel room. What can one say about German reunification? It's already *happened*.

Coughed all night. Called the publisher this morning, then the publicist. It's such a shame to cancel my appearance on the panel, but I must save my voice for my readings. The publisher sent me more flowers. The publicist brought me a package of cough drops—"with organically grown Swiss alpine herbs." Now I can cough through my interviews with my breath smelling of lemon balm and wild thyme. I've never been happier to have a cough.

On the elevator, there was the tragicomic Englishwoman; from the look of her, she'd doubtless awakened with the recovered memory of yet another rape.

At lunch in the Hessischer Hof, there was (at another table) the German novelist who does it with chickens; he was being interviewed by a woman who interviewed me earlier this morning. My interviewer at lunch was a man with a bigger cough than mine. And when I was alone, just sipping coffee at my table, the young German novelist looked at me whenever I coughed—as if I had a feather caught in my throat.

I truly love my cough. I can take a long bath and think about my new novel.

In the elevator, like a small man inflated to grotesque size—with helium—there is the atrocious American male, the Unbearable Intellectual. He seems offended when I step into the elevator with him.

"You missed the panel. They said you were sick," he tells me.

"Yes."

"Everyone gets sick here—it's a terrible place."

"Yes."

"I hope I don't catch something from you," he says.

"I hope not."

"I'm probably already sick—I've been here long enough," he adds. Like his writing, it's unclear what he means. Does he mean he's been in *Frankfurt* long enough to catch something, or does he mean he's been in the *elevator* long enough to have been exposed to what I've got?

"Are you still not married?" he asks me. It's not a pass; it's a signature non sequitur of the kind the Unbearable Intellectual is renowned for.

"Still not married, but maybe about to be," I answer.

"Ah—good for you!" he tells me. I'm surprised by his genuine fondness for my answer. "Here's my floor," he says. "Sorry you weren't on the panel."

"Yes." Ah, the little-heralded chance encounter between world-famous authors—is there anything that compares with it?

The woman writer should meet the strawberry-blond boyfriend at the Frankfurt Book Fair. The bad boyfriend is a fellow fiction writer—very minimalist. He's published only two books of short stories—fragile tales, so spare that most of the story is left out. His sales are small, but he has been compensated by the kind of unqualified critical adoration that often accompanies obscurity.

The woman novelist should be a writer of "big" novels. They are a parody of the proverbial wisdom that opposites attract. In this case, they can't stand each other's writing; their attraction is strictly sexual.

He should be younger than she is.

They begin an affair in Frankfurt and he comes with her to Holland, where she is going after the book fair to promote a Dutch translation. He doesn't have a Dutch publisher—and he has been far less in the limelight in Frankfurt than *she* has been. Although she hasn't noticed this, *he* has. He hasn't been in Amsterdam since he was a student—a summer abroad. He remembers the prostitutes; he wants to take her to see the prostitutes. Maybe a live-sex show, too.

"I don't think I want to see a live-sex show," the woman novelist says. It could be *his* idea to pay a prostitute to let them watch. "We could have our *own* live-sex show," the short-story writer says. He seems almost indifferent to the idea. He implies that she might be more interested in it than he is. "As a *writer*," he says. "For *research*."

And when they're in Amsterdam, and he's escorting her through the red-light district, he keeps up a casual, lighthearted banter. "I wouldn't want to see *her* do it—she looks inclined to bondage." (That kind of thing.) The minimalist makes her think that watching a prostitute will be merely a naughty bit of hilarity. He gives her the impression that the most difficult part of it will be trying to contain their laughter—because, of course, they can't reveal their concealed presence to the customer.

But I wonder how the prostitute would hide them so that they could see without being seen?

That will be *my* research. I can ask my Dutch publisher to walk with me through the red-light district—after all, it's a thing tourists do. He probably is asked by all his women authors; we all want to be *escorted* through the seedy, the sordid, the sexual, and the deviant. (The last time I was in Amsterdam, a journalist walked with me through the red-light district; it was *his* idea.)

So I will get a look at the women. I remember that they don't like it when women look at them. But I'm sure I'll find one or two who don't absolutely terrify me—someone I can go back to, alone. It will have to be someone who speaks English, or at least a little German.

One prostitute might be enough, as long as she is comfortable about talking to me. I can imagine the act without seeing it, surely. Besides: it is what happens to the woman in hiding, the woman writer, that most concerns me. Let's presume the bad boyfriend is aroused, even that he masturbates while they're hiding together. And she can't protest, or even make the slightest move to get away from him—without the prostitute's customer knowing that he's being watched. (Then how can he masturbate? That's a problem.)

Maybe the irony is that the prostitute has at least been paid for how she's used, but the woman writer is used, too; she has spent her money to be used. Well. Writers must have thick skins. No irony there.

Allan called. I coughed for him. Now that there is no immediate possibility for us to have sex—given the ocean between us—naturally I felt like having sex with him. Women are perverse!

I didn't tell him about the new book, not a word. It would have spoiled the postcards.

[In another postcard to Allan, which was an aerial view of the Frankfurt Book Fair, boasting some 5,500 publishers from some 100 countries.]

NEVER AGAIN WITHOUT YOU.

LOVE,
RUTH

On the KLM flight from Frankfurt to Amsterdam: both my cough and my black eye are barely with me. The cough exists only as a tickle at the back of my throat. The eye and my right cheekbone remain vaguely discolored—chartreuse, a yellowish green. There's no swelling, but the color suggests that I have been sick for a long time, and that the sickness, like my cough, is lingering.

It's the right look for someone who's about to approach a prostitute. I appear to have an old disease to share.

My guidebook for Amsterdam informs me that the red-light district, known as *de Walletjes* ("the little walls"), was officially sanctioned in the fourteenth century. There are tittering references to the district's "scantily clad girls in their shop windows."

Why is it that most writing about the seedy, the sordid, the sexual, and the deviant is always so unconvincingly superior in tone? (Amusement is as strong an expression of superiority as indifference is.) I think that any expression of amusement *or* indifference toward the unseemly is usually false. People are either attracted to the unseemly or disapproving of it, or both; yet we try to sound superior to the unseemly by *pretending* to be amused by it or indifferent to it.

"Everyone has a sexual hang-up, at least one," Hannah once said to me. (But if *Hannah* has one, she never told me what it is.)

There are the usual obligations ahead of me in Amsterdam, but I have enough free time for what I need to do. Amsterdam isn't Frankfurt; nothing is as bad as Frankfurt. And, to be honest, I can't wait to meet my prostitute! There is the thrill of something like shame about this "research." But of course I *am* the customer. I'm prepared—indeed, I'm fully expecting—to pay her.

[In another postcard to Allan, which she mailed from Schiphol Airport and which—not unlike the earlier postcard she mailed to her father, of the German prostitutes in their windows on the Herbertstrasse—was of *de Walletjes*, the red-light district of Amsterdam: the neon from the bars and sex shops reflecting in the canal; the passersby, all men in raincoats; the window in the foreground of the photograph, framed in lights of a purplish red, with the woman in her underwear in the window . . . looking like a misplaced mannequin, like something on loan from a lingerie shop, like someone *rented* for a private party.]

FORGET EARLIER QUESTION. THE TITLE IS *MY LAST BAD BOY-FRIEND*—MY FIRST FIRST-PERSON NARRATOR. YES, SHE'S ANOTHER WOMAN WRITER. BUT TRUST ME!

LOVE,

RUTH

The First Meeting

The publication of *Niet voor kinderen,* the Dutch translation of *Not for Children,* was the principal reason for Ruth Cole's third visit to Amsterdam, but Ruth now thought of the research for her prostitute story as the all-consuming justification for her being there. She'd not yet found the moment to speak of her new excitement to her Dutch publisher, Maarten Schouten, whom she affectionately referred to as "Maarten with two *a*'s and an *e*."

For the translation of *The Same Orphanage*—in Dutch, *Hetzelfde weeshuis,* which Ruth had struggled in vain to pronounce—she had stayed in a charming but run-down hotel on the Prinsengracht, where she'd discovered a sizable stash of marijuana in the small bedside drawer she'd selected for her underwear. The pot probably belonged to a previous guest, but such was Ruth's nervousness on her first European book tour that she was certain the marijuana had been planted in her room by some mischievous journalist intent on embarrassing her.

The aforementioned Maarten with two *a*'s and an *e* had assured her that possession of marijuana in Amsterdam was barely a noticeable offense, much less an embarrassment. And Ruth had loved the city from the beginning: the canals, the bridges, all the bicycles, the cafés, and the restaurants.

On her second visit, for the Dutch translation of *Before the Fall of Saigon*—she was pleased that she could at least say *Voor de val van Saigon*—Ruth stayed in another part of town, on the Dam Square, where her hotel's proximity to the red-light district had led an interviewer to take it upon himself to show Ruth the prostitutes in their windows. She'd not forgotten the blatancy of the women in their bras and panties at midday, or the "SM Specials" in the window of a sex shop.

Ruth had spotted a rubber vagina suspended from the ceiling of the shop by a red garter belt. The vagina resembled a dangling omelet, except for the tuft of fake pubic hair. And there were the whips; the cowbell, attached by a leather strap to a dildo; the enema bulbs, in a variety of sizes; the rubber fist.

But that was five years ago. Ruth had not yet had the opportunity to see whether the district had changed. She was now staying in her third hotel, on the Kattengat; it was not very stylish, and it suffered from a number of graceless efforts to be orderly. For example, there was a breakfast room that was strictly for the guests on Ruth's floor. The coffee was cold, the orange juice was warm, and the croissants lay in a litter of crumbs—suitable only for taking to the nearest canal and feeding to the ducks.

On its ground floor and in the basement, the hotel had spawned a health club. The music favored for the aerobics classes could be detected in the bathroom pipes for several floors above the exercise facility; the plumbing throbbed to the ceaseless percussion. In Ruth's estimation, the Dutch—at least while exercising—preferred an unrelenting and unvarying kind of rock music, which she would have categorized as an unrhymed form of rap. A tuneless beat repeated itself while a European male, for whom English was very much a foreign language, reiterated a single sentence. In one such song, the sentence was: "I vant to have sex vit you." In another: "I vant to fook you."

Her firsthand inspection of the gym had quickly dashed any tentative interest she might have had in it. A singles' bar in the guise of an exercise facility was not for her. She also disliked the self-consciousness of the exercise. The stationary bikes, the treadmills, the stair-climbing devices—they were all in a row, facing the floor for the aerobics classes. No matter where you were, you could not escape seeing the leaping and the gyrations of the aerobic dancers in the plethora of surrounding mirrors. The best you could hope for would be to witness a sprained ankle or a heart attack.

Ruth decided to take a walk. The area around her hotel was new to her; she was actually closer to the red-light district than she realized, but she began walking in the opposite direction. She crossed the first canal she came to and turned onto a small, attractive side street—the Korsjespoortsteeg—where, to her surprise, she encountered several prostitutes.

In what seemed to be a well-kept residential area were a half-dozen windows with working women in their lingerie. They were white women, prosperous-looking if not in every case pretty. Most of them were younger than Ruth; possibly two of them were her age. Ruth was so shocked that she actually stumbled. One of the prostitutes had to laugh.

It was late morning, and Ruth was the only woman walking on the short street. Three men, each of them alone, were silently window-shopping. Ruth had not imagined that she could find a prostitute who might talk to her in a place that was less seedy and less conspicuous than the red-light district was; her discovery encouraged her.

When she found herself on the Bergstraat, once again she was un-prepared—there were more prostitutes. It was a quiet, tidy street. The first four girls, who were young and beautiful, paid no attention to her. Ruth was aware of a slowly passing car, the driver intently looking over the prostitutes. But this time Ruth wasn't the only woman on the street. Ahead of her was a woman dressed much as Ruth was—black jeans, black suede shoes with a stacked, medium-high heel. The woman, also like Ruth, wore a short, mannish leather jacket, but in dark brown and with a silk paisley scarf.

Ruth was walking so quickly that she nearly overtook the woman, who, on her arm, carried a canvas shopping bag from which a large bot-tle of mineral water and a loaf of bread protruded. The woman looked casually over her shoulder at Ruth; she gazed mildly into Ruth's eyes. The woman wore no makeup, not even lipstick, and was in her late for-ties. As she passed them by, she waved or smiled to each of the prosti-tutes in their windows. But near the end of the Bergstraat, at a ground-floor window where the curtains were drawn, the woman abruptly stopped to unlock a door. She instinctively looked behind her before stepping inside, as if she were accustomed to being followed. And again she gazed at Ruth—this time with a more searching curios-ity, and with what struck Ruth as something wantonly flirtatious in her at-first-ironic and then seductive smile. The woman was a prostitute! She was just now going to work.

Ruth once more walked past the prostitutes on the Korsjespoort-steeg. She was aware of more men on the street, none of whom would look at her or at one another. She recognized two of them; they had made the same circle she had. How many times would they return for a longer look? This, too, Ruth wanted to know; it was a necessary part of her research.

While it would be easier for her, alone, to interview a prostitute on a pleasant, unthreatening street such as this one, or on the Bergstraat, Ruth believed that the character in her novel—that *other* woman writer with her bad boyfriend—had best suffer *her* encounter in one of the worst of the rooms in the red-light district. After all, if the awful experience was to degrade and humiliate her, wouldn't it be more appropriate—not to mention more atmospheric—if it happened in the sleaziest environment imaginable?

This time the prostitutes on the Korsjespoortsteeg regarded Ruth with wary stares and a barely detectable nod or two. The woman who'd laughed at Ruth when she'd stumbled gave her a cool, unfriendly appraisal. Only one of the women made a gesture that could have been construed as either beckoning or scolding. She was a woman of Ruth's age, but much heavier; her blond hair was dyed. The woman pointed an index finger at Ruth and lowered her eyes in exaggerated disapproval. It was a schoolmarmish gesture, although there was no small amount of wickedness in the heavy woman's smirking smile—she might have thought Ruth a lesbian.

When she again turned onto the Bergstraat, Ruth walked slowly in the hope that the older prostitute would have had time to dress herself—or to *un*dress herself, as the case might be—and to position herself in her window. One of the younger, more beautiful prostitutes winked openly at Ruth, who felt strangely exhilarated by such a mockingly salacious proposition. The pretty girl's wink was so distracting that Ruth nearly walked by the older prostitute without recognizing her; in truth, the prostitute's transformation was so complete that she was an altogether different woman from the plain person with a shopping bag whom Ruth had seen on the street only minutes ago.

In the open doorway stood a vivacious, red-haired whore. Her wine-red lipstick matched her claret-colored bra and panties, which were all she wore except for a gold wristwatch and a pair of jet-black slingbacks with three-inch heels. The prostitute was now taller than Ruth.

The window curtains were open, revealing an old-fashioned bar-stool with a polished brass base, but the prostitute was in the midst of a domestic pose: she stood in her doorway with a broom, with which she had just swept from her threshold a single yellow leaf. She held the broom at the ready, offering a challenge to more leaves, and she care-fully looked Ruth over, from her hair to her shoes—as if Ruth were standing in the Bergstraat in her underwear and high heels and the prostitute were a conservatively dressed housewife dutifully attending to her chores. That was when Ruth realized that she'd stopped walking, and that the red-haired prostitute had nodded to her with an inviting smile, which—as Ruth had not yet found the courage to speak—was growing quizzical.

"Do you speak English?" Ruth blurted.

The prostitute seemed more amused than taken aback. "I don't have a problem with English," she said. "I don't have a problem with les-bians, either."

"I'm not a lesbian," Ruth told her.

"That's all right, too," the prostitute replied. "Is it your first time with a woman? I know what to do about that."

"I don't want to *do* anything," Ruth quickly stated. "I just want to talk with you."

The prostitute became uncomfortable—as if "talk" were in a cate-gory of aberrant behavior, short of which she drew the line. "You have to pay more for that," the redhead said. "Talk can go on for a long time."

Ruth was nonplussed by the attitude that seemingly any sexual ac-tivity would be preferable to conversation. "Oh, of course I'll pay you for your time," Ruth told the redhead, who was scrutinizing Ruth meticulously. But it was not Ruth's body that the prostitute was assess-ing; what interested her was how much money Ruth had paid for her clothes.

"It costs seventy-five guilders for five minutes," the redhead said; she had correctly estimated that Ruth wore unimaginative but expensive clothes.

Ruth unzipped her purse and peered into her wallet at the unfamil-iar bills. Was seventy-five guilders about fifty dollars? It struck Ruth as a lot of money for a five-minute conversation. (For what the prostitute *usually* provided—in the same amount of time, or less—it seemed in-sufficient compensation.)

"My name is Ruth," Ruth said nervously. She extended her hand, but the redhead laughed; instead of shaking hands, she pulled Ruth into her small room by the sleeve of her leather jacket. When they were both inside, the prostitute locked the door and closed the window curtains; her strong perfume in such a confined area was nearly as overpowering as the redhead's near-nakedness.

The room itself was all in red. The heavy curtains were a shade of maroon; the rug, a blood-red broadloom, gave off the faded odor of carpet cleaner; the bedspread, which neatly covered a twin-size bed, was of an old-fashioned, rose-petal pattern; the pillowcase for the solitary pillow was pink. And the towel, which was the size of a bath towel and a different shade of pink from the pillowcase, was folded perfectly in half and covered the center of the bed—no doubt to protect the bedspread. On a chair beside the tidy, serviceable bed stood a stack of these pink towels; they *looked* clean, if slightly shabby—just like the room.

The small red room was ringed with mirrors; there were almost as many mirrors, at as many unwelcome angles, as there were at the hotel's health club. And the light in the room was so dim that, each time Ruth took a step, she saw a shadow of herself either retreating or advancing—or both. (The mirrors, of course, also reflected a multitude of prostitutes.)

The prostitute sat down on her bed in the exact center of the towel, without needing to look where she was sitting. She crossed her ankles, supporting her feet by the spikes of her heels, and leaned forward with her hands on her thighs; it was a pose of long experience, which pushed her pert, well-formed breasts forward, exaggerated her cleavage, and allowed Ruth a view of her small, purplish nipples through the claret-colored mesh of her demi-bra. Her bikini panties elongated the narrow V of her crotch and exposed the stretch marks on the prostitute's pouting stomach; she'd clearly had children, or at least one child.

The redhead indicated a lumpy easy chair, where Ruth was supposed to sit. The chair was so soft that Ruth's knees touched her breasts when she leaned forward; she needed to cling to the armrests with both hands in order to avoid the appearance of lolling on her back.

"The chair works better for blow jobs," the prostitute told her. "My name is Dolores," the redhead added, "but my friends call me Rooie."

"Rooie?" Ruth repeated, trying not to think of the number of blow jobs that had been performed in the cracked-leather chair.

"It means 'Red,' " said Rooie.

"I see," Ruth said, edging herself forward in the blow-job chair. "As it turns out, I'm writing a story," Ruth began, but the prostitute quickly stood up from her bed.

"You didn't say you were a journalist," Rooie Dolores said. "I don't talk to journalists."

"I'm *not* a journalist!" Ruth cried. (My, how that accusation stung!) "I'm a *novelist.* I write *books,* the kind one makes up. I just need to be sure the details are right."

"*What* details?" Rooie asked. She wouldn't sit down on the bed; she paced. Her movements allowed the novelist to see some additional aspects of the prostitute's carefully appointed workplace. A small sink was mounted to an interior wall; beside it was a bidet. (There were several more bidets in the mirrors, of course.) On a table between the bidet and the bed was a box of tissues and a roll of paper towels. A white-enameled tray with a hospital aura held both the familiar and some *un*familiar lubricants and jellies, and a dildo of an uncomfortable size. Like the tray, of a similar hospital or doctor's-office whiteness, was a wastebasket with a lid—the kind that was opened by stepping on a foot pedal. Through a partially open door, Ruth saw the darkened WC; the toilet, with a wooden seat, was flushed with a pull chain. And by the standing lamp with the scarlet stained-glass shade, a table next to the blow-job chair held a clean, empty ashtray and a wicker basket full of condoms.

These were among the details that Ruth needed, together with the shallowness of the room's wardrobe closet. The few dresses and nightgowns, and a leather halter top, could not hang at right angles to the closet's back wall; the clothes were twisted diagonally on their hangers, as if they were prostitutes attempting to show themselves at a more flattering angle.

The dresses and the nightgowns, not to mention the leather halter top, were entirely too youthful for a woman of Rooie's age. But what did Ruth know about dresses or nightgowns? She rarely wore the former, and she preferred to sleep in a pair of panties and an oversize T-shirt. (As for a leather halter top, she'd never considered wearing one of those.)

Ruth began her story. "Suppose a man and a woman came to you and offered to pay you to allow them to watch you with a customer? Would you do that? Have you ever done that?"

"So *that's* what you want," Rooie said. "Why didn't you say so? Sure I can do that—of course I've done that. Why didn't you bring your boyfriend?"

"No, no—I'm not here with a boyfriend," Ruth replied. "*I* don't want to watch you with a customer—I can imagine that. I just want to know how you arrange it, and how common or uncommon it is. I mean, how often are you asked by *couples*? I would think that men, alone, would ask you more frequently than couples. And that women, alone, were... well, rare."

"That's true," Rooie answered. "Mostly it's men, alone. *Some* couples, maybe once or twice a year."

"And women alone?"

"I can do that, if that's what you want," Rooie said. "I do that from time to time, but not often. Most men don't mind if another woman watches. It's the *women* who are watching who don't want to be seen."

It was so warm and airless in the room, Ruth longed to take her leather jacket off. But, in present company, it would be too brazen of her to be wearing just her black silk T-shirt. Therefore, she unzipped her jacket but kept it on.

Rooie walked over to the wardrobe closet. There was no door. A chintz curtain—in a pattern of fallen autumn leaves, mostly red—hung from a wooden dowel. When Rooie closed the curtain, it concealed the contents of the closet—except for the shoes, which she turned around so that their toes were pointed out. There were a half-dozen pairs of high-heeled shoes.

"You would just stand behind the curtain with the toes of your shoes pointed out, like the other shoes," Rooie said. She stepped through the part in the curtain and concealed herself. When Ruth looked at Rooie's feet, she could hardly tell the shoes that Rooie was wearing from the other shoes; Ruth needed to be *looking* for Rooie's ankles in order to see them.

"I see," Ruth said. She wanted to stand in the wardrobe closet to see what her view of the bed would be; through the narrow part in the curtain, it might be difficult to see the bed.

It was as if the prostitute had read her mind. Rooie stepped out from behind the curtain. "Here, you try it," the redhead said.

Ruth could not avoid brushing against the prostitute when she slipped through the parted curtain. The entire room was so small that it was next to impossible for two people to move in it without touching.

Ruth fit her feet between two pairs of shoes. Through the narrow slit where the curtain was parted, she had a clear view of the pink towel centered on the prostitute's bed. In an opposing mirror, Ruth could also see the wardrobe closet; she had to look closely to recognize her own shoes among the shoes below the bottom hem of the curtain. Ruth could not see herself through the curtain—not even her own eyes, peering through the slit. Not even a portion of her face, unless she moved, and even then she could detect only some undefined movement.

Without moving her head, just her eyes, Ruth could take in the sink and bidet; the dildo in the hospital tray (together with the lubricants and jellies) was clearly visible. But Ruth's view of the blow-job chair was blocked by one armrest and the back of the chair itself.

"If the guy wants a blow job and someone's watching, I can give him a blow job on the bed," Rooie said. "If that's what you're thinking ..."

Ruth hadn't been in the wardrobe closet for more than a minute; she'd not yet noticed that her breathing was irregular, or that her contact with the gold-colored dress on the nearest hanger had made her neck begin to itch. She was aware of a slight discomfort in her throat when she swallowed—the last vestiges of her cough, she thought, or the coming of a cold. When a pearl-gray negligee slipped off a hanger, it was as if her heart had stopped and she had died where she always imagined she would: in a closet.

"If you're comfortable in there," Rooie said, "I'll open the window curtains and sit in the window. But this time of day it might take a while to get a guy to come in—maybe half an hour, maybe as much as forty-five minutes. Of course, you'll have to pay me another seventy-five guilders. This has already taken a lot of my time."

Ruth stumbled on the shoes as she rushed out of the wardrobe closet. "No! I don't *want* to watch!" the novelist cried. "I'm just writing a *story*! It's about a *couple*. The woman is my age. Her boyfriend talks her into it—she's got a bad boyfriend."

Ruth saw, with embarrassment, that she'd kicked one of the prostitute's shoes halfway across the room. Rooie retrieved the shoe; then she knelt at her wardrobe closet, straightening up the other shoes. She returned them all to the usual, toes-in position—including the shoe that Ruth had kicked.

"You're a weird one," the prostitute said. They stood awkwardly beside the wardrobe closet, as if they were admiring the newly arranged shoes. "And your five minutes are up," Rooie added, pointing to her pretty gold watch.

Ruth again unzipped her purse. She took three twenty-five-guilder bills out of her wallet, but Rooie was standing close enough to look inside Ruth's billfold for herself. The prostitute deftly picked out a fifty-guilder bill. "Fifty is enough—for five more minutes," the redhead said. "Save your small bills," she advised Ruth. "You might want to come back ... after you think about it."

So quickly that Ruth didn't anticipate it, Rooie pressed closer to Ruth and nuzzled Ruth's neck; before Ruth could react, the prostitute lightly cupped one of Ruth's breasts as she turned away and again seated herself dead-center on the towel protecting her bed. "Nice perfume, but I can hardly smell it," Rooie remarked. "Nice breasts. *Big* ones."

Blushing, Ruth tried to lower herself into the blow-job chair without letting the chair claim her. "In my story ..." the novelist started to say.

"The trouble with your story is that nothing happens," Rooie said. "So the couple pays me to watch me do it. So what? It wouldn't be the first time. So what happens *then*? Isn't that the story?"

"I'm not sure what happens then, but that *is* the story," Ruth answered. "The woman with the bad boyfriend is humiliated. She feels degraded by the experience—not because of what she sees, but because of the boyfriend. It's the way *he* makes her feel that humiliates her."

"That wouldn't be the first time, either," the prostitute told her.

"Maybe the man masturbates while he's watching," Ruth suggested. Rooie knew it was a question.

"It wouldn't be the first time," the prostitute repeated. "Why would the woman be surprised at that?"

Rooie was right. And there was another problem: Ruth didn't know everything that could happen in the story because she didn't know enough about who the characters were and what their relationship was. It wasn't the first time that she'd made such a discovery about a novel she was beginning; it was just the first time that she'd made the discovery in front of another person—not to mention a stranger and a prostitute.

"Do you know what *usually* happens?" Rooie asked.

"No, I don't," Ruth admitted.

"The watching is just the beginning," the prostitute told her. "With couples, especially—the watching just leads to something else."

"What do you mean?" Ruth asked her.

"The next time they come back, they don't want to watch—they want to *do* something," Rooie said.

"I don't think my character would come back a second time," Ruth replied, but she considered the possibility.

"Sometimes, after the watching, the couple wants to do things immediately—like right then," Rooie said.

"What kind of things?" Ruth asked.

"All kinds," Rooie said. "Sometimes the guy wants to watch me with the woman—he wants to see me get the woman hot. Usually I start with the guy, and the woman watches."

"You *start* with the guy...." Ruth said.

"Then the woman," Rooie said.

"That's actually happened?" Ruth asked.

"*Everything's* happened," the prostitute said.

Ruth sat in the scarlet-tinged light, which now cast an intensifying, reddish glow throughout the small room; the pink towel on the bed, where Rooie sat, was doubtless a deeper shade of pink because of the scarlet color of the stained-glass lamp shade. The only other light in the room was the muted light that found its way through the window curtains and a dim overhead light that was trained on the door to the street.

The prostitute leaned forward in the flattering light; in so doing, her breasts appeared ready to slip out of her demi-bra. While Ruth held tightly to the armrests of the blow-job chair, Rooie softly covered Ruth's hands with her own. "You want to think about what happens and come see me again?" the redhead asked.

"Yes," Ruth said. She hadn't meant to whisper, nor could she take her hands out of the prostitute's hands without falling backward in the awful chair.

"Just remember—*anything* can happen," Rooie told her. "Anything you want."

"Yes," Ruth whispered again. She stared at the prostitute's exposed breasts; it seemed safer than staring into her clever eyes.

"Maybe if you watched me with someone—I mean you, alone—you'd get some ideas," Rooie said in a whisper of her own.

Ruth shook her head, aware that the gesture conveyed far less conviction than if she'd said sharply, "No, I don't think so."

"Most of the women alone who watch me are young girls," Rooie announced in a louder, dismissive voice.

Ruth was so surprised at this that she looked into Rooie's face without meaning to. "Why young girls?" Ruth asked. "Do you mean they want to know what having sex is like? Are they *virgins?*"

Rooie let go of Ruth's hands; she pushed herself back on her bed and laughed. "They're hardly *virgins!*" the redhead said. "They're young girls who are thinking about being prostitutes—they want to see what being a *prostitute* is like!"

Ruth had never been so shocked; not even the knowledge that Hannah had fucked her father had been this astonishing.

Rooie pointed to her wristwatch and stood up from her bed exactly at the same time Ruth stood up from the difficult chair. Ruth had to contort herself in order not to make contact with the prostitute.

Rooie opened the door to a midday sunlight of such sudden brightness that Ruth realized she'd underestimated the dimness of the lighting in the prostitute's red room. Turning away from the light, Rooie dramatically blocked Ruth's exit while she bestowed on Ruth's cheeks three kisses—first on Ruth's right cheek, then on her left, and then on her right again. "The Dutch way—three times," the prostitute said cheerfully, with an affection more suitable for old friends.

Of course Ruth had been kissed this way before—by Maarten and by Maarten's wife, Sylvia, whenever they'd said their hellos and goodbyes—but Rooie's kisses had lingered a little longer. And Rooie had also pressed her warm palm against Ruth's belly, causing Ruth to instinctively tighten her stomach muscles. "What a flat tummy you have," the prostitute told her. "Have you had any babies?"

"No, not yet," Ruth replied. The doorway was still blocked.

"I've had one," Rooie said. She hooked her thumbs inside the waistband of her bikini panties and lowered them in a flash. "The hard way," the prostitute added, in reference to the highly visible scar from a cesarean section; the scar was not nearly as surprising to Ruth, who'd already noted Rooie's stretch marks, as the fact that the prostitute had shaved off her pubic hair.

Rooie let go of the waistband of her panties, which made a snap. Ruth thought: If I'd rather be *writing* than what I'm doing, imagine how *she* feels. After all, she's a *prostitute;* she would probably rather be *being* a prostitute than flirting with me. But she also enjoys making me uncomfortable. Irritated with Rooie now, Ruth just wanted to go. She tried to edge around Rooie in the doorway.

"You'll be back," Rooie told her, but she let Ruth slip into the street without further physical contact. Then Rooie raised her voice, so that anyone passing in the Bergstraat, or a neighboring prostitute, could hear her. "You better zip up your purse in this town," the redhead said.

Ruth's purse was open, an old failing, but her wallet and passport were in place, and—at a glance—whatever else should be there. A tube of lipstick and a fatter tube of colorless lip gloss; a tube of sunscreen and a tube of moisturizer for her lips.

Ruth also carried a compact that had belonged to her mother. Face powder made Ruth sneeze; the powder puff had long ago been lost. Yet at times, when Ruth looked in the small mirror, she expected to see her mother there. Ruth zipped her purse closed while Rooie smiled ironically at her.

When Ruth struggled to return Rooie's smile, the sunlight made her squint. Rooie reached out and touched Ruth's face with her hand. She was staring at Ruth's right eye with a keen interest, but Ruth misunderstood the reason. After all, Ruth was more used to people spotting the hexagonal flaw in her right eye than she was used to being punched.

"I was born with it ..." Ruth started to say.

But Rooie said, "Who hit you?" (And Ruth had thought her bruise had healed.) "About a week or two ago, it looks like ..."

"A bad boyfriend," Ruth confessed.

"So there *is* a boyfriend," Rooie said.

"He's not here. I'm alone here," Ruth insisted.

"You're only alone until the next time you see me," the prostitute replied. Rooie had only two ways of smiling, ironically and seductively. Now she was smiling seductively.

All Ruth could think of saying was: "Your English is surprisingly good." But this barbed compliment, however true, had a much more profound effect on Rooie than Ruth had anticipated.

The prostitute lost every outward manifestation of her cockiness. She looked as if an old sorrow had returned to her with near-violent force.

Ruth almost said she was sorry, but before she could speak, the redhead responded bitterly: "I knew somebody English—for a while."

Then Rooie Dolores went back inside her room and closed the door. Ruth waited, but the window curtains did not open.

One of the younger, prettier prostitutes was scowling resentfully at Ruth from across the street, as if she were personally disappointed that Ruth should spend her money on an older, less attractive whore.

There was only one other pedestrian on the tiny Bergstraat—an older man with his eyes cast down. He would not look at any of the prostitutes, but he raised his eyes sharply to Ruth as he passed by. She glared back at the man, whose eyes were fixed on the cobblestones as he walked on.

Then Ruth walked on, too. Her personal but not professional confidence was shaken. Whatever the possible story was—the most probable story, the best story—she had no doubt that she would think of it. She hadn't thought enough about her characters; that was all. No, the confidence she'd lost was something moral. It was at the center of herself *as a woman,* and whatever "it" was, Ruth marveled at the feeling of its absence.

She would go back to see Rooie again, but that was not what bothered her. She felt no desire to have *any* sexual experience with the prostitute, who had certainly stimulated her imagination but who had *not* aroused her. And Ruth still believed that there was no necessity for her, either as a writer *or* as a woman, to watch the prostitute perform with a customer.

What bothered Ruth was that she *needed* to be with Rooie again—just to see, as in a story, what would happen next. That meant that Rooie was in charge.

The novelist walked quickly back to her hotel, where—before her first interview—she wrote only this in her diary: "The conventional wisdom is that prostitution is a kind of rape for money; in truth, in prostitution—maybe *only* in prostitution—the woman seems in charge."

Ruth had a second interview over lunch, and a third and fourth after lunch. She should have tried to relax then, because she had an early-evening reading, followed by a book-signing and then a dinner. But instead, Ruth sat in her hotel room, where she wrote and wrote. She developed one possible story after another, until the credibility of each felt strained. If the woman writer watching the prostitute perform was going to feel humiliated by the experience, whatever came of the experience sexually had to happen to the woman writer; somehow, it had to be *her* sexual experience. Otherwise, why would *she* feel humiliated?

The more Ruth made an effort to involve herself in the story she was *writing,* the more she was delaying or avoiding the story she was *living.* For the first time, she knew what it felt like to be a character in a novel instead of the novelist (the one in charge)—for it was as a *character* that Ruth saw herself returning to the Bergstraat, a character in a story she *wasn't* writing.

What she was experiencing was the excitement of a *reader* who needs to know what happens next. She knew she wouldn't be able to keep herself away from Rooie. Irresistibly, she wanted to know what would *happen.* What would Rooie suggest? What would Ruth allow Rooie to do?

When, if only for a moment, the novelist steps out of the creator's role, what roles are there for the novelist to step into? There are only creators of stories and characters in stories; there are no other roles. Ruth had never felt such anticipation before. She felt she had absolutely no will to take control of what happened next; in fact, she was exhilarated *not* to be in charge. She was happy *not* to be the novelist. She was not the writer of *this* story, yet the story thrilled her.

Ruth Changes Her Story

Ruth stayed after her reading to sign books. Then she had dinner with the sponsors of the signing. And the following evening in Utrecht, after her reading at the university there, she also signed books. Maarten and Sylvia helped Ruth with the spelling of the Dutch names.

The boys wanted their books inscribed, "To Wouter"—or to Hein, Hans, Henk, Gerard, or Jeroen. The girls' names were no less foreign to Ruth. "To Els"—or to Loes, Mies, Marijke, or Nel (with one *l*). And then there were those readers who wanted their last names included in the inscription. (The Overbeeks, the Van der Meulens, and the Van Meurs; the Blokhuises and the Veldhuizens; the Dijkstras and the De

Groots and the Smits.) These book-signings were such arduous exercises in spelling that Ruth left both readings with a headache.

But Utrecht and its old university were beautiful. Before her reading, Ruth had had an early dinner with Maarten and Sylvia and their grown sons. Ruth could remember when they'd been "little" boys; now they were taller than she was and one of them had grown a beard. To Ruth, still childless at thirty-six, one of the shocks of knowing couples with children was the disquieting phenomenon of how the children grew.

On the train back to Amsterdam, Ruth told Maarten and Sylvia of her lack of success with boys the age of their sons—that is, when she'd been their age. (The summer she'd come to Europe with Hannah, the more attractive boys had always preferred Hannah.)

"But now it's embarrassing. *Now* boys the age of your boys *like* me."

"You're very popular with young readers," Maarten said.

"That's not what Ruth meant, Maarten," Sylvia told him. Ruth admired Sylvia: she was smart and attractive; she had a good husband and a happy family.

"Oh," Maarten said. He was very proper—he actually blushed.

"I don't mean that *your* boys are attracted to me in that way," Ruth quickly told him. "I mean some boys their *age.*"

"I think *our* boys are probably attracted to you in that way, too!" Sylvia told Ruth. She was laughing at how shocked her husband had been; Maarten hadn't noticed the number of young men surrounding Ruth at both her book-signings.

There'd been many young women, too, but they were attracted to Ruth as a role model—not only as a successful writer, but also as an unmarried woman who'd had several boyfriends and yet still lived alone. (Why this seemed glamorous, Ruth didn't know. If only they'd realized how little she liked her so-called personal life!)

With the young men, there was always one boy—at least ten but sometimes fifteen years Ruth's junior—who made a clumsy effort to hit on her. ("With an awkwardness that approaches heartbreaking proportions," was the way Ruth put it to Maarten and Sylvia.) As a mother of boys that age, Sylvia knew exactly what Ruth meant. As a father, Maarten had paid closer attention to his sons than to the unknown young men who'd been falling all over themselves around Ruth.

This time there'd been one in particular. He'd stood in line to have his book autographed after her reading in Amsterdam *and* in Utrecht;

she'd read the same passage on back-to-back nights, but this young man had not appeared to mind. He'd brought a well-worn copy of one of her paperbacks to the reading in Amsterdam, and in Utrecht he'd held out the hardcover of *Not for Children* for her signature—both were English editions.

"It's Wim with a *W,*" he told her the second time, because Wim was pronounced "Vim"—the first time she'd signed a book for him, Ruth had written his name with a *V.*

"Oh, it's *you* again!" she told the boy. He was too pretty, and too obviously smitten with her, for her to forget him. "If I'd known you were coming, I would have read a different passage." He lowered his eyes, as if it pained him to look at her when she looked back.

"I go to school in Utrecht, but my parents live in Amsterdam. I grew up there." (As if this explained everything about his attendance at both her readings!)

"Aren't I speaking in Amsterdam again tomorrow?" Ruth asked Sylvia.

"Yes, at the Vrije Universiteit," Sylvia told the young man.

"Yes, I know—I'll be there," the boy replied. "I'll bring a third book for you to sign."

While she signed more books, the captivated boy stood off to one side of the line and looked longingly at her. In the United States, where Ruth Cole almost always refused to sign books, the young man's worshipful gaze would have frightened her. But in Europe, where Ruth usually agreed to book-signings, she never felt threatened by the lovestruck gazes of her young-men admirers.

There was a questionable logic to how nervous Ruth felt at home and how comfortable abroad; Ruth doubtless romanticized the slavish devotion of her European *boy* readers. They existed in an irreproachable category, these smitten boys who spoke English with foreign accents, and who'd read every word she'd written—they'd also made her the older-woman fantasy in their tortured young minds. They'd now become *her* fantasy, too, which—on the train back to Amsterdam—Ruth was able to joke with Maarten and Sylvia about.

It was too short a train trip for Ruth to tell them everything about the new novel that was on her mind, but in laughing together about the available young men, Ruth realized that she wanted to change her story. It should *not* be another writer whom the woman writer meets at the Frankfurt Book Fair, and then brings with her to Amsterdam. It should be one of her *fans*—a wannabe writer and a would-be young lover. The woman writer in the new novel should be considering that it is high time for her to be married; she should even, also like Ruth, be weighing the marriage proposal of an impressive older man whom she is deeply fond of.

The unbearable beauty of the boy named Wim made him hard to put out of her mind. If Ruth hadn't only recently suffered her miserable encounter with Scott Saunders, she would even have been tempted to enjoy (or embarrass) herself with Wim. After all, she was alone in Europe; she was probably going home to get married. A no-regrets fling with a young man, with a *much* younger man ... wasn't that the kind of thing that older women who were about to marry even older men *did*?

What Ruth did tell Maarten and Sylvia was that she'd like a tour of the red-light district, recounting that part of the story, or as much as she knew: how a young man talks an older woman into paying a prostitute to watch her with a customer; how *something happens;* how the woman is so humiliated that she changes her life.

"The older woman gives in to him in part because she thinks *she's* in control—and because this young man is exactly the sort of beautiful boy who was unattainable to her when she was his age. What she doesn't know is that this boy is capable of causing her pain and anguish—at least I *think* that's what happens," Ruth added. "It all depends on what happens with the prostitute."

"When do you want to go to the red-light district?" Maarten asked.

Ruth spoke as if the idea were so new to her that she hadn't yet thought of the particulars. "When it's most convenient for you, I guess...."

"When would the older woman and her young man go to the prostitute?" Maarten asked.

"Probably at night," Ruth answered. "It's likely that they're a little drunk. I think *she* would have to be, to have the nerve."

"We could go there now," Sylvia said. "It's a roundabout way back to your hotel, but it's only a five- or ten-minute walk from the station."

Ruth was surprised that Sylvia would even consider accompanying them. It would be after eleven, close to midnight, when their train arrived in Amsterdam. "Isn't it dangerous this late at night?" Ruth asked.

"There are so many tourists," Sylvia said with distaste. "The pickpockets are the only danger."

"You can get your pocket picked in the daytime, too," Maarten said.

In *de Walletjes*—or *de Wallen*, as the Amsterdammers called it—it was much more crowded than Ruth anticipated. There were drug addicts and drunken young men, but the small streets were teeming with other people; there were many couples, most of them tourists (some of whom were visiting the live-sex shows), and even a tour group or two. If it had been just a little earlier in the night, Ruth would have felt safe to be there alone. There was mostly a tireless seediness on display— and the people who, like her, had come there to *gawk* at the seediness. As for the men who were involved in the usually prolonged act of choosing a prostitute, their furtive searching was conspicuous in the midst of the unembarrassed sex-tourism.

Ruth decided that her older woman writer and her young man would not find the time and place conducive to approaching a prostitute, although from the confines of Rooie's room it had been apparent that, once one was in a prostitute's chamber, the outside world quickly slipped away. Either Ruth's couple would come to the district in the predawn hours—when everyone except the serious drug addicts (and sex addicts) had gone to bed—or they would come in the early evening or daytime.

What had changed about the red-light district, since Ruth's previous visit to Amsterdam, was that so many of the prostitutes were not white. There was a street where almost all the women were Asian—probably Thais, because of the number of Thai massage parlors in the neighborhood. Indeed, they *were* Thais, Maarten told her. He also told her that some of them had formerly been men; they'd allegedly had their sex-change operations in Cambodia.

On the Molensteeg, and in the area of the old church on the Oude-kerksplein, the girls were all brown-skinned. They were Dominicans and Colombians, Maarten told her. The ones from Suriname, who'd come to Amsterdam at the end of the sixties, were all gone now.

And on the Bloedstraat there were girls who looked like men, tall girls with big hands and Adam's apples. Maarten told Ruth that most of them *were* men—Ecuadoran transvestites who had a reputation for beating up their customers.

There were, of course, some white women, not all of them Dutch, in the Sint Annenstraat and the Dollebegijnensteeg, and also in the street where Ruth wished that Maarten and Sylvia had *not* taken her. The Trompettersteeg was not only too narrow for an alley; it was too narrow for an upstairs hall. The air was trapped in there, and a war of odors raged unceasingly: urine and perfume, so richly commingled that the result resembled bad meat. There was also a dry, scorched smell—from the whores' hair dryers—and this stink of something burnt seemed incongruous because the alley, even on a rainless night, was wet. The air never moved enough to dry the puddles on the stained pavement.

The walls, dirty and damp, marked the backs and chests and shoulders of the men's clothes—for the men had to press themselves against the walls in order to pass one another. The prostitutes in their windows, or in their open doorways, were near enough to smell and touch, and there was nowhere to look—except into the face of the next one, and the one after that. Or into the faces of the browsing men, which were the worst faces of all—alert, as they were, to the prostitutes' hands flitting into the alley, making contact, and making contact again. The Trompetterssteeg was a buyer's market; the contact was too face-to-face for mere window-shopping.

Ruth realized that, in *de Wallen*, one needn't pay a prostitute to see someone having sex—the motivation for that had to come from the particular young man himself, and/or from the character of the older woman writer. There would need to be something, or something missing, in *their* relationship. After all, in the Erotic Show Centre, one could rent video cabins. SIMPLY THE BEST, the advertisement read. Or at the Live Porno Show, the promised sex was REAL FUCKING LIVE. And in another spot: REAL FUCKING ONSTAGE. One did not have to make any great or special effort to be a voyeur here.

A novel is always more complicated than it seems at the beginning. Indeed, a novel *should be* more complicated than it seems at the beginning.

There was at least some consolation to Ruth in seeing that the "SM Specials" in the sex-shop window had not changed. The rubber vagina that resembled an omelet was once again suspended from the ceiling of the shop, although the garter from which it hung was now black, not red. And no one had bought the comic dildo with the cowbell attached by a leather strap. The whips were still on display, and the enema bulbs were presented in the same (or a similar) selection of sizes. Even the rubber fist had endured the passage of time untouched—as defiant and unwanted as ever, Ruth thought ... that is, she *hoped*.

It was half past midnight when Maarten and Sylvia returned Ruth to her hotel. Ruth had paid careful attention to the route they'd taken. In the lobby of her hotel, she kissed them both good night. The Dutch way—three times—but more quickly, more matter-of-factly, than Rooie had kissed her. Then Ruth went to her room and changed her clothes. She put on an older, faded pair of blue jeans and a navy-blue sweatshirt that was too big for her; it was not flattering to her figure, but it almost hid her breasts. She also put on the most comfortable shoes she'd brought with her, black suede loafers.

She waited in her room for fifteen minutes before leaving the hotel. It was a quarter to one in the morning, but she was not even a five-minute walk from the nearest of the prosperous streets for prostitutes. Ruth wasn't thinking of visiting Rooie again at this hour. But she did want a glimpse of Rooie Dolores in her window. Maybe I could watch her lure a customer inside, Ruth thought. She'd go back for a real visit the next day, or the following one.

Thus far Ruth Cole's experience with prostitutes should have been a lesson to her: Ruth's capacity to anticipate what might happen next in the world of prostitution was clearly not as developed as her skills as a novelist; one might wish that Ruth had developed at least a degree of wariness regarding her unpreparedness among women of this walk of life—for there on the Bergstraat, in what should have been Rooie's window, sat a much coarser, much younger woman than Rooie. Ruth recognized the leather halter top that had hung in Rooie's shallow wardrobe closet. It was black, the décolletage fastened by silver snaps, but the girl was too bosomy for the halter to be entirely closed. Beneath her deep cleavage, under the halter top, the girl's flabby stomach over-hung her black half-slip, which was torn. The waistband was ripped; the white elastic contrasted with the black of the slip and the roll of sallow flesh from the fat girl's ample belly. She might have been pregnant, but the gray hollows under the young prostitute's eyes revealed a degree of inner damage that suggested her capacity for conception was minimal.

"Where's Rooie?" Ruth asked. The fat girl got off her stool and opened the door a crack.

"With her daughter," the tired girl said.

Ruth was walking away when she heard a dull thump against the window glass. It was not the familiar tapping of a fingernail, or a key or

a coin, which Ruth had heard from the windows of several other prostitutes. The fat girl was hitting the window with the big pink dildo that
Ruth had earlier seen in the hospital tray on the table by Rooie's bed.
Once the young prostitute had got Ruth's attention, she stuck the end
of the dildo in her mouth and gave it an unfriendly tug with her teeth.
Then she nodded indifferently to Ruth, and at last she shrugged, as if
her remaining energy allowed her only this limited promise: that she
would *try* to make Ruth as happy as Rooie could make her.

Ruth shook her head *no,* but she gave the young prostitute a kindly
smile. In return, the pathetic creature repeatedly slapped the dildo
against the palm of her hand, as if marking time to music only she
could hear.

That night Ruth had a frightfully arousing dream about the beautiful
Dutch boy named Wim. She awoke embarrassed, and with the conviction that the bad boyfriend in her novel-in-progress should *not* be a
strawberry blond; she even doubted that he should be entirely "bad." If
the older woman writer was going to suffer a humiliation that would
cause her to change her life, it should be *she* who is bad; one doesn't
change one's life because *someone else* has been bad.

Ruth was not easily persuaded by the belief that women were victims; or, she was convinced that women were as often victims of themselves as they were of men. On the evidence of the women she knew
best—herself and Hannah—this was certainly true. (Of course Ruth
didn't know her mother, but she suspected that Marion probably *was* a
victim—one of her father's *many* victims.)

Furthermore, Ruth had had her revenge on Scott Saunders; why
drag him, or a look-alike strawberry blond, into a novel? In *Not for Children,* the widow novelist, Jane Dash, had made the correct decision,
which was *not* to write about her antagonist Eleanor Holt. Ruth had already written about that! ("As a novelist, Mrs. Dash despised writing
about real people; she found it a failure of the imagination—for any
novelist worthy of the name ought to be able to invent a more interesting character than any real person. To turn Eleanor Holt into fiction, even for the purpose of derision, would be a kind of flattery.")

I should practice what I preach, Ruth told herself.

Given the unsatisfactory pickings in the breakfast room, and the fact
that her only interview of the day was also a lunch, Ruth swallowed

half a cup of lukewarm coffee and an orange juice of a similarly unappealing temperature; then she went forth to the red-light district. At nine in the morning, it was advisable not to walk through the district with a *full* stomach.

She crossed the Warmoesstraat within sight of the police station, which she didn't notice. What first caught her eye was a young, drug-addicted street prostitute who was squatting at the corner of the Enge Kerksteeg. The young addict was having difficulty maintaining her balance; she could keep herself from falling only by resting the palms of both hands on the curb as she urinated in the street. "For fifty guilders, I can do anything a man can do for you," the girl said to Ruth, who ignored her.

At nine o'clock, only one window prostitute was working on the Oudekerksplein beside the old church. At first appearance, the prostitute could have been one of the Dominican or Colombian women Ruth had seen the night before, but this woman was much darker-skinned; she was very black, and very fat, and she stood with hearty confidence in her open doorway, as if the streets of *de Wallen* were surging with men. In fact, the streets were virtually empty—except for the street cleaners, who were picking up the previous day's litter.

In the unoccupied cubicles for the prostitutes, many cleaning women were busily at work, their vacuum cleaners presiding over their occasional small talk. Even in the narrow Trompetterssteeg, where Ruth wouldn't venture, a cleaning woman's cart, containing her pail and mop and bottles of cleaning solvent, protruded from a room into the alley. There was also a laundry bag of soiled towels, and a bulging plastic bag of the kind that fits in a wastebasket—no doubt filled with condoms, paper towels, and tissues. Only new-fallen snow could make the district look truly clean in the penetrating morning light—maybe on a Christmas morning, Ruth thought, when not even one prostitute would be working there. Or would there be?

On the Stoofsteeg, where the Thai prostitutes had been dominant, only two women were soliciting from their open doorways; they were, like the woman by the old church, very black and very fat. They were chatting to each other in a language like no other Ruth had ever heard—and because they interrupted their conversation to give Ruth a neighborly and courteous nod, she dared to stop and ask them where they were from.

"Ghana," one of the women said.

"Where *you* from?" the other one asked Ruth.

"The United States," Ruth replied. The African women murmured appreciatively; rubbing their fingers together, they made the universal request for money.

"You want anything we can give you?" one of them asked Ruth.

"You want to come inside?" the other asked.

Then they laughed uproariously. They suffered from no illusion that Ruth was truly interested in having sex with them. It was simply that the well-known *wealth* of the United States made it impossible for them not to try to entice Ruth with their abundant wiles.

"No, thank you," Ruth said to them. Still smiling politely, she walked away.

There were only cleaning women in evidence where the Ecuadoran men had strutted their stuff. And on the Molensteeg, where last night there had been more Dominicans and Colombians, there was another African-looking prostitute in a window—this one was very lean—and yet another cleaning woman in another of the cubicles.

The desertion of the district gave it more of the atmosphere that Ruth had always had in mind; the look of abandonment, which was the look of unwanted sex, was better than the nonstop sex-tourism of the district at night.

In her all-consuming curiosity, Ruth wandered into a sex shop. As in a traditional video store, each category was afforded its own aisle. There was the spanking aisle, and the aisles for oral and anal sex; Ruth did not explore the excrement aisle, and the red light over the door to a closed "video cabin" prompted her to leave the shop before the customer exited the private viewing box. Ruth was willing merely to *imagine* his expression.

For a while she thought she was being followed. A compact, powerful-looking man in blue jeans and dirty running shoes was always behind or across the street from her—even after she'd circled the same block twice. He had a tough face with the stubble of two or three days' growth of beard, and a haggard, irritable expression. He wore a loose-fitting windbreaker cut like a baseball warm-up jacket. He didn't look as if he could afford a prostitute; yet he followed her as if he thought she *was* one. At last he disappeared and she stopped worrying about him.

She walked in the district for two hours. By eleven o'clock, some of the Thais had returned to the Stoofsteeg; the Africans were gone. And around the Oudekerksplein, the one fat black woman, possibly also from Ghana, had been replaced by a dozen or more brown-skinned women—the Colombians and the Dominicans again.

By mistake, Ruth turned into a dead-end alley off the Oudezijds Voorburgwal. The Slapersteeg quickly narrowed and ended at three or four prostitutes' windows, the access to which was a single door. In the open doorway, a big brown prostitute with what sounded like a Jamaican accent grabbed Ruth by her arm. A cleaning woman was still at work inside the rooms, and two other prostitutes were readying themselves in front of a long makeup mirror.

"Who are you looking for?" the big brown woman asked.

"No one," Ruth said. "I'm lost."

The cleaning woman kept sullenly to her task, but the prostitutes at the makeup mirror—and the big one who held fast to Ruth's arm—laughed.

"*I'll* say you're lost," the big prostitute said, leading Ruth out of the alley by her arm. The prostitute firmly squeezed and squeezed Ruth's arm; it was in the manner of an unasked-for massage, or like the affectionate, sensual kneading of dough.

"Thank you," Ruth said, as if she'd truly been lost—as if she'd truly been rescued.

"No problem, sugar."

This time, when Ruth again crossed the Warmoesstraat, she noticed the police station. Two uniformed policemen were in conversation with the compact, powerful-looking man in the windbreaker who'd been following her. Oh, good—they've arrested him! Ruth thought. Then she guessed that the thuggish man was a plainclothes cop; he appeared to be giving orders to the two cops in uniform. Ruth was ashamed and hurried on—as if she were a criminal! *De Wallen* was a small district; in one morning, she'd stood out—she'd looked suspicious.

And as much as Ruth preferred *de Wallen* in the morning to what the district became at night, she doubted that it was the right place or time of day for her characters to approach a prostitute and pay her to allow them to watch her with a customer. They might wait all morning for the first customer!

But now there was barely time to continue past the area of her hotel to the Bergstraat, where Ruth expected to find Rooie in her window; it was just before midday. This time, the prostitute had undergone a milder transformation. Her red hair had a less orange, coppery tone; it was darker, more auburn—almost maroon—and her demi-bra and bikini panties were an off-white, like ivory, which accentuated the whiteness of Rooie's skin.

By leaning over, Rooie could open her door without getting off her barstool; thus she was able to sit in her window seat while Ruth poked her head inside. (Ruth made a point of not crossing the threshold.) "I haven't time to stop and see you now," Ruth said, "but I want to come back."

"Fine," Rooie said, shrugging. Her indifference surprised Ruth.

"I looked for you last night, but someone else was in your window," Ruth went on. "She said you were spending the night with your daughter."

"I spend every night with my daughter—every weekend, too," Rooie replied. "The only time I'm here is when she's in school."

In an effort to be friendly, Ruth asked: "How old is your daughter?"

"Look," the prostitute sighed, "I'm not getting rich talking to you."

"I'm sorry." Ruth stepped back from the doorway as if she'd been pushed.

Before Rooie leaned over and closed her door, she said: "Come see me, when you have the time."

Feeling like a fool, Ruth chastised herself for having had such high expectations of a prostitute. Of course *money* was the main thing on Rooie's mind—if not the *sole* thing. Here Ruth was trying to treat the woman as a friend, when all that had really happened was that Ruth had *paid* her for their first conversation!

After so much walking without any breakfast, Ruth was ravenous at lunch. She was sure that she gave a disorganized interview. She couldn't answer a single question regarding *Not for Children,* or her two earlier novels, without changing the subject to some element of her novel-in-progress: the excitement of starting her first novel in the first-person voice; the compelling idea of a woman who, in an instant of bad judgment, humiliates herself to a degree that she embarks on a whole new life. But as Ruth talked about this, she caught herself thinking: Who am I kidding? This is *all* about me! Haven't *I* made some bad decisions? (At least one, just recently...) Aren't *I* about to embark on a whole new life? Or is Allan merely the "safe" alternative to a life I'm afraid to pursue?

At her late-afternoon lecture at the Vrije Universiteit—it was her *only* lecture, really; she kept revising it, but in essence it stayed the same— her speech sounded disingenuous to her. Here she was, espousing the purity of imagination as opposed to memory, extolling the superiority of the *invented* detail as opposed to the merely autobiographical. Here she was, singing the virtues of creating wholly imagined characters as opposed to populating a novel with personal friends and family members—"ex-lovers, and those other limited, disappointing people from our actual lives"—and yet the lecture had worked well again. Audiences loved it. What had begun as an argument between Ruth and Hannah had served Ruth, the novelist, very well; the lecture had become her credo.

She asserted that the best fictional detail was a *chosen* detail, not a remembered one—for fictional truth was not only the truth of observation, which was the truth of mere journalism. The best fictional detail was the detail that *should have* defined the character or the episode or the atmosphere. Fictional truth was what *should have* happened in a story—not necessarily what *did* happen or what *had* happened.

Ruth Cole's credo amounted to a war against the *roman à clef*, a put-down of the autobiographical novel, which now made her feel ashamed because she knew she was getting ready to write her most autobiographical novel to date. If Hannah had always accused her of writing about a Ruth character and a Hannah character, what was Ruth writing about now? Strictly a Ruth character who makes a bad, Hannah-like decision!

And so it was painful for Ruth to sit in a restaurant and listen to the compliments of her sponsors from the Vrije Universiteit; they were well-meaning but mostly academic types, who favored theories, and theoretical discussions, to the more concrete nuts and bolts of storytelling. Ruth hated herself for providing them with a theory of fiction about which she now had sizable doubts.

Novels were not arguments; a story worked, or it didn't, on its own merits. What did it matter if a detail was real or imagined? What mattered was that the detail *seemed* real, and that it was absolutely the *best* detail for the circumstances. That wasn't much of a theory, but it was all Ruth could truly commit herself to at the moment. It was time to retire that old lecture, and her penance was to endure the compliments for her *former* credo.

It wasn't until (in lieu of dessert) she asked for another glass of red wine that Ruth knew she'd had too much to drink. At that instant she also remembered not seeing the beautiful Dutch boy Wim in line for her autograph after her successful but mortifying speech. He'd said he would be there.

Ruth had to admit that she'd been looking forward to seeing young Wim again—and perhaps drawing him out a little. Truly she *hadn't* been planning to flirt with him, at least not in earnest, and she had already decided *not* to sleep with him. She'd wanted only to arrange a time to be alone with him—possibly a coffee in the morning—to discover what his interest in her was; to *imagine* him as her admirer, and maybe as her lover; to absorb more of the *details* of which the beautiful Dutch boy was composed. And then he hadn't shown up.

I guess he finally got tired of me, Ruth thought. She could sympathize with him if he had; she had never felt so tired of herself.

Ruth refused to allow Maarten and Sylvia to accompany her to her hotel. She'd kept them up late the night before; everyone was in need of an early night. They put her in a cab and instructed the driver. Across the street from her hotel, at the taxi stand on the Kattengat, she saw Wim standing under a streetlight—like a lost boy who'd been separated from his mother in a crowd, which had since dispersed.

Mercy! Ruth thought, as she crossed the street to claim him.

Not a Mother, Not Her Son

At least she didn't sleep with him—not exactly. They did spend the night together in the same bed, but she did not have sex with him—not really. Oh, they had kissed and cuddled; she *did* permit him to touch her breasts, but she made him stop when he got too excited. And she'd slept the whole night in her panties and a T-shirt; she'd not been naked with him. It wasn't her fault that he'd taken all his clothes off. She'd gone into the bathroom to brush her teeth, and to change into the panties and the T-shirt, and when she'd come back into the bedroom, he'd already undressed and crawled into bed.

They'd talked and talked. His name was Wim Jongbloed; he'd read every word she'd written, over and over again. He wanted to be a writer like her, but he'd not approached her after her lecture at the Vrije Universiteit; he'd been devastated by what she'd had to say. He wrote nonstop autobiographical logorrhea—he'd never "imagined" a story or a character in his life. All he did was record his miserable longings, his wretchedly ordinary experience. He'd left her lecture wanting to kill himself, but instead he'd gone home and destroyed all his writing. He'd thrown his diaries—for that's all he'd written—into a canal. Then he'd called every first-class hotel in Amsterdam until he found out where she was staying.

They'd sat talking in the hotel bar until it was obvious that the bar was closing; then she'd taken him to her room.

"I'm no better than a journalist," Wim said, brokenhearted.

Ruth winced to hear her own phrase recited to her; it was a line right out of her lecture. What she'd said was: "If you can't make something up, you're no better than a journalist."

"I don't know *how* to make up a story!" Wim Jongbloed complained.

He probably couldn't write a decent sentence to save his soul, either, but Ruth felt totally responsible for him. And he was so pretty. He had thick, dark-brown hair and dark-brown eyes with the longest eyelashes. He had the smoothest skin, a fine nose, a strong chin, a heart-shaped mouth. And although his body was too slight for Ruth's taste, he had broad shoulders and a wide chest—he was still in the process of growing into his body.

She began by telling him about her novel-in-progress; how it kept changing, how *that* was what you did to make up a story. Storytelling was nothing more than a kind of heightened common sense. (Ruth wondered where she'd read that; she was sure she hadn't thought it up.)

Ruth even confessed that she'd "imagined" Wim as the young man in her novel. That *didn't* mean she would have sex with him; in fact, she wanted him to understand that she would *not* have sex with him. It was enough for her to have fantasized about it.

He told her that *he* had fantasized about it, too—for years! He'd once masturbated to her book-jacket photograph. Upon hearing this, Ruth went into the bathroom and brushed her teeth, and changed into a pair of clean panties and a T-shirt. And when she came out of the bath-room, there he was—naked in her bed.

She'd not once touched his penis, although she felt it poking against her when they hugged; it felt good to hug the boy. And he'd been aw-fully polite about masturbating, at least the first time. "I just have to do it," he'd told her. "May I?"

"All right," she said, turning her back to him.

"No, looking at you," he begged her. "Please ..."

She turned over in bed to face him. Once she kissed his eyes, and the tip of his nose, but not his lips. He stared at her so intently that Ruth could almost believe she was his age again. And it was easy for her to imagine that this was how it had been with her mother and Eddie O'Hare. Eddie hadn't told her this part, but Ruth had read all of Eddie's novels. She knew perfectly well that Eddie hadn't *invented* the masturbation scenes; poor Eddie could invent next to nothing.

When Wim Jongbloed came, his eyelids fluttered; Ruth kissed him on the lips then, but it was not a lingering kiss—the embarrassed boy ran to the bathroom to wash his hand. When he trotted back to bed, he fell asleep so quickly, his head on her breasts, that she thought: I might have liked to have tried my hand at that, too!

Then she decided she was glad she *hadn't* masturbated. If she had, it would have been more like having sex with him. Ruth found it ironic that she needed to make her own rules and her own definitions. She wondered if her mother had needed to similarly restrain or measure herself with Eddie. If Ruth had *had* a mother, would she have found herself in such a situation as this?

She only once pulled back the sheets and looked at the sleeping boy. She could have gone on looking at him all night, but she even re-strained or measured how long she looked. It was a good-bye look—and chaste enough, under the circumstances. She resolved that she wouldn't let Wim in her bed again, and in the early morning Wim made her more determined to keep her resolution. When he thought she was still asleep, he masturbated beside her again, this time sneaking his hand under her T-shirt and holding fast to one of her bare breasts. She pretended to continue sleeping while he ran to the bathroom to wash his hand. The little goat!

She took him out to a café for breakfast, and then they went to what he called a "literary" café on the Kloveniersburgwal—for more coffee.

De Engelbewaarder was a dark place with a farting dog sleeping under one table, and—at the only tables that got any window light—a half-dozen English soccer fans were drinking beer. Their shiny blue soccer shirts lauded a brand of English lager, and when another two or three of their mates would wander in and join them, they would, in salutation, break into a fragment of a rousing song. But not even these desultory outbursts of singing could rouse the dog from its sleep, or keep it from farting. (If de Engelbewaarder was Wim's idea of a "literary" café, Ruth would have hated to see what he called a lowlife bar.)

Wim seemed less depressed about his writing in the morning. Ruth believed she'd made him happy enough for her to expect some further research assistance from him.

"What kind of 'research assistance'?" the young man asked the older woman writer.

"Well."

Ruth remembered her shock upon reading that Graham Greene, as a student at Oxford, had experimented with Russian roulette—that suicidal game with a revolver. The information had jarred her image of Greene as a writer who had the greatest control of himself. At the time of his dangerous game, Greene was in love with his younger sister's governess; the nanny was twelve years older than young Graham and already engaged to be married.

While Ruth Cole could imagine a young idolater like Wim Jongbloed playing Russian roulette over her, what did she think *she* was doing when she went with Wim to the red-light district, and almost at random approached first this and then that prostitute with the proposition that she allow them to watch her with a customer? While Ruth had explained to Wim that she was posing this question *hypothetically*—that she did not truly want to see a prostitute perform the act (or acts)—the prostitutes whom Ruth and Wim talked to either misunderstood or deliberately misinterpreted the proposition.

The Dominican and Colombian women who dominated the windows and doorways in the area of the Oudekerksplein did not appeal to Ruth because she suspected they had a poor understanding of English, which was the case; Wim confirmed that they had a worse grasp of Dutch. There was a tall, stunning blonde in an open doorway off the

Oudekennissteeg, but she spoke neither English nor Dutch. Wim said that she was Russian.

Finally they found a Thai prostitute in a basement room on the Barndesteeg. She was a heavyset young woman with flabby breasts and a potbelly, but she had an amazing moon-shaped face, a lush mouth, and wide, beautiful eyes. At first her English seemed passable, as she led them through a warren of underground rooms where a virtual village of Thai women regarded them with the utmost curiosity.

"We're just here to *talk* to her," Wim said unconvincingly.

The solid prostitute led them to a dimly lit room with nothing in it but a double bed that was covered by an orange and black bedspread of a roaring tiger. The center of the bedspread, which was the tiger's open mouth, was partially covered by a green towel that was bleach-stained in spots, and slightly wrinkled—as if the heavyset prostitute had only moments ago been lying on it.

All the rooms off the underground hall were partitioned by walls that didn't reach the ceiling; the light from other, more brightly lit rooms crept over these thin partitions. The surrounding walls trembled when the prostitute lowered a bamboo curtain that covered the doorway; under the curtain, Ruth could see the bare feet of the other prostitutes padding past in the hall.

"Which one of you will watch?" the Thai woman asked.

"No, that's *not* what we want," Ruth told her. "We want to ask you about what experiences you've had with couples paying you to watch you with a customer." There was nowhere in the room where anyone could be hidden, so Ruth asked: "And how would you do it? Where would you put someone who wanted to watch?"

The thickset Thai undressed. She wore a sleeveless orange sheath of some thin, slinky material. It had a zipper down the back, which she undid very quickly; she slipped her shoulders out of the straps and wriggled the dress down over her hips to the floor. She was naked before Ruth could say another word. "You can sit on this side of the bed," the prostitute told Ruth, "and I lie down with him on the other side."

"No ..." Ruth began again.

"Or you could stand, anywhere you want," the Thai told her.

"What if we *both* want to watch?" Wim asked, but this only further confused the prostitute.

"You *both* want to watch?" the solid woman asked.

"Not exactly," Ruth said. "*If* we both wanted to watch, how would you arrange that?"

The naked woman sighed. She lay down on the towel on her back; she took up the whole towel. "Which one wants to watch first?" the prostitute asked. "It should cost a little more, I think..." Ruth had already paid her fifty guilders.

The big Thai opened her arms to them, beseechingly. "You want *both* to do *and* watch?" she asked them.

"No, no!" Ruth scolded her. "I just want to know if anyone has ever watched you *before*, and *how* they watched you."

The perplexed prostitute pointed toward the top of the wall. "Somebody watching us *now*—is *that* how you want to do it?" Ruth and Wim looked at the partition that served as a partial wall on the near side of the double bed. Near the ceiling, the face of a smaller, older Thai woman grinned down at them.

"My God!" Wim said.

"This isn't working," Ruth announced. "It's a language problem." She told the prostitute that she could keep the money; they'd seen all they wanted.

"No watching, no doing?" the prostitute asked. "What is wrong?"

Ruth and Wim were navigating the narrow hall with the naked woman following them—she was asking them if she was too fat, if *that* was what was wrong—when the smaller, older Thai prostitute, the woman who'd been grinning down at them, blocked their exit from the hall.

"You want something *different*?" she asked Wim; she touched his lips with her fingers, and the boy drew back from her. The little, older woman winked at Ruth. "*You* know what this boy likes, I bet," she said, fondling Wim's crotch. "Oooh!" the small Thai cried. "He got a *beeeg* one—he wants *something*, all right!" Wim, in a panic to protect himself, covered his crotch with one hand and his mouth with the other.

"We're leaving now," Ruth said firmly. "I've already paid." The little prostitute's clawlike hand was reaching for Ruth's breast when the big, naked Thai who was following behind them pushed her way between Ruth and the aggressive older whore.

"She is our very best sadist," the heavyset prostitute explained to Ruth. "*That's* not what you want, is it?"

"No," Ruth said; she felt Wim at her side, like a clinging child.

The bigger prostitute said something in Thai to the smaller one, who backed into an unlit room. Ruth and Wim could still see her; she was sticking her tongue out at them as they hurried along the hall toward the welcome daylight.

"You had an *erection?*" Ruth asked Wim, when they were safely on the street again.

"Yes," the boy confessed.

What *wouldn't* give the boy a hard-on? Ruth wondered. And the little goat had squirted *twice* the night before! Were there men who ever had enough? But it occurred to Ruth that her mother must have liked Eddie O'Hare's amorous attention. The concept of *sixty times* had new meaning.

It was one of the South American prostitutes on the Gordijnensteeg who said to Wim: "Half-price for you with your mother." At least her English was good. And because it was better than her Dutch, Ruth did the talking.

"I'm *not* his mother, and we just want to talk with you—just talk," Ruth said.

"It costs the same, whatever you do," the prostitute said. She was wearing a sarong with a matching demi-bra—a floral pattern meant to represent tropical vegetation. She was tall and slender, her skin a kind of coffee-with-cream color, and although her high forehead and pronounced cheekbones gave her face an exotic aspect, there was something too prominent about the bones in her face.

She led Wim and Ruth upstairs to a corner room; the curtains were sheer, and the light from outside gave the sparsely furnished room a rural atmosphere. Even the bed, which had a pine headboard and a quilted bedspread, had the look of something one would find in the spare bedroom of a farmhouse. Yet dead-center in the queen-size bed was the expected towel. No bidet, no sink—no place to hide, either.

To one side of the bed were two straight-backed wooden chairs—the only place to put one's clothes. The exotic prostitute removed her bra, which she put on the seat of one chair, and she unwrapped her sarong; she was wearing nothing but a pair of black panties when she sat on the towel. She patted the bed on either side of her, inviting Wim and Ruth to join her.

"You don't have to undress," Ruth told her. "We're just *talking* with you."

"Whatever you want," the exotic woman replied.

Ruth sat on the edge of the bed beside her. Wim, who was less cautious, plopped himself down a little closer to the prostitute than Ruth liked. He probably already has a hard-on! Ruth was thinking. That instant it became clear to her what should happen in her story.

What if the older woman writer felt that the younger man was insufficiently attracted to her? What if he seemed almost indifferent to having sex with her? Of course he *did* it. And it was clear to her that he *could* do it all day and all night; yet he always left her with the feeling that he never got very excited. What if he made her feel so self-conscious about her sexual attractiveness that she never entirely dared to show *her* excitement (lest she make a fool of herself)? This would be a boy quite different from Wim in *that* regard—an utterly superior sort of boy. Not as much of a slave to sex as the older woman writer would have liked . . .

But when they watch the prostitute together, the young man very slowly, very deliberately, lets the older woman know that he's *really* aroused. And he gets *her* so aroused that she can scarcely keep still in the wardrobe closet; she can't wait for the prostitute's customer to be gone. And when the customer leaves, the older woman has to have the young man right there, on the prostitute's bed, with the prostitute watching her with a kind of bored contempt. The prostitute might touch the woman writer's face, or her feet—or even her breasts. And the woman writer is so consumed by the passion of the moment that she can do nothing but let everything happen.

"I've got it," Ruth said aloud. Neither Wim nor the prostitute knew what she was talking about.

"Got what? What's it going to be?" the prostitute asked. The shameless woman had her hand in Wim's lap. "Touch my breasts. Go on, touch them," the prostitute told the boy. Wim looked uncertainly at Ruth, like a child seeking his mother's permission. Then he put a tentative hand on one of the prostitute's small, firm breasts. He withdrew his hand the instant he touched her, as if her skin were unnaturally cold or unnaturally hot. The prostitute laughed. It was like a man's laugh, harsh and deep.

"What's wrong with you?" Ruth asked Wim.

"*You* touch them!" the boy said. The prostitute turned invitingly to Ruth.

"No, thank you," Ruth told her. "Breasts are not miracles to me."

"*These* are," the prostitute told her. "Go on—touch them."

The novelist may have known her story, but her curiosity—if nothing else—was aroused. She put a careful hand on the woman's nearest breast. It was as hard as a flexed biceps muscle, or a fist. It was as if the woman had a baseball under her skin. (Her breasts were no bigger than baseballs.)

The prostitute patted the V of her panties. "You want to see what I've got?" The disconcerted boy looked beseechingly at Ruth, but this time it was not her permission to touch the prostitute that he wanted.

"Can we go now?" Wim asked Ruth.

As they were groping their way down the dark stairs, Ruth asked the prostitute where she or he was from.

"Ecuador," the prostitute informed them.

They turned onto the Bloedstraat, where there were more of the Ecuadoran men in the windows and in the doorways, but these prostitutes were bigger and more obviously male than the pretty one had been.

"How's your hard-on?" Ruth asked Wim.

"Still there," the young man told her.

Ruth felt she didn't need him anymore. Now that she knew what she wanted to happen, she was bored with his company; for the story she had in mind, he was the wrong boy, anyway. Yet the question remained of *where* the older woman writer and her young man would feel most at ease about approaching a prostitute. Maybe *not* in the red-light district ...

Ruth herself had been more comfortable in the more prosperous part of town. It wouldn't hurt to walk with Wim on the Korsjespoort-steeg and on the Bergstraat. (The idea of letting Rooie have a look at the beautiful boy struck Ruth as a kind of perverse provocation.)

They needed to pass by Rooie's window on the Bergstraat twice. The first time Rooie's curtain was drawn; she must have been with a customer. When they circled the Bergstraat a second time, Rooie was in her window. The prostitute showed no signs of recognizing Ruth—she just stared at Wim—and Ruth neither nodded nor waved; she didn't even smile. All Ruth did was ask Wim—casually, in passing—"What do you think of *her*?"

"Too old," the young man said.

Ruth felt *certain* that she was through with him. But although she had dinner plans for that evening, Wim told her that he would be waiting for her after dinner at the taxi stand on the Kattengat, opposite her hotel.

"Shouldn't you be in school?" she asked him. "What about your classes in Utrecht?"

"But I want to see you again," he pleaded.

She warned him that she would be too tired for him to spend the night. She needed to sleep—to *really* sleep.

"I'll just meet you at the taxi stand, then," Wim told her. He looked like a beaten dog who wanted to be beaten again. Ruth couldn't have known then how glad she would be to see him waiting for her later. She had no idea that she was *not* through with him.

Ruth met Maarten at a gym on the Rokin that he'd told her about; she wanted to see if it would be a good place for the woman writer and her young man to meet. It was perfect, meaning it wasn't too fancy. There were a number of serious weight lifters. The young man Ruth was thinking of—a much cooler, more detached young man than Wim— would be a devoted bodybuilder.

Ruth told Maarten and Sylvia that she'd "virtually spent the night" with that devoted young admirer of hers. He'd been useful; Ruth had persuaded him to "interview" a couple of prostitutes in *de Wallen* with her.

"But how did you ever get rid of him?" Sylvia asked.

Ruth confessed that she wasn't *finally* rid of Wim. When she said he'd be waiting for her after dinner, both Maarten and Sylvia laughed. Now, if they took her to her hotel after dinner, Ruth wouldn't have to explain Wim to them. Ruth reflected that everything she'd wanted had fallen into place. All that remained was for her to visit with Rooie again. Hadn't Rooie been the one to tell her that *anything* could happen?

In lieu of lunch, Ruth went with Maarten and Sylvia to a signing at a bookstore on the Spui. She ate a banana and drank a small bottle of mineral water. Afterward, she would have most of the afternoon to herself—to see Rooie. Ruth's only concern was that she didn't know when Rooie left her window to pick up her daughter from school.

There was an episode at the book-signing that Ruth might have taken as an omen that she should *not* see Rooie again. A woman Ruth's age arrived with a shopping bag—evidently a reader who'd brought her entire library to be autographed. But in addition to the Dutch *and* English editions of Ruth's three novels, the contents of the shopping bag also included the Dutch translations of Ted Cole's world-famous books for children.

"I'm sorry—I don't sign my father's books," Ruth said to her. "They're *his* books. I didn't write them. I shouldn't sign them." The woman looked so stunned that Maarten repeated in Dutch what Ruth had said.

"But they're for my children!" the woman said to Ruth.

Oh, why not just do what she wants? Ruth thought. It's easier to do what everyone wants. Besides, as Ruth signed her father's books, she felt that *one* of them was hers. There it was: the book she had inspired. *A Sound Like Someone Trying Not to Make a Sound.*

"Say it in Dutch for me," Ruth asked Maarten.

"It's god-awful in Dutch," he told her.

"Say it anyway," she asked him.

"Het geluid van iemand die geen geluid probeert te maken." Even in Dutch, the title gave Ruth the shivers.

She should have taken it as a sign, but she looked at her watch instead. What was she worrying about? There were fewer than a dozen people still standing in line. Ruth would have plenty of time to see Rooie.

The Moleman

By midafternoon at that time of year, only small patches of sunlight lingered on the Bergstraat; Rooie's room was in the shade. Rooie was smoking. "I do it when I get bored," the prostitute told Ruth, gesturing with her cigarette as Ruth came inside.

"I brought you a book—it's something else to do when you get bored," Ruth said. She'd brought an English edition of *Not for Children.* Rooie's English was so excellent that a Dutch translation would have been insulting. Ruth intended to inscribe her novel, but she'd not yet written anything in the book—not even her signature—because she didn't know how to spell Rooie's name.

Rooie took the novel from her. She turned it over, paying close attention to Ruth's jacket photo. Then she put the book down on the table by the door, where she kept her keys. "Thanks," the prostitute said. "But you'll still have to pay me."

Ruth unzipped her purse and peered into her wallet. She needed to let her eyes adjust to the dim light; she couldn't read the denominations on the bills.

Rooie had already sat down on the towel in the middle of her bed. She had forgotten to draw the window curtains, possibly because she'd presumed that she *wouldn't* be having sex with Ruth. There was a matter-of-factness about Rooie today that suggested that she had given up the idea of trying to seduce Ruth. The prostitute had become resigned to the fact that all Ruth wanted to do was *talk*.

"That was a darling boy I saw you with," Rooie told Ruth. "Is he your boyfriend or your son?"

"He's neither," Ruth replied. "He's not young enough to be my son. Not unless I had him when I was fourteen or fifteen."

"It wouldn't be the first time someone had a baby at that age," Rooie said. Remembering the open curtains, she got up from the bed. "He was young enough to be *my* son," the prostitute added. She was closing the window curtains when something or someone out on the Bergstraat caught her eye. Rooie closed the curtains only three quarters of the way. Before she moved to the outside door, the prostitute turned to Ruth and whispered: "Just a minute ..." She opened the door a crack.

Ruth had not yet sat down in the blow-job chair; she was standing in the darkened room, with one hand on the armrest of the chair, when she heard a man's voice speaking English out on the street.

"Should I come back later? Should I wait?" the man asked Rooie. He spoke English with an accent that Ruth couldn't quite place.

"Just a minute," Rooie told him. She closed the door. She closed the curtains the rest of the way.

"Do you want me to leave? I can come back later..." Ruth whispered, but Rooie was standing beside her, covering her mouth with her hand.

"How's this for perfect timing?" (The prostitute also whispered.) "Help me turn the shoes." Rooie knelt by the wardrobe closet, turning the shoes from toes-in to toes-out. Ruth stood, frozen, by the blow-job chair. Her eyes had not adjusted to the weak light; she still couldn't see well enough to count out Rooie's money.

"You can pay me later," Rooie said. "Hurry up and help me. He looks nervous—maybe it's his first time. He won't wait all day."

Ruth knelt beside the prostitute; her hands were shaking and she dropped the first shoe she picked up. "Let me do it," Rooie responded crossly. "Just get in the closet. And *don't move*! You can move your eyes," the prostitute added. "Nothing but your eyes."

Rooie arranged the shoes on either side of Ruth's feet. Ruth could have stopped her; she could have raised her voice, but she didn't even whisper. Ruth later thought—for about four or five years—that she hadn't spoken up because she was afraid that Rooie would be disappointed in her. It was like responding to a childhood dare. One day Ruth would realize that being afraid you'll look like a coward is the worst reason for doing anything.

Ruth instantly regretted that she'd not unzipped her jacket; it was stifling in the wardrobe closet, but Rooie had already admitted her customer to the small red room. Ruth didn't dare move; besides, the zipper would have made a sound.

The man seemed disconcerted by all the mirrors. Ruth had only the briefest glimpse of his face before she deliberately looked away. She didn't *want* to see his face; there was something inappropriately bland about it. Ruth watched Rooie instead.

The prostitute removed her bra; today it was black. She was about to remove her black panties, but the man stopped her. "It's not necessary," he said. Rooie appeared to be disappointed. (Probably for *my* benefit, thought Ruth.)

"It costs the same, whether you look or touch," Rooie told the bland-faced man. "Seventy-five guilders." But her customer apparently knew what it cost—he had the money in his hand. He'd been carrying the bills in his overcoat pocket; he must have taken the money out of his wallet before he came into the room.

"No touching—just looking," the man said. For the first time, Ruth thought that he spoke English with a German-sounding accent. When Rooie reached for his crotch, he sidestepped her hand; he didn't let her touch him.

He was bald and smooth-faced with an egg-shaped head and a non-descript body—not very big. His clothing was nondescript, too. The charcoal-gray trousers of his suit were loose-fitting, even baggy, but the pants were crisply pressed. The black overcoat had a bulky appearance, as if it were a size too large. The top button of his white shirt was unbuttoned, and he'd loosened his tie.

"What do you do?" Rooie asked him.

"Security systems," the man mumbled. "SAS," Ruth thought he added—she couldn't be sure. Did he mean the airline? "It's a good business," Ruth heard him say. "Lie on your side, please," he told Rooie.

Rooie curled herself up on the bed like a little girl, facing him. She drew her knees up to her breasts, hugging herself, as if she were cold, and gazing at the man with a coquettish smile.

The man stood over her, looking down. He'd dropped his heavy-looking briefcase in the blow-job chair, where Ruth could no longer see it. It was a misshapen leather briefcase of the kind a professor or a schoolteacher might carry.

As if in reverence of Rooie's curled figure, the man knelt on the rug beside her bed, his overcoat trailing on the broadloom. A long sigh escaped him. It was then that Ruth heard him wheeze; his breathing was distinguished by a bronchial-sounding whistle. "Straighten your legs, please," the man said. "And reach over your head, as if you're stretching. Pretend you're just waking up in the morning," he added, almost breathlessly.

Rooie stretched—fetchingly, Ruth thought—but the asthmatic wasn't satisfied. "Try yawning," he suggested. Rooie faked a yawn. "No, a *real* yawn—with your eyes closed."

"Sorry—I don't close my eyes," Rooie told him. Ruth realized that Rooie was afraid. It was as sudden as knowing a door or a window had been opened because of a change in the air.

"Perhaps you could kneel?" the man asked, still wheezing. Rooie seemed relieved to kneel. She knelt on the towel on her bed, resting her elbows and her head on the pillow. She peered sideways at the man; her hair had fallen a little forward, partially hiding her face, but she could still see him. She never took her eyes off him.

"Yes!" the man gasped enthusiastically. He clapped his hands, just twice, and swayed from side to side on his knees. "Now shake your head!" the man told Rooie. "Toss your hair all around!"

In an opposing mirror, on the far side of the prostitute's bed, Ruth caught a second, unwanted glimpse of the man's flushed face. His small, squinty eyes were partially closed; it was as if his eyelids were growing over his eyes—like the blind eyes of a mole.

Ruth's own eyes darted to the mirror opposite the wardrobe closet; she was afraid she would see some movement behind the slightly parted curtain, or that there would be a detectable tremble in her shoes. The clothes in the closet seemed to gather themselves around her.

Rooie, as instructed, shook her head—her hair falling over her face. For not more than a second—*maybe* two or three—her hair covered her eyes, but that was all the time the moleman needed. He lunged forward, his chest dropping on the back of Rooie's head and neck, his chin on her spine. He clamped his right forearm across her throat; then he grabbed hold of his right wrist with his left hand, and squeezed. He slowly got off his knees, coming to his feet with the back of Rooie's head and neck pressed to his chest—his right forearm crushing her throat.

Several seconds passed before Ruth realized that Rooie couldn't breathe. The man's bronchial whistle was the only sound Ruth could hear. Rooie's thin arms flailed silently in the air. One of her legs was bent beneath her on the bed, and the other leg kicked straight out behind her so that her left high-heeled shoe shot off her foot and struck the partially open door to the WC. The sound got the strangler's attention; he wheeled his head around, as if he expected to see someone sitting on the toilet. At the sight of Rooie's far-flung shoe, he smiled with relief; he returned his attention to suffocating the prostitute.

A rivulet of sweat ran between Ruth's breasts. She thought of bolting for the door, but she knew the door was locked and she had no idea how to unlock it. She could imagine the man pulling her back into the room, his forearm collapsing *her* windpipe, too, until her arms and legs were as limp as Rooie's.

Involuntarily, Ruth's right hand opened and closed. (If only she'd had a squash racquet, she would later think.) But Ruth's fear so immobilized her that she did nothing to help Rooie—a memory of herself that she would never forget or forgive. It was as if the clothes in the prostitute's closet had held her.

By now Rooie was no longer kicking. The ankle of her one bare foot dragged on the rug as the wheezing man appeared to dance with her. He'd released her throat so that her head was thrown back in the crook of his arm; his mouth and nose nuzzled the side of her neck as he shuffled back and forth with her in his arms. Rooie's arms hung at her sides, her fingers brushing her bare thighs. With an extreme gentleness, as if he were doing his utmost not to wake a sleeping child, the moleman returned Rooie to her bed and once more knelt beside her.

Ruth could not help feeling that it was with intense recrimination that the prostitute's wide-open eyes stared at the narrow part in the wardrobe-closet curtain. Apparently the murderer didn't like the look in Rooie's eyes, either. He delicately closed them with his thumb and index finger. Then he took a tissue from the box on Rooie's bedside table, and, with the tissue as a barrier between himself and some imagined disease, he poked the prostitute's tongue back inside her mouth.

The problem was that the dead prostitute's mouth would not stay shut; her lips had remained parted, and her chin had dropped down to her chest. The wheezing man impatiently turned Rooie's face to one side, propping up her chin with the pillow. The unnaturalness of the prostitute's pose obviously vexed him. He sighed a short, irritated sigh, followed by a high-pitched, rasping wheeze, and then he tried to attend to the matter of Rooie's sprawling limbs. But he could not bend her into the position he desired. Either an arm slid here or a leg flopped there. At one point, the moleman became so exasperated that he sunk his teeth into Rooie's bare shoulder. His bite broke the skin, but Rooie bled very little—her heart had already stopped.

Ruth held her breath; almost a minute later, she realized that she shouldn't have. When she needed to breathe again, she had to take a *big* breath; and for several breaths thereafter, she virtually gasped for air. By the way the murderer stiffened, Ruth could tell that he'd heard her; at least he'd heard *something*. The killer instantly stopped fussing over Rooie's most desirable pose; he stopped wheezing, too. He held his own breath and listened. Although Ruth had not coughed for several days, her cough was now threatening to come back; there was a telltale tickle at the back of her throat.

The moleman slowly stood up, scanning all the mirrors in the red room. Ruth knew very well what the killer thought he had heard: he'd heard the sound of someone trying not to make a sound—*that's* what he'd heard. And so the murderer held his breath, and stopped wheezing, and looked all around. The way his nose twitched, it appeared to Ruth that the moleman was *sniffing* for her, too.

To calm herself, Ruth didn't look at him; instead, she stared at the mirror opposite the wardrobe closet. She tried to see herself in the narrow slit where the curtain was parted; she picked out her shoes among the shoes pointed toes-out beneath the curtain. After a while, Ruth could make out the bottom hem of her black jeans. If she looked hard enough, she could see her feet in one pair of those shoes. And her ankles and shins ...

Suddenly the killer began to cough; he made a terrible, sucking sound that convulsed his entire body. By the time the moleman stopped coughing, Ruth had regained control of her own breathing.

The secret to absolute stillness is absolute concentration. "In the whole rest of your life," Eddie O'Hare had told her when she was a little girl, "if you ever need to feel brave, just look at your scar." But Ruth couldn't see her right index finger without moving either her head or her hand. Instead she concentrated on *A Sound Like Someone Trying Not to Make a Sound.* Of her father's stories, all of which she knew by heart, she knew this one best. There was also a moleman in it.

"Imagine a mole twice the size of a child, but half the size of most adults. This mole walked upright, like a man, and so he was called the moleman. He wore baggy pants, which hid his tail, and old tennis shoes that helped him to be quick and quiet."

The first illustration is of Ruth and her father coming in the front door of the Sagaponack house; they are holding hands as they cross the threshold into the front hall, which is flooded with sunlight. Ruth and her father don't even glance at the coat tree in the corner. Standing there, partially hidden by the coat tree, is the big mole.

"The moleman's job was hunting little girls. He liked to catch them and carry them back underground with him, where he kept them for a week or two. The little girls didn't like it underground. When the moleman finally let them go, they would have dirt in their ears and dirt in their eyes—and they would need to wash their hair every day for ten days before they stopped smelling like earthworms."

The second illustration is a medium close-up of the moleman hiding under a standing lamp in the dining room while Ruth and her father are eating their supper. The moleman has a curved head that comes to a point, like a spade, and no external ears. The small, vestigial eyes are nothing but subtle indentations in his furry face. The five broad-clawed toes of his forepaws make his paws resemble paddles. His nose, like the nose of a star-nosed mole, is composed of twenty-two pink tentacle-like touch organs. (The pink of the moleman's star-shaped nose is the only color other than brown or black in any of Ted Cole's drawings.)

"The moleman was blind, and his ears were so small that they fit inside his head. He couldn't see the little girls, and he could barely hear them. But he could smell them with his star-shaped nose—he could smell them especially well when they were alone. And his fur was velvety—you could brush it in any direction without resistance. If a little girl stood too close to him, she could not resist touching his fur. Then, of course, the moleman would know she was there.

"When Ruthie and her daddy finished dinner, Ruthie's daddy said: 'We're out of ice cream. I'll go to the store and get some ice cream, if you clear our dishes from the table.'

" 'Okay, Daddy,' Ruthie told him.

"But that meant she would be alone with the moleman. Ruthie didn't realize that the moleman was in the dining room until after her daddy had gone."

The third illustration is of Ruth carrying some dishes and silverware into the kitchen. She keeps a wary eye on the moleman, who has emerged from under the standing lamp, his star-nosed snout thrust forward—sniffing for her.

"Ruthie was careful not to drop a knife or a fork, because even a mole can hear a sound as loud as that. And although she could see him, she knew that the moleman couldn't see her. At first Ruthie went straight to the garbage; she tried putting old eggshells and coffee grounds in her hair, so that she wouldn't smell like a little girl, but the moleman heard the eggshells cracking. And besides, he *liked* the smell of coffee grounds. Something smells like earthworms! the moleman thought, sniffing closer and closer to Ruthie."

There is a fourth illustration of Ruth running up the carpeted stairs, the coffee grounds and eggshells falling out of her hair behind her. At the foot of the stairs, staring blindly after her—his star-nosed snout pointed up the stairwell—is the moleman. One of his old tennis shoes has already crept onto the bottom step of the stairs.

"Ruthie ran upstairs. She had to get rid of the coffee grounds and eggshells. She had to try to smell like her daddy instead! And so she dressed herself in his unwashed laundry, she put his shaving cream in her hair. She even rubbed her face with the soles of his shoes, which she realized was a bad idea. Moles like dirt. She scrubbed the dirt off and put on more shaving cream, but she had to hurry—it would be a *very* bad idea to be trapped upstairs with the moleman. And so she tried to sneak past him on the stairs."

The fifth illustration: on the center landing of the stairs, the moleman is halfway up; Ruth—in her father's old clothes, and covered with shaving cream—is halfway down. They are close enough to touch each other.

"The moleman smelled an adult sort of smell, which he shrank away from. But Ruthie had got some shaving cream up her nose. She needed to sneeze. Even a mole can hear a sneeze. Ruthie tried to stop a sneeze three times, which is no fun—it makes your ears feel awful. And each time she made a small sound that the moleman could faintly hear. He cocked his head in her direction.

"What was that sound? he was thinking. How he wished he had external ears! It had been a sound like someone trying not to make a sound. He went on listening. He went on sniffing, too, while Ruthie didn't dare move. She just stood there, trying not to sneeze. She also had to try hard not to touch the moleman. His fur looked so velvety!

"What *is* that smell? the moleman kept thinking. Boy, did some guy need to change his clothes! The same guy must have been shaving three times a day. And somebody had touched the bottom of a shoe. Somebody had broken an egg, too—and spilled some coffee. Someone is a *mess*! the moleman thought. But somewhere, in all of that, there was a little girl who smelled *almost* alone. The moleman knew this because he could smell her baby powder. After her bath, the moleman was thinking, she puts baby powder in her armpits and between her toes. This was one of those wonderful things that impressed the moleman about little girls.

"His fur looks so soft, I think I'll faint—or sneeze, Ruthie thought."

In the sixth illustration, a close-up of Ruth and the moleman on the center landing of the stairs, his paddle of a forepaw is reaching out to her; a long claw is about to touch her face. Her small hand is reaching out to him, too—her hand is about to stroke the velvety fur on the moleman's chest.

" 'It's me—I'm home!' Ruthie's daddy cried. 'I got two flavors!'

"Ruthie sneezed. Some of the shaving cream was sprayed on the moleman. He hated shaving cream. And it's not easy to run when you're blind. The moleman bumped into the newel post at the bottom of the stairs. He tried to hide behind the coat tree in the front hall again, but Ruthie's daddy saw him and grabbed him by the seat of his baggy pants, where his tail was, and threw him out the front door.

"Then Ruthie got a special treat. She was allowed to eat two flavors of ice cream and take a bath at the same time, because no one should go to bed smelling of old laundry and shaving cream and eggshells and coffee grounds—and only a little bit of baby powder. Little girls should go to bed smelling of *lots* of baby powder, and nothing else."

In the seventh illustration—"one for every day of the week," Ted Cole had said—there is Ruth tucked into her bed. Her father has left the door open to the master bathroom, so that its night-light is visible. Through a part in the window curtain, we can see the black of night and a distant moon. And on the outside window ledge, the moleman is curled up—as snugly asleep as if he were underground. His paddle-shaped paws with their broad claws hide his face, all but the fleshy-pink star of his nose; at least eleven of the twenty-two pink tentacle-like touch organs are pressed against the glass of Ruth's bedroom window.

For months—among the *other* models posing for her father—a succession of dead star-nosed moles had made Ted's workroom as unapproachable as the squid ink had ever made it. And once, in a plastic bag, Ruth had found a star-nosed mole in the freezer, where she'd gone looking for a Popsicle.

Only Eduardo Gomez hadn't seemed to mind—for the gardener had an implacable hatred of moles of any kind. The job of providing Ted with sufficient numbers of star-nosed moles had soothed Eduardo's disposition noticeably.

That had been the long fall after Ruth's mother and Eddie O'Hare had left.

The story had been written, and rewritten, over the summer of '58, but the illustrations had come later. All of Ted Cole's publishers—and his translators, too—had begged Ted to change the title. They'd wanted him to call the book *The Moleman*, of course, but Ted had insisted that the book be called *A Sound Like Someone Trying Not to Make a Sound*, because his daughter had given him the idea.

And now—in the small red room with Rooie's murderer—Ruth Cole tried to calm herself by thinking about the brave little girl named Ruthie who had once shared the center landing of the stairs with a mole that was twice her size. At last Ruth dared to move her eyes, just her eyes. She wanted to see what the murderer was doing; his wheezing was driving her crazy, but she could also hear him moving around, and the dim room had become slightly dimmer.

The killer had unscrewed the lightbulb from the standing lamp beside the blow-job chair. It was such a low-wattage bulb that the loss of light was less noticeable than the fact that the room was markedly less red. (The murderer had removed the scarlet stained-glass lamp shade, too.)

Then, from the big briefcase in the blow-job chair, the moleman withdrew some kind of high-wattage floodlight, which he screwed into the socket of the standing lamp. Now Rooie's room was ablaze with light. Neither the room nor Rooie was improved by this new light, which illuminated the wardrobe closet, too. Ruth could clearly see her ankles above her shoes. In the narrow part in the curtain, she could also see her face.

Fortunately, the murderer had ceased his survey of the room. It was strictly how the light fell on the prostitute's body that interested him. He pointed the ultrabright light more directly at Rooie's bed, taking care to light his subject as brightly as possible. He impatiently slapped Rooie's unresponsive right arm, for it had failed to stay where he'd placed it; he seemed disappointed that her breasts had gone so slack, but what could he do? He liked her best on her side, with one but not both of her breasts in view.

In the glaring light, the killer's bald head was gleaming with sweat. There was a grayness to his skin, which Ruth hadn't noticed before, but his wheezing had lessened.

The murderer appeared more relaxed. He proceeded to scrutinize Rooie's posed body through the viewfinder of his camera. It was a camera Ruth recognized: a Polaroid of the old-fashioned, large-format kind—the same camera that her father used to take pictures of his models. The resultant black-and-white print had to be preserved with the bad-smelling Polaroid print coater.

The killer wasted little time in taking one picture. Thereafter, he couldn't have cared less about Rooie's pose; he rolled her roughly off the bed so that he could use the towel under her to unscrew the flood-light, which he returned to his big briefcase. (The floodlight, although it had been on for only a short time, was clearly hot.) The murderer also used the towel to wipe his fingerprints off the small lightbulb he'd earlier unscrewed from the standing lamp; he wiped his prints off the stained-glass lamp shade, too.

He kept waving the developing film in one hand. The film was about the size of a business envelope. The killer didn't wait more than twenty or twenty-five seconds before he opened the film; then he went to the window seat and parted the curtains slightly, so that he could judge the quality of the print in natural light. He seemed very satisfied with the picture. When he came back to the blow-job chair, he returned his camera to the big briefcase. As for the photograph, he carefully wiped it with the bad-smelling print coater; then he waved the photo in the air to dry.

In addition to his wheezing, which now was light, the murderer hummed an unfollowable tune—as if he were making a sandwich he was looking forward to eating alone. Still waving the already-dry print, the killer walked once to the door to the street, tested how to unlock it, and—opening the door a crack—peered briefly outside. He'd touched both the lock and the doorknob with his hand in the sleeve of his over-coat, leaving no fingerprints.

When he closed the door, the killer saw Ruth Cole's novel *Not for Children* on the table where the prostitute had left her keys. He picked up the book, turned it over, and studied the author's photograph. Then, without reading a word of the novel, he opened the book in the middle and placed the photograph between the pages. He put Ruth's novel in his briefcase, but the briefcase sprang open when he picked it up from the blow-job chair. With the standing lamp unlit, Ruth couldn't see which of the contents of the briefcase had fallen out on the rug, but the murderer dropped to all fours; picking things up and returning them to the briefcase affected his wheezing, which was once more at whistle-pitch when he finally stood up and clasped the briefcase firmly closed.

The murderer gave a last look at the room, then. To Ruth's surprise, he gave no last look at Rooie. It was as if the prostitute now existed only in the photograph. Then, almost as quickly as he'd killed her, the gray-faced mole departed. He opened the door to the street without pausing to see if anyone was passing in the Bergstraat—or if a neigh-boring prostitute was standing in her open doorway. Before he closed the door, he bowed to Rooie's doorway, as if Rooie herself were standing only a few feet inside. He again covered his hand in his coat sleeve when he touched the door.

Ruth's right foot was asleep, but she waited a minute or more in the wardrobe closet, in case the killer came back. Then Ruth stumbled over the shoes as she limped out of the closet; she also dropped her purse, which, typically, was unzipped, forcing her to grope around on the dark, poorly lit rug, searching by touch for anything that might have fallen out. She could feel, inside her purse, everything that she knew was important to her (or had her name on it). On the rug, her hand encountered a tube of something too fat to be her lip gloss, but she put it in her purse, anyway.

What she would later consider as her shameful cowardice—her craven immobility in the wardrobe closet, where she'd been frozen with fear—was now matched by a cowardice of another kind. Ruth was already covering her tracks, at once wishing and then *pretending* that she'd never been there.

She couldn't bring herself to take a last look at Rooie. She did pause at the door to the street, and for an eternity she waited inside the room with the door ajar—until she couldn't see a prostitute in any of the other doorways, and there were no pedestrians on the Bergstraat. Then Ruth walked briskly into the late-afternoon light, which she liked so much in Sagaponack but which here had only the chill of a waning fall day about it. She wondered who would notice when Rooie didn't pick up her daughter after school.

For ten, maybe twelve minutes, Ruth tried to convince herself that she was *not* running away; that's how long it took her to walk to the Warmoesstraat police station in *de Wallen*. Once she was back in the red-light district, Ruth's pace slowed considerably. Nor did she approach the first two policemen she saw; they were on horseback—they towered above her. And at the door to the police station, at 48 Warmoesstraat, Ruth balked at going inside. She found herself returning to her hotel. She was beginning to realize not only what a coward but what an inadequate eyewitness she was.

Here was the world-famous novelist with her penchant for detail; yet, in her observations of a prostitute with a customer, she had failed to come away with the most important detail of all. She could never identify the murderer; she could barely describe him. She'd made a point of not looking at him! The quality of his vestigial-like eyes, which had so forcefully reminded her of the moleman, was hardly an identifying characteristic. What Ruth had best retained of the killer was what was ordinary about him—his blandness.

How many bald businessmen with big briefcases were there? Not all of them wheezed or had large-format Polaroid cameras—nowadays, surely, the camera was at least one defining detail. Ruth guessed it was a system of photography of interest only to professionals. But how much did that narrow the field of suspects?

Ruth Cole was a novelist; novelists are not at their best when they go off half-cocked. She believed that she should *prepare* what she was going to tell the police—preferably in *writing*. But by the time she'd returned to her hotel, Ruth was aware of the precariousness of her position: a renowned novelist, an extremely successful (but unmarried) woman, is the cringing witness to the murder of a prostitute while hiding in the prostitute's closet. And she would ask the police (and the public) to believe that she was observing the prostitute with a customer for "research"—this from a novelist on record as saying that real-life experience was second-rate in comparison to what one could imagine!

Ruth could easily foresee the response to *that*. At last she'd found the humiliation she was looking for, but of course this was one humiliation that she wouldn't write about.

By the time she'd taken a bath and readied herself for her dinner with Maarten and Sylvia and the book-club people, she'd already written some notes about what to tell the police. Yet, by her degree of distraction at the book-club dinner, Ruth knew that she'd failed to convince herself that merely writing her account of the murder was as correct as going to the police in person. Long before the conclusion of the meal, she was feeling responsible for Rooie's daughter. And as Maarten and Sylvia drove her back to her hotel, Ruth felt more and more guilty; by then she knew that she had no intentions of *ever* going to the police.

The details of Rooie's room, from the intimate point of view of the wardrobe closet, would stay with Ruth far longer than it would take the novelist to capture the appropriate atmosphere of a working prostitute's chamber. The details of Rooie's room would remain as near to Ruth as the moleman curled on the ledge outside her childhood window, his starry nose pressed against the glass. Her horror and fear of her father's stories for children had come to life in an adult form.

"Well, there he is—your never-ending admirer," Maarten said, when he saw Wim Jongbloed waiting at the taxi stand on the Kattengat.

"Oh, how tedious," Ruth said wearily, thinking that she'd never been as glad to see anyone in her life. She knew what she wanted to tell the police, but she didn't know how to tell them in Dutch. Wim would know. It was merely a matter of making the foolish boy think he was doing something else. When Ruth kissed Maarten and Sylvia good night, she was aware of the questioning look that Sylvia gave her. "No," Ruth whispered, "I'm *not* going to sleep with him."

But the lovestruck boy had come to her with his own expectations. He'd brought some marijuana, too. Did Wim actually think he was going to seduce her by getting her stoned first? Naturally she got him stoned instead. Then it was easy to get him laughing.

"You have a funny language," she began. "Say something in Dutch to me, anything at all."

Whenever he spoke, she tried to repeat what he said—it was as simple as that. He found her pronunciation hysterical.

"How do you say, 'The dog ate this'?" she asked. She made up a number of sentences before she slipped in one she truly wanted. " 'He is a bald, smooth-faced man with an egg-shaped head and a nondescript body—not very big.' I'll bet you can't say that fast," she told him. Then she asked him to write it out so that she could try saying it herself.

"How do you say, 'He doesn't have sex'?" Ruth asked the boy. "You know, like you," she added. Wim was so stoned that he even laughed at that. But he told her. And he wrote out whatever she asked him to. She kept telling him to spell the words clearly.

He still thought he was going to have sex with her later on. But, for the time being, Ruth was getting what she wanted. When she went into the bathroom to pee, she looked in her purse for her lip gloss and found the tube of Polaroid print coater, which she'd apparently taken from the floor of Rooie's room by mistake. In the dim light of the prostitute's room, Ruth had thought it had fallen out of her purse, but it was something that had fallen out of the murderer's briefcase. It had his fingerprints on it, and hers. But what would hers matter? Because it was the only real evidence from Rooie's room, the tube of print coater had to be given to the police. Ruth came out of the bathroom and coaxed Wim through another joint, which she only pretended to inhale. " 'The murderer dropped this,' " she told him then. "Say that. Write it out, too."

What saved her from having to have sex with him, or having to allow him to masturbate beside her again, was that Allan called. Wim could tell that Allan was somebody important.

"I miss you more than I ever have," Ruth told Allan, truthfully. "I should have made love to you before I left. I want to make love to you as soon as I'm back—I'm coming back the day after tomorrow, you know. You're still meeting me at the airport, aren't you?"

Even stoned, Wim got the message. The boy looked around the hotel room as if he'd misplaced half his life in it. Ruth was still talking to Allan when Wim left. He could have made a scene, but he wasn't a bad boy—just an ordinary one. The only peevish gesture he made in leaving was to take a condom out of his pocket; he dropped it beside Ruth where she sat on the bed, still talking to Allan. It was one of those special condoms that come in flavors—this one claimed to be banana-flavored. Ruth would bring the condom to Allan. A little present from the red-light district, she would tell him. (She already knew she wouldn't tell him about Wim, *or* Rooie.)

The novelist sat up transcribing what Wim had written into an orderly message, in her own handwriting—her own *printing*, to be exact. She carved every letter of the foreign language with the utmost care; she didn't want to make any mistakes. The police would doubtless conclude that there'd been a witness to Rooie's murder, but Ruth didn't want them to know that the witness wasn't Dutch. This way the police might presume that the witness was another prostitute—possibly one of Rooie's neighbors on the Bergstraat.

Ruth had a plain manila envelope, manuscript-size, which Maarten had given her with her itinerary. She put her notes for the police in this envelope, together with the tube of Polaroid print coater. When she handled the tube, she touched it only by the ends, holding it between her thumb and index finger; she knew she'd touched the body of the tube when she'd picked it up off Rooie's rug, but she hoped she hadn't marred the killer's fingerprints.

She hadn't the name of a policeman, but she assumed she could safely address the envelope to the police station at 48 Warmoesstraat. First thing in the morning, before she wrote anything on the envelope, she went downstairs to the lobby of the hotel and got the correct postage from the concierge. Then she went out looking for the morning newspapers.

It was the front-page story in at least two Amsterdam papers. She bought the newspaper that had a picture under the headline. It was a photo of the Bergstraat at night, not very clear. A police barrier had enclosed the sidewalk immediately in front of Rooie's door. Behind the barrier, someone who looked like a plainclothes cop was talking to two women who looked like prostitutes.

Ruth recognized the cop. He was the compact, powerful-looking man in the dirty running shoes and the baseball-type warm-up jacket. In the picture, he appeared to be clean-shaven, but Ruth had no doubt that it was the same man who'd followed her for a while in *de Wallen;* clearly both the Bergstraat and the red-light district were his beat.

The headline read: MOORD IN DE BERGSTRAAT

Ruth didn't need to know Dutch to figure that out. While there was no mention of "Rooie"—the prostitute's nickname—the article did mention that the murder victim was one Dolores de Ruiter, age forty-eight. The only other name mentioned in the article—it was also in the caption of the photograph—was the policeman's, Harry Hoekstra, and he was referred to by two different titles. In one place he was a *wijkagent,* in another a *hoofdagent.* Ruth determined that she wouldn't mail her envelope until she'd had time to ask Maarten and Sylvia about the newspaper story.

She brought the article in her purse to dinner; it would be her last dinner with them before leaving Amsterdam, and Ruth had rehearsed how she would casually bring up the story of the murdered prostitute: "Is this a story about what I think it is? I've actually walked on this street."

But she didn't have to bring it up. Maarten had already spotted the story and clipped it from the paper. "Have you seen this? Do you know what it is?" When Ruth pretended ignorance, Maarten and Sylvia told her all the details.

Ruth had already assumed that the body would be discovered by the younger prostitute who used Rooie's room at night—the girl she'd seen in the window in the leather halter top. The only surprise in the article was that there was no mention of Rooie's daughter.

"What's a *wijkagent?*" Ruth asked Maarten.

"The cop on the beat, the district's officer," he told her.

"Then what's a *hoofdagent?*"

"That's his rank," Maarten replied. "He's a senior police officer—not quite what you call a sergeant."

Ruth Cole left Amsterdam for New York on a late-morning flight the following day, having had the taxi take her to the nearest post office en route to the airport. At the post office, she mailed the envelope to Harry Hoekstra, who was almost a sergeant in the Amsterdam police force—District 2. It might have surprised Ruth to know the motto of the 2nd District, which was inscribed in Latin on the police officers' key rings.

ERRARE
HUMANUM
EST

To err *is* human, Ruth Cole knew. Her message, together with the Polaroid print coater, would tell Harry Hoekstra much more than Ruth had meant to say. The message, in carefully printed Dutch, was as follows:

1. *De moordenaar liet dit vallen.*
   [The murderer dropped this.]
2. *Hij is kaal, met een glad gezicht, een eivormig hoofd en een onopvallend lichaam—niet erg groot.*
   [He is a bald, smooth-faced man with an egg-shaped head and a nondescript body—not very big.]
3. *Hij spreekt Engels met, denk ik, een Duits accent.*
   [He speaks English with, I think, a German accent.]
4. *Hij heeft geen seks. Hij neemt één foto van het lichaam nadat hij het lichaam heeft neergelegd.*
   [He doesn't have sex. He takes one photograph of the body after he has posed the body.]
5. *Hij loenst, zijn ogen bijna helemaal dichtgeknepen. Hij ziet eruit als een mol. Hij piept als hij ademhaalt. Astma misschien ...*
   [He has squinty eyes, almost totally closed. He looks like a mole. He wheezes. Asthma, maybe ...]
6. *Hij werkt voor SAS. De Scandinavische luchtvaartmaatschappij? Hij heeft iets te maken met beveiliging.*
   [He works for SAS. The Scandinavian airline? He has something to do with security.]

That, together with the Polaroid print coater, was Ruth's complete eyewitness account. It might have worried her, a week or so later, to hear Harry Hoekstra's comment to a colleague in the Warmoesstraat police station.

Harry was not a detective; more than a half-dozen detectives were already looking for Rooie's murderer. Harry Hoekstra was just a street cop, but the red-light district and the area of the Bergstraat had been Harry's beat for more than thirty years. No one in *de Wallen* knew the prostitutes and their world better than he did. Besides, the eyewitness account had been addressed to Harry. It had at first seemed safe to assume that the witness was someone who *knew* Harry—most likely a prostitute.

Harry Hoekstra, however, never *assumed*. Harry had his own way of doing things. The detectives had made the murderer their job; they'd left the lesser matter of the witness to Harry. When asked if he was making any progress with his investigations concerning the prostitute's murder—was he any closer to finding the killer?—almost-a-sergeant Hoekstra replied: "The killer isn't my job. I'm looking for the *witness*."

Followed Home from the Flying Food Circus

If you're a writer, the problem is that, when you try to call a halt to thinking about your novel-in-progress, your imagination still keeps going; you can't shut it off.

Thus Ruth Cole sat on the plane from Amsterdam to New York, composing opening sentences in spite of herself. "I suppose I owe at least a word of thanks to my last bad boyfriend." Or: "His awfulness notwithstanding, I am grateful to my last bad boyfriend." And so on, as the pilot made some mention of the Irish coast.

She would have liked to linger over the land a little longer. With nothing but the Atlantic beneath her, Ruth discovered that if she stopped thinking about her new book, even for a minute, her imagination plunged her into more inhospitable territory—namely, what would happen to Rooie's daughter? The now-motherless girl might be as young as seven or eight, or as old as Wim, or older—but not if Rooie had still been picking her up after school!

Who would take care of her now? The prostitute's daughter ... the very idea occupied the novelist's imagination like the title of a novel she wished she'd written.

To stop herself from obsessing any further, Ruth looked through her carry-on bag for something to read. She'd forgotten about the books that had traveled with her from New York to Sagaponack, and then to Europe. She'd read enough (for the time being) of *The Life of Graham Greene*—and, under the circumstances, she couldn't bear to reread Eddie O'Hare's *Sixty Times*. (The masturbation scenes alone would have pushed her over the edge.) Instead, Ruth again began the Canadian crime novel that Eddie had given her. After all, hadn't Eddie told her that the book was "good airplane reading"?

Ruth resigned herself to the irony of reading a murder mystery; but, at the moment, Ruth would have read *anything* to escape her own imagination.

Once more Ruth was irritated by the purposeful obscurity of the author photo; that the unknown author's name was a nom de plume also irked her. The author's pen name was Alice Somerset, which meant nothing to Ruth. However, if Ted Cole had seen that name on a book jacket, he would have looked at the book—and especially at the author photo, as obscure as it was—very closely.

Marion's maiden name was Somerset, and Alice was Marion's mother's name. Mrs. Somerset had opposed the marriage of her daughter to Ted Cole. Marion had always regretted her estrangement from her mother, but there had been no way to put an end to it. And then, before the deaths of Thomas and Timothy, her mother had died; Marion's father died shortly thereafter, also before the deaths of Marion's beloved boys.

On the back flap of the book jacket, all it said about the author was that she'd emigrated to Canada from the United States in the late fifties; and that, during the time of the Vietnam War, she'd served as a counselor to young American men who were coming to Canada to evade the draft. "While she would hardly claim it as her first book," the back flap said about the author, "Ms. Somerset is rumored to have made her own contribution to the invaluable *Manual for Draft-Age Immigrants to Canada*."

The whole thing put Ruth off: the coy back flap, the sneaky author photo, the precious nom de plume—not to mention the title. *Followed Home from the Flying Food Circus* sounded to Ruth like the title of a country-western song she would never want to hear.

She couldn't have known that the Flying Food Circus had been a popular restaurant in Toronto in the late seventies, or that her mother had worked as a waitress there; in fact, it had been something of a triumph for Marion, who was then a woman in her late fifties, to be the only waitress in the restaurant who wasn't a *young* woman. (Marion's figure had still been that good.)

Nor could Ruth have known that her mother's first novel, which had not been published in the United States, had been modestly successful in Canada. *Followed Home from the Flying Food Circus* had been published in England, too; it, and two subsequent novels by Alice Somerset, had also enjoyed several *very* successful publications in foreign languages. (The German and the French translations, especially—Marion had sold many more copies of her novels in German and in French than she'd sold in English.)

But Ruth would need to read to the end of Chapter One of *Followed Home from the Flying Food Circus* before she realized that Alice Somerset was the nom de plume for Marion Cole, her modestly successful mother.

Chapter One

A salesgirl who was also a waitress had been found dead in her apartment on Jarvis, south of Gerrard. It was an apartment within her means, but only because she had shared it with two other salesgirls. The three of them sold bras at Eaton's.

For the dead girl, the department-store position had been a step up. She'd formerly sold lingerie in a shop called the Bra Bar. She used to say that the Bra Bar was so far out Avenue Road that it was halfway to the zoo, which was an exaggeration. She once joked to her roommates that the customers at the Bra Bar were more often from the zoo than from Toronto, which of course was an exaggeration, too.

Her roommates said that the dead girl had had a great sense of humor. She'd moonlighted as a waitress, her roommates reported, because she used to say that you didn't meet many guys while you were selling bras. For five years she'd worked nights at the Flying Food Circus, where she'd been hired—like the other women who worked there—because she looked good in a T-shirt.

The waitresses' T-shirts at the Flying Food Circus were tight and low-cut, with a hamburger in the bottommost part of the décolletage. The hamburger had wings, which were spread over the waitresses' breasts. When her roommates found her body, that was all the dead young woman was wearing: the tight, low-cut T-shirt with the flying hamburger covering her breasts. Moreover, the T-shirt had been put on her after she'd been murdered. There were fourteen stab wounds in the dead girl's chest, but not one hole in the flying-hamburger T-shirt.

Neither of the victim's roommates believed that the murdered salesgirl had been "seeing anyone" at the time. But the apartment had not been broken into—the young woman had let someone in. She'd offered whoever it was a glass of wine, too. There were two full glasses of wine on the kitchen table—no lip marks on either glass, and the only fingerprints on both glasses were hers. There was no fabric of any kind in any of the stab wounds—in other words, she'd been naked when she was stabbed. Either she'd let someone into the apartment when she was naked, in which case it must have been someone she'd known rather well, or she'd been talked out of her clothes without an apparent struggle—possibly at knifepoint. If she'd been raped, it was without her offering any detectable resistance—probably at knifepoint, too—or else she'd had sex willingly, which seemed less likely. In either case, she had had sex shortly before she was killed.

Whoever it was hadn't worn a condom. The murdered girl's roommates told the policewoman who first talked to them that their dead friend always used a diaphragm. She hadn't used it this time, which was further indication that she'd been raped. And the flying-hamburger T-shirt pointed to someone who knew her from the Flying Food Circus—not someone who'd met her at Eaton's, or at the Bra Bar. After all, the murderer had not stabbed the salesgirl and then dressed her in a bra.

The homicide detectives who were partners for this investigation had not been partners for long. The man, Staff Sergeant Michael Cahill, had come to Homicide from the critical-incident team. Although Cahill liked it in Homicide, he was at heart a critical-incident kind of man. He had a still-life mentality, which naturally inclined him to investigate things—not people. He would rather search for hairs on a rug, or semen stains on a pillowcase, than talk to anyone.

The woman, Cahill's partner, was well matched with him. She'd started as a constable in uniform, with her shoulder-length auburn hair, which had since turned gray, tucked up under her cap. Detective Sergeant Margaret McDermid was good at talking to people and finding out what they knew; she was a virtual vacuum cleaner when it came to sucking up information.

It was Staff Sergeant Cahill who found the congealed trickle of blood in a fold of the shower curtain. He deduced that the murderer had calmly taken the time to have a shower after he'd murdered the salesgirl and had dressed her in the flying-hamburger T-shirt. Detective Cahill also found a bloodstain on the soap dish—it was a smudged print that had been made by the heel of the murderer's right hand.

It was Detective Sergeant Margaret McDermid who talked to the roommates. She focused on the Flying Food Circus, which anyone would have focused on. The detective was fairly sure that the principal suspect would turn out to be a man with a special feeling for the waitresses in those winged T-shirts—at least he would turn out to be someone who'd had a special feeling for one of them. Perhaps he'd been a co-worker of the dead girl's, or a frequent customer. Maybe a new boyfriend. Yet clearly the murdered salesgirl had not known the murderer as well as she thought.

From the restaurant, it was too far to walk to the waitress's apartment. If the murderer had followed her home from work to learn where she lived, he would have had to follow her taxi by car—or in another taxi. (The murdered waitress always took a taxi home from the Flying Food Circus, her roommates said.)

"It must have been messy fitting her into that T-shirt," Cahill told his partner.

"Hence the shower," Margaret said. She was liking Homicide less and less, but it wasn't because of Cahill's unnecessary remarks. She liked Cahill well enough. What she wished was that she'd had a chance to talk to the murdered salesgirl.

Sergeant McDermid always found herself more interested in the victim than in the murderer—not that finding the murderer was without gratification for her. She just would rather have had the opportunity to tell the salesgirl not to let whoever it was in her door. These were unsuitable or at least impractical sentiments for a homicide detective to have, Margaret knew. Maybe she would be happier in Missing Persons, where there was some hope of finding the person before he or she became a victim.

Margaret concluded that she would rather look for *potential* victims than for murderers. When she told Cahill her thoughts, the staff sergeant was phlegmatic. "Maybe you should try Missing Persons, Margaret," he told her.

Later, in the car, Cahill said that the sight of that blood-soaked flying hamburger was enough to make a vegetarian out of him, but Margaret didn't allow herself to be distracted by the remark. She was already imagining herself in Missing Persons, looking for someone to save instead of someone to catch. She speculated that many of the missing would be young women, and that more than a few of these would turn out to be homicides.

In Toronto, women who were abducted were rarely found in the city. The bodies would turn up somewhere off the 401, or—after the ice had broken up in Georgian Bay, and the snow had melted in the forests—the human remains would be discovered off Route 69 between Parry Sound and Pointe au Baril, or nearer Sudbury. Maybe a farmer would find something in a field off the 11th Line in Brock. In the States, someone snatched in a city would often be found in the same city—in a Dumpster, say, or a stolen car. But in Canada there was all this land.

Some of the young women who were missing would turn out to be runaways. From rural Ontario, they would likely end up in Toronto, where many of them were easily found. (Not infrequently, they would have become prostitutes.) But the missing persons who would interest Margaret the most would be children. What Detective Sergeant McDermid was unprepared for was how much of the business of Missing Persons would entail studying the photographs of children. She was also unprepared for how much the photographs of these missing children would haunt her.

Case by case, the photographs were filed, and as the unfound missing children grew older than their last available photographs, Margaret would mentally revise their appearance. Thus she learned that you needed a good imagination in order to have any success in Missing Persons. The photographs of the missing children were important, but they were only the first drafts—they were pictures of children-in-progress. The ability that the sergeant shared with the parents of these missing children was truly a special but torturous gift: namely, that of seeing, in the mind's eye, what the six-year-old would look like at the age of ten or twelve, or what the teenager would look like in his or her twenties—"torturous," because to imagine your missing child grown older, or even entirely grown up, is one of the more painful things that the parents of missing children do. The parents can't help themselves—they have to do it. But Sergeant McDermid discovered that she had to do it, too.

If this gift made her good at her job, it also kept her from having much of a life. The children she couldn't find became *her* children. When they were no longer an active case in Missing Persons, she took their photos home.

Two boys especially haunted her. They were Americans who had disappeared during the Vietnam War. The boys' parents thought that they'd escaped to Canada in 1968—probably the midpoint of Vietnam "war resisters," as they were called, coming across the border. At the time, the boys would have been seventeen and fifteen. The seventeen-year-old was a year away from being eligible for the draft, but a student deferment would have kept him safe for at least another four years. His younger brother had run away with him—the boys had always been inseparable.

The seventeen-year-old's flight was probably a mask to hide his deeper disillusionment with his parents' divorce. To Sergeant McDermid, both boys were more the victims of the hatred that had developed between their parents than they were victims of the war in Vietnam.

Anyway, the boys' case in Missing Persons was no longer under active investigation. If that seventeen-year-old and fifteen-year-old were alive today, they would be in their early thirties! Yet their case was not "retired" for either of their parents, or for Margaret.

The father, who'd said he was "something of a realist," had provided Missing Persons with the boys' dental records. The mother had sent the photographs that Sergeant McDermid had taken home.

That Margaret was unmarried, and past the age of ever having children of her own, doubtless contributed to her obsession with the handsome boys she saw in those photographs—and to her equally enduring obsession with what might have become of them. If they were alive, where were they now? What did they look like? What women might have loved them? What children of their own might they have fathered? What would their lives be like? If they still lived ...

Over time, the bulletin board on which Margaret tacked the boys' photos had been moved from the combination living-dining room in her apartment—where it had occasionally drawn comment from dinner guests—to her bedroom, which no one but Margaret ever saw.

Sergeant McDermid was almost sixty, although she could still successfully lie about her age. In a few years, she would be as retired as the case of the missing young Americans. In the meantime, she was past the age of inviting anyone to see her bedroom, where the bulletin board with the unfound boys' pictures was the principal view from her bed.

There were times, when she couldn't sleep at night, that she regretted moving the many images of those boys this close to her. And the alternately anxious and grieving mother still sent photographs. Of these, the mother would comment: "I know they don't look like this anymore, but there's something about William's personality that comes through in this picture." (William was the older of the boys.)

Or the mother would write: "I realize you can't see their faces clearly in this one—I mean, you can't see their faces at all, I know—but there is something about Henry's mischievousness that might be useful to you in your search." The particular photograph that accompanied this note was of the mother herself as a young, attractive woman.

She's in bed, in a hotel room somewhere. From the look of it, Margaret guessed that the hotel was in Europe. The young mother is smiling, perhaps laughing, and both her boys are in bed with her—only they're under the covers. All you can see of the boys is their bare feet. *She thinks I can identify them by their feet!* Margaret thought despairingly. Yet she could not stop looking at the photograph.

Or at the one of William as a little boy, playing doctor to Henry's knee. Or the one where the boys, at the ages of about five and seven, are both dismantling lobsters—William with a certain technical ease and zeal, while Henry is finding the task both gruesome and beyond his abilities. (To their mother, this also demonstrated the boys' different personalities.)

But the best photograph of the boys, taken near the time of their disappearance, was after a hockey game—presumably at the boys' school. William is taller than his mother—he's holding a hockey puck in his teeth—and Henry is still shorter than his mom. Both boys are wearing their hockey uniforms, but they have traded their skates for high-top basketball shoes.

It had been a popular photograph among Margaret's colleagues in Missing Persons—when the case was still active—not only because the mother was pretty but because both boys, in their hockey uniforms, looked so Canadian. Yet to Margaret there was something identifiably American about these missing boys, a kind of cocksure combination of mischief and unstoppable optimism—as if each of them thought that his opinion would always be unchallengeable, his car never in the wrong lane.

But it was only when she couldn't sleep, or when she'd looked too often and too long at these photographs, that Sergeant McDermid ever regretted leaving Homicide for Missing Persons. When she'd been looking for the murderer of the young waitress in the flying-hamburger T-shirt, Margaret had slept very well. Yet they'd never found that murderer, or the missing American boys.

When Margaret would run into Michael Cahill, who was still in Homicide, it was natural for her to ask him, as a colleague, about what he was working on—as he asked her. When they had cases that weren't going anywhere—cases that had "unsolved" written all over them, from the start—they would express their frustration in the same way: "I'm working on one of those followed-home-from-the-Flying-Food-Circus kinds of cases."

Missing Persons

Ruth could have stopped reading right there, at the end of Chapter One. There was no question in her mind that Alice Somerset was Marion Cole. The photographs that the Canadian writer had described could not be coincidental—not to mention the *effect* of the photographs on the haunted detective in Missing Persons.

That her mother was still preoccupied with the photos of her missing boys came as no surprise to Ruth, nor did the fact that Marion must have obsessed on the subject of what Thomas and Timothy would have looked like as grown men—and what their lives would have been like, had they lived. The surprise to Ruth, after the initial shock of establishing her mother's existence, was that her mother had been able to write indirectly about what most haunted her. Simply that her mother was a *writer*—if not a good one—was the greatest shock to Ruth of all.

Ruth had to read on. There would be more photographs described, of course, and Ruth could remember each one. The novel was true to the genre of crime fiction only in that it eventually pursued a single case of Missing Persons to its solution: two little girls, sisters, are safely recovered from their abductor, who turns out to be neither a sex fiend nor a child molester (as one first fears) but a barely less terrible estranged father and divorced husband.

As for the waitress found in the flying-hamburger T-shirt, she remains a metaphor for the unsolved or unsolvable crime—as do the missing American boys, whose images (both real and imagined) are still haunting Detective Sergeant McDermid at the end of the novel. In this sense, *Followed Home from the Flying Food Circus* succeeds beyond the genre of crime fiction; it establishes Missing Persons as a psychological condition. Missing Persons becomes the permanent state of mind of the melancholic main character.

Even before she finished reading her mother's first novel, Ruth desperately wanted to talk to Eddie O'Hare—for she assumed (correctly) that Eddie knew something about Marion's career as a writer. Surely Alice Somerset had written more than this one book. *Followed Home from the Flying Food Circus* had been published in 1984; it was not a long novel. By 1990, Ruth guessed, her mother might have written and published a couple more.

Ruth would soon learn from Eddie that there *were* two more, each of them entailing additional casework in the field of Missing Persons. Titles were not her mother's strength. *Missing Persons McDermid* had a certain alliterative charm, but the alliteration seemed strained in *McDermid Reaches a Milestone.*

The principal story in *Missing Persons McDermid* details Sergeant McDermid's efforts to find a runaway wife and mother. In this case, a woman from the States abandons her husband and child; the husband, who is looking for her, is convinced that his wife has run away to Canada. In the course of setting out to find the missing wife and mother, Margaret uncovers some unseemly incidents involving the husband's myriad infidelities. Worse, the detective realizes that the distraught mother's love for a previous child (who was killed in a plane crash) has made her run away from the fearful responsibility of loving a *new* child—that is, the child she has abandoned. When Sergeant McDermid finds the woman, who was formerly a waitress at the Flying Food Circus, the policewoman is so sympathetic toward her that she allows her to slip away. The bad husband never finds her.

"We have reason to suspect that she's in Vancouver," Margaret tells the husband, knowing full well that the runaway woman is in Toronto. (In this novel, the photographs of those missing American boys retain their place of prominence in the detective's monastic bedroom.)

In *McDermid Reaches a Milestone*, Margaret—who has been "almost sixty, although she could still lie about her age," over the course of two novels—*finally* becomes a sexagenarian. Ruth would instantly understand why Eddie O'Hare was particularly impressed by the third of Alice Somerset's novels: the story concerns the return of a former lover of the sixty-year-old detective.

When Margaret McDermid had been in her forties, she'd been deeply committed to volunteer counseling of young American men coming to Canada to escape the Vietnam War. One of the young men falls in love with her—a boy not yet in his twenties with a woman already in her forties! The affair, described in frankly erotic terms, is quickly over.

Then, as Margaret turns sixty, her "young" lover comes to her—again in need of her help. This time, it is because his wife and child are missing—presumed kidnapped. He's now a man in his thirties, and Sergeant McDermid is distracted by wondering if he still finds her attractive. ("But how *could* he? Margaret wondered—an old hag like me.")

"*I* would still find her attractive!" Eddie would tell Ruth.

"Tell *her*—not *me*, Eddie," Ruth would say.

In the end, the former young man is happily reunited with his wife and child, and Margaret consoles herself by once more imagining the lives of those missing American boys whose pictures stare back at her in her lonely bedroom.

391 of the British

Ruth would relish a jacket blurb on *McDermid Reaches a Milestone:* "the best living crime writer!" (This from the president of the British Crime Writers Association, although it was not a widely held opinion.) And *Missing Persons McDermid* was awarded the so-called Arthur for Best Novel. (The Crime Writers of Canada named the award after Arthur Ellis, which was the name adopted by Arthur English, the Canadian hangman from 1913 until 1935; his uncle John Ellis was the hangman in England at that same period of time. Subsequent Canadian hangmen took the name "Arthur Ellis" as their nom de travail.)

However, it was not uncommon that success in Canada—and an even more measurable success in her French and German translations—did *not* mean that Alice Somerset was similarly well known or even well published in the United States; indeed, she had barely been published in the States. A U.S. distributor for her Canadian publisher had tried unsuccessfully to promote *McDermid Reaches a Milestone* in a modest way. (The third of the three novels was the only one of sufficient interest to the Americans for them to publish it at all.)

Eddie O'Hare was envious of Alice Somerset's foreign sales, but he was no less proud of Marion for her efforts to convert her personal tragedy and unhappiness to fiction. "Good for your mother," Eddie would tell Ruth. "She's taken everything that hurt her and turned it into a detective series!"

But Eddie was unsure if he was the model for the young lover who re-enters Margaret McDermid's life when she's sixty, or if Marion had taken *another* young American as her lover during the Vietnam War.

"Don't be silly, Eddie," Ruth would tell him. "She's writing about you, only you."

About Marion, Eddie and Ruth would agree on the most important thing: they would let Ruth's mother remain a missing person for as long as she wanted to be. "She knows where to find us, Eddie," Ruth would tell her newfound friend, but Eddie bore the unlikelihood of Marion ever wanting to see him again like a permanent sorrow.

Arriving at JFK, Ruth expected to find Allan waiting for her when she passed through customs; that she found Allan waiting with Hannah was a surprise. To Ruth's knowledge, they had never met before; the sight of them together caused Ruth the most acute distress. She *knew* she should have slept with Allan before she left for Europe—now he'd slept with Hannah instead! But how could that be? They didn't even know each other; yet there they were, looking like a couple.

In Ruth's view, they looked "like a couple" because they seemed to possess some terrible secret between them—they appeared stricken with remorse when they saw her. Only a novelist could ever have imagined such nonsense. (In part, it was because of her perverse ability to imagine *anything* that in this instance Ruth failed to imagine the obvious.)

"Oh, baby, baby…" Hannah was saying to her. "It's all my fault!" Hannah held a mangled copy of *The New York Times;* the newspaper was in a lumpy roll, as if Hannah had wrung it to death.

Ruth stood waiting for Allan to kiss her, but he spoke to Hannah: "She doesn't know."

"Know *what?*" Ruth asked in alarm.

"Your father's dead, Ruth," Allan told her.

"Baby, he killed himself," Hannah said.

Ruth was shocked. She'd not thought her father capable of suicide, because she'd never thought him capable of blaming himself for anything.

Hannah was offering her the *Times*—or, rather, its wrinkled remains. "It's a shitty obit," Hannah said. "It's all about his bad reviews. I never knew he had so many bad reviews."

Numbly, Ruth read the obituary. It was easier than talking to Hannah.

"I ran into Hannah at the airport," Allan was explaining. "She introduced herself."

"I read the lousy obit in the paper," Hannah said. "I knew you were coming back today, so I called the house in Sagaponack and talked to Eduardo—it was Eduardo who found him. That's how I got your flight number, from Eduardo," Hannah said.

"Poor Eduardo," Ruth replied.

"Yeah, he's a fucking wreck," Hannah said. "And when I got to the airport, of course I was looking for Allan. I assumed he'd be here. I recognized him from his photo…"

"I know what my mother is doing," Ruth told them. "She's a writer. Crime fiction, but there's more to it than that."

"She's in denial," Hannah explained to Allan. "Poor baby," Hannah told her. "It's my fault—blame *me,* blame *me!*"

"It's *not* your fault, Hannah. Daddy didn't give you a second thought," Ruth said. "It's *my* fault. *I* killed him. First I kicked his ass at squash, then I killed him. You had nothing to do with it."

"She's angry—it's *good* that she's angry," Hannah said to Allan. "Outward anger is good for you—what's bad for you is to *implode*."

"Go fuck yourself!" Ruth told her best friend.

"That's good, baby. I mean it—your anger is good for you."

"I brought the car," Allan told Ruth. "I can take you into the city, or we can drive out to Sagaponack."

"I want to go to Sagaponack," Ruth told him. "I want to see Eddie O'Hare. First I want to see Eduardo, then Eddie."

"Listen—I'll call you tonight," Hannah told her. "You might feel like unloading a little later. I'll call you."

"Let me call you first, Hannah," Ruth said.

"Sure, we could try that, too," Hannah agreed. "You call me, or I'll call you."

Hannah needed a taxi back to town, and the taxis were in one place, Allan's car in another. In the wind, in the awkward good-bye, *The New York Times* became more disheveled. Ruth didn't want the newspaper, but Hannah insisted that she take it.

"Read the obit later," Hannah said.

"I've already read it," Ruth replied.

"You should read it again, when you're calmer," Hannah advised her. "It will make you really angry."

"I'm already calm. I'm already angry," Ruth told her friend.

"She'll calm down. Then she'll get *really* angry," Hannah whispered to Allan. "Take care of her."

"I will," Allan told her.

Ruth and Allan watched Hannah cut in front of the line waiting for taxis. When they were sitting in Allan's car, Allan finally kissed her.

"Are you okay?" he asked.

"Strangely, yes," Ruth replied.

Oddly enough, there was an absence of feeling for her father; what she felt was *no* feeling for him. Her mind had been dwelling on missing persons, not expecting to count him among them.

"About your mother..." Allan patiently began. He'd allowed Ruth to collect her thoughts for almost an hour; they had been driving for that long in silence. He really *is* the man for me, Ruth thought.

It had been late morning by the time Allan learned that Ruth's father was dead. He could have called Ruth in Amsterdam, where it would have been late afternoon; Ruth would then have had the night alone, and the plane ride home, to think about it. Instead Allan had counted on Ruth not seeing the *Times* before she landed in New York the following day. As for the prospect of the news reaching her in Amsterdam, Allan had hoped that Ted Cole wasn't *that* famous.

"Eddie O'Hare gave me a book my mother wrote, a novel," Ruth explained to Allan. "Of course Eddie knew who'd written the novel—he just didn't dare tell me. All he said about the book was that it was 'good airplane reading.' I'll say!"

"Remarkable," Allan said.

"Nothing strikes me as remarkable anymore," Ruth told him. After a pause, she said: "I want to marry you, Allan." After another pause, Ruth added: "Nothing is as important as having sex with you."

"I'm awfully pleased to hear that," Allan admitted. It was the first time he'd smiled since he saw her in the airport. Ruth needed no effort to smile back at him. But there was still that absence of feeling for her father that she'd felt an hour ago—how strange and unexpected it was! Her sympathy was stronger for Eduardo, who had found her father's body.

Nothing stood between Ruth and her new life with Allan. There would need to be some sort of memorial service for Ted. It would be nothing very elaborate—nor would many people be inclined to attend, Ruth thought. Between her and her new life with Allan, there was really only the necessity of hearing from Eduardo Gomez exactly what had happened to her father. The prospect of this was what made Ruth realize how much her father had loved her. Was she the only woman who'd made Ted Cole feel remorse?

The Standoff

Eduardo Gomez was a good Catholic. He was not above superstition, but the gardener had always controlled his inclination to believe in fate within the strict confines of his faith. Fortunately for him, he'd never been exposed to Calvinism—for he would have proven himself a ready and willing convert. Thus far, the gardener's Catholicism had kept the more fanciful of his imaginings—in regard to his own predestination—in check.

There had been that seemingly unending torture when the gardener had hung upside down in Mrs. Vaughn's privet, waiting to die of carbon-monoxide poisoning. It had crossed Eduardo's mind that *Ted Cole* deserved to die this way—but not an innocent gardener. At that helpless moment, Eduardo had seen himself as the victim of another man's lust, and of another man's proverbial "woman scorned."

No one, certainly not the priest in the confessional, would fault Eduardo for having felt that way. The hapless gardener, hung up to die in Mrs. Vaughn's hedge, had every reason to feel unjustly done-in. Yet, over the years, Eduardo knew that Ted was a fair and generous employer, and the gardener had never forgiven himself for thinking that Ted *deserved* to die of carbon-monoxide poisoning.

Therefore it wreaked havoc on Eduardo's superstitious nature—not to mention strengthened his potentially rampant fatalism—that the luckless gardener should have been the one to find Ted Cole dead of carbon-monoxide poisoning.

It was Eduardo's wife, Conchita, who first sensed that something was wrong. She'd picked up the mail at the Sagaponack post office on her way to Ted's house. Because it was her day of the week to change the beds and do the laundry and the general housecleaning, Conchita arrived at Ted's ahead of Eduardo. She deposited the mail on the kitchen table, where she couldn't help noticing a full bottle of single-malt Scotch whiskey; the bottle had been opened, but not a drop had been poured. It sat beside a clean, empty glass of Tiffany crystal.

Conchita also noticed Ruth's postcard in the mail. The picture of the prostitutes in their windows on the Herbertstrasse, the red-light district in the St. Pauli quarter of Hamburg, disturbed her. It was an inappropriate postcard for a daughter to send her father. Yet it was a pity that the mail from Europe had been slow to arrive, for the message on the postcard might have cheered Ted—had he read it. (THINKING OF YOU, DADDY. I'M SORRY ABOUT WHAT I SAID. IT WAS MEAN. I LOVE YOU! RUTHIE.)

Worried, Conchita nonetheless began cleaning in Ted's workroom; she was thinking that Ted might still be upstairs asleep, although he was usually an early riser. The bottommost drawer of Ted's so-called writing desk was open; the drawer was empty. Beside the drawer was a large dark-green trash bag, which Ted had stuffed with the hundreds of black-and-white Polaroids of his nude models; even though the bag was tied closed at the top, the smell of the Polaroid print coater escaped from the bag when Conchita moved it out of the way of her vacuum cleaner. A note taped to the bag said: CONCHITA, PLEASE THROW THIS TRASH AWAY BEFORE RUTH COMES HOME.

This so alarmed Conchita that she stopped vacuuming. She called upstairs from the bottom of the stairwell. "Mr. Cole?" There was no reply. She went upstairs. The door to the master bedroom was open. The bed had not been slept in; it was still neatly made, just as Conchita had left it the morning before. Conchita wandered down the upstairs hall to the room Ruth now used. Ted (or someone) had slept in Ruth's bed last night, or he had at least stretched out on it for a little while. Ruth's closet and her chest of drawers were open. (Her father had felt the need to take a last look at her clothes.)

By now, Conchita was worried enough to call Eduardo—even before she came downstairs—and while she was waiting for her husband to arrive, she took the large dark-green trash bag from Ted's workroom and carried it out to the barn. There was a code panel that opened the garage door to the barn, and Conchita keyed in the proper code. When the garage door opened, Conchita saw that Ted had piled up some blankets along the barn floor, thus sealing the crack under the garage door; she also realized that Ted's car was running, although Ted wasn't in the car. The Volvo was chugging away in the barn, which reeked of exhaust fumes. Conchita dropped the trash bag in the open garage doorway. She waited in the driveway for Eduardo.

Eduardo shut off the Volvo before he went looking for Ted. The tank was less than a quarter full—the car had probably run most of the night—and Ted had slightly depressed the accelerator pedal with an old squash racquet. It was one of Ruth's old racquets, and Ted had pressed the racquet head against the accelerator and wedged the handle under the front seat. This had kept the car idling high enough so that it hadn't stalled.

The trap door to the squash court on the second floor of the barn was open, and Eduardo climbed the ladder; he was scarcely able to breathe, because the exhaust fumes had risen to the top of the barn.

Ted was dead on the floor of the squash court. He was dressed to play. Maybe he'd hit the ball for a while, and run around a little in the court. When he got tired, he lay down on the floor of the court, perfectly positioned on the T, the spot on the court he'd always told Ruth to take possession of—to occupy, as if her life depended on it, because it was *the* position on the court from which you could best control the play of your opponent.

Later Eduardo regretted that he opened the large dark-green trash bag and examined the contents before he threw the bag in the trash. His memory of the many drawings of Mrs. Vaughn's private parts had never left him, although he'd seen her private parts in shreds and tatters. The black-and-white photographs were a grim reminder to the gardener of Ted Cole's fascination with demeaned and demoralized women. Feeling sick to his stomach, Eduardo deposited the photographs in the trash.

Ted had left no suicide note, unless one counts the note on the trash bag—CONCHITA, PLEASE THROW THIS TRASH AWAY BEFORE RUTH COMES HOME. And Ted had anticipated that Eduardo would use the telephone in the kitchen, for there on the notepad, by the kitchen phone, was another message: EDUARDO, CALL RUTH'S PUBLISHER, ALLAN ALBRIGHT. Ted had written down Allan's number at Random House. Eduardo made the call without hesitation.

But as grateful as Ruth would be to Allan for taking charge, she could not stop searching the Sagaponack house for the note she was hoping that her father had left for *her*. That there *was* no note confounded her; her father had always been able to say something self-justifying—he'd been tireless in defending himself.

Even Hannah was hurt that he'd left no word for her, although Hannah would convince herself that a hang-up on her answering machine must have been a call from Ted.

"If only I'd been there when he called!" Hannah would say to Ruth.

"If only ..." Ruth had said.

The memorial service for Ted Cole was conducted in an impromptu fashion at the public school for grades one through four in Sagaponack. The school board, and the past and present teachers at the school, had called Ruth and offered her the premises. Ruth hadn't realized the degree to which her father had been a benefactor of the school. He'd twice bought them new playground equipment; every year he donated art supplies for the children; he was the principal provider of children's books for the Bridgehampton library, which was the library used by the schoolchildren in Sagaponack. Moreover, unbeknownst to Ruth, Ted had frequently read to the children during Story Hour, and, at least a half-dozen times during each school year, he came to the school and gave the children drawing lessons.

Thus, in an atmosphere of undersize desks and chairs, and with the surrounding walls displaying children's drawings of the most notable themes and characters from Ted Cole's books, a local remembrance was held for the famous author and illustrator. A most beloved retired teacher at the school spoke fondly of Ted's dedication to the entertainment of children, although she confused his books with one another; she thought that the moleman was a creature who lurked under the terrifying door in the floor, and that the indescribable sound like someone trying not to make a sound was that of the misunderstood mouse crawling between the walls. From the children's drawings on the walls, Ruth saw sufficient numbers of mice and molemen to last her a lifetime.

Except for Allan and Hannah, the only noticeable out-of-towner was the gallery owner from New York who'd made a small fortune selling Ted Cole's original drawings. Ted's publisher couldn't come—he was still recovering from a cough he'd caught at the Frankfurt Book Fair. (Ruth thought she knew the cough.) And even Hannah was subdued—they were all surprised to see so many children in attendance.

Eddie O'Hare was there; as a Bridgehampton resident, Eddie was no out-of-towner, but Ruth hadn't expected to see him. Later she understood why he'd come. Like Ruth, Eddie had imagined that Marion might show up. After all, it was one of those occasions at which Ruth dreamed that her mother *might* make an appearance. And Marion was a writer. Weren't all writers drawn to endings? Here was an ending. But Marion wasn't there.

It was a raw, blustery day with a wet wind blowing from the ocean; instead of lingering outside the schoolhouse, people hurried to their cars when the makeshift service was over. All but one woman, whom Ruth judged to be about her mother's age; she was dressed in black, she even wore a black veil, and she hovered in the vicinity of her shiny black Lincoln as if she couldn't bear to leave. When the wind lifted her veil, her skin appeared to be stretched too tightly over her skull. The woman whose skeleton was threatening to break through her skin stared at Ruth so intently that Ruth jumped to the conclusion that the woman must be the angry widow who'd written her that hateful letter—the so-called widow for the rest of her life. Taking Allan's hand, Ruth alerted him to the woman's presence.

"I haven't lost a husband yet, so she's come to gloat over the fact that I've lost a father!" Ruth said to Allan, but Eddie O'Hare was within hearing distance.

"I'll take care of this," Eddie told Ruth. Eddie knew who the woman was.

It was not the angry widow—it was Mrs. Vaughn. Eduardo had spotted her first, of course; he'd interpreted Mrs. Vaughn's presence as another reminder of the fate to which he was doomed. (The gardener was hiding in the schoolhouse, hoping his former employer would miraculously disappear.)

It was not that her skeleton was breaking through her skin; rather, her alimony had included a sizable allotment for cosmetic surgery, of which Mrs. Vaughn had partaken to excess. When Eddie took her arm and helped her in the direction of the shiny black Lincoln, Mrs. Vaughn did not resist.

"Do I know you?" she asked Eddie.

"Yes," he told her. "I was a boy once. I knew you when I was a boy." Her bird's-feet fingers were like claws on his wrist; her veiled eyes eagerly searched his face.

"You saw the drawings!" Mrs. Vaughn whispered. "You carried me into my house!"

"Yes," Eddie admitted.

"She looks just like her mother, doesn't she?" Mrs. Vaughn asked Eddie. She meant Ruth, of course, and Eddie disagreed, but he knew how to talk to older women.

"In some ways, yes—she does," Eddie replied. "She looks a little bit like her mother." He helped Mrs. Vaughn into the driver's seat. (Eduardo Gomez would not leave the schoolhouse until he saw the shiny black Lincoln drive safely away.)

"Oh, I think she looks *a lot* like her mother!" Mrs. Vaughn told Eddie.

"I think she looks like her mother and father *both*," Eddie tactfully replied.

"Oh, no!" Mrs. Vaughn cried. "*No one* looks like her father! He was one of a kind!"

"Yes, you could say that," Eddie told Mrs. Vaughn. He closed her car door and held his breath until he heard the Lincoln start; then he rejoined Allan and Ruth.

"Who was she?" Ruth asked him.

"One of your father's old girlfriends," Eddie told her. Hannah, who heard him, looked after the departing Lincoln with a journalist's fleeting curiosity.

"I had a dream they'd all be here, *all* his old girlfriends," Ruth said.

Actually, there *was* one other, but Ruth never knew who she was. She was an overweight woman who'd introduced herself to Ruth before the service in the schoolhouse. She was plump and fiftyish, with a contrite expression. "You don't know me," she'd said to Ruth, "but I knew your father. Actually, my mother and I knew him. My mother committed suicide, too, so I'm very sorry—I know how you must feel."

"Your name is ..." Ruth had said, shaking the woman's hand.

"Oh, my maiden name was Mountsier," the woman said in a self-deprecating way. "But you wouldn't know me...." Then she'd slipped away.

"Gloria—I think she said that was her name," Ruth told Eddie, but Eddie didn't know who she was. (*Glorie* was her name, of course—the late Mrs. Mountsier's troubled daughter. But she'd slipped away.)

Allan insisted that Eddie and Hannah join him and Ruth at the Sagaponack house for a drink after the service. By then it had begun to rain, and Conchita had finally freed Eduardo from the schoolhouse and taken him home to Sag Harbor. For once (or once again) there was something stronger than beer and wine in the Sagaponack house; Ted had bought an excellent single-malt Scotch whiskey.

"Maybe Daddy bought the bottle because he was thinking of this occasion," Ruth said. They sat at the dining-room table, where, once in a story, a little girl named Ruthie had sat with her daddy while the moleman waited in hiding under a standing lamp.

Eddie O'Hare had not been in the house since the summer of '58. Hannah had not been in the house since she'd fucked Ruth's father. Ruth thought of this, but she refrained from comment; although her throat ached, she didn't cry.

Allan wanted to show Eddie his idea for the squash court in the barn. Since Ruth had given up the game, Allan had a plan to convert the court into either an office for himself or an office for Ruth. That way,

one of them could work in the house—in Ted's former workroom—
and the other could work in the barn.

Ruth was disappointed that *she* didn't get to go off with Eddie alone,
because she could have talked all day to him about her mother. (Eddie
had brought with him Alice Somerset's other two novels.) But with
Eddie and Allan in the barn, Ruth was left alone with Hannah.

"You know what I'm going to ask you, baby," Hannah told her friend.
Of course Ruth knew.

"Ask away, Hannah."

"Have you had sex yet? I mean with Allan," Hannah said.

"Yes, I have," Ruth replied. She felt the good whiskey warming her
mouth, her throat, her stomach. She wondered when she would stop
missing her father, or *if* she would stop missing him.

"And?" Hannah asked.

"Allan has the biggest cock I've ever seen," Ruth said.

"I didn't think you *liked* big schlongs, or is it someone else who said
that?" Hannah asked.

"It's not *too* big," Ruth said. "It's just the right size for me."

"So you're fine? And you're getting married? You're gonna try to
have a kid? The whole deal, right?" Hannah asked her.

"I'm fine, yes," Ruth replied. "The whole deal, yes."

"But what *happened?"* Hannah asked her.

"What do you mean, Hannah?"

"I mean, you're so calm—something must have *happened*," Hannah
said.

"Well. My best friend fucked my father, then my father killed himself, and I found out that my mother is a journeyman sort of writer—
is that what you mean?"

"All right, all right—I deserve that," Hannah said. "But what happened to *you?* You're *different.* Something *happened* to you."

"I've had my last bad boyfriend, if that's what you mean," Ruth
replied.

"Okay, okay. Keep it to yourself," Hannah said. *"Something* happened.
But I don't care. Go on and keep it to yourself."

Ruth poured her friend a little more of the single-malt Scotch
whiskey. "This is good, isn't it?" Ruth asked.

"You're a weird one," Hannah told her. It struck a chord. It was what
Rooie had told Ruth the first time Ruth refused to stand in the
wardrobe closet among the shoes.

"Nothing *happened,* Hannah," Ruth lied. "Don't people simply come to a point when they want their lives to change, when they want a new life?"

"Yeah ... I wouldn't know," Hannah answered. "Maybe they do. But only because something *happens* to them."

Ruth's First Wedding

Allan Albright and Ruth Cole were married over the long Thanksgiving weekend, which they spent at Ruth's house in Vermont. Hannah, together with a bad boyfriend, was a weekend-long houseguest, as was Eddie O'Hare, who gave the bride away. (Hannah was Ruth's maid of honor.) With Minty's help, Eddie had identified that George Eliot passage about marriage—Ruth wanted Hannah to read it at her wedding. Of course Minty couldn't resist a small lecture upon his success in locating the passage.

"You see, Edward," Minty informed his son, "a passage of this kind, which is a summation—both in its content and in its tone—is certain to be an opening passage to a chapter or, more likely, a concluding passage. And as it suggests some deeper finality, it is more likely a passage to be found near the end of a book than it is to be found near the beginning."

"I see," Eddie said. "What book is it from?"

"The hint of irony gives it away," Minty intoned. "That, and its bittersweet quality. It's like a pastoral, but more than a pastoral."

"Which novel is it, Dad?" Eddie begged his father.

"Why, it's *Adam Bede,* Edward," the old English teacher told his son. "And it's well suited for your friend's wedding, which is a November wedding, the same month Adam Bede himself was married to Dinah— 'on a rimy morning in parting November,' " Minty quoted from memory. "That's from the first sentence of the last chapter, not counting the Epilogue," the old English teacher added.

Eddie felt exhausted, but he'd identified the passage, as Ruth had asked him to.

At Ruth's wedding, Hannah read from George Eliot with a lack of conviction, but the words themselves were alive for Ruth.

"What greater thing is there for two human souls, than to feel that they are joined for life—to strengthen each other in all labor, to rest on each other in all sorrow, to minister to each other in all pain, to be one with each other in silent unspeakable memories at the moment of the last parting?"

What greater thing is there, indeed? Ruth wondered. She thought she had only begun to love Allan; she believed she was already loving him more than she'd ever loved anyone else, except her dad.

The civil ceremony, which was conducted by a local justice of the peace, was held in Ruth's favorite bookstore in Manchester, Vermont. The booksellers, a man and his wife who were old friends of Ruth's, were kind enough to close their store for a couple of hours on one of the busiest shopping weekends of the year. After the wedding, the bookstore opened its doors to business-as-usual, but there seemed to be more than the expected numbers of book buyers waiting to be served. Among them were some curiosity seekers. As the new Mrs. Albright (which Ruth Cole would never be *called*) left the store on Allan's arm, she averted her eyes from the bystanders.

"If there are any journalists, I'll handle them," Hannah had whispered to Ruth.

Eddie was looking all around for Marion, of course.

"Is she here? Do you see her?" Ruth asked, but Eddie just shook his head.

Ruth was looking for someone else, too. She was half-expecting that Allan's ex-wife would show up, although Allan had scoffed at her fears. The subject of children had been a bitter one between Allan and his former wife, but their divorce had been a joint decision. Harassment was not a part of his ex-wife's nature, Allan had said.

On that busy Thanksgiving weekend, they'd had to park at some distance from the bookstore. As they passed a pizza restaurant and a store that sold candles, Ruth realized that they were being followed; notwithstanding that Hannah's bad boyfriend had the appearance of a bodyguard, someone was following the small wedding party. Allan took Ruth's arm and hurried her along the sidewalk; they were now near the parking lot. Hannah kept turning to look at the elderly woman who was following them, but the woman was not one to be stared down.

"She's not a journalist," Hannah said.

"Fuck her—she's just some old lady," Hannah's bad boyfriend said.

"I'll handle this," said Eddie O'Hare. But this older woman was immune to Eddie's charms.

"I'm not talking to you. I'm talking to *her*," the elderly woman told Eddie; she was pointing at Ruth.

"Look, lady—it's her wedding day. Take a fucking hike," Hannah said.

Allan and Ruth stopped walking and faced the old lady, who was out of breath from hurrying after them. "It's *not* my ex-wife," Allan whispered, but Ruth knew this as surely as she knew that the old woman wasn't her mother.

"I wanted to see your face," the elderly lady said to Ruth. In her own way, she was as nondescript as Rooie's murderer. She was just another older woman who'd let herself go. And with that thought, even before the woman spoke again, Ruth suddenly knew who she was. Who else but a widow for the rest of her life would be so inclined to let herself go?

"Well, now you've seen my face," Ruth told her. "What next?"

"I want to see your face again, when you're a widow," the angry widow said. "I can't wait for that."

"Hey," Hannah told the elderly lady, "by the time she's a widow, you'll be dead. You look like you're dying already."

Hannah took Ruth's arm out of Allan's hand and started pulling her toward their car. "Come on, baby—it's your wedding day!"

Allan briefly glared at the old woman; then he followed Ruth and Hannah. Hannah's bad boyfriend, although he *looked* like an enforcer, was actually an ineffectual wimp. He just scuffed his feet and glanced at Eddie.

And Eddie O'Hare, who'd never met an older woman who couldn't (or wouldn't) be charmed, thought he would try again with the angry widow, who was staring after Ruth as if she were memorizing the moment.

"Wouldn't you agree that weddings are sacred, or that they should be?" Eddie began. "Aren't they among those days that we are meant to remember all our lives?"

"Oh, *yes*—I agree!" the old widow said eagerly. "She'll surely remember this day. When her husband's dead, she'll remember it more than she wants to. There's not an hour that goes by that I don't remember *my* wedding day!"

"I see," Eddie said. "Can I walk you to your car?"

"No, thank you, young man," the widow told him.

Eddie, defeated by her righteousness, turned away and hurried after the wedding party. All of them were hurrying, perhaps because of the rawness of the November weather.

There was a small dinner party in the late afternoon. The local booksellers came, and Kevin Merton (Ruth's caretaker) with his wife. Allan and Ruth had arranged no honeymoon. As for the new couple's plans, Ruth had told Hannah that they would probably use the Sagaponack house more frequently than they would get to Vermont. Eventually they would have to choose between Long Island and New England, which—once they had a child—would be an obvious choice, Ruth had said. (When the child was old enough to go to school, she would want the child to be in Vermont.)

"And when will you know if there's gonna be a kid?" Hannah had asked Ruth.

"When I get pregnant, or when I don't," Ruth had replied.

"But are you *trying?*" Hannah had asked.

"We're going to start trying after the New Year."

"So soon!" Hannah said. "You're not wasting any time."

"I'm thirty-six, Hannah. I've wasted enough time."

The fax machine in the Vermont house rang throughout her wedding day, and Ruth kept leaving her dinner party to check the messages. (Congratulations from her foreign publishers, for the most part.) There was a sweet message from Maarten and Sylvia in Amsterdam. (WIM WILL BE BROKENHEARTED! Sylvia had written.)

Ruth had asked Maarten to keep her informed of any developments in the case of the murdered prostitute. Maarten had told Ruth that there was no news about the prostitute's murder. The police weren't talking about it.

"Did she have any children?" Ruth had earlier faxed Maarten. "I wonder if that poor prostitute had any children." But there had been nothing in the news about the prostitute's daughter, either.

Ruth had got on an airplane, she'd crossed an ocean, and what had happened in Amsterdam had all but vanished. Only in the dark, when she lay awake, did she feel the touch of a dress on a hanger or smell the leather of the halter top that had hung in Rooie's closet.

"You're gonna tell me when you're pregnant, aren't you?" Hannah asked Ruth, when they were doing the dishes. "You're not gonna try to keep *that* a secret, too, are you?"

"I have no secrets, Hannah," Ruth lied.

"You're the biggest secret I know," Hannah told her. "The only way I know what's going on with you is the only way everyone else knows it. I just have to wait and read your next book."

"But I don't write about myself, Hannah," Ruth reminded her.

"So you say," Hannah said.

"Of course I'll tell you when I'm pregnant," Ruth said, changing the subject. "You'll be the first to know, after Allan."

When she went to bed with Allan that night, Ruth felt only half at peace with herself; she also felt exhausted.

"Are you okay?" Allan asked her.

"I'm okay," Ruth told him.

"You seem tired," Allan said.

"I *am* tired," Ruth admitted.

"You seem *different,* somehow," Allan told her.

"Well. I'm married to you, Allan," Ruth replied. "*That's* different, isn't it?"

By the end of the first week of January 1991, Ruth would be pregnant, which would be different, too.

"Boy, that was fast!" Hannah would remark. "Tell Allan not every guy his age is still shooting live ammunition."

Graham Cole Albright—seven pounds, ten ounces—was born in Rutland, Vermont, on October 3, 1991. The boy's birthday coincided with the first anniversary of German reunification. Although she hated to drive, Hannah drove Ruth to the hospital. She'd been staying with Ruth for the final week of Ruth's pregnancy, because Allan was working in New York; he drove to Vermont on the weekends.

It was two in the morning when Hannah left Ruth's house for the hospital in Rutland, which was about a forty-five-minute drive. Hannah had called Allan as they were leaving for the hospital. The baby wasn't born until after ten in the morning. Allan arrived in plenty of time for the actual delivery.

As for the baby's namesake, Graham Greene, Allan remarked that he hoped *his* little Graham would never share the novelist's reputed habit of frequenting brothels. Ruth, who for more than a year had been bogged down near the end of volume one of *The Life of Graham Greene*, felt a far greater anxiety about one of Greene's other habits: his inclination to travel to the world's trouble spots in search of firsthand experience. This was nothing Ruth would wish upon *her* little Graham, nor would she ever again seek such experiences for herself. After all, she'd seen a prostitute murdered by her customer, and it appeared that the murderer had got away with it.

Ruth's novel-in-progress would suffer a yearlong hiatus. She moved with her baby boy back to Sagaponack, which meant that Conchita Gomez could be Graham's nanny. This also made the weekends easier for Allan. He could take the jitney or the train from New York to Bridgehampton in half the time it took him to drive from the city to Vermont; he could also work on the train.

In Sagaponack, Allan used Ted's former workroom for an office. Ruth claimed that the room still smelled of squid ink, or of a decomposing star-nosed mole—or of the Polaroid print coater. The photographs were gone now, although Ruth said she could still smell them, too.

But what could she smell (or otherwise detect) in *her* office on the second floor of the barn—the remodeled Sagaponack squash court, which Ruth chose as *her* workroom? The ladder and trap door had been replaced by a normal flight of stairs and a normal door. Ruth's new office had baseboard heating; there was a window where the dead spot on the front wall of the squash court had been. When the novelist sat typing on her old-fashioned typewriter, or—as she more often did—writing by hand on the long yellow pads of lined paper, she never heard the reverberation that the squash ball used to make against the telltale tin. And the T on the former court, which she'd been taught to take possession of (as if her life depended on it), was carpeted now. Ruth couldn't see it.

She *could* smell, from time to time, the exhaust fumes from the cars that were still parked on the ground floor of the old barn. It wasn't a smell that bothered her.

"You're a weird one!" Hannah would say to her, again. "It would give me the creeps to work here!"

But, at least until Graham was old enough to go to preschool, the Sagaponack house would be fine for Ruth; it was fine for Allan and for Graham, too. They would go to Vermont for the summers, when the Hamptons were overrun—and when Allan didn't so much mind the long drive from the city and back. (It was a four-hour drive from New York to Ruth's house in Vermont.) Ruth would worry, then, about Allan driving such a distance at night—there were deer on the roads, and drunken drivers—but she was happily married; and, for the first time, she loved her life.

Like any new mother—especially, like any new *older* mother—Ruth worried about her baby. She'd been unprepared for how much she was going to love him. But Graham was a healthy child. Ruth's anxieties about him were entirely the product of her imagination.

At night, for example, when she thought that Graham's breathing was strange or different—or worse, when she couldn't hear him breathing—she would rush from the master bedroom to the nursery, which had been her own bedroom as a child. There, Ruth would often curl up on the rug beside the crib. She kept a pillow and a quilt in Graham's closet for such occasions. Allan would often find her on the floor of the nursery in the mornings—sound asleep beside her sleeping child.

And when Graham was no longer sleeping in a crib, and he was old enough to climb in and out of his bed by himself, Ruth would lie in the master bedroom, hearing her child's feet padding across the floor of the master bathroom on his way to her. It was exactly how Ruth had crossed that bathroom floor as a child, padding on her way to her mother's bed . . . no, to her *father's* bed, more often, except for that memorable night when she'd surprised her mother with Eddie.

This is closure, if there ever is closure, the novelist thought to herself. Something had come full circle. Here was an ending *and* a beginning. (Eddie O'Hare was Graham's godfather. Hannah Grant was the boy's godmother—a more responsible and reliable godmother than one might have thought.)

And on those nights when she lay curled on the nursery floor, listening to her child breathe, Ruth Cole would be thankful for her good luck. Rooie's murderer, who had clearly heard the sound of someone trying not to make a sound, had not found her. Ruth often thought of him. She not only wondered who he was, and if he had a habit of killing prostitutes; she wondered if he'd read her novel—for she'd seen him take Rooie's copy of *Not for Children*. Maybe he'd only wanted the book as a place to keep his Polaroid picture of Rooie safe from harm.

On those nights, curled on the rug beside Graham's crib (later, his bed), Ruth surveyed the dimly lit nursery in the glow of the feeble night-light. She saw the familiar part in the window curtain; through the narrow slit, a black streak of night sky was visible—sometimes starry, sometimes not.

Usually it was a catch in Graham's breathing that would make Ruth get up off the floor and look closely at her sleeping son. Then she would peek through the part in the curtain to see if the moleman was where she half-expected him to be: curled asleep on the window ledge with some of the pink tentacles of his star-shaped nose pressed against the glass.

The moleman was never there, of course; yet Ruth would sometimes wake with a start, because she was sure she'd heard him wheeze. (It was only Graham, who'd made a curious sigh in his sleep.)

Then Ruth would fall back to sleep—often wondering why her mother hadn't made an appearance, now that her father was dead. Didn't she want to see the baby? Ruth would wonder. Not to mention *me*!

It made her so angry that she tried to stop wondering.

And because Ruth was often alone with Graham in the Sagaponack house—at least on those nights when Allan was staying in the city— there were times when the house made peculiar sounds. There was the mouse-crawling-between-the-walls sort of sound, and the sound-like-someone-trying-not-to-make-a-sound sort of sound, and the whole range of sounds between those sounds—the opening-of-the-door-in-the-floor sort of sound, and the absence of sound that the moleman made when he held his breath.

He was out there, somewhere, Ruth knew; he was still waiting for her. In the moleman's eyes, she was still a little girl. Trying to sleep, Ruth could see the moleman's small, vestigial eyes—the furry dents in his furry face.

As for Ruth's new novel, it was waiting for her, too. One day she wouldn't be a new mother, and she would write again. So far, she'd written only about a hundred pages of *My Last Bad Boyfriend*. She hadn't yet come to the scene when the boyfriend persuades the woman writer to pay a prostitute to watch her with a customer—Ruth was still working up to it. That scene was waiting for her, too.

III

FALL
1995

The Civil Servant

Sergeant Harry Hoekstra, formerly *hoofdagent* or almost-a-sergeant Hoekstra, was avoiding the task of cleaning out his desk. His office, on the second floor of the District 2 police station, overlooked the Warmoesstraat. Harry, while he did nothing about his desk (which had never been cleaned out before), distracted himself by regarding the changes in the street—for the Warmoesstraat, like the rest of the red-light district, had undergone some changes. As a street cop who was now looking forward to an early retirement, Sergeant Hoekstra knew that very little had ever escaped his attention.

Opposite the station, there'd once been a flower shop, the Jemi, but the shop had moved to the corner of the Enge Kerksteeg. Still within Harry's view was a place called La Paella, and an Argentinean restaurant called Tango, but the Jemi flower shop had been replaced by Sanny's Bar. Were Harry as prescient as many of his colleagues thought he was, he might have seen sufficiently into the future to know that, within a year of his retirement, Sanny's Bar would itself be replaced by the unfortunately named Café Pimpelmée. But even the powers of a good policeman do not extend into the future with such specific detail. Like many men who choose to retire early, Harry Hoekstra believed that most of the changes in his neighborhood of business were not changes for the better.

It was in '66 when the hashish had first come to Amsterdam in noticeably larger amounts. In the seventies, the heroin came; first with the Chinese, but by the end of the Vietnam War, the Chinese had lost the heroin market to the Golden Triangle in Southeast Asia. Many of the addicted prostitutes were couriers for the heroin.

Nowadays, more than sixty percent of the addicts were known to the health department—and there were Dutch police officers stationed in

Bangkok. But more than *seventy* percent of the prostitutes in the red-light district were illegal aliens; basically, there was no keeping track of the "illegals."

As for the cocaine, it had come from Colombia via Suriname in small planes. The Surinamese brought it to the Netherlands in the late sixties and early seventies. The Surinamese prostitutes had not been that much of a problem, and their pimps had caused only a little trouble; the problem had been the cocaine. Now the Colombians themselves brought it, but the Colombian prostitutes were not a problem, either, and their pimps made even less trouble than the Surinamese pimps.

In his more than thirty-nine years of service on the Amsterdam police force, thirty-five of which he'd spent in *de Wallen*, Harry Hoekstra had only once had a gun pointed at him. It was Max Perk, a Surinamese pimp, who'd pointed the gun at Harry, which had prompted Harry to show Max *his* gun. Had there been a shootout of the quick-draw variety, Harry would have lost—Max had drawn his gun first. But the display of weapons was more in the nature of a show of force, which Harry had won. Harry's gun was a Walther nine-millimeter.

"It's made in Austria," Harry had explained to the pimp from Suriname. "The Austrians really know their guns. This will blow a bigger hole in you than yours will blow in me, and mine will blow more holes in you in a hurry." Whether this was true or not, Max Perk had put down his gun.

Yet, notwithstanding Sergeant Hoekstra's *personal* experiences with the Surinamese, he believed that the days ahead were fairly certain to be worse. Criminal organizations were bringing young women from the former Soviet bloc into Western Europe; *thousands* of women from Eastern Europe were now working involuntarily in the red-light districts of Amsterdam, Brussels, Frankfurt, Zurich, Paris, and other Western European cities. The owners of nightclubs, striptease joints, peep shows, and brothels commonly traded these young women for a fee.

As for the Dominicans, the Colombians, the Brazilians, and the Thais, most of these young women knew what they were coming to Amsterdam *for*; they understood what they were going to *do*. But the young women from Eastern Europe often were under the impression that they were going to be waitresses in respectable restaurants. They had been students and shop girls and housewives before they'd accepted these misleading job offers in the West.

Among these newcomers to Amsterdam, the window prostitutes were the best off. But now the girls in the windows were being undersold by the girls on the streets; everyone was more desperate for work. The prostitutes whom Harry had known the longest were either retiring or threatening to retire—not that prostitutes didn't often threaten to retire. It was a business of what Harry called "short-term thinking." The hookers were always telling him that they were stopping "next month" or "next year"—or else one of the women would say, "I'm taking next *winter* off, anyway."

And now, more than ever, many prostitutes had admitted to Harry that they'd had what they called a moment of doubt; this meant that they'd let in the wrong man.

There were simply more wrong men than there used to be.

Sergeant Hoekstra remembered one Russian girl who'd accepted a so-called waitressing job at the Cabaret Antoine. The Cabaret Antoine was no restaurant. It was a brothel, and the brothel owner had immediately seized the Russian girl's passport. She was told that even if a customer didn't want to use a condom, she couldn't refuse to have sex with him—unless she wanted to find herself out on the street. Her passport had been phony, anyway, and she soon found a seemingly sympathetic client, an older man, who procured another phony passport for her. But by then her name had been changed—in the brothel, they'd reduced her name to Vratna because her real name was too difficult to pronounce—and her first two months of "salary" were withheld because her so-called debts to the brothel had to be deducted from her earnings. The alleged "debts" were described to her as agency fees, taxes, food, and rent.

Shortly before the brothel was raided by the police, Vratna accepted a loan from her sympathetic client. The older man paid her share of the rent for a window room, which she used with two other girls from Eastern Europe, and so she became a window prostitute. As for the "loan," which Vratna could never repay, her seeming sympathizer became her most privileged client; he visited her often. Naturally she charged him no fee; in fact, he'd become her pimp without her knowing it. Soon she was paying him half her earnings from her other clients. As Sergeant Hoekstra later thought of him, he was her *not*-so-sympathetic client.

He was a retired executive named Paul de Vries, who'd taken up pimping for these illegal Eastern European girls as a kind of sport and pastime. It was no more than an amusing game for him: to fuck young girls, at first for a price but later for free. Eventually, of course, they would be paying *him*—and he would *still* be fucking them!

One Christmas morning—one of only a few recent Christmases that Harry had *not* taken off—Harry had ridden his bicycle through the new snow in *de Wallen;* he had wanted to see if any of the prostitutes were working. He'd had an idea, not unlike Ruth Cole's, that in the new snow of a Christmas morning even the red-light district might look pristine. But Harry had been, uncharacteristically, more sentimental than that: for those few girls who might be working in their window rooms on Christmas morning, Harry had bought some simple presents. Nothing fancy or expensive, just some chocolates and a fruitcake and not more than half a dozen Christmas-tree ornaments.

Harry knew that Vratna was religious, or at least she'd told him that she was, and for her—just in case she was working—he'd bought a present of slightly more value. Still, he'd paid only ten guilders for it in a secondhand jewelry shop; it was a cross of Lorraine, which the salesgirl had told him was especially popular with young people of unconventional tastes. (It was a cross with two crosspieces, the upper shorter than the lower.)

It had been snowing hard, and there were almost no visible footprints in *de Wallen;* some tracks surrounded the one-man urinal by the old church, but in the untracked snow on Vratna's small street, the Oudekennissteeg, there were no footprints at all. And Harry had been relieved to see that Vratna *wasn't* working; her window was dark, her curtain closed, the red light off. He was about to ride on, with his rucksack of humbly inspired Christmas presents, when he noticed that the door to Vratna's window room was not properly closed. Some snow had drifted inside, and the snow made it difficult for Harry to close the door.

He'd not meant to look into her room, but he needed to open the door wider before he could close it. He was scuffing the snow off the threshold with his foot—it was not the best weather for his running shoes—when he saw the young woman hanging from the ceiling-light fixture. With the door to the street open, the wind rushed in and caused her hanging body to sway. Harry stepped inside and closed the door against the blowing snow.

She'd hanged herself that morning, probably a little after the first light of day. She was twenty-three. She was dressed in her old clothes—what she'd worn to the West for her new waitressing job. Because she was not dressed (which is to say, *un*dressed) as a prostitute, Harry hadn't at first recognized her. Vratna had put on all her jewelry, too—what there was of it. It would have been superfluous for Harry to have given the girl another cross. There were a half-dozen crosses around her neck; there were nearly as many crucifixes, too.

Harry didn't touch her, or anything in her room. He merely noted that, from the chafe marks at her throat—not to mention the damage to the ceiling plaster—she must not have suffocated right away. She had thrashed for a while. A musician rented the apartment above Vratna's window room. Normally he might have heard the hanging girl—at least the falling plaster and the presumed grinding of the ceiling-light fixture—but the musician went away every Christmas. Harry usually went away for Christmas, too.

On his way to the police station to report the suicide—for he already knew it was not a murder—he'd looked back at the Oudekennissteeg only once. In the new-fallen snow, the tire marks from his bicycle were the sole evidence of life on the tiny street.

Opposite the old church, there was only one woman working as a window prostitute that Christmas morning; she was one of the fat black women from Ghana, and Harry paused to give her all his presents. She was happy to have the chocolates and the fruitcake, but she told him she had no use for the Christmas-tree ornaments.

As for the cross of Lorraine, Harry had kept it for a while. He even bought a chain for it, although the chain cost him more than the cross had. Then he'd given the cross and the chain to a girlfriend of the moment, but he made the mistake of telling the girlfriend the whole story. It was one of those things he was always misjudging about women. He'd thought she would take the cross *and* the story as a compliment. After all, he'd been genuinely fond of the Russian girl; this particular cross of Lorraine had some sentimental value for him. But no woman likes to hear how *cheap* a piece of jewelry was, *or* that it was purchased for another woman—not to mention for an illegal alien, a Russian whore who'd hanged herself in her place of business.

The girlfriend of *that* moment had given Harry back his gift; it was of no sentimental value to *her*. At the moment Harry didn't have a girl-friend, nor did he imagine that he would ever be inclined to bestow his cross of Lorraine on another woman—even if there *were* another woman.

Harry Hoekstra had never suffered from a shortage of girlfriends. The problem, if it was a problem, was that he always had this or that girl for only a moment. He was not a libertine. He never cheated on his girls—he had them only one at a time. But whether they left him or he left them, they didn't last.

Now, stalling at the task of cleaning out his desk, Sergeant Hoek-stra—at fifty-seven and fully intending to retire later in the fall, when he would be fifty-eight—wondered if he would always be "unat-tached." Surely his attitude toward women, and theirs toward him, was at least partially job-related. And at least part of the reason why Harry had opted for an early retirement was that he wanted to see if his as-sumption was true.

He'd been eighteen when he'd first gone to work as a cop on the street; at fifty-eight, he would have put in forty years of service. Natu-rally Sergeant Hoekstra would be given a slightly smaller pension than if he waited until the standard retirement age of sixty-one, but as an unmarried man with no children, he wasn't in need of a bigger pension. And the men in Harry's family had all died fairly young.

While Harry was in excellent health, he was taking no chances on his genetic predisposition. He wanted to travel; he also wanted to try liv-ing in the country. Although he'd read a lot of travel books, he'd taken few trips. And although Harry liked travel books, he liked novels still more.

Looking at his desk, which he was loath to open, Sergeant Hoekstra thought: It's about time for a new novel by Ruth Cole, isn't it? It must have been five years since he'd read *Not for Children*. How long did it take her to write a novel, anyway?

Harry had read all of Ruth's novels in English, for Harry's English was quite good. And in the streets of the red-light district, in "the little walls," English was increasingly becoming the language of the pros-titutes and their customers—*bad* English was the new language of *de*

Wallen. (Bad English, Harry thought, would be the language of the next world.) And as a man whose next life was about to begin at fifty-eight, Sergeant Hoekstra, a soon-to-be-retired civil servant, wanted *his* English to be good.

The Reader

Sergeant Hoekstra's women usually complained about his indifference to shaving; that he was clearly not vain may have attracted the women in the first place, but eventually they took his lack of attention to his face as a sign that he was indifferent to *them.* When the stubble on his face began to resemble a beard, he shaved; Harry didn't like beards. Sometimes he would shave every other day, sometimes only once a week; other times he would get up in the night and shave, so that the woman he was with would wake up to a different-looking man in the morning.

Harry exhibited a similar indifference toward his clothes. Harry's job was walking. He wore sturdy, comfortable running shoes; jeans were the only pants of necessity. He had short, bandy legs, a flat stomach, and the nonexistent bum of a young boy. From the waist down, he was built a lot like Ted Cole—compact, all function—but his upper body was more developed. He went to a gym every day—he had the well-rounded chest of a weight lifter—but because he generally wore long-sleeved, loose-fitting shirts, the casual observer never knew how muscular he was.

These shirts were the only colorful part of his wardrobe; most of his women commented that they were *too* colorful, or at least too busy. He liked shirts "with a lot going on," he used to say. They were the kind of shirts you could never wear with a tie, but Harry almost never wore a tie, anyway.

He rarely wore his police uniform, either. He was as familiar to everyone in *de Wallen* as the most flamboyant and long-in-residence of the window prostitutes were; he walked the district for at least two or three hours every working day or night.

For a jacket, he preferred windbreakers or something water-repellent—always in dark, solid colors. He had an old leather jacket that was lined with wool flannel for the cold weather, but all his jackets, like his shirts, were loose-fitting. He didn't want his Walther nine-millimeter, which he carried in a shoulder holster, to make a visible lump. Only if it was raining hard would he wear a baseball cap; he didn't like hats, and he never wore gloves. One of Harry's ex-girlfriends had described his mode of dress as "basic thug."

His hair was dark brown but turning gray, and Harry was as indifferent to it as he was to shaving. He had it cut too short; then he let it grow too long.

As for his police uniform, Harry had worn it much more frequently in his first four years, when he'd served in the west of Amsterdam. He still had his apartment there, not because he was too lazy to move but because he liked the luxury of having *two* functioning fireplaces—one in his bedroom. His chief indulgences were firewood and books; Harry loved reading by a fire, and he owned so many books that it would have been a chore for him to move *anywhere*. Besides, he liked bicycling to work and home again; he believed in putting some distance between himself and *de Wallen*. As familiar as he was with the red-light district, and as recognizable a figure as he was in its crowded streets—for *de Wallen* was his real office, "the little walls" were the well-known drawers of his *real* desk—Harry Hoekstra was a loner.

What Harry's women also complained about was how much he remained *apart*. He would rather read a book than listen. And regarding talk: Harry would rather build a fire and go to bed and watch the light flickering on the walls and on the ceiling. He also liked to read in bed.

Harry wondered if only *his* women were jealous of books. It was their principal preposterousness, he believed. How could they be jealous of *books*? He found this all the more preposterous in the cases of those women he'd met in bookstores. Harry had met a lot of women in bookstores; others, although fewer lately, he'd met in his gym.

Harry's gym was the one on the Rokin where Ruth Cole's publisher, Maarten Schouten, had taken her. At fifty-seven, Sergeant Hoekstra was a little old for most of the women who went there. (Young women in their twenties telling him that he was in terrific shape "for a guy his age" would never be the high point of his day.) But he'd recently dated one of the women who worked at the gym, an aerobics instructor.

Harry hated aerobics; he was strictly a weight lifter. In a day, Sergeant Hoekstra walked more than most people walked in a week—or in a month. And he rode his bicycle everywhere. What did he need aerobics for?

The instructor had been an attractive woman in her late thirties, but she was given to missionary zeal; her failure to convert Harry to her exercise of choice had hurt her feelings, and no one in Harry's recent memory had so resented his reading. The aerobics instructor had not been a reader, and—like all of Harry's women—she'd refused to believe that Harry had never had sex with a prostitute. Surely he'd at least been tempted.

He was "tempted" all the time—although, with each passing year, the temptation grew less. In his almost forty years as a cop, he'd been "tempted" to kill a couple of people, too. But Sergeant Hoekstra *hadn't* killed anybody, and he hadn't had sex with a prostitute.

Yet there was no question that Harry's girlfriends were uniformly uneasy about his relationships with those women in the windows— and, in ever-increasing numbers, on the streets. He was a man of the streets, Harry was, which may have immeasurably contributed to his fondness for books and fireplaces; that he'd been a man of the streets for almost forty years *definitely* contributed to his desire to try living in the country. Harry Hoekstra had had it with cities—with *any* city.

Only one of his girlfriends had liked to read as much as Harry did, but she read the wrong books; among the women Harry had slept with, she was also the closest to being a prostitute. She was a lawyer who did volunteer work for a prostitutes' organization, a liberal feminist who'd told Harry that she "identified" with prostitutes.

The organization for prostitutes' rights was called De Rode Draad (The Red Thread); at the time Harry met the lawyer, The Red Thread enjoyed an uneasy alliance with the police. After all, both the police and The Red Thread were concerned for the prostitutes' safety. Harry always thought that it should have been a more successful alliance than it was.

But, from the beginning, the board members of The Red Thread had rubbed him the wrong way: in addition to the more militant prostitutes and ex-prostitutes, there were those women (like his lawyer friend) who'd struck him as *impractical* feminists—concerned mainly with making the organization an emancipation movement for prostitutes. Harry had believed, from the beginning, that The Red Thread should be less concerned with manifestos and more concerned with protecting the prostitutes from the dangers of their profession. Yet he'd preferred the prostitutes and the feminists to the *other* members of the board—the labor-union types, and what Harry called the "how-to-get-subsidized people."

The lawyer's name was Natasja Frederiks. Two thirds of the women who worked for The Red Thread were prostitutes or ex-prostitutes; at their meetings, the nonprostitutes (like Natasja) were not allowed to speak. The Red Thread paid only two and a half salaries to four people; everyone else involved there was a volunteer. Harry had been a volunteer, too.

In the late eighties, there'd been more interaction between the police and The Red Thread than there was now. For one thing, the organization had failed to attract the foreign prostitutes—not to mention the "illegals"—and there were hardly any *Dutch* prostitutes left in the windows or on the streets.

Natasja Frederiks wasn't doing volunteer work for The Red Thread anymore; she'd become disillusioned, too. (Natasja now called herself an "ex-idealist.") She and Harry had first met at a regular Thursday-afternoon meeting for first-time prostitutes. Harry thought these meetings were a good idea.

He sat in the back of the room and never spoke unless asked a direct question; he was introduced to the first-time prostitutes as "one of the more sympathetic members of the police force," and the new girls were encouraged to talk with him after the usual business of the meeting was over. As for the "usual business," there was often an older prostitute who told the first-timers what to be careful of. One of the old-timers was Dolores de Ruiter, or "Red" Dolores, as Harry and everyone in the red-light district knew her. Rooie Dolores had been a hooker in *de Wallen*, and later on the Bergstraat, a lot longer than Natasja Frederiks had been a lawyer.

What Rooie always told the new girls was to make sure the customer had a hard-on. She wasn't kidding. "If the guy's in the room with you— I mean the *second* he puts his foot in the door—he should have an erection." If he didn't, Rooie warned the new girls, maybe he hadn't come for sex. "And never shut your eyes," Rooie always admonished the new girls. "Some guys like you to shut your eyes. Just *don't.*"

There'd been nothing unpleasant or even disappointing in his sexual relationship with Natasja Frederiks, but what Harry most vividly remembered was how they had argued about books. Natasja had been born to
argue, and Harry didn't like to argue; but he enjoyed having a girlfriend
who read as much as he did, even if she read the wrong books. Natasja
read nonfiction of the change-the-world variety; she read *tracts*. They
were mostly books of leftist-leaning wishful thinking—Harry didn't
believe that the world (or human nature) could be changed. Harry's job
was to understand and accept the existing world; maybe he made the
world a little safer, he liked to think.

He read novels because he found in them the best descriptions of
human nature. The novelists Harry favored never suggested that even
the worst human behavior was alterable. They might morally disap-
prove of this or that character, but novelists were not world-changers;
they were just storytellers with better-than-average stories to tell, and
the good ones told stories about believable characters. The novels
Harry loved were complexly interwoven stories about real people.

He didn't enjoy detective novels or so-called thrillers. (Either he figured out the plot too soon or the characters were implausible.) He
would never have marched into a bookstore demanding to be shown
the classics or the newest literary fiction, but he ended up reading
more "classics" and more "literary" novels than any other kind—although they were all novels of a fairly conventional narrative structure.

Harry didn't object to a book being funny, but if the writer was *only*
comic (or merely satirical), Harry felt let down. He liked social real-
ism, but not if the writer was without *any* imagination—not if the story
wasn't enough of a story to keep him guessing about what was going to
happen next. (A novel about a divorced woman who spends a weekend
at a resort hotel, where she sees a man she *imagines* having an affair
with—but she doesn't; she just goes home again—was not enough of a
novel to satisfy Sergeant Hoekstra.)

Natasja Frederiks said that Harry's taste in novels was "escapist," but
Harry adamantly believed it was Natasja who was escaping the world
with her idiotic nonfiction of idle wishfulness about how to *change* it!

Among contemporary novelists, Sergeant Hoekstra's favorite was
Ruth Cole. Natasja and Harry had argued about Ruth Cole more than
about any other author. The lawyer who'd volunteered her services to
The Red Thread because she said she "identified" with prostitutes as-

serted that Ruth Cole's stories were "too bizarre"; the lawyer who was a champion of rights for prostitutes, but who was not allowed to speak at any of the organization's meetings, claimed that the plots of Ruth Cole's novels were "too unlikely." What's more, Natasja didn't like plot. The *real* world (which she so fervently sought to change) was without a discernible plot of its own, Natasja said.

Natasja, who (like Harry) would one day quit volunteering for The Red Thread because the prostitutes' organization represented fewer than a *twentieth* of the active prostitutes in the city of Amsterdam, accused Ruth Cole of being "too unrealistic" for her tastes. (At the time both Harry and Natasja would quit their volunteer work for The Red Thread, the Thursday-afternoon meetings for first-time prostitutes drew less than five percent of the first-time prostitutes working in *de Wallen.*)

"Ruth Cole is more realistic than *you* are," Harry had told Natasja.

They'd broken up because Natasja said Harry lacked ambition. He didn't even *want* to be a detective—he was content to be "just" a cop on the beat. It was true that Harry needed to be on the streets. If he wasn't out there walking, in his *real* office, he didn't feel like a policeman at all.

On the same floor where Harry's *official* office was, the detectives had their own office; it was full of computers, at which they spent too much time. Harry's best friend among the detectives was Nico Jansen. Nico liked to tease Harry that the last murder of a prostitute in Amsterdam, which was the murder of Dolores de Ruiter in her window room on the Bergstraat, had been solved by his computer in the detectives' computer room, but Harry knew better.

Harry knew it was the mystery witness who'd *really* solved the prostitute's murder; it had been Harry's analysis of the eyewitness account, which, after all, had been addressed to him, that had eventually told Nico Jansen what to look for in his overpraised computer.

But theirs was a friendly argument. The case was solved—that was the main thing, Nico said. However, it was the *witness* who still interested Harry, and he didn't like it that his witness had slipped away. It was all the more maddening to him because he was absolutely certain that he'd seen her—he'd actually *seen* her—and she'd *still* got away!

The middle drawer of Sergeant Hoekstra's desk heartened him; there was nothing in it that he needed to throw away. There were a dozen old pens and a few keys that Harry didn't recognize, but his replacement might derive some satisfying curiosity from speculating what the keys were *for*. There was also a combination bottle opener and corkscrew—even in a police station, one could never have enough of *those*—and there was a teaspoon (not too clean, but one could always clean it). You never knew when you might get sick and need a teaspoon to take your medicine, Harry thought.

He was about to close the drawer, leaving the contents undisturbed, when an item of even more remarkable usefulness caught his eye. It was the broken handle to the desk's bottommost drawer, and no one but Harry knew what a truly useful little tool it was. It fit perfectly between the treads of Harry's running shoes; he used it to scrape the dogshit off his soles, if and when he stepped in any. However, Harry's replacement would not necessarily realize the broken handle's value.

Using one of the pens, Harry wrote a note, which he put in the middle drawer before closing it. DON'T FIX BOTTOMMOST DRAWER, BUT SAVE BROKEN HANDLE. EXCELLENT FOR GETTING DOGSHIT OFF SHOES. HARRY HOEKSTRA.

Thus encouraged, Harry took the three side drawers of the desk in order, starting at the top. In the first of them was a speech he'd written but had never delivered to the members of The Red Thread organization. It concerned the matter of underage prostitutes. Harry had reluctantly assented to the position taken by the prostitutes' organization that the legal age for prostitutes be lowered from eighteen to sixteen.

"No one *likes* the idea of minors working in prostitution," Harry's speech had begun, "but I like less the idea of minors working in dangerous places. Minors are going to be prostitutes, anyway. Many brothel owners won't care if their prostitutes are only sixteen-year-olds. What's important is that the sixteen-year-olds can make use of the same social services and health-care facilities that the older prostitutes use, *without* being afraid that they will be turned over to the police."

It was not cowardice that had prevented Harry from giving his speech; Harry had contradicted the "official" police position before. It was that he hated the whole idea of allowing sixteen-year-olds to be prostitutes only because you couldn't stop them from being prostitutes. On the issue of *accepting* the real world and making an educated guess about how to make it marginally safer, even a social realist like Harry Hoekstra would have admitted that certain subjects depressed him.

He had not given the speech because, in the long run, it would have been of no practical help to the underage prostitutes—just as the Thursday-afternoon meetings for first-time prostitutes were of no *practical* help to the vast majority of *them*. They didn't or wouldn't attend the meetings; in all likelihood, they didn't know that the meetings *existed*—or if they *had* known, they wouldn't have cared.

But perhaps the speech would be of some practical use to the next cop who sat at his desk, Harry thought, and so he left the speech where it was.

In regard to the middle of the three side drawers, Harry was at first alarmed to see that it was empty. He stared into the drawer with the dismay of a man who'd been robbed in a police station; then he recalled that the drawer had been empty for as long as he could remember. The desk itself was a testimony to how little Sergeant Hoekstra had used it! In truth, the alleged "task" of cleaning it out was entirely focused on the unfinished business that—for five years now—Harry had faithfully kept in the bottommost drawer. In his view, it was the *only* police business that stood between him and his retirement.

Since the handle to the bottommost drawer had broken off and become Harry's tool of choice for removing dogshit from his shoes, he now had to pry the drawer open with his pocketknife. The file on the witness to the murder of Rooie Dolores was disappointingly thin, which belied how often and how closely Sergeant Hoekstra had read and reread it.

Harry appreciated a complicated plot, but he had a stodgy preference for chronological stories. It was ass-backward storytelling to find the murderer before you found the witness. In a proper story, you found the witness first.

Ruth Cole had more than a policeman searching for her. She had an old-fashioned *reader* on her case.

The Prostitute's Daughter

Rooie had started as a window prostitute in *de Wallen* during Harry's first year as a street cop in the red-light district. She was five years younger than he was, although he'd suspected her of lying about her age. In her first window room, on the Oudekennissteeg—the same small street where Vratna would later hang herself—Dolores de Ruiter had looked younger than eighteen. But that was how old she was. She'd been telling the truth. Harry Hoekstra had been twenty-three.

In Harry's opinion, "Red" Dolores had generally *not* told the truth, or she'd told mostly half-truths.

On her busiest days, Rooie had worked in her window room for ten or twelve hours straight, during which time she'd accommodated as many as fifteen clients. She made enough money to buy a ground-floor room on the Bergstraat, which she rented part-time to another prostitute. By then she'd lightened her workload to only three days a week, five hours a day, and she could still afford two vacations a year. She usually spent Christmas at some ski resort in the Alps, and every April or May she went somewhere warm. She'd once been in Rome for Easter. She'd been to Florence, too—and to Spain, and Portugal, and the south of France.

Rooie had a habit of asking Harry Hoekstra where she should go. After all, he'd read those countless travel books. Although Harry had never been to any of the places Rooie wanted to go, he'd researched all the hotels; Harry knew that Rooie preferred to stay in "moderately expensive" surroundings. He also knew that, while her warm-weather holidays were important to her, Rooie took greater pleasure from the ski resorts at Christmastime; and even though she would take a few private ski lessons every winter, she never got beyond the beginner level. When she'd finished with the lessons, she would ski only half-days by herself—and only until she met someone. Rooie always met someone.

She'd told Harry it was fun to meet men who didn't know she was a prostitute. Occasionally they were well-off young men who skied hard and partied harder; more often they were quiet, even somber men who were no better than intermediate skiers. Her particular fondness was for divorced fathers who got to spend only every other Christmas with their children. (Generally speaking, the fathers with sons were easier to seduce than the fathers with daughters.)

It always gave Rooie a pang to see a man and a child in a restaurant together. They were often not talking, or their conversation was awkward—usually about the skiing or the food. She could detect in the fathers' faces a kind of loneliness that was different from but similar to the loneliness in the faces of her colleagues on the Bergstraat.

And a romance with a father who was traveling with his child was always delicate and secretive. For someone who didn't have many *real* romances in her life, Rooie believed that delicacy and secrecy were enhancing to sexual tension; also, there was nothing quite like the carefulness required when one had to take into consideration the feelings of a child.

"Aren't you afraid that these guys will want to come see you in Amsterdam?" Harry had asked. (She'd been to Zermatt that year.) But only once had someone insisted on coming to Amsterdam. Usually she'd managed to discourage it.

"What do you tell them you *do*?" Harry had asked her another time. (Rooie had just returned from Pontresina, where she'd met a man who was staying with his son at Badrutt's Palace in St. Moritz.)

"Red" Dolores always told the fathers a comfortable half-truth. "I make a modestly good living from prostitution," Rooie would begin, watching the shock settle in. "Oh, I don't mean *I'm* a prostitute!" she then would say. "I'm just an impractical landlady who *rents* to prostitutes...."

If pressed, she would elaborate on the lie. Her father, a urologist, had died; she'd converted his office to a prostitute's window room. Renting to prostitutes, though less profitable, was "more colorful" than renting office space to doctors.

She loved to tell Harry Hoekstra the stories she'd made up. If Harry had been, at best, a vicarious traveler, he had also vicariously enjoyed Rooie's little romances. And he knew why there was a urologist in Rooie's story.

An *actual* urologist had been Rooie's constant admirer, *and* her most regular client, well into his eighties—before dropping dead in the prostitute's room on the Bergstraat one Sunday afternoon. He'd been such an unfailing sweetheart that he often forgot to have the sex he'd paid for. Rooie had been very fond of the dear old man, Dr. Bosman, who swore to her that he loved his wife, his children, and his innumerable grandchildren—the family photos of whom he showed to Rooie with unflagging pride.

The day he died, he sat fully clothed in the blow-job chair, complaining that he'd eaten too much for lunch—even for a Sunday. He asked Rooie to fix him a bicarbonate of soda, for which he confessed to having an even greater need (at the moment) than he had for what he called her "inestimable physical affections."

Rooie was forever grateful that her back was turned to him when he expired in the chair. After she'd fixed the sodium bicarbonate, she turned to face him, but old Dr. Bosman was dead.

Rooie's penchant for half-truths had betrayed her then. She'd called Harry Hoekstra and told him that an old man was dead in her window room, but that at least she'd saved him from dying in the street. She'd seen him looking decidedly unwell, half-staggering on the Bergstraat, and she'd brought him into her room and sat him down in a comfortable chair, where he'd begged her for a bicarbonate of soda.

" 'Tell my wife I love her!' were the old man's last words," Rooie had informed Harry. She'd *not* told Harry that the dead urologist had been her oldest and most regular client; she'd genuinely wanted to spare Dr. Bosman's family the knowledge that their beloved patriarch had died with his long-standing whore. But Harry had figured it out.

There was something about how peaceful Dr. Bosman looked in "Red" Dolores's blow-job chair—that, and how noticeably upset Rooie had been. In her own way, she'd *loved* the old urologist.

"How long had he been seeing you?" Harry immediately asked her. Rooie burst into tears.

"He was always so *nice* to me!" Rooie had cried. "No one was ever as nice to me. Not even *you*, Harry."

Harry had helped Rooie work on her story. It was basically the lie she'd first told him, but Harry helped her get the details right. Exactly *where* on the Bergstraat had Rooie first noticed that the old doctor was "half-staggering," as she'd put it; exactly *how* had she got him to come inside her room? And didn't she have to help him to the chair? And when the dying urologist had asked the prostitute to tell his wife that he loved her, had his voice been strained? Was his breathing restricted?

Had he been in any obvious *pain*? Surely Dr. Bosman's wife would want to know.

The widow Bosman had been so grateful to Rooie Dolores that the merciful prostitute had been invited to the old urologist's memorial service. Everyone in Dr. Bosman's family had spoken to Rooie of their deep gratitude to her. Over time, the Bosmans had made the prostitute a virtual member of their family. They developed the habit of inviting Rooie to their Christmas and Easter dinners, and to other family gatherings—weddings, anniversaries.

Harry Hoekstra had often reflected that Rooie's half-truth about Dr. Bosman was probably the best lie he'd ever been associated with. "How was your trip?" Harry would always ask the prostitute, whenever she'd been away. But the rest of the time he asked her: "How are the Bosmans?"

And when Dolores de Ruiter had been murdered in her window room, Harry had notified the Bosmans straightaway; there was no one else he needed to inform. Harry also trusted that the Bosmans would bury her; in fact, Mrs. Bosman organized and paid for the prostitute's funeral. Quite a sizable representation of the Bosman family was in attendance, together with a scattering of policemen (Harry among them) and a similarly small number of women from The Red Thread. Harry's ex-girlfriend Natasja Frederiks was there, but by far the most impressive turnout came from Rooie's *other* family—namely, the prostitutes, who'd attended in droves. Rooie had been popular among her colleagues.

Dolores de Ruiter had lived a life of half-truths. And what was *not* the best of her lies—indeed, what Harry thought of as one of the most painful lies he'd ever been associated with—became evident at the funeral. One after another, the prostitutes who'd known Rooie took Harry aside to ask him the same question.

"Where's the daughter?" Or, looking over the multitude of old Dr. Bosman's grandchildren, they would ask: "Which one is she? Isn't the daughter here?"

"Rooie's daughter is dead," Harry had to tell them. "In fact, she's been dead for quite a number of years." In *truth*, only Harry knew, the prostitute's daughter had died before she was born. But that had been Rooie's well-kept secret.

————

Harry had first heard of Rooie's Englishman after the prostitute returned from a ski holiday in Klosters. On Harry's advice, she'd stayed at the Chesa Grischuna, where she'd met an Englishman named Richard Smalley. Smalley was divorced and spending Christmas with his six-year-old son, a neurasthenic wreck of a boy whose perpetual nervousness and exhaustion Smalley blamed on the boy's overprotective mother. Rooie had been touched by the two of them. The boy clung to his father, and he slept so fitfully that it had been impossible for Richard Smalley and Rooie to have sex. They'd managed "some stolen kisses," as Rooie had told Harry—"and some pretty intense fondling."

She'd had all she could do to keep Smalley from coming to Amsterdam to see her in the ensuing year. The next Christmas, it was the ex-wife's turn with the neurasthenic son. Richard Smalley returned to Klosters alone. Over the course of the year, in letters and in phone calls, he'd persuaded Rooie to join him for Christmas at the Chesa—a dangerous precedent, Harry had warned Rooie. (It was the first time she'd spent a second Christmas at the same ski resort.)

She and Smalley had fallen in love, the prostitute informed Harry upon her return to Amsterdam. Richard Smalley wanted to marry her; he wanted Rooie to have his child.

"But does the Englishman know you're a prostitute?" Harry had asked. It turned out that Rooie had told Richard Smalley she was an *ex*-prostitute; she'd come halfway to the truth, which she hoped would be far enough.

That winter she rented her window room on the Bergstraat to two more girls; with three girls paying her rent for the room, Rooie could almost match what she'd earned as a prostitute. It would at least be enough for her to live on until she married Smalley—and more than enough "supplementary income" after she was married.

But when she married (and moved in with) Smalley, in London, Rooie became an absentee landlady to three window prostitutes in Amsterdam; while Rooie had been careful not to rent to drug addicts, she couldn't oversee how the girls were treating her old place on the Bergstraat. Harry had tried to keep an eye on the room, but Rooie's tenants took liberties; soon one of the girls was subletting to a fourth prostitute, and quickly there was a fifth—one of them was a drug addict. Then one of Rooie's original tenants left; she'd skipped two months' rent before Rooie even knew she was gone.

Rooie was pregnant when she returned to Amsterdam to assess the condition of her room on the Bergstraat. Some instinct made her hang on to the place, which was barely breaking even—and after a few necessary repairs and some serious cleaning bills, the room was probably costing her money. The Englishman wanted her to sell it. But Rooie found two ex-prostitutes, both of them Dutch, who wanted to get back into the business; by renting exclusively to them, Rooie thought she could meet the maintenance costs. "The hell with trying to make a profit," she'd told Harry. "I just want to keep the place, in case things don't work out in England."

She must have known then, when she was seven months pregnant, that things weren't going to "work out" with Richard Smalley. She'd eventually gone into labor in London, and it had been a bad birth from the beginning. Despite an emergency C-section, the fetus was stillborn. Rooie never saw her dead daughter. It was then that Smalley had started in with the predictable recriminations. There was something wrong with Rooie, which had caused the stillbirth; and *what* was wrong with her had something to do with her past life as a prostitute—she must have done too much fucking.

One day, unannounced, Rooie was back in her window on the Bergstraat; that was when Harry learned about the end of Rooie's marriage, and her stillborn daughter. (By then, of course, Rooie's English was pretty good.)

The next Christmas, she'd gone again to Klosters and stayed once more at the Chesa Grischuna, but that would be her last holiday in a ski town. Although neither Richard Smalley nor his neurasthenic son was there, some word of who Rooie was must have got around. In unpredictable situations, which she couldn't foresee, she was aware that she was being treated as an ex-prostitute—not as an ex-wife.

She swore to Harry that she'd overheard someone on a gondola whispering the words "Smalley's whore." And in the Chesa—where she ate every evening alone—a small, bald man in a velvet dinner jacket with a flaming-orange ascot had propositioned her. A waiter had brought Rooie a complimentary glass of champagne from the bald man, together with a note in hand-printed English capitals.

HOW MUCH? the note had asked. She'd sent back the champagne.

Shortly after this final visit to Klosters, Rooie had stopped working in her window on weekends. Later still, she stopped working nights, and soon she was leaving her window in midafternoon—in time to pick her daughter up from school. That was what she told everyone.

The other prostitutes on the Bergstraat would occasionally ask to see pictures. Naturally they understood why they'd never seen the alleged daughter in the vicinity of the Bergstraat; most prostitutes kept their work a secret from their younger children.

The prostitute with whom Rooie shared her window room was the most curious, and Rooie had a photograph that she liked to show. The little girl in the photo was about five or six; she was happily seated on Rooie's lap at what looked like a family dinner party. She was one of Dr. Bosman's grandchildren, of course; only Harry Hoekstra knew that the photograph had been taken at one of the Bosmans' Easter dinners.

So *that* was the prostitute's daughter, whose absence had never been as noticeable as it was at Rooie's funeral. At that confused gathering, some of the prostitutes had asked Harry to remind them of the missing daughter's name; it wasn't a common name. Did Harry remember what it was?

Of course he did. It was Chesa.

And following Rooie's funeral, at what amounted to the wake—for old Mrs. Bosman, who was paying, believed in wakes—the name of the dead daughter had been sufficiently repeated among the prostitutes so that the old widow herself approached Harry. (He was awkwardly attempting to dispose of a hard-boiled egg that he didn't want to eat; the egg had some kind of caviar on it.) "Who's *Chesa?*" old Mrs. Bosman asked.

Harry then told her the whole story. The story moved Mrs. Bosman to tears, but the old lady was no fool. "Of course I knew that my dear husband was visiting the prostitute," she confided to Harry. "But the way I see it, she did me a kindness—and she *did* keep him from dying in the street!"

Only a few years before her murder, Rooie Dolores had reduced her annual vacations to one warm-weather holiday in April or May. She'd spent her last Christmases with the Bosmans; there were so many grandchildren that Rooie had a lot of presents to buy. "It's still cheaper than going skiing," she'd told Harry. And one dark winter—it was the winter before she was killed—Rooie had asked Harry to join her on her warm-weather holiday on a fifty-fifty basis.

"You're the one with the travel books," she'd teased him. "*You* pick the place and I'll go with you." Whatever had been the charm of those divorced fathers, taking perpetual vacations with their subdued children, it had finally worn thin with her.

Harry had *imagined* taking a trip with Rooie for a long time, yet her invitation both surprised and embarrassed him. The first place he'd thought of being with her was Paris. (Imagine being in Paris with a prostitute!)

Harry had started writing in the margins of his travel books, and underlining key sentences about the appropriate hotels. One of the first hotels Harry considered staying in was the Hôtel du Quai Voltaire, the same hotel where Ted had taken the photograph of Marion with Thomas's and Timothy's *feet*. But the Hôtel du Quai Voltaire was not as highly recommended as the Hôtel de l'Abbaye or the Duc de Saint-Simon. Harry had decided that he wanted to stay somewhere in Saint-Germain-des-Prés, but he believed that the choice of their hotel should be left to Rooie.

Harry brought his Paris guidebooks, replete with his underlinings and marginalia, to Rooie's room on the Bergstraat. He'd had to linger in the street until she finished with a customer.

"Oh, Harry!" she'd cried. "You want to take an old whore to *Paris*? April in Paris!"

Neither of them had ever been to Paris. It would never have worked out. Harry could imagine Rooie liking Notre-Dame and the Tuileries, and the antique shops that he'd only read about; he could see her happily on his arm in the gardens of the Luxembourg. But he couldn't quite picture her at the Louvre. After all, she lived in Amsterdam and she'd not once been to the Rijksmuseum! How could Harry have taken her to Paris?

"Actually, I don't think I can get away," he hedged. "April gets busy in *de Wallen*."

"Then we'll go in March," Rooie told him. "We'll go in *May*! What's it matter?"

"I don't think I can really do it, Rooie," Harry had admitted to her.

Prostitutes are familiar enough with rejection; they handle it pretty well.

After he'd got the call that Rooie had been murdered, Harry looked around her room on the Bergstraat for the guidebooks, which Rooie hadn't returned. They were stacked on the narrow reading table in the WC.

He also noted that the murderer had bitten Rooie, and that the way her body had been carelessly pushed off the bed made it seem there had been nothing ritualistic about the killing. She'd most likely been strangled, but there were no thumbprint or fingerprint bruises at her throat; this pointed to her being choked with a forearm, the *hoofdagent* had thought.

That was when he saw the wardrobe closet with the shoes pointed toes-out; a pair of them had been kicked out of alignment with the others, and there was a space in the middle of the row where another pair of shoes would have fit.

Shit! There was a *witness*! Harry had known then. He knew that Rooie had been one of the few prostitutes who went out of her way to do a kindness for the first-timers. He also knew the way she did it: she let the first-timers watch her with a customer, just to see how it was done. She'd hidden a lot of girls in her wardrobe closet. Harry had heard about Rooie's method at one of the meetings for first-time prostitutes at The Red Thread. But Rooie hadn't gone to those meetings for quite some time; Harry wasn't even sure if The Red Thread still *held* meetings for first-time prostitutes.

In the open doorway to Rooie's window room, the sniveling girl who'd found Rooie's body sat sobbing. Her name was Anneke Smeets. She was a recovered heroin addict—at least she'd convinced Rooie that she was recovered. Anneke Smeets was not dressed for working in the window; usually she wore a leather halter top, which Harry had seen hanging in the closet.

But in the doorway Anneke looked plain and disheveled. She wore a baggy black sweater with stretched-out elbows and jeans that were ripped in both knees. She had no makeup on, not even lipstick, and her hair was dirty and stiff. The only suggested wildness, amid everything that was plain about her, was that Anneke Smeets had a tattoo of a lightning bolt (albeit a small one) on the inside of her right wrist.

"It appears that someone might have been *watching* from the wardrobe closet," Harry began.

Still sobbing, the girl nodded her head. "It looks like it," she agreed.

"Was she helping out a first-timer?" Harry asked Anneke.

"Nobody I knew!" said the sobbing girl.

And so Harry Hoekstra suspected—even before Ruth Cole's eye-witness account arrived at the Warmoesstraat station—that there'd been a witness.

"Oh, God!" Anneke suddenly cried. "Nobody picked her daughter up from school! Who's going to tell her daughter?"

"Somebody already picked her up," Harry lied. "Somebody already told the daughter."

But he told the truth, a few days later, when his best friend among the detectives, Nico Jansen, wanted a word with Harry—in private. Harry knew what the "word" would be about.

There were the Paris guidebooks on Jansen's desk. Harry Hoekstra wrote his name in all his books. Nico Jansen opened one of the travel books to the part about the Hôtel Duc de Saint-Simon. Harry had written in the margin: *The heart of the Faubourg Saint-Germain, a great location.*

"Isn't that your handwriting, Harry?" Jansen asked him.

"My name's in the front of the book, Nico. Did you miss my *name?*" Harry asked his friend.

"Were you planning a trip with her?" Detective Jansen asked. Harry had been a cop for more than three decades; at last he knew how it felt to be a suspect.

Harry explained that Rooie took a lot of trips—all Harry did was read the travel books. He'd long been in the habit of lending her his guidebooks, Harry said. She'd been accustomed to asking him where she should stay and what she should see.

"But you didn't have a *relationship* with Rooie, did you, Harry?" Nico asked. "You never actually took a trip with her, did you?"

"No, I never did," Harry replied.

It was generally a good idea to tell the cops the truth. Harry *hadn't* had a relationship with Rooie; he'd never taken a trip with her, either. That much was true. But the cops didn't have to know *everything.* It wasn't necessary for Nico Jansen to know that Harry had been tempted. Oh, how he'd been tempted!

Sergeant Hoekstra Finds His Witness

Nowadays, Sergeant Hoekstra wore his police uniform only on those occasions when the red-light district was overrun with tourists or out-of-towners. (He'd worn it to Rooie's funeral, too.) And when it came to giving tours, Harry was the 2nd District's cop of choice—not only because he spoke better English (and German) than any other policeman in the Warmoesstraat station but also because he was the acknowledged expert on the red-light district, and he loved to take people there.

He'd once shown *de Wallen* to a group of nuns. He not infrequently showed "the little walls" to schoolchildren. The window prostitutes would calmly look the other way when they saw the children coming, but once a woman in a window had abruptly closed her curtain; later she told Harry that she'd recognized her own child among the group.

Sergeant Hoekstra was also the 2nd District's cop of choice when it came to talking to the media. Because false confessions were common, Harry had quickly learned never to give the exact details of a crime to the press; on the contrary, he often provided the journalists with *false* details—this tended to expose the crazies in a hurry. In the case of "Red" Dolores's murder, he'd managed to draw out a couple of false confessions by telling the journalists that Rooie had been strangled after "a violent struggle."

The two false confessions were from men who said they'd choked Rooie to death with their hands. One of them had persuaded his wife to scratch his face and the backs of his hands; the other had convinced his girlfriend to kick him repeatedly in the shins. In both cases, the men *looked* as if they'd been party to "a violent struggle."

As for the actual method of Rooie's murder, the detectives had wasted no time at their computers; they'd conveyed the necessary information to Interpol in Wiesbaden, Germany, whereupon they discovered that there'd been a similar slaying of a prostitute in Zurich about five years earlier.

All Rooie had been able to do was to kick off one of her shoes. The prostitute in the area of the Langstrasse in Zurich had managed a little more resistance; she'd broken a fingernail in what must have been a brief struggle. Some fabric, presumably from the killer's suit pants, was caught under the prostitute's broken nail; it was a high-quality fabric, but so what?

The most convincing connection between the Zurich murder and Rooie's murder in Amsterdam was that in Zurich there'd also been a standing lamp with the lamp shade and the lightbulb removed but undamaged. The Zurich police hadn't known the part about photographing the victim. The murder in Zurich hadn't had a witness; nor had anyone mailed the Zurich police a tube of Polaroid print coater with a perfect print of the presumed killer's right thumb.

None of the prints taken from the prostitute's room off the Langstrasse in Zurich had matched the Amsterdam thumbprint, however, and in Wiesbaden there was no matching thumbprint in the Interpol file, either. The second print on the tube was a clear, *small* print of a right index finger. It indicated that the probable witness had picked up the print coater with "her" thumb and index finger at either end. (The witness *must* have been a woman, everyone had decided, because the fingerprint was so much smaller than the print of the probable murderer's thumb.)

Another small but clear print of the witness's right index finger had been taken from one of the shoes pointed toes-out in Rooie's wardrobe closet. And the same right index finger had touched the inside doorknob of Rooie's window room—doubtless when the witness had let herself out on the street, after the murderer had gone. Whoever she was, she was right-handed, and she had a glass-thin, perfectly centered scar on her right index finger.

But Interpol had no match for the probable witness's right index finger, either—not that Harry had expected Interpol to match *that* print. He was sure that his witness wasn't a criminal. And after a week of talking to the area's prostitutes, Harry was also sure that his witness wasn't a prostitute. She was probably a goddamn sex-tourist!

In a short period of time, less than a week, every prostitute on the Bergstraat had seen the likely witness as many as a half-dozen times! And Anneke Smeets had *talked* to her. The mystery woman had asked for Rooie one night, and Anneke—in her leather halter top, and brandishing a dildo—had told the tourist Rooie's alleged reason for not working at night. Rooie was with her daughter, Anneke had said.

The prostitutes on the Korsjespoortsteeg had seen the mystery woman, too. One of the younger whores told Harry that his witness was a lesbian, but the other prostitutes had disagreed; they'd been wary of the woman because they couldn't tell what she wanted.

As for the men who walked and walked past the window prostitutes— always looking, always horny, but never making a decision—they were called *hengsten* ("stallions"), and the prostitutes who'd seen Ruth Cole walking past their windows called her a female *hengst*. But of course there is no such thing as a female stallion, which is why the mystery woman made the prostitutes uneasy.

One of them said to Harry: "She looked like a reporter." (Reporters made the prostitutes *very* uneasy.)

A foreign journalist? Sergeant Hoekstra had rejected the possibility. Most of the foreign journalists who came to Amsterdam with a professional interest in prostitution were told to talk to *him*.

From the prostitutes in *de Wallen*, Harry discovered that the mystery woman hadn't always been alone. There'd been a younger man with her, maybe a university student. While the witness Harry was looking for was in her thirties and had spoken only English, the boy had definitely been Dutch.

That had answered one question for Sergeant Hoekstra: If his missing witness was an English-speaking foreigner, who had written the eyewitness account in Dutch? And some additional information shed a little light on the carefully printed document that the witness had mailed to Harry. A tattooist whom Harry regarded as a handwriting expert had looked at the meticulous lettering and concluded that the text had been *copied*.

The tattooist's name was Henk, and he did most of the lettering at the tattoo museum in the red-light district, the so-called House of Pain. (His specialty was a poem—any poem you wanted—tattooed in the shape of a woman's body.) According to him, the witness's pen had paused too long on every letter; only someone copying a foreign language would have written each letter so slowly. "Who has to work this hard not to make a spelling mistake?" Henk had asked Harry. "Someone who doesn't know the language—that's who."

The prostitutes in *de Wallen* did not think Harry's witness and the Dutch boy had been a sexual couple. "It was not just the age difference," said the Thai prostitute whom Ruth and Wim had visited on the Barndesteeg. "I could tell they'd never had sex with each other."

"Maybe they were working up to it," Harry had suggested. "Maybe they were *going to* have sex."

"I didn't think so," the Thai prostitute said. "They couldn't even tell me what they wanted. They just wanted to *watch*, but they didn't even know *what* they wanted to watch!"

The other Thai prostitute who remembered the unusual couple was the old sadist with a reputation for terrorizing her clients. "The Dutch boy had a *beeeg* one," she declared. "He really wanted to do it. But his *mommy* wouldn't let him."

"That boy was ready to fuck anything, except me," the transvestite from Ecuador told Harry. "The woman was merely curious. She wasn't going to have sex. She just wanted to *know* about it."

If the Dutch boy had been with the mystery woman in Rooie's closet, Harry was sure the two of them would have tried to stop the killing. And, almost from the beginning, Harry had doubted that the witness was a first-time prostitute; unless she'd been an "illegal," even a first-timer would have gone to the police. And if she'd been an "illegal," who would she have found to write her eyewitness account in such perfect Dutch?

A Jamaican prostitute on the Slapersteeg also remembered Ruth Cole. "She was small. She said she was lost," the Jamaican told Harry. "I took her out of the alley by her arm. I was surprised she had such a strong right arm."

That was when Sergeant Hoekstra realized that he had seen the mystery woman himself! He suddenly recalled the woman he'd followed through *de Wallen* one early morning; she'd had an athletic way of walking. She was small, but she looked strong. She certainly hadn't looked "lost." She'd looked purposeful, and Harry had followed her not only because she seemed out of place, but also because she was strikingly attractive. (Not to mention vaguely familar! It's a wonder Harry failed to recognize her from her book-jacket photos.) When he became aware that she'd noticed him following her, Harry had gone back to the Warmoesstraat station.

He'd spoken to the two fat prostitutes from Ghana last. The unknown tourist had paused on the Stoofsteeg long enough to ask the prostitutes where they were from; in turn they'd asked Ruth Cole where *she* was from, and she'd told them she was from the United

States. (What Harry had learned from the prostitutes from Ghana—namely, that his witness was an American—would turn out to be a more important bit of information than he'd first thought.)

Nico Jansen had come to a dead end on his computer. The Polaroid print coater with the azure-blue cap could have been purchased in either Amsterdam or Zurich. That (according to the mystery witness) the murderer looked like a mole, that he wheezed, that he had squinty eyes ("almost totally closed") . . . of what use was this without a fingerprint in Zurich that matched the thumbprint on the tube of Polaroid print coater in Amsterdam?

And that the witness had thought the murderer worked for SAS, the Scandinavian airline, proved to be a false lead. Despite the examination of the prints of every male employee working in security for SAS, a matching thumbprint could not be found.

Only because Harry Hoekstra knew English so well, and German a little, was the murderer ever caught. It turned out that the most important piece of information in the eyewitness's account was the observation that the murderer spoke English with what might have been a *German*-sounding accent.

It was the day after Nico Jansen told Harry that the detectives had come to a dead end in regard to Rooie's murder. Harry had gone back to the eyewitness account again. Suddenly he saw what he'd been missing. If the murderer's first language was German, SAS might *not* be SAS—in the German alphabet, as in the Dutch, *a* is pronounced as *ah*. In the German alphabet, *e* is pronounced as *ay*. And to an *American* witness, S*E*S would have *sounded* like S*A*S. The murderer had nothing to do with the Scandinavian airline. The murderer had something to do with security for a company called SES!

Harry didn't need Nico Jansen's computer to find out what SES was. The International Chamber of Commerce was happy to help Harry find a company with those initials in a German-speaking city, and in less than ten minutes Harry had identified the murderer's employer. The venerable Schweizer Elektronik- und Sicherheitssysteme (SES) was located in Zurich; the company designed and installed security alarms for banks and museums all over Europe.

It gave Harry some small pleasure to find Nico Jansen in the detectives' room, where the computers always bathed the faces of the detectives in an unnatural light and bombarded them with unnatural sounds.

"I've got something for you to feed into your computer, Nico," Harry had said. "If you want me to talk to your colleague in Zurich, my German's better than yours."

The detective in Zurich was named Ernst Hecht; he was getting ready to retire. He'd presumed he would never find out who had killed a Brazilian prostitute in the area of the Langstrasse almost six years before. But the Schweizer Elektronik- und Sicherheitssysteme was a small but important security-alarm company; for insurance reasons, every employee of the company who'd ever designed or installed a security system for a bank or a museum had been fingerprinted.

The thumb that matched the thumbprint on the Polaroid print coater belonged to a former employee, a security-alarm engineer named Urs Messerli. Messerli had been in Amsterdam in the fall of 1990 to prepare an estimate for the expense of a fire- and motion-detection system in an art museum. He'd routinely traveled with an old Polaroid camera that used 4X5 Land film, type 55, whose black-and-white prints were preferred by all the engineers at SES. They were large-format prints, with negatives. Messerli had taken over six dozen photographs of the interior of the art museum in Amsterdam in order to know how many fire- and motion-detection devices would be needed and exactly where they should be installed.

Urs Messerli was no longer working for SES because he was very ill. He was hospitalized, presumed to be dying of a lung infection related to his emphysema, which he'd had for fifteen years. (Harry Hoekstra thought that someone suffering from emphysema probably *sounded* a lot like an asthmatic.)

The Universitätsspital in Zurich was famous for its care of emphysema patients. Ernst Hecht and Harry didn't have to worry about Urs Messerli slipping away before they could talk to him, not unless Messerli slipped away into death; the patient was on oxygen most of the time.

And Messerli suffered from another, more recent misfortune. His wife of some thirty years was divorcing him. While he lay dying, literally gasping for breath, Messerli's wife was also insisting that she *not* be written out of her husband's will. She'd discovered several photographs of naked women in his home-office. Shortly after he'd been hospitalized, he'd asked her to look for some important papers— namely, a codicil to his will. Frau Messerli had come upon the photographs quite innocently.

By the time Harry flew to Zurich, Frau Messerli was still innocent of the most important content of those photographs of naked women, which she'd given to her divorce lawyer. Neither she nor her lawyer realized that they were photographs of prostitutes who were dead; that the women were *naked* was all that concerned them.

Harry had no difficulty identifying Rooie's photograph in Ernst Hecht's office; and Hecht had easily recognized the murdered Brazilian prostitute from the area of the Langstrasse. What had surprised both policemen was that there were a half-dozen *other* photographs.

The Schweizer Elektronik- und Sicherheitssysteme company had sent Urs Messerli all over Europe; he'd killed prostitutes in Frankfurt and in Brussels, in Hamburg and The Hague, in Vienna and Antwerp. He hadn't always killed them in the same efficient way, nor had he always lit his subjects with the same floodlight from his big leather briefcase, but he *had* always posed his dead girls in a similar fashion: lying on their sides with their eyes closed, and with their knees drawn up to their chests in a modest, little-girlish posture, which was why Messerli's wife (and his wife's lawyer) had never suspected that the naked women were *dead*.

"You must congratulate your witness," Ernst Hecht had told Harry. They were en route to the Universitätsspital to see Urs Messerli before he died—Messerli had already confessed.

"Oh, I *will* thank her," Harry had said. "When I find her."

Urs Messerli's English was exactly as the mystery-woman witness had described it: Messerli spoke English well, but with a German-sounding accent. Harry chose to speak to Messerli in English—especially since Ernst Hecht's English was pretty good, too.

"In Amsterdam, on the Bergstraat ..." Harry had begun. "She had auburn hair and a good figure for a woman her age, but fairly small breasts..."

"Yes, yes—I know!" Urs Messerli had interrupted him.

A nurse had to pull off the oxygen mask in order for Messerli to be able to speak; then he would gasp—he made a sucking sound—before the nurse covered his mouth and nose with the mask again.

His grayness was far in advance of how gray he'd been when Ruth Cole had seen him and likened him to a mole; now his skin resembled ash. The enlarged air spaces in his lungs made a sound of their own, which was separate from his ragged breathing; it was as if you could hear the damaged tissue that lined the walls of the air spaces breaking away.

"You had a *witness* in Amsterdam," Harry told the murderer. "I don't suppose you got a look at her."

For once, the vestigial-like eyes opened wider—like a mole discovering sight. The nurse removed the oxygen mask again. "Yes, yes—I *heard* her! Someone *was* there!" Urs Messerli gasped. "She made a small sound. I *almost* heard her." A paroxysm of coughing overcame him. The nurse once more had to cover his mouth and nose with the mask.

"She was in the wardrobe closet," Harry told Messerli. "All the shoes had been turned—they were pointed toes-out—and she was standing among the shoes. You probably could have seen her ankles, if you'd looked."

Urs Messerli was inexpressibly saddened by this news, as if he would have enjoyed at least *meeting* the witness—if not killing her.

This happened in April '91, six months after Rooie's murder—one year after Harry Hoekstra had almost taken Dolores de Ruiter to Paris. That night in Zurich, Harry wished he *had* taken Rooie to Paris. He didn't have to spend the night in Zurich; he could have flown back to Amsterdam at the end of that same day, but for once he wanted to do something that he'd only read about in a travel book.

He declined Ernst Hecht's invitation to dinner. Harry wanted to be alone. Thinking of Rooie, he was not *entirely* alone. He'd even chosen a hotel that he thought Rooie would have liked. Although it was not the most expensive hotel in Zurich, it was too expensive for a cop. But Harry had traveled so little that he'd saved a fair amount of money. He didn't expect the 2nd District to pay for his room at the Hotel Zum Storchen, not even for one night, yet that was where he wanted to stay. It was a charmingly romantic hotel on the banks of the Limmat, and Harry chose a room that looked across the river at the floodlit Rathaus.

Harry took himself to dinner at the Kronenhalle, across the Limmat. Thomas Mann had eaten there—and James Joyce. There were two dining rooms with original paintings by Klee, Chagall, Matisse, Miró, Picasso. Rooie wouldn't have cared, but she would have liked the *Bündnerfleisch* and the shredded calf's liver with *Rösti*.

Harry usually drank nothing stronger than beer, but that night at the Kronenhalle he had four beers and a whole bottle of red wine by himself. He was drunk when he returned to his hotel room. He fell asleep with his shoes on, and only the phone call from Nico Jansen forced him to wake up and properly undress for bed.

"Tell me about it," Jansen said. "It's finished, right?"

"I'm drunk, Nico," Harry replied. "I was asleep."

"Tell me about it, anyway," Nico Jansen said. "The bastard killed eight hookers—each one in a different city, right?"

"That's right. He'll be dead in a couple of weeks—his doctor told me," Harry said. "He has a lung infection. He's had emphysema for fifteen years. It sounds like asthma, I guess."

"You seem cheerful," Jansen said.

"I'm drunk," Harry repeated.

"You should be a *happy* drunk, Harry," Nico told him. "It's finished, right?"

"All but the witness," Harry Hoekstra said.

"You and your witness," Jansen said. "Let her go. We don't need her anymore."

"But I *saw* her," Harry said. He didn't realize until he said it, but it was because he'd *seen* her that he couldn't get her out of his head. What had she been *doing*? She'd been a better witness than she probably knew, Harry thought. But all he said to Nico Jansen was: "I just want to congratulate her."

"Jesus, you *are* drunk!" Jansen told him.

Harry tried to read in bed, but he was too drunk to comprehend what he was reading. The novel, which had been halfway-decent airplane reading, was too challenging to read when he'd been drinking. It was the new novel by Alice Somerset, her fourth. It would be the last of her Margaret McDermid detective novels—the title was *McDermid, Retired*.

Notwithstanding his usual disdain for crime fiction, Harry Hoekstra was a big fan of the elderly Canadian author. (While Eddie O'Hare would never have thought of seventy-two as "elderly," that's how old Alice Somerset, alias Marion Cole, was in April '91.)

Harry liked the so-called Margaret McDermid mysteries because he thought that the Missing Persons detective possessed a convincingly accurate amount of melancholy for a cop. Also, Alice Somerset's novels weren't really "mysteries"; they were psychological investigations into the mind of a lonely policewoman. For Harry, the novels believably demonstrated the *effect* of those missing persons on Sergeant

McDermid—meaning, of course, those missing persons whom the detective could never find.

Although, at the time, Harry was at least four and a half years away from retiring, it didn't help him to read about a policewoman who *had* retired—especially since the point of the novel was that, even after she'd retired, Sergeant McDermid went on thinking like a cop.

She becomes a prisoner of those photographs of the forever-missing American boys. She can't bring herself to destroy the photos, even though she knows the boys will never be found. "One day she would find the courage to destroy them, she hoped." (That was the end of the novel.)

She *hoped*? Harry thought. That's *it*? She just *hoped*? Shit! What kind of an ending was that? Thoroughly depressed and still awake, Harry looked at the author photo. He was irritated that you could never get a good idea of what Alice Somerset looked like. There was the matter of her face, turned away; and she always wore a hat. The hat *really* pissed Harry off. A nom de plume was one thing, but what was she—a criminal?

And because Harry couldn't get a good look at Alice Somerset's face, her hidden face reminded him of his missing witness. He'd not got a good look at her face, either. Naturally he'd noticed her breasts, and there'd been an attitude of alertness to her whole body; but what had also impressed him was the way she'd seemed to *study* everything. That was part of the reason he'd been drawn to study *her*. Harry realized that it wasn't only because she was *the witness* that he wanted to see her again; whoever she was, she was a woman he wanted to meet.

That April '91, when the newspapers in Amsterdam carried the story of the capture of the prostitute-killer, there was something anticlimactic about the murderer being deathly ill. Urs Messerli would never leave the Universitätsspital—he would die that same month. A serial killer of as many as eight prostitutes should have generated more of a sensation, but the story was headline news for less than a week; by the end of May, it was gone from the news altogether.

Maarten Schouten, Ruth Cole's Dutch publisher, was attending the Bologna Children's Book Fair in Italy when the story broke. (It was not news in Italy because none of the murdered prostitutes had been Italian.) And from Bologna, every year, Maarten traveled to New York; now that their boys were grown up, Sylvia went with him to both places. And because Maarten and Sylvia missed the news about finding Rooie's killer, Ruth missed hearing about it, too. She would go on thinking that the moleman had got away with it—that he was still *out there.*

It was four and a half years later, in the fall of 1995, when Harry Hoekstra, who was pushing fifty-eight and *almost* retired, saw the new Ruth Cole novel in the window of that bookshop on the Spui, the Athenaeum. He immediately bought it.

"It's about time she wrote another novel," Sergeant Hoekstra said to the salesgirl.

All the booksellers in the Athenaeum knew Harry. His fondness for Ruth Cole's novels was nearly as familiar to them as the gossip that Sergeant Hoekstra had met more of his girlfriends in the Athenaeum, while browsing for books, than anywhere else. The booksellers at the Athenaeum liked to tease him. While they didn't doubt his fondness for reading travel books and novels, they also enjoyed telling the sergeant that they suspected he came to their bookshop not only to *read.*

My Last Bad Boyfriend, which Harry bought in English, had a god-awful title in Dutch—*Mijn laatste slechte vriend.* The salesgirl who waited on Harry, and who was quite a knowledgeable young bookseller, explained to him the possible reasons why Ruth Cole had needed five years to write what didn't appear to be a very long book. "It's her first novel in the first-person voice," the young bookseller began. "And I understand she had a baby a few years ago."

"I didn't know she was married," Harry said, looking more closely at Ruth's jacket photo. She didn't *look* married, Harry thought.

"Then her husband died, about a year ago," the bookseller said.

So Ruth Cole was a widow, Sergeant Hoekstra supposed. He studied the author photo. Yes, she looked more like a widow than she looked married. There was something sad in one of her eyes, or else it was some kind of flaw. She stared warily at the camera, as if her anxiety were an even more permanent part of her than her grief.

And to think that Ruth Cole's previous novel was *about* a widow—and now she *is* one! Sergeant Hoekstra thought.

The trouble with author photos, Harry mused, was that they were always so posed. And the authors never seemed to know what to do with their hands. There were a lot of clasped hands and folded arms and hands in pockets; there were hands on chins and hands in the hair. They should just keep their hands by their sides or in their laps, Harry believed.

The other problem with author photos was that they were often composed of no more than heads and shoulders. Harry wanted to see what the writers' bodies looked like. In Ruth's case, you couldn't even see her breasts.

On his days off, Harry often left the Athenaeum and sat reading in one of the cafés on the Spui, but he felt inclined to read Ruth Cole at home.

What could be better? A new Ruth Cole novel and two days off!

When he got to the part of the story about an older woman with a younger man, he was disappointed. Harry was almost fifty-eight; he didn't want to read about a woman in her thirties with a *younger* man. Nevertheless, Harry was intrigued by the Amsterdam setting. And when he got to the part about the younger man persuading the older woman to pay a prostitute to watch her with a customer... aha, one can imagine Sergeant Hoekstra's surprise. "It was a room all in red, which the stained-glass lamp shade made redder," Ruth Cole had written. Harry knew the room she had in mind.

"I was so nervous that I wasn't of much use," Ruth Cole wrote. "I couldn't even help the prostitute turn the shoes toes-out. I picked up only one of the shoes, and I promptly dropped it. The prostitute scolded me for being such a nuisance to her. She told me to hide myself behind the curtain; then she lined up the rest of the shoes, on either side of my own. I suppose my own shoes must have been moving a little, because I was trembling."

Harry could imagine her trembling, all right. He marked the place in the novel where he stopped reading; he would finish the book tomorrow. It was already late at night, but what did it matter? He had the whole next day off.

Sergeant Hoekstra rode his bicycle from the west of Amsterdam to *de Wallen* in record time. He'd paused only to take a pair of scissors and remove Ruth Cole's photo from the book jacket; there was no reason for anyone else to know who his witness was.

He found the two fat women from Ghana first. When he showed them the picture, Harry had to remind them of the mystery woman from the United States who'd paused on the Stoofsteeg and asked them where they were from.

"That was a long time ago, Harry," one of the women said.

"Five years," he said. "Is it her?"

The prostitutes from Ghana stared at the photograph. "You can't see her breasts," one of them said.

"Yeah, she had nice breasts," the other one said.

"Is it her?" Harry asked them again.

"It's been five years, Harry!" the first one said.

"Yeah, it's been too long," the other one said.

Harry next found the young, heavyset Thai prostitute on the Barndesteeg. The older one, the sadist, was asleep, but Harry had more trust in the younger prostitute's judgment, anyway.

"Is it her?" he asked again.

"It *could* be," the Thai slowly said. "I remember the boy better."

Two younger policemen, in uniform, were on the Gordijnensteeg, breaking up a brawl outside one of the Ecuadorans' window rooms. There was always a lot of fighting where the Ecuadoran transvestites were. In another year, they would all be deported. (They'd been deported from France a few years before.)

The young cops seemed surprised to see Sergeant Hoekstra; they knew he had the night off. But Harry told them he had a little business to attend to with the man with the rock-hard breasts the size of baseballs. The Ecuadoran transvestite sighed deeply when he looked at Ruth Cole's picture.

"It's a pity you can't see her breasts—she had nice ones," he told Harry.

"Then it's her—you're sure?" Harry asked him.

"She looks older," the prostitute said with disappointment.

She *is* older, Harry knew. And she'd had a baby, and her husband had died; there was a lot to account for why Ruth Cole looked older.

Harry couldn't find the Jamaican prostitute who'd led Ruth by her arm out of the Slapersteeg; she was the one who'd said that Harry's witness had a strong right arm for such a small woman. Is she some kind of *athlete*? Harry was thinking.

The Jamaican prostitute was sometimes missing for a week or more at a time. She must have had some other life that was giving her trouble, maybe in Jamaica. But it didn't matter—Harry didn't need to see her.

He pedaled his bicycle over to the Bergstraat last. He had to wait for Anneke Smeets to be finished with a customer. Rooie had left her window room to Anneke in her will. It had probably helped to keep the overweight young woman off heroin, but the luxury of Anneke *owning* Rooie's room had done a lot of damage to Anneke's diet. She was too fat to fit into the leather halter top anymore.

"I want to come in," Harry told Anneke, although he generally preferred to talk to her in the open air of the street; he had never liked how Anneke smelled. And it was now very late at night; Anneke smelled awful when she was ready to call it quits and go home.

"Is this a business call, Harry?" the overweight young woman asked. "Your business or mine?"

Sergeant Hoekstra showed her the author photo.

"That's her. Who is she?" Anneke asked.

"Are you sure?"

"Of course I'm sure—it's her. But what do you want with her? You got the killer."

"Good night, Anneke," Harry said. But when he stepped outside on the Bergstraat, he saw that someone had stolen his bicycle. This small disappointment was in the nature of the missing Jamaican prostitute being missing again. What did it really matter? Harry had the whole day off tomorrow: time enough to finish Ruth Cole's new novel *and* buy a new bicycle.

There were no more than twenty or thirty murders in Amsterdam a year, most of them not domestic, but whenever the police dragged one of the canals (looking for a body), they found *hundreds* of bicycles. Harry couldn't have cared less about his stolen bicycle.

Near the Hotel Brian, on the Singel, there were girls in window rooms where there had never been girls in the windows before. More "illegals," but Harry was off duty; he left the girls alone and went into the Brian to ask the man at the reception desk to call him a taxi.

In a year's time, the police would crack down on the "illegals"; soon there would be empty window rooms around the red-light district. Maybe *Dutch* women would once more be working in the windows. But by then Harry would be retired—it hardly mattered to him anymore.

Back in his apartment, Harry built a fire in his bedroom. He couldn't wait to read the rest of Ruth Cole's novel. With some Scotch tape, Sergeant Hoekstra stuck Ruth's author photo on the wall beside his bed. The firelight flickered there as he read into the night; he only occasionally got out of bed, to build up the fire. In the flickering light,

Ruth's anxious face seemed more alive to Harry than it had seemed on the back of her book. He could see her purposeful, athletic walk, her alert presence in the red-light district, where he'd followed her with at first fleeting, then renewed interest. She had nice breasts, Harry remembered.

At last, five years after his friend's murder, Sergeant Hoekstra had found his witness.

In Which Eddie O'Hare Falls in Love Again

As for Alice Somerset's fourth and apparently final Margaret McDermid mystery—*McDermid, Retired*—if Harry Hoekstra had been disappointed in the ending, Eddie O'Hare had been devastated. It was not merely what Marion had written about the photographs of her lost boys: "One day she would find the courage to destroy them, she hoped." More depressing was the overall fatalism of the retired detective. Sergeant McDermid was resigned to the permanence of the boys being lost. Even Marion's effort to breathe a *fictional* life into the death of her sons had deserted her. Alice Somerset sounded as if she was finished with writing; *McDermid, Retired* struck Eddie O'Hare as an announcement that the *writer* in Marion had retired, too.

At the time, all Ruth had said to Eddie was: "Lots of people retire *before* they're seventy-two."

But now, four and a half years later, in the fall of '95, there'd been no word from Marion—Alice Somerset had not written, or at least not published, another book—and neither Eddie nor Ruth gave half as much thought to Marion as they used to. It sometimes seemed to Eddie that Ruth had written her mother off. And who could blame her?

Ruth was unquestionably (and deservedly) angry that neither Graham's birth nor any of his subsequent birthdays had prompted an appearance from her mother. And Allan's death a year ago, which *might* have inspired Marion to come forward and offer her condolences, had resulted in another no-show.

Although Allan had never been religious, he'd left very careful and specific instructions regarding what he wanted done in the event of his death. He wanted to be cremated and he'd asked to have his ashes scattered in Kevin Merton's cornfield. Kevin, their Vermont neighbor and the caretaker for Ruth's house in her absence, had a lovely, rolling cornfield—it was the principal view from Ruth's master bedroom.

Allan hadn't considered that Kevin and his wife might object; the cornfield was not Ruth's property. But the Mertons had raised no objections. Kevin philosophized that Allan's ashes would be *good* for the cornfield. And Kevin had told Ruth that if he ever had to sell his farm, he would sell her or Graham the cornfield first. (It was typical of Allan to have presumed on Kevin's kindness.)

As for the house in Sagaponack, in the year that followed Allan's death, Ruth would often think of selling it.

Allan's memorial service was held at the New York Society for Ethical Culture, on West Sixty-fourth Street. His colleagues at Random House made all the arrangements. A fellow editor spoke first—a fond remembrance of Allan's often intimidating presence at the venerable publishing house. Then four of Allan's authors spoke; as his widow, Ruth was not among the speakers.

She'd worn an unfamiliar hat with a more unfamiliar veil. The veil had frightened Graham; she'd needed to beg the three-year-old's permission before he allowed her to wear it at all. The veil had seemed essential to her—not out of reverence or because of tradition, but to mask her tears.

The majority of mourners and friends who'd come to pay their respects to Allan were of the opinion that the child clung to his mother throughout the service, but it was more the case that his mother clung to him. Ruth had held the three-year-old on her lap. Her tears were probably more disturbing to him than was the reality of his father's death—at three, his sense of death was inexact. After several pauses in the memorial service, Graham whispered to his mother: "Where is Daddy *now?*" (It was as if, in the child's mind, his father were away on a journey.)

"It's gonna be okay, baby," Hannah, who was seated next to Ruth, whispered throughout the service. This irreligious litany was a surprisingly welcome irritation to Ruth. It distracted her from her grief. The mindlessness of Hannah's repetition made Ruth wonder if Hannah thought she was consoling the child who'd lost his father or the woman who'd lost her husband.

Eddie O'Hare had been the last to speak. Allan's colleagues had not chosen him, nor had Ruth.

Given Allan's low opinion of Eddie as a writer *and* speaker, it frankly astonished Ruth that Allan had designated a role for Eddie at the memorial service. Just as Allan had chosen the music and the location—the latter for its nonreligious atmosphere—and just as emphatically as Allan had insisted on *no flowers* (he'd always hated the smell of flowers), Allan had left instructions that Eddie should speak last. Allan had even told Eddie what to say.

As always, Eddie was a little faltering. He fumbled about for some sort of introduction, which made it clear that Allan hadn't told him *everything* that he was supposed to say—Allan hadn't anticipated that he would die so young.

Eddie explained that, at fifty-two, he was only six years younger than Allan had been. The age factor was important, Eddie struggled to say, because Allan had left instructions for Eddie to read a certain poem—Yeats's "When You Are Old." What was embarrassing was that Allan had imagined that Ruth would already be an old woman when he died. He'd quite correctly assumed that, given the eighteen-year difference in their ages, he would die before she would. But, typical of Allan, he'd never imagined that he would die and leave his widow still a *young* woman.

"Jesus, this is excruciating," Hannah had whispered to Ruth. "Eddie should just read the fucking poem!"

Ruth, who already knew the poem, would have been happier *never* to hear it. The poem always made her cry—even removed from the context of Allan's death and Ruth herself being left a widow. She had no doubt that it would make her cry now.

"It's gonna be okay, baby," Hannah whispered again, as Eddie finally read the Yeats poem.

> When you are old and grey and full of sleep,
> And nodding by the fire, take down this book,
> And slowly read, and dream of the soft look
> Your eyes had once, and of their shadows deep;

How many loved your moments of glad grace,
And loved your beauty with love false or true,
But one man loved the pilgrim soul in you,
And loved the sorrows of your changing face;

And bending down beside the glowing bars,
Murmur, a little sadly, how Love fled
And paced upon the mountains overhead
And hid his face amid a crowd of stars.

Understandably, everyone in attendance assumed that Ruth cried so bitterly because of how much she'd loved her husband. She *had* loved Allan, or at least she'd learned to. But even more, Ruth had loved her *life* with him. And while it pained her that Graham had lost his father, it was at least better for Graham that the boy was young enough not to be permanently scarred. In time, Graham would hardly remember Allan at all.

But Ruth had been so angry with Allan for dying, and when Eddie read the Yeats poem, it only made her angrier to hear how Allan had *assumed* she would be an old woman when he died! Ruth, of course, had always *hoped* she would be an old woman when Allan died. Now here she was, just turned forty—and with a three-year-old son.

And there was yet a meaner, more selfish reason for Ruth's tears. It was that reading Yeats had discouraged her from even *trying* to be a poet; hers were the tears a *writer* cried whenever a writer heard something better than anything he or she could have written.

"Why is Mommy crying?" Graham had asked Hannah—for the hundredth time, because Ruth had been on-and-off inconsolable since Allan's death.

"Your mommy's crying because she misses your daddy," Hannah whispered to the child.

"But where is Daddy *now*?" Graham asked Hannah; he'd not yet had a satisfactory answer from his mother.

After the service, a crush of people had pressed around Ruth; she lost count of the number of times her arms were squeezed. She kept her hands clasped at her waist; most people didn't try to touch her hands—just her wrists and her forearms and her upper arms.

Hannah had carried Graham, Eddie slinking alongside them. Eddie looked especially sheepish, as if he regretted having read the poem—

or else he was silently berating himself in the belief that his introduction should have been longer and clearer.

"Take off the pail, Mommy," Graham had said.

"It's a *veil*, baby—not a pail," Hannah told the boy. "And Mommy wants to keep it on."

"No, I'll take it off now," Ruth said; she'd finally stopped crying. A numbness enclosed her face; she felt impervious to crying or to any form of showing how upset she was. Then she remembered that dreadful old woman who'd called herself a widow for the rest of her life. Where was she now? Allan's memorial service would have been the perfect place for her to reappear!

"Do you remember that terrible old widow?" Ruth asked Hannah and Eddie.

"I'm on the lookout for her, baby," Hannah had replied. "But she's probably dead."

Eddie was still in the throes of being overcome by the Yeats poem, yet he'd never stopped being the constant observer. Ruth was looking for Marion, too; then she thought she saw her mother.

The woman wasn't old enough to be Marion, but Ruth didn't realize this at first. What struck Ruth was the woman's elegance, and what had seemed to be her heartfelt sympathy and concern. She was looking at Ruth not in a threatening or invasive way, but with both pity and an anxious curiosity. She was an attractive older woman, only Allan's age—not even sixty. Also, the woman *wasn't* looking at Ruth at all as closely as she appeared to be looking at *Hannah*. That was when Ruth realized that the woman wasn't really looking at Hannah, either; it was *Graham* who was drawing the woman's attention.

Ruth touched the woman's arm and asked, "Excuse me ... do I know you?"

The woman, embarrassed, averted her eyes. But whatever had shamed her passed; she gathered her courage and squeezed Ruth's forearm.

"I'm sorry. I know I was staring at your son. It's just that he doesn't look at all like Allan," the woman said nervously.

"Who *are* you, lady?" Hannah asked her.

"Oh, I'm sorry!" the woman said to Ruth. "I'm the *other* Mrs. Albright. I mean the *first* Mrs. Albright."

Ruth didn't want Hannah to be rude to Allan's ex-wife, and Hannah looked as if she were about to ask: "Were you invited?"

Eddie O'Hare saved the day.

"I'm so glad to meet you," Eddie said, squeezing the ex-wife's arm. "Allan always spoke so highly of you."

The ex–Mrs. Albright was stunned; she was easily as overcome as Eddie had been by the Yeats poem. Ruth had never heard Allan speak "highly" of his ex-wife; sometimes he'd spoken *pityingly* of her—specifically, because he felt certain she would rue her decision never to have children. Now here she was, staring at Graham! Ruth was sure that the ex–Mrs. Albright had come to Allan's memorial service *not* to pay her respects to Allan, but to get a look at his child!

But all Ruth said was: "Thank you for coming." She would have gone on, babbling insincerities, but Hannah stopped her.

"Baby, you look better with the veil on," Hannah whispered. "Graham, this is an old friend of your daddy's," Hannah told the boy. "Say 'Hello.' "

"Hello," Graham said to Allan's ex-wife. "But where *is* Daddy? Where is he *now?*"

Ruth slipped the veil back on; her face felt so numb that she was unaware she was crying again.

It was for children that one wanted heaven, Ruth thought. It was only for the sake of being able to say: "Daddy's in *heaven,* Graham," which was what she'd said then.

"And heaven is nice, isn't it?" the boy began. They'd had many discussions of heaven, and what it was like, since Allan had died. Possibly heaven meant more to the boy because the discussion of it was so new; as neither Ruth nor Allan was religious, heaven had not been a part of Graham's first three years on earth.

"I'll tell you what heaven is like," the ex–Mrs. Albright said to the boy. "It's like your best dreams."

But Graham was of an age where he more frequently had nightmares. Dreams were not necessarily heaven-sent. Yet if the boy was to believe the Yeats poem, he would be forced to envision his daddy *pacing the mountains overhead and hiding his face in a crowd of stars!* (Is that heaven or a nightmare? Ruth would wonder.)

"She's not here, is she?" Ruth suddenly said to Eddie, through her veil.

"I don't see her," Eddie admitted.

"I know she's not here," Ruth said.

"Who's not here?" Hannah asked Eddie.

"Her mother," Eddie replied.

"It's gonna be okay, baby," Hannah whispered to her best friend. "Fuck your mother."

In Hannah Grant's opinion, *Fuck Your Mother* would have been a more appropriate title for Eddie O'Hare's fifth novel, *A Difficult Woman*, which was published that same fall of '94 when Allan died. But Hannah had given up on Ruth's mother long ago, and—not yet being an older woman herself, at least not in her own mind—Hannah was sick to death of Eddie's younger-man-with-older-woman theme. Hannah was thirty-nine—as Eddie had pointed out, exactly the age Marion had been when he'd fallen in love with her.

"Yeah, but you were sixteen, Eddie," Hannah reminded him. "That's one category I've eliminated from my sexual lexicon—I mean fucking teenagers."

While Hannah had accepted Eddie as Ruth's newfound friend, there was more about Eddie that troubled Hannah than the natural jealousy that friends often feel toward friends of friends. She'd had boyfriends who were Eddie's age, and older—Eddie was fifty-two in the fall of '94—and while Eddie was hardly Hannah's cup of tea, he was nonetheless a physically attractive older man who was not a homosexual; yet he'd never made a pass at her. Hannah found this more than troubling.

"Look—I *like* Eddie," she would say to Ruth, "but you've got to admit that there's something wrong with the guy." What Hannah found "wrong" was that Eddie had eliminated younger women from *his* sexual lexicon.

Ruth still found Hannah's "sexual lexicon" more disturbing than Eddie's. If Eddie's enduring attraction to older women was weird, at least it was weird in a selective way.

"I suppose I'm some kind of sexual shotgun—is that what you mean?" Hannah asked.

"Different folks, different strokes," Ruth replied tactfully.

"Look, baby, I saw Eddie on Park Avenue and Eighty-ninth—he was pushing an old woman in a wheelchair," Hannah said. "I also saw him one night in the Russian Tea Room—he was with an old lady in a *neck brace!*"

"They might have had accidents. They didn't necessarily succumb to old age," Ruth responded. "*Young* women break their legs—the one in the wheelchair might have been skiing. There are automobile accidents. There's always whiplash...."

"Baby," Hannah pleaded. "This old woman was *confined* to a wheelchair. And the one with the neck brace was a walking *skeleton*—her neck was too *thin* to hold up her head!"

"I think Eddie's sweet," was all Ruth would say. "You're going to get old, too, Hannah. Wouldn't you like to have someone like Eddie in your life *then?*"

But even Ruth had to confess that she found *A Difficult Woman* a serious stretch of the so-called *willing* suspension of her disbelief. A man in his early fifties, who bears remarkable similarities to Eddie, is the doting lover of a woman in her late seventies. They make love amid a daunting host of medical precautions and uncertainties. Not surprisingly, they meet in a doctor's office, where the man is anxiously awaiting his first sigmoidoscopy.

"What are you here for?" the older woman asks the younger man. "You look healthy enough." The younger man admits his anxiety concerning the procedure he is about to undergo. "Oh, don't be silly," the older woman tells him. "Heterosexual men are such cowards when it comes to being penetrated. There's really nothing to it. I must have had a half-dozen sigmoidoscopies. Mind you, be prepared—they do give you a little gas."

A few days later, the two encounter each other at a cocktail party. The older woman is so beautifully dressed that the younger man doesn't recognize her. Moreover, she approaches him in an alarmingly coquettish manner. "I last saw you when you were about to be penetrated," she whispers to him. "How'd it go?"

Stammering, he replies: "Oh, very well, thank you. And you were right. It was nothing to be afraid of!"

"I'll show you something to be afraid of," the woman whispers to him, which begins their disturbingly passionate love story, which is over only when the older woman dies.

"For God's sake," Allan had said to Ruth about Eddie's fifth novel. "You've got to hand it to O'Hare—nothing embarrasses him!"

Despite his ongoing habit of calling Eddie by his last name, which Eddie intensely disliked, Allan had developed a genuine affection for him, if not for his *writing*—and Eddie, although Allan Albright was the antithesis of his kind of man, had grown far more fond of Allan than he had thought possible. They'd been good friends when Allan died, and Eddie had not taken his responsibilities at Allan's memorial service lightly.

Eddie's relationship with Ruth—especially the limited degree to which he understood her feelings for her mother—was a different matter.

While Eddie had observed the enormous changes in Ruth upon her becoming a mother, he'd not realized how being a mother had persuaded her to take an even more unforgiving view of Marion.

Simply put, Ruth was a good mother. At the time of Allan's death, Graham would be only a year younger than Ruth had been when Marion had left her. Ruth could not conceive of the *lack* of love Marion had felt for her daughter. Ruth would sooner *die* than leave Graham; she could never *imagine* leaving her son.

And if Eddie was obsessed with Marion's state of mind—or what he could fathom of it from *McDermid, Retired*—Ruth had read her mother's fourth novel with impatience and disdain. (There is a point when sorrow becomes self-indulgent, she thought.)

As a publisher, Allan had done his homework on Marion; he'd found out as much as he could about the Canadian crime writer who called herself Alice Somerset. According to her Canadian publisher, Alice Somerset was not enough of a success in Canada to support herself from her book sales within her own country; however, her French and German translations were far more popular. She made quite a comfortable living from her translations. In addition to maintaining a modest apartment in Toronto, Ruth's mother spent the worst months of the Canadian winter in Europe. Her German and French publishers were happy to find her suitable apartments to rent.

"An agreeable woman, but somewhat aloof," Marion's German publisher had told Allan.

"Charming in a standoffish way," the French publisher had said.

"I don't know why she bothers with the nom de plume—she just strikes me as a very private person," Marion's Canadian publisher told Allan; the publisher also provided Allan with Marion's Toronto address.

"For God's sake," Allan would repeatedly say to Ruth; in fact, he'd had one such conversation with Ruth only a few days before he died. "Here's your mother's address. You're a writer—just write her a letter!"

You could even go see her, if you wanted to. I'd be happy to go with you, or you could go alone. You could take Graham—surely she'd be interested in *Graham!*"

"*I'm* not interested in *her!*" Ruth had said.

Ruth and Allan had come into New York for Eddie's publication party, which was held on an October evening not long after Graham's third birthday. It had been one of those warm, sunny days that felt like summer—and when the evening came, the night air brought a contrasting coolness that epitomized the very best of autumn. "An unbeatable day!" Ruth would remember Allan saying.

They'd taken a two-bedroom suite at the Stanhope; they'd made love in their bedroom while Conchita Gomez had taken Graham to the hotel restaurant, where the boy was treated like a little prince. They'd all driven into the city from Sagaponack, although Conchita protested that she and Eduardo were too old to spend even a single night apart; one of them might die, and it would be terrible for a happily married person to die alone.

The spectacular weather, not to mention the sex, had made such a favorable impression on Allan that he'd insisted on walking the fifteen blocks to Eddie's publication party. In retrospect, Ruth would think that Allan had looked a little flushed upon their arrival; but she'd thought at the time it was only a sign of good health or the effect of the cool fall air.

Eddie had been his usual self-deprecating self at the party: he gave a silly speech wherein he thanked his old friends for giving up whatever more entertaining plans they had had for the evening; he gave an overly familiar synopsis of the plot of his new novel; then he assured his audience that they needn't bother to read the book, now that they already knew the story. "And the main characters will be fairly recognizable...from my previous novels, that is," Eddie had mumbled. "They've just grown a little older."

Hannah was there with an undeniably awful man, a former professional hockey goalie who'd just written a memoir about his sexual exploits—and who took an unsavory pride in the unimpressive fact that he'd never been married. His terrible book was called *Not in My Net*, and his humor was principally demonstrated by his charmless habit of referring to the women he'd slept with as *pucks*, thus enabling him to crack the joke "She was a great puck."

Hannah had met him when she'd interviewed him for a magazine article she was writing; her subject was what jocks did when they retired. As far as Ruth could tell, they tried to be either actors or writers; she'd remarked to Hannah that she liked it better when they tried to be actors.

But Hannah was increasingly defensive on the matter of her bad boyfriends. "What does an old married lady know?" Hannah would ask her friend. Nothing, Ruth would have been the first to admit. Ruth just knew that she was happy. (She knew she was lucky to be happy, too.)

Even Hannah would have acknowledged that Ruth's marriage to Allan had worked. If Ruth would never have confessed that their sex life had been only tolerable at the start, she later would have described even this aspect of her life with Allan as something she'd learned to enjoy. Ruth had found a companion she could talk to, and he was someone she liked to listen to as well; furthermore, he was a good father to the only child she would ever have. And the child . . . ah, her whole life had changed because of Graham, and for that, too, she would always love Allan.

As an older mother—she was thirty-seven when Graham was born—Ruth worried about her son's safety more than younger mothers did. She also spoiled Graham, but it had been her choice to have an only child. What are only children for, if not for spoiling? To dote on Graham had become the most sustaining part of Ruth's life. The boy was two before Ruth went back to being a writer.

Now Graham was three. His mother had finally finished her fourth novel, although she continued to describe the novel as *un*finished—for the expressed reason that she'd not yet thought the book was finished enough to show to Allan. Ruth was being disingenuous, even to herself, but she couldn't help it. She was worried about Allan's reaction to the novel—for reasons that had nothing to do with how finished or *un*finished the book was.

It had long been her understanding with Allan that she would never show him anything she'd written until *she* believed it was as finished as she could make it. Allan had always urged his authors to do this. "I can best be an editor only when *you* think you've done everything you can," he'd tell his writers. (How could he urge an author to take another step if the author was still walking? Allan always said.)

If she'd fooled Allan into accepting that her novel was not yet ready to show him because she *said* it was not quite finished, Ruth hadn't fooled herself. She'd already rewritten the novel as much as she could; she sometimes doubted she could re*read* the book, much less pretend that she was still re*writing* it. Nor did she doubt that it was a good novel; she believed it was her best work.

In truth, the only thing that bothered Ruth about her newest novel, *My Last Bad Boyfriend,* was her fear that the book would insult her husband. The main character of the book was entirely too close to one aspect of Ruth herself before she was married: her main character was prone to involving herself with the wrong sort of man. Furthermore, the titular bad boyfriend in her novel was an unlikely and unlikable combination of Scott Saunders and Wim Jongbloed. That this sexual lowlife persuades the Ruth character (as Hannah would doubtless call her) into watching a prostitute with a customer might be less disturbing to Allan than the fact that the so-called Ruth character is uncontrollably overcome with sexual desire. And the resultant shame she feels—for sexually losing control of herself—is what convinces her to accept a marriage proposal from a man who is sexually unexciting to her.

How could Allan *not* be insulted by what Ruth's new novel implied about the *author's* reasons for marrying *him*? That her marriage to Allan had been the happiest four years of her life, which Allan surely knew, did not mitigate what Ruth feared was her novel's more cynical message.

Ruth had fairly accurately imagined everything that Hannah would conclude from *My Last Bad Boyfriend:* namely, that her less adventurous friend had had a fling with a Dutch boy, who'd fucked her brains out while a prostitute *watched*! It was a brutally humiliating scene for *any* woman, even for Hannah. But Ruth wasn't worried about Hannah's reaction; Ruth had a history of ignoring or rejecting Hannah's interpretations of her fiction.

Yet here Ruth was: she'd written a novel that would surely offend many readers and critics—especially the *women* among them—but so what? The *only* person she cared about not offending, Allan, might be the very person whom *My Last Bad Boyfriend* was most likely to offend!

The night of Eddie's publication party struck Ruth as the best possible time for her to confess her fears to Allan. She had even gone so far as to imagine that she was getting up the nerve to tell Allan what had happened to her in Amsterdam. Ruth believed her marriage was that unassailable.

"I don't want to have dinner with Hannah," she whispered to her husband at Eddie's party.

"Aren't we having dinner with O'Hare?" Allan asked her.

"No, not even with Eddie—not even if he asks us," Ruth had replied. "I want to have dinner with you, Allan—just you."

From the party, they'd caught a cab uptown to the restaurant where Allan had so gallantly left her alone with Eddie O'Hare—that seemingly long-ago night after her reading at the 92nd Street Y, and Eddie's never-ending introduction.

There was no reason for Allan *not* to drink a lot of wine; they'd already had sex, and neither of them had to drive. But Ruth silently wished that her husband wouldn't get drunk. She didn't want him to be drunk when she told him about Amsterdam.

"I'm dying for you to read my book," she began.

"I'm dying to read it—when you're ready," Allan told her. He was so relaxed. It really was the perfect time to tell him everything.

"It's not just that I love you and Graham," Ruth said. "It's that I will appreciate forever the life you've spared me *from*, the life I *had*..."

"I know—you've told me." He sounded slightly less patient with her now, as if he didn't want to hear her say, again, how she'd repeatedly got herself in trouble as a single woman; how, until Allan, her judgment (when it came to men) was not to be trusted.

"In Amsterdam..." she tried to say, but then she thought that, to be honest, she should begin with Scott Saunders and the squash game—not to mention the après-squash game. But her voice had stopped. "It's just more difficult to show you this novel," she began again, "because your opinion means so much more than it ever did, and your opinion has always meant a lot." Already she was evading what she wanted to say! She felt as crippled by cowardice as she had in Rooie's wardrobe closet.

"Ruth, *relax*," Allan told her, holding her hand. "If you think having *another* editor would be better for you—I mean for our relationship..."

"No!" Ruth cried. "That's *not* what I mean!" She'd not meant to pull her hand away, but she had. Now she tried to take back his hand, but he'd put it in his lap. "I mean that it's all because of you that I've had *my* last bad boyfriend—it's not just a *title*, you know."

"I know—you've told me," he said again.

What they'd ended up talking about was the scary and oft-repeated subject of who Graham's guardian should be, should anything happen to both of them. It was so unlikely that anything could happen to both of them that would leave Graham an orphan; Graham went absolutely everywhere with them. If their plane crashed, the boy would die, too.

But it was a matter that Ruth couldn't let rest. As it stood, Eddie was Graham's godfather, Hannah his godmother. Neither Ruth nor Allan could imagine Hannah as anybody's mother. Her devotion to Graham notwithstanding, Hannah had a life that made being a parent unthinkable. While she'd impressed both Ruth and Allan by her attentiveness to Graham—in that eager manner that women who've chosen not to have children of their own can sometimes exhibit with other people's children—Hannah was *not* a good choice for Graham's guardian.

And if Eddie had shunned younger women, he seemed not to know (in the slightest) what to do with children. He behaved awkwardly, even foolishly, in Graham's company. Eddie was so nervous around Graham that he made Graham nervous, and Graham was not a nervous child.

By the time they got back to the Stanhope, Allan and Ruth were both drunk. They kissed their baby boy good night. (Graham was asleep on a roll-away bed in their bedroom.) They bid Conchita Gomez good night, too. Before Ruth had finished brushing her teeth and readying herself for bed, Allan was already sleeping soundly.

Ruth noticed that he'd left the window open. Even if the air that night was special, it was never a good idea to leave a window open in New York—the noise of the early-morning traffic would wake the dead. (It would not wake Allan.)

In every marriage there are designated chores; there is always someone who is largely responsible for putting out the trash, and someone who is principally in charge of not running out of coffee or milk or toothpaste or toilet paper. Allan was in charge of *temperature:* he opened and closed the windows, he fiddled with the thermostat, he built up the fire or he let it die down. And so Ruth left the window open in their bedroom at the Stanhope. And when the early-morning traffic woke her at five, and when Graham crawled into bed between his parents, because he was cold, Ruth said: "Allan, if you close the window, I think we can *all* go back to sleep."

"I'm cold, Daddy," Graham said. "Daddy's *really* cold," the child added.

"We're *all* really cold, Graham," Ruth replied.

"Daddy's colder," Graham said.

"Allan?" Ruth started to say. She knew. She reached cautiously around Graham, who was cuddled against her, and touched Allan's cold face without looking at him. She slipped her hand under the covers, where her own body and Graham's were warm, but even under the covers Allan was cold to her touch—as cold as the bathroom floor in Vermont on a winter morning.

"Sweetie," Ruth said to Graham, "let's go in the other room. We'll let Daddy sleep a little more."

"I want to sleep a little more, too," Graham told her.

"Let's go in the other room," Ruth repeated. "Maybe you can sleep with Conchita."

They traipsed through the living room of the suite, Graham dragging his blanket and his teddy bear, Ruth in her T-shirt and panties; not even marriage had altered what she wore to bed. She knocked on the door of Conchita's bedroom, waking the old woman.

"I'm sorry, Conchita, but Graham would like to sleep with you," Ruth told her.

"Sure, honey—you just come on in," Conchita said to Graham, who marched past her to her bed.

"It's not as cold in here," the child observed. "It's so cold in our room—Daddy is freezing."

"Allan is dead," Ruth whispered to Conchita.

Then, alone in the living room of the suite, she worked up the nerve to go back into her bedroom. She closed the bedroom window before she went into the bathroom, where she hastily washed her hands and face, and brushed her teeth, ignoring her hair. She then stumbled into her clothes without once looking at Allan or touching him again. Ruth didn't want to see his face. For the rest of her life, she would prefer to imagine him as he'd looked when he was alive; it was bad enough that she would take to her grave the memory of his unnatural coldness.

It was not yet six in the morning when she called Hannah.

"You better be a friend of mine," Hannah said when she answered the phone.

"Who the fuck is it?" Ruth heard the ex-goalie ask.

"It's me. Allan's dead. I don't know what to do," Ruth told Hannah.

"Oh, baby, baby—I'll be right there!" Hannah said.

"Who the fuck *is* it?" the former hockey star asked again.

"Oh, go find yourself another *puck*!" Ruth heard Hannah tell him. "It's none of your fucking business who it *is*...."

By the time Hannah arrived at the Stanhope, Ruth had already called Eddie at the New York Athletic Club. Between them, Eddie and Hannah made all the arrangements. Ruth didn't have to talk to Graham, who'd fortunately fallen back to sleep in Conchita's bed; the child didn't wake up until after eight, by which time Allan's body had already been removed from the hotel. Hannah, who took the boy to breakfast, was amazingly resourceful in answering Graham's questions about where his father was. It was too soon for Allan to be in heaven, Ruth had decided; she meant it was too soon to have the heaven conversation, which there would be so many of later. Hannah stuck to more practical untruths: "Your daddy went to the office, Graham"; and, "Your daddy might have to take a trip."

"A trip where?" Graham asked.

Conchita Gomez was a wreck. Ruth was just numb. Eddie volunteered to drive them all back to Sagaponack, but Ted Cole had not taught his daughter to drive for nothing. Ruth knew that she could drive in or out of Manhattan whenever she had to. It was enough that Eddie and Hannah had spared her having to deal with Allan's *body*.

"I can drive," Ruth told them. "Whatever happens, I can drive." But she couldn't bear to search through Allan's clothes for the car keys. Eddie found the keys. Hannah packed Allan's clothes.

In the car, Hannah sat in back with Graham and Conchita. Hannah was in charge of conversing with Graham—that was her role. Eddie sat in the passenger seat. It was unclear to everyone, Eddie included, what *his* role was, but he occupied himself by staring at Ruth's profile; Ruth never took her eyes off the road, except to look in the side-view or rearview mirror.

Poor Allan—it must have been cardiac arrest, Eddie was thinking. It was; he got that right. But what Eddie got *wrong* was more interesting. What he got wrong was that he imagined he'd fallen in love with Ruth, just by staring at her sorrowful profile; what he didn't realize was how much, at that moment, she had forcefully reminded him of her unhappy mother.

Poor Eddie O'Hare! What had befallen him was most unkind: the bewildering illusion that he was now in love with the daughter of the only woman he'd ever loved! But who can distinguish between falling in love and *imagining* falling in love? Even *genuinely* falling in love is an act of the imagination.

"Where is Daddy *now*?" Graham began. "Is he still at the office?"

"I think he has a doctor's appointment," Hannah told the child. "I think he went to see the doctor because he wasn't feeling very well."

"Is he still cold?" the boy asked.

"Maybe," Hannah replied. "The doctor will know what's wrong with him."

Ruth's hair remained unbrushed—it looked slept-on—and her pale face had no makeup. Her lips were dry, and the crow's-feet at the corners of her eyes were more prominent than Eddie had ever seen them. Marion had had crow's-feet, too, but Eddie had momentarily lost sight of Marion; he was transfixed by Ruth's face, with its emanating sadness.

Ruth at forty was in the first numbness of mourning. Marion at thirty-nine, when Eddie had last seen her, had been grieving for five years; *her* face, which her daughter's face now so closely resembled, had reflected an almost eternal grief.

As a sixteen-year-old, Eddie had fallen in love with Marion's sadness, which seemed a more permanent part of her than her beauty. Yet beauty is remembered after beauty leaves; what Eddie saw reflected in Ruth's face was a *departed* beauty, which was another measure of the love Eddie truly felt for Marion.

But Eddie didn't know that he was still in love with Marion; he truly believed that he'd fallen in love with Ruth.

What the hell is the matter with Eddie? Ruth was thinking. If he doesn't stop staring at me, I'm going to drive off the road!

Hannah had also noticed that Eddie was staring at Ruth. What the hell is the matter with Eddie? Hannah was thinking. Since when did the asshole take an interest in a *younger* woman?

Mrs. Cole

"She'd been a widow for one year," Ruth Cole had written. (A mere four years before she became a widow herself!) And a year after Allan's death—just as she'd written of her fictional widow—Ruth was still struggling "to keep her memories of the past under control, as any widow must."

How had she known almost everything about it? the novelist now wondered—for although she'd always claimed that a good writer could imagine *anything* (and imagine it truly), and although she'd often argued that real-life experience was overvalued, even Ruth was surprised by how *accurately* she'd imagined being a widow.

A whole year after Allan's death, *exactly* as she'd written of her fictional widow, Ruth was "as prone to being swept away by a so-called flood of memories as she was on that morning when she'd awakened with her husband dead beside her."

And where was the angry old widow who'd assaulted Ruth for writing *un*truthfully about being a widow? Where was the harpy who'd called herself a widow for the rest of her life? In retrospect, Ruth was disappointed that the old witch had not made an appearance at Allan's memorial service. Now that she was a widow, Ruth *wanted* to see the miserable old hag—if only to shout in her face that everything she'd written about being a widow was *true*!

The evil old woman who'd tried to spoil her wedding with her hateful threats, the resentful old harridan who'd so shamelessly let herself go . . . where was she now? Probably she was dead, as Hannah had declared. If so, Ruth felt cheated; now that the conventional wisdom of the world granted her the authority to speak, Ruth would have liked to give the bitch a piece of her mind.

For hadn't the hag bragged to Ruth about the superiority of *her* love for *her* husband? The very idea of someone saying to someone else, "You don't know what grief is," or, "You don't know what love is," struck Ruth as outrageous.

This unforeseen anger toward the old widow without a name had provided Ruth with an inexhaustible fuel for her first year as a widow. In the same year, also unforeseen, Ruth had experienced a softening in her feelings toward her mother. Ruth had lost Allan, but she still had Graham. With her heightened awareness of how much she loved her only child, Ruth found herself sympathizing with Marion's efforts *not* to love another child—since Marion had already lost *two*.

How her mother had managed not to take her own life was a matter of amazement to Ruth, as was how Marion had even been *able* to have another child. All at once, why her mother had left her began to make sense. Marion hadn't wanted to love Ruth because she couldn't stand the idea of losing a third child. (Ruth had heard all this from Eddie, five years ago, but until she'd had a child and lost a husband, she didn't have either the experience or the imagination to believe it.)

Yet Marion's Toronto address had sat for a year in a prominent place on Ruth's desk. Pride and cowardice—now *there* was a title worthy of a long novel!—prevented Ruth from writing to her. Ruth still believed that it was Marion's role to reintroduce herself to her daughter, since Marion had been the one who had left. As a relatively new mother and an even newer widow, Ruth was a newcomer to both grief and the fear of an even greater loss.

It was Hannah's suggestion that Ruth give her mother's Toronto address to Eddie.

"Let her be Eddie's problem," Hannah said. "Let *him* agonize over whether to write her or not."

Of course Eddie *would* agonize over whether or not to write Marion. Worse, he had on several occasions *tried* to write her, but none of his efforts had made it into the mail.

"Dear Alice Somerset," he'd begun, "I have reason to believe that you are Marion Cole, the most important woman in my life." But that struck him as too jaunty a tone, especially after almost forty years, and so he'd tried again, taking a more straightforward approach. "Dear Marion: For Alice Somerset could only be you—I have read your Margaret McDermid novels with"—uh, with *what*? Eddie had asked himself, and that had stopped him. With fascination? With frustration? With admiration? With despair? With all of the above? He couldn't say.

Besides, after carrying a torch for Marion for thirty-six years, Eddie now believed he had fallen in love with Ruth. And after a year of imagining he was in love with Marion's daughter, Eddie still didn't realize that he'd never stopped loving Marion; he *still* believed he loved Ruth. Thus Eddie's efforts to write Marion became tortured in the extreme. "Dear Marion: I loved you for thirty-six years before I fell in love with your daughter." But Eddie couldn't even bring himself to say that to *Ruth*!

As for Ruth, in her year of mourning, she often wondered what had happened to Eddie O'Hare. Yet her grief, and her constant concerns for young Graham, distracted Ruth from Eddie's obvious but puzzling agonies. She'd always thought he was a sweet, odd man. Was he now a sweet man who'd grown odder? He could spend an entire dinner party in her company without uttering more than monosyllables; yet whenever she so much as looked at him, he was staring at her. Then, always, he would instantly look away.

"What *is* it, Eddie?" she'd asked him once.

"Oh, nothing," he'd replied. "I was just wondering how you were doing."

"Well, I'm doing all right—thank you," Ruth had said.

Hannah had her own theories, which Ruth dismissed as absurd. "He looks like he's fallen in love with you, but he doesn't know how to hit on *younger* women," Hannah had said. For a year, the thought of *anyone* hitting on her had struck Ruth as grotesque.

But, that fall of '95, Hannah would say to her: "It's been a year, baby—it's time you got back in circulation again."

The very idea of being "back in circulation" repelled Ruth. Not only was she still in love with Allan and her memory of their life together, but Ruth felt chilled at the prospect of confronting her own bad judgment *again*.

As she'd written in the very first chapter of *Not for Children*, who knew when it was time for a widow to re-enter the world? There was no such thing as a widow re-entering the world "safely."

The publication of Ruth Cole's fourth novel, *My Last Bad Boyfriend*, was delayed until the fall of 1995, which was the earliest possible date that Ruth could conceive of making her first public appearance since her husband's death—not that Ruth was as available as her publishers would have liked. She'd agreed to a reading at the 92nd Street Y, where she'd not read since Eddie O'Hare's marathon introduction in 1990, but Ruth had refused to give any interviews in the U.S.—on the grounds that she was spending only one night in New York, en route to Europe, and that she *never* wanted to conduct any interviews at her home in Vermont. (Since the first of September, the Sagaponack house had been on the market.)

Hannah maintained that Ruth was crazy to isolate herself in Vermont; according to Hannah, Ruth should sell the Vermont house instead. But Allan and Ruth had agreed: Graham should grow up in Vermont.

Besides, Conchita Gomez was too old to be Graham's principal nanny. And Eduardo was too old to be a caretaker. In Vermont, Ruth would have available babysitters close to home. Kevin Merton had three daughters of babysitting age; one of them, Amanda, was a high-school student who was permitted a limited amount of travel. (The high school had agreed that a book tour with Ruth Cole fell into the category of an educational trip; hence Ruth was taking Graham and Amanda Merton with her to New York and Europe.)

Not all of her European publishers were satisfied by Ruth's plans to promote *My Last Bad Boyfriend.* But Ruth had fairly warned everyone: she was still in mourning, and she would go nowhere without her four-year-old son; moreover, neither her son nor his nanny should be kept out of school for longer than two weeks.

The trip Ruth planned would be as easy on herself and Graham as possible. She was flying to London on the Concorde, and she would fly back to New York from Paris—again on the Concorde. Between London and Paris, she would bring Graham and his babysitter to Amsterdam; she couldn't *not* go to Amsterdam, she'd decided. The novel's partial setting there—that humiliating scene in the red-light district—made the book of special interest to the Dutch; and Maarten was her favorite European publisher.

It was not Amsterdam's fault that Ruth now dreaded going there. Surely she could promote her new novel for Maarten without visiting the red-light district. Every unoriginal journalist who interviewed her, not to mention every photographer assigned to take her picture, would insist on Ruth returning to *de Wallen*—the setting of the novel's most notorious scene—but Ruth had resisted the lack of originality in journalists and photographers before.

And perhaps it was a form of penance that she should have to go back to Amsterdam, the novelist thought—for wasn't her fear a form of penance? And why wouldn't she be afraid every second she was in Amsterdam—for how could the city *not* remind her of the eternity of her hiding in Rooie's closet? Wouldn't the wheezing of the moleman be the background music in her sleep? *If* she could sleep . . .

In addition to Amsterdam, the only part of Ruth's book tour that she was dreading was her one night in New York, and she was dreading that only because, once again, Eddie O'Hare was introducing her before her reading at the 92nd Street Y.

She'd unwisely chosen to stay at the Stanhope; she and Graham had not been there since Allan's death, and Graham remembered the last place he'd seen his father better than Ruth had thought he would. They were not staying in the same two-bedroom suite, but the configuration of the rooms and the decor were strikingly similar.

"Daddy was sleeping on *this* side of the bed, Mommy on *that* side," the boy explained to his babysitter, Amanda Merton. "The window was open," Graham went on. "Daddy had left it open, and I was cold. I got out of my bed..." Here the boy stopped. Where *was* his bed? With Allan gone, Ruth hadn't asked the hotel to provide a roll-away for Graham; there was more than enough room in her king-size bed for her and her small son. "Where's *my* bed?" the boy now asked.

"Sweetie, you can sleep with me," Ruth told him.

"Or you can sleep in *my* bedroom, with *me*," Amanda offered helpfully—anything to get Graham off the subject of his father's death.

"Okay. Fine," Graham said in the tone of voice he used when something was wrong. "But where is Daddy *now*?" His eyes welled with tears. For half a year, or more, he hadn't asked that question.

Oh, how *stupid* of me to bring him *here*! Ruth thought, hugging the child while he cried.

Ruth was still in the bathtub when Hannah came to the suite, bringing with her a lot of presents for Graham of the kind *not* suitable for taking on a plane to Europe: an entire village of interlocking blocks, and not just one stuffed animal, but a whole family of apes. They would have to ask the Stanhope to keep the village and the apes for them, which would make it a major inconvenience if they chose to stay in a different hotel.

But Graham seemed completely recovered from how the hotel had triggered his memory of Allan's death. Children were like that— suddenly heartbroken, and then as quickly over it—whereas Ruth now felt resigned to the memories that being in the Stanhope evoked in *her*. She kissed Graham good night; the child was already discussing the room-service menu with Amanda when Ruth and Hannah left for Ruth's reading.

"I hope you're gonna read the good part," Hannah said.

The "good part" to Hannah was the deeply disturbing sex scene with the Dutch boyfriend in the prostitute's window room. Ruth had no intention of *ever* reading that scene.

"Will you see him again, do you think?" Hannah asked her, en route to the Y. "I mean, he's gonna read the book...."

"Will I see *whom* again?" Ruth asked, although she knew very well the "him" Hannah had meant.

"The Dutch boy, whoever he is," Hannah replied. "And don't tell me there wasn't a Dutch boy!"

"Hannah, I never had sex with a Dutch boy."

"My bet is, he's gonna read the book," Hannah went on.

By the time they got to Ninety-second Street and Lexington Avenue, Ruth was almost looking forward to Eddie O'Hare's introduction—at least that would put an end to her having to listen to Hannah.

Of course Ruth had considered that Wim Jongbloed would read *My Last Bad Boyfriend;* she was prepared to be as icy to him as she had to be. *If* he approached her . . . But what had both surprised and relieved Ruth, albeit in an anticlimactic fashion, was that Maarten had informed her that Rooie's murderer had been caught in Zurich. Soon after his capture, the killer had *died*!

Maarten and Sylvia had mentioned this to Ruth rather casually. "I don't suppose they ever found that prostitute's killer, did they?" Ruth had asked them, with feigned indifference. (She'd put the question to them in a recent weekend phone call, together with the usual questions regarding the itinerary for her upcoming trip.) Maarten and Sylvia had explained how they'd missed the news: they were away from Amsterdam—thus the story was secondhand for them—and by the time they heard the details, they'd forgotten that Ruth had been interested in the story.

"In Zurich?" Ruth had asked. So *that* had been the moleman's German-sounding accent—he'd been *Swiss*!

"I think it was Zurich," Maarten had replied. "And the guy had killed other prostitutes, all over Europe."

"But only one in Amsterdam," Sylvia had said.

Only one! Ruth had thought. She'd struggled to make her interest in the case seem enduringly offhand. "I wonder how they caught him," she'd mused aloud.

But the details weren't fresh in Maarten's or Sylvia's memory; the killer had been caught, and then he'd died, a number of years ago.

"A number of *years*!" Ruth had repeated.

"I think there was a witness," Sylvia said.

"I thought there were fingerprints, too—and the guy was very sick," Maarten added.

"Was it asthma?" Ruth asked, suddenly not caring if she gave herself away.

"I think it was emphysema," Sylvia said.

Yes, that could have been it! Ruth thought, but all that really mattered to her was that the moleman had been caught. The moleman was *dead*! And his death made it bearable for Ruth to revisit Amsterdam—the scene of the crime. It was *her* crime, as she remembered it.

Eddie O'Hare was not only on time for Ruth's reading; he was so early that he sat for over an hour in the greenroom, alone. He was much preoccupied with the events of the past few weeks, in which both his mother and father had died—his mother of cancer, which had mercifully moved swiftly, and his father (not as suddenly) upon the occurrence of his fourth stroke within the past three years.

Poor Minty's third stroke had rendered him almost blind, his view of a page narrowed to what he described as "the world as seen through a telescope if you look through the wrong end." Dot O'Hare had read aloud to him before the cancer took her away; thereafter Eddie had read aloud to his father, who complained that his son's diction was inferior to his late wife's.

There was no question regarding *what* to read aloud to Minty. His books were dutifully marked, the pertinent passages underlined in red, and the books themselves were so familiar to the old teacher that no plot summary was necessary. Eddie merely leafed through the pages, reading only the underlined passages. (In the end, the son had *not* escaped the father's soporific method in the classroom.)

Eddie had always believed that the long opening paragraph of *The Portrait of a Lady*, in which Henry James describes "the ceremony known as afternoon tea," was entirely too ceremonious for its own good; yet Minty declared that the passage deserved countless rereadings, which Eddie accomplished with the same shut-down portion of his brain he'd once called upon to get him through his first sigmoidoscopy.

And Minty adored Trollope, who Eddie thought was a sententious bore. Minty loved this passage from Trollope's autobiography best of all: "I do believe that no girl has risen from the reading of my pages less modest than she was before, and that some may have learned from them that modesty is a charm well worth preserving."

Eddie believed that no girl had ever *risen* from reading Trollope at all; he was sure that every girl who fell into Trollope never rose again.

An *army* of girls had perished while reading him—all of them dying in their *sleep*!

Eddie would forever remember walking his father to the bathroom and back after his father couldn't see. Since his third stroke, Minty's fuzzy slippers were held to his unfeeling feet with rubber bands; they squeaked on the floor under his flattened insteps. The slippers, which were pink, had belonged to Eddie's mom, because Minty's feet had shrunk to the degree that his own slippers could not be kept on his feet—not even with rubber bands.

There then came the last sentence of Chapter 44 of *Middlemarch*, which the old schoolteacher had underlined in red, and which his son read aloud in a gloomy voice. Eddie was thinking that George Eliot's sentence might apply to his feelings for Marion or Ruth—not to mention their imagined feelings for *him*. "He distrusted her affection; and what loneliness is more lonely than distrust?"

So what if his father had been a boring teacher? At least he'd marked all the pertinent passages. A student could have done a lot worse than to have taken a course from Minty O'Hare.

The memorial service for Eddie's father, which was held in the non-denominational church on the academy campus, was better attended than Eddie had expected. Not only did Minty's colleagues come—the doddering emeriti among the faculty, those hearty souls who'd out-lasted Eddie's father—but there were two generations of Exeter students on hand. They might have *all* been bored by Minty, at one time or another, but their humble presence suggested to Eddie that his father had been a pertinent passage in all their lives.

Eddie was glad to have found, among his father's uncountable un-derlinings, a passage that seemed to please Minty's former students. Eddie chose the last paragraph from *Vanity Fair*, for Minty had always been a Thackeray man. "Ah! *Vanitas Vanitatum!* which of us is happy in this world? Which of us has his desire? or, having it, is satisfied?—come, children, let us shut up the box and the puppets, for our play is played out."

Then Eddie returned to the matter of his parents' small house; they'd bought it upon Minty's retirement from the academy, when he and Dot (for the first time) had been forced out of faculty housing. The nondescript house was in a part of town Eddie was unfamiliar with—a narrow, claustrophobic street that might have been any street in any small town. His parents must have been lonely there, away from the academy's impressive architecture and the old school's sweeping grounds. The nearest neighbors' house had an unmown lawn, strewn with castaway children's toys; a giant, rusted corkscrew, to which a dog had once been chained, was screwed into the ground. Eddie had never seen the dog.

It seemed cruel to Eddie that his parents had spent their twilight years in such surroundings—their nearest neighbors did not appear to be Exonians. (Indeed, the domestic squalor of the offending lawn had often suggested to Minty O'Hare that his neighbors were the very embodiment of that which the old English teacher most abhorred: a subpar secondary-school education.)

In packing up his father's books—for he'd already put the house up for sale—Eddie discovered his own novels, which were unsigned; he'd neglected to inscribe them to his own parents! The five of them were on a shelf together; it pained Eddie to note that his father hadn't underlined a single passage. And beside his life's work, on the same shelf, Eddie spotted the O'Hare family's copy of Ted Cole's *The Mouse Crawling Between the Walls,* which the clam-truck driver had autographed to near perfection.

It's no wonder Eddie was a wreck when he arrived in New York for Ruth's reading. It had also been a burden to him that Ruth had given him Marion's address. Inevitably, he'd at last reached out to Marion. He had sent her his five novels, which he'd failed to inscribe to his parents; instead he inscribed them to *her,* as follows: "To Marion—Love, Eddie." And with the package, together with the little green form he'd filled out for Canadian customs, he enclosed a note.

"Dear Marion," Eddie wrote, as if he'd been writing her his whole life, "I don't know if you've read my books, but—as you can see— you've never been far from my thoughts." Under the circumstances— namely, that he believed he was in love with Ruth—that was all Eddie had mustered the courage to say, but it was more than he'd said in thirty-seven years.

Upon his arrival in the greenroom at the 92nd Street Y, the loss of his parents, not to mention his pathetic effort to make contact with Marion, had left Eddie virtually speechless. He already regretted sending Marion his books; he was thinking that it would have been more than enough to send her just the titles. (The titles alone now struck him as wretched excess.)

Summer Job
Coffee and Doughnuts
Leaving Long Island
Sixty Times
A Difficult Woman

When Eddie O'Hare finally stepped up to the microphone onstage and addressed the jam-packed Kaufman Concert Hall, he astutely interpreted the reverential hush of the audience. They worshiped Ruth Cole, and the consensus was that *this* book was her best. The audience also knew that this was Ruth's first public appearance since her husband's death. Lastly, Eddie interpreted, there was an *anxious* hush throughout the audience—for there were many souls in the enormous crowd who knew how Eddie could go on and on.

Therefore, Eddie said: "Ruth Cole needs no introduction."

He must have really meant it. He walked forthwith off the stage and took the seat that had been saved for him in the audience, beside Hannah. And throughout Ruth's reading, Eddie stared stoically straight ahead, his gaze falling twelve or fifteen feet to the left of the podium, as if the only way he could endure to look at Ruth was to keep her in the periphery of his vision.

And he never stopped crying, Hannah would say later; Hannah's right knee had got wet because she'd held his hand. Eddie had wept silently—as if every word Ruth uttered was a blow to his heart that he accepted as his due.

He was nowhere to be seen in the greenroom afterward; Ruth and Hannah went out to dinner alone.

"Eddie looked absolutely suicidal," Ruth said.

"He's gaga over you—it's cracking him up," Hannah told her.

"Don't be silly—it's my mother he's in love with."

"Christ! How *old* is your mother?" Hannah asked.

"Seventy-six," Ruth replied.

"It would be obscene to be in love with a seventy-six-year-old!" Hannah said. "It's *you*, baby. Eddie's gaga over you—he *is*!"

"*That* would be obscene," Ruth said.

A man eating dinner with someone who appeared to be his wife kept staring at their table. Ruth said he was staring at Hannah, but Hannah said he was staring at Ruth. In either case, they agreed it was no way for a man eating with his wife to behave.

As they were paying the bill, the man awkwardly approached their table. He was in his thirties, younger than Hannah and Ruth, and he was good-looking despite his hangdog expression, which seemed to affect even his posture. The closer he came to them, the more he stooped. His wife still sat at their table, her head in her hands.

"Jesus! He's gonna hit on you in front of his fucking wife!" Hannah whispered to Ruth.

"Excuse me," the miserable wretch said.

"Yeah, what is it?" Hannah asked. She kicked Ruth under the table— an I-told-you-so sort of kick.

"Aren't you Ruth Cole?" the man asked.

"No shit," Hannah said.

"Yes," Ruth replied.

"I'm embarrassed to bother you," the wretched man mumbled, "but it's my wife and my anniversary, and you're my wife's favorite writer. I know you don't sign books, but I gave my wife your new novel for an anniversary present and we just happen to have it with us. I feel terrible asking you, but would you sign it?" (The wife, abandoned at their table, was on the verge of utter mortification.)

"Oh, for God's sake ..." Hannah started to say, but Ruth jumped to her feet. She wanted to shake the man's hand—and his wife's hand, too. Ruth even smiled as she signed her book. She couldn't have been less like herself. But in the taxi, back to the hotel, Hannah said something to her—leave it to Hannah to make Ruth feel unready to re-enter the world.

"It may have been his anniversary, but he was looking at your breasts," Hannah said.

"He was not!" Ruth protested.

"Everyone does, baby. You better get used to it."

Later, in her suite at the Stanhope, Ruth resisted calling Eddie. Besides, at the New York Athletic Club, they probably refused to answer the phone after a certain hour. Or else they would demand to know, when you called, if you were wearing a coat and tie.

Instead Ruth wrote a letter to her mother, whose Toronto address had become fixed in her memory. "Dear Mommy," Ruth wrote, "Eddie O'Hare still loves you. Your daughter, Ruth."

The Stanhope stationery lent to the letter a formality, or at least a distance, that she hadn't intended. Such a letter, Ruth thought, should begin "Dear Mother," but "Mommy" was what she'd called her mother; and it was what Graham called Ruth, which meant more to Ruth than anything else in the world. She knew she'd re-entered the world the instant she handed the letter to the concierge at the Stanhope—just before leaving for Europe.

"It's to *Canada*," Ruth pointed out. "Please be sure you use the right postage."

"Of course," the concierge said.

They were in the lobby of the Stanhope, which was dominated by an ornate grandfather's clock; it had been the first thing Graham recognized when they'd come into the hotel from Fifth Avenue. Now the porter was wheeling their luggage past the imposing face of the clock. The porter's name was Mel. He'd always been especially attentive to Graham; he'd also been the porter on duty when Allan's body had been removed from the hotel. Probably Mel had helped with the body, but Ruth didn't really want to remember *everything*.

Graham, holding Amanda's hand, followed their luggage out of the Stanhope, onto Fifth Avenue, where their limousine was waiting.

"Good-bye, clock!" Graham said.

As the car was pulling away, Ruth called good-bye to Mel.

"Good-bye, Mrs. Cole," Mel replied.

So *that's* who I am! Ruth Cole decided. She'd never changed her name, of course—she was too famous to change her name. She'd never actually become Mrs. Albright. But she was a widow who still felt married; she was *Mrs.* Cole. I'll be Mrs. Cole forever, Ruth thought.

"Good-bye, Mel's hotel!" Graham called.

They drove away from the fountains in front of the Met, and the flapping flags, and the dark-green awning of the Stanhope, under which a waiter was rushing to attend to the only couple who didn't find the day too cold to be sitting at one of the sidewalk tables. From Graham's view, sunk into the backseat of the dark limo, the Stanhope reached into the sky—maybe even to heaven itself.

"Good-bye, Daddy!" the little boy called.

Better Than Being in Paris
with a Prostitute

Traveling internationally with a four-year-old requires a devout attention to basic idiocies that may be taken for granted at home. The taste
(even the color) of the orange juice demands an explanation. A croissant is not always a *good* croissant. And the device for flushing a toilet,
not to mention exactly how the toilet flushes or what sort of noise it
makes, becomes a matter of grave concern. While Ruth was fortunate
that her son was toilet-trained, she was nonetheless exasperated that
there were toilets the boy didn't dare sit on. And Graham could not
comprehend jet lag, yet he had it; the boy was constipated, but he
couldn't understand that this was a direct result of what he refused to
eat and drink.

In London, because the cars were on the wrong side of the street,
Ruth would not let Amanda and Graham *cross* a street, except to go to
the small park nearby; beyond this unadventuresome expedition, the
boy and his nanny were confined to the hotel. And Graham discovered
that there was starch in the bedsheets at the Connaught. Was starch
alive? he wanted to know. "It *feels* alive," the child said.

As they left London for Amsterdam, Ruth wished that, in London,
she'd been half as courageous as Amanda Merton. The forthright girl
had achieved a measurable success: Graham was over his jet lag, he was
*un*constipated, and he was no longer afraid of foreign toilets—whereas
Ruth had reason to doubt that she'd re-entered the world with even a
vestige of her former authority on display.

While she'd previously taken her interviewers to task for not bothering to read her books before they talked to her, this time Ruth had suffered the indignity in silence. To spend three or four years writing a
novel, and then to waste an hour or more talking to a journalist who
hadn't taken the time to *read* it ... well, if this didn't demonstrate a sizable lack of self-esteem, what did? (And *My Last Bad Boyfriend* wasn't a
long novel, either.)

With a meekness that was most uncharacteristic, Ruth had also tolerated an oft-repeated and utterly predictable question, which had nothing to do with her new novel: namely, how was she "coping" with being a widow, and had she found anything in her actual experience of widowhood to contradict what she'd written about being a widow in her previous work of fiction?

"No," said Mrs. Cole, as she'd begun to think of herself. "Everything is just about as bad as I imagined it."

In Amsterdam, not surprisingly, a *different* "oft-repeated and utterly predictable question" was a favorite among the Dutch journalists. They wanted to know how Ruth had conducted her research in the red-light district. Had she actually hidden in a window prostitute's wardrobe closet and watched a prostitute have sex with a customer? (No, she had *not*, Ruth replied.) Had *her* "last bad boyfriend" been Dutch? (*Absolutely not*, the author declared. But even as she spoke, she was on the lookout for Wim—she was certain he would put in an appearance.) And why was a so-called literary novelist interested in prostitutes in the first place? (She wasn't *personally* interested in prostitutes, Ruth answered.)

It was a shame, most of her interviewers said, that she had singled out *de Wallen* for such scrutiny. Had nothing else about the city caught her attention?

"Don't be provincial," Ruth told her interrogators. "*My Last Bad Boyfriend* is not *about* Amsterdam. The main character isn't *Dutch*. There is simply an *episode* that takes place here. What happens to the main character in Amsterdam compels her to change her life. It's the story of her life that interests me, especially her desire to *change* her life. Many people encounter moments in their lives that convince them to change."

Predictably, the journalists then asked her: What such moments have *you* encountered? And: What changes have you made in *your* life?

"I'm a novelist," Mrs. Cole would say then. "I haven't written a memoir—I've written a novel. Please ask me about my novel."

Reading her interviews in the newspapers, Harry Hoekstra wondered why Ruth Cole put herself through such tedium and trivia. Why be interviewed at all? Surely her books didn't *need* the publicity. Why didn't she just stay at home and start another novel? But I suppose she likes to travel, Harry thought.

He'd already heard her give a reading from her new novel; he'd also seen her on a local television show, and he'd watched her at a book-signing at the Athenaeum, where Harry had cleverly positioned himself behind a bookshelf. By removing no more than a half-dozen titles from the shelf, he could closely observe how Ruth Cole handled her fans. Her most avid readers had formed a line for her autograph, and while Ruth sat at a table signing and signing, Harry had a largely unobstructed view of her profile. Through the window he'd made in the bookshelf, Harry saw that there *was* a flaw in Ruth's right eye—as he'd guessed from her book-jacket photo. And she really *did* have great breasts.

Although Ruth signed books for more than an hour without complaint, there was one mildly shocking occurrence. It suggested to Harry that Ruth was a lot less friendly than she'd at first appeared; indeed, at some level, Ruth struck Harry as one of the angriest people he'd ever seen.

Harry had always been attracted to people who contained a lot of anger. As a police officer, he'd found that *un*contained anger was nothing but a menace to him. Whereas *contained* anger greatly appealed to him, and he believed that people who weren't angry at all were basically unobservant.

The woman who caused the trouble was in line for an autograph; she was elderly, and at the outset she appeared innocent of any wrongdoing, which is only to say she'd done nothing wrong that Harry could *see*. When it was her turn, she presented herself at the front of the line and put on the table an English edition of *My Last Bad Boyfriend*. A shy-looking (and equally elderly) man stood beside her. He was smiling down at Ruth—the old woman was smiling down at Ruth, too. The problem seemed to be that Ruth failed to recognize her.

"Should I inscribe this for you, or for someone in your family?" Ruth asked the old lady, whose smile lessened noticeably.

"To me, please," the old woman said.

She had an innocuous American accent. But there was a false sweetness to the "please." Ruth waited politely ... no, perhaps a *little* impatiently ... for the woman to tell her what her name was. They went on looking at each other, the recognition *not* coming to Ruth Cole.

"My name is Muriel Reardon," the old lady finally said. "You don't remember me, do you?"

"No, I'm sorry," Ruth said. "I don't."

"I last spoke to you at your wedding," Muriel Reardon continued. "I'm sorry for what I said at the time. I'm afraid I wasn't myself."

Ruth went on looking at Mrs. Reardon, the color in her right eye changing from brown to amber. She hadn't recognized the terrible old widow who'd been so certain of herself in her attack, five years ago, for two understandable reasons: she'd had no expectations of ever running into the harpy in *Amsterdam,* and the old hag had remarkably improved her appearance. Quite the opposite of being dead, as Hannah had declared, the wrathful widow had restored herself very nicely.

"It's one of those coincidences that can't be merely a coincidence," Mrs. Reardon was saying, in a way that suggested she was newly religious. She was. In the five years since she'd assaulted Ruth, Muriel had met and married *Mr.* Reardon, who was still beaming beside her, and both Muriel *and* her new husband had become avid Christians.

Mrs. Reardon continued: "Begging your forgiveness was strangely foremost on my mind when my husband and I came to Europe—and here, of all places, I find you! It's a miracle!"

Mr. Reardon overcame his shyness to say: "I was a widower when I met Muriel. We're on a tour to see the great churches and cathedrals of Europe."

Ruth went on looking at Mrs. Reardon in what seemed to Harry Hoekstra an increasingly *un*friendly way. As far as Harry was concerned, Christians always wanted something. What Mrs. Reardon wanted was to dictate the terms of her own forgiveness!

Ruth's eyes had narrowed to the point where no one could have spotted the hexagonal flaw in her right eye. "You remarried," she said flatly. It was the voice she read aloud in—curiously deadpan.

"Please forgive me," Muriel Reardon said.

"What happened to being a widow for the rest of your miserable life?" Ruth asked.

"Please . . ." Mrs. Reardon said.

Mr. Reardon, after fumbling in the pocket of his sports jacket, produced an assortment of note cards with handwriting on them. He seemed to be searching for a specific card, which he couldn't find. Undaunted, he began to read spontaneously. "'For the wages of sin is death,'" Mr. Reardon read, "'but the gift of God is eternal life. . . .'"

"Not *that* one!" Mrs. Reardon cried. "Read her the one about *forgiveness!*"

"I *don't* forgive you," Ruth told her. "What you said to me was hateful and cruel and untrue."

"'For to be carnally minded is death; but to be spiritually minded is life and peace,'" Mr. Reardon read from another card. Although it was not the quotation he was looking for, either, he felt obliged to identify the source. "These are from Paul's letter to the Romans."

"You and your *Romans,*" Mrs. Reardon snapped.

"Next!" Ruth called—for the next person in line had every reason to be impatient with the delay.

"I don't forgive you for not forgiving me!" Muriel Reardon cried out, an *un*-Christian venom in her voice.

"Fuck you and *both* your husbands!" Ruth shouted after her, as her new husband struggled to lead her away. He'd returned the biblical quotations to his jacket pocket—all but one. Possibly it was the quotation he'd been searching for, but no one would ever know.

Harry had assumed that the somewhat shocked-looking man seated beside Ruth Cole was her Dutch publisher. When Ruth smiled at Maarten, it wasn't a smile Harry had seen on Ruth's face before, but Harry correctly interpreted the smile as indicative of a renewed self-confidence. Indeed, it was evidence that Ruth had re-entered the world with *some* of her former assertiveness intact.

"Who was *that* asshole?" Maarten asked her.

"Nobody worth knowing," Ruth replied. She paused then, in mid-signature, and looked around as if she were suddenly curious about who might have overheard her uncharitable remark—meaning *all* her uncharitable remarks. (Was it Brecht who said that sooner or later we begin to resemble our enemies? Ruth thought.)

When Harry saw that Ruth was looking at him, he withdrew his face from the window he'd made in the bookshelf, but not before she'd seen him.

Shit! I'm falling in love with her! Harry thought. He'd not fallen in love before; at first he suspected he was having a heart attack. He abruptly left the Athenaeum; he preferred to die on the street.

When the line for Ruth Cole's autograph had dwindled to only two or three remaining diehards, one of the booksellers asked: "Where's Harry? I saw him here. Doesn't he want his books signed?"

"Who's Harry?" Ruth inquired.

"He's your biggest fan," the bookseller told her. "He also happens to be a cop. But I guess he's gone. It's the first time I've seen him at a signing, and he hates readings."

Ruth sat quietly at the table, signing the last copies of her new novel.

"Even *cops* are reading you!" Maarten said to her.

"Well ..." Ruth replied. She couldn't say more. When she looked at the bookshelf, where she'd seen his face, the window that had been opened amid the books was closed. Someone had replaced the books. The cop's face had vanished, but it was a face she'd never forgotten—the plainclothes cop who'd followed her through the red-light district was following her still!

What Ruth liked best about her new hotel in Amsterdam was that she could get to the gym on the Rokin very easily. What she liked least about it was its proximity to the red-light district—she was less than half a block from *de Wallen*.

And it was awkward for Ruth when Amanda Merton asked if she could take Graham to see the Oude Kerk. (Amsterdam's oldest church, which is thought to have been built in about 1300, is situated in the middle of the red-light district.) Amanda had read in a guidebook that the climb to the top of the Oude Kerk tower was recommended for children—the tower afforded a splendid view of the city.

Ruth had postponed an interview in order to accompany Amanda and Graham on the short walk from their hotel; she'd also wanted to see if climbing the church tower was safe. Most of all, Ruth had wanted to guide Amanda and Graham through *de Wallen* in a way that would provide her four-year-old son with the *least* opportunity of seeing a prostitute in her window.

She thought she knew how to do it. If she crossed the canal at the Stoofsteeg, and then walked nearer the water than the buildings, Graham could scarcely glimpse those narrow side streets where the women in their windows were close enough to touch. But Amanda wanted to buy a souvenir T-shirt that she'd spotted in the window of the Bulldog café; hence Graham got a good look at one of the girls, a prostitute who had briefly left her window on the Trompetterssteeg to buy a pack of cigarettes in the Bulldog. (A very surprised Amanda Merton got an inadvertent look at her, too.) The prostitute, a petite brunette, wore a lime-green teddy with a snap crotch; her high heels were a darker shade of green.

"Look, Mommy," Graham said. "A lady, still getting dressed."

The view of *de Wallen* from the tower of the Oude Kerk was indeed splendid. From the high tower, the window prostitutes were too far away for Graham to discern that they were wearing only their underwear, but even from such a height Ruth could pick out the perpetually loitering men.

Then, as they were leaving the old church, Amanda turned the wrong way. On the horseshoe-shaped Oudekerksplein, several South American prostitutes were standing in their doorways, talking to one another.

"More ladies getting dressed," Graham said absently; he couldn't have cared less about the near-nakedness of the women. Ruth was surprised by his lack of interest; the four-year-old was already of an age where Ruth would no longer let him take a bath with her.

"Graham won't leave my breasts alone," Ruth had complained to Hannah.

"Like everyone else," Hannah had said.

For three consecutive mornings, in his gym on the Rokin, Harry had watched Ruth work out. After she'd spotted him in the bookshop, he'd been more careful in the gym. Harry kept himself busy with the free weights. The heavier barbells and dumbbells were at one end of the long room, but Harry could keep track of Ruth in the mirrors; he knew what her routine was.

She did a series of abdominal exercises on a mat; she did a lot of stretching, too. Harry hated stretching. Then, with a towel around her neck, she rode a stationary bike for half an hour, working up a pretty good sweat. When she was finished with the bike, she did some light lifting, never anything heavier than the two- or three-kilo dumbbells. One day she would work her shoulders and arms, her chest and back the next.

All in all, Ruth worked out for about an hour and a half—a moderately intense, sensible amount of exercise for a woman her age. Even without knowing her squash history, Harry could tell that her right arm was a lot stronger than her left. But what particularly impressed Harry about Ruth's workout was that nothing distracted her, not even the awful music. When she was riding the bike, she had her eyes closed half the time. When she worked out with the weights and on the mat, she seemed to be thinking of nothing at all—not even her next book. Her lips would move as she counted to herself.

In the course of her workout, Ruth drank a liter of mineral water. When the plastic bottle was empty, she never threw it in the trash without screwing the cap back on—a small but distinguishing feature of a compulsively neat person. Harry had no trouble getting a clear fingerprint of her right index finger from one of the water bottles she'd thrown away. And there it was: the perfectly vertical slash. No knife could have cut her so cleanly; it had to have been glass. And the cut was so small and thin that it had almost disappeared; she must have done it when she'd been much younger.

At forty-one, Ruth was ten or more years older than any of the other women in the Rokin gym—nor did Ruth wear the stretched-tight workout gear that the younger women favored. She wore a tucked-in T-shirt and the kind of loose-fitting athletic shorts that are made for men. Ruth was conscious of having more of a belly than she'd had before Graham was born, and her breasts were lower than they used to be, although she weighed exactly what she had when she was still playing squash.

Most of the men in the gym on the Rokin were at least ten years younger than Ruth, too. There was only one older guy, a weight lifter whose back was usually turned to her; what she'd seen of his tough-looking face was partial, briefly glimpsed in the mirrors. He was very fit-looking, but he needed a shave. On the third morning, she recognized him as she was leaving the gym. He was her cop. (Since seeing him in the Athenaeum, Ruth had begun to think of him as her very own policeman.)

Thus—in the lobby of the hotel, upon returning from the gym— Ruth was ill prepared to encounter Wim Jongbloed. After three nights in Amsterdam, she'd almost stopped thinking about Wim; she'd begun to believe he might leave her alone. Now here he was, with what appeared to be a wife and a baby, and he was so *fat* that she'd not known who he was until he spoke. When he tried to kiss her, she made a point of shaking his hand instead.

The baby's name was Klaas. He was in the blob phase of babyhood, his bloated face like something left underwater. And the wife, who was introduced to Ruth as "Harriët with an umlaut," was similarly swollen; she carried some excess fat from her recent pregnancy. The stains on the new mother's blouse indicated that she was still nursing, and that her breasts had leaked. But Ruth quickly judged that Wim's wife had been made *more* wretched by this meeting. Why? Ruth wondered. What had Wim told his wife about Ruth?

"You have a beautiful baby," Ruth lied to Wim's unhappy-looking wife. Ruth remembered how wrecked she'd felt, for a full year after Graham was born. Ruth had great sympathy for any woman with a new baby, but her lie about Klaas Jongbloed's alleged beauty had no discernible effect on the baby's miserable mother.

"Harriët doesn't understand English," Wim told Ruth. "But she's read your new book in Dutch."

So *that* was it! Ruth thought. Wim's wife believed that the bad boyfriend in Ruth's new novel was *Wim*, and Wim had done nothing to discourage this interpretation. Since—in Ruth's novel—the older woman writer is overcome with desire for her Dutch boyfriend, why would Wim have discouraged his wife from believing *that*? Now here was the overweight Harriët with an umlaut, with her leaking breasts, standing beside a very trim and fit Ruth Cole—a very *attractive* older woman, who (Wim's wretched wife believed) was her husband's former lover!

"You told her we were lovers. Is that it?" Ruth asked Wim.

"Well, weren't we—in a way?" Wim replied slyly. "I mean, we slept in the same bed together. You let me do certain things..."

"We never had sex, Harriët," Ruth said to the uncomprehending wife.

"I *told* you—she doesn't understand English," Wim said.

"*Tell* her, damn it!" Ruth said.

"I've told her my own version," Wim replied, smiling at Ruth. Claiming to have had sex with Ruth Cole had evidently given Wim some sort of power over Harriët with an umlaut. Her downcast appearance gave Harriët a suicidal aura.

"Listen to me, Harriët—we were never lovers," Ruth tried again. "I've *not* had sex with your husband—he's lying."

"You need your Dutch translator," Wim told Ruth; he was openly laughing at her now.

That was when Harry Hoekstra spoke to Ruth. She'd been completely unaware that he'd followed her into the hotel lobby, as he had every morning. "I can translate for you," Harry told Ruth. "Just tell me what you want to say."

"Oh, it's *you*, Harry!" Ruth said, as if she'd known him for years and he was her best friend. It wasn't only from the mere mention of Harry the cop at the bookstore that she knew his name; she also remembered it from the newspaper account of Rooie's murder. Besides, she'd *written* his name (taking pains to spell it properly) on the envelope that had contained her eyewitness account.

"Hello, Ruth," Harry said.

"Tell her I never had sex with her lying husband," Ruth said to Harry, who began to speak in Dutch to Harriët—much to Harriët's surprise. "Tell her I let her husband masturbate beside me—that was all," Ruth said. "And he beat off again when he thought I was asleep."

As Harry went on translating, Harriët seemed cheered. She handed the baby to Wim; she said something in Dutch to her husband as she started to leave. When Wim followed her, Harriët said something more.

"She said, 'You hold the baby—he's wet,'" Harry translated for Ruth. "Then she asked him: 'Why did you want me to meet her?'"

As the couple with their baby were leaving the hotel, Wim said something plaintive-sounding to his angry wife. "The husband said, 'I was in her book!'" Harry translated.

Once Wim and his wife and baby were gone, Ruth was left alone with Harry in the lobby—except for a half-dozen Japanese business-men standing at the registration desk, where they'd been mesmerized by the translation exercise they'd overheard. What they'd compre-hended of it was unclear, but they stared in awe at Ruth and Harry— as if they'd just witnessed an example of cultural differences that would be hard to explain to the rest of Japan.

"So ... you're *still* following me," Ruth said slowly to her cop. "Do you mind telling me what I've done?"

"I think you know what you've done. It's not too bad," Harry told her. "Let's take a little walk."

Ruth looked at her watch. "I have an interview here in forty-five minutes," she said.

"We'll be back in time," Harry replied. "It's just a short walk."

"A walk *where*?" Ruth asked him, but she thought she knew.

They left their gym bags with the concierge. Instinctively, Ruth took hold of Harry's arm as they turned onto the Stoofsteeg. It was still early enough in the morning for the two fat women from Ghana to be working there.

"That's her, Harry—you got her," one of them said.

"That's her, all right," the other prostitute agreed.

"Remember *them*?" Harry asked Ruth. She still held his arm as they crossed the canal onto the Oudezijds Achterburgwal.

"Yes," she answered in a small voice.

She'd showered and washed her hair at the gym. Her hair was a little wet, and she was aware that her cotton T-shirt was not quite warm enough for the weather; she'd dressed only for the walk back to her hotel from the Rokin.

They turned onto the Barndesteeg, where the young, moon-faced Thai prostitute stood shivering in her open doorway in an orange slip; she'd grown heavier in the past five years.

"Remember *her*?" Harry asked Ruth.

"Yes," Ruth answered again.

"That's the one," the Thai told Harry. "All she want to do is watch."

The transvestite from Ecuador had left the Gordijnensteeg for a window on the Bloedstraat. Ruth instantly recalled the feel of his baseball-size breasts. But this time there was something so obviously male about him that Ruth couldn't believe she'd ever thought he was a woman.

"I told you she had nice breasts," the transvestite said to Harry. "It took you long enough to find her."

"I stopped looking for a few years," Harry replied.

"Am I under arrest?" Ruth whispered to Harry.

"Of course not!" Harry told her. "We're just taking a little walk."

It was a fast walk—Ruth was no longer cold. Harry was the first man she'd ever been with who walked faster than she did; she almost had to jog to keep up with him. When they turned onto the Warmoesstraat, a man in the doorway of the police station called after Harry—Harry and the man soon were shouting back and forth to each other in Dutch. Ruth had no idea if they were talking about her or not. She guessed not, because Harry never so much as slowed his pace during the short conversation.

The man in the doorway of the police station was Harry's old friend Nico Jansen.

"Hey, Harry!" Jansen had called. "Is this how you're going to spend your retirement, walking around with your girlfriend in your old place of business?"

"She's not my girlfriend, Nico," Harry had called back. "She's my *witness*!"

"Holy shit—you found her!" Nico had shouted. "What are you going to *do* with her?"

"Maybe marry her," Harry had replied.

Harry held her hand across the Damrak, and Ruth took his arm again when they crossed the canal over the Singel. They weren't far from the Bergstraat when she got up the nerve to say something to him.

"You missed one," Ruth told Harry. "There was another woman I talked to—I mean, back in the district."

"Yes, I know—on the Slapersteeg," Harry said. "She was a Jamaican. But she got into some trouble. She's gone back to Jamaica."

"Oh," Ruth replied.

On the Bergstraat, the curtain was drawn across the window to Rooie's room; although it was only midmorning, Anneke Smeets was with a customer. Harry and Ruth waited on the street.

"How did you cut your finger?" Harry asked her. "Was it on some glass?"

Ruth started to tell him the story, then interrupted herself. "But the scar is so small! How did you see it?" He explained that the scar showed up very clearly on a fingerprint, and that—in addition to the Polaroid print coater—she'd touched one of Rooie's shoes, and the doorknob, and a water bottle in the gym.

"Oh," Ruth said. As she went on with the story of how she'd cut herself—"It was the summer when I was four"—she showed him her right index finger with the tiny scar. In order to see it, he had to hold her hand steady in both his hands—she was trembling.

Harry Hoekstra had small, square fingers; he wore no rings. There was almost no hair on the backs of his smooth, muscular hands.

"You're *not* going to arrest me?" Ruth asked again.

"Of course not!" Harry told her. "I just wanted to congratulate you. You were a very good witness."

"I could have saved her if I'd done something," Ruth said, "but I was too afraid to move. I might have made a run for it, or I could have tried hitting him—with the standing lamp, maybe. But I did nothing. I was too afraid to move—I couldn't *move*," she repeated.

"You're lucky you *didn't* move," Harry told her. "He would have killed you both—at least he would have tried to. He was a murderer—he killed eight prostitutes. He didn't kill all of them as easily as he killed Rooie, either. And if he'd killed you, we wouldn't have had a witness."

"I don't know," Ruth said.

"*I* know," Harry told her. "You did the right thing. You stayed alive. You were a witness. Besides, he *almost* heard you—he said there was a moment when he heard *something*. You must have moved a little."

It made the hairs on the backs of Ruth's arms stand up to remember how the moleman had thought he'd heard her—he *had* heard her!

"You talked to him?" Ruth asked quietly.

"Just before he died, yes," Harry said. "Believe me. It's a good thing you were afraid."

The door to Rooie's room opened, and an ashamed-looking man glanced furtively at them before he entered the street. It took Anneke Smeets a few more minutes to pull herself together. Harry and Ruth waited until she'd positioned herself in her window. As soon as she saw them, Anneke opened her door.

"My witness is feeling guilty," Harry explained to Anneke in Dutch. "She thinks she might have saved Rooie, if she hadn't been too afraid to leave the closet."

"The only way your witness could have saved Rooie was to be her *customer*," Anneke replied, also in Dutch. "I mean, she should have been the customer *instead of* the customer Rooie chose."

"I know what you mean," Harry said, but he saw no reason to translate any of this for Ruth.

"I thought you were retired, Harry," Anneke said to him. "How come you're still working?"

"I'm not working," Harry told Anneke. Ruth couldn't even guess what they were talking about.

On their way back to the hotel, Ruth observed: "She's put on a lot of weight, that girl."

"Food is better for you than heroin," Harry replied.

"Did you know Rooie?" Ruth asked.

"Rooie was a friend of mine," Harry told her. "Once we were going to take a trip together, to Paris, but it never happened."

"Did you ever have sex with her?" Ruth dared to ask him.

"No. But I *wanted* to!" Harry admitted.

They crossed the Warmoesstraat again and re-entered the red-light district by the old church. Only a few days earlier, the South American prostitutes had been sunning themselves, but now only one woman was standing in her open doorway. Because of the cooler weather, she'd wrapped a long shawl around her shoulders, yet anyone could see that she wore nothing but a bra and a pair of panties underneath. The prostitute was from Colombia, and she spoke the creative English that had become *de Wallen*'s principal language.

"Holy Mother, Harry! Are you arrestin' dot woman?" the Colombian called.

"We're just taking a little walk," Harry said.

"You said me you was *retired!*" the prostitute called after them.

"I *am* retired!" Harry called back to her. Ruth let go of his arm.

"You're retired," Ruth said to him in the voice she used for reading aloud.

"That's right," the ex-cop answered. "After forty years ..."

"You didn't tell me you were retired," Ruth said.

"You didn't ask," the former Sergeant Hoekstra replied.

"If it's not *as a cop* that you've been interrogating me, in exactly what capacity *have* you been interrogating me?" Ruth asked him. "Just what authority do you have?"

"No authority," Harry said happily. "And I haven't been interrogating you. We've just been taking a little walk."

"You're retired," Ruth repeated. "You look too young to be retired. How old are you, anyway?"

"I'm fifty-eight."

It made the hair stand up on the backs of her arms again, because it was the same age Allan had been when he died; yet Harry had struck her as much younger. Harry didn't look fifty, and Ruth already knew he was very fit.

"You tricked me," Ruth said.

"In the wardrobe closet, when you were looking through the curtain," Harry began, "was it *as a writer* that you were interested, or as a woman—or both?"

"Both," Ruth answered. "You're still interrogating me."

"My point is: it was *as a cop* that I first followed you," Harry told her. "Later, it was as a cop *and* as a man that I was interested in you."

"As a *man?* Are you trying to pick me up?" Ruth asked him.

"It was as a *reader,* too," Harry continued, ignoring her question. "I've read everything you've written."

"But how did you know I was the witness?"

"'It was a room all in red, which the stained-glass lamp shade made redder,'" Harry quoted to her, from her new novel. "'I was so nervous that I wasn't of much use,'" he continued. "'I couldn't even help the prostitute turn the shoes toes-out. I picked up only one of the shoes, and I promptly dropped it.'"

"Okay, okay," Ruth said.

"Your fingerprints were on only one of Rooie's shoes," Harry added.

They were back at the hotel when Ruth asked him: "*Now* what are you going to do with me?"

Harry looked surprised. "I don't have a plan," he admitted.

In the lobby, Ruth easily spotted the journalist who would conduct her last interview in Amsterdam. After that she had a free afternoon; she was going to take Graham to the zoo. She'd made a tentative date to have an early dinner with Maarten and Sylvia before leaving for Paris in the morning.

"Do you like the zoo?" Ruth asked Harry. "Have you ever been to Paris?"

In Paris, Harry chose the Hôtel Duc de Saint-Simon; he had read too much about it *not* to stay there. And he'd once imagined being there with Rooie, which he confessed to Ruth. Harry found that he could tell Ruth everything—even that he'd bought the cross of Lorraine (which he'd given her) for very little money, and that he'd originally bought it for a prostitute who hanged herself. Ruth told him that she loved the cross all the more *because of* the story. (She would wear the cross every day and night they were in Paris.)

Their last night in Amsterdam, Harry had shown her his apartment in the west of the city. Ruth was amazed at how many books he had, and that he liked to cook, and shop for food, and build a fire in his bedroom at night—even when it was warm enough to sleep with the window open.

They lay in bed together with the firelight flickering on the bookshelves. The outside air stirred the curtain; the breeze was both mild and cool. Harry asked about her bigger, stronger right arm, and she told him everything about her history with the sport of squash, which included her penchant for bad boyfriends—the story of Scott Saunders; the story of what kind of man her father was, and how he died.

Harry showed her his Dutch edition of *De muis achter het behang. The Mouse Crawling Between the Walls* had been his favorite book as a child— before his English was good enough to permit him to read almost every author who *wasn't* Dutch in English. He'd read *A Sound Like Someone Trying Not to Make a Sound* in Dutch, too. In bed, Harry read the Dutch translation aloud to her, and she recited it in English for him—from memory. (Ruth knew everything about the moleman by heart.)

When Ruth told Harry the story of her mother and Eddie O'Hare, it didn't surprise her that Harry had read all the Margaret McDermid mysteries—she'd assumed that crime fiction was the *only* fiction that cops ever read—but it astonished her that Harry had read everything by Eddie O'Hare, too.

"You've read my whole family!" Ruth told him.

"Is everyone you know a *writer*?" Harry asked her.

That night, in the west of Amsterdam, she fell asleep with her head on Harry's chest—all the while remembering how he'd played so naturally with Graham at the zoo. First they'd imitated the expressions of the animals, and the sounds the birds made; then they'd described what was different about each creature's smell. But even with her head on Harry's chest, Ruth woke up when it was still dark; she wanted to be back in her own bed before Graham woke up in Amanda's room.

In Paris, it was not a long walk from Harry's hotel on the rue de Saint-Simon to where Ruth was officially staying—at the Lutetia on the boulevard Raspail. In the courtyard of the Duc de Saint-Simon, someone turned on a garden hose early every morning; the sound of the water woke her and Harry. They would quietly get dressed, and Harry would walk with her to her hotel.

While Ruth was interviewed nonstop in the lobby of the Lutetia, Harry would walk Graham to the playground in the Luxembourg gardens, giving Amanda the mornings off—to shop, or to explore on her own; to go to the Louvre, which she did twice, or the Tuileries or Notre-Dame or the Eiffel Tower. After all, the justification for Amanda missing two weeks of school was that accompanying Ruth Cole on a book tour would be educational. (As for what Amanda thought of Ruth staying out all night, Ruth hoped that this was also "educational.")

Not only did Ruth find her French interviewers very agreeable, in part because they'd *all* read *all* her books—and in part because the French journalists *didn't* think it strange (or unnatural or bizarre) that

Ruth Cole's main character was a woman who'd been persuaded to watch a prostitute with her customer—but Ruth also felt that Graham had never been in safer hands than when he was with Harry. (Graham's only complaint about Harry was that, if Harry was a policeman, where was his gun?)

It was a warm, damp evening when Ruth and Harry passed by the red awning and the white stone façade of the Hôtel du Quai Voltaire. There was no one in the tiny café-bar; and on the plaque outside, beside the wrought-iron lamp, the short list of the famous guests who'd stayed in the hotel did not make mention of Ted Cole's name.

"What do you want to *do*, now that you're retired?" Ruth asked the former Sergeant Hoekstra.

"I'd like to marry a rich woman," Harry said.

"Am I rich enough?" Ruth asked him. "Isn't this better than being in Paris with a prostitute?"

In Which Eddie and Hannah Fail to Reach an Agreement

By the time his KLM flight arrived in Boston, the former Sergeant Hoekstra was looking forward to putting a little distance between himself and the ocean. He'd lived his whole life in a country that was below sea level; Harry thought that the mountains of Vermont might be a welcome change.

It had been only a week since Harry and Ruth had parted company in Paris. As a best-selling author, Ruth could afford the dozen or more transatlantic phone calls that she'd made to Harry; yet, given the length of their conversations, it was already an expensive relationship—even for Ruth. For Harry, although he'd not made more than a half-dozen calls from the Netherlands to Vermont, a long-distance relationship that required this much dialogue would soon bankrupt him; at the very least, he feared his retirement would be short-lived. Thus, even before

Harry arrived in Boston, he'd already proposed to Ruth—in his anti-climactic fashion. It was Harry's first proposal of marriage; he had no experience with it.

"I suppose we should get married," he'd told her, "before I'm completely broke."

"Okay—if you really mean it," Ruth had replied. "Just don't sell your apartment, in case it doesn't work out."

Harry had thought this was a sensible idea. He could always rent his apartment to a fellow policeman; especially from an absentee landlord's perspective, the former Sergeant Hoekstra believed that cops would be more reliable than most other tenants.

In Boston, Harry had to pass through U.S. Customs; not seeing Ruth for a week, and now this rite of passage in a foreign country, gave him his first twinge of doubt. Not even *young* lovers got married in the giddy aftermath of fucking their brains out for only four or five days, and then missing each other for only a week! And if *he* was having doubts, what was *Ruth* feeling?

Then his passport was stamped and handed back to him. Harry saw a sign that said the automatic door was out of order, but the door opened nonetheless, admitting him into the New World, where Ruth was waiting for him. The instant he saw her, his doubts vanished, and in the car she said to him: "I was having second thoughts, until I saw you."

She was wearing a fitted olive-green shirt; it clung to her in the manner of a long-sleeved polo shirt, but it was more open at the throat, where Harry could see the cross of Lorraine that he'd given her—the two crosspieces glinting in the brilliant autumn sun.

They drove west for close to three hours, across most of Massachusetts, before turning north into Vermont. That mid-October, the fall foliage was at its peak in Massachusetts, but the colors were more muted—just past their prime—as Ruth and Harry headed north. It struck Harry that the low, wooded mountains reflected the melancholy of the changing season. The faded colors heralded the coming dominance of the bare, mouse-brown trees; soon the evergreens would be the only color against the mouse-gray sky. And in six weeks or less, the changing fall would change again—soon the snow would come. There'd be days when shades of gray would be the only colors amid a prevailing whiteness, which would be brightened by intermittent skies of purplish slate or blue.

"I can't wait to see the winter here," Harry told Ruth.

"You'll see it soon enough," she replied. "The winter here feels like forever."

"I'll never leave you," he said.

"Just don't die on me, Harry," Ruth told him.

Because Hannah Grant hated to drive, she had been involved in more than one compromising relationship. She also loathed spending her weekends alone, which meant that she'd often left Manhattan on a weekend, to visit Ruth in Vermont, in the company of one bad but car-driving boyfriend or another.

At the moment, Hannah was between boyfriends, a condition she rarely tolerated for long, and so she'd asked Eddie O'Hare to be her designated driver for the weekend, even though he would first have to come into Manhattan to pick her up. Hannah believed she was justified in asking Eddie to drive her to Vermont—Hannah *always* believed she was justified. But Ruth had invited her *and* Eddie for the weekend, and Hannah had long believed that there was no such thing as a detour too prolonged or inconvenient to suggest.

She'd been surprised at how easily Eddie was persuaded, but Eddie had a reason of his own to think that a four-hour drive in the same car with Hannah might be beneficial—even providential. Naturally the two friends (if you could call Hannah and Eddie "friends") were dying to talk to each other about what had befallen their *mutual* friend, for Ruth had sincerely shocked both Hannah and Eddie by her announcement that she was in love with a Dutchman, whom she intended to marry—not to mention that the Dutchman was an ex-cop, whom she'd known for less than a month!

When she was between boyfriends, Hannah dressed what she called "down," which is to say she dressed almost as plainly as Ruth, who would never have described Hannah as dressing down. But Eddie noted that Hannah's lank hair had an atypically oily, unwashed look to it, and she wasn't wearing any makeup, which was a sure sign that Hannah was between boyfriends. Eddie knew that Hannah would never have called him and asked him for a ride if she'd had a boyfriend—*any* boyfriend.

At forty, Hannah had lost little of her sexual rawness, which her tired-looking eyes only enlarged. Her tawny, amber-blond hair had turned ash-blond (with Hannah's help), and the pale hollows under her prominent cheekbones served to exaggerate her aura of a constant, predatory hunger. It was a decidedly *sexual* hunger, Eddie thought, glancing sideways at Hannah in the car. And that it had been a while since she'd waxed her upper lip was sexually enhancing. The blond down on her upper lip, which Hannah had the habit of exploring with the tip of her tongue, gave her an animalistic power that provoked in Eddie an unexpected and unwanted sense of arousal.

Eddie O'Hare had never been sexually attracted to Hannah Grant, nor was he attracted to her now; but when Hannah paid less attention to her appearance, her sexual presence announced itself with more brutal force. She'd always been long-waisted and thin, with high, small, shapely breasts, and when she gave in to her slovenliness, it heightened that aspect of herself of which she was (finally) least proud: chiefly, Hannah looked *born* to be in bed with someone—and with someone else, and someone else—again and again. (All in all, she was sexually terrifying to Eddie—and never so much as she was when she was between boyfriends.)

"A fucking Dutch cop! Can you imagine?" Hannah asked Eddie.

All that Ruth had told the two of them was that she'd first seen Harry at one of her book-signings, and that he'd later introduced himself to her in the lobby of her hotel. It infuriated Hannah that Ruth had been nonchalant about Harry being a retired policeman. (Ruth had been more expressive on the subject of Harry being a *reader*.) He'd been a street cop in the red-light district for forty years, but all that Ruth had said was that Harry was *her* cop now.

"Exactly what kind of relationship does a guy like that have with those hookers?" Hannah asked Eddie, who just kept driving, as best he could; he found it impossible not to look at Hannah from time to time. "I hate it when Ruth lies to me, or when she doesn't tell the whole truth, because she's such a *good* liar," Hannah said. "It's her fucking business to make up lies, isn't it?"

Eddie stole another look at her, but he would never interrupt her when she was angry—Hannah angry was a sight that Eddie loved to behold.

Hannah slouched in her seat, the seat belt noticeably parting her breasts while at the same time flattening her right breast into virtual nonexistence. Glancing at her sideways again, Eddie saw that Hannah wasn't wearing a bra. She had on a slinky, soft-looking silk pullover, which was frayed at both cuffs—the turtleneck had lost what elasticity it had ever had. Hannah's thinness was exaggerated by how the turtleneck drooped around her throat. The outline of her left nipple was clearly visible where the seat belt stretched the pullover against her breast.

"I've never heard Ruth sound so happy," Eddie said unhappily; his memory of how positively ecstatic she'd been on the phone nearly caused him to shut his eyes in pain, but he remembered he was driving. To him, the burnt-ochre color of the dead and dying leaves was a morbid reminder that the foliage season was over. Was his love for Ruth dying, too?

"So she's gaga about the guy—that's fucking obvious," Hannah said. "But what do we know about him? What does *Ruth* really know about him?"

"He could be one of those male gold diggers," Eddie suggested.

"No shit!" Hannah cried. "Of *course* he could be! Cops don't make any money unless they're corrupt."

"And he's as old as Allan was," Eddie said. Hearing Ruth sound that happy had half-convinced Eddie that he *wasn't* in love with her, or that he'd fallen out of love with her. It was confusing. Eddie wouldn't really know how he felt about Ruth until he saw her with the Dutchman.

"I never went out with a *Harry*," Hannah said. "It's not like I'm utterly without standards."

"Ruth said that Harry was truly excellent with Graham," Eddie countered. "Whatever that means." Eddie knew that he'd failed Ruth in his insufficient efforts with Graham. He was Graham's godfather in name only. (Ever since he'd spent a whole day with Ruth when *she* was a child, and doubtless because it was also the day Ruth's mother left, Eddie had felt completely devastated in the presence of children.)

"Ruth could be seduced by *anyone* who was 'truly excellent' with Graham," Hannah rejoined, but Eddie doubted that the tactic would ever have worked for him—even if he could have mastered the tactic.

"I understand that Harry has taught Graham how to kick a soccer ball," Eddie offered, in faint praise.

"American kids should learn to *throw* balls," Hannah replied. "It's those fucking Europeans who like to *kick* them."

"Ruth said that Harry was very well read," Eddie reminded her.

"I know that," Hannah said. "What *is* he—a writers' *groupie?* At her age, she shouldn't be vulnerable to that!"

At *her* age? thought Eddie O'Hare, who was fifty-three but looked older. The problem was partly his height—more accurately, his posture—which made him appear slightly stooped. And the crow's-feet at the corners of his eyes extended across the pale indentations of his temples; while Eddie's hairline had not receded, his hair was entirely silver-gray.

In a few years, Eddie's hair would turn white.

Hannah looked sideways at him and his crow's-feet; the latter gave Eddie the appearance of someone who was chronically squinting. He had kept himself thin, but Eddie's thinness added to his age. He was nervously thin, unhealthily thin. He looked like someone who was too worried to eat. And that he didn't drink caused Hannah to think of Eddie as the epitome of boredom.

Still, she would have liked it if he *occasionally* made a pass at her; that he didn't struck Hannah as indicative of his sexual apathy. I must have been nuts to ever imagine Eddie was in love with Ruth! Hannah now thought. Maybe the unfortunate man was in love with old age itself. For how long had he ridiculously carried a torch for Ruth's mother?

"How old would Marion be now?" Hannah asked Eddie, seemingly out of the blue.

"Seventy-six," Eddie answered, without needing to think about it.

"She might be dead," Hannah suggested cruelly.

"Certainly not!" Eddie said, with more passion than he expressed on most subjects.

"A fucking Dutch cop!" Hannah exclaimed again. "Why doesn't Ruth just *live* with him for a while? Why does she have to *marry* the guy?"

"Search me," Eddie replied. "Maybe she wants to be married because of Graham."

Ruth had waited almost two weeks—that is, with Harry actually *in* the Vermont house—before she'd allowed Harry to fall asleep in her bed. She'd been nervous about Graham's reaction to finding Harry there in the morning. She'd wanted the boy to get to know Harry first. But when Graham had finally found Harry in his mother's bed, the boy had matter-of-factly climbed in between them.

"Hi, Mommy and Harry!" Graham had said. (It broke Ruth's heart, because of course she could remember when the boy had said, "Hi,

Mommy and Daddy!") Then Graham had touched Harry and reported to Ruth: "Harry's not cold, Mommy."

Of course, Hannah was jealous in advance of Harry's alleged success with Graham; in her own way, Hannah was good at playing with Graham, too. In addition to Hannah's distrust of the Dutchman, Hannah's innate competitiveness had been aroused by the very idea of a *cop* capturing her godson's trust and affection—not to mention that the cop had captured *Ruth's* trust and affection, too.

"God, isn't this drive fucking *interminable?*" Hannah now asked.

Because he'd started in the Hamptons, Eddie thought of saying that the drive was two and a half hours *more* fucking interminable for him, but all he said was: "I've been thinking about something." Indeed he had!

Eddie had been preoccupied with the thought of buying Ruth's house in Sagaponack. For all the years Ted Cole had lived there, Eddie had studiously avoided Parsonage Lane; he'd not once driven past the house, which was a landmark of the most exciting summer of his life. But after Ted's death, Eddie had gone out of his way to drive on Parsonage Lane. And since the Cole house had been for sale, and Ruth had enrolled Graham in preschool in Vermont, Eddie had taken every opportunity he had to turn onto the lane, where he slowed his car to a crawl. He was not above riding his bicycle past Ruth's Sagaponack house, too.

That the house hadn't yet been sold gave him only the slimmest hope. It was a prohibitively expensive piece of property. Real estate on the ocean side of the Montauk Highway was too pricey for Eddie, who could afford the Hamptons only if he continued to live on the *wrong* side of the highway. To make matters worse, Eddie's two-story, gray-shingled house on Maple Lane was not more than a couple of hundred yards from the remnant of the Bridgehampton railroad station. (While the trains were still in service, all that remained of the station house was the foundation.)

Eddie's view was of his neighbors' porches and their browning lawns, their competing outdoor barbecues and their children's bicycles; it was hardly an ocean view. Eddie couldn't hear the thump of the surf as far inland as Maple Lane. What he heard were screen doors slamming and children fighting and parents shouting angrily at their children; what he heard were dogs, barking dogs. (In Eddie's opinion, there were entirely too many dogs in Bridgehampton.) But what Eddie heard, most of all, were the trains.

The trains passed so near to his house, on the north side of Maple Lane, that Eddie had given up using his small backyard; he kept his barbecue on the front porch, where a grease fire had scorched a section of shingles and blackened the porch light. The trains passed so near that Eddie's bed shook when he was sound asleep, which he rarely was, and he'd installed a door on the cabinet where he kept his wineglasses, because the vibrations caused by the trains would shake the glasses off the shelves. (Although he drank nothing but Diet Coke, Eddie preferred his Diet Coke in a wineglass.) And the trains passed so near to Maple Lane that the neighborhood dogs were always being killed; yet these dogs were replaced with seemingly louder, more aggressive dogs, who barked at the trains with a keener level of complaint than the dead dogs had ever managed.

Compared to Ruth's house, Eddie owned a kennel by the railroad tracks. How it grieved him: not only that Ruth was moving away, but that the monument to the sexual zenith of his life was for sale and he couldn't buy it. He would never have presumed on Ruth's friendship or her sympathy; he hadn't even dreamed of asking her, as a personal favor, to lower her price.

What Eddie O'Hare *had* dreamed about—what had preoccupied his waking hours, too—was asking Hannah to buy the house with him. This dangerous combination of fantasy and desperation was sadly in keeping with Eddie's character. He didn't like Hannah, nor did she like him; yet Eddie wanted the house badly enough that he was about to propose sharing it with her!

Poor Eddie. He knew that Hannah was a slob. Eddie detested messiness to the degree that he paid a cleaning woman not only to clean his modest house once a week but also to *replace* (not merely wash) the pot holders when they were stained. The cleaning woman was also instructed to wash *and iron* the dish towels. And Eddie hated Hannah's boyfriends, long in advance of those predictable moments when Hannah herself would grow to hate them.

He'd already envisioned Hannah's clothes (not to mention her *under*clothes) deposited everywhere about the house. Hannah would swim naked in the pool and use the outdoor shower with the door open. Hannah would throw away or eat Eddie's leftovers in the refrigerator—

while *her* leftovers would grow green and fuzzy before Eddie would take it upon himself to get rid of them. Hannah's half of the phone bill would be appalling, and Eddie would have to pay it all because she would be on assignment in Dubai (or some such place) whenever *any* of the bills arrived. (Besides, Hannah's checks would bounce.)

Hannah would also fight with Eddie over the use of the master bedroom, and win—on the grounds that she needed the king-size bed for her boyfriends and the extra closet space for her clothes. But Eddie had rationalized that he would be happy to use the larger of the guest bedrooms at the end of the upstairs hall. (After all, he'd slept with Marion there.)

And given the advanced age of most of Eddie's female friends, Eddie assumed that he would have to convert what was once Ted Cole's workroom (and later Allan's office) into a *downstairs* bedroom—for some of Eddie's more fragile and infirm older women could not be expected to climb stairs.

Eddie intuited that Hannah would allow him to use the former squash court in the barn as his office; that it had been Ruth's office appealed to him. Since Ted had killed himself in the squash court, the barn was off-limits to Hannah. It wasn't that Hannah had a conscience, but she was superstitious. Besides, Hannah would use the house only on weekends or in the summer, whereas Eddie would live there full-time. That Eddie hoped Hannah would be away *a lot* was the main reason he could delude himself into thinking that he could share the house with her at all. But what an enormous risk he was taking!

"I said I've been thinking about something," Eddie said again. Hannah hadn't been listening.

As she looked at the passing landscape, Hannah's expression hardened from an abject indifference to an overt hostility. When they crossed the border into Vermont, Hannah glared at the very memory of her undergraduate years at Middlebury, as if both the college and the State of Vermont had done her some unpardonable disservice—although Ruth would have said that the chief cause of Hannah's four years of turmoil and depression at Middlebury had been Hannah's promiscuity.

"Fucking Vermont!" Hannah said.

"I've been thinking about something," Eddie repeated.

"Me, too," Hannah told him. "Or did you think I was taking a nap?"

Before Eddie could respond, they glimpsed their first sight of the war memorial in Bennington; it rose like an inverted spike, high above the buildings of the town and the surrounding hills. The Bennington Battle Monument was a flat-sided, chiseled needle that marked the defeat of the British by the Green Mountain Boys. Hannah had always hated it.

"Who could live in this fucking town?" she asked Eddie. "Every time you turn around, there's that giant phallus standing over you! Every guy who lives here has gotta have a big-cock complex."

A big-cock complex? Eddie thought. Both the stupidity and the vulgarity of Hannah's remark offended him. How could he ever have contemplated sharing a house with her?

The current older woman in Eddie's life—a platonic relationship, but for how much longer?—was Mrs. Arthur Bascom. She was still known to everyone in Manhattan as Mrs. Arthur Bascom, although her late husband, the philanthropic Arthur Bascom, had long ago passed away. Mrs. Arthur Bascom—"Maggie" to Eddie, and to her innermost circle of friends—had continued her late husband's philanthropy; yet she was never seen at a black-tie function (the perpetual fund-raisers) without the companionship of a much younger, unmarried man.

In recent months, Eddie had played the role of Maggie Bascom's escort. He'd presumed that Mrs. Bascom had selected him for his sexual inactivity. Lately he wasn't so sure; maybe it was Eddie's sexual *availability* that had attracted Mrs. Arthur Bascom after all, because—especially in his last novel, *A Difficult Woman*—Eddie O'Hare had described, in loving detail, the sexual attentions paid to the older-woman character by the character of the younger man. (Maggie Bascom was eighty-one.)

Regardless of Mrs. Arthur Bascom's exact interest in Eddie, how could Eddie have imagined that he could ever invite her to his *and Hannah's* house in Sagaponack if Hannah was actually *there*? Not only would Hannah be swimming nude, but she would probably invite discussion of the color differences between the ash-blond hair on her head and her darker-blond pubic hair—Hannah had heretofore left the latter alone.

"I suppose I should dye my fucking pubes, too," Eddie could imagine Hannah saying to Mrs. Arthur Bascom.

What *had* he been thinking? If Eddie sought the company of older female friends, he surely did so (in part) because they were reliably more refined than women Eddie's age—not to mention women *Hannah's* age. (By Eddie's standards, not even Ruth was "refined.")

"So what have *you* been thinking about?" Hannah then asked him. In half an hour, or less, they'd be seeing Ruth and meeting her cop.

Maybe I should consider this a little more carefully, Eddie thought. After all, at the end of the weekend, he faced a four-hour drive back to Manhattan with Hannah; there would be time enough to broach the subject of them sharing a house together *then*.

"I forgot what it was I was thinking about," Eddie told Hannah. "It'll come back to me, I'm sure."

"I guess it couldn't have been one of your more overpowering brainstorms," Hannah teased him, although the very idea of sharing a house with Hannah impressed Eddie as one of the *most* overpowering brainstorms he'd ever had.

"On the other hand, maybe it *won't* come back to me," Eddie added.

"Maybe you were thinking about a new novel," Hannah suggested. With the tip of her tongue, she touched the dark-blond down on her upper lip again. "Something about a younger man with an older woman ..."

"Very funny," Eddie said.

"Don't get defensive, Eddie," Hannah told him. "Let's forget, for a moment, your interest in older women...."

"That's fine with me," Eddie said.

"There's another aspect to it that interests me," Hannah continued. "I wonder if the women you see—I mean the ones in their fucking *seventies* or *eighties*—are still sexually active. I mean, do they *wanna* be?"

"*Some* of them are sexually active. Some of them want to be," Eddie answered warily.

"I was afraid you'd say that—that really gets to me!" Hannah said.

"Do you imagine that *you* won't be sexually active in your seventies or eighties, Hannah?" Eddie asked.

"I don't even wanna think about it," Hannah declared. "Let's get back to *your* interest. When you're with one of these old gals—Mrs. Arthur Bascom, say ..."

"I haven't had sex with Mrs. Bascom!" Eddie interrupted.

"Okay, okay—not *yet*, you haven't," Hannah said. "But let's say you do, or you *will*. Or let's say you do it with some other old lady, some old dame in her seventies or eighties. I mean, what are you *thinking*? Are you really *looking* at her and feeling *attracted*? Or are you thinking of someone else when you're with her?"

Eddie's fingers ached; he was gripping the steering wheel harder than he needed to. He was thinking of Mrs. Arthur Bascom's apartment on Fifth Avenue and Ninety-third Street. He was remembering all the photographs—of her as a child, as a young girl, as a young bride, as a young mother, as a not-so-young bride (she was married three times), and as a youthful-looking *grand*mother. Eddie couldn't look at Maggie Bascom and not envision her as she was at every phase of her long life.

"I try to see the whole woman," Eddie said to Hannah. "Of course I recognize that she's old, but there are photographs—or the equivalent of photographs in one's imagination of anyone's life. A *whole* life, I mean. I can picture her when she was much younger than I am— because there are always gestures and expressions that are ingrained, ageless. An old woman doesn't always see herself as an old woman, and neither do I. I try to see her whole life in her. There's something so moving about someone's whole life."

He stopped talking, not only because he'd embarrassed himself but also because Hannah was crying. "No one will ever see *me* that way," Hannah said.

It was one of those moments when Eddie *should* have lied, but he couldn't speak. No one ever *would* see Hannah that way. Eddie tried to imagine her at sixty, not to mention seventy or eighty, when her raw sexuality would be replaced by ... well, by *what*? Hannah's sexuality would *always* be raw!

Eddie took one hand off the steering wheel and touched Hannah's hands. She was wringing them in her lap, and when Eddie touched her, she said: "Keep two hands on the fucking wheel, Eddie. I'm just be- tween boyfriends, at the moment..."

Sometimes it was his capacity for pity that got Eddie into trouble. In a dangerously enlarged part of his heart, Eddie believed that what Hannah truly needed was not another boyfriend but a *good* friend.

"I've been thinking that we might try sharing a house together," Eddie proposed. (It was a good thing he was at the wheel, and not Hannah—she would have driven off the road.) "I was thinking that, together, we could buy Ruth's house in Sagaponack. Of course I don't imagine that we would ... um, *overlap* there together very much of the time."

Naturally Hannah was unsure of exactly *what* Eddie was proposing. In her vulnerable state of mind, Hannah's first reaction was that Eddie was making more than a pass; it sounded to her as if he wanted to *marry* her. But the more Eddie went on, the more confused Hannah became.

" *'Overlap'?*" Hannah asked him. "What does fucking *'overlap'* mean?"

Eddie, seeing her confusion, could not suppress his panic. "You could have the master bedroom!" he blurted. "I'd be happy in the bigger of the guest bedrooms, the one all the way down the hall. And what used to be Ted's workroom, and Allan's office, could very well become a *downstairs* bedroom. I'd be happy with that, too." He paused only for a breath before blurting on: "I know your feelings about the barn, the former squash court. I could work there—that is, make it my office. But the rest of the house—you know, the *whole* house—we'd share. Of course, in the summer we'd have to haggle about weekend guests. You know—your friends or mine! But if you basically liked the idea of a house in the Hamptons, I think that—between the two of us—we could afford it. And *Ruth* would be happy." He was babbling now. "After all, she and Graham could come visit us. It would mean—for *Ruth,* I mean—that she wouldn't have to give up the house altogether. Ruth and Graham *and* the cop, I mean," Eddie added, because he couldn't tell from Hannah's stricken expression if she was still confused by his suggestion or suddenly carsick.

"You mean we'd be fucking *roommates?*" Hannah asked.

"Fifty-fifty!" Eddie cried out.

"But you'd live there full-time, wouldn't you?" Hannah asked, with a shrewdness that Eddie was unprepared for. "How do you figure it's 'fifty-fifty' if I come out for the summer, and for occasional weekends, and you live there fucking full-time?"

I should have known! Eddie thought. Here he'd tried to regard Hannah as a friend and she was already *negotiating* with him! It would never work! If only he'd kept his mouth shut! But what he said was: "I couldn't afford it if you didn't pay half. Probably *both* of us can't afford it, anyway."

"That stupid house can't be worth *that* much!" Hannah said. "What's it cost?"

"A lot," Eddie replied, but he didn't know the answer. More than he could afford by himself—that was all he knew.

"You wanna buy it and you don't know how much it costs?" Hannah asked.

At least she'd stopped crying. Hannah probably made much more money than he did, Eddie reflected. She was increasingly successful as a journalist, if not renowned; many of her topics were too trashy to bring her *renown*. She'd recently done a cover story for a major magazine (not that Eddie believed *any* magazine was "major") about the failure to rehabilitate the inmates in state and federal prisons. In addition to the controversy created by the article, Hannah had been briefly involved with an ex-convict; in fact, the ex-convict had been *Hannah's* last bad boyfriend, which possibly explained her present wrecked condition.

"You could probably afford to buy the whole house by yourself," Eddie told Hannah morosely.

"What would I want with that house?" she asked him. "It's not exactly a fucking treasure trove of memorabilia for *me*!"

I'll never get the house, but at least I won't have to live anywhere with *her*! Eddie was thinking.

"Jesus, you're weird, Eddie," Hannah said.

It was only the first weekend in November, but all along the dirt road that led uphill past Kevin Merton's farm to Ruth's house, the trees had lost their leaves. The bare branches of the stone-gray maples and the bone-white birches seemed to be shivering in anticipation of the coming snow. It was already cold. When they got out of the car in Ruth's driveway, Hannah stood hugging herself while Eddie opened the trunk. Their suitcases *and* their coats were in the trunk; they'd not needed their coats in New York.

"Fucking Vermont!" Hannah said again, her teeth chattering.

The sound of someone splitting wood drew their attention. Two or three cords of unsplit hardwood were dumped in the yard by the kitchen entrance; beside them was a smaller, neater woodpile-in-progress. At first Eddie thought that the man splitting wood and stacking the split logs was Ruth's caretaker, Kevin Merton—that's who Hannah thought he was, too, until something about the wood-splitter invited her to give him a closer look.

He was so intent on his task that he'd not noticed the arrival of Eddie's car. The man, in just a pair of jeans and a T-shirt, was working hard enough so that he didn't feel the cold; in fact, he was sweating. And he had a system for splitting and stacking the wood. If a log wasn't too big around, he would set it vertically on the chopping block and split it lengthwise with an ax. If it was too big—and he knew this at a glance—he would set the log on the block and then split it with a wedge and a maul. Although handling the tools seemed to be second nature to him, Harry Hoekstra had been splitting wood for only a week or two; he'd never done it before.

Harry loved doing it. With each powerful stroke of his ax or his maul, he envisioned the fires he would build. And he appeared to Hannah and Eddie to be both strong enough and sufficiently engaged by his task to have gone on splitting wood all day. He looked as if he could go on doing *anything* all day—or all night, Hannah thought. She suddenly wished she'd waxed her lip, or at least washed her hair and put on a little makeup; she wished she'd worn a bra, and some better clothes.

"It must be the Dutchman, Ruth's cop!" Eddie whispered to Hannah.

"No shit," Hannah whispered back. She momentarily forgot that Eddie didn't know her private game with Ruth. "Didn't you hear that sound?" Hannah asked Eddie, who looked bewildered—as usual. "My panties, sliding to the ground," Hannah told him. "*That* sound."

"Oh," Eddie said. What a vulgar woman Hannah was! Thank God he wouldn't be sharing a house with her!

Harry Hoekstra had heard their voices. He dropped his ax and approached them; they stood like children, afraid to stray from the car, as the ex-cop walked up and took Hannah's suitcase from her shivering hand.

"Hello, Harry," Eddie managed to say.

"You must be Eddie and Hannah," Harry said to them.

"No shit," Hannah said, but her voice was uncharacteristically little-girlish.

"Ruth said you'd say that!" Harry told her.

Okay, *now* I get it—who *wouldn't* get it? Hannah was thinking. I wish I'd met him first! Hannah was *really* thinking. But a part of her, which always undermined her outward and only *seeming* self-confidence, told Hannah that even if she *had* met Harry first, he wouldn't have been interested in her—at least not for more than one night.

"It's nice to meet you, Harry," was all that Hannah was able to say.

Eddie saw Ruth coming outside to greet them, her arms wrapped around herself in the cold. She'd spilled some flour on her jeans, and there was a touch of flour on her forehead, where she'd pushed aside her hair with the back of her hand.

"Hi!" Ruth called to them.

Hannah had never seen Ruth look like this; it was something beyond being happy.

It's what love is, Eddie realized; he'd never felt so depressed. Looking at Ruth, Eddie wondered what had ever made him think she resembled Marion—how had he even imagined he could be in love with her?

Hannah glanced back and forth; at first covetously, at Harry—then enviously, at Ruth. They're in fucking love! she realized, hating herself.

"You've got flour on your forehead, baby," Hannah told Ruth, kissing her. "Did you hear that sound?" Hannah whispered to her old friend. "My panties, sliding to the ground—no, actually *hitting* the ground!"

"Mine, too," Ruth told her, blushing.

Ruth's got it, Hannah thought—the life she's always wanted. She's got it. But all Hannah said to Ruth was: "I gotta wash my hair, baby. And maybe put on a little makeup." (Hannah had stopped looking at Harry—she simply couldn't look at him.)

Then Graham burst out the kitchen door and ran to them. He grabbed Hannah around her hips, almost knocking her down; it was a welcome distraction. "Who's this brat?" Hannah cried. "This can't be my very own *godkid*—he's too big! Who *is* this brat!"

"It's me! It's *Graham*!" Graham yelled.

"*You* can't be Graham—you're too *big*!" Hannah told him, picking him up and kissing him.

"Yeah, it's me—it's Graham!" Graham shouted.

"Say 'yes' not 'yeah,' baby," Hannah whispered to the boy.

"Yes, it's me—it's Graham!" the boy repeated.

"Come show me to my room, Graham," Hannah said to him. "And help me turn on the shower, or the bathtub—I gotta wash my hair."

"Have you been crying, Hannah?" the boy asked. Ruth looked at Hannah, who looked away. Harry and Eddie were standing by the kitchen door, admiring Harry's woodpile-in-progress.

"Are you okay?" Ruth asked her friend.

"Yeah. Eddie just asked me to live with him, only he didn't mean it that way," Hannah added. "He just wanted me to be his roommate."

"That's odd," Ruth remarked.

"Oh, you don't know the half of it!" Hannah told her, kissing Graham again.

Graham felt heavy in Hannah's arms—she wasn't used to carrying a four-year-old. Hannah turned toward the house to find her room, to take a shower or a bath, to soak herself in her freshest memory of what love looked like—just in case it might one day happen to her.

It wouldn't happen, Hannah knew.

A Happy Couple,
Their Two Unhappy Friends

Ruth Cole and Harry Hoekstra were married on Thanksgiving morning in the hardly used living room of Ruth's Long Island house. Ruth could think of no better way to say good-bye to the house than to get married in it. The front and upstairs halls were lined with stacks of cardboard boxes, which were labeled for the movers. Every piece of furniture was tagged with either a red or a green tag; red meant that the movers should leave it, green meant they should take it to Vermont.

In the event that the Sagaponack house was still not sold by the summer, Ruth would rent it. She'd tagged most of the furniture to stay; she didn't even *like* most of it. The house in the Hamptons had never been a happy one for Ruth, except when she'd lived there with Allan. (She rarely associated Allan with the Vermont house, which was just as well.)

Eddie saw that all the photographs had been taken down from the walls; they must have been packed in some of the cardboard boxes. Unlike the last time Eddie had seen the house stripped of photographs, the picture hooks had also been removed; the holes in the walls had been filled, and the walls had been freshly painted over or newly wall-papered. A potential buyer would never know how many photographs had once hung there.

Ruth told Eddie and Hannah that she'd "borrowed" the minister for the wedding service from one of the Bridgehampton churches. He was a big, baffled-looking man with a hearty handshake and a booming baritone voice, which resonated throughout the downstairs of the house and caused the settings on the dining-room table to rattle. Conchita Gomez had already set the table for Thanksgiving dinner.

Eduardo gave the bride away. Eddie was Harry's best man. Hannah was Ruth's maid of honor, which she'd now been twice. At Ruth's first wedding, it had been Eddie who'd given the bride away; he was relieved not to do so again. Eddie preferred being best man; even though he'd known Harry for less than a month, Eddie had grown very fond of the Dutchman. Hannah was also very fond of Harry, but she still had trouble looking at him.

Harry had picked a poem to read. Not knowing that Allan had instructed Eddie to read a Yeats poem at Allan's own memorial service, Harry chose a Yeats poem for his and Ruth's wedding. Although the poem made Ruth and Hannah *and* Eddie cry, Ruth loved Harry all the more for it. It was the poem about "being poor," which (compared to Ruth) Harry certainly was; and Harry read it with the uncompromising vigor with which a first-time policeman might read a criminal his rights.

The poem was called "He Wishes for the Cloths of Heaven," and Eduardo and Conchita held hands during Harry's recitation—as if they were being married all over again.

> Had I the heavens' embroidered cloths,
> Enwrought with golden and silver light,
> The blue and the dim and the dark cloths
> Of night and light and the half-light,
> I would spread the cloths under your feet:
> But I, being poor, have only my dreams;
> I have spread my dreams under your feet;
> Tread softly because you tread on my dreams.

Graham was the ring bearer, but he'd misheard the word. The boy expected to be the ring *burier*. Thus, when it came time for him to hand over the rings, Graham was outraged that an important part of the wedding had been forgotten. When was he supposed to *bury* the rings, and where? After the service, since Graham was in despair over what he believed was the botched symbolism of the rings, Ruth let the boy bury her and Harry's rings at the roots of the privet that towered over the swimming pool. Harry paid close attention to the burial site, so that after a certain solemn passage of time, Graham could be shown where to dig the rings up.

Otherwise, Ruth's second wedding went without a hitch. Only Hannah noticed that neither Ruth nor Eddie seemed to be on the lookout for Ruth's mother. If Marion was on their minds, they weren't showing it. Marion had rarely been much on Hannah's mind; Hannah, of course, had never met Ruth's mother.

The Thanksgiving turkey, which Ruth and Harry had brought from Vermont, would have fed another family in addition to Ruth and Harry and Hannah and Eddie and Eduardo and Conchita; Ruth sent Eduardo and Conchita home with half the leftovers. Graham, suspicious of turkey, demanded a grilled-cheese sandwich instead.

In the course of the long dinner, Hannah casually inquired of Ruth how much she was asking for the Sagaponack house. The sum was so staggering that Eddie spilled a generous portion of cranberry sauce in his lap, whereas Hannah coolly said to Ruth: "Maybe that's why you haven't sold it yet. Maybe you oughtta drop the price down, baby."

Eddie had already given up hope that the house would ever be his; he'd certainly given up wanting to share it with Hannah, who was still "between boyfriends" but who nonetheless managed to make herself beautiful for the entire Thanksgiving weekend. (Ruth had noticed that Hannah went to considerable efforts to make herself pretty around Harry.)

Now that Hannah was once more paying attention to her appearance, Eddie ignored her—her prettiness meant little to him. And Ruth's unmistakable happiness had dampened Eddie's yearlong ardor for her; he was back in love with Marion, where he belonged. But what hope had he of seeing or even hearing from Marion? It had been about two months since he'd sent her his books—he'd not heard a word. Eddie had given up expecting to hear from Marion, as had Ruth. (Marion also hadn't answered Ruth's letter.)

Yet, after almost forty years, what was there to expect? That Marion would deliver a testimonial to her conduct in Toronto? That she would send them an essay on her experiences with expatriation? Surely not even Ruth and Eddie could have *expected* Marion to show up for Ruth's second wedding. "After all," as Hannah whispered to Harry while he refilled her wineglass, "she didn't show up for the first one."

Harry knew when to leave a subject alone. He simply began, in his best impromptu fashion, a kind of unstoppable ode to firewood. No one knew how to respond. All that anyone could do was listen. In fact, Harry had borrowed Kevin Merton's pickup truck and hauled a half-cord of Vermont hardwood to Long Island.

Harry was a trifle obsessed with firewood, Eddie had observed. Eddie had not been exactly fascinated by Harry's wood discussion, which Harry had carried on, at length, over what remained of Thanksgiving dinner. (Harry was still talking about firewood when Eduardo and Conchita went home.) Eddie vastly preferred it when Harry talked about books. Eddie hadn't met many people who'd read as many books as Harry had—excepting Eddie's departed father, Minty.

After dinner, while Harry and Eddie did the dishes, and Hannah got Graham ready for bed and prepared to read him a bedtime story, Ruth stood outside under the stars by the swimming pool; the pool had been partially drained and covered for the coming winter. In the darkness, the U-shaped border of privet that surrounded the pool served as a vast window frame that enclosed her view of the stars.

Ruth could scarcely remember when the swimming pool and the encircling hedge hadn't been there, or when the lawn had been the unmown field that her father and mother had argued about. Now it occurred to Ruth that, on other cold nights—when someone else was doing the dishes, and her father or a babysitter had been putting *her* to bed with a story—her mother must have stood in this yard, under these same pitiless stars. Marion would not have looked to the heavens and thought herself as lucky as her daughter was.

Ruth knew she'd been lucky. My next book should be about fortune, she thought: about how fortune and misfortune were unequally distributed, if not at birth then in the course of circumstances beyond our control; and in the seemingly random pattern of colliding events—the people we meet, when we meet them, and if or when these important people might chance to meet someone else. Ruth had had only a *little misfortune*. Why was it that her mother had had such *a lot*?

"Oh, Mommy," Ruth said, to the cold stars, "come enjoy your grandson while you still can."

Upstairs in the master bedroom—in fact, on the same king-size bed where she'd made love to the late Ted Cole—Hannah Grant was still *trying* to read a bedtime story to the grandson Ted never knew. Hannah hadn't made much progress; the rituals of teeth-brushing and pajama-choosing had taken longer than she'd expected. Ruth had told Hannah that Graham was crazy about the Madeline books, but Graham wasn't so sure.

"Which one am I crazy about?" Graham inquired.

"All of them," Hannah said. "Pick the one you want and I'll read it."

"I don't like *Madeline and the Gypsies,*" Graham informed her.

"Good. We won't read that one, then," Hannah said. "I don't like it, either."

"Why?" Graham asked her.

"For the same reason you don't like it," Hannah answered. "Pick one you like. Pick a story, any story."

"I'm tired of *Madeline's Rescue,*" Graham told her.

"Fine. I'm sick of it, too, actually," Hannah said. "Pick one you like."

"I like *Madeline and the Bad Hat,*" the boy decided, "but I don't like Pepito—I really don't like him."

"Isn't Pepito in *Madeline and the Bad Hat?*" Hannah asked.

"That's what I don't like about it," Graham answered.

"Graham, you gotta pick a story you *do* like," Hannah said.

"Are you getting frustrated?" Graham asked her.

"Me? Never," Hannah said. "I got all day."

"It's night," the boy pointed out. "The day's over."

"How about *Madeline in London?*" Hannah suggested.

"Pepito's in that one, too," Graham said.

"How about just plain old *Madeline,* the original *Madeline?*"

"What's 'original' mean?" Graham asked.

"The first one."

"I've heard that one too many times," Graham said.

Hannah hung her head. She'd had a lot of wine with dinner. She truly loved Graham, who was her only godchild, but there were times when he confirmed Hannah's decision to never have children.

"I want *Madeline's Christmas,*" Graham finally announced.

"But it's only Thanksgiving," Hannah said. "You wanna Christmas story on Thanksgiving?"

"You said I could pick any one I wanted."

Their voices carried downstairs to the kitchen, where Harry was scrubbing the roasting pan. Eddie was drying a spatula by absently waving it in the air. He'd been speaking to Harry on the subject of tolerance, but he appeared to have lost his train of thought. Their conversation had begun with the issue of *in*tolerance (largely racial and religious) in the United States, but Harry sensed that Eddie had drifted into a more personal area of discussion; in fact, Eddie was on the verge of confessing his intolerance of *Hannah*, when Hannah's very own voice, in her dialogue with Graham, distracted him.

Harry knew about tolerance. He would not have argued with Eddie, or with one of Eddie's fellow citizens, that the Dutch are more tolerant than most Americans, but Harry believed this to be the case. He could sense Hannah's intolerance of Eddie, *not only* because (in her view) Eddie was pathetic, and because of the sameness of his infatuation with older women, but also because Eddie wasn't a famous writer.

There is no intolerance in America that compares to the peculiarly American intolerance for lack of success, Harry thought. And while Harry had no fondness for Eddie's writing, he liked Eddie a lot, especially because of Eddie's abiding affection for Ruth. Admittedly, Harry was puzzled by the *nature* of Eddie's adoration; the source of it must be the missing mother, Harry guessed—for the ex-cop could tell that what Ruth and Eddie had most in common was Marion's absence. Her absence was a fundamental part of their lives, like Rooie's daughter.

As for Hannah, she called for more tolerance than even the Dutchman was accustomed to bestowing. And Hannah's affection for Ruth was less certain than Eddie's. Moreover, in the way that Hannah looked at Harry, the former Sergeant Hoekstra saw something too familiar. Hannah had the heart of a hooker—and a prostitute's heart, Harry knew, was *not* the proverbial heart of gold. A prostitute's heart was chiefly a calculating heart. An affection that was calculated was never trustworthy.

It's not the easiest thing to meet the friends of someone you've fallen in love with, but Harry knew how to keep his mouth shut and when to be just an observer.

While Harry set a stockpot to boil on the stove, Eddie inquired of the former policeman what plans he had for enjoying his retirement— for it still puzzled Eddie (and Hannah) as to what Harry might find to *do* with himself. Would something in law enforcement in Vermont ever interest him? Harry was such an eager yet discriminating reader— might he try to write a novel himself one day? And it was evident that he liked to work with his hands. Would some sort of outdoor job appeal to him?

But Harry told Eddie that he hadn't retired to look for another job. He wanted to read more; he wanted to travel, but only when Ruth was free to travel with him. And although Ruth was a halfway-decent cook—that was her own description—Harry was a better cook, and he was the one in the family who had the time to do the grocery shopping. Moreover, Harry was looking forward to doing a lot of things with Graham.

It was exactly what Hannah had privately confided to Eddie: Ruth had married a housewife! What writer wouldn't want to have his or her own housewife? Ruth had called Harry her very own policeman, but Harry was really Ruth's very own *housewife*.

When Ruth came in from outside, her hands and face were cold, and she warmed herself by the stockpot, which had begun to bubble.

"We'll have turkey soup all weekend," Harry told her.

When the dishes were done, Eddie sat with Ruth and Harry in the living room, where the couple had been married only that morning but where Eddie was given the impression that Ruth and Harry had known each other forever; they *would* know each other forever, Eddie felt certain. The newlyweds sat on the couch—Ruth sipping her wine, Harry drinking his beer. Upstairs they could hear Hannah reading to Graham.

> It was the night before Christmas
> And all through the house
> Not a creature was stirring
> Not even the mouse.

> For like everyone else in that house which was old
> The poor mouse was in bed with a miserable cold.
> And only
> Our brave little Madeline
> Was up and about
> And feeling
> Just fine.

"That's how I feel," Harry said. "Just fine."

"Me, too," Ruth said.

"To the lucky couple," said Eddie O'Hare, toasting them with his Diet Coke.

The three friends raised their glasses. There was the odd, ongoing pleasure of Hannah's voice, reading to Graham. And Ruth thought again of how lucky she'd been, how she'd suffered only a *little misfortune.*

Over that long Thanksgiving weekend, the happy couple dined only once more with Hannah and Eddie, their two unhappy friends.

"They've been fucking all weekend—I'm not kidding," Hannah whispered to Eddie, when he came to dinner Saturday night. "I swear, they invited me so that I could look after Graham while they snuck off and *did* it! No wonder they didn't go on a honeymoon—they didn't *need* to! Making me the maid of honor was just an excuse!"

"Maybe you're imagining things," Eddie said, but Hannah truly had been put in an unusual position, at least "unusual" for her. She was in Ruth's house without a boyfriend, and Hannah was keenly aware that if Ruth and Harry *weren't* having sex every minute, they obviously *wanted* to.

In addition to a beet salad, Harry had made a terrific turkey soup; he'd baked some cornbread, too. To everyone's surprise, Harry persuaded Graham to try a little of the soup, which the boy ate with a grilled-cheese sandwich. They were still eating when Ruth's hardworking real estate agent knocked on the door, bringing with her a bitter-looking woman who was introduced to them all as a "potential buyer."

The agent apologized to Ruth for not calling first, not to mention not making an appointment, but the so-called potential buyer had just heard that the house was on the market and she'd insisted on seeing it; she was on her way back to Manhattan that very night.

"To beat the traffic," the potential buyer said. Her name was Candida and her sourness emanated from her pinched-together mouth, which was so tightly closed around itself that it must have hurt her to smile—laughter was unthinkable, from such a mouth. Candida might have been as pretty as Hannah once—she was still as thin, and as fashionably attired—but she was now at least Harry's age, although she looked older; and she seemed more interested in assessing the people at the dining-room table than in the house.

"Is someone getting divorced?" Candida asked.

"Actually, they just got married," Hannah said, pointing to Ruth and Harry. "And we've never been divorced *or* married," Hannah added, indicating Eddie and herself.

Candida glanced questioningly at Graham. In Hannah's answer, there'd been no explanation regarding where *Graham* had come from. And no explanation would be forthcoming, Hannah decided, staring the sour-looking woman down.

On the dining-room sideboard, where the remains of the salad course attracted a further look of disapproval from Candida, there was also a copy of the French translation of *My Last Bad Boyfriend*, which was of great sentimental value to Ruth and Harry—for they looked upon *Mon dernier voyou* as a fond memento of their falling in love in Paris. The way Candida looked at the novel implied her disapproval of French, too. Ruth hated her. Probably the real estate agent also hated her, and right now the agent was embarrassed.

A hefty woman who was inclined to chirp, the agent apologized again for intruding on their dinner. She was one of those women who rush into real estate after their children have flown the nest. She had a shrill, insecure eagerness to please that was more in keeping with the endless providing of peanut-butter-and-jelly sandwiches than with the selling or buying of houses; yet her enthusiasm, if fragile, was not feigned. She truly wanted everyone to like everything, and since this happened rarely, the real estate agent was easily given to sudden tears.

Harry offered to turn the lights on in the barn, so that the potential buyer could see the office space on the second floor, but Candida announced that she wasn't looking for a house in the Hamptons because she wanted to spend time in a barn. She wanted to look around upstairs—she was most interested in bedrooms, Candida said—and so the agent traipsed off with her. Graham, who was bored, went after them.

"My fucking underwear's all over the guest-room floor," Hannah whispered to Eddie, who could imagine it—who had *already* imagined it.

When Harry and Ruth went into the kitchen to fuss with the dessert, Hannah whispered to Eddie: "You know what they do in bed together?"

"I can *imagine* what Ruth and Harry do in bed together," Eddie whispered to Hannah, in response. "I'm sure I don't need to be *told*."

"He *reads* to her," Hannah whispered. "It goes on for *hours*. Sometimes she reads to him, but I can hear him better."

"I thought you said they fucked all the time."

"I meant all day. At night, he *reads* to her—it's sick," Hannah added.

Once more, Eddie was overcome with envy and longing. "Your average housewife doesn't do that," he whispered to Hannah, to which she responded with a drop-dead glare.

"What are you two whispering about?" Ruth called from the kitchen.

"Maybe we're having an affair," Hannah answered, which caused Eddie to cringe.

They were eating the apple pie when the real estate agent brought Candida back into the dining room—Graham trailing malevolently behind them. "It's too much house for me," Candida announced. "I'm divorced." The agent, in hurrying after her departing client, gave Ruth a look full of imminent tears.

"Did she have to *say* she was divorced?" Hannah asked. "I mean, who couldn't tell she was divorced?"

"She looked at one of the books Harry is reading," Graham reported. "And she stared at your bra and your underpants, Hannah."

"There are people who do that, baby," Hannah said.

That night Eddie O'Hare fell asleep in his modest house on the north side of Maple Lane, where the tracks of the Long Island Rail Road ran not more than two hundred feet from the headboard of his bed. He was so tired—for tiredness often overcame him when he was depressed—that he was not awakened by the passing of the eastbound 3:21. At that hour of the morning, the eastbound train usually woke him, but on this particular Sunday morning he slept right through ... that is, until the westbound passage of the 7:17. (On weekdays, Eddie was awakened earlier than this every morning—by the westbound 6:12.)

Hannah called him when he was still making coffee.

"I gotta get outta here," Hannah whispered. She'd tried to get a seat on the jitney, but the buses were booked solid. She had earlier planned to leave that evening on the westbound 6:01 to Penn Station. "But I gotta leave sooner than that," Hannah informed him. "I'm going nuts—the lovebirds are driving me crazy. I figured you knew the trains."

Oh, yes—Eddie knew the trains. As for an afternoon train, there was a westbound 4:01 on Saturdays, Sundays, and holidays. You could almost always get a seat in Bridgehampton. Nevertheless, Eddie warned Hannah that if the train was unusually crowded, she might have to stand.

"You think some guy won't offer me his seat, or at least let me sit in his lap?" Hannah asked. The thought of this further depressed Eddie, but he agreed to pick up Hannah and drive her to the Bridgehampton station. The foundation, which was all that remained of the derelict station, was virtually next door to Eddie's house. And Hannah told Eddie that Harry had already promised to take Graham for a walk on the beach in the late afternoon—at the exact same time Ruth had declared she wanted to take a long bath.

There was a cold rain that Sunday at the end of the Thanksgiving weekend. In her bath, Ruth remembered that it was the anniversary of the night her father had made her drive him to the Stanhope, where Ted had taken so many of his women. En route he'd told her the story of what had happened to Thomas and Timothy, while Ruth had kept her eyes on the road. Now Ruth stretched out in her bath, hoping that Harry had dressed himself and Graham properly for their walk on the beach in the rain.

When Eddie picked up Hannah, the Dutchman and the boy were getting into Kevin Merton's pickup truck in their oilskin slickers and their broad-brimmed sou'wester hats. Graham also wore a knee-high pair of rubber boots, but Harry had on his familiar running shoes, which he never cared about getting wet. (What had worked for him in *de Wallen* would suffice for the beach.)

Because the weather was bad, only a modest number of New Yorkers were returning to the city on the late-afternoon train; many more of them had left earlier. By the time it arrived in Bridgehampton, the westbound 4:01 was less than packed.

Hannah said: "At least I won't have to give up my virginity or something, just to get a fucking seat."

"Take care of yourself, Hannah," Eddie told her—with genuine concern, if not total affection.

"You're the one who should take care of himself, Eddie."

"I know how to take care of myself," Eddie protested.

"Let me tell you something, my funny friend," Hannah said. "Time doesn't stop." She took his hands and kissed him on both his cheeks. It was what Hannah did, instead of a handshake. Sometimes she'd fucked people instead of shaking their hands.

"What do you mean?" Eddie asked.

"It's been almost forty years, Eddie. It's time you got over it!"

Then the train left and took her away. The westbound 4:01 left Eddie standing in the rain, where Hannah's remarks had turned him to stone. Her remarks were of the nature of such a long-standing sorrow that Eddie carried them with him throughout the inattentive cooking and eating of his Sunday-night supper.

"Time doesn't stop" echoed in Eddie's mind long after he'd plopped a marinated tuna steak on his outdoor grill. (The gas barbecue, on the front porch of Eddie's unimpressive house, was at least protected from the rain.) "It's been almost forty years, Eddie." Eddie repeated this to himself while he ate his tuna steak, together with a boiled potato and a handful of boiled frozen peas. "It's time you got over it!" he said aloud, as he washed his one dish and his wineglass. When he wanted another Diet Coke, Eddie was so despondent that he drank straight from the can.

The house trembled at the passing of the westbound 6:01—the later but not the latest of the westbound Sunday trains. "I hate trains!" Eddie shouted, for not even his nearest neighbor could have heard him above the noise of the clattering train.

The whole house shook again for the passing of the 8:04, which was indeed the last of the westbound Sunday trains. "Fuck you!" Eddie yelled pointlessly.

No kidding—it was time he got over it. But he would never get over Marion. Eddie knew he would never get over her.

Marion at Seventy-Six

Maple Lane, appropriately, is lined for half its length by dozens of old maple trees. A few other types of trees—an oak or two, some decorative Bradford pears—are mixed in with the maples. Approaching from the east, one forms a primary impression that is favorable. Maple Lane seems to be a well-shaded, small-town street.

Cars are parked in driveways—some residents park on the street, under the trees—and the presence of children is indicated by the occasional bike or trike or skateboard. Everything speaks of a comfortable if not grand middle-class population. The dogs, unfortunately, speak for themselves—and loudly. Indeed, the dogs watch over what is the heart of Eddie O'Hare's neighborhood with a protectiveness that suggests to the outsider or passerby that these modest-looking houses must be vastly more chock-full of wealth than they appear to be.

Moving west on Maple Lane, Chester Street goes off to the south, revealing more pleasant, charmingly shaded houses. But then, almost exactly halfway along the lane—at that point where Corwith Avenue also heads south, to Main Street—the whole aspect of Maple Lane abruptly changes.

The north side of the street turns entirely commercial. From Eddie's front porch, both a NAPA Auto Parts and a John Deere dealership are visible—they share a long, ugly building with the replete charmlessness of a utility shed. There's also Gregory Electric, in an arguably less offensive frame building, and Iron Horse Graphics, which occupies a fairly good-looking modern structure. The small brick building (Battle Iron and Bronze) is positively handsome, but for the fact that in front of it—in front of *all* these buildings—is a wide, unkempt, continuous parking area, monotonously composed of gravel. And behind these commercial buildings is, finally, the defining feature of Maple Lane: the tracks of the Long Island Rail Road, which run parallel to the lane and lie within a stone's throw north of it.

In one open lot, an unsteady-looking pile of track sections is stacked, and beyond the tracks are mounded heaps of sand, topsoil, and gravel—the storage area for Hamptons Materials, Inc., which is marked by a very prominent sign.

On the south side of Maple Lane, only a few private homes are squeezed alongside more commercial property—including the office for the Hampton Tank and Gas Service. Thereafter, the south side of the lane falls apart altogether. There are some seedy bushes, dirt, more gravel, and—especially in the summer months, or on holiday weekends—a line of cars parked at right angles to the street. Albeit rarely, the line of parked cars might extend for a hundred yards or more, but now—on a desolate Sunday night at the end of the long Thanksgiving weekend—only a few cars are parked there. It has the appearance of a neglected used-car lot. However, in the absence of cars, the parking area looks worse than abandoned—it seems hopeless. All the more so for its proximity to the unhappy structure on the north side and poorer end of the street—the aforementioned relict of the *former* Bridgehampton railroad station.

The foundation is cracked. Two small, prefabricated shelters stand in mock replacement of what the station house used to be. There are two benches. (On this cold, wet Sunday night in late November, no one is sitting on either bench.) A hedge of ill-tended privet has been planted in an apologetic effort to disguise the degeneration of the once-prosperous railroad. The forlorn remnant of the station, an unsheltered telephone box, and a tarred platform that runs for fifty yards along the tracks... alas, for the predominantly well-to-do village of Bridgehampton, this passes for a rail-transportation site.

Along this sorry stretch of Maple Lane, the surface of the street is patchy asphalt that has been laid over the original cement. The verges are gravelly and ill defined; there are no sidewalks. And on this particular November night, there is no traffic. Busy traffic conditions don't often occur or long prevail on Maple Lane, not only because the town of Bridgehampton is served by surprisingly few passenger trains but also because the trains themselves are cinder-stained relics. The passengers must disembark the old-fashioned way—namely, by clambering down the rusted steps at the end of each car.

Ruth Cole, and most travelers to and from New York who were in her income bracket, never took the train; Ruth took the jitney instead. Eddie, although he was decidedly *not* in Ruth's income bracket, usually took the jitney to and from New York, too.

In Bridgehampton, not even a half-dozen local taxis await the arrival of those trains likely to have more than one or two off-loading passengers—for example, the Friday evening Cannonball Express, which arrives at 6:07 sharp (following a 4:01 departure from Penn Station). But, generally speaking, the west end of Maple Lane is a scruffy, sad, deserted place. The cars and taxis rushing east on the lane or south on Corwith Avenue, after a train's brief appearance at the station platform, seem to be in a big hurry to get away from there.

Is it any wonder that Eddie O'Hare wanted to get away from there, too?

———

Of all the Sunday nights in the year—in the Hamptons, particularly—
the Sunday night that marks the end of the long Thanksgiving weekend is conceivably the loneliest. Even Harry Hoekstra, who had every
reason to be happy, could feel the loneliness of it. At fifteen minutes
past eleven on that Sunday night, Harry was indulging in a favorite,
newfound pastime. The retired police officer was pissing on the lawn
behind Ruth's Sagaponack house. The former Sergeant Hoekstra had
seen several street prostitutes and drug addicts pissing on the streets of
the red-light district; yet until he'd experienced the Vermont woods
and fields, and the lawns of Long Island, Harry hadn't known how entirely satisfying an outdoor act of urination could be.

"Are you peeing outside again, Harry?" Ruth called.

"I'm looking at the stars," Harry lied.

There were no stars to look at. Although the rain had finally
stopped, the sky was black and the air had turned much colder. The
storm had blown out to sea, but the northwest wind was sharp; whatever weather the wind was bringing, the sky was still overcast. It was a
dreary night, by anyone's standards. The faint glow on the northern
horizon was caused by the headlights of those cars carrying the few
New Yorkers who'd not already returned to New York; the Montauk
Highway, even in the westbound lane, had remarkably little traffic for
any Sunday night. The foul weather had sent *everyone* home early. Rain
is the best policeman, Harry remembered.

And then the train whistle made its mournful sound. It was the whistle for the eastbound 11:17, the last train of the night. Harry shivered
and went back inside the house.

It was *because of* the eastbound 11:17 that Eddie O'Hare had not gone
to bed; he'd waited up because he couldn't stand to be lying awake in
his trembling bed when the train arrived and then departed. Eddie always went to bed *after* the eastbound 11:17.

Since the rain had stopped, Eddie had dressed himself warmly and
stood outside on his porch. The arrival of the 11:17 attracted the ca-
cophonous attention of the neighborhood dogs, but not a single car
passed. Who would be taking an eastbound train to the Hamptons at
the end of the Thanksgiving weekend? Nobody, Eddie thought, although he heard one car leave the parking area at the west end of
Maple Lane; it drove off in the direction of Butter Lane—it didn't pass
Eddie's house.

Eddie continued to stand in the cold on his porch, listening to the departing train. After the dogs stopped barking and the train could no longer be heard, he tried to enjoy the brief tranquillity, the unusual quietude.

The northwest wind was definitely bringing the winter with it. The cold air blew over the warmer water in the puddles that dotted Maple Lane. Out of the resultant fog, Eddie suddenly heard the sound of wheels, but they were like the wheels on a child's toy truck—they gave off a barely audible sound, although by now the sound of the wheels had got the attention of a dog or two.

A woman was making her way through the fog. Behind her, she was pulling one of those suitcases you see most frequently in airports—a suitcase on little wheels. Given the broken surface of the street—the cracked pavement, the gravelly verge, not to mention the puddles— the woman was struggling with her suitcase, which was better equipped for airports than the wrong end of Maple Lane.

In the darkness and the fog, the woman appeared to be of no specific age. She was of above-average height—quite thin, but not exactly frail; yet even in her shapeless raincoat, which she'd gathered tightly around her in the cold, her body was still shapely. It was not like an *elderly* woman's body at all, although Eddie could now discern that she *was* an older woman—albeit a beautiful one.

Not knowing if the woman saw him standing in the darkness of his porch—and being, therefore, as careful as he could be not to startle her—Eddie said: "Excuse me. May I help you?"

"Hello, Eddie," Marion said. "Yes, you certainly *may* help me. I've been thinking about how much I would like you to help me for what seems like the longest time."

What did they talk about, after thirty-seven years? (If it had happened to you, what would you have talked about *first?*)

"Grief can be contagious, Eddie," Marion told him, as he took her raincoat and hung it in his front-hall closet. It was only a two-bedroom house. The single guest room was small and airless, and at the top of the stairs—near the equally small room that Eddie used for his office. The master bedroom was downstairs; one could look into it from the living room, where Marion now sat on the couch.

As Eddie started upstairs with her suitcase, Marion stopped him by saying: "I'll sleep with you, Eddie—if it's all right. I'm not terribly good on stairs."

"Of course it's all right," Eddie told her, taking her suitcase into his bedroom.

"Grief *is* contagious," Marion began again. "I didn't want you to catch my grief, Eddie. I *really* didn't want *Ruth* to catch it."

Had there been other young men in her life? One can't blame Eddie for asking her. Younger men had always been attracted to Marion. But who among them could ever have matched her memory of those two young men she lost? There hadn't been one younger man who'd even matched her memory of *Eddie*! What Marion had begun with Eddie had ended with him.

One can't blame Eddie for then asking her if she had known *older* men. (After all, he was more familiar with that kind of attraction.) But when Marion had accepted the companionship of older men— widowers primarily, but divorcés and intrepid bachelors as well— she'd discovered that even older men found mere "companionship" insufficient; naturally they'd wanted sex, too. And Marion *didn't* want sex—after Eddie, she honestly hadn't wanted it.

"I'm not saying sixty times was enough," she told him, "but you *did* set a standard."

At first Eddie thought it must have been the happy news of Ruth's second wedding that had finally drawn Marion out of Canada, but although Marion was pleased to learn of her daughter's good fortune, she confessed to Eddie that she'd not heard a word about Harry Hoek- stra until Eddie told her.

Naturally it then occurred to Eddie to ask Marion why she'd come back to the Hamptons *now*. When Eddie considered all the times that he *and* Ruth had half-expected Marion to make an appearance ... well, why *now*?

"I heard the house was for sale," Marion told him. "It was never the *house* I had to get away from—it was never you, either, Eddie."

She'd kicked off her shoes, which were wet, and through her sleek pantyhose, which were tinted a pale-tan color, her toenails were painted the fiery pink of the beach roses that grew wild behind the dreaded Mrs. Vaughn's Southampton estate.

"Your former house is an *expensive* house, nowadays," Eddie ventured to say. He couldn't bring himself to mention the exact amount that Ruth wanted.

As always, he loved what Marion was wearing. She had on a long skirt, which was a dark charcoal-gray, and a crewneck cashmere sweater of salamandrine-orange, an almost tropical pastel color, similar to that pink cashmere cardigan she'd been wearing when Eddie first met her— the sweater that he'd been so obsessed with, until his mother gave it away to some faculty wife.

"How much *is* the house?" Marion asked him.

When Eddie told her, Marion sighed. She'd been away from the Hamptons too long; she had no idea how the real estate market had flourished. "I've made a fair amount of money," Marion said. "I've done better than I deserve to have done, considering what I've written. But I haven't made *that* much money."

"I haven't made very much money from my writing at all," Eddie admitted, "but I can sell this house anytime I want to." Marion had politely made a point of not looking at her somewhat shabby surroundings. (Maple Lane was Maple Lane, and the years of Eddie's summer rentals had taken their toll *inside* the house, too.)

Marion's long, still-shapely legs were crossed; she sat almost primly on the couch. Her pretty scarf, which was the pearl-gray color of an oyster, perfectly separated her breasts, which Eddie could see were enduringly well formed. (Perhaps it was her bra.)

Eddie took a deep breath before he rushed into what he had to say. "How about we split Ruth's house, fifty-fifty? Actually," he added quickly, "if you can afford to pay two thirds, I think one third might be more realistic for me than half."

"I *can* afford two thirds," Marion told him. "Also, I'm going to die and leave you, Eddie. Eventually I'll leave my two thirds to *you!*"

"You're not dying *now*, are you?" Eddie asked her—for it panicked him to think it might have been Marion's impending death that had brought her back to him, just to say good-bye.

"Goodness, no! I'm fine. At least I'm not dying of anything I *know* about, except old age...."

This was their inevitable conversation; Eddie had anticipated it. After all, he'd written this conversation so many times that he knew the dialogue by heart. And Marion had read all his books; she knew what the character of the devoted younger man said to the older-woman character in *all* of Eddie O'Hare's novels. The younger man was eternally reassuring.

"You're not old, not to *me*," Eddie began. For so many years—and five books!—he had rehearsed this moment. Yet he was still anxious.

"You're going to have to take care of me, maybe sooner than you think," Marion warned him.

But for thirty-seven years Eddie had *hoped* that Marion would let him take care of her. If Eddie felt astonished, it was only because he'd been right the very first time—he'd been *right* to love Marion. Now he had to trust that she'd come back to him as soon as she could. Never mind that it had taken her thirty-seven years. Maybe she'd needed that long to make peace with her grief for Thomas and Timothy—not to mention making peace with whatever degree of ghost Ted had doubtless conjured up, just to haunt her.

Here was a whole woman—for, true to her character, Marion had brought Eddie her entire life to contend with *and* to love. Was there anyone as capable of the task? The fifty-three-year-old author had loved her both in the literal *and* in the literary sense for all these years!

One can't blame Marion for telling Eddie all the times of the day and the week she avoided. For instance, when children got out of school—not to mention all museums, all zoos. And parks in any decent weather, when the children would be sure to be there with their nannies or their parents; and every daytime baseball game—all Christmas shopping, too.

What had she left out? All summer and winter resorts, the first warm days of the spring, the last warm days of the fall—and every Halloween, of course. And on her list of things never to do: she never went out for breakfast, she gave up ice cream... Marion was always the well-dressed woman alone in a restaurant—she would ask for a table at the latest time they served. She ordered her wine by the glass and ate her meals with a novel.

"I hate eating alone," Eddie commiserated with her.

"Eating with a novel is not eating alone, Eddie—I'm mildly ashamed of you," she told him.

He couldn't help but ask her if she'd ever thought of picking up the phone.

"Too many times to count," Marion replied.

And she'd never expected to make even a modest living from her books. "They were only therapy," she said. Before the books, she had got from Ted what her lawyer had demanded: enough to live on. All Ted had wanted in return was that she let him have Ruth to himself.

When Ted died, it had been *too* tempting to call. Marion had had her telephone disconnected. "And so I gave up the phone," she told Eddie. "It was no harder to give up than weekends." She'd stopped going out on weekends long before she gave up the phone. (Too many children.) And whenever she traveled, she tried to arrive after dark—even on Maple Lane.

Marion wanted a drink before she went to bed. And she didn't mean a Diet Coke—a can of which Eddie had been clutching in one hand, although it was empty. There was an open bottle of white wine in Eddie's refrigerator, and three bottles of beer (in case someone stopped by). There was also a bottle of better stuff, a single-malt Scotch whiskey, which Eddie kept under the kitchen sink—for those more favored guests and his only occasional female company. He'd first and last had a drink of the good stuff in Ruth's Sagaponack house, following Ted's memorial service; on that occasion, he'd been surprised by how much he'd enjoyed the taste. (He kept a little gin on hand, too, although even the smell of gin made him gag.)

In any case—in a wineglass, which was Eddie's only glassware— Eddie offered Marion a drink of the single-malt whiskey. He even had a drink himself. Then, as Marion used the bathroom first and readied herself for bed, Eddie scrupulously washed the wineglasses in warm water and dish detergent (before redundantly putting the glasses in the dishwasher).

Marion, in an ivory-white slip, and with her hair unpinned—it was shoulder-length, and of a whiter shade of gray than Eddie's—surprised him in the kitchen by putting her arms around his waist and hugging him while his back was turned to her.

For a while, this was the chaste position they maintained in Eddie's bed, before Marion allowed her hand to stray to Eddie's erection. "Still a boy!" she whispered, while she held him by what Penny Pierce had once called his "intrepid penis"—long ago, Penny had also made reference to his "heroic cock." Marion would never have been so silly or so crass.

Then they faced each other in the dark, and Eddie lay, as he'd once lain with her, with his head against Marion's breasts; her hands ran through his hair as she clasped him to her. Thus they fell asleep, until the westbound 1:26 woke them.

"Merciful heavens!" Marion cried, because the westbound early-morning train was probably the loudest of all the trains. Not only is one often *dead* asleep at twenty-six minutes past one in the morning, but the westbound train passed Eddie's house before it reached the station. One not only felt the bed shake, and heard the rumbling of the train—one also heard the brakes.

"It's just a train," Eddie reassured her, holding her in his arms. So what if her breasts had shriveled and sagged? Only a little! And at least she still *had* breasts, and they were soft and warm.

"How can you get a penny for this house, Eddie? Are you sure you can sell it?" Marion asked.

"It's still the Hamptons," Eddie reminded her. "You can sell anything out here."

In the pitch-dark night, and now that they were wide-awake again, Marion's fears about seeing Ruth surfaced. "Does Ruth hate me?" Marion asked him. "I certainly have given her every reason to...."

"I don't think Ruth hates you," Eddie told her. "I think she's just angry."

"Anger is all right," Marion said. "You can get *over* anger more easily than you can get over some other things. But what if Ruth doesn't want us to have the house?"

"It's still the Hamptons," Eddie said again. "Regardless of who she is, and who you are, Ruth is still looking for a buyer."

"Do I snore, Eddie?" Marion asked him—seemingly apropos of nothing.

"Not yet, not that I've heard," he told her.

"Please tell me if I do—no, *kick* me if I do. I've had no one to tell me if I do or don't," Marion reminded him.

Marion indeed snored. Naturally Eddie would never tell her *or* kick her. He slept blissfully through the sound of her snoring, until the eastbound 3:22 woke them again.

"Dear God, if Ruth won't sell us the house, I'll take you to Toronto. I'll take you anywhere but here," Marion said. "Not even love could keep me here, Eddie. How do you stand it?"

"My mind has always been somewhere else," he confessed. "Until now." He was amazed that her scent, where he lay at her breasts, was the same one he remembered; the scent that had long evaporated from Marion's lost pink cashmere cardigan—the same scent that was on her underwear, which he had taken with him to college.

They were sound asleep again when the westbound 6:12 woke them.

"That one was westbound, wasn't it?" Marion asked.

"Correct. You can tell by the brakes."

After the 6:12, they made love very carefully. They'd fallen back to sleep when the eastbound 10:21 wished them a sunny, cold, clear-skied good morning.

It was Monday. Ruth and Harry had a reservation on a Tuesday-morning ferry sailing from Orient Point. The real estate agent—that hefty woman easily given to tears of failure—would let the movers in and lock up the Sagaponack house after Ruth and Harry and Graham were back in Vermont.

"It's now or never," Eddie said to Marion, over breakfast. "They'll be gone tomorrow." He could tell that Marion was nervous by how long she took to get dressed.

"Who does he look like?" Marion asked Eddie, who misunderstood her; he thought she meant who did *Harry* look like, but Marion was asking about Graham. Eddie had understood that Marion was afraid of seeing Ruth, but Marion was also afraid of seeing Graham.

Fortunately (in Eddie's opinion), Graham had been spared Allan's lupine appearance; the boy definitely looked more like Ruth.

"Graham looks like his mother," Eddie said, but that wasn't what Marion had meant, either. She'd meant which of *her* boys did Graham resemble, or did he resemble either of them? It wasn't Graham himself whom Marion was afraid of seeing—it was any reincarnation of Thomas or Timothy.

The grief over lost children never dies; it is a grief that relents only a little. And then only after a long while. "Please be specific, Eddie. Would you say that Graham looks more like Thomas or like Timothy? I just need to be prepared for him," Marion said.

Eddie wished he could say that Graham looked like *neither* Thomas *nor* Timothy, but Eddie had a better memory of the photographs of Ruth's dead brothers than Ruth had. In Graham's round face, and in his widely spaced dark eyes, there was that babylike sense of wonder and expectation that Marion's younger son had reflected.

"Graham looks like Timothy," Eddie admitted.

"Just *a little* like Timothy, I suppose," Marion said, but Eddie knew it was another question.

"No, a lot. He looks *a lot* like Timothy," Eddie told her.

This morning Marion had chosen the same long gray skirt, but a different cashmere crewneck; it was burgundy-colored, and in place of a scarf she wore a simple necklace—a thin platinum chain with a single bright-blue sapphire that matched her eyes.

First she'd put her hair up; now she let it down on her shoulders, with a tortoiseshell band to keep it off her face. (It was a windy day, cold but beautiful.) Finally, when she thought she was ready for the meeting, Marion refused to wear a coat. "I'm sure we won't be standing outside for long," she said.

Eddie tried to distract her from the momentousness of the meeting by discussing how they might remodel Ruth's house.

"Since you don't like stairs, we could convert Ted's former workroom into a downstairs bedroom," Eddie started to say. "The bathroom across the front hall could be enlarged, and if we made the kitchen entrance the main entrance to the house, then the downstairs bedroom would be pretty private." He wanted to keep talking—anything to distract her from imagining how much Graham might resemble Timothy.

"Between climbing the stairs and sleeping in Ted's so-called *work-room* ... well, I'll have to think about that," Marion told him. "It might *eventually* feel like a personal triumph, to be sleeping in the very room where my former husband seduced so many unfortunate women—not to mention where he drew them and photographed them. That might be most *pleasurable*, now that I think of it." Marion had suddenly brightened to the idea. "To be *loved* in that room—even, later, to be *cared for* in that room. Yes, why not? Even to *die* in that room would be okay with me. But what do we do with the goddamn squash court?" she then asked him.

Marion hadn't known that Ruth had already converted the second floor of the barn—Marion also hadn't known that Ted had died there. She'd known only that he'd committed suicide in the barn, by carbon-monoxide poisoning; she'd always assumed that he'd been in his *car,* not in the goddamn squash court.

These and other trivial details preoccupied Eddie and Marion as they turned off Ocean Road in Bridgehampton; they took Sagaponack Road to Sagg Main Street. It was almost midday, and the sun fell on

Marion's fair skin, which was still remarkably smooth; the sun caused her to shade her eyes with her hand, before Eddie reached across her and lowered the sun visor. The bright-yellow hexagon of incalculable light shone like a beacon in her right eye; in the sun, this spot of gold turned her right eye from blue to green, and Eddie knew that he would never again be separated from her.

"Till death do us part, Marion," he said.

"I was just thinking the same thing," Marion told him. She put her thin left hand on his right thigh, and kept it there while Eddie turned right off Sagg Main onto Parsonage Lane.

"Good Lord!" Marion said. "Look at all the new houses!"

Many of the houses were not all that "new," but Eddie couldn't imagine how many so-called new houses had been built on Parsonage Lane since 1958. And when Eddie slowed his car at the driveway of Ruth's house, Marion was shocked by the towering privet; the hedges loomed behind the house and surrounded the swimming pool, which she couldn't see from the driveway but which she assumed was there.

"The bastard put in a pool, didn't he?" she asked Eddie.

"Actually, it's sort of a nice pool—no diving board."

"And of course there's an outdoor shower, too," Marion guessed. Her hand trembled against Eddie's thigh.

"It's going to be okay," he assured her. "I love you, Marion."

Marion sat in the passenger seat and waited for Eddie to open the car door for her; because she'd read all his books, she knew it was the kind of thing that Eddie liked to do.

A handsome but rough-looking man was splitting wood outside the kitchen door. "Goodness, he looks strong!" Marion said, as she got out of the car and took Eddie's arm. "Is that Ruth's policeman? What's his name?"

"Harry," Eddie reminded her.

"Oh, yes—*Harry*. It doesn't sound very Dutch, but I'll try to remember it. And the little boy's name? My own grandson, and I can't even remember his name!" Marion exclaimed.

"It's Graham," Eddie told her.

"Yes, *Graham*—of course." On Marion's still-exquisite face, which was as monumentally chiseled as the face of a Greco-Roman statue, there was a look of inestimable grief. Eddie knew the photograph that Marion must have been remembering. Timothy at four, at the wasted Thanksgiving dinner table, holding an uneaten turkey drumstick, which he viewed with a distrust comparable to that suspicion with which *Graham* had regarded Harry's presentation of the roast turkey only four days before.

In Timothy's innocent expression, there was nothing that even remotely forecast how the boy would be killed in a mere eleven years—not to mention that, in dying, Timothy would be separated from his leg, which his mother would discover only when she tried to retrieve her dead son's shoe.

"Come on, Marion," Eddie whispered. "It's cold outside. Let's go in and meet everybody."

Eddie waved to the Dutchman, who instantly waved back. Harry then hesitated. The ex-cop didn't recognize Marion, of course, but he'd heard all about Eddie's reputation with older women—Ruth had told him. And Harry had read all of Eddie's books. Therefore, Harry gave a tentative wave to the older woman on Eddie's arm.

"I've brought a buyer for the house!" Eddie called to him. "An *actual* buyer!"

That got the former Sergeant Hoekstra's attention. He sunk his ax into the chopping block—that way Graham couldn't cut himself on it. He picked up the splitting wedge, which was also sharp; Harry didn't want Graham to cut himself on the wedge, either. He left the maul lying on the ground. The four-year-old could barely have lifted the maul.

But Eddie and Marion were already entering the house—they hadn't waited for Harry.

"Hello? It's me!" Eddie called from the front hall.

Marion was staring at Ted's workroom with a renewed enthusiasm—more accurately, with an enthusiasm she'd never known she had. But the bare walls in the front hall had also caught her attention; Eddie knew that Marion must have been remembering every photograph that *used to* hang there. Now there were no photos, no picture hooks, no *anything*. Marion also saw the cardboard boxes stacked on top of one another—not entirely unlike the way the house must have looked when she'd last seen it, in the company of *her* movers.

"Hello!" they heard Ruth call, from the kitchen.

Then Graham ran into the hall to greet them. It must have been hard for Marion to meet Graham, but Eddie thought she managed it well. "You must be Graham," Marion said. The child was shy around strangers; he stood beside and a little behind Eddie—at least he knew Eddie.

"This is your grandmother, Graham," Eddie told the boy.

Marion held out her hand. Graham shook it with an exaggerated formality. Eddie kept looking at Marion; she seemed to be holding herself together.

Graham, unfortunately, had never known any grandparents. What he knew about grandmothers, he knew from books, and in books the grandmothers were always very old. "Are you very old?" the boy asked his grandmother.

"Oh, yes—I certainly am!" Marion told him. "I'm seventy-six!"

"Do you know what?" Graham asked her. "I'm only four, but I already weigh thirty-five pounds."

"Goodness!" Marion said. "Once I used to weigh a *hundred* and thirty-five pounds, but that was quite a while ago. I've lost a little weight...."

The front door opened behind them, and Harry stood sweating in the doorway, holding his beloved splitting wedge. Eddie would have introduced Marion to Harry, but suddenly—at the kitchen-end of the front hall—there was Ruth. She'd just washed her hair. "Hi!" Ruth said to Eddie. Then she saw her mother.

From the doorway, Harry said: "It's a buyer for the house. An *actual* buyer." But Ruth didn't hear him.

"Hello, honey," Marion said to Ruth.

"Mommy ..." Ruth managed to say.

Graham ran to Ruth. The four-year-old was still the age for clinging to her hips, which he did, and Ruth instinctively bent to pick him up. But her whole body stopped; she simply didn't have the strength to lift him. Ruth rested one hand on Graham's small shoulder; with the back of her other hand, she made a halfhearted attempt to wipe away her tears. Then she stopped trying—she let the tears come.

In the doorway, the artful Dutchman didn't move. Harry knew better than to move.

Hannah was wrong, Eddie knew. There are moments when time does stop. We must be alert enough to notice such moments.

"Don't cry, honey," Marion told her only daughter. "It's just Eddie and me."

ABOUT THE AUTHOR

JOHN WINSLOW IRVING was born in Exeter, New Hampshire, in 1942. He is the author of nine novels, among them *The World According to Garp, The Hotel New Hampshire, The Cider House Rules, A Prayer for Owen Meany,* and *A Son of the Circus.* Mr. Irving is married and has three sons; he lives in Toronto and in southern Vermont.

ABOUT THE TYPE

The text of this book was set in Janson, a misnamed typeface designed in about 1690 by Nicholas Kis, a Hungarian
in Amsterdam. In 1919 the matrices became the property
of the Stempel Foundry in Frankfurt. It is an old-style
book face of excellent clarity and sharpness. Janson serifs
are concave and splayed; the contrast between thick and
thin strokes is marked.